# HE'S VERY GOOD . . .

She looked in her mirror and her hopes fell. "Our friend is behind us again and he's coming up fast. Closing the distance."

"Then he knows we're on to him."

"Christ! He's got a gun, Red! He's stuck his arm out the window."

"Don't worry," Red told her. "Shooting a pistol left-handed from a moving car at another moving car at sixty miles an hour at this distance? Hell, he'd be lucky to hit that mountain."

There was a sharp crack and the rear window distintegrated into flashing shards. Something buzzed in the air between them and smashed into the tapedeck. Fee howled and ducked into his console.

"Unless," Red continued thoughtfully, "that's Orvid Crayle behind us. He's very good."

# IN THE COUNTRY OF THE BLIND

## MICHAEL FLYNN

# IN THE COUNTRY OF THE BLIND

This is a work of fiction. All the characters and events portrayed in this book are fictional, and any resemblance to real people or incidents is purely coincidental, except for some friends and relatives who make cameo appearances.

Portions of this book have appeared in different form in *Analog* magazine.

A Baen Books Original

Baen Publishing Enterprises
260 Fifth Avenue
New York, N.Y. 10001

ISBN: 0-671-69886-9

Cover art by John Rheaume

First printing, July 1990

Distributed by
SIMON & SCHUSTER
1230 Avenue of the Americas
New York, N.Y. 10020

Dedication:

For Dennis Harry Flynn
(1948–1964)
who would have been co-author

Dedication

For Dennis Harry Flynn
(1943–1964)
who would have been co-author

# PART 1

# HORSESHOE NAILS

# Then

The rain fell in torrents, beating a staccato rhythm on the cobblestoned street. It created rivers and oceans on the paving and formed a curtain beyond which only vague shapes could be seen. The man waited beneath the hissing gas lamp in the middle of the block. The rain ran off his broad-brimmed hat and down the back of his neck. It was a hot, sticky rain; not a bit of coolness in it, and he endured it stoically. He hitched the waterproof leather briefcase under his arm, changing his grip for the hundredth time. Far off to the south he heard booming; but whether of guns or of thunder, he didn't know.

*A drumming of hooves from G Street.* The man turned expectantly; but it was only a troop of cavalry that turned the corner: horses stepping high, striking sparks off the paving with their hooves. Leather straps and belts gleamed wetly in the dusk and the metal of sabers and spurs and bits jangled like an Arabian belly dancer.

He read their cap badges as they rode by: Third Pennsylvania. He raised his arm and huzzahed and their captain saluted him smartly with his quirt.

He watched them fade out of sight as they vanished once more behind the curtain of rain, headed for the Potomac bridges and who knew what fate? When he turned his attention back to the street, the landau was there in front of him. The nigh horse, no more than three feet away, blew his breath out and rolled his eyes at him. Startled, the man took a step backward into a puddle, while the driver, a shapeless lump on the lazyboard, pulled on his reins to calm the beast.

The door opened and Isaac poked his head out, smiling sourly. "Well, Brady," he asked in his broad New England accent, "will you climb in, or do you like the rain so much?"

Brady didn't bother to answer. He stepped into the cab and sat beside the older man. The upholstery inside the landau smelled dank and musty; the hint of mold in every breath. Everything in Washington smelled that way. It was an awful town. What did people say about it? That it had all the charm of a Northern city; and all the efficiency of a Southron one. Brady shook the rain off his hat, and wiped his face with his neckerchief. The carriage started with a jerk.

He saw Isaac glance covertly at the briefcase, and snorted. "Impatient, Isaac?" he asked. His Indiana voice twanged like a Jew's harp. "My train arrived two hours ago. You could have met me then, at the station."

"Ayuh," Isaac agreed readily. "Could have. Didn't."

Brady grunted and looked out at the passing houses, colorless and gray in the pouring rain. They were headed toward Georgetown. Abruptly, the texture of the ride changed. The bouncing and rattling gave way to a sticky, sucking sound. The horses' hooves slapped the muddy road. Brady smiled. "I see they haven't finished paving the streets yet."

"Ayuh. Nor finished the Capitol Dome, neither." Isaac looked at him, then looked away. "Great many things still unfinished."

Brady let that lie and they rode awhile in silence.

"Town's danged spy-crazy," said Isaac after a while. "Too many comin's and goin's. Draws attention. I was followed last week, I think. Naught to do with the Society, but the Council thought 'twere best we not meet at the station."

Brady looked at him. That was as close to an apology as he was ever going to get from the New Englander. He sighed. " 'Tain't important," he said.

Isaac leaned over and tapped the briefcase with his index finger. "But this is," he said. "This is. Tell me square, Brady, and on the level. Is it what we expected?"

Brady didn't answer him directly. He stroked the leather with his palm, feeling the wetness. The metal clasps were cold to his touch. "Three weeks of calculations," he said. "Three weeks, even with Babbage engines, and six of us, working in two teams around the clock. We used numerical integration and some of that new theory that's come from Galois' papers. When we were done, we switched over and

4

checked the other team's work." He shook his head. "There's no mistake."

"Then he must die."

Brady jerked his head around and looked at Isaac. The New Englander was drawn and pale. The age-spots were dark against his parchmentlike skin. Brady nodded once, and Isaac shut his eyes.

"Well, that be news should please some on the Council," he said, gazing on some inner landscape. "Davis and Meechum. Phineas, too. His mills are idled, with no cotton coming North."

Brady frowned. "Are they allowing their personal interests to—"

"No, no. They are guided by the equations, just as we. Slavery had to go. We all agreed, even our Southron members. The equations . . . They showed us what would come to pass if it didn't." Isaac shivered, remembering. "That was why we . . . took measures." The old man's face closed up tighter. "They will see the need for this action, as well."

He opened his eyes and fixed Brady with a stare. "And if they bow to necessity with smiles and we, with sorrow; why, what difference?"

"Damnation, Isaac! It should never have come to this!" Brady slapped the briefcase, a sharp sound that made Isaac blink.

"Don't want his blood on your hands, do you? Well, theah's blood enough already. This war—"

"Was an accident. A miscalculation. Douglas should have won. He knew how to make deals. He could have ended slavery and made the South love him for it. Popular sovereignty and the Homestead Act. That would have done for it."

"Maybe," Isaac allowed. "But Buchanan vetoed the Homestead Act out of personal spite for Douglas, something we couldn't foresee. And we didn't know then how determined Yancey and the other secessionists were. After that fiasco at the Charleston convention, the election was thrown wide open; and the Republicans—"

"That backwoods buffoon!" said Brady angrily. "His winning changed everything! Panicked the South into secession. But how could we have calculated it? The man failed at everything he ever attempted. He failed twice in business; had a nervous breakdown; was defeated for House Speaker, then for re-election; was defeated for *land-officer*, of all things.

5

He ran for the Senate twice and the vice presidency once and lost the nomination all three times. Hell's bells, Isaac! He even lost the presidential election!"

"Not in the electoral college," Isaac pointed out. "And he did have a plurality."

"The man is a statistical anomoly!"

Isaac chuckled. "That's what really bothers you, isn't it?"

Brady framed a tart reply, then thought better of it. Beating a dead horse wouldn't make it run faster. He slouched in his seat. "Be that as it may be. The war was an accident, *this* is different!" He slapped the briefcase again. "A calculated act; not a calculated risk."

Isaac nodded slowly. "Though I doubt a corpse cares much whether 'twere done in by accident or design. Still, needn't worry about yourself. We never act directly. A word heah. A word theah. Washington's always been Confederate in her heart. Someone will act."

"Aye. But we will bear the guilt."

"Why, so we will! Was there ever any doubt? Did you doubt it when you took the Oath?"

Brady looked away, out the window. "No."

They were silent again, listening to the carriage wheels rolling through the mud. The rain drummed the roof of the landau.

"And what if he does *not* die?"

Isaac just wouldn't let it be. Brady scowled at him.

"And what if he does not die?" Isaac persisted.

Brady sighed. He hefted his briefcase, then dropped it into Isaac's lap. "Read it yourself. It's all there. The secondary path from the fifteenth yoke. We have clandestine medical reports on him and his whole family. And on Ann Rutledge, as well. His old law partner, Billy Herndon, has been dropping sly hints to whomever will listen. His wife is certifiably insane, save no one has the guts to say so aloud. It's congenital in at least two of his sons. Damn!" He closed his eyes tight. His hands clenched into fists. "I have never liked any task less than the reading of those reports." He relaxed slowly and looked at Isaac. "There's no mistake. He will go mad before his new term expires. Already he has . . . bizarre dreams.

"And the madness, and the disease it springs from, will discredit his reconciliation program."

"Aye. Leading to victory for the Radicals and probable

6

impeachment. There will be permanent military occupation of the South, stifling of technological progress there, growing resentment among the whites, sporadic rioting and racial pogroms, followed by repression and a new Rebellion in 1905 that will be overtly supported by at least two European Powers. That, too, is in the calculations."

Isaac smiled without humor. "Then, 'tain't so much a matter of blood on our hands, but how much, and whose."

Brady chewed on his knuckle. The skin there was frayed, almost raw. Isaac watched him thoughtfully for a moment, then turned his attention to the window. The silence between them lengthened.

"Gloomy night," said Isaac finally, still gazing at the dark outside the landau. "Fittin' somehow."

"We haven't built Utopia, have we, Isaac?"

Isaac shook his head. "Not yet. Give it time, boy. Give it time. Rome weren't built in one day, neither. The Society's too small yet to move the world by much; but it will be bigger someday, *if* we persevere." He turned and faced Brady, his eyes sharp and piercing. "Just remember, Brady. Famines. Worldwide wars. Weapons deadlier nor any Gatling gun and ironclad. It's all theah on the chahts. You've seen 'em. In less than a century there will be explosive shells more powerful than 20,000 *tons* of guncotton, or of this new stuff, dynamite. God's wounds! The Petersburg mine held only 8,000 *pounds* of black powder! Imagine five-thousand such mines exploded at once!" He shook his head. "I faired those curves m'self, Brady. They're exponential. If we've any hope of tempering them in time, we must act; and act *now!*"

For Isaac, that was quite a speech. Brady stared at the older man and, with a sudden rush of compassion, laid his hand upon his arm and squeezed. Isaac looked at the hand, then at Brady. Then the driver called to his horses and the landau pulled up before a modest Georgetown brick house. After a moment, Brady released Isaac's arm and opened the door. He made to step out, but Isaac restrained him.

"Theah's something else, isn't theah, Brady Quinn? I know you well, and you're concealing something."

The wind blew the rain into the cab. Brady would not look at Isaac. "Don't make me tell you, Isaac."

Isaac backed away from him. "What is it, Brady? Has it to do with the Society?" There was uncertainty in his voice, and the beginnings of fear.

"Isaac, you've been like a father to me for twenty years. Please, don't ask me."

Isaac squared his shoulders. "No. My life is in this work. I built the Society, Brady. Phineas and I and old Jed Crawford. We read between the lines of Babbage's book. Saw what could be done. Saw what *must* be done. We laid out the first ten yokes. If you have found something that—" He shook his head suddenly, violently. "I must know!"

Brady sighed and looked away from him. He had known that this moment would come; had dreaded it. He had known that he would tell Isaac everything. But that did not make it any the less unpleasant. "Young Carson has developed a new algorithm," he said. "Based on a children's game, of all things. It . . . Well, it changes after the twenty-ninth yoke."

Isaac scowled, not understanding. "The twenty-ninth? . . . I don't know what you mean. If everything after the— No! Tell me, Brady!"

Brady told him and the old man stared, openmouthed. Brady closed his eyes briefly in heartache, then he left the landau and walked to the front door of the townhouse. He looked back once, through the rain, and saw the old man weeping.

8

# Now
# I

Sarah looked at the window and decided that it was too damned dirty to look *through*. Glancing around the empty room, she saw a rag in a corner. It was probably just as filthy as everything else in the old house. There were mouse droppings scattered about, cobwebs, fragments of plaster. In some places, the ribs of the walls showed through the broken plaster.

With a sigh of disgust, she walked over and picked up the rag and shook it. A spider crawled out, and she watched it go its way.

"Just how long has this house been vacant?" she asked.

"Five, six years." That was Dennis, her architect. He was rapping on the walls, looking for the supporting beams. He paused and studied the door frame; ran his fingers over the miter joints and nodded in approval. "Good, solid work, though. They sure knew how to build back then."

"The good old days," said Sarah absently. "When women knew their place."

Dennis looked at her. "They still do," he said. "Just more places, is all."

She snorted. Returning to the window, she ran the rag over it. The grime was stubborn. It had had years in which to settle in. She managed to clear a circle in the middle of the pane and peered out at Emerson Street. "Can we refurbish the place? Bring it up to Code and all. That's what I need to know. This neighborhood's going to be the next to boom, and I want to be here first." She had been late getting in on

9

Larimer and Auraria. She was going to be first here, by God. Let the other developers follow *her* for a change.

She could look straight across the street at the second-floor windows there. Those houses had been built on the same basic plan as this one. One-time mansions turned rental apartments. There was a man standing in one of the windows, stripped to the waist, drinking something out of a can. He saw her looking and waved an invitation.

She ignored him and craned her neck to the left, pressing her cheek against the glass. She could just make out the dome of the state capitol, gleaming gold in the afternoon sun. The downtown skyscrapers, though, blocked her view of the mountains. No matter, she thought. The Brown Cloud blocks it for everyone. She watched the traffic at the corner, counting cars-per-minute.

She stood away from the window and clapped the dust from her hands. Dennis had left the room. She could hear him tapping away down the hall.

"How does it look?" she called. She found her clipboard and jotted a few notes.

"Utilities look good," she heard him answer. "No computer ports, naturally; but we can put those in when we upgrade the rest of the wiring."

She followed his voice down the hall and found him in one of the other bedrooms. He was poking at a hole in the wall. "There's still piping in the walls for the old gas mantles." He looked at her and shook his head. "This must have been a swank place a hundred years ago, before they messed it up. There's even a separate servants' stairwell down the end of the hall." He pointed vaguely.

"I know. I've got a list of all the previous owners in my PC at home. One of the old-time silver barons built the place; but the Panic came along a few years later and he had to sell out."

"Easy come; easy go."

"But, you're right. The workmanship in this building was superb! If I could find the sonofabitch who painted over the parquet flooring on the main staircase . . ." That *did* make her mad. She loved good workmanship, no matter what the job; and that staircase had been the work of a master joiner. This area had once been upper class; though not so high-tone as "Humboldt Island" over by Cheesman Park on the "good" side of Colfax. It was funny how neighborhoods went in cycles like that.

10

Dennis nodded. "I know what you mean. When they made this place into a boarding house and subdivided the rooms, they paneled right over the original walls. Can you imagine that? You should *see* the wainscoting! Here."

He pulled on a section of drywall and it came away. Bits of plaster and gypsum fell to the floor, along with some nails and loose scraps of paper. The original wall behind it was in bad shape. The wainscoting was partially destroyed and there were holes in the plaster; but Sarah could well imagine what it must have looked like when it had been new.

The papers on the floor caught her eye and she stooped and picked them up. Habit. It was silly to think about tidying up a dump like this, but habits were self-booting programs. She glanced at the scraps. A yellowed newspaper clipping and a torn sheet of foolscap with a handwritten list of dates.

"What are those?" asked Dennis, brushing his hands and standing up.

"Just trash. Looks like someone's crib notes for a history test and . . ." She read the headline on the clipping. "An 1892 story from the old *Denver Express.*" She handed the foolscap to Dennis and read through the rest of the news story. "A gunfight," she told him. "Two cowboys on Larimer Street. Neither one was scratched; but a bystander was killed. An old man named Brady Quinn."

She frowned. Quinn? Now where had she seen that name before? It had been recently, she was sure. It nibbled at the edge of her memory. Well, never mind. It would come back to her eventually. Probably at three in the morning.

"Odd sort of crib notes."

"Hmm?" She glanced at Dennis. He was scowling over the foolscap. "What do you mean?"

"Well, the entries here are in two different handwritings, for one thing. The earlier items are in the old Spencerian style."

"Someone started the list," said Sarah. "Then someone else continued it."

"And this, up at the top. What does it say? Biological? Diological?"

She glanced where he pointed. "Cliological. Cliological something. It's smudged. I can't make it out."

"That's a big help. What's 'cliological?'"

She shrugged. "Beats me. I never heard the word before."

"And the mixture of entries is odd, too. Famous events and

obscure events all jumbled together. How does the nomination of Franklin Pierce, or the election of Rutherford Hayes, or Winfield Scott's military appointments belong on the same list as the election of Abraham Lincoln or his assassination, or the sinking of the Lusitania? Or . . . Hello!"

"What?" She moved behind him and read over his shoulder. He pointed. "Brady Quinn murdered," she read.

"Yep, your friend Quinn is right in there with Lincoln and Teddy Roosevelt. And with von Kluck's Turn, whatever that was. 1914. Must have been World War I."

"No kidding? And 'Frederick W. Taylor, fl. ca. 1900.' Who was he?"

Dennis shook his head. "There are a half dozen entries here that I never heard of."

"Well, that's modern education for you. They don't teach things anymore that our great-great-grandparents took for granted. Personally, I think it started with Thomas Dewey's whole-word method of reading." She tapped Dewey's name on the list with her fingernail. "English isn't Chinese and you can't teach it that way. It just doesn't work. No wonder half the kids in this country grow up functionally illiterate. My own teachers—some of them, anyway—were damn near illiterate themselves."

"I'll bet they all had education degrees, though."

She snorted. "Which meant they knew all there was to know about teaching, except the subject."

"When I was in graduate school," Dennis remembered, "the education prof across the hall from us told me that that wasn't important." She looked at him and he shrugged. "True story."

"That's the way folks are. 'If'n I don't know about it, it ain't important.' Ask any engineer about writing sonnets; or ask any poet about stress and shear. You'll get the same answer." She wondered, as she often did, that her own life had been so different.

Dennis chuckled and pointed to the list. "Or ask any architect about factor analysis. There's a note at the bottom, where it's torn. 'Try orthogonal factor analysis . . .' "

"Orthogonal factor analysis? Oh, I learned about that in sociology. It's a statistical method they use to define socioeconomic groups. Each group is defined by a cluster of mutually correlated traits in an n-dimensional space. I think they use it in physical anthropology, too."

12

Dennis raised one eyebrow and looked at her. "Oh, yeah?" He studied the sheet. "Each entry here is marked with a 1, 2, or 3. Maybe those are three 'orthogonal factors.'" He folded the list and tucked it in his shirt pocket. "Well, maybe I'll check some of this out. Find out what the list means."

They took the servants' stairs to the main floor. It was dark in the stairwell and their shoes crunched on dirt and broken plaster.

"Tell me," Dennis said on the way down, "if education is so lousy, how did you get to be so smart?"

She stopped and looked at him. In the dimness the architect was only an indistinct shadow. "Because I wouldn't *let* them cheat me!" she snapped. "I've had to fight for everything I've ever had. Because of my sex. Because of my color. I wouldn't *accept* a second-rate education!"

"I didn't mean to sound patronizing," Dennis said. "Christ, you know me, Sarah. I had . . . Well, not the same problems, obviously; but at prep school, they didn't expect the idle rich to want to tackle anything 'hard.'"

"Yeah, I know," she answered. "It ain't yo' fault yo' was bo'n white and rich."

"Hey, I said I was sorry. It's just that you seem to know more things about more things than anybody else I've ever met."

"Jack of all trades; master of none," she snorted. "You're right. I'm sorry I took it the wrong way." She turned away from him. "I guess I just have a bump for curiosity."

But it hadn't always been that way, she remembered. Once, she had been as content as her playmates to coast through school, and life. Putting in the time, because the Law and her mother and her father said she had to. "It was in the fifth grade, I suppose." She ran a finger along the dirty bannister. "Our class took a field trip to the Museum of Science and Industry. That was . . . oh, more years ago than I care to remember." *Oh Lord, the South Side of Chicago.* She could see herself careening wide-eyed from exhibit to exhibit; a little girl in cornrows who could barely read. There had been an exhibit of calculating machines, ranging from the old key-set mechanisms all they way up to the latest in mini-desktops. There had been a walk-through model of a human heart. There had been a rock that had been brought back from another world!

13

"It was like being doused with ice water," she told him. That trip had awakened her with a shock; and even now, through the telescope of years, she could feel the shiver of excitement she had felt then. "There was an enormous and fascinating world out there, *and my teachers were not telling me about it!* So . . ." And she shrugged self-consciously. "I explored it on my own. I began cutting classes, sneaking off to the public library; later on, even to the University of Chicago library." She'd had to con her way in there: no one would believe a little black girl had come there to *read*.

And she had read everything. African music, physics, law, medicine, Chinese history, statistics, German philosophy, computers. Everything. Some of her friends who knew what she was doing had asked her what good it all was. What would she ever use it for? She had treated the question with the same scorn she felt for the apathy behind it. Use it? She wasn't looking for training, she was looking for an education.

She had passed all her school classes, of course. She made certain she took all the tests. Most of her teachers, she was convinced, had deeply resented her success, because she had achieved it in spite of them. But there had been two . . . Ah, *those* had been teachers!

"Habits are hard to break, I suppose." Dennis' voice broke into her memories.

"Hmm? What do you mean?"

They had reached the ground floor, where it was light. She could see the smile on Dennis' face. "How many seminars and classes have you taken in the few years we've known each other?"

"Realty law. Creative writing. A dozen programming classes. I think the hacking was the most fun. I don't know. I've lost count."

"See what I mean?" he said. "I admire you. You haven't stopped; you're still stretching yourself. Sometimes I wish I had your curiosity about things. I must have a score of books at home that I've always meant to read. I bought them all with good intentions; but, I never seem to find the time for them. My journals and technical reading seem to take up all my spare time."

"You can always make the time. It's a matter of setting your priorities."

Dennis ran his hand across his shirt pocket. "Yes. I suppose curiosity is like everything else. It comes with practice."

*   *   *

They paused on the sidewalk outside the building while Dennis sketched some ideas on his pad. She knew better than to try and peek. He'd throw away a dozen good concepts before he kept a single great one to show her. Over the years she had learned to trust his judgment.

Sarah brushed at the dirt on her clothing. Cars lined the entire block, both sides. She would have to do something about parking when she developed the area.

Dennis tossed the sketchpad into the back seat of his Datsun. "Friday for lunch?"

She nodded absently. She was wondering how much of the block she could buy up before anyone else noticed what was happening and the prices jumped. Maybe she could run it through a couple of dummy corporations.

"Got a name for it."

"Hmm? For what?"

"The project. Brady Quinn Place. We can tie in the histori- cal aspect. The turn of the century with the turn of the century. The 1890s meet the 1990s. Solidness and elegance combined with efficiency and technology."

She thought it over. "Not bad," she admitted.

"Not bad? It's a natural. There's a real nostalgia in this town for that era. Cowboys. Baby Doe Tabor. Mattie Silks. Sheriff Dave Cook."

"I'll think about it," she said. "Find out who this Brady Quinn character was. We wouldn't want to use his name if he was only some two-bit tin-horn."

"Why not? Mattie Silks was a madam."

"Ah, but in a woman, sleaze is respectable."

She drove her Volvo through the diagonal streets of down- town Denver, past the steel-and-glass towers of the energy and telecommunications companies. She wondered what would happen to such complexes when networking out of the home became common. Her projected renovation included access- ing each unit to the DataNet as well as to a community satellite dish. The technoyups would love that!

She had planned to take Colfax Avenue home because she liked to watch for commercial property possibilities; but at the last minute she changed her mind and cut down Speer to the Sixth Avenue Expressway. That was a straight run west, non-

15

stop practically to the Hogback, with the Front Range dead ahead the whole way. It was a sight she never tired of.

A few years ago she had taken one of those executive survival courses. Rock climbing. Shooting rapids. Living in the wilderness. From high tech to low tech. She had learned how to handle knives and bows. For graduation, they had dropped her off somewhere in the High Country with nothing but the clothes on her back. She had learned a lot about who she was during those two grueling days. And she had grown to love the mountains. They were her refuge when the stress of business grew too great. She promised herself a few days in the High Country after the Emerson Street project was finished.

The afternoon clouds were rolling over the mountains, so close she felt she could touch them. She gauged the sky thoughtfully, estimating the chance of rain, then she opened the sunroof anyway. What the hell. She liked the feel of the breeze and, if it did rain, she could close it up fast enough. She was a risk-taker from way back.

Later, in her home, sipping a brandy in front of the fire, Quinn's name finally clicked. She remembered where she had seen it before. She set her snifter to the side and pushed herself out of the sofa. A log in the fire snapped, sending a wave of pine scent through the room. Feline P. Cat, her Manx, followed her to the terminal desk and watched intently as she called up a file and scrolled through it. When she finally found the entry she sought, she nodded in self-satisfaction.

Once, a very long time ago, Brady Quinn had owned the house on Emerson Street. He had bought it from the silver baron in 1867, and sold it in 1876 to a man named Randall Carson. From there, through several intermediate owners, it had come to her.

"That makes him some sort of 'ancestor' of mine," she told the cat. "Maybe Dennis is right and we can use him as a hook for the project. If he is anything more than a poor jerk who got caught in the crossfire of someone else's argument."

Feline blinked his agreement.

"Maybe the files at the *News* or the *Post* can help me. What do you think, Fee?"

The cat yawned.

"You're right. The *Express* and the *Times* aren't around any more. Maybe the Western History Room at the DPL has something. And the tax records at the City and County Build-

16

ing." She jotted some notes to herself. She'd always hated doing research during her reporter days. Now she was actually looking forward to it. It was a break in the routine. When it's your *job*, she thought, it's never *fun*. She decided to real-time the various repositories, since most of the material she was interested in hadn't been databased into the Net yet. Nobody was about to use up valuable bytes with hundred-year-old real estate records!

# II

When Sarah walked into the city room of the *Rocky Mountain News* the next morning she saw Morgan Grimes hunched over his desk. She stepped off the elevator and walked around the pillars past the reception desk, and there he was. The city room was a study in mauve, burgundy, and gray, with the reporters' desks arranged in "pods" of six. There was no one else in the room except the copy editor, who glanced up briefly from her station at the head of the U of copy desks before bending back to her work.

Morgan was talking on the phone, his face twisted in concentration, holding the earpiece with his left shoulder while he tapped notes into his terminal. When he saw her coming he said something into the phone, then covered the mouthpiece with his hand.

"Yes, young lady, may I help you?"

"Stuff it, Morgan. I came to use the library for a while. Is that all right with you?"

"Library," he groused. "It's a morgue, dammit. I don't care who says different." He looked her over. "So that's all? Just using our morgue? Not looking for your old job back?"

She laughed. "Not even on a bet. Give up the office suite, the Volvo, the tailored dresses, the condo in Aspen? For what?"

"For the thrill," he answered. "For the glamour. *The Front Page. All the President's Men.* That sort of thing."

"Sure, I remember the glamour. Obituaries. Press conferences. Media 'opportunities.' Staged demonstrations. Not to mention coolie wages, unpredictable work hours, and last-

18

minute assignments out of town. No, thanks." She tried to peek at his VDT but he hit a button and it went blank.

"Uh-uh," he said. "That's a no-no."

"What are you working on, Morgan?"

"The Pulitzer, of course."

She looked at him, unsure if he were kidding. Morgan Grimes had the straightest face in the business and could wear sincerity the way most men wore cologne. During the days when they had teamed up together, she had never been able to tell when he was putting her on or not; a fact that he used against her mercilessly. *I wonder if he's still using the same access code.* She had cracked it years ago, just for practice; but she had never actually used it to enter his files. Now, though, she thought about tapping into his files through the Net. *Leave him a sarcastic message. Teach him not to play cute with me.* She thought she could hack it, even though the reporters' terminals were not always connected to the Net. There were ways to mouse into any system.

She looked around the city room. "Everybody out on assignment?"

"Uh-huh. Except Kevin. He's on another book promotion tour. Should be back next week. I suppose you heard about his latest best seller."

"Yeah. Follow-up to *The Silent Brotherhood*, isn't it? Easy life. Well, tell everyone I stopped by and said hello."

"They will be thrilled beyond words. Actually, it has been good seeing you again. You always were a pretty good—"

"*Don't say it, Morgan!*"

"—news-hen. The morgue's still where it always was; but everything's on discs now, not microfilm. That wouldn't bother you, though, would it?"

"Sure wouldn't," she said as she left. She swung her body with mock sassiness. "I was born with a microchip on my shoulder."

Dennis' appointment was at 15:00 hours and he arrived at the offices of the DU history department precisely at 14:59. A series of doors opened off of a central reception area. No one was at the reception desk, although an open can of pop hinted at someone's imminent return. He looked around uncertainly until a plump, moon-faced woman stuck her head out of one of the doors.

"Mr. French?" she asked.

19

"Yes, are you Professor Llewellyn?" He headed in her direction. "Thank you for seeing me. I know how busy you folks are."

"Not at all. The semester is over now and I have some spare time. It's just such a surprise when a non-student makes an appointment. Come in and sit down." She guided him into her office. "Gwynneth Llewellyn is my name."

They shook hands. Llewellyn's grip was surprisingly firm. Dennis sat in a worn, high-back chair, pulling up his pants legs so they wouldn't bag. He sat erect, with his hands folded across his middle.

Llewellyn planted herself behind her desk and leaned forward on her beefy arms. Her skin was pale, spotted red with freckles. Her cheeks were plump and round. She reminded Dennis of someone's aunt and he half-expected cornbread muffins and cocoa; so he was quite surprised when she took up a corncob pipe and lit it.

She blew a smoke ring, gauging his reaction with a twinkle in her eye. "So what can I do for you, Mr. French?"

He came right to the point. Neither his time nor the professor's was something to be wasted. "I am trying to discover the rationale behind this list of historical events." He reached into his vest pocket and pulled out the scrap of foolscap that he and Sarah had found in the Emerson Street house.

He had spent all day Tuesday and Wednesday reading history and talking to some people he knew at Metro and CU. Making time, he supposed Sarah would say. He was convinced there was a common theme running through all the items on the list. Some principle that defined what went on the list and what didn't. He was annoyed that he couldn't simply glance at the entries and know what that common factor was; like he could glance at a building and know what principles the architect had used to make his design decisions. He wasn't sure if that represented a problem with his education, with his own abilities, or with the list itself; but the problem niggled at him, like a stone in his shoe.

He unfolded the sheet and handed it over to Professor Llewellyn. She pulled out a pair of old-fashioned bifocals and perched them on her nose. She gave him a quick apologetic smile and focused on the page, her head tilted slightly back and her lips thrust forward in a pout.

When she had finished, she took off her glasses and looked

20

at him. "I take it, you're not interested in knowing what these events are. You can find most of them referenced in any good history text."

He nodded. "And I have been reading to the extent I have time. I am an architectural consultant and I'm afraid I've simply not the freedom to pursue these things to the depth I suspect may be necessary. The people I've talked with so far have given me facts, details. All fascinating. Much of it I hadn't known. By now I feel as if I've actually met some of the people on that list. Like Thomas B. Reed. He was quite a character. The serenely sarcastic New England Buddha, they called him."

"He was the most brilliant man in politics in his day," Llewellyn told him. "He should have been nominated for President."

"But I want more than facts. I am searching—for want of a better word—for insight. Some of those entries concern well-known people or events. Others are obscure. The sinking of the battleship *Maine* and the nomination of Franklin Pierce don't exactly pop into one's mind together."

She smiled. "No, they surely do not." She scanned through the list again. "Insight is a perfectly good word, Mr. French; and it is exactly what you are looking for. The same thought bothered me as I read this, too. If these are the answers to a quiz or an examination, it would be a very strange unit of study. I'm afraid even I don't know what some of these entries are, let alone what they might mean. I know about Ambrose Bierce disappearing in Mexico, of course; but who was this Brady Quinn fellow, or Davis Belleau, or Agatha Penwether?"

"Murder victims."

She nodded testily. "Yes, I can read; but what are they doing here with Teddy Roosevelt and Lincoln; or with Edison, Dewey, Ford, and Taylor?" She laid the foolscap on her desk and leaned back in the swivel chair. The springs creaked. She puffed on her pipe, staring pensively at the ceiling. "I may be getting an idea," she told him. "Tell me, Mr. French. Do you know who said this? 'Under our system a worker is told just what he is to do and how to do it. Any improvement he makes upon the orders given him is fatal to his success.'"

Dennis shrugged. "I don't know. Lenin? Mao?" He did not see the relevance of her question.

"No, it was Frederick Taylor," she said, indicating the

21

list. Dennis remembered the item. *Frederick W. Taylor, fl. ca. 1900.*

"Ah. And Taylor was? . . ."

She aimed the stem of her pipe at him. "He was an engineer who lived at the turn of the century. American industry at the time was faced with a tide of poorly educated immigrant laborers, and Taylor developed a system to boost productivity by separating the planning and the execution of work. Engineers and managers made the plans; foremen and workers carried them out. It ended the old craftsman system, in which the worker planned his own work; and it's been the basis of American business philosophy ever since."

Dennis laughed. "Oh, no! And I thought it was Lenin or Mao? That's priceless!"

She smiled thinly. "Don't forget that Engels was a factory owner himself; and he was not necessarily the junior partner of the team. He thought that entire nations could be run rationally, the way factories were."

"I've yet to encounter a business that was run rationally," Dennis interjected.

Llewellyn grunted, but ignored the interruption. "Socialism, after all, is simply the culmination of capitalism. The pinnacle—if that's the right word—of what I like to call the Managed Society. If you want to see Lenin's state in embryo, study Henry Ford's company. His Sociological Department 'inspectors' could barge in unannounced on employees in their homes and question them on their marriages, their finances, their private lives; and Harry Bennett's 'outside squads' were just small-time Brown Shirts. Oh, certainly, both Ford and Lenin had the best of intentions: to improve the lot of the common man; but the management system they developed—"

"Now, wait a minute! Lenin wanted power!"

"And Ford didn't?"

"Henry Ford never had anyone executed," Dennis protested.

"Though Bennett's goons *did* beat up and harrass 'dissidents.' And other employers during the class war did not shrink from killing union organizers. Sometimes with private armies, but more often with the aid of government troops. The difference between Ford and Lenin was more a matter of scale than anything else, Mr. French. Lenin organized his entire country into one vast Company Town, with all that implies. In plain language, the Soviet Union is the largest

22

capitalistic organization on the planet. The Party members are the stockholders; and the Politburo is the Board of Directors. The average citizen or employee has no effective say in how the organization is run. A centralized bureaucracy makes five-year plans that never work. Internal criticism is not allowed, although suggestions for improvements are encouraged, provided they are not truly revolutionary. Everyone must be a 'team player,' by which they mean: 'follow the boss's orders' rather than genuine teamwork. Troublemakers are exiled to Siberia or to meaningless jobs. Or they are terminated." Dr. Llewellyn smiled humorlessly. "An interesting choice of words, that."

"Don't forget the hostile takeovers," said Dennis.

Professor Lllewellyn laughed. "That's the spirit!"

"You know, I never thought of it before," Dennis admitted, "but a large corporation is run like a socialist state."

"Vice versa, actually. Don't forget which came first."

"Thanks to Frederick W. Taylor."

Llewellyn nodded. "He wasn't the only harbinger; but he was the catalyst."

"So your point is . . ." He let the sentence hang.

"Oh, yes, your list. Now this is purely off the cuff, understand. But the items I am familiar with seem to be historical turning points of a rather subtle kind. The events themselves were small—by that I mean that few people were involved —but they had disproportionate consequences. Do you recall the George Herbert poem? 'For want of a nail, the shoe is lost. For want of a shoe, the horse is lost.' And so on. In the end a kindgom is lost. Had Richard III not lost his horse, Bosworth Field might have gone the other way, it was that near a thing. And what then? No Tudors, perhaps; and English history becomes something quite different. Well, these events are like that. You see, most individual events have little impact on the overall course of history; but some build, like an avalanche, into consequences that only become evident in hindsight."

"I see. Like Mr. Taylor's attempts to boost factory productivity led to your Managed Society."

"It's not *my* society," she said a trifle huffily. "I objected to the trend in the 60s and I still object to it. The idea that Those In Charge Know Better . . . those who say that government should be run more like a business should study the Soviet Union; or better yet, some of our own large corporations."

23

Dennis grinned. "Just between you and I, I've never had too much respect for the way large corporations are run. That's why I'm in business for myself. What about the other items on the list? He laid the list flat on her desk and they both huddled over it.

"How about . . . Oh, Winfield Scott's military appointments? How was that a horseshoe nail?"

She looked at him and took her pipe from her teeth. "A horseshoe nail," she repeated, smiling. "I like that. Perhaps I will use it in my classes next semester, with your permission."

"My permission?" Dennis was surprised. "Certainly."

"Thank you. I would say that Scott's appointments added a few years to the Civil War. He named mostly Southerners to key posts, you know; which wasn't surprising, since he himself was a Virginian. As a result, the Confederacy wound up with more experienced officers. Of course, at the time, no one knew there would be a civil war; and Scott was, and remained, a staunch Unionist. So it wasn't as though he planned it that way."

"There seem to be a number of Civil War items on the list. What does this mean? *Jan/Feb, 1861. The Twiggs Affair: his orders delayed, but not his return.*"

Llewellyn shook her head. "I don't know. I am not an encyclopedia. The name seems vaguely familiar; but I do not remember the context. I suggest you find a good history of the Civil War, or the events leading up to it."

"Yes, I will. If I have time." He studied the list. "I suppose then that Theodore Roosevelt's nomination for vice-president was a small thing that led to the trust-busting and other progressive reforms."

Llewellyn drew on her pipe and sent a cloud toward the ceiling. She looked uncertain. "Perhaps. But then why not list his accession to the presidency instead? Did you know that his nomination for vice-president was actually arranged by his political enemies, who were trying to finish his career by burying him in a dead-end job?"

"Things didn't quite work out the way they expected," Dennis commented.

"No, they didn't. The best laid plans of mice and men gang aft agly, as Bobby Burns once wrote." She folded the list and handed it back to Dennis. "Perhaps the Roosevelt nomination was a horseshoe nail that was 'hammered back in,' so to speak."

"By McKinley's assassination. I see." Somehow, he had always thought of history as something solid. Something inevitable. But the way Llewellyn had explained things, history was nothing more than the chance combination of random causes. A multiplication of unlikely coincidences that could have turned one way as easily as another. Horseshoe nails. He felt as if he had been viewing a cathedral for a long time, admiring the arches and spires and groined vaulting, when suddenly the angle of the lighting had changed and the appearance of the structure had been transfigured. It was an odd feeling—oddly exhilarating—to see the familiar from a new perspective. He rose. "I'd like to thank you again for your time. You've been a considerable help."

"Not at all," she demurred, shaking his hand.

He turned to go and paused. "Oh. One last thing, if you will. The word in the heading. Cliological. Do you know what it means?"

"Cliological?" she frowned. "No, I never— Oh!" She laughed. "What is it?"

"Clio was the Greek muse of history. Apparently, the writer, or someone, coined the term as a parallel to biology or sociology, meaning 'a science of history.' Perhaps the writer was a science student taking a history course."

Dennis thought about his meeting with Llewellyn as he drove homeward down University Avenue. A scientific approach to history. How could that be, when one considered how great was the role of random chance? Well, the fact that some college student a hundred years ago had thought it was possible didn't mean that it was. College students were notorious for their flights of fancy. Why, when he had been in school, he had . . . Well, that was of no consequence now. He had switched from linguistics to architecture. [Now there was a switch for you!] And his artificial 'language' was mummifying in a drawer somewhere.

What was it that had been written at the bottom of the list? *Try orthogonal factor analysis?* The list was in his pocket, but he did not remove his hand from the wheel to take it out. Try orthogonal factor analysis. Yes, that was it. Now that sounded terribly scientific. Then he remembered that the list was written in two different hands. Two different 'cliologists?' And one hand had been much older than the other, he recalled now. He wondered what that might mean.

# III

After three years on the Net Watch, Red Malone still did not know the name of his teammate. They had played countless games of rummy and pinochle. They had swapped lies about the women they had known (and a few that they hadn't). They had monitored intelligence during scores of quiet crises, the kind that *never* appeared in the newspapers. And still Red did not even know which of the Agencies 'Charlie' worked for.

And 'Charlie,' of course, knew as little about Red.

It made sense, in a way. Redundancy. They had learned that from the reliability engineers. Two agents on watch at all times, to guard against moles, or rogues running unauthorized ops. The chances that *both* agents would be turned or doubled were far less than for one. And in an age when wars were fought with information—or sometimes disinformation—the security of "holes" like the Net Watch was as critical as that of the missiles holes.

So each of them was there to keep the other honest; and that made it necessary that they be strangers to one another.

Red picked up the clipboard and scanned the log entries for the last two shifts. Most of them were in codes he was not supposed to know. Other Watchkeepers from other Agencies. Idly, he wondered which codes Charlie could read. Everyone had his own code. Red amused himself by trying to crack them. It was better than crosswords. He whistled *East Virginia*, off-key, as he read.

Sometimes he wondered what would happen if he were to insert some sort of disinformation program into the Net. Not that he could write such a program; but he knew people who could. It was his business to know People Who Could. It would be great fun, a real knee-slapper; and remembering the prank would help him while away the hours in Leavenworth.

He sighed. Rules took the fun out of life. He wondered sometimes about those who made the rules their life. Then he remembered what his own job was and he laughed aloud, earning him an odd stare from 'Charlie.'

The air conditioner hissed a cold draft through the gray-painted room. Red always wore his suit-jacket in the Watch-room. He couldn't figure how his companion could sit there in his shirtsleeves. He shook his head and put down the clipboard. Why couldn't they at least team him with someone who had the same metabolism? He reached into his jacket pocket and pulled out a well-worn deck of cards. He hated Saturday duty. He cut the deck and riffed the two halves together.

The machines hummed in the background. Lights winked on and off. Disc readers buzzed intermittently. Relays clicked. It reminded him of that time he had gone camping. (When had that been? Two years ago. He and— *That* long ago?) The nighttime forest had made noises just like the Watch-room, except that it had been insects and animals making them. When he had mentioned the similarity to the other campers, they had looked at him strangely.

Now here he sat. Camped out in the electronic jungle. Listening for the sounds of predators. He riffed the deck of cards once more; tapped them on the console desk.

An alarm rang: a soft, insistent beep, and a winking red light on the console. He sat upright, suddenly alert, the cards forgotten. Charlie reached out and hit the cut-off. "What is it?" he asked.

Red played the keyboard and checked the intelligence he called up on his screen. "It's a tripwire. Someone's accessing files that an Agent wanted flagged."

"Yeah? Well, they leave the bait out there and wait to see who nibbles. Who do we notify?"

Red checked his list. "Umm. Someone named Foxhound."

"Must be a code name."

"No shit?"

Charlie gave him a sour look. "Don't give me any grief. What's the flag and where'd it go up?" He was already busy entering the notification code. The computer would compare his entry to Red's to see if they matched. Not so much to guard against deliberate disinformation as against inadvertent keystroke errors.

Red scrolled the information on his screen. He read off a Net Access Code and Charlie read it back to him. Active and passive checking, both ways.

"The watchword is . . . uh, 'Quinn,' " he told Charlie. *Quinn?* he thought. *Well, well.* "Says here that this is the third time this week it's been tripped by the same User. Well, third time's the charm, right? That's what triggers the signal. Sounds to me like someone running an op."

"Never mind that crap. What were the CPU codes? All three of them."

Red called off the numbers and Charlie confirmed them.

"That last one is where the User is now?" Charlie asked.

"Yeah. Know where it's located?"

"No, and I don't care. Neither should you."

"Yeah. Well, the eighteen-prefix means it's a self-contained system tapping into the DataNet, but not a regular part of it. Then the next nine digits are a cipher for the ZIP. The rest of it identifies the port on the System where the modem hooked in. Not too hard to de-crypt once you know what it is."

"Listen to Sherlock Holmes. Look, all we know is the code number for the port. Foxhound or his Handler will have the address where it's located. That's their worry. An Agent wants to flag a file, he's got his reasons. All we do is watch the Net and see if anyone accesses it. We don't know who the Agent is. We don't know who the User is. We don't know where the terminal is located or what the watchword means."

Red chuckled. "Is there anything we *do* know?"

Charlie swiveled his chair around. "Yeah. I know how to play rummy and you don't. You've shuffled those cards enough to wear the pips off 'em. So, deal."

Red flicked the cards with the ease of long practice. "This has been the most excitement we've had in two weeks. My heart is pounding."

Charlie grunted. "Most folks go on the Net, they don't nose around where they shouldn't. You decided yet what you're doing on your vacation?"

Red set the remainder of the deck down between them. He turned over the top card. It was a queen. "Yeah. Camping."

Charlie picked off the deck. "Camping? Thought you hated that stuff."

"I do. That's why I'm going. Self-discipline. It builds character to do something you hate."

Charlie looked baffled for a moment. Then he shook his head sadly. "Next thing, you'll be roasting rats for lunch. You're weird. I ever tell you that? You're weird."

Sarah was in the Western History Room at the Denver Public Library when her beeper went off. It was Monday and she had spent the entire day at the public terminals there. Her eyes felt dry and dusty from staring at computer records. Brady Quinn was an elusive man. She had hunted for him through one file after another without success. After selling the Emerson Street house, he had not bought another one, at least not in Denver. In fact, except for a second news article that mentioned him only incidentally, Quinn had left no trace at all in the local records between the sale of his house and his death, sixteen years later.

Well, that was a lot easier to do a hundred years ago than it was today. Back then a citizen could live her entire life without more than a handful of encounters with the government. Today you couldn't sneeze without leaving a trace in a file somewhere.

However, the second news article had contained a clue that she had followed into the National Archives, where she finally hit pay dirt. She was just reading the printout when her beeper went off. The other patrons turned and looked at her. She smiled an apology and went downstairs to the public phones and called her service.

The message was from Dennis. If she was downtown and in the mood, give him a buzz and they'd have dinner together. His treat, at the Augusta.

She never could resist a free meal. She called him at his office and confirmed the time. Then she climbed the stairs back to the third floor to pack her things away.

She stopped in the doorway. There was a man standing by her briefcase, reading her notes. For a moment she was too astonished to do anything but gape. Of all the nerve! "Can I help you?" she asked sarcastically.

The man turned and looked at her. He was tall and rangy, with a thin, prominent nose. There was no embarrassment or surprise in his face. His eyes were dead, without expression. He looked at her with no more interest than if he had looked at the furniture.

29

"No," he said. "You can't." Only his mouth spoke. The rest of his face remained uninvolved. There was an air of menace about him; an aura of barely restrained violence. It was in his bearing, in the lines of his face. Sarah caught her lower lip between her teeth. Was he a crazy off the street? Perhaps she should call the police.

"I'll thank you to leave my things alone," she said, wondering if he would become violent.

The man smiled. It was a cold smile, a brief contortion of the lips into an unwonted configuration. Then it was gone. That smile chilled her more than any threat could have done. No, he wasn't crazy. Not exactly.

"I will," he said, "but you won't."

Then he left. He walked straight toward the door and Sarah hastily stepped aside, lest he come too close. He paid her no attention as he walked by.

Sarah looked after his departing figure until he had vanished down the stairwell. Then she let out a shaky breath.

"He gone?"

Sarah turned, startled. One of the other library patrons stood there. A small, nut-brown woman of indeterminate age, with a wind-weathered face, and wearing a denim jacket.

"I tol' him to leave yore things alone," she said, "but he just looked at me like I was some kinda bug."

Sarah shook her head. "Who was he?"

A shrug. "Ain't never seen him in here before. Acts like a New Yorker, yuh ask me."

"A weirdo."

"Mebbe. Young lady, it mebbe ain't none of my business, but . . . The way he looked at yuh?"

It chilled her just to remember. "What about it?"

"I seen that look once before. Riding fences on my spread out to Buffalo Creek. Saw me a diamondback a-staring down a bird. A lark bunting, it was. That snake stared at that bird the same way that there fella looked at you."

Sarah swallowed. The ranch woman's description was very apt, she thought. The man had been very much like a snake. "Thanks for your concern," she said. "I'm meeting a friend for dinner; so, if you don't mind, I'll . . ." She walked to the table where her briefcase lay and gathered up her papers. She fumbled them inside and snapped it shut. When she was leaving, though, the ranch woman stopped her again.

"Missy? That snake. Ah didn't stop it. It's nature's way and even snakes have to eat. But, the bird . . ."

"What about the bird?"

"That poor bird just a-stood there and waited. Never even tried to git away. Just a-stood there and let that snake strike it." She smiled at her. "Yuh be careful, Missy, y'hear?"

Sarah thought about the man in the library as she rode the electric bus down the 16th Street Mall. She was still thinking about him when she entered the restaurant. She saw Dennis wave to her from across the room.

Dennis stood while the waiter seated her, then he resumed his own seat. "A Bristol cream sherry for Ms. Beaumont," Dennis told the waiter, "and Jameson's, neat, for myself." The waiter left and Dennis turned to her. "What's wrong? You look upset."

"Oh, nothing. Just a little run-in at the library." She told him about the stranger and he shook his head sympathetically.

"The West is getting more and more like the East," he said. "Here, this will take your mind off it." He reached down and brought up his sketch pad. "I thought you might like to look at a few concepts I've come up with for Brady Quinn Place."

Brady Quinn Place. She had almost forgotten why she had been researching Quinn's life at all. *I should have been working on the project,* she thought. *I've spent a whole week doing nothing but research.* It made her feel guilty, having fun like that while Dennis was working his heart out.

She took the sketch pad from him and looked at the drawings he had made. They were good. Dennis' ideas usually were. She especially liked the roof-to-ground atrium on the south wall, with the mezzanine balcony on the second floor.

They batted ideas back and forth for awhile over their drinks. Then, after the waiter had taken their dinner orders, the talk turned to Brady Quinn. "I finally discovered who he was," she told him. "It wasn't easy, but I finally tracked him down. He was a statistician in the Interior Department for a number of years before and during the Civil War."

"Didn't you tell me yesterday that you couldn't find a trace of him anywhere?"

"That's right. Until I came across a news story—not the one we found in the house, but another one. It gave me the clue I needed; and made me think that . . . Well, you tell me. I'll read it to you." She unsnapped her briefcase and

31

pulled out a photocopy. "This was in the *Rocky Mountain News* for Monday, July 18th, 1881."

> *A daring train robbery by masked men occurred on Saturday, July 16th, on the Chicago, Rock Island, and Pacific Rail Road, at Winston, near Cameron, Mo. The robbers were six in number and were supposed to be under the leadership of Jesse James. The men boarded the train at Cameron. At Winston, when the train stopped, they stood up in the aisle of a car with drawn revolvers. One of the bandits advanced with a revolver in each hand toward Wm. Westfall, the conductor, and ordered him to hold up his hands. The conductor was slow in complying and was shot through the heart. One of the other bandits shot through the head John McCullogh, a stonecutter of Wilton Junction, who turned in his seat. The same man then shot and wounded Brady Quinn, retired, a government clerk during the late War. The bandits then went to the express car and overpowered the Express Messenger, who was intimidated into opening the safe, from which $3,000 was taken."*

She handed him the facsimile printout. "There's more. The James Gang went after the engineer, too; but he set the brake and crawled out into the pilot and hid."

"Ah, the wild and woolly west," said Dennis. He looked at the photocopy. "Some folks have tried to make the James brothers into heroes. Sure doesn't sound too heroic."

"We only make people into legends after they're dead, so they won't embarrass the legend-makers." She pointed. "Well, the story said that Quinn was a government clerk during the war. I figured that must have been the Civil War, so I hacked into the DataNet from the Library and accessed the National Archives in Washington."

Dennis sipped his drink. "Isn't that illegal?" he asked. He placed his glass down precisely where he had picked it up, exactly matching the wet ring on the table cloth.

"Of course it's illegal," Sarah said, "it wouldn't be any fun if it weren't. Those files are tough to get into and you *can't* alter or erase them." She paused for a moment while the waiter set their food down. London broil for Dennis; lobster for her. "Anyway, to make a long story short, I found Brady Quinn's employment file. Interior Secretary McClelland appointed him to the post of statistician for special investigations in 1853, on the recommendation of one Isaac Shelton of Massachussetts. His appointment was renewed by each succeeding Secretary down to Usher. After the war, he retired from public life, first to his native Muncie, then to Denver. The Pension Office lost track of him in 1876. In fact, I couldn't find *any* trace of him at all between 1876 and 1881, when he was shot on the train in Missouri."

He arched his eyebrows. "Yes, and then shot again in, what? 1892? Shot *twice* as an innocent bystander? In two separate incidents?"

"Right. That was my own reaction. Someone wanted to kill him, but wanted it to look like an accident. Our Mister Quinn is becoming quite the mystery man. He evidently went into hiding in 1876. From whom? Why?"

"A statistician in the Interior Department," mused Dennis. "I can see where a man in such a position would make a lot of enemies." He grinned at his own joke. "Well, it was more than a hundred years ago. Whatever it was all about is long over."

Sarah snorted. "Of course it is, but we want to use his name as a theme, not just a label. We can't call the project Brady Quinn Place without telling people why. It might as well be John Doe Place. No, whatever the mystery is surrounding him, *that* is what we want to hang the theme on."

"I know it," he said. She watched him cut his steak into careful slices, spear one on his fork and transfer the fork to his right hand. She had long ago taught herself to use knife and fork the European way and had tried in vain to convince Dennis that his way was inefficient. "If I could discover why his death was included on that list of historical events," he said thoughtfully, "that might give us a lead. It seems so out of place." He looked at her. "There *was* a common theme that ran through most of the items, you know. They were all horseshoe nails."

"Horseshoe nails? What do you mean?"

He smiled. "A private joke. I was talking to a professor at DU last Thursday. About the list that we found. That was her analysis. She said that these were instances when the actions of a relative handful of people had disproportionate consequences: changed the course of history, sometimes obvi-

33

ously, sometimes subtly." Briefly, he summarized his meeting with Professor Llewellyn.

She nodded as she saw his point. Secretly, she was amused to discover that Dennis, too, had been spending his time on "extracurricular" activities. She didn't feel so embarrassed at wasting a whole week now. "I suppose she knows what she's talking about. It's her specialty, after all. But she credits this Taylor fellow with creating communism? That seems a pretty big accomplishment for an industrial engineer."

"No, no. She only said that Taylor, Ford, Lenin and the others were part of a trend toward the Managed Society, with decision-making authority vested in a professional, managerial class. You know what I'm talking about. Just follow the procedures. Anything not compulsory is forbidden." He looked at his steak, frowned, and cut it vigorously. "Bureaucrats," he said, bitterly, and looked back at Sarah. "Did I ever tell you? When I was working as a civil engineer, before I took my architecture degree, my company was swallowed by a conglomerate. One of those hostile takeovers they used to have. The new owners sent in new managers to run things; their own people, not a single one of whom was an engineer."

"Let me guess. They were MBA's with financial backgrounds."

"Bingo. My own *supervisor* didn't know the first thing about strength of materials or Proctor density. You know what he said? 'A professional manager can manage any business or function, wherever good management is needed.' Straight out of the textbooks."

Sarah grunted. "It reminds me of that education prof you told me about. The one who said that teachers only need to know teaching, not the subject matter. So, what happened?"

"What do you think? Efficiency went down; waste went up. There was 100 percent personnel turnover within the year. The company went from a money-maker to a loser. Gutted. Just so a corporate staff miles away could hold all the reins of power in their hot little fast-track hands." He shook his head. "Funny. I guess I'm still bitter about it, even after all these years."

"If centralization worked that well, Russia would export wheat."

He chuckled. "Well put. Come to think of it, Professor Llewellyn did say Russia was run like a corporation. But, tell me. Do you notice the similarities between teachers and managers? They've both dropped their adjectives."

"Come again?"

"When teachers and managers became *professional* teachers and *professional* managers, they forgot how to be *history* teachers or *engineering* managers."

"Judging by the results," Sarah laughed, "someone wants us to be ignorant and unproductive. Maybe Thomas Dewey and Frederick Taylor were part of a conspiracy."

"There are two problems with the list, though, that I still don't have straight in my mind. There are plenty of 'turning points of history' that are not on the list."

"And Brady Quinn is."

"Right. That's the big puzzle. The one that concerns us and our project. What sort of 'image' will Brady Quinn Place have? How did his death—or the deaths and disappearances of other unknowns—change the course of history?"

"Little events with big consequences," she mused, dipping her lobster into the melted butter.

"Well, not all of them," admitted Dennis. "Professor Llewellyn thought that one or two failed to come off. They could have had big consequences, but something else unexpected happened that derailed them. 'Hammered back the nail,' she said."

An idea struck her and she pointed her fork at Dennis. "Wait a minute! Nothing important happened because Quinn was killed."

He looked puzzled. "Well, yes. That is the problem."

"No, that's the *answer!* Nothing important happened *because* Quinn was killed. Sure, that must be it. Take . . . oh, take the *Challenger* disaster of a while back. It was pretty straightforward to trace the sequence of cause and effect. All the way back to your friends, the 'professional managers.' Remember how that one vice president told his engineering manager to 'take off your engineering hat and put on your management hat!'? But suppose those rocket engineers had been listened to. You know, the ones who warned against launching. Suppose the launch was postponed. Everyone gripes about it. Later, when the weather is warmer, they launch successfully. Because the warning is heeded, no disaster happens. A small action with a big consequence."

"Okay. But that creates a different sort of problem."

"What's that?"

"*How did those events get on the list?* It's easy to say that because Brady Quinn was killed, or because Ambrose Bierce

35

disappeared, something important failed to materialize; but how did anyone know it? How do you trace the fault-tree of something that never occurred? Have you ever tried to prove something from the absence of negative evidence?"

"Professional managers do it all the time. That's why they launched *Challenger*, remember? The engineers couldn't *prove* that anything bad would happen." She dabbed at her lips with her napkin and looked at her watch. "Look, Dennis, I hate to eat and run, but I've got a property I want to look at down by Union Station."

"Union Station?" He blinked at the sudden change of subject.

"Yes. I've had it in the back of my head to buy into that area. There's been a lot of renewed talk about building a convention center down there, so I thought, why not? I'm stopping there on the way home to look it over."

Dennis rolled his eyes. "Another project. Oh, good. I don't have enough work as it is."

"Don't worry," she said, laughing. Dennis loved to gripe; but he thrived on work. "I won't be developing it right away. Maybe nothing will come of the convention center talk; but, just in case, I want to have a key property in my purse." She chuckled again. "In an odd way, though, it is a sort of spin-off of this Brady Quinn business."

"How so?"

"The building I'm going to look at was once owned by Randall Carson, the same fellow who bought Quinn's Emerson Street house. I was searching through some old real estate records, looking for Quinn. Handwritten on index cards, if you can imagine. I guess when the county microfiched their records back in the 1980s they didn't think these were worth doing. Anyway, I was looking for Quinn's name, but you know how that goes. Carson's name just caught my eye."

# IV

The building sat near the Union Pacific tracks. It was under the viaduct, on a small side street off of Fifteenth. Sarah parked by the Post Office Annex and walked from there. The street under the viaduct was already dark, even though the sun hadn't set yet. Fragments of sunlight found their way between the old warehouses and created a spiderweb of shadows out of the abutments and steel girders. It reminded Sarah of the streets under the El in Chicago. The Fifteenth Street traffic ran across the viaduct overhead, and Sarah could hear the hum of the tires above her. The street below was deserted.

Her heels clicked on the pavement and the roadbed overhead echoed the sound back to her half a beat behind. Click(ick); Click(ick). Then a strange double echo: Click(ick)(tap). She stopped and turned. It was an automatic reaction and it was a moment before she realized she had done so.

*There's someone there*, she thought, peering into the shadows. A bum. A wino. The railyard was nearby. This was a good place to hop a freight.

She turned and resumed walking. The images of a thousand late night movies flashed through her mind. The lone woman walking the deserted street at night. Don't go. Everyone knows the alien/monster/mad slasher is waiting, but the stupid woman goes anyway. The audience is always so much wiser.

There probably wasn't anyone there. It was just a freak echo caused by the viaduct. No aliens/monsters/mad slashers.

Of course, isn't that what they always say in the movies?

37

The next time she heard the double echo it took an act of will not to bolt and run.

The trend nowadays was to preserve the building's shell, regardless of what was done with the interior. Historical preservation. Conserving the unique character of the neighborhood or city. Sarah stood on the street outside and looked over the building's exterior. Solid, red brick construction. There were three rows of windows, the upper two dark. Widener's Restoration Handicrafts, she recalled from the real estate records, occupied only the first floor of the old building. The other two were unused. She nodded in satisfaction. This one might do.

She entered the building and looked for the second-shift foreman. Widener's was one of several small employers of the handicapped. The company collected used or secondhand items and refurbished them for resale to the poor. She paused for a few moments in the broad, open first-floor room and watched while the men and women painted, soldered, sewed, and wired. It wasn't like an assembly line: no two items were alike. It took skill to diagnose and repair the faults of each one.

She found the foreman in his office. Binders and catalogs sat strewn every which way on shelves and atop file cabinets. Papers littered the desk. Dirt and trash had accumulated in the corners of the room. Paul Abbot, the foreman, sat amidst this splendor, leaning back in an old wooden desk chair, his feet propped up on the desk, reading a magazine. Sarah wrinkled her nose.

"Mr. Abbot? I'm Sarah Beaumont. We spoke on the phone yesterday. About seeing the building?"

Abbot looked at her, waited a beat, then put both his feet on the floor. He laid the magazine face up on the desk, so Sarah could see that it contained pictures of naked women. The foreman looked from the magazine to her. He smiled, but said nothing, letting his gaze wander over her appraisingly. He grunted his approval and shifted the toothpick in his mouth from the left side to the right. He stuck his hands behind his neck and linked his fingers together. "Yeah?"

"Yes," she answered. "I'm thinking of buying this building . . ."

"What, ya gonna throw me an' my feebs out on the street?"

Almost, Sarah was amazed that this creature possessed the gift of speech. "Nothing like that, I assure you. I simply wish to inspect the premises."

"Inspect the premises," he mimicked. "Jeez, lady. Why'n'cha just rub my nose in it? Ya wanna look the joint over, be my guest; but ya don't hafta go put on airs." He reached out a foot, hooked a drawer handle and jerked it open. "There's a flashlight in there. You'll need it upstairs. We don't use them floors, so there's no lights up there."

Obviously, he wasn't going to hand her the light, so she bent over and fished it out herself. It was a large industrial size flashlight. "Thanks," she said sarcastically.

"No, thank *you*," he replied, grinning.

She realized that, in reaching into the desk drawer, she had given him a perfect view down the front of her blouse. Her face burned and she took a deep breath to calm herself. What was it her mother had always said? Some people were no better than they should be. She had never known what that meant before.

"Which way are the stairs?" she asked.

He roused himself from his chair. "C'mon, I'll take you." Stepping past her, he held the door open for her. Surprised at this act of chivalry, she walked through, but as she did so, he brushed his hand up against her rear.

She spun and struck out with the flashlight. It caught him just above the elbow. He howled. "Hey! Watchit, lady, willya!"

"No, sucker. *You* watch it. You try that shit on me again and you're dead meat. You got that?"

"Look. I make a pass, sure. I ask do you wanna do it. You know how it is. Sometimes they say yes. What the hell." He rubbed his elbow.

When they reached the stairway to the second floor, she recalled what Abbot had said about the lighting. The last thing she wanted was to wander around upstairs in the dark with this lecher. She stopped and wagged the flashlight at him. "I think I'd rather look around myself."

He shrugged. "Suit yourself."

She climbed the stairs. The air in the stairwell was hot and stale. The runners creaked beneath her feet. At the top, she flicked her light on. The beam was dim but wide. She played it in a circle around the room and saw old manufacturing machinery, sitting in dust-shrouded ranks. The tang of old metal filled the air.

She approached the nearest machine and looked more closely. A metal stamping press, she decided. The drivebelt on the flywheel was long rotted; the metal, pitted with rust. A patina

39

covered the brass fittings. She rubbed the brass nameplate with her thumb. Bliss Company, it read, followed by a parade of patent numbers and dates.

She toured the room, checking the flooring and rafters. In one corner, in what had once been a gauging laboratory, she found a musty old bed. It was nothing but a shapeless mattress thrown on the floor. Nearby was a stack of girlie magazines.

She returned to the stairwell and climbed to the top floor. The room was much like the one below, except that the machines were smaller and more varied and, if that were possible, in even worse shape. The smell of rust and of ancient machine oil was heavy. The flashlight cast a circle of light, throwing the nearest machine into sharp relief, a patchwork of lights and shadows, projections and cavities, like some crazed lunar landscape. Beyond it, other machines crouched in the dark. She wondered why the equipment had been abandoned. It was surely worth money, even today.

On the far side of the room were the lavatories. She stepped in and looked around. Ancient and corroded fixtures greeted her, lined up like the statues on Easter Island. Rusty water seeping from a broken pipe had formed a puddle from which a stalagmite was growing. She had turned and was leaving when an odd shadow in the corner caught her eye.

She walked closer and found a blind, dog-leg turn with a broken doorway. A shower stall? A closet? There were three boards nailed across it. An old sign with faded lettering was stapled to the boards. Stairway condemned.

A stairway? In the lavatory? A back stairwell, maybe. She aimed her flashlight through the door. Sure enough, there was a flight of stairs. But they led up, not down. Funny. From the outside, she had seen only three rows of windows; and the main staircase had ended on this floor.

Well, she thought, nothing ventured . . . The stairs looked to be in no worse shape than the others she had already climbed. There were no footprints in the thick dust that carpeted them. *To boldly go where no one has gone before* . . . She pulled the boards away and stepped through the broken doorway.

She was wrong about the steps. They were in worse shape. The sixth one gave way when she put her weight on it. Her right foot plunged through the rotted board and the splintered edges raked her ankle and calf. Pain shot up her leg.

She grabbed the bannister to keep from falling, but it came loose from the wall. The flashlight dropped from her hand and rolled down two steps, leaving her in semi-darkness.

"Damn!" She tried to pull her leg out, but it was caught. Like in one of those "Chinese handcuffs" she had played with as a child. She winced in pain and a high-pitched sound escaped her throat. *Calm down*, she told herself.

She forced herself to listen. The silence was palpable. It covered her like a cloak. Within the silence were tiny sounds that served only to accentuate it. The old building murmured and whispered. Drafts sighed and timbers creaked. She could barely discern the muted rumble of the viaduct outside. Somewhere nearby water dripped slowly into a pool. It was a lonely, solitary echo. A steady, measured cadence. Plunk . . . Plunk . . . She felt as if she were deep inside some cave.

She thought briefly of calling for help. But Abbot was two floors down and unlikely to hear. And even if he did come, he would use the opportunity to grope her while freeing her leg. Besides, she had never needed help. She could handle her own rescue.

Bending over, she probed the hole with her fingers. Splinters pointed straight downward like miniature spears. If she were to pull her leg straight up, they would impale her ankle. She reached in and broke off the pieces, slowly enlarging the hole. After a few minutes of patient work, it was big enough to pull her foot out.

She turned and sat down on the step, rubbing her ankle. It was scraped raw. She supposed her nylons were ruined. She stood tentatively and tested the ankle. It hurt, but she could stand on it. She gritted her teeth and retrieved the flashlight. It was flickering. She smacked it sharply with the flat of her hand and the light brightened.

She aimed the light down the stairs, then up the stairs. Then she grimly resumed climbing, testing each step carefully before putting her weight on it.

Lacking windows, the fourth floor was pitch black, without even the promise of light. She played the beam around the room, picking out nondescript wooden furniture. A row of oaken filing cabinets lined one wall; five ancient roll-top desks, another. In the center of the room were heavy oaken tables with ungainly-looking machines atop them. Everything was covered with a thick layer of dust. There were rodent tracks in the dust, but no footprints.

An eerie feeling stole over her as she made a circuit of the room. Each piece of furniture stood out briefly in the circle of her flashlight, like an actor taking his moment on the stage. She was the first human being to enter this room in who knew how many years. From the looks of things, this floor had been abandoned long before the others. What sort of ghosts haunted manufacturing plants?

She tried to open one of the roll tops, but it was stuck tight. She grunted and pulled and it gave just a fraction of an inch. When it did so, however, a feeling of unaccountable dread stole over her and she backed away and caught her breath. She played the light over the crack she had opened up; but she knew that under no circumstances would she try to look through it.

The darkness is getting to me, she thought. *How long before I start imagining that someone else is up here with me?*

She walked to the center tables and inspected the machines there more closely. They were full of cams and cogs, ratchet wheels and rods. Notched bars jutted out at odd angles. Each machine had a keyboard with lever keys, like an old-style manual typewriter. There were ten rows and ten columns of keys in the center of the board. She rubbed away the dust and saw that each column was numbered from zero to nine. She reached out curiously to depress a key, but it was frozen in place.

They were obviously primitive calculating machines. As a computer buff, she had always been fascinated by such machines. She remembered the exhibit of early key-set and key-driven mechanisms she had seen so long ago in Chicago. Dorr's *Comptometer* had come out in 1885; the Burroughs in 1911. The styling and ornamentation of these machines seemed even older. The cams looked as if they had been fashioned individually, by hand. She looked for a nameplate, but she couldn't find one. *Maybe I can check the patent office*.

She brushed off the other keys and recognized the standard arithmetic symbols. There were also keys marked with the < and > signs. And other symbols that were totally strange to her. What did ¬ mean? Or ∉? Or ⊗ and ⊕?

She gave it up and turned her attention to the filing cabinets. Most of the drawers she pulled out were empty, but a few contained loose pages filled with mathematical computations. Her light picked out the title on one torn fragment. *On the Eventual Bifurcation of Highly-connected Dynamic Sets.* Great stuff.

One drawer was locked. She yanked on it hard and heard the metal pins give way, the wood splinter. Another yank and the pins bent. The drawer slid out with a protest of shot bearings and warped and swollen wood. Inside were two thick file folders. She tried to read the tabs in the dim light. The ink was old, faded; the handwriting, ornate.

*Index.* She pulled the smaller folder out of the drawer and took it to the table. Holding the flashlight in her left hand, she opened it and tried to read some of the titles in the dim light. *An Optimal Policy for Commodity Purchases Using Integral Simplices. A Branch-and-Bound Approach to the Job Shop Problem. On the n-Space Graph Structure of Iroquois Matrilinearity. Applications of Green's Function to Queues in Semi-Closed Networks. The Dynamical Equations of Ideon Contagion.*

What was all this? Mathematical research? No, not entirely. Some of the titles, she saw, dealt with anthropology or economics. Applied mathematics, then. A peculiar mix; and what an odd place for it! The dates written next to the titles of the papers ran through 1892. The earliest one was 1833: a real wowser entitled *Some Stochastic Processes with Absorbing Barriers* by someone named Jedediah Crawford. Her light wandered up and down the filing cabinets. Sixty years of mathematical papers? A college hidden on the fourth floor of a manufacturing plant?

She pulled out the other folder from the drawer and peered at it in the dim light. *Maintenance and Repair of Babbage Analytical Engines.*

That stopped her. Charles Babbage had been Lucasian Professor of Mathematics at Cambridge University from 1828 to 1839. Any real computer buff knew about him. He had once described a new kind of calculating machine, far advanced over the simple add/subtract models then available. His Analytical Engine would supposedly carry out an entire sequence of operations without a human being keying each one in. It would also have the capability of running either of two alternative sequences, depending on the results of previous calculations.

The storage was to be purely mechanical, using wheels and punched cards, but Babbage had in effect described the digital computer. Unfortunately, the actual construction of such "engines" had been beyond the state of mid-nineteenth century engineering art. None had ever been built.

A ball of ice formed in the pit of her stomach. She turned and stared at the darkness where the machines sat. None had ever been built.

Humming the old *Twilight Zone* theme song, she carried the folder to the table and flipped through it. There was page after page of mechanical drawings, with detailed specifications and callouts. A Rube Goldberg nightmare. Definitely the machine on the table, though. More pages, of handwritten instructions in ornate Spencerian script.

It was too much to look at here in the darkness. She decided to take it home with her. Just as she was closing the folder, a note caught her eye. It was written sideways in the margin of one of the drawings.

*"Discussed possible electrification with Thomas while in Menlo Park. Not presently feasible. B. Quinn. 21 July 1881."*

She arched her eyebrows in surprise. B. Quinn. Brady Quinn? Well, well. Had Carson been more than the buyer of Quinn's house? Had he and Quinn been business associates?

And associates of Edison, as well. At least, she knew of no other Thomas in Menlo Park in 1881 with whom one would discuss "electrification."

*Now we're onto something*, she thought. "Brady Quinn Place" was sounding better and better. Quinn was a local figure. He knew Edison on a first-name basis. And he was apparently involved somehow with the world's first computers.

This could be *big!* The dust on the floor and tables was thick. No one had been in the room in years. In decades. *No one else knows about these machines*, she thought. And when I buy the building, the machines will be mine, too.

Her flashlight dimmed and she smacked it again. This time it did not brighten. She didn't like the idea of finding her way back down in the dark. She closed the folder and tucked it and the Index folder under her arm. *I'll come back later, with better light.* At the door, she paused for one last look.

She played the light over the black, shadowy mechanisms. The world's first computers. Yet, here they sat, long abandoned and forgotten. Odd. With an invention like that, they should have made history.

When she returned the flashlight, Abbot noticed the folders under her arm and smirked. "Lootin', hunh? Why'n'cha take some of the copper and brass off'n the stampin' presses? They sell for a good piece of cash down t' the scrapyard."

Sarah reminded herself that Abbot had never been up the hidden stairwell. She hoped he would not wonder where she had found file cabinets. Best if he worried about something else. "Does Widener know you're stealing his property and selling it?"

"Widener? Hell, he ain't never set foot in the place. Me and Babs, that's the daytime forelady, we got a good thing goin'. None of the feebs can climb stairs, so they don't even know what a bonanza is up there. An' you ain't gonna tell, lady, 'cause then I'll say how you walked off with some stuff yourself." He leaned back in his chair and folded his arms smugly.

She smiled tolerantly. "I'm afraid you've got me."

"Damned right." He nodded vigorously. "You ain't no better'n Babs and me. I—" His eyes dropped to her ankle. "Hey! You hurt yourself up there? You okay?"

"Well . . ."

"Cause I tolja it was dangerous up there. I offered to come wit' ya but you insisted to go alone. You ain't gonna sue or nothin, are you?" The toothpick in his mouth danced nervously from side to side.

For one brief moment she had thought his concern had been for her. In a way, it was nice to know his self-absorption was universal. A burst of altruism would have been a flaw in his otherwise seamless character.

"No," she told him. "I ain't gonna sue or nothin'." The last thing she wanted was a troop of lawyers and claims investigators wandering around upstairs.

The sun had set by the time she left the building and the street outside was black. The streetlamps created oases of light at the corner with Wynkoop. Otherwise, it was pitch dark, not unlike the room on the fourth floor. Suddenly, remembering her dread in the dark room, she wished she had parked closer.

She walked briskly toward the corner and the Post Office Annex. Once again she thought she could hear ghost-footsteps behind her.

It's only a trick of acoustics, she told herself. No one's following me. Years of rational training insisted on that; but millenia of instinct won. The bogey men have always lived in the dark. She quickened her footsteps.

Just as she turned the corner, one of the big loading dock doors on the Postal Annex rolled up with a metalic clangor that made her jump. A gang of mailhandlers began moving large postal bags onto the dock. They were laughing and talking. The footsteps behind her (if there really had been footsteps, she scolded herself) stopped.

She looked at the men and recognized their supervisor. She had met him at a party once, during her newspapering days. He was the brother of one of the other reporters. He had taken her for a ride on his Suzuki. What was his name?

"Hey, Pat!" she called, suddenly remembering . "Still riding that bike of yours?"

Pat turned, surprised. "Who? . . . Oh." He snapped his fingers. "Wait, don't tell me. Sue . . . No. Sarah, right? Yeah, Kevin told me how you quit the paper. Went into real estate or something. Wheeling and dealing, he said."

"That's right. I was inspecting a property around the corner." She looked back into the darkness of Fifteenth Street. "I may be wrong, but I think someone was following me. Could you hang around and watch until I get into my car? I'm parked right over there."

"Sure. No problem."

It was irrational, she knew; but she felt relieved. Someone who knew her knew she had been there. The other men were waiting, not really interested; but they would remember, too.

The first thing she did when she got in the car was to lock the doors. Then she took a deep breath. *And what if he's already in the car?* She jerked around and looked in the back seat.

It was empty. Sarah let out her breath. She felt monumentally foolish. She relaxed in the seat and laid her head on the backrest, eyes closed. *I'm spooked,* she thought. The desolate air on the top floor of the Widener Building. The emptiness of the street under the viaduct. Too many late night movies. There probably hadn't been anyone following her at all.

She sat up, started the car, and put it in gear. Unbidden, the thought arose. *I wonder if it was the man from the library.*

It was a troubled sleep she slept that night, haunted by darkness and footsteps and tall, cadaverous strangers. In it, she opened the desk in the Widener building and saw the man from the library. He smiled at her and hissed and his

46

tongue slipped in and out of his mouth, a black, ropelike
tongue with a fork at its tip.

She gasped and awoke to find her nightgown damp and
smelling of fear. Her pulse tripped in her ears, and her eyes
darted around the dark bedroom, seeing shapes in the shadows. *You're being silly*, she told herself; but she twisted and
turned the bedside lamp on to low. Then she settled back on
the pillows and allowed sleep a reluctant return.

# V

In the morning, as she drank her breakfast of black coffee
and thought about what to do next, her night fears faded. The
coffee was strong and hot and by the time she had finished
half a cup she had half convinced herself that the man in the
library was simply a nosy and offensive person. And, of course,
no one had been following her under the viaduct.

She laid the two folders she had taken from the file cabinet
on the kitchen table and skimmed through them while the
caffeine did its work. She spared only a glance or two for the
Index, with its incomprehensible titles; noting only some of
the dates and names. It was the manual for the Babbage
machines that really interested her.

She didn't know enough about blueprints and mechanical
engineering to decipher the drawings; but the intended function of the machine was clear from the write-ups. It was
definitely a mechanical computer, and it looked just like the
three that she had seen in the room atop the Widener Building. She thought about the dust-shrouded machines—Babbage
engines—and the thought excited her. This was a discovery
of tremendous historical importance. It was a chance for her
to be remembered for something significant. To be more than
Sarah Beaumont, upwardly mobile developer and ex-reporter.

Brady Quinn had jotted several amendments and marginal
notes in the instructions. So had Randall Carson and a man
named Dayton Black. She took the folder to her computer
terminal and shooed Fee off the desk. She found a pad of
paper and a pen and made a list of the names she wanted to
search. Then she thought some more and added further key-

words. Babbage engines. Isaac Shelton. Thomas Edison. Charles Babbage. Denver. Menlo Park. Jedediah Crawford.

*I shouldn't be spending so much time on this.* The name of the project was surely its least important feature. She realized that she had already spent an entire week researching Quinn. It was a week ago today that she had visited Morgan Grimes at the *News. I really should be costing the renovations on the Emerson Street house*, she thought, *not meandering through the DataNet.* There was a kilotonne of work to do. She had to PERT out the schedules. Talk to contractors. Get things moving. The Quinn business had waited a hundred years. It could wait a while longer.

She promised herself she would spend time with REAL-TOR, her expert program, organizing her buyout of the rest of the block. She could write a mouse that would search out connections between Quinn, Carson, and the others. Let the computer do the grunt work. She would give the mouse the keywords and let it run for a couple of days to see what information was on the Net. Then she could look the results over to see if she needed to realtime anything herself.

She sat in front of the terminal and flexed her fingers, like a pianist about to play. Friends in college had sometimes asked her why, with her obvious skills, she hadn't become a programmer. Computers were useful tools, she had responded, but she didn't want to be a toolmaker. That had shocked some of the "propeller heads." They had never thought of themselves in so prosaic a fashion.


Dennis was reading in his favorite chair when he heard the key fumbling at the apartment door. *That must be Jerry with the groceries*, he thought. He marked his place with a bookmark and laid his book down and went to open the door.

Jeremy Collingwood was balancing two grocery bags in his hands and trying to unlock the door at the same time. Dennis took one of the bags. "You could have knocked," he said. "You might have dropped everything."

"Sorry."

"No harm. Did you get everything on the list?"

"Of course I got everything on the list. Have I ever forgotten to get anything on the list?"

Jerry seemed a bit touchy tonight. Dennis wondered if he had had another run-in at the grocery store. He carried the bag to the kitchenette and began putting the cans away, setting them in the rear of the cabinets, behind the cans already there. Jerry had put the pantry on a kanban reorder system using a FIFO inventory policy. The older materials were always in front and as soon as enough cans were removed to expose the stars pasted on the shelves, Jerry or Dennis would go out and buy more.

"Say, Jerry," he asked while they worked. "Do you have any books about the Civil War?"

Jeremy closed the freezer door. "I think I have the Bruce Catton set. Why?"

Dennis folded the grocery sacks and put them in the paper recycling bin. He saw that the stack was nearly up to the line, which meant it was almost time for another trip to the Tricycle center. He wondered what the market price for paper was this week. Jerry would know. He was an accountant.

"Oh, I've been reading a little history the past week."

"Really? That's not like you."

Dennis was nettled but tried not to let it show. "A man can have more than one interest," he said.

Jerry looked at him. "Indeed he may. Look on the second shelf of the third bookcase. Probably toward the middle of the shelf."

The bookcases lined two walls of the front room. Dennis searched where Jerry had indicated. "Catton, did you say? There are three volumes here. Which one would cover February of 1861?"

"Don't you know?" Jerry sounded amused.

"I said I was reading a little history. If I already knew the answers, I wouldn't need to do the reading, would I?"

"Alright, Dennis. Don't get bitchy. You want *The Coming Fury*."

Dennis pulled the big, white volume off the shelf and carried it to his favorite bergeré chair and opened it to the index.

"Most people start in the front of the book."

"I'm not most people. It's only one particular event that interests me. I'm not about to read the entire . . ." He checked the numbers. "The entire 500 odd pages."

Jeremy shrugged. "It's your loss."

Dennis ignored him. He ran his forefinger down the index entries. Trescott. Trumbull. Twiggs. There it was. Twiggs, David Emanuel. He turned to page 226 and began to read.

The section was entitled "Colonel Lee Leaves Texas."

Brigadier General Twiggs, he quickly discovered, had been commander of the Department of Texas. A seventy-year-old Georgian "with heavy white hair and an ear-to-ear beard," his sympathies had lain entirely with the secessionists; unlike his second-in-command, Colonel Lee, who had written that "secession is nothing but revolution."

Orders relieving Twiggs of command had been issued on 28 January; but for some unaccountable reason, they had been sent by ordinary mail and did not reach San Antonio until 15 February, at which time the relieving commander, Colonel Carlos Waite of the First Infantry, was sixty miles away, on the Indian frontier. Twiggs was already in conference with the Texas state commissioners, negotiating the surrender of all army property, including the surrender of all officers and men.

The Texans tried to arrest Lee, who was passing through San Antonio under orders on his way to Washington; but Lee had argued that, since he had already been detached from Twiggs' command and ordered to Washington, he should not have been on the list of surrendered officers.

*Interesting*, thought Dennis. This must have been during the crisis months before Fort Sumter. Apparently, Scott had offered the command of the Union armies to Lee in case of hostilities; but Lee had declined on the grounds that Virginia might also secede. He despised the secessionists, but he would not fight against his own state. But how was the Twiggs affair a horseshoe nail? If the orders had arrived earlier, would Something Big have happened? Or, remembering Sarah's remark at dinner the evening before, because the orders arrived late did Something Big *not* happen?

He found an answer of sorts further down the page:

> "A fascinating 'if' develops at this point. A few months earlier, in Twiggs' absence, Lee had been acting commander of the Department of Texas. If the secession crisis had come to a head then, or if Twiggs' return had been delayed past mid-winter, it would have been Lee and not Twiggs on whom the Texas commissioners would have made their demand for the surrender of government property. Without question, Lee would have given them a flat refusal—in which case it might easily have been Lee, and not Major Robert Anderson, who first received and returned the fire of the secessionists, with

51

*San Antonio, rather than Fort Sumter, as the scene of
the fight that began a great war. Subsequent history
could have been substantially different."*

If Lee had resisted the Texans, Jefferson Davis would surely
never have offered him the Confederate command. Yes, surely,
subsequent history would have been different.

*Twiggs' orders delayed, but not his return,* the list had
said.

Delayed by whom? he wondered.

For the next few days Sarah sweated over her project,
putting in bids on a half dozen properties in the area, spacing
them so that no one else could develop the area without her
cooperation. Location was everything in the real estate game.
She routed the deals through a complex arrangement of dummies and fronts. There was no way to conceal the volume of
activity; but she didn't want anyone to know that she was the
one behind it all.

She priced the renovations through several contractors she
knew, keeping the discussions tentative and basing her estimates on the house she and Dennis had inspected. She made
a note to meet with Dennis and firm up the details on the
proposed renovations. She was looking for the lowest costs
and was experienced enough to know that that did not always
mean the lowest price.

She also put in a bid on the Widener Building. It hadn't
been on the market, but realtors knew that every property
had its price. If you made the right offer.

It was not until noon on Friday that she decided to take a
break. She closed her real estate files and put a ragtime disc
on the CD player. She went to the kitchen and made herself
some coffee and, when she returned to the terminal, called in
her mouse. Time to see what it had learned about Quinn and
the Babbage engines. She had told Dennis about the strange,
primitive computers and he had been quite pleased with
himself. His intuition had been vindicated. *Brady Quinn Place,*
named after a man involved with the world's forgotten first
computer, made perfect sense for a project that treated information as a utility and data ports as essential as water taps and
electrical outlets.

The disc began playing *Creole Belles* while she scrolled

through her findings. She hummed along with it. "My Creole belle, I know her well . . ."

Naturally, there was a mass of information on both Edison and Babbage. They were famous historical figures. But there was nothing that connected them with Quinn or Carson or the machines on the hidden fourth floor. She did learn that Thomas Edison used to meet regularly with Henry Ford, Harvey Firestone, and John Burroughs "to discuss the direction of the country." They went on nature hikes in Ford's private preserve in Michigan. Well, businessmen were always grouching how the country was going to hell in a handbasket. Burroughs, she found when she had looked him up, was a naturalist. One of the first ecologists.

"That explains the nature hikes, then," she said aloud. She laughed at the thought of three tycoons of industry slogging through the fields looking at mushrooms and butterflies. The idea that Henry Ford "stopped to smell the roses" bordered on the ludicrous.

As for Babbage, it was amusing, but hardly germane, to learn that he had hated organ grinders and had led several campaigns to ban them from the streets. It was more interesting that he actually started work on a "difference engine," a prototype of his proposed mechanical computer. But, after spending £23,000, including £6,000 of his own money, he had abandoned the project incomplete.

Babbage had co-founded the Analytical Society and had popularized the concept of life insurance, "a business based on the notion that unpredictable events can form predictable patterns." In 1832 he had written *On the Economy of Machinery and Manufactures*, anticipating much of what was now called operations research and systems analysis. Altogether a remarkable man.

There was also a curious note in the 1833 *Proceedings of the New York Academy of Sciences*, placed by Jedediah Crawford, announcing an open meeting to discuss the import of Babbage's theories, with a view to forming a Babbage Society to propogate them. She remembered that Crawford had been the author of the earliest paper listed in the Index she had found in the locked drawer. The mouse had identified him as *quondam* Professor of Mathematics at Yale in the 1820s and 30s. Had he actually formed his Society? It fit. Such a society would surely try to build Babbage engines.

Her mouse had found no other references in the Net to a

"Babbage Society"; but the Net was young and many databases were not yet in it. It would be nice to dig into some offline material and see what she could turn up.

She sat for a minute, tapping her fingers on the desk top. The CD was playing Botsford's 1908 *Black and White Rag* and her fingers beat time with it. She really should get back to work on the project. But it was already three o'clock in the afternoon, on a Friday. She did have some business to conduct at the City and County Building and, while she could do it by phone and modem, driving downtown would give her an excuse to drop in at the newspaper and at the library. She fought the temptation, not too doggedly, then gave in. There was still work waiting to be done on her project, but digging after Quinn and the Babbage Society was just too much fun. She picked up the phone and made an appointment to see the County Assesor that afternoon.

She didn't expect to find anything about the Babbage Society in the *News* morgue and she wasn't disappointed. The *News*, after all, had not started publication until 1859. But Morgan promised he would ask around for her. He had a friend on the *New York Times*. The *Times* was not much older than the *News* but, being in the East, would have been more likely to pick up stories about Crawford's society.

She finished her business with the Assesor's office and, leaving the City and County Building, decided to cut across Civic Center Park to the library. She jaywalked across Bannock to the Park and passed slowly through the afternoon crowds, deep in thought. There were young people lounging around the Park. Some were loafing on the steps of the Greek Theatre. Frisbees leaped from the crowd like locusts from a meadow.

*I'll need help,* she thought. She remembered the titles in the Index. Gibberish. Although she recognized some of them as dealing with operations research problems, another tie to Babbage. And the drawings in the Babbage Engine Manual. *A mechanical engineer, at least. And a mathematician. Maybe an historian, as well.* She hated the idea of sharing her discovery. The experts would take over and she would be politely ushered aside. *Thank you, Ms. Beaumont, but we'll take it from here.*

She had gone it alone her whole life, asking help from no one, making it on her own. The thought of being excluded

54

disturbed her. It wasn't just that the publicity over the machines would help sales at Brady Quinn Place. That would happen whether she was personally involved in the investigation or not. But, dammit, that wasn't the point! She *wanted* to be part of it! She wanted to be known as the discoverer.

She was passing the Greek Theatre when her right heel caught on a crack in the paving and, because her ankle was still sore from the accident on the stairs, she stumbled. Something whined and hit the stone column next to her and rock fragments stung her cheek.

"Hey! What the hell do you think you're doing?"

She turned at the sound of the voice. A big, burly man wearing an unbuttoned sport shirt was stalking across the park, hollering. Beyond him, she could see a park policeman reaching for his holster. Some of the kids were turning to look.

What was going on? She turned her head. There was a man on the other side of the reflecting pool holding a pistol. Two-handed stance. Feet spread wide. The gun was pointed at her. *The gun was pointed at her!*

She didn't stop to think. Reflexes took over. She ducked between two pillars of the Greek Theatre and dropped flat to the ground on the other side. *This isn't happening!* There was another spat and whine as a bullet ricocheted off the stone. People were screaming. She crawled to the end of the temple-like colonnade. Her heart was pounding. Dared she peek? He might be waiting for her to poke her head out. But he might already be running toward her position! Hide or run? She had to know. Cautiously, she peered around the end of the colonnade.

She saw the man with the gun turn and fire at the big man who was bearing down on him. The bullet took the big man through the open mouth and the back of his head exploded in a shower of flesh, blood and bone. The impact flipped the man over backward and he lay sprawled, eyes staring at the sky overhead.

The gunman turned and looked at Sarah. People were running in all directions. He brought his gun up. The park policeman shouted an order. He had his own weapon out, already pointed at the gunman. The gunman turned, lightning quick, and fired. The policeman staggered back, squeezing off two fast shots as he did so. The gunman spun and crumpled and the policeman dropped to his knees, holding his stomach.

55

There were sirens in the distance, growing louder.

Holding to the stone pillar for support, Sarah stood and surveyed the park. There was a confusion of people. Some were still running; others had stopped. A woman was holding the body of the first man, wailing and pressing him to her. He was dead for sure. He had probably saved her life by distracting the gunman, she thought. What had possessed him to charge an armed man like that? He probably had not been aware of the gun at all. It had been silenced.

She looked in the gunman's direction. He lay still. A young man walked up to him and stared at the body. A blue and white bird flapped down from the sky, cocked its head left, then right; then pecked at the face of the dead man.

Sarah felt the sourness rise in her throat. She turned her head aside and retched. It was a great, heaving, stomach-twisting convulsion. When she had finished, she fished in her briefcase for a handkerchief and wiped her mouth. There was blood on the handkerchief from her cheek, where the stone fragments had struck.

She felt numb. Without sensation. The tableau on the park seemed distant; as if seen through a telescope the wrong way. The sounds were muted. She turned her back on it and began walking down 14th Street. In a walled-off corner of her mind she knew she should stay and wait for the police. *You're in shock*, the voice said. *You're not yourself.*

She'd crossed Cherokee and was passing behind the Mint when a car pulled up and braked sharply next to her. The tires squealed. Sarah spun, her whole body tensed, and her heart skipped a beat.

Morgan rolled down his window. "Quick," he said. "Jump in."

She stared at him, then walked around his car and slid into the passenger seat. Morgan drove an old Chevy of indeterminate year and color. She slammed the door closed and hunched over in the seat, hugging herself.

Morgan shook her shoulder. "Take your jacket off. And the big red bow."

"What . . .?"

"Just do it." He put the car into gear without waiting to see if she was complying. Dumbly, she shrugged out of her suit and loosened the bow. She looked at it. It was bright red, the color of arterial blood. She began shaking.

Morgan shoved a clipboard at her. "Put the sunglasses on

56

and stick the pencil behind your ear. Try not to look like a well-dressed black businesswoman."

She looked at him. "Why? . . ."

"Because that's what came over the police radio. Some maniac was taking potshots at people in the park, and the description of one of the targets sounded a lot like someone who had just been in to see me."

Fourteenth Street was one-way eastbound. Sarah saw that they were headed back toward the Civic Center. She felt her stomach tighten and she began to shake her head.

"I figured you'd be in no kind of shape, so I came looking."

"Uh, thanks."

"Sure thing."

The police had erected a barricade and were waving all the traffic onto Bannock. Morgan grunted and turned. He rolled down the window and called to one of the officers. "Hey, what's going on here?" Sarah turned her face away. She could feel the bleeding starting again on her cheek.

"There's been a shooting in the park, sir," the officer answered.

"Anyone hurt?"

"I couldn't say."

"The *News* have anyone there?"

"Yes, sir. A reporter and photographer just arrived."

"Okay. Thanks." Morgan rolled the window up and continued down Bannock.

"You didn't tell him who I was."

"He didn't ask."

"They're looking for me."

"Then they'll find you; but tomorrow is soon enough for that."

"Morgan, why did you come looking for me?"

He turned his head and smiled at her. "To get the scoop, of course. A firsthand, eyewitness account of the biggest story this year."

"A scoop. Is that all?"

This time he wouldn't look at her. "Sure. That's all."

"Morgan, what would you have done if the policeman had said that no one from the *News* was there?"

"Why, I'd've stuck a press card in my hat and you and me'd go cover the story together. Just like old times."

"Morgan, if we'd have gone in there, someone would have recognized me!"

57

He looked at her, his mouth agape. "Really? I thought all you people looked alike!"

She couldn't help herself. It took her back to their first reporting days together, when they used to ride each other unmercifully. The *Black and White Rag*. She started to laugh, but the laughter turned to tears.

Morgan Grimes' apartment was on Capitol Hill in a rambling old apartment building that had gone condo back in the 70s. He took her through a side entrance, three flights up and down the hall. It was like the inside of a maze. He let her inside his apartment and locked the door behind them.

Sarah walked to the sofa and sat down. She stared at the wall. There were prints hanging there: long, thin Japanese paintings with their strange vertical perspective. Chrysanthemums and pagodas. Mountains loomed out of misty cloud banks. Faerie waterfalls plunged over steep cliffs. Her tears blurred the pictures, making the waterfalls more real.

Suddenly, there was a glass in front of her. Morgan was pressing a drink on her. She took it and drank it without tasting anything. She shoved the empty glass back into his hands.

"Another one?" he asked.

"Yes. Please."

"Want to talk about it?" He wandered over to his bar and poured something amber straight out of a bottle.

"Yes. No. Not yet. I'm still shaky. Morgan, that man was trying to kill me."

"A maniac. He shot three or four people. I heard on the police radio. One dead. One serious. Two slightly wounded. You were just there at the wrong time. You're okay now."

"No, dammit! He was shooting at *me!* The others, they were just bystanders."

"I know it probably seemed that way, but—"

"Morgan, I *know*. He looked straight at me." She thought back, remembering. The scene had played itself out in slow motion. Every word, every gesture was etched in her memory. "He looked straight at me. God help me, he smiled."

"Like I said. A maniac."

"Maniacs don't use silencers. They don't strike stances like they were on a target range." Morgan handed her a refill and she gulped it down. She remembered how the first bullet had struck the stone column next to her. Inches away. If she

58

hadn't stumbled, she'd be dead now. Her skull blown apart. One moment: the smell of the grass and the trees, the cries of children playing, the shining gold of the Capitol dome at the far end of the Civic Center; the next moment, nothing; not even blackness. No more Sarah Beaumont. She began to shiver.

"Here," said Morgan. She turned. He was holding out a long flannel bathrobe, blue and white plaid. "You threw up. It's on your clothing. Go in my bedroom and get out of those clothes. I'll take them downstairs to the laundry room. Then I'll take care of that cheek. There's iodine in the medicine cabinet."

She did as he said. After she had handed him her soiled clothing she sat on the edge of the bed, her arms wrapped tightly around herself, and waited. An immeasurable time went by. When he returned from the laundry, she stood up and went to him. "Hold me, Morgan," she said.

He looked at the robe and frowned. "Sarah, I don't think . . ."

"Hold me," she repeated, letting the robe fall open.

He flushed. His ears burned a bright red and he turned his face away. "I never thought I'd hear myself say this, but . . ." He bit his lip, reached out, and pulled the folds of the robe together. "Look, Sarah, you were this close to being dead. Now you want to prove you're alive. This isn't you talking. Another day, if you're still willing, God knows I'll be; but not now, not tonight. I've got my standards, low as they might be."

"Morgan." She put her arms around him. "I'm shaking so bad I need to hold onto something solid. Just that. Nothing more."

Awkwardly, he put his arms around her and she felt herself relax at last. Drowsy. The drinks were catching up with her. She willed sleep to come and with it, forgetfulness.

# VI

In the morning she awoke in a strange bed. There was a moment of disorientation and her eyes searched the walls, finding nothing familiar. She sat up and noticed she was wearing a strange bathrobe but was otherwise naked. She saw her clothing carefully hung on the back of the bedroom door. *Where?* . . .

She remembered. The Civic Center. The shootings. But, already yesterday's events seemed remote. Something seen on the TV news. Film at ten. A self-defense mechanism, she decided. The mind distanced itself from the horror or went mad.

She rose and dressed. She remembered Morgan holding her. She had kissed him and, after a moment, he had kissed her back. *Poor Morgan*, she thought. It must have been agony for him. Morgan had always been a hand with the ladies, and she had felt his desire.

She found him asleep on the recliner in the living room. He was twisted into an uncomfortable-looking position and his clothing was wrinkled. She shook her head. He liked to come on like a tough, cynical reporter, but sometimes the real Morgan Grimes showed through. She wondered why the two of them had never made it as a news team.

In the kitchen, she hunted up some eggs, chili, and other things and set about making *huevos rancheros*. She was shredding the Monterey Jack when he walked in. He looked at what she was doing, grunted, and walked out again. After a minute, she heard the shower start.

\*       \*       \*

Later, Sarah stood by his apartment window and gazed out at the city. Behind the buildings, miles away but still dwarfing them, the Rockies showed dimly through the haze. There were places there, not too far away, where a woman could be alone, with no other humans for miles. With a shiver of *frisson*, she remembered staring out the window of the house on Emerson Street not quite two weeks ago. It had even been about the same time of day and not too far from where she stood now. The scene lay unchanged, yet there was a wall between the two events. That had been another Sarah, another life; and she thought it was odd to remember something that had happened to someone else. She wondered if everyone who faced death felt the same way: reborn through some terrible baptism of blood. Perhaps that was why the Japanese had made a sacrament of suicide.

"So, you believe the gunman was after you specifically."

She turned and faced Morgan. The newsman was sitting in his recliner, a steno pad balanced on his knee. "Yes, I'm certain. Do they know who it was yet?"

"No. I called the paper this morning. He had no ID on him. Nothing. They're going through mug shots and showing his face on the tube. Someone will recognize him and call in." He looked at her with narrowed eyes. "*You* don't know who he was, do you?"

She shook her head emphatically. "No, of couse not."

"Then, if he wasn't a madman, why was he trying to kill you?"

"I don't know!"

"Don't you think you deserve to?"

She laughed. It was her first real laugh since the shooting. "I suppose if anyone deserves to know, I do. But he's in no shape to tell me now."

"There are only eight reasons for murder. We can go through the list, if you like."

"Only eight? I would have thought there'd be as many reasons as there are victims."

"No, only eight. It's the details, not the basic motives, that differ from killing to killing."

She shrugged. "So what are they?"

He held up his fingers and counted off with his pen. "There are the impersonal, the emotional, and the rational. As far as the impersonal reasons go, you've already ruled out homicidal mania. What about someone making a political statement?"

She hesitated. "A terrorist or assassin? But what sort of statement would he make by shooting *me*?"

"They pick victims at random, don't they? Don't forget he also shot four other people and killed one. They think the policeman will live."

"No, that was—I don't know. Window dressing. He didn't shoot at anyone else until I was behind a stone wall."

"Which means . . ."

"He didn't want anyone to know that I was the target."

"If you know, then he failed."

"A failure. Yes. He should have taken up another line of work."

Morgan looked at her oddly, then he shrugged. "Alright. He was a professional hit man and it was important that no one probe too deeply into his reasons for singling you out. Who hired him?"

"If I knew that—"

"And why? What about rage or revenge? Two of the emotional reasons."

She shook her head. "No. Revenge for what? For bringing off a sharp business deal? That doesn't make sense. Realtors don't hire hit men for things like that."

"Do evicted tenants?"

"Morgan, I've never hurt anyone that badly."

"A grudge doesn't have to be reasonable. It doesn't even have to be real. And all it takes is one person with a grudge. Okay, what about jealousy?"

"Who has time for romance? Abe and I split years ago—"

"Professional jealousy?"

"No, dammit! I get along fine with everyone."

"As far as you know, anyway. It's like revenge. Who knows what might excite someone else to jealousy? You're pretty well off. Some may resent a woman, and an attractive black one at that, being so successful. Or old friends might be jealous of your success."

Chicago's Old Town flashed through her mind. Hyde Park. Faces she had played with in childhood; faces she hadn't even thought of in too many years. Where were they now? Still in Old Town, probably. Friends left far behind, on another planet. Did they hate her that she had left and never come back? That she had never even looked back? "Christ, Morgan, you'll have me paranoid."

"Even paranoids have enemies."

62

Anger swept over her like a wave on a beach and she let it break on him. "What is this, an interrogation?" She turned her back on him and stared out the window once more. But, this time she saw Chicago, not Denver. She leaned her arms against the window sill.

"I'm glad you trust me, at least."

She faced him again. "What do you mean?"

"We were poor starving reporters together, remember? Now you're rich and I'm still poor and starving. For a while, anyway. I might be insanely jealous, for all you know; but you turned your back on me."

She smiled crookedly. "Thanks, Morgan. You're a pal. I won't do it again."

His face was serious. "I mean it. If you're right. If you're not just imagining things, *don't sit with your back to the room*. That's how they got Hickock."

"All right. I'm sorry I got mad. You're just a reporter doing your job."

He looked at her for a long moment, then his eyes dropped to his notepad. "Yeah." He tapped his notebook rhythmically with his pen. "Well, folks with an emotional reason for murder usually do it themselves; so let's concentrate on the rational reasons. To gain something you possess. You do not haf zee Maltese Falcon, do you?" He delivered the last line in a pinched Peter Lorre accent.

"He didn't try to rob me, Morgan; and . . . and I'm cutting him out of my will as of today." She started laughing. Morgan frowned and started to rise from his chair. She waved him back. "No, I'm alright. God! I can joke about it now. I just never realized there were so many goddamn reasons to kill."

Morgan smiled, without humor. "Only eight, remember? Number seven: To cover up for another crime. You're not a witness to anything, are you? I suppose a detective or a reporter or a secret agent might be sniffing around the edges of some dreadful secret and not realize it; but a real estate broker? Not likely."

"You've really made a science out of this, haven't you?"

"But what have you been sniffing around lately?"

She hesitated. She didn't want word of her Emerson Street project to leak out yet, least of all on the front page of the *News*. She had asked his help in researching the Babbage Society, but she hadn't told him why. "Nothing important," she told him. "Certainly nothing dangerous." Then, swearing him off-the-record, she told him about Emerson Street, Brady Quinn, and the 100-year-old Babbage engines. He listened and made notes.

"You're right. It doesn't sound too promising, but I'll look into it. Who else knows about it? You said Paul Abbot was the foreman you talked to? And Dennis French has the paper you found in the wainscoting?" He jotted down the names. "I'll go see them both later today, if I have time."

"Abbot doesn't know about the Babbage engines, and I don't want him to know. He'd take them apart and sell them for scrap metal."

Morgan smiled at her. "I will be the soul of discretion. Maybe Abbot is afraid you'll turn him in for looting and hired a killer to silence you. Okay. Eighth and final reason: To protect themselves from you."

"Self-defense?! Morgan, are you nuts? I'm no threat to anyone. I don't even step on spiders."

"Maybe you should; some are poisonous. But self-defense is like any other motive. It's in the other person's mind. You might not even know it. You may have done something somewhere that someone somehow perceived as a threat."

"Oh, that really pins it down, Morgan! Let's go arrest the son-of-a-bitch!"

"Sarah, I'm trying to help."

"You're trying to get a story!"

"Yeah. Right."

"Besides, why not just warn me off? Why shoot me down in broad daylight?"

"Maybe the warning itself would have been too revealing."

"You've been reading too many spy thrillers." Then she remembered the man in the library and her feeling later that she was being followed. Had they been warnings? And if so, of what? She told Morgan about them.

He nodded. "This may be something. The man in the library," he said. "He wasn't the same one who shot at you."

"No."

"Hmm. Then if there is a connection between the two events, it implies that there's an organization, not an individual trying to kill you."

"If there is. I don't know. I've never been shot at, let alone by the Klan or the Arab Brotherhood."

"An organization." He sat back and tapped his teeth with

64

his pen. "Tell me," he said casually, "what do you know about John Benton or Genevieve Weil?"

She shook her head. "Never heard of them."

"Daniel Kennison?"

"Just what I read in the papers. What has Kennison Demographics got to do with my being shot at?"

"Maybe nothing. Maybe everything. And if it does, I don't know why; but it's probably more pertinent than your Brady Quinn. Let me check things out and I'll get back to you."

She waited, but he didn't explain further. She had the distinct impression that Morgan knew more than he was saying and that he thought it was important. He saw a possible tie-in with a story he was working on, but he wasn't about to say what it was. Morgan had always played his stories close to his vest, one reason why their team had been so short-lived.

He was going to check things out. She'd have to be satisfied with that.

Sarah stood on the balcony of her house, perched high on the side of South Table Mountain, and stared down at the night. She swirled the brandy in her snifter from time to time. Behind her, all the house lights had been extinguished. Only the fire shed any light, its faint, red glow accentuating the shadows, making them dance. She liked to stand alone in the night. It was peaceful. Although sometimes the loneliness seeped into her and caused an ache somewhere at the base of her throat.

The black was seamless. Who could say where earth ended and sky began? The lights close below were laid out in geometric precision, like gems on a black velvet cloth; but farther away, urban order gave way to rural disorder, and the lights grew progressively more random, until they blended imperceptibly into the chaos of the night sky.

The shopping center at 32nd and Youngfield might well be a stellar cluster. Some of the lights moved; but were they meteors or automobiles? To her left, the looming mass of Lookout Mountain was a dark nebula, black against black, with only a few lights showing on it.

She took a swallow of brandy. The police had been sympathetic when she had gone to see them after leaving Morgan's apartment. They had even understood why she hadn't come in immediately. Shock, they had said. But they hadn't bought her theory that she had been singled out deliberately; that the other victims had been camouflage. The maniac theory was too attractive, too tidy.

*Beam me up, Scotty,* she thought. *There's no intelligent life down here.*

No, that wasn't fair. She'd been unable to supply them with a plausible motive for being the chosen target. Only an intuition. A knowledge that passed between the killer's eyes and her own, in that most intimate of all relationships. The police had nodded knowingly. The greatest fear was the fear of a meaningless death, of what Morgan had called the impersonal motives. The randomness of terrorism strips its victims of individuality; and the victim often has a need to find a reason, any reason, as long as it is something personal. But they hadn't looked into the man's eyes. They hadn't seen for themselves.

She was marked for death and she didn't know why. That was the real terror. The look the gunman had given her. It was impossible to describe, but it left no doubt in her mind. It was recognition and satisfaction and anticipation all at once. Thinking back, she could see that he had been a man who enjoyed his work.

Her survival classes had saved her. She had dived behind shelter automatically, without thinking. But even afterward, she had not resumed thinking; and that bothered her. All her life she had been *making* choices, not *taking* choices. But not yesterday. She remembered telling Morgan how she needed to hold him, and her cheeks burned at the memory. She couldn't remember ever telling anyone that. She had never needed anyone.

When you stood alone, you never had illusions about responsibility. She had always despised those around her who blamed their friends, their circumstances, their bad luck, anything but themselves for their failures. But yesterday, in a way, she had been one of them: reacting, not acting; moved by circumstances beyond her control; stunned by the surprise, the viciousness, and, most of all, the feeling of utter powerlessness.

Powerlessness. That's what sucked the heart out of anyone. Perhaps all along, all those other people had simply had lower thresholds of psychological pain.

*Introspective tonight, aren't we?* A faint smile played on her lips while she watched the traffic hurtle along I-70. Folks heading for the mountains. Saturday night at the Old Dillon

66

Inn. No one hunting them. She thought about joining them; of jumping into her Volvo [no, her Blazer] and heading for the High Country. She knew places where no one could ever find her. Places where she couldn't even find herself. The Summit was only an hour's drive away; but she knew places even closer, in the Foothills.

Run and hide. That had been Morgan's parting advice. But running had never been her style. (Except running from Old Town, a voice in her head reminded her.) She wasn't helpless. She knew how to take care of herself. The streets of Chicago had been no safe haven; nor the mountains of Colorado. She was prepared now.

*They won't get me the way they got Brady Quinn.*

Why, what a peculiar thought that was! That business had been over with for a hundred years.

She reentered the house and slid the glass door shut behind her. She walked four steps across the firelit room and paused. What was it? A sound subliminally heard? A smell lingering in the air? A shadow rock-solid among the shifting shadows thrown by the fire? She dropped the brandy snifter and it shattered on the parquet flooring.

*There's someone else in the room!*

A part of her wanted to roll up into a tight ball and make the world go away. I can't take any more of this! But the other part of her was angry. I *won't* take any more of this!

Two quick strides and she was at the fireplace, with the heavy, wrought-iron poker gripped tightly in her hands. She kept her back to the wall. *Like Wild Bill Hickock should have done.*

"It's a bad idea," said a voice in the darkness. "Standing in front of a fire like that. It silhouettes you." It was a man's voice. It sounded amused.

"Who are you?"

"A friend."

"Sure. All my friends are into breaking and entering."

He turned on the table lamp and she blinked at the sudden glare. When her eyes had adjusted, she saw that he held a gun. She felt her stomach drop out of her, but she didn't move. She was figuring distances. It was a small caliber gun. It wouldn't pick her up and knock her down. Or would it?

He pointed the gun straight up. The cylinder popped out and the cartridges dropped to the floor.

"There," he said. "Now I'm helpless."

She looked him over. "Somehow, I doubt that."

He grinned. "I like you. You've got a sense of humor. But you've got to admit that if I were here to kill you, you'd've been dead and down the mountainside an hour ago. So I'm not an enemy and, who knows? Maybe I am a friend, after all."

She relaxed a little. He was right. He wasn't here to kill her. But she did not release her grip on the poker, nor did she leave her position by the wall.

He was a stocky man with a brush cut of red hair. His fingers were short and stubby. He had ruddy cheeks. He sat totally at ease in her sofa, as if he were a long-familiar neighbor. There was a smile on his face. Sarah decided from his laugh lines that he spent a lot of his time smiling.

Which proved nothing. The killer had smiled, too.

"Who are you and what do you want?" she demanded.

"I'm a friend—"

"Friends have names."

He looked at her for a long moment, then he nodded. "Call me Red," he said.

"Alright, Red. Let's see some identification."

He shrugged and pulled out his wallet. He flipped through the cardholder, extracted an identification card, and held it out to her.

"Put it on the table; then sit on your hands."

He grinned and did as he was told. Sarah stepped up and snatched the card from the coffee table. It was a photo ID card, issued by Utopian Research Associates. It gave his name as Red Malone and his occupation as Adjustor. The photograph matched. "How many different identification cards like this do you carry?" she asked, putting it back on the table.

He grinned again. "Who counts?"

She sighed. She was getting tired of standing. She walked to the side of the room opposite the sofa and sat in the stuffed chair facing him. "So, tell me, Red. Old friend. Why have you broken into my home?"

"To warn you that you may be in danger."

"You're too late. I already know."

He looked sheepish. "Yes, I heard. It was my fault. I didn't know They had local assets, so I didn't move fast enough. Deep programming is damned hard to uncover. The man himself didn't even know he was one of Theirs, so how could

68

we? A phone call with the trigger phrase spoken, a description of the op, and he was off and running before anyone knew it. Good news in one way, though."

"Good news."

"Sure. It means that They're spread thin around here. There are better ways to take out targets than launching an assassin. That means They were panicked and used the first disposable asset that was handy. It was really stupid on Their part."

"They were stupid," she repeated. "Oh, good. I feel much better now."

"You're alive and he's dead," he pointed out, "You're feeling better than he is."

"That was plain luck, pure and simple. If I hadn't hurt my ankle—"

"Panic is *always* stupid. But you can't blame Them. They were scared. They knew you were running an op on them. They saw the signs all around, but never anything that could be traced. Then, when you queried the Brady Quinn file, you slipped up and used your own Net Access Code." He wagged a finger at her. "That was careless of you."

"I still don't understand," she replied testily. "Who are 'they'? What's so important about Brady Quinn? And where do you fit in?"

Red's smile faded. He looked puzzled. "You're not kidding me, are you?" He stared at her intently. "If you don't know what I'm talking about, then why were you poking into Brady Quinn's life?"

"Poking into? . . . What's wrong with that? He once owned a house I just bought. My architect and I found an old newspaper clipping about his being shot, and we thought Brady Quinn Place had a nice ring to it." She almost went on to mention Quinn's connection with the Babbage engines, but stopped herself. It was bad enough that Dennis and Morgan both knew. She could trust them. She wasn't about to tell a total stranger about the machines or her project.

He looked worried now. "You weren't investigating the murders of Kenny Robertson or Alice McAuliffe?" He frowned as he said the last name.

"I don't know who they are."

He bit his lip. "I think there's been a mistake."

"A mistake?" The word outraged her. "A mistake!" she cried. "Someone just tried to kill me, mister! He shot four other people and killed one just to cover it up. And you call it a *mistake?*"

He looked at her. "Mistakes needn't be trivial. Terrible deeds have been done in error." There was a strange look in his eye when he said that.

"Now I really feel great! I was almost killed; but it's okay because it was stupid and it was a mistake. Do you have any other good news? Are you going to tell me what's going on, or are we going to sit here and trade banalities?"

"It would be safer if we traded banalities."

"I'm not safe now!"

He pursed his lips and considered. "I can tell you a little bit. Will that satisfy you?"

"Try me."

"You're in no position to bargain, you know. I can walk out right now, and you wouldn't be any the wiser."

"I already know you work for the CIA."

That surprised him. She could see it in his eyes: the way they widened for a moment. Then they shaded over again and he grinned at her. "What makes you say that?"

"The way you talk. 'Running an op.' The assassin was an 'asset.' That's spook talk. And the guy in the park. Brainwashed and hypnotized, you said. Programmed to kill me and be thrown away. That's straight out of some old Robert Ludlum thriller."

"So I read a lot of old thrillers. You're just guessing."

"Yeah, but I guessed right, didn't I?"

He was irritated. "Just for the record, I do *not* work for the CIA. You can call Langley and ask them. They'll tell you they never heard of me."

"I'm sure they will," she agreed. "Now, tell me what I've gotten mixed up in. Dammit, I *deserve* to know."

Red stood suddenly and began to pace, back and forth across the room. He did not approach her, but she instinctively gripped the poker tighter. He stopped and faced her. "Look," he said. "If you really don't know what's going on, it's best if we keep it that way. If I can convince Them that you're harmless, They'll leave you alone."

"I don't understand why anyone would want to kill me. I've never hurt anyone. And why should Brady Quinn matter?"

He shook his head. "I shouldn't have said anything; but I thought you already knew. Damn." He resumed pacing. Sarah watched him. Back and forth. Back and forth.

"There's Us and Them," he said after a while. "Never mind who We are or who They are. They have a dirty little secret. So do We; and we both want it kept secret. They'll stop at nothing to keep it that way."

"And you?"

He stopped pacing and looked at her sadly. "We'll stop. At some things." He resumed his pacing. "About three months ago They began getting indications that someone was running an op—" He paused, looked at her, and twisted his lip in a grimace. "I really should watch my phraseology," he admitted ruefully. "Someone was snooping around Their operations," he continued. "Someone very careful. Call him the Intruder. He was asking questions that were better left unasked. Tying together bits and pieces that should have remained unconnected. He was in and out of data bases, accessing files that must never see the light of day. They began to get very, very nervous. It would mean the nearest tree or lamppost for Them if it ever got out. And for Us, too, come to that. They told Us what was happening, of course; but We didn't know any more about it than They did."

He stood still and faced her. "Then you tripped the Brady Quinn alarm on the DataNet. They thought that meant the Intruder was close to unravelling the whole thing. So They panicked."

She was bitter. "I suppose it's my fault I was shot at. What should I do, apologize?"

He seemed not to notice her sarcasm. "No, it was unintentional. The point is, They didn't know any better Themselves. It simply never occured to Them that you weren't who They thought you were."

"So, if They'd shot the real Intruder, They'd have been justified?"

"Justified? Whose Justice? Is a cornered rat justified when it bites? Organizations are like organisms. If they perceive a threat, they'll try to protect themselves. It's simply a natural law of living systems. It doesn't matter one whit if the system is a rat, the Mafia, or the Boy Scouts."

"The Boy Scouts don't shoot their enemies," she retorted.

He jabbed a finger at her. "They would if the alternative were being lynched themselves! I'm trying to tell you what's natural and you keep talking about what's moral. We're on two different wavelengths. When I say a response is natural, I mean just that. I don't have to like it any better than you do.

71

The kind of response depends on the kind of threat, that's all. And for them, the threat is deadly."

"And for you?"

He didn't answer her. Instead, he returned to the sofa and sat down. When he spoke, it was almost to himself. "You can always run from a threat. Fight or flight. Sometimes that doesn't work, either." There was a strange faraway look on his face. Then his eyes focused on her. "Look. None of this helps you. Just lay off this Quinn business. You don't *need* it for your project, do you? Drop it and what have you lost? A few hours wasted in the libraries and the databases, that's all. I'll talk to Them. Try to convince Them you aren't the one They want."

Red had risen from the sofa and was picking up his bullets, putting them back in his gun. "Do me a favor," he said. "And yourself, too. Stay far away from Brady Quinn and everything connected with him. Alright? Just stick to real estate."

"That was how I started onto Quinn in the first place," she reminded him.

He looked at her bleakly, then walked to the door. Sarah followed.

"When will you tell me?"

He turned at the door. "Tell you what?"

"Whether They agree not to kill me."

He shook his head. "You'll know."

"No. You come back and tell me. I deserve that much."

He gave her a long look. "Alright," he said slowly, "you do at that. But only if you promise not to hit me with that poker."

She looked down, surprised, and found she still gripped the iron poker that she had taken from the fireplace. "Fair enough," she replied. "If you agree to ring the doorbell like a civilized human being."

He grinned. "It's a date, then."

72

# VII

After he had gone, Sarah went to her desk and sat down, with her hands clasped in a ball on the desk top. She listened to the silence. The antique grandfather's clock was a steady metronome beat in the hallway; but that only emphasized the silence. Her mother's house had always been full of sounds.

*Tick*. She wondered where Fee was. He was nowhere in sight. Too damned independent. That was the problem with cats. They came and went as they pleased.

*Tick*. Funny. She had never noticed before how *alone* she was. *Tick*. She could name business associates by the score; but where were her friends, her family? She had always prided herself on her independence, her self-reliance; but when had she slipped over the line from independence to loneliness? *Tick*.

That damned clock! She stood and walked briskly to the entrance hallway, where she opened the front of the case and pulled the counterweight down. The clock hesitated, skipped a beat, then stopped.

Sarah closed the door and leaned her forehead against it. The glass felt cool on her skin. After a moment, she stepped back and looked at her reflection. It was her mother's face. A bit younger and more rounded than she remembered her mother; but she could see the resemblance in the eyes and chin.

She listened, trying to hear the sounds of her mother's house. The sounds she dimly remembered from her past. And for an instant they were there: the hiss of the teakettle on the old gas range; the *basso profundo* rumble of her father's snores whenever he was home from the road; the gentle drone of her mother as she hummed her beloved ragtime; the screams of her brothers as they chased each other from room to room. *Why did I ever want to escape from that?*

Then the spell faded and it was only her own face in the glass and the only thing she saw in her eyes was fear.

She walked slowly back to her study. It was past time she took hold of herself. *You're master of your own fate,* she told herself. *No one else.* She felt as if she were in the middle of a mine field. Somehow, by dumb luck, she had gotten as far as she had; but she didn't know which way to go from here. *I know too much,* she thought, *but I don't know enough.*

A little knowledge is a dangerous thing.

The cliché made her laugh, it was so literally true. And what can you do? You can't forget the little you know; you can only try to learn more. Enough to be safe.

She put a CD on the player, setting the volume low; loud enough to hear but not loud enough to distract. The first cut, though, turned out to be the *New Orleans Hop Scop Blues,* and she almost turned around and rejected it, its melody was so unbearably sad. Then, on second thought she let it play, because underneath the melody was that unconquerable raggy beat. You may beat me; but you can't defeat me.

She sat down at her desk and pulled a notepad in front of her. Taking a pen from the deskholder, she paused in thought. Red had warned her to stay away from anything touching on Quinn. But, if she stayed off the DataNet, how would anyone know what she did in the privacy of her home?

She looked around the study. Light wood paneling. Cathedral ceiling. Hanging plants. She wondered if the place was bugged. Red would have had the opportunity. How long had he been in the house while she stood innocently on the balcony? The thought made her shiver. How had he gotten in without her hearing? What if his intentions had been lethal? She would be dead now, without ever knowing why.

And that made her angry. Not the dying. That was only fear. But the not knowing.

The walls were silent; the quiet, ominous. In the background, the ragtime blues wailed. She turned her back on it all and hunched over her desk, concentrating on the pad where it sat in a pool of light from the desk lamp. *Let's take stock,* she told herself. *What is it that I know?*

I know that someone is trying to kill me. She wrote that at

the top of the sheet and drew a box around it. Staring at the words, she gripped her pen tightly and chewed on her lower lip. Then she took a deep breath and continued jotting notes.

*Why do They want to kill me?* Because They think I'm close to uncovering Their secret. *Why?* Because They think I'm the Intruder. *Why?* Because my research into Brady Quinn tied in with whatever it was the Intruder was doing. From what Red had told her, that involved the deaths of two people named Kenny Robertson and Alice McAuliffe. She drew a double-headed arrow connecting Brady Quinn with the other two names. *Why should those deaths worry Them?* Unless They had killed them. Had Robertson and McAuliffe been two others who had stumbled on the deadly secret?

She wrote her thoughts down in schematic fashion, using the fault tree symbols that Abe had taught her years ago. People too often argued in circles, or overlooked possibilities, or even forgot some of their own ideas. Sarah had found that diagramming her thoughts in an orderly way helped to organize her thinking. Abe had called it a fault tree, but she called it a why-why diagram, which had always annoyed him. He had scoffed at her use of the method for what he called "soft" problem solving.

Funny. She hadn't thought about Abe for a long time. What had stirred up that memory? She wondered where he was now; how he had made out as a reliability engineer. He had never struck her as having the kind of drive he needed to reach the top. Not like the drive she had. They'd had some good times, the two of them; but in the end, he'd left and she'd never been quite sure why.

*Never mind that now,* she told herself. The point of this exercise is to get at the root cause of my problem, not to reminisce pointlessly over things that didn't matter any more. If they ever did matter.

She made a marginal note: *KR & AMcA. Find out who.*

Sarah tapped her teeth with her pen. This branch seemed a dead end. Without further data, she was no closer to the root cause. Except, she had a hint—only a supposition on her part, really—that she wasn't the first victim.

*What about Quinn?* That's what had actually triggered the attack. What had she learned about him that was so dangerous? He had been a "special-project" statistician for the government before and during the Civil War; and had resigned abruptly afterwards. She toyed for the moment with a "CIA" scenario, like that old movie *Three Days of the Condor*. Quinn's resignation from "special projects" had not been accepted. "The only way to leave is feet first." Only, there hadn't been a CIA back then. There had barely been a Secret Service to bodyguard the President. (And not very well, as it had turned out.) They didn't play spook games in those days.

Or did they? She caught herself before she scratched out that line of reasoning. What *had* those special projects been? Something best kept quiet? Something the government wanted kept quiet even a hundred years later? She shook her head. Considering the skeletons that had come jitterbugging out of the closets of recent history, she doubted that any scandal from the Civil War era could be that threatening.

Besides, from the way Red had talked about Us and Them, she'd had the distinct impression that he was not talking about the government.

That was only an impression. She might be wrong; so she allowed the branch to remain on her diagram.

There was also Quinn's association with the putative Babbage Society. If there was anything extraordinary about Quinn, the Society and its curious machines were certainly tied in with it. Yet, that had also been long ago. How could it have anything to do with the attack on her yesterday?

*Hold it.* She remembered the foolscap sheet with the list of "horseshoe nails." The one Dennis had kept. There had been several murders noted on it, hadn't there? Quinn and two others. She hadn't been interested in the others before, they'd had nothing to do with her Emerson Street project; but now she wondered if they might not also be part of the pattern that had drawn so tightly around her. What had their names been? She thought for a moment, wishing she had kept a copy of the list. Davis something. Bellows? And Agnes, no Agatha . . . What? Penwether. That was it, Agatha Penwether. And Ambrose Bierce. He had disappeared, but it seemed to fit in with the murders, somehow.

She wrote the names on her diagram. As she recalled, Bellows had been killed some years before Quinn. 1876? Hey! Wasn't that the year Quinn had disappeared? Perhaps that was why he had gone into hiding in the first place! Excitedly, she jotted a note on the diagram. She'd have to call Dennis and check the date. Penwether, she thought, was killed later, about 1915 or 16. A quick check of the encyclopedia told her that Bierce had disappeared in Mexico in 1913. She made another note: *Robertson, McA: when?*

She scanned her diagram, reading what she had written, and a cold knot of dread stole over her. Jesus! Were the people after her the same ones who had killed Quinn? Quinn had hidden himself for sixteen years, but they had found him in the end. Would she spend the rest of her life looking over her shoulder? She shivered despite the fire in the fireplace. Bellows, Quinn, Penwether, Bierce, Robertson, McAuliffe. And how many others? *How many others?*

A new sense of urgency gripped her. What was the connection between the murders and the Babbage Society? Quinn had been a member—maybe. Had the other victims been members as well? Was someone hunting them down?

No. Quinn had gone underground, but his partner, Carson, had not. Evidently, the other man had not felt exposed to the same danger. And Edison. He had been associated with them in some way. Then she remembered something that her mouse had told her. How Edison had met regularly with Ford and the others. *A cell of the Society?* No one had tried to kill them.

So, being a member of the Society was not a sufficient condition to become a victim. Was it a *necessary* condition? Did the victims form a subset of the Society?

She opened the center drawer of her desk and pulled out the Index folder that she had taken from the fourth-floor file cabinets. The papers of the Babbage Society? She scanned the names of authors, chewing on her pen. Jedediah Crawford. The founder. Phineas Hammondton. Isaac Shelton. Hmmm. Wasn't it Shelton who had gotten Quinn his job in the Interior Department? The papers written by all three bore similar dates: the 1830s and 40s. Charter members?

Yes, there was Brady Quinn, too. But his papers bore later dates, so he was not an original member. She went through the names again, more carefully this time. There! Davis Belleau. Not Bellows, after all. His papers were also written in the 1830s and 40s—another Founder. Excited now, she looked for the names of the other victims. And . . .

No, Penwether and the others were not listed. So, either they were not members of the Society or else they became members after 1892, the last year in the Index.

And there was another coincidence: 1892 was the year Quinn was killed. Was that when the office in the Widener

Building had been abandoned? Was that, in fact, the reason why it had been abandoned?

She remembered how thick the dust in the office had been. How the machines had sat silent and rusting on their heavy, ancient tables for a hundred years. How the stairway to the fourth floor had been concealed; the machine shop below, an apparent front. How, after the brief notice of its foundation, there had been no public record of the Society.

She made another note: *Babbage Society secret*. Their offices, their analytical engines, even their very existence. Was that The Secret? The existence of the Babbage Society? But what difference could that make today?

Unless They were the Babbage Society; still secret, still deathly afraid of losing that secrecy.

But that only pushed the question further back. Why had the Society been secret?

She cupped her chin in her hands and stared at the wall. Such a long trail of death. And there was no reason to suppose she had all the names. She wondered how many of the other authors in the Index had met untimely ends. Something else to check up on.

Absently, she chewed on the end of her pen. But what about Randall Carson, who was Quinn's associate? Carson had *not* gone into hiding.

*They didn't know about Carson*. Could that be it? She scanned the Index again, looking for Carson's name. She didn't know exactly what she expected to find. Some pattern. Something *different* about Randall Carson. A special cause, Abe had once told her, always produces a special pattern in the data.

A subconscious impression formed and bobbed to the surface of her mind. Carefully, she went back through the Index and verified it. There were no papers attributed to Randall Carson until after 1867, when Quinn came west. In fact, as a few minutes of additional study showed, except for Quinn himself, the names of the authors before and after 1867 formed two disjoint sets. Now what did that mean?

Wait a minute. She took the pen from her mouth and stared into space. Us and Them, Red had told her. Two groups with the same secret. Two disjoint sets. What if the Society had split and one faction had gone after the other?

Sure! Quinn had broken with the Society in 1867 when he came west. Started his own rival society. That's why the names on the *post-bellum* papers were all different.

Great. But when a professional society splits, they usually don't go gunning after each other.

Unless one faction is afraid the other will spill The Secret.

The picture was becoming clearer: Quinn works in the Interior Department as a "mole" for the Babbage Society, Lord knows why. At the end of the Civil War, he quits abruptly, goes West and starts his own group. Then Belleau is killed—and maybe others, too. Quinn goes underground and becomes a hunted man. The Widener Building offices she had found were Quinn's, hidden for the same reason as the man himself. Carson, a man unknown to the others, is the front man. But then, when Quinn is killed, they close up shop.

Then she recalled how the file cabinets had been emptied, apparently in haste. The doorway, boarded up. *Maybe they didn't close up. Maybe they just moved elsewhere.*

It was all starting to make a terrible kind of sense! A thrill ran through her limbs. She was so elated that it took her a moment to realize that she had still not discovered the root cause. She was still looking at symptoms. The tremblors and uplifts and shattered buildings that marked a great earthquake. She had not found the fault line yet. What had set the whole thing in motion? What was The Secret?

The Society had built mechanical computers. Babbage engines.

*So what?* Why keep the machines secret? Especially in such a technophilliac era as the Victorian Age? Babbage had actually begun public construction of one, but had given it up as impractical. (Or had he?)

Answer: It wasn't the machines themselves, but the way they used them.

To do academic research. Why keep that secret?

It was getting late. Her notepad was filling up with ideas and questions and speculations. Yawning, she flipped the sheet over and started a fresh page. Red had implied a great public outrage; so it wasn't your ordinary, garden-variety secret.

Answer: Not the research *per se*, but the purpose of the research, demanded secrecy.

Question: What purpose?

Answer: Where did the list of trigger events fit in?

That wasn't an answer. That was another question. She had almost forgotten the list that Dennis had kept. Except that

79

Brady Quinn's murder had appeared on it, it hadn't seemed particularly relevant. Now she wondered. Was there a connection between the "horseshoe nails" on the list and the researches of the Babbage Society? She wrote *Call Dennis* on her pad and underlined it three times.

She read through the Index once more, this time studying the titles rather than the authors and dates, searching for some sense of their intentions. Most of the titles were gibberish to her. There were frequent references to "yokes" and "ideons." *On the Effects of the Deletion of "Stovepipe" from the Fifteenth Yoke.* That was one of Quinn's. 1864. *Reinforcement of the Ideon Complex Relative to Incandescent Lighting.* Carson, 1871.

She looked up "ideon" in the dictionary, but found nothing. However, "ideo-" was given as a prefix meaning "idea."

On the second page, she found another odd word; but one that she remembered. A paper by Phineas Hammondton entitled *A Cliological Analysis of Outlandish Settlements.* (Outlandish didn't count as odd. She remembered from her language arts classes that the term "Outlands" had originally referred to the lands west of the Mississippi.) But "cliological" she remembered from Dennis' list. His professor friend had said the word would mean "science of history." *Answer: They were using Babbage's embryonic system analysis to study history.*

Yes. That made sense. But still, what was the big deal? Why the secrecy? Sure, looking for scientific laws at work in history would have been controversial. After all, look at the fuss people had made over Darwin! But the Victorians had prided themselves on their scientific progress. They wouldn't have reacted any worse to the notion of a cultural science than they had to that of a biological science.

Patiently, she continued to read. Something would click. The titles couched in mathematical jargon, she ignored. There was no chance that she would understand their meaning. But scattered among them were a few titles in plain English. Or almost in plain English. *The Impact of the Zoopraxiscope on Live Theatre,* 1879. *Rate of Change of the Powers Accorded the General Govt. vis a vis the Sev'ral States & its Significance Regarding the 15ᵗʰ and 23ʳᵈ Yokes,* Meechum Clark, 1836. *Dates of Incorporation for the Various Mexican Territories,* Crawford, 1834. *Effect of Wireless Telegraphy on the Propogation of Ideons,* Shelton, 1847. *A Geological Apprecia-*

*tion of the Sierra Country and it's Likely Effect on the Peopling of the Californias*, J. C. Frèmont, 1841. *Speculations, Stemming from John Hyatt's Artificial Billiard Balls, on the Non-Chemical Nature of the Ultimate Explosive*, Carson, 1871. *Ideons Required for the Encouragement of Aerial Flight*, 1862. *On the Replacement of Rail Roads by Autonomously Directed Vehicles. Expected Results of the General European War, ca. 1910-1915*. That one, by a man named F. P. Hatch, was written in 1882. *The Desirability of the Third Sub-branch Off the 35th Yoke and the Ideons Required for its Realization*, 1853.

An uneasy feeling stole over her as she read. There was something peculiar about some of those titles. Some of them were written long before the events they appeared to describe. *Well, it's a science's business to predict, isn't it?* And if they had been studying history scientifically . . . Yet, another tone rang through. Something in the choice of words. Something her literary ear picked out. A sense of mastery and challenge. The anticipation of action, not simply of observation. Of requirements to be met.

*They weren't scientists. They were engineers.*

The thought rose unbidden in her mind, and it was a moment or two before she realized what it meant. When she did, the implication stunned her. They hadn't been trying to study cultural systems at all; they had been trying to control them!

She dropped the Index folder to the desk and stared into space, her mouth slightly parted. *Could that be it?* Had the Babbage Society been trying to manipulate the course of history behind-the-scenes? The list that Dennis had taken. Horseshoe nails, he had said. Times when the actions of a handful of people had had disproportionate consequences. Turning points of history. And some shadowy people with great clunking computers had identified them and made them turn the way they wanted. What else could it be? *What else could it be?*

That would certainly explain Their fear of discovery. Slavery, exploitation, wars, recessions. Lincoln's assassination, for God's sake! She remembered that from the list. History was a trail of sorrow and tragedy. If people discovered that a specific group were somehow responsible . . . Oh, yes. The nearest lamppost would not be near enough.

She remembered all the things she had longed to forget.

All the symbols of failure. How hard it had been for her father to find jobs; how the real estate agent had steered them away from certain neighborhoods, forcing them to live among the drug addicts and the gangs that had finally swallowed her baby brother; how her mother had died all too young because she couldn't afford the medicine she needed. Sarah clenched her teeth. So, They feared lynching, did They? Well, she might just give a hand with the rope herself.

But, on the other hand, if They were directing history, why not credit Them with the good, as well? The inventions that made life easier; the liberation movements of the last few decades; child labor laws, social security, the safety net of laws and regulations that protected the helpless from at least the worst exploitations.

No, it was all too absurd. History was too complex to master.

But was it too complex to *try* to master? And trying, with a secretly suppressed scientific breakthrough, might they not have succeeded, at least a little? And having succeeded just a little, might they not have killed to protect the secret of that success? It made sense. It made an awful, terrifying sense.

She gripped the desk top to keep the room from spinning. *So, I'm master of my own fate, am I?* she thought bitterly. When Crawford, Quinn and the others had scripted things out 150 years ago? What a grand illusion! A charade. A Potemkin village. History was folk tales, its heroes and heroines capering fools.

Her past was suddenly askew. She was cast adrift, and nothing meant what it seemed to mean. It was as if her mother's face had slipped just a bit, showing itself to be a mask; and behind the loved and familiar features was another person; a stranger, and not her mother at all.

She sat in the dimly lit study, in the pool of light cast by her desk lamp, and shivered while the dying flames in the fireplace cast jeering ghosts upon the walls. In her ears, the cheerful rag *War Clouds,* was a mockery. She had never felt more alone.

82

# VIII

*What else could it be?* Dennis put his finger between the pages to mark his place and stared pensively into the distance. What else could it be? He could hear Jeremy whistling in the bedroom as he tied his tie.

Dennis glanced again at the newspaper where it lay on the coffee table. MAD KILLER IN PARK, the headline shrieked. And the sidebar: A BRUSH WITH DEATH, by Morgan Grimes. Exclusive interview with well-known developer Sarah Beaumont. Bullet missed by inches. How does it feel to brush so close to death? A file photo of an impossibly cheerful Sarah.

Dennis shuddered. He had been calling her all day, ever since he had heard the awful news; but there had been no answer. He had left a message on her answering machine.

Jeremy walked out of the bedroom, tugging on the knot in his tie. "How do I look?"

Dennis spared him a glance. "You look fine."

Jeremy tsk'ed and rolled his eyes up. "A fashion critic you are not. I suppose you are going to the play dressed just the way you are." He turned to go.

"Jerry, wait. I want you to listen to something." He opened the book he had been reading. *Cultural Literacy*, by E. D. Hirsch, Jr. He found his place, cleared his throat and read. ". . . although Noah Webster's spellers, readers, and dictionaries enjoyed uniquely large sales, they were not unique in any other respect. In fact . . . the contents of American schoolbooks of the nineteenth century were so similar and interchangeable that their creators might seem to have participated in a conspiracy to indoctrinate young Americans with

83

commonly shared attitudes, including a fierce national loyalty and pride."

He closed the book and looked at Jeremy. "Well?" Jeremy looked puzzled and shrugged. Dennis sighed. "Never mind, then."

Jeremy returned to the bedroom, shaking his head. "Are you ready? We're leaving in a few minutes."

Dennis laid the book atop the newspaper. *Mad Gunman, my foot.* He thought again about the list that he had been studying. Davis Belleau murdered. Brady Quinn murdered. Ambrose Bierce disappeared. Agatha Penwether murdered. No, not a madman.

"*. . . participated in a conspiracy to indoctrinate young Americans.*"

"*. . . maybe Taylor and Dewey were part of a conspiracy.*"

"*Horseshoe nails . . .*"

"*1860—Lincoln's election.*"

"*A statistician in the Interior Department . . . Shot twice as an innocent bystander?*"

Fragments of conversation echoed in his memory. Fragments of text. They resonated with one another. They shifted like a kaleidoscope into new and startling mosaics.

"*Horseshoe nails . . .*"

"*Edison, Ford, and the others used to meet regularly to discuss the course of the country.*"

"*1896—Tho°. B. Reed loses nomination.*"

"*The actions of a handful of individuals that had consequences all out of proportion.*"

"*1865—Lincoln's assassination.*"

"*. . . changed the course of history, sometimes obviously, sometimes subtly.*"

"*1914—von Kluck's Turn.*"

"*. . . some events build, like an avalanche, into consequences that only become evident in hindsight . . .*"

"*1865—Twiggs's orders were delayed . . .*" By whom?

"*Maybe someone hammered the nail back in.*"

"*1900—The°. Roosevelt made VP.*"

"*. . . turning points of a rather subtle kind . . .*"

"*fl. ca. 1900—Frederick W. Taylor.*"

"*. . . part of a conspiracy.*"

"*Cliology . . . means a 'science of history.' *"

Quinn. Carson. Secret room. Babbage engines.

"*. . . try orthogonal factor analysis . . .*"

84

*"Cliology . . . means a 'science of history.' "*

*Davis Belleau murdered. Brady Quinn murdered. Ambrose Bierce disappeared. Agatha Penwether murdered.*

*" . . .change the course of history . . ."*

What else could it be? The list no longer seemed a nagging puzzle to be solved. He had found the logic behind it, and it was a frightening logic.

*Davis Belleau murdered. Brady Quinn murdered. Ambrose Bierce disappeared. Agatha Penwether murdered. Sarah Beaumont . . .*

Why Sarah? he wondered. Why only her. We both discovered the list. Why not me, as well?

Why not, indeed? He began to shake. Why not?

Well, he had wanted to develop his curiosity, hadn't he? He had worked at it all week, like a body builder. And what was it they said about curiosity and cats?

There had to be a reason why they had attacked Sarah and not him. They knew about Sarah; but not about him. That was one possibility. The second possibility, of course, was that they just hadn't gotten around to him. Yet.

Sarah was a hacker. She did most of her work on the DataNet. That could be it. Dennis did not know a great deal about computers. In fact, he mistrusted them. He refused to patronize ATM machines; and never used debit cards. But he knew enough to realize that one program could monitor another; could watch to see what information one "accessed." No one could possibly monitor public libraries and book stores and archives and private conversations.

*In that case, they might be on to her, but not me.*

*Then I should be safe.*

He let out a shaky breath. *They couldn't know about me.*

The thought comforted him, warmed him, restored the security he had lost when he had first realized what the list really meant. *I've got to warn Sarah.* He reached a hand toward the phone, then paused. Telephones could be tapped, couldn't they? If he called her and warned her, and these people—whoever they were—were listening, they would know that he knew.

Bullet missed by inches.

How does it feel to brush so close to death?

*It feels shitty, Morgan Grimes, that's how it feels.*

The heroic thing, he knew, would be to call Sarah anyway. To warn her, despite the danger to himself.

But she hadn't answered her phone this morning. Maybe she's hiding, like Brady Quinn. Perhaps she's figured it out herself by now. Then, if he tried to warn her, he would only expose himself to no purpose.

Slowly, he withdrew his hand. He looked at it where it lay in his lap. It was trembling; but not with fear. He had just discovered something about himself; and he did not particularly like it.

Sarah awoke with a start the next morning, slumped over her desk. Her neck and arms were stiff. She had vague recollections of a nightmare, now thankfully forgotten. *I must have fallen asleep at the terminal last night. How late did I work?* She stretched and pushed herself out of the chair. Stumbling to the window, she pulled the curtains open and blinked at the morning sun.

She found her way to the kitchen and turned the coffee on staring at it numbly until it had started to perk. On her way to the front door, she noticed that the grandfather's clock was stopped. *Must've forgot to wind it.* She yawned and opened the front door and stooped and picked up the morning *News*.

As she did so, she remembered that she had stopped the clock herself, and that she had spent hours thinking over what she knew about Quinn, and that she had reached a frightening conclusion, and that someone was trying to kill her.

The nightmare returned. She stepped back and slammed the door and leaned against the wall, breathing fast. *Damn! That was careless, Sarah.* There could have been a sniper out there, waiting for her to grab her paper. She remembered opening the curtains. She had stood directly in front of the window, in plain view of anyone farther down the mountain-side. Anyone with a telescopic sight.

*Shooting uphill is difficult,* she reminded herself. The shots would fall short. And there wasn't any place for a sniper to hide except on her neighbors' properties. She peered through the peephole in her door and stared at the driveway. Nothing. Nothing she could see. The ornamental bushes that lined the walk now seemed sinister places of concealment; a squad of assassins could hide among them.

She closed her eyes and let her breath out slowly. Then she sidled back to the window and, back against the wall, drew the curtains. The room darkened.

Returning to the kitchen, she threw the paper down on the

table and tried to pour herself a cup of coffee. Her hand wobbled and the first drops hit the saucer. *Calm yourself, Sarah,* she chided herself. *Panic is always stupid.* She waited a moment, breathing evenly, then filled the cup. Then she sat and deliberately forced herself to review her situation.

A secret society—the Babbage Society—trying to direct the course of history? Madness. How was it even possible? And yet it fit. Babbage and his embryonic system analysis. The mechanical computers. The papers in the Index. The "horseshoe nails." The man in the library. Red's visit. If anything, it seemed even more likely than it had last night.

So, what was she to do about it? Red had warned her to do nothing. Sit tight and he would fix things. But who was Red, that she should put her faith in him? He hadn't killed her and he had certainly had the means and the opportunity. But that was hardly the basis for trust and friendship. *Have you met my good friend, Red Malone? He didn't kill me when he had the chance.*

And yet, what else could she do but sit tight? Should she call Dennis? She had tried last night, after she had realized what the Babbage Society was; but there had been no answer. He and Jeremy had probably gone out. They often did on Saturday nights. Dennis distrusted gadgets like answering machines and the phone had rung and rung, until she had finally hung up in frustration.

Now, in the morning's light, it seemed less a good idea. Whatever Dennis knew or didn't know, he had not gone on the DataNet. And if that were so, he was safe, at least temporarily. While, if she called him to warn him, and the Babbage people were tapping her phone—and that seemed an elementary conclusion—it would endanger him.

*Morgan!*

She had gone to see Morgan on Friday, before the incident in the Park, to ask for his help in locating old news items about the Babbage Society. She had spent the evening with him after the attempt on her life and told him everything about Quinn. She hadn't known then, of course, that the knowledge was dangerous; or that it had anything to do with the attack in the Park. But he had promised to check into the Babbage Society for her. He was going to ask questions. He would have no idea what he was walking into. She had to warn him!

She was punching up the City Room at the News when the

incoming line rang. She hesitated, unsure whether to answer. Then she thought it might be Malone or Dennis and clicked the phone hook once to switch lines.

"Yes?"

"Sarah! Thank God!"

"Morgan? I was just going to call you. I—"

"Never mind that. I'll be out there in two shakes. Don't go anywhere. Don't open the door for anyone until I get there."

"Morgan, what's the matter with you? I've never heard you sound so—"

"You're in danger. Worse than I ever thought. Have you seen page seven in this morning's *News?*"

"No."

"Read it."

The line went dead. A moment later, the dial tone sounded in her ear. She hooked the phone. Then she laughed. She had tried to call Morgan to warn him; and he had called her to warn her! That was priceless.

So what was on page seven that was so important? She returned to the kitchen table and picked up her coffee cup. Her gaze rested on the newspaper she had thrown on the table. Giant block letters on the front page shrieked her name; but she had no desire to relive those events, so she flipped open to the inside pages. She hardly glanced at the stories. Trivia. Play-acting. None of them meant anything. Politics and business and trade talks. She wondered how much of the day's news had been engineered by Them.

She felt almost lighthearted. Morgan was coming. It would be good to have him with her. She was still frightened; but the load was not so heavy now. She was not alone.

At first, the headline on page seven did not register. COUPLE SLAIN IN LOVE TRIANGLE. That sort of thing happened somewhere every day. A man named Joseph Dawson had trailed his wife, Barbara, to a West Colfax motel. There he had shot her and her lover, Paul Abbot, a co-worker, before turning the gun on himself. A lurid scandal. The kind that would grace the front page of a New York tabloid. Sex and violence.

But . . . Paul Abbot? The foreman at Widener's? She set her cup down shakily and re-read the story. A sordid affair, like hundreds of others. Adultery. Jealousy. Rage. Murder and suicide. And she didn't believe it for a moment.

*Poor Babs,* she thought. And her poor husband. She even

88

found a shred of sympathy for Paul Abbot. He had been an odious lecher, but he had been a human being. He hadn't deserved what had happened to him. She wondered if They had lured Dawson into doing the deed, or whether They had simply killed all three of them and set it up to look like a sex triangle.

That must have been what Morgan meant. He had drawn the same conclusion. But why had They killed Abbot? And Barbara Dawson, the other foreman? She barely knew Abbot; and Dawson, she knew not at all. Yet, it must have something to do with the Babbage Society. It was too much of a coincidence. She took her coffee and ran to the computer desk where she began hacking.

Someone *had* been following her, after all, that day under the viaduct. She had spent a long time in the Widener building. Had They drawn some mad conclusion about her and Abbot? Or had They gone there Themselves and found the secret room and the Babbage engines? If so, they could be killing anyone who might know about them.

But the police records, when she moused into them, revealed no assault on Ernst Widener, the owner, or on any of the other employees. Nor were there any reports of burglary or vandalism at the Widener Building. Surely, if They had discovered the secret room, They would not leave the machines there for others to find.

Then why kill Abbot and Dawson? They had tried to assassinate her because of what they thought she knew. But Abbot was totally in the dark.

But did They know that? They must think that she had told him something. Why They would think so, God alone knew. But then why the delay? She had gone to the building on Monday and the attack hadn't been until Friday. Why hadn't they acted immediately against her and her supposed "accomplice?"

Perhaps They hadn't been sure about her at first. After all, any casual researcher might show a passing interest in Quinn for any number of innocuous reasons. Something else must have happened in the meantime to convince Them otherwise. But what?

*Her mouse!* It was running in the Net, hunting for connections between Quinn, the Babbage Society, analytical engines, and a half dozen other things. Oh Lord! Nosing into Brady Quinn's life wasn't motive enough. By itself, it might have made Them suspicious; but that mouse must have scared Them silly. No wonder there had been no attempt to warn her off. *Based on what They thought I already knew, it was long past time for warnings.*

The mouse had been running for several days before They acted; so They hadn't noticed it right away. That meant They weren't omniscient. And Malone had said that They were frightened of exposure. For the first time, she thought of Them as human beings rather than as an impersonal force. They weren't infallible; They made mistakes. Deadly mistakes. *They might be just as uncertain of Their next step as I am!*

She activated her terminal and recalled the mouse. It was much too late to matter. Red was going on a fool's errand. He would never be able to convince Them that she wasn't the Intruder now. In fact, once Red found out about the mouse, he might begin to have doubts himself.

*I know what* They *do in such matters.* When in doubt, kill. *But what do Red's people do?* He hadn't actually said they wouldn't kill her. ("Terminate with extreme prejudice," she imagined Red saying.) With a sudden chill, she wondered what sort of "adjusting" Red did.

She picked up the paper again and looked at the headline. COUPLE SLAIN IN LOVE TRIANGLE. Now, it seemed, They were backtracking her activities, eliminating anyone else she may have talked to.

She stood up so suddenly that she jarred the desk; spilling the coffee. *Anyone else she might have talked to?!* There was no question now of endangering him. She ran to the phone and punched Dennis' number. The phone was preprogrammed, so she only had to hit two buttons. Still, she managed to miss one in her haste. She cursed, cut the connection, and punched again.

The phone rang. "Come on," she muttered through clenched teeth. "Come on . . ."

Jeremy answered. Dennis' friend.

"Jerry, this is Sarah. Is Dennis there? I need to talk to him right away. It's important." *I might be wrong. I probably am. I hope I am.*

"You mean you haven't heard?" Jerry answered. His voice sounded distraught, as if he'd been crying. That was likely. Jerry was high-strung and sensitive. "Oh, it's terrible. It's simply awful."

90

Her heart stopped and her hand tightened on the receiver. "What is? What happened?"

"Dennis. He was struck by a car last night. A hit-and-run. We were on our way home from the DCPA and . . . They took him to Porter. They were operating all night."

"Oh, no! Will he . . . Is he alright now?"

"I . . . don't know," Jerry admitted. "I've been calling and calling. Making a frightful pest of myself. They won't know until later today. They say his condition is critical. They've got nurses watching him; and he's hooked up to all sorts of equipment, so the doctors will know if there's any change."

*Thank God for the space program,* Sarah thought. *It boosted medical technology a century ahead. They save people routinely now who would have been lost only a few decades ago.* She was trying to reassure herself, she knew. Operations weren't miracles; and medicine was not theology. But "critical" wasn't "DOA," either. There was still a chance. A good one.

*They must have more assets in place, now,* she thought. *A hit-and-run late at night was a lot smoother take-out than a mad gunman in the Park. The police would ask fewer questions.*

"Who did it, Jerry? Do they know?"

"Who? No one knows. Teeners high on mothers' tears or something. The police have a bulletin out; but they'll never catch them."

*No,* thought Sarah, *they never will. They won't even know to look.*

"And what damned difference will it make if they do?"

Privately, Sarah agreed. But she told Jerry some banal platitudes about having hope and how Dennis would pull through, and how everything would turn out for the best. She tried to sound very confident. She wasn't sure she believed it, and she didn't suppose Jerry did, either.

She was surprised to discover that the injury of another could affect her as much as the trauma she herself had been through. Ah, Dennis. She sobbed softly. If only she had called last night. He might not have gone out. He might have stayed home and They would not have gotten him.

Or, perhaps They would have gone to his apartment; and instead of being in critical condition, Dennis would be dead, and Jeremy as well. It wasn't any use accepting the responsibility for another's act. It wasn't her fault that Dennis had been run over. It was Their fault. It was Their vicious paranoia, not her researches, nor her failure to call. And rather than sorrow, what she should feel most of all was anger.

When would Morgan get here? She looked impatiently at the clock. It was a twenty-five minute drive from Downtown to Applewood. There shouldn't be much traffic; not on a Sunday morning.

A new thought struck her with the suddeness of a slap. Morgan had said yesterday that he would call on Paul Abbot and on Dennis. Now, both had been attacked. Could it be that . . . ?

A cold unreasoning fear chilled her.

Red Malone had implied that people could be programmed, without their knowledge or consent. Drugs. Hypnosis. The killer in the Park had been programmed, he said. So why not Morgan? They could have aimed him at Dennis, at Abbot and launched him as easily as a Stinger missile.

And who was to say that it was programming? He could just as easily be a witting tool. What was the word? A mole?

*No, not Morgan! It wasn't in him!*

Yet how did she know that? How close had she ever gotten to him? Never past the surface. Never past the *Hi, how are you, sure is good to see you, have you heard the latest*. She had never known Morgan Grimes; only the face that he kept for her to see. Now Morgan was on his way here. To kill her? That was crazy.

*Even paranoids have enemies.*

But they never could have friends, could they? Morgan had told her not to turn her back on him. Had he been trying to warn her, despite conditioning? In retrospect, his questions seemed more sinister. He had been pumping her to find out what she knew. And she had had the impression even then that he knew more than he was letting on.

She noticed that the light was blinking on her answering machine. How long had it been like that? How long had it been since she had checked? Since yesterday? Mechanically, she played it back.

It was Dennis. He wanted to know how she was. He had heard about the shooting and was concerned. For a sliver of an instant she thought she was listening to him speak in real time and almost started to answer. Then she remembered and she hit the cut-off. She stared silently at the machine for a few moments, then she rewound the tape and played the message

92

again and then again. *Oh, Dennis, what have we stumbled into?*

Run and hide.

Sound advice, indeed; but running was serious business, not to be undertaken lightly. Where would she go? You can't hide by checking into a motel. It would have to be in the forest. Up in the High Country.

The garage smelled of oil and gasoline. It was a large garage, oversized even for two cars, and rows of bright red storage cabinets lined two walls. The old, white, mud-splattered Blazer sat on the far side. For the next several minutes she busied herself in loading it. No point in running without good equipment. It felt good to be in motion, any kind of motion, even running. Anything was better than standing still.

Down sleeping bag. It got *cold* at night in the High Country, even in the summer. Geological Survey maps. Compass. Kerosene lantern. Flashlight, with extra bulbs and batteries. Matches, the kind that struck anywhere. (In a pinch, she could start a fire with a bow drill; but why go out of your way to make things hard on yourself?) Fishing line and hooks. Wire and wire cutters. Hunting knife and strop.

She pulled the knife from its scabbard. The blade gleamed wickedly in the light of the bare bulb suspended from the garage ceiling. She turned it this way and that, seeing her reflection weirdly distorted. She remembered her "final exam" in wilderness survival. The knife was perfectly balanced. It would make a complete revolution in thirty feet, a handy thing to know, as several rabbits had discovered to their sorrow. You could starve to death on rabbit meat, she remembered. Too lean; not enough fat. Survival trivia. Next to *real* survival, it had all been play-acting.

She turned and jerked her arm and the knife planted itself in the center panel of the garage door. She grunted and recovered the blade, stuffing it into her rucksack.

In the bedroom, she changed into sensible hiking clothes. Bush jacket. Heavy trousers to protect her legs. Sturdy boots. A change of clothing in case she got wet. She was lacing up her boots when she remembered something Red Malone had said. *You can always run from a threat. Sometimes that doesn't work, either.* She wondered what he had meant by that.

She had climbed into the Blazer and was about to open the garage door when the dashboard clock caught her eye. Nine-

93

fifty. Was that right? She checked her wrist watch. Yes, it was. Morgan was late.

Or was he outside, waiting for her to open the door? Had his call been intended to panic her into running? She left the garage and returned to the front door where she looked through the peephole again.

Still nothing. But then, what could she expect to see? A man with a rifle? They wouldn't be so clumsy this time. A second try for the same victim in the same way would raise too many questions. Even the police might notice.

What should she do? Stay put or run for it? A sitting duck, or a duck on the wing?

The phone rang as she passed back through the kitchen and she stared at it as if it had suddenly come alive. After three rings her answering machine cut in. Hello, she heard herself say. I can't come to the phone right now.

She groped around under the breakfast bar and pulled out a stool. She sat on it and stared at the recorder.

"Sarah? This is Kevin, at the *News*. Call me right away. It's an emergency."

She twisted her fingers together. *Kevin?* A vague sense of foreboding stole over her. She snatched the telephone and punched up the City Room. She asked for Kevin. "Tell him Sarah Beaumont is returning his call."

Kevin was on the line within moments. "Sarah. I'm sorry to have to tell you this; but your old partner, Morgan Grimes, was stabbed to death in the parking lot just a half hour ago."

Sarah felt as if a massive electric current had gone through her. Morgan? Morgan couldn't possibly be dead. He was a fixture, like Mount Evans. Always there. She remembered how they had traded insults during her cub reporter days. How he had shared bylines with her. How he had taken care of her the day she had been shot at.

She remembered how she had suspected him, feared his coming here, and was ashamed. Her eyes burned. It had been a crazy paranoid thought.

"God, no!" she said. "Do they know who did it?" She knew. It was Them. They were making a clean sweep of it. Morgan was dead, and it was all her fault. Once fear had seized you, you did stupid, foolish things. Evil had not done half the harm in the world as foolishness.

"A doper," said Kevin. "There was a packet of mothers' tears under his body and a thick wad of bills in his coat

94

pocket. The police think he was scoring some dope and the deal went sour."

"Kevin, you know that isn't true!"

"Hey, I knew Morg' as well as anyone. I know that wasn't his scene. But it looks bad."

What could she tell him? That there were four easily-explained assaults in the last two days that were not so easily explained? A mad sniper; a love triangle; a hit-and-run; and a dope deal. The police would see no connection. And if she told Kevin, it would only mark him as another target.

"Sarah. The reason I called . . . His last words were for you. He said, 'Tell Sarah the Pulitzer isn't worth this.' " He waited for her to say something. When she didn't reply, he asked, "Does that mean anything to you?"

"I—No. No, it doesn't." She thanked him for calling and hung up quickly.

She couldn't think of anything else to do so she walked to the kitchen table and sat there. The remnants of her coffee were cold and stale. She didn't bother to clear it away. She shoved it aside and laid her head in her arms. *I never did repay him for how he helped me. Instead, I let him get killed. I could have warned him, but I was afraid. I was afraid and I didn't trust him. I should have known him better. I should have let myself get closer to him, back when we worked together.*

*"Should have" cuts no ice. What happened to the Sarah that was in charge of herself?*

She's gotten an awful fright, that's what. She found out she's not in charge, after all.

*Bullshit. So the circumstances aren't the best. They're dangerous. Fine. You can't choose your circumstances. The three billion odd other people in the world do that for you. But you can choose how you face those circumstances.*

That's easy for you to say. A very dear friend of mine is lying in a hospital mashed into Jell-o. Another one is in the morgue. (*Morg' is in the morgue*, gibbered a mad portion of her mind.) And I don't suppose They'll stop at one try at me, either.

*No, I don't suppose They will. So what are you going to do, give up? Giving up is the only solid-gold, guaranteed way to fail. They won't have to beat you, because you'll have already beaten yourself.*

So what can I do?

95

*Hit back!*

At who, sucker? I don't even know who They are.

*You don't have to know that.*

She straightened. No, I don't, she realized. She set her jaw. She could pay Morgan back now. It wasn't enough. It would never be enough; but he would need a coin for the ferryman. She went to her terminal and set to work.

# IX

"Is the line secure?"

Red Malone sat in the motel bed propped up on the pillows. It was the regular motel phone, voice channel only, going through the regular switchboard, over the regular AT&T lines. "Sure, it's secure," he said. "Have I ever lied to you?" He popped a can of 7-Up with his left hand and took a sip.

"Why have you contacted us?"

"Why, Cousin Daniel, to hear the sweet sound of your voice." He grinned at the phone. "To gossip a little, maybe. How are tricks over on your side of the fence? Kill any innocent women and children lately?" He always enjoyed baiting Kennison. There were few things in life that gave him such undiluted pleasure.

"No," Kennison's voice answered him. "None that were innocent."

Red heard the edge in the other's reply. He put the can aside. "Explain."

"I owe you no explanations. If there are debts, perhaps you owe us one, of gratitude."

"Gratitude." He said it through clenched teeth.

"Yes, a little cabal that had stumbled onto the Secret. Fortunately, we have nipped it in the bud."

"You didn't get her. She escaped."

"A temporary inconvenience. We have gotten her organization, however."

"You fool! She doesn't have an organization. She's a naif. No connection with the Intruder. She stumbled on Quinn by accident, because of a real estate deal she's putting together.

97

But she doesn't know his significance. I told her to lay off."

"Indeed?"

"Yeah, indeed."

"Then, you spoke with her. That hardly seems politic."

"Sure. But *We* like to ask questions first."

"In cases like this one, it is better to be safe. He who hesitates is lost."

"Fools rush in, you—" Red bit his tongue. He was going to call Kennison a son of a bitch; but he didn't want trouble with the ASPCA. "I talked to her and I believe her."

"Ah, well, Cousin Malone. You always did have a weakness in that way. I suppose she is pretty."

Kennison had a lot of nerve raking over that particular sore. He liked to talk about debts? Well, the chit was still out on that one. "She could be as ugly as you and it wouldn't matter. Will you call off your dogs?"

"On your say so? I am afraid not. That is a Council decision."

"Well, network your damned Council and tell them what I told you. We're sharing information on this one, and that's my information."

"Information that hardly seems supported by the facts, my dear fellow."

"Facts? What do you mean?"

Kennison tsk'ed and Red glared at the phone in irritation. Then Kennison told him about the mouse and Red listened in silence. He closed his eyes. "You're sure of that?" he asked when he had finished.

"We were able to trace the mouse directly back to her home terminal."

"That doesn't make sense. Why would she be so careless? The Intruder never slipped up like that."

"Even Jove nods."

Red stared at the window of the motel. The highway traffic whipped by. The window rattled. The soda on the nightstand fizzed. He felt like a monumental fool. "Yeah, I guess he does at that."

"You are on the scene, are you not? Perhaps you can take care of business for us."

"I don't work for you."

"No, but the Secret protects us both. It is in our joint interest to secure this leak before it becomes public."

"Not a chance. This is a Council matter." He liked throwing Kennison's words back at him.

"You will not attempt to impede our instrument, will you?"

"I'll do what I damn well please." He slammed the phone down so hard he knocked over the soda can. The soda splashed his shirt and pants. "Damn it!" He leapt from the bed and dabbed at his clothes with his handkerchief. It did no good. His pants looked like he had wet himself. "Damn it!" he repeated. He grabbed the can and threw it across the room. It left a trail behind on the carpet and the bedclothes. He hated being wrong; and he hated looking like a fool. He would have to pay another visit to Ms. Beaumont.

Sarah spent the entire day in front of the screen, composing a worm. It was rough going, even for her: a bi-level program, with the second program encrypted in the code of the first. On the surface, it would look like normal NetMail: billboard chatter on the hacker network. It could boot from terminal to terminal without arousing suspicion.

Buried deep within the harmless chatter was a cryptogrammic algorithm. The cryptogram was self-booting and would trigger the second level program.

The second level was an anagram of the first. Embedded like a complex crossword puzzle in several dimensions, it would create a self-replicating worm. Whenever an off-line database suckled on the Net, the worm would inject a clone into the outside system. Once there, it would hunt for references to Sarah Beaumont, Dennis French, Paul Abbot, Morgan Grimes, Brady Quinn, Charles Babbage, and the names from the Babbage Society Index. If it found them, or even a significant fraction of them, the clone would send word back through a complex relay of Network nodes, then scramble the database. Otherwise it would erase itslf. She used JUGGERNAUT for the scrambler. She had used it years ago, playing "Core Wars." It was crude, but effective; and They wouldn't be expecting it.

It might take a while, but eventually her worm would locate Their databases. An operation of that magnitude had to be on computer these days. Sooner or later, They would tap into the Net. When They did, she would know who and where They were, and she would have the satisfaction of destroying Their files. The odds were against any database but Theirs containing that particular collection of names, but at the moment she didn't much care if she scrambled the telephone directory.

She was almost finished when she realized what an idiot she was. She cursed herself for a fool. There was only one way to be safe when you knew someone's deadly secret, and she had overlooked it. Grimly, she set to work adding another subprogram.

When she was finally done, she stretched and looked at the clock. It was two in the morning. She had been at the terminal steadily for almost sixteen hours. *Not even time-and-a-half for overtime.* But she felt a satisfaction. She was fighting back, the only way she knew how. She wasn't a victim anymore. She might lose yet, still get killed; but at least she'd go down like John Henry, with a hammer in her hand. There was even something exhilarating about the thought. Sooner or later, everyone went down into darkness. What mattered was how you went: cringing like a slave; or defiant, like Nat Turner.

God, she was hungry. She hadn't realized how late it was. She hadn't eaten all day. Just a half cup of coffee in the morning.

She yawned and wandered into the kitchen and began to fix herself a sandwich. It was dark in the kitchen. The refrigerator cast a lonely circle of light around her. Everyone around her was being struck down. But she didn't feel helpless anymore.

*Tell Sarah the Pulitzer isn't worth this.*

Those had been Morgan's last words. She remembered the day she had visited the *News*, when Morgan had been talking on the phone. That first day, when she had started looking into Quinn's life. Only twelve days ago? It seemed like twelve lifetimes. What are you working on? The Pulitzer, of course.

She leaned on the refrigerator door. Morgan must have meant that the knifing had to do with the story he'd been chasing. He had been trying to get a message through, to one person who would understand. Morgan had wanted her to read his story file.

She closed the refrigerator and ran to the terminal, her sandwich forgotten. She hacked into the *News* system, again using a roundabout method, and keyed in Morgan's secret code, the one she had cracked years ago. A message appeared on the screen.

100

*Hello, Sarah. I know it's you because no one else could have broken this particular code. I hope you're not reading this, because if you are, then I'm dead and never reached your house. I know you wouldn't hack into here just for fun. You're honest. A character defect in a reporter, but one I always liked in you.*

"I liked it in you, too, Morgan," she whispered. Why was it we never told our friends these things while it mattered?

*The file you want is codenamed* DEATHLIST. *It's the story that will win me that Pulitzer, if I ever finish it. When I first stumbled onto it, I didn't know what I'd found. It was just a thread. Later I found another thread. I followed them and, somehow, they tied together. Then they tied in with a third item, and I had the hint of a pattern. It was just a hint, but it frightened me. Now, that business you asked me to check out for you? The Babbage Society? It seems to be still another thread. I wouldn't have realized except for Dennis' list, but now it all seems to fit. Sarah, there are a group of men and women operating in this country who make Murder, Inc. look like Mahatma Gandhi. There's no doubt in my mind that they have arranged killings, nation-wide for many, many years.*

What Morgan had uncovered, Sarah found as she read the file, was a series of seemingly unrelated deaths. Most of them had appeared accidental, or easily explained. A suicide here; a barroom quarrel there. Car accidents. Crazed snipers in towers. The world, it seemed, was populated by innocent bystanders.

But there had been odd little connections. Two victims, widely separated in time and space, had been working independently on biographies of William Harrison Hatch, a little-known statistician of the 1920s. That odd coincidence had made Morgan curious. Gradually, he had unearthed other circumstances linking two or more of the victims until, finally, he had a closed set of mutually connected deaths.

*Orthogonal factor analysis,* she remembered.

An odd twist: statisticians, ecologists, newspaper reporters, system analysts, policemen and certain other specialties had been represented among the victims far in excess of their numbers among the general public. Morgan had wondered, in a sardonic gloss, whether the insurance companies had known.

At first, Morgan thought of it as a human interest piece: the strange synergies of a small world. Later, he became convinced that the coincidences were more sinister. For a while, according to his notes, he had thought that he had found the most bizarre serial murderer yet. But the killings went on too long. No one person could have committed them all; unless he had started as a child and continued the grisly work well into old age. It had to be the work of more than one person.

He had followed a gossamer web of hints, remarks, half-world gossip. The trail was faint, and sometimes he lost it amid a confusing tangle of pseudonyms and anonymous phone calls. But Morgan was good at what he did. Sarah had always admired his dogged persistence and his native caution. He always found the trail again.

Eventually, it had led him to a small group of people whose sole remarkable feature was that, with few exceptions, they were unremarkable. John Benton, Genevieve Weil, Daniel Kennison, and some others. Except for Kennison, who ran a well-known polling firm, they managed to stay out of newspapers; and they appeared to have nothing to do with one another. Sarah remembered that Morgan had asked her about them that time in his apartment.

All of them were wealthy, so wealthy that they were never mentioned by *Forbes*, or *Fortune*, or *Town* and *Country*. It was the kind of wealth that *never* advertised itself. All of them had increased already-considerable inheritances through good fortune in the stock market and foreign investments. As Morgan's note put it: "They bought Xerox before it became a verb."

His interview with Sarah was in the file as well. He hadn't been sure at the time that the attack in the Park belonged on his list; but he had had a hunch. If it did, it might give him a chance to learn their motive: Why would these wealthy people take such risks to kill total strangers? Until he knew that, he didn't have a story. No wonder he had been so interested in categorizing the different reasons for murder.

At the very end, there was a curious note. *Autocopy to Q-File.* What did that mean? Who else had Morgan sent the information to?

Sarah finished reading his notes and waited for the hard

copy to print. It was all clear to her now. Morgan Grimes was the Intruder. In his list of fifty-odd murder victims were the names of Kenneth Robertson and Alice McAuliffe, the two people that Red had mentioned. It was Morgan's snooping into the murders that had made Them nervous in the first place. More than fifty killings? No wonder They had been nervous about discovery!

Morgan hadn't realized at first that the Brady Quinn mystery and his own serial murders had been linked. They belonged to different centuries. Then he had seen Dennis' list. Agatha Penwether, the latest name on Dennis' list, was also the earliest name on his own. No wonder Morgan had been so excited when he had called her. Dennis' information had extended his list of killings back to 1876, the year of Davis Belleau's murder.

But it also meant he had exposed himself. Because he hadn't known about the connection, he hadn't exercised his usual caution. His inquiries into the murders had been quite discreet. If nothing else, the prominence of newspaper reporters among the victims assured that. But, like Sarah, he had asked about Quinn and the Babbage Society openly, on the Net and on the phone. That must have alerted Them. By the time Morgan realized that there was a connection, it was too late.

His friendship with Sarah had been the clincher. They were already convinced she was "running an op" on Them; that she was, in fact, the Intruder. In a tragic irony, They must have figured Morgan for a partner. Immediately after the encounter in the library, Sarah had met with both Dennis and Paul Abbot. Then, after the shooting in the Park, she'd spent the night with Morgan and the next day Morgan had visited the same two men. So, rather than take chances, They had gone after all three of her "co-conspirators."

That explained why They had killed Paul Abbot, a man with only the most tenuous connection to her. She could understand now how it must have looked to Them. But she hated Them for the Dawsons and the man in the park, who had been killed only for window dressing.

So much violence. Across so many years. All to protect the one vital secret: that They had been quietly directing the course of history for the last 160 years.

That was only a guess, that part about directing history; but it was the only guess that seemed to make sense. She wished

103

that she had never deduced it. She wished that she could forget it; that everything could go back to the way it was, where history was something that simply happened.

It was futile. Like a bird flapping against a window pane, nothing she did mattered because an anonymous little group had been quietly setting the limits for everyone else. She wondered if the bird would be any happier knowing about glass.

*What you don't know can't hurt you.* There was a folk saying for everything. A comforting formula to take the place of thought.

It was wrong. Ignorance always was. What you don't know can *kill* you. She remembered once seeing a sparrow die after flying at full speed into the side of one of the glass towers downtown. It had fallen to the pavement just in front of her. The memory still saddened her. She could see herself quite clearly as that sparrow, rushing full tilt—like how many others before her?—into an unseen barrier.

Even if she could somehow forget everything she had learned, it would only be the illusion of freedom. The walls would still be there, even if she never beat her wings against them; all the more powerful, because you can never demolish a wall that you don't know exists.

But knowing that the walls were there, knowing that they had been built by others, that did cause pain. An angry pain. *My whole life I fought so I wouldn't be just another victim. And now I discover we're all victims.* Like a prisoner who finally escapes from his cell only to find himself in a larger cell.

# X

The doorbell woke her up.

The insistent chimes repeated themselves like a stuck record. She put her hands over her ears. "Oh, shut up."

She always woke up hard. Abe, her old roommate, had made fun of that. He'd been the sort who jogged in the morning, and ate "hearty" breakfasts. Bacon (broiled, not fried) and eggs (soft-boiled, of course). While she struggled with her coffee. Their relationship had been doomed from the start.

She had crashed on the sofa early that morning, after spending all night on the terminal writing her program and reading Morgan's files. Now she looked blearily at the clock on the fireplace mantle, where it sat just under the portrait of Dr. King. Noon. The day half gone. Dr. King gazed into the distance, looking impossibly noble. "Free at last . . ." Freedom, what an irony! How could there be freedom when—

The doorbell rang again and she wondered if she were going to answer it. Yesterday she had packed for hiding in the mountains; when she had believed, crazily, that Morgan was coming to kill her. Then, last night, she had finally taken steps to fight back. This morning (no, this afternoon) did she still plan to run?

Well, that might depend on who was ringing her doorbell.

Feline leaped up on the back of the sofa and prowled back and forth. He yawned at her. "Yaaaow."

Sarah held up her hands and Fee jumped into them. "How are you, Fee?" she asked him. "I haven't seen you for a while. Out tomcatting, I'll bet. Where were you when I needed

105

you?" She remembered vividly the feelings of loneliness she'd had . . . What? Two nights ago? Her time sense was all screwed up. Saturday. And today was Monday. Two weeks to the day—almost to the hour—since she had found the papers in the house on Emerson Street.

Fee looked her in the eye.

"Miaaou."

"No, you're right. I shouldn't blame you. After all, where was I when you needed me, right?" Being shot at. Going catatonic at Morgan's apartment. She scratched Fee in his special place, just behind the skull. The door chimes rang again. She sighed. "Well, let's see who's so anxious to meet us."

She rolled off of the sofa and got to her feet. Remembering how carelessly she had gone to the door yesterday morning, she first went to the fireplace and grabbed the poker. Then she went to the door and peered through the peephole.

It was Red Malone. Dressed as a plumber, complete with a plumber's van parked in the road. He held a clipboard stuffed with ragged and official-looking papers. She watched him fidget from foot to foot, then reach out and stab the doorbell again.

Sarah opened the door. Red stood for a moment, then stepped in. "It's about time you opened the damned—"He scowled. "What's so funny?"

Wordlessly, she held out the poker. He looked at it, then at her; and grunted. "At least I kept my part of the bargain. I rang your damned bell."

He walked past her into the living room and planted himself in the same sofa he had occupied before. Sarah followed and leaned against the archway that separated the living room from the entrance foyer. She laid the poker on the end table and folded her arms across her chest. Red looked at her and shook his head.

"Sarah, Sarah, what am I going to do with you? You diddled me good. You know that? I really believed you when you said you weren't the Intruder. Can you imagine how stupid I felt when They told me about your mouse? You've been a busy little lady." He didn't smile when he said it. Red had smiled so much on his previous visit that his serious demeanor now seemed ominous.

"I can explain that."

106

He nodded gravely. "Oh, good!" He stuck his arms behind his head. "I can hardly wait to hear."

"Don't you get flip with me, mister 'Adjuster!' Every word I told you last time was the truth!"

Red leaned forward and stabbed a finger at her. "Sure. Every word was true; but you didn't tell me all the words, did you? You knew a hell of a lot more than you let on. A little mouse told you. Don't play games with me! The stakes are too high for game playing."

"Games? My God! A very dear friend of mine is dead, and another one may die, and some people I never knew at all are dead . . ." (Morgan was dead. Every now and then that knowledge intruded on her thoughts and stopped them cold. And he *had* been a friend; perhaps a better one than she had known. Brusquely, she shoved the memory aside. She couldn't allow it to hamper her now. Later, maybe, there would be time for mourning.) "Dead," she repeated. "And you accuse me of playing games?"

He leaned forward and rested his arms on his knees. "No, that won't wash," he said stonily. "That mouse of yours proves you were up to something. Who are you?"

"I'm Sarah Beaumont. I'm a businesswoman. My God, is that so sinister? Of course, I didn't tell you ev didn't want my plans to leak to my competitors. I was re-searching Brady Quinn because he looked like a good hook for a real estate project. That's all."

"No, that's not all. How did you make the connection with Babbage, Edison, and the others?"

"I—"

When she hesitated, Red snapped at her. "Come on! This is no time to be coy. It's your life we're talking about, not your damned balance statement. *I* know you wouldn't be stupid enough to use your own access code, but *They* are in a panic." He grimaced and looked away. "But I guess you know that already."

She pursed her lips and looked him in the eye. Could she trust Red Malone? He certainly acted as if he were trying to help her, but how could she be certain? She stared at him for a time without speaking and he stared steadily back. Then she took a deep breath and made a decision.

She retrieved the two folders from her terminal desk and carried them back. "Here," she said, and dropped them in

Red's lap. He looked at her, looked at the folders, and looked back at her.

"Go ahead, read them."

He frowned. Then he read the folder tabs and his face went white. He paged rapidly through the sheets, exclaiming to himself. Then he looked up at her. "Do you know what this stuff means?"

"I think so."

Red's shoulders slumped and he sagged back on the sofa. She told him everything she had deduced the night before; about Quinn, about Carson, about the Babbage Society. She told Red what had happened to Dennis, Morgan, and the Widener people; but for some reason—perhaps a residual of mistrust—she did not tell him about the worm she had written in revenge. It might be that he wouldn't try to stop it; but if she didn't tell him, he *couldn't* stop it. For now, silence seemed the best strategy.

Red listened closely. After she was finished, he sat silently for a long moment, rubbing his hands together. The pine logs crackled in the fireplace. Then he shook his head and laughed sadly. "What irony," he said. "The most closely-held secret in history unraveled by a complete naif." He looked at her. "Congratulations," he said sourly. He opened one of the folders and flipped the pages. "Where did you find these?"

"In an old building down near the train station. Off of Fifteenth."

He looked into the distance. "So that's where it was," he said quietly. He dropped the folders to the coffee table. "We knew Carson had been headquartered somewhere in the old downtown; but we didn't know where. And we didn't know he had left anything behind when he moved, so nobody ever bothered to go back and look." He smiled apologetically. "There was a lot of confusion at the time, or so they say. If Carson had been more careful evacuating the place, there wouldn't have been anything up there for you to find. That was bad luck, your stumbling on those machines like that."

"Someone would have found them, sooner or later."

"Sure, and sold them for scrap without ever knowing what they were. That would have been best, I suppose."

"What happens now?"

He ignored her question and made a steeple with his fingers. "Where is that worksheet you say you found? The cliological analysis."

"As far as I know, the list was either on Dennis at the time he was run down or it's in his office at home."

He grunted disapproval. "It should never have been there, in the house. Worksheets should never have been taken off-site. They knew that, even back then, before everybody became so security-conscious." Red pushed himself out of the sofa and walked past her into the kitchen. He picked up the telephone and looked at her. "Mind if I make a call?"

"Can I stop you?"

"Yes," he said seriously and waited for an answer.

She waved an arm. "Go ahead."

Red punched up a number, shielding the phone with his body so she couldn't see it. Then he covered the mouthpiece and spoke into it for a few minutes. He listened a while, nodding. "Fine," he said. "Make it so." Then he hung up and faced Sarah.

"We're bringing some of our assets down to keep an eye on your friend. It'll be a while until they get there; but I don't think They'll try anything at the hospital. Someone will watch that history professor you mentioned, too; but I doubt she's in any danger."

"Thanks."

"What? Oh, you're welcome. But We're doing it for Ourselves as much as for your friend." He smiled. "Damage containment. Maybe we can find that list and destroy it."

Sarah grabbed him by the arm as he came through the archway. "I've told you what I know," she said. "Now it's your turn. Tell me what you know. How much of what I guessed is right? About the Babbage Society, I mean."

He pried her fingers off his arm. "There is no more Babbage Society," he told her. "It died a long time ago." He returned to the sofa and looked at his watch.

"You didn't answer my question."

"I know. I didn't intend to." He stared at his hands, turning them this way and that. "Old habits, they die hard," he said. "But I suppose there's no point in concealing things from you any more. It's too late and it won't change anything." He shrugged and waved her to a seat next to him. "Sit down. I'm going to tell you the damnedest story you ever heard."

She wouldn't sit next to him, which seemed to amuse him. Instead she took the same chair she had taken the last time.

109

She sat there and gripped the arms of the chair and waited. She crossed her legs.

Red paused, licking his lips and squinting into the distance. "Start the way Crawford and the others started. They were interested in mass behavior. How many acres were planted in wheat versus corn. How many miles of railroad track were in operation. How many telegraph stations. And so on. Data collection was all the rage back then, during the second quarter of the nineteenth century. Reformers like Adolphe Quetelet, the Belgian astronomer, were trying to create a scientific basis for a progressive social policy. They compiled all sorts of figures on population, climate, trade, poverty, education, crime, you name it.

"Then along came Babbage's book, with its rudimentary system theory. Crawford started a small philosophical society to discuss and speculate on Babbage's ideas, and someone got the idea of applying the techniques to the social data they had been collecting. What the Founders discovered was that the data followed predictable mathematical curves." He traced a curve in the air with his arm. "And, once the underlying equations were solved—using those Babbage engines you saw—the trajectory could be predicted within statistical limits." He paused a moment and frowned. "They developed theories to try to explain what they saw. They weren't always right. Sometimes their errors were ludicrous. After all, it was a brand new technology; and the data wasn't always the best; and their understanding was still too shallow. But they were persistent. Whenever a prediction failed, they went back and studied their models to discover what had been overlooked. Over the decades they became more accurate and precise. It took a long time. Even today, we sometimes get taken by surprise. It's a complex problem."

She shook her head. "Complex? It sounds damned impossible. Like predicting the motion of a mobile with a million parts."

Red grinned again. "Ah, but we don't pay attention to most of them. The Pareto Principle comes into play. Twenty percent of those variables account for 80% of what happens. If you don't believe me, find out what percentage of authors contribute most of the science journal articles; or how many running backs account for most of the yardage gained in football. It's a matter of simplifying the system. We don't need to know what the fifth decimal place is going to be fifty years from now, as long as we know the trend. We'll add the decimal places as we go along."

"Then I was right. The Babbage Society meant to control the course of history, didn't it?"

He leaned forward and clasped his hands together, staring at a point halfway across the room. He didn't look at her. "Yes," he said. "And no. You're overstating the case. We don't control history. We can't. No one can. Do you have any idea what an impossible task that would be? How much cultural energy would be required to alter the trajectory of a major industrial society? As well try to sweep back the tide. No, something like that would take generations of careful nudging; it would require a constancy of purpose over many lifetimes." He turned and looked her in the eye. "We gave it up long ago."

She frowned. There was something in the way Red had spoken. A tone of voice. She couldn't quite put her finger on it, but she had a feeling that he was talking to himself as much as to her. "You gave it up. Then what are you doing?" she asked.

He shrugged and looked away. "What else? Getting rich."

"Getting rich," she repeated.

"That's right. No grandiose plans to rule the world or control history. Disappointed?"

Sarah didn't answer him; but oddly enough, she *was* disappointed. A secret cabal planning to rule the world had a mad kind of grandeur to it. A secret cabal for personal gain seemed merely sordid.

"We don't try to change the tides of history, but we do try to surf on them." He chuckled. "As undignified as that may sound. We don't try to stop the flow; we go with the flow. It's much easier to modulate an existing trend than it is to start or stop one. So we make a few minor adjustments here and there to enhance our portfolios. That's all. No major surgery. Just knowing what the future holds in store," he said, "is a big help in the markets."

"I'm sure it is," she said wryly. "Isn't 'insider' trading illegal, though?"

He laughed. "I don't think the law covers our situation. No, I'm talking about a grander scale. Plans that don't mature for decades. Think, for example, what an advantage it was to know decades in advance that isolationism would keep the U.S. out of World War II. That all the other industrial nations

111

would be flattened and American companies would have no serious rivals for twenty years. It opened up all sorts of investment opportunities."

"Investment opportunities?" she said, appalled. "You take millions of deaths pretty cold-bloodedly."

He shook his head. "How else should I take it? We didn't start the war. We didn't start isolationism. *It would have happened anyway!* Only, we had advance knowledge. Why not take advantage of it? Why is that so wicked?" He spread his hands in appeal.

"You could have tried to stop it!"

He cocked his head at her and grinned. "Really? How?"

"I don't know. That's your department."

He snorted. "Look, there's a lot you don't know; so just hold off on the moral judgements, will you? It's not that easy."

"No, I don't suppose it is. Should I shed tears? You did try it, didn't you? You tried directing history. Once, a long time ago."

Red clenched his hands together and rested his chin on them. His eyes were unfocused, as if he were seeing those long-ago days. "It wasn't the Founders' intentions, either. Not at first. But as the data accumulated, they found their curves converging on disaster: a general world-wide collapse in the early 1940s."

Sarah jerked her head around and stared at him. "They were wrong, then."

"Were they?" Red wondered. "Or was their nudging successful? How would you ever know? *I* know, of course. But if you didn't believe the math . . ." A shrug. "They saw a confluence of several trends: the unification of the Germanies and their rise as a scientific and industrial power; the compression of population on her resources after the mid-1800s, leading to a 'breakout' cycle. But, with all the easy overseas colonies taken by then, the breakout would be against literate and well-armed European nations rather than, ah, 'less sophisticated' opponents. Meanwhile, explosives were becoming exponentially more powerful. Put them all together and . . . Well, suppose Germany had had atomic bombs in 1939?"

She shook her head, not wanting to believe him. "It never happened. Maybe their equations were wrong. You said yourself that they weren't always right."

He wouldn't look at her. "What would you have done? Stood by, because the forecast might be wrong? Or taken action, because the forecast might be right? You can't stop an exponential trend at the last moment. They did what they had to do. Small seeds. They planted small seeds that they hoped to nurture through the generations. The Society was small and it only operated in the U.S. Their activities didn't carry much socio-kinetic energy . . ." He smiled as if in apology for the jargon. " . . . so they looked for focal points—fulcra, they called them; yokes were the mathematical operators—times where they could get enough leverage over large scale events. They aimed to build the U.S. into a technological counter-weight to Germany, to bleed off some of the pressures that were building there. Slavery was stifling our technology, so slavery had to go. The South was a poor, feudalistic, agrarian backwater in a rich, industrial world; but, because of the Constitution, she had a virtual veto over anything the Congress considered. *No* to 'internal improvements.' *No* to a Pacific railroad. *No* to protection for industry. They did what they had to do," he repeated.

A strange feeling went through her. They'd ended slavery? But it had been for all the wrong reasons! Not freedom or human dignity, but economics and technological progress. She remembered some of the tales her grandfather had told her about his grandfather. Economics be damned! "How did they do that?" she asked. "End slavery, I mean. The Babbage Society started the Civil War?"

Red rose from the sofa and stuffed his hands in his pockets. "Not on purpose. That was one of the mistakes. You see, slavery was already dying, for economic reasons. New Mexico had been open to slavery for decades, yet only a score of slaves had been taken there. Seward gave the 'peculiar institution' fifty years at most before it expired naturally. No, the Society simply tried to hurry it along the way to its grave."

"How?"

"How? By nurturing the economic forces that were killing it. The Society didn't go out and foment Abolition. They used their power and resources to push hard for the Homestead Bill and Popular Sovereignty. Those did more harm to slavery than *Uncle Tom's Cabin* or *The Impending Crisis in the South*. A society of yeoman farmers has no use for slavery or great plantations. Crawford and the others, they never planned on a war."

"But they got one anyway."

Red grimaced and looked away. "The kindling was there

and they were playing with matches. We're a lot smarter nowadays."

"Oh, I just bet you are."

He looked at her. "We are because we don't try to do it as often. That's smarter, isn't it? Not unless we're very, very sure that we know what we're doing. Not until we've studied the proposal from twenty different directions. Only then will we try an adjustment."

Sarah grunted. "And you're an Adjustor."

Red grinned. "Yeah, that's me." He twisted his hands like he was turning knobs.

"A country isn't like a TV set," Sarah protested. "There aren't any knobs on people."

"No? Not even on that womanizing communist you think so much of?"

She scowled. "What? Who?"

"Him." He pointed to the portrait over the mantle. "That sonuvabitch who tried to wreck the country."

She stood out of her chair. "*Don't you dare say that about a man like Dr. King!*"

Malone said nothing. He simply sat there on the sofa, grinning at her. Slowly, she sank back into her seat. "You bastard. Why did you say that?"

"Just to show you that people do have buttons. I figured from the photograph that he was one of yours."

"Then, you don't believe what you just said, do you?"

"I don't have to. All I need to know is that if I need you to be angry, I can push that button. When you're not expecting it, of course," he added. Red put his arms out, palm up. "Ideas are the key, you see. Ideas—we call them memes— cause learned behavior the way genes cause instinctive behavior."

"Memes." Something went click. Some of the titles she had read in the Index. "You used to call them ideons, didn't you?"

He blinked in surprise and looked at her respectfully. "Yes. Elementary ideas. Like elementary particles. Protons, electrons . . . and ideons. The analogies were all physical back then. Later, when Darwin's and Mendel's works became better known, biological analogies seemed more appropriate. In a way, ideas are like viruses. People 'catch' them from each other through communication media. It's a process very much like epidemics. I could write the equations for you, if you like."

She stood from the chair and walked to the window where she stared down the mountainside at her neighbors' homes. She couldn't imagine that people were going about their normal lives just a few hundred yards away. "Cause behavior?" she said with her back to him. "*Cause?* No, it just doesn't sit right with me. People are killing each other over it and I just don't understand how it's possible!" She clenched her hands into fists at her side. "How can you say that behavior is caused by a set of equations, like a . . . Like a goddam pendulum?" She turned and faced him and dared him to answer.

He shook his head. "You've got it backwards. It's not the equations that cause behavior. It's the behaviors that cause the equations. Get the difference? There's no compulsion. The process isn't deterministic; it's probablistic. Like predicting the weather."

"An eighty percent chance of coups today across South America," she said waving at an imaginary weather map.

Red chuckled. "Something like that."

"But you can't mint an idea and plant it in people's heads!"

"No?" Red smiled. "Ever hear of Pet Rocks?"

"People aren't robots, dammit. You can't program them!"

"Oh, hell, Sarah. I've known people who weren't half as flexible as robots, and you have, too. There was a gal in Las Vegas who— Well, never mind. That's not important. It's free will that makes cliology possible, anyway."

She stared at him. "What?"

"Sure. A free choice is predictable."

"No, I can't buy that."

"It's the *irrational* choice that's unpredictable. That's what makes madmen so frightening. A free choice is rational more often than not."

"But how do you know that someone won't make an irrational choice?"

"We don't," he replied happily. "But we don't have to. *Because it works out on the average.* Behavior is an action, and action triggers reaction—by other people and by the environment—recognition, money, security, self-esteem, whatever's appropriate on Maslow's Hierarchy. We call them 'biopsychological benefits.' That feedback reinforces the behavior, positively or negatively. People naturally want to repeat behaviors that benefit them or imitate ones that seem to benefit others. So we can forecast the frequency distribution

115

of people who will choose a behavior by studying the reinforcement it provides."

She shook her head. "That's too simplistic. Complex issues don't have simple answers!"

"Really?" He smiled in a patronizing manner. "*Who told you that?* That's a prime example of a meme that's flourishing in our culture. People pass it along to each other like a bad cold. But have you ever wondered who planted that particular meme, and why? Is there a better way to prevent people from even *trying* to discover so-called laws of history?" He grinned smugly.

She frowned and turned away from him again. She pressed her lips together. She saw where it all was leading. She could see how they could steer society any way they wanted it to go. "So, you figure out what behaviors will give the results you want; then you encourage those through positive feedback and reinforcement." Sign up for Psychology 101 and rule the world.

"That's right. We reward the people who behave the way we want. We've got the wealth and influence nowadays to make it effective. And enough leverage in the communications industry to . . ."

The anger boiled up and over. She turned and jabbed a finger at him. "Goddamn it!" she spat out. "People aren't puppets!"

"Did I say they were? You're not listening. I only said that we publicize and reward the behavior we want. *We don't coerce it!* But people aren't stupid. If they think that a certain behavior will benefit them, a predictable percentage of them will imitate it voluntarily. That's why we have so many people in communications—editors, speech-writers, programming directors; people behind the scenes. To make sure the right memes are publicized. Free will does the rest." He smiled ironically. "The statistics only work when people can choose freely. And besides," he added accusingly, "what else is a commercial supposed to do? Or a sermon? Or an office supervisor? Aren't they all attempts to encourage certain behaviors by holding out the promise of rewards?"

Sarah swallowed her response. Red did have a point. But she wondered at what point the power to reward became the power to coerce. Manipulation was more subtle than force, but the results were much the same. And force, at least, had the one benefit of being open and honest.

Red waited a moment. His eyes flicked to his watch and he grunted. "No answer, right? Because Madison Avenue is doing the same thing we're doing. We're better at it because we know *which* behaviors to cultivate. It's not always obvious, you know. That's where Babbage's theories came into the picture. It helped us discover which knobs to twist. You see, every action has unintended spin-offs. For example, the liberation of educated, white, suburban females meant unemployment for uneducated, black, urban males. And it doesn't matter that that wasn't anyone's intention!" he interjected, stifling her protest. "After all, proponents of defense spending never intended to hand the consumer electronics market over to the Japanese, either. But that's what happened when the cream of our engineering talent was lured into armaments and aerospace. Every engineer working on better bombs was an engineer *not* working on better TV's or stereos."

"So, what's your point?" she asked coldly. "That women's lib was bad? That defense spending should have been cut?"

Red waved his hand and made a sound of contempt. "Don't give me that crap. Just because an action has consequences you like, you think it can't have other consequences, as well. And bad things can have good spin-offs, as far as that goes. Tell me who is better off today, the descendants of the blacks who were brutally kidnapped into slavery? Or the descendants of the ones who were left behind?"

"That's no justification for the slave trade!" she said.

"Who said it was? *Justice has nothing to do with it.* Look, I was born an American, and I'm thankful; but I'm not thankful that a million people starved to death in the potato famine or on the 'coffin ships' trying to get here. It's not a matter of what's right or what's wrong, just or unjust. The system doesn't *care*. Change one component and the rest of the system reacts, maybe years later and in ways you don't expect. In ways you won't even *like*. That's what we go for. The effect we want is usually one of those hidden side-effects; it's hardly ever the alleged purpose of the act. Besides, I told you that all we do these days is tinker a little bit."

"Fine. That's just great. You and your friends tinker with other people's destinies, but not to worry, because you only tinker a little!"

"A tinker is someone who fixes things."

"No. Keep your hands off other people's lives."

"Ah! *Laissez faire.* You're like businessmen or environmen-

117

talists. You've got the Humans Should Not Interfere With the System meme."

She did not care for the way he phrased it. He made it sound as if her beliefs were only things that she had "caught" from others, like a disease. "Deliberate interference by humans is unnatural," she said. "It upsets the economic or ecological balance. History should run free. Like a wild river!" She threw her arm out as she said it.

He laughed. He threw back his head and roared and slapped his knee.

"What's so funny?" she asked suspiciously.

"That people like you think human behavior is unnatural. Just what do you think history *is*, Ms. Beaumont? It's nothing *but* human intervention! People are constantly trying to change history—or keep it from changing. Napoleon, Jesus Christ, Dr. King. All of them had a vision of the future and tried to arrange things so it would come about. Why, you yourself are doing the very thing you condemn Us for."

She felt her cheeks flush. "What do you mean by that crack?" she demanded.

He beckoned with his hand. "Tell me again about your Emerson Street project. Trying to change the history of Capitol Hill, weren't you? Buying and selling houses to alter the settlement patterns. Changing the course of people's lives, without their knowledge or consent. Would the residents there *want* your new gentrified neighborhood? Maybe they like things just the way they are."

"Now, wait a—"

"And you're doing it in secret for personal gain, just like Us," he went on over her objections; "because if anyone found out, your plan wouldn't work and you wouldn't make a big bundle. The only difference between what you do and what We do is that *We're better at it!* We use statistics and the scientific method. But everyone is tinkering with history, every day. So don't get on your moral high horse with me. Is it morally superior to tinker ignorantly and haphazardly like the rest of you? How is it better to go at it blindly?"

"It *is* different!" she said, choking the words out.

He folded his arms. "Really? Tell me how."

"The rest of us don't kill people!"

He froze. Then he grimaced and dipped his head in acknowledgement. "There is that," he admitted. "Although I could argue that stumbling blindly through history has killed more people than They ever will. Things went wrong for the Society a long time ago, terribly wrong." He rubbed his hands together. "Look, when Crawford and the others formed the Babbage Society, they never intended anything like what's happened. Remember, they were trying to save the world."

"Good for them," she said sarcastically.

He looked hurt. "They were," he insisted. "Oh, I'm not saying no one was harmed. People died because of things they did. The War Between the States . . . We still don't know why that happened. Something was overlooked in the equations. But people would have died anyway. Only rarely did the Founders ever feel compelled to delete specific individuals."

"Let's tell the Vatican. Maybe they'll be canonized."

He screwed his face up. "I'm not making excuses for them. They weren't saints by any means. They did what they felt was necessary, and the choices often meant personal agony. They never authorized a deletion lightly or simply to protect themselves. It was all for a greater good. To prevent what they saw coming. Genevieve is . . . different."

"Genevieve? Genevieve Weil?"

He looked at her shrewdly. "Yes. I see you've heard of her. She's Their chairman. To be honest, I don't think she's quite sane. I think the fear of discovery has driven her mad. Her mother's fault. The old bitch never kept anything from her, even as a child; and she used to imagine angry mobs coming to their house to tear them limb from limb because they had discovered Mommy's Secret. Her mother used the fear as a lazy way to discipline her. 'Do as I say or I'll tell the newspapers about us and people will come and kill us all.' Can you imagine saying that to a six-year-old child?"

"Am I supposed to feel sorry for her because she had a difficult childhood? I'm sorry, I don't." But she couldn't help imagining the tiny child; afraid to have friends; afraid of saying the wrong thing; constantly terrified of exposure for things she did not understand and had no part in starting. Her mother had been cruel and abusive. Beatings would have been kinder.

"Sorry?" mused Red. "No. Understanding, perhaps. So that, if someday you have to kill her, you can do it without hate. Kennison and the others, they're a little afraid of her themselves; but her family has been recruiting and promoting people for a long time now and they're all her willing followers. Natural selection, I suppose. It was her great-grandfather who realized how he could use the Society's own tools to manipulate the Society itself. A ruthless bastard. I don't know how he ever got past his recruiter. It would have worked, too, if it hadn't been for Quinn. He and Carson foresaw the *coup*. Not Weil specifically, of course. It was years and years before it happened, and Grosvenor Weil hadn't even been recruited at the time. But they could see it coming in their equations. So they took steps to preserve something of the original Society. It broke old Isaac Shelton's heart when Quinn told him."

The telephone rang and they both started at the sound. Sarah glanced from the phone to Red. "Go ahead," she told him. "You've been waiting for it to ring."

He cocked an eyebrow at her and she pointed to his wrist. "Because you keep looking at your watch every few minutes. That's how. Go on. Answer it."

Red went to the kitchen and took the phone off the wall. He listened without saying anything. Then he smiled and bowed to her. Before he could complete the bow, however, his smile froze and a look of surprise crossed his face. He turned his back on her. "Say again," she heard him whisper.

Whatever the message was, she decided, it was not what he had expected. Now he was making plans. Plans for her. Sarah wondered what her own best move should be. Red was personable and his arguments were well-reasoned; but she wasn't about to succumb to them. Or to let him decide things for her. She remembered that she had packed her Blazer with survival gear and it was ready and waiting for her.

Red hung the phone up and faced her grimly. "Your friend has vanished. He's not in the hospital; and Porter's computer never heard of him. According to their records, he was never even admitted."

His words were like ice water in the face. She had been using his lecture and her anger as novocaine against the pain of reality. Now it was reality's turn. She gasped. "Dennis? But he was! Jerry spoke to them! He was in the critical care unit!" Somehow, she had thought him safe from further harm in the hospital. There was a bitter taste in her mouth. Despite Red's assurances, They had gotten Dennis after all. Red tried to stammer an apology but she barely heard him. Too many shocks. Too many shocks.

A hand shook her shoulder and she looked into Red's face.

"Come on," she heard him say. "There's been a change in plans. We've got to move."

Immediately, she became cautious. Fee rubbed against her pants leg and she reached down and picked him up. He settled into the crook of her left arm and she stroked him absently—and perhaps a little firmly, because he twisted in her grip. "What do you mean? Where are you taking me?"

"Why, to Our place, of course. We're supposed to meet Janie at Falcon Castle. She'll take you from there."

"The Walker Mansion ruins? Isn't that a bit melodramatic?"

He lifted his hands. "She picked the spot. It's close by, and not many folks know about it."

"Suppose I don't want to come with you?"

"You don't have to. We never interfere with free choice. You can come with Us, or stay here and get killed."

"Free choice!" she muttered.

# XI

Red laughed when he saw her well-stocked Blazer. "You won't need all that paraphernalia where we're going," he said.

"I haven't decided whether I'm going with you," she answered. "Going with you isn't the only alternative to staying here."

He pursed his lips and nodded. "Maybe not, but it's the smart move."

"So you say."

"My plumber's van is less conspicuous."

"A four by four is hardly conspicuous in Colorado."

"I didn't mean that. I meant that They probably know what cars you drive."

Her patience had worn thin. Red acted as if the whole business was one big game. "Will you quit that Us and Them crap!" she snapped. They're the Babbage Society and you're . . . What? Utopian Research Associates?"

He nodded. "Yes. But We never call Them the Babbage Society. Men like Crawford and Shelton and Hammondton, were men of the highest ideals. Grosvenor Weil perverted those ideals. Nowadays there's practically nothing left of the original memes of the Society."

*Men of the highest ideals*, she thought. Trying to save the world. And they had killed people and accidentally set off the Civil War in the process. Maybe that was the trouble with high ideals. From such a height, ordinary people begin to look small and unimportant. "Have it your way," she said, "but I plan to keep my options open." She climbed into the cab of the Blazer and slammed the door. Fee settled into his

122

usual place in the center console. She'd removed the lid to it when she bought the car and had made a kind of padded cat-seat out of it. "See you around," she said and hit the garage door opener. She started the engine and put the Blazer in reverse, but before she could back out, Red yanked open the passenger's door and hopped in beside her.

She braked sharply and looked at him. He was buckling his seat belt. "What do you think you're doing?"

"Well, if you won't come with me," he said reasonably, "I'll have to come with you. Maybe I can answer some more questions for you. Maybe I can still convince you to come to Falcon Castle. Janie'll be sore as hell if we don't show up."

"My heart bleeds for her. Who is Janie, anyway? Your wife?"

He looked startled. "Wife? Me? Are you kidding? I'm the wild and independent sort. No, Jane Addams Hatch runs the local safe house. She was sure you'd opt to join the Good Guys."

Carefully, she backed down the steep dirt driveway to Foothills Road, twisting in her seat to watch. "I know that They're the Bad Guys," she told him over her shoulder, "but I'm not convinced that you folks are the Good Guys."

"We're the enemy of your enemy," he said.

"That doesn't make you my friend. You're doing the same thing as the Babbage people, aren't you? You're simply not as ruthless about it."

Once on Foothill Road, she looked both ways for traffic. There were only a few cars parked alongside the road near the houses. She shifted into forward and headed toward Eldridge Street.

"You know," he said after a few moments' silence, "wild rivers only seem like a good thing if you don't live downstream."

For an instant, she couldn't figure out what he was talking about. Then she recalled what she had said earlier, comparing history to a wild river. "But if you dam the river to help the folks downstream," she told him, "you'll flood the folks upstream."

"With the river of history, we've no choice. Like it or not, we're all going to be living downstream."

"Don't play semantic games. You know what I mean."

He shrugged. "Sure I do. But that's my whole point. If you dam the river, you flood the folks upstream. If you *don't* dam the river, then it's the downstream folks who get flooded. No matter what you do, someone suffers. You can't make an omelette without breaking eggs."

"Spoken like a chef. What if you're one of the eggs instead? That whole bit about the good of the group— What about the rights of the individual? Is the group free to trample on them?"

He looked at her. "Would you sacrifice the safety of the group to the whims of individuals? What were Typhoid Mary's rights?"

"That's a loaded question!"

"What good is an unloaded one?" he snapped. He chewed his lip and watched the passing houses. "Maybe it'll make you think."

"Maybe. Shouldn't it make you think, as well?"

He grunted. "Let's not quarrel. We both have the same enemy; only we look at Them in different ways. To you, the Society's manipulations deny the rights of individuals. So you don't see much difference between Them and Us. Well, I see plenty of difference. They are the individuals; and They are destroying the group in pursuit of Their own gain."

Something in the way he spoke chilled her. She braked at the stop sign and looked at him. "How?" she asked.

He stared straight ahead through the windshield. "They're breeding a nation of peasants," he said, his voice tight and low. "Technopeasants. They encourage any meme that downplays thoughtful analysis or encourages docility or self-indulgence or uniformity."

She glanced at him again; downshifted; and drove through the stop sign. She remembered how she and Dennis had discussed the same subject—but she didn't want to think about Dennis just now. "Damn. You don't make it easy on me, do you? That's a trend I've fought and argued against for years. I even ran for a seat on the Jeffco school board."

"To do a little cliological tinkering?"

She tightened her lips. "To do some open and aboveboard politicking."

"Did you win?"

She snorted. "What do you think? My opponent pointed out that I have no children; let alone any in the public schools. As if childbearing made one an effective manager."

"It might. Managing a houseful of brats is a lot like running a schoolboard." He chuckled. "Tell me. Do you want to help fight that trend? Effectively, I mean. Public hearings and debates and Full Participation by All Concerned Parties never accomplishes anything."

"What? Are you offering me a job?" Of all the things that Red had told her today, that was the most surprising. And the most frightening. A chance to fight the things she had always hated. Using methods that she despised.

"Yes. Help me get the Associates off their *laissez faire* duffs. We've got to do something to blunt Their program. A uniform, docile society is more predictable; and the forecasts would be simpler and more precise. But it can't last, any more than domestic sheep could last in the wild. It's long-term suicide. But, for the first time in history," he continued, "the old Society is run by people who just don't give a damn beyond their own lifetimes. Even Grosvenor Weil, to give the old devil his due, had the long-term perspective. He wanted his children and grandchildren to live well. Genevieve, she has no children."

The eastbound traffic on 32nd Street was heavy. The day shift at Coors was letting out. She stopped at the intersection and waited for a break in the traffic. "Do you mean to tell me that the only reason the Babbage Society is domesticating us is to make their computations easier? Shit."

What she saw happening around her was bad enough. In what other society did people use "smart" and "wise" as insults? Or tell people "don't get smart"; and call them "nerds" if they did?

All that was bad enough. To know that the trend had been nurtured and encouraged by a secret elite was worse. But to know that they had done so for no more reason than to simplify their goddam arithmetic! It was the ultimate in arrogance.

She saw an opening in the traffic and went for it, turning sharp right. The oncoming car braked and honked. In her rearview mirror she saw the driver shake his fist.

"Does that mean you'll take the job?"

"Are you kidding? I'm against everything you're for. I think your methods are despicable. The whole concept is repulsive."

He grinned. "Wouldn't you say that makes you the ideal recruit? The last kind of person I'd want in the Associates is one who enjoyed the power."

Sarah opened her mouth to say something, then changed her mind. "I don't get you, Red. One minute you talk like you want to free the puppets; the next minute, like you want to be a puppeteer."

"We're all puppeteers, whether we like it or not. It's just a matter of learning which strings to pull."

"No!"

"When you're dealing with culture, what's natural and what's human intervention is a moot point. Ninety-nine percent of us are constantly making changes. Yanking on the puppet strings. What was Thomas Jefferson trying to do? Or Ronald Reagan? Or the NAACP? Or the Ku Klux Klan, for that matter? Trying to shape the future a little closer to their hearts' desires. Everyone's changing the future, every day. Haphazardly. Blindly. With their eyes fixed only on their own, intended goal; with no notion of interaction, spin-off, or the long-term effects. Maybe a few advertisers, preachers, and the like, have a vague grasp of some principles; but that's as far as it goes. Maybe sometimes we don't see things so clearly, either. But," he grinned at her, "in the country of the blind, the one-eyed man is king."

"Yeah? Well, you people have been tinkering with history for what? Almost a century and a half? You know what bothers me most?" She made another sharp right at the church and headed up the ramp onto westbound I-70.

"No, what?"

"The shoddy workmanship."

He turned and gave her a startled look, then he laughed. "I suppose it seems that way to you. But what new technology has ever been put into practice without a few blunders? Hell, we must be doing something right, because, after all, we do make money at it."

"Yeah. Good for you," she said acidly.

He didn't answer her and she spared him a covert glance as she drove. He was leaning his elbow on the door window, his fist propping his head up, watching the houses go by.

"Here's a puzzle for you," he announced suddenly. "Suppose you saw a young boy about to be run over by a bus. Would you try to save him?"

She glanced at him, then back at the road. "What? Sure, if I could."

"Good. But now suppose you knew that if the boy lived he would grow up into another Hitler. Millions would die because of him. Would you still try to save him?"

She scowled and would not look at him. "How could I know something like that?"

"Grant me the supposition. You know it. ESP. Whatever. What would you do?"

"That's no choice."

"Yes it is. No one ever promised you that the choices would be easy, or pleasant."

She clamped her jaws shut, refusing to answer. She saw what Red was getting at.

"Of course, *not* deciding is also a decision," he told her. "You will have to do one or the other. Save him or not." Red waited a while, watching her. "What really makes it agonizing," he said at length, "is that you *know* the boy personally. He delivers your morning paper."

She closed her face up tighter and kept her attention firmly on her driving.

"And now take the supposition one step further. This child, who, beyond any hope of doubt, will kill millions of other innocent people . . . What if he's *not* standing in front of a bus? Would you push him?"

"Jesus Christ!" she whispered harshly. The words escaped from her involuntarily. She looked at him and there wasn't a trace of a smile on his face.

"I don't know if even He could help. Knowing the future is a mixed blessing. Maybe we foresee a disaster coming. To avoid it requires terrible measures. People will suffer; some will die. But if we do nothing, then we allow the original disaster to happen. We're responsible either way. Cliology has created new problems for decision-makers."

She grunted. "It sounds like an old problem to me. Do the ends justify the means?"

He shook his head. "It's not that simple." He looked away from her, out the window. "It's a philosophical trap," he said. "Where does responsibility end? No matter what we do or don't do, there will be pain. A different set of people suffer and die, is all. It's knowing about it in advance that changes things. What can we do, but try our best, knowing our best isn't good enough."

They drove in silence after that, only the tires making any comment. She kept the Blazer at the speed limit and cars passed them constantly, their drivers sparing her dirty looks. *This is crazy*, she thought. She couldn't go into hiding with Red tagging along; and she could hardly keep him prisoner. She would have to dump him somewhere soon.

"Do you know how to get to Falcon Castle?" Red asked.

127

"What? Sure. Out Turkey Creek Canyon to Parmalee Gulch Road. I've hiked most of the Foothills around here. But I'm not going there."

"Yes, you are."

She turned and looked at him. His revolver was trained on her. Red's gaze was as steady as his gun. She held his gaze for a moment then turned her attention back to the road and ignored him. She concentrated fiercely on her driving, wondering if she had judged Red rightly. She could feel the sweat in her armpits.

Then she heard him sigh and put the gun back in its holster. "You saw the safety was on, didn't you?"

Actually, she hadn't seen. Who knew from safeties? She smiled to herself. She had known that Red wouldn't shoot her because it just wasn't in him to do it. At least not in cold blood.

From the corner of her eye, she watched him stare through the window at the passing scenery. It was barren country they were passing through, all browns and no greens. Scrub brush and buffalo grass, with a few evergreens spotted here and there. There were a few scattered houses, and a trailer park off in the distance on the right. Green Mountain hulked on their left. "Where do you plan to drop me?" he asked abruptly.

Sarah checked the rearview mirror and pulled into the right hand lane. "There's a foot trail from Morrison up to the castle," she told him. "I'll drop you there. It's a three-mile hike, about 2,000 feet up. You up to it?"

He shrugged. "Sure."

They went through the cut in the Hogback, with its odd sign: Point of Geological Interest. When the Interstate had been dug through the high thin ridge that paralleled the Foothills, it had exposed the colorful folds of ancient seabeds, set like diagonal stripes beside the roadbed. A parking area and path had been built so that people could "walk back through time." Red stared curiously at the sightseers.

"Ever been out this way before?" she asked him.

"What? Oh, a couple times. Camping. The Associates have a ranch southwest of here."

They pulled down the exit ramp and Sarah turned left onto Morrison Road. The Interstate banked above them, curving up Mount Vernon Canyon toward Georgetown and Silver Plume. The High Country. Sarah longed to be up there, in that wild and beautiful land along the timberline, among the krummholz and tundra flowers. Alone and free. But to be alone, she had to dump Red. To be free . . . Well, that was another issue entirely. To be free, she had to tear down the walls the Society and the Associates had built. Yes, and maybe the walls she had built, as well.

The road to Morrison ran south between the Hogback and Mount Morrison. Ahead on the right, Sarah could see Red Rocks Park, with its sandstone formations weirdly carved by millenia of winds. She checked her mirror again, made a snap decision, and turned sharply into the park.

Red looked at her. "Someone's following us, right? You keep looking in your mirror."

"A dark blue sedan," she told him. "It got on the Interstate right after we did and stayed behind us, even though I deliberately drove slow. He got off at Mount Vernon with us, and , . ." Another glance in the mirror. "Now he's decided to visit Red Rocks, too. If you've got another explanation, I'd be glad to hear it."

The blue car was hanging way back. To be less conspicuous, she supposed. That gave her an idea. She kept to the high road through the park. On the lower road, she would be clearly visible to him; but the high road twisted its way in and around the sandstone and the sight distance was limited. Maybe she could lose him.

The park had its usual quota of weekday visitors. Cars were parked along the roadside and people were hiking and rock climbing. One man with a beard was strumming an acoustical guitar to a circle of admirers. *Too many witnesses here*, she thought. Whoever was chasing them wouldn't dare try anything. Then she remembered what had happened in the Civic Center and felt fear. Who knew what They would dare? She had been foolish and reckless to come through the park.

No help for it now. Past Ship Rock and the Amphitheater she came to a fork in the road. She checked behind her. The blue car was still out of sight behind the rocks. She made a sharp right at the fork and floored the gas pedal. The Blazer spun on loose gravel, then the tires gripped and they shot through the narrow roadway past Creation Rock. If she could be out of sight before her pursuer reached the fork, he would probably assume that she had continued straight through. The road she was taking now had fewer turns. She could gain some distance on him; maybe throw him off their track.

A few minutes later, they came down from the Rocks past

the mouth of Bear Creek Canyon and into the town of Morrison. There was no sign of the blue car. She wondered if their pursuer knew yet that she was aware of him. She turned right onto Route 8 and headed south again.

Red twisted in his seat and looked behind them. "Didn't you say you were going to drop me in Morrison?"

"The trailhead's up ahead yet," she told him. "But I've changed my mind. It's too risky. I don't know if I shook our friend back there and I'd rather not get caught in the parking lot there. Besides, the first mile or so of the trail is across open meadow. If our friend has a gun, we'd be sitting ducks."

"We?"

Sarah took a deep breath. Decision had come quietly, without her knowledge. "We," she admitted. "I guess I do need your help after all."

"It's not disgraceful to need someone's help, you know."

"It is for me."

Mount Falcon rose on their right. Like most of the Foothills, it was a low, broad mountain. The peak was a shade over two miles away, rising to just over 7800 feet, 1800 feet higher than the roadbed.

She looked in her mirror and her hopes fell. "Our friend is behind us again and he's coming up fast. Closing the distance."

"Then he knows we're on to him."

"Christ! He's got a gun, Red! He's stuck his arm out the window."

"Don't worry," Red told her. "Shooting a pistol left-handed from a moving car at another moving car at sixty miles an hour at this distance? Hell, he'd be lucky to hit that mountain."

There was a sharp crack and the rear window distintegrated into flashing shards. Something buzzed in the air between them and smashed into the tapedeck. Fee howled and ducked into his console.

"Unless," Red continued thoughtfully, "that's Orvid Crayle behind us. He's very good." He zipped open his repairman's coveralls and retrieved his revolver. He checked the action, then unbuckled his seat belt. "Well, Orvid and I were bound to cross swords someday." He looked at her and smiled. "I'm pretty good myself."

"I bet you are."

Red climbed over the seat and made his way to the back of the Blazer. "I think you've met Orvid already," he commented. "Tall, thin fellow. Looks like death warmed over?"

Sarah recalled her encounter in the library. "Yes. I think I have. Pleasant kind of guy?"

"That's the one. Orvid's Their Station Chief here in Colorado. You know what that means, don't you?"

"Sure. More good news. You don't send management out on a job unless you're shorthanded and there's no one else available. I don't know how much more good news I can take."

Red laughed. "That's the spirit." He braced himself against the back seat and, with his feet on the tailgate, he drew a bead through the shattered rear window. "Try not to hit any bumps for a while," he said.

"Right," Sarah muttered to herself, and floored the gas pedal. Crayle probably had the edge on them in speed, but there was no point in making it easier for him to close the distance. Unfortunately, Route 8 was relatively straight through this stretch of country, between the Hogback and the Foothills. No twists or turns to confuse the aim. She wished Red would hurry up and get it over with.

Two cars approached from the opposite direction and, glancing in the mirror, she saw that Crayle had pulled his gun in. *He's not going to throw himself away,* she thought, *like he did the man in the Civic Center.* Crayle was at least as interested in getting away as he was in getting the job done. He wasn't a fanatic or an automaton. That might give them an edge. "Hey," she said. "What we should do is just drive around until we find a police car. Crayle won't dare try anything then."

"Sure he would," Red's voice replied. "He'd gun us down and flash a badge. CIA or something like that. Claim we were fugitives. Local cops would buy it, because, whatever badge it was, it'd be legit."

"Can't you flash a badge, too?"

"Not with a half-dozen bullet holes in me." Red paused, then added thoughtfully. "I'm sure he'd rather not use his cover if he could avoid it. He might get away with killing us in front of the police; but his superiors would hear and know that it wasn't a Company operation. The word would get around the Community that maybe he'd been turned or had gone rogue."

*Bang!* The noise was loud inside the Blazer and the car swayed as Sarah jerked convulsively. "Hold the car still," Red demanded. She realized that Red had squeezed off a shot. "Did you get him?" she asked. No answer. He fired twice

131

more and Sarah flinched at the sound. "Did you get him?" she asked again, a slight edge to her voice.

"Yes and no," he told her as he climbed back into the passenger's seat. "I got his radiator and his front tires. Bigger targets than his pointy head. His tires are flat and he's losing water. His engine'll overheat and seize up."

She closed her eyes briefly and breathed a sigh of relief. They were going to get away and Red hadn't had to kill anyone. She didn't like Crayle. She *hated* Crayle; but she was glad Red hadn't killed him. "Then we're going to make it," she said.

There was another loud bang and the Blazer veered sideways. In a panic, she fought the steering as they skidded zig-zag down the road.

"Unless," Red said calmly, "he shoots out our tires, too."

Sarah spared him an exasperated glance.

Red shook his head in reluctant admiration. "Damn, he's good."

She managed to bring the Blazer down to a managable speed without spinning out. Both rear tires were making floppy sounds. She took a shaky breath and was amazed to discover how calm she was. Uncertainty breeds fear, she thought. There were no uncertainties now.

Behind them she saw Crayle already stopped by the roadside. Steam poured from under his car's hood. Crayle stepped out, dressed in a long, tan overcoat too warm for the weather. His left hand was jammed in his pocket. He looked from his car to them, kicked the car once, then started after them on foot. He didn't run, but he took long, quick strides, the kind that ate miles.

"He's persistent, too," she told Red. Crayle knew that, with their back tires gone, they weren't going far. Certainly there was no chance of making it to the entrance to Falcon Park around the back side of the mountain. And once they were all afoot, Crayle only needed to close to within pistol range. With his aim, he'd have them.

She tried to picture the Geological Survey map in her mind. She'd been over this area before, about a year ago. There was a dirt road that led from Route 8 to the base of the mountain. They could climb from there. It wouldn't be hard. Just hands and feet. Once they reached the trail on top and the rendezvous point, Janie could drive them to safety. Crayle, on foot, would be helpless to stop them. If only they could gain enough of a lead on him.

She came on the turn suddenly and jerked hard to the right. The Blazer slewed and wobbled and she winced at the abuse the wheels were taking. She could see hunks of rubber behind them. They'd be riding on the rims shortly.

"If you're thinking about stopping to change the tire," Red remarked dryly, "I wouldn't recommend it." He pointed to where Crayle was cutting diagonally across the meadow. He was following Strain Gulch, trying to head them off.

"Yeah. Where's the Indianapolis pit crew when you really need them," she said. Red snorted. "Besides," Sarah tapped the gas gauge, "this needle's dropping faster than usual on this gas hog. I think one of those shots got the tank or the gas line." She nibbled on her lower lip. A spark might have caused it to burst into flame; turned the Blazer into a giant Molotov cocktail.

The road came to an end. Sarah braked and turned the engine off. She reached around behind her and snagged her back pack. "End of the line," she told Red, kicking the door open. "We walk from here."

Red hopped out. "Up there?" he asked, staring at the mountain.

"You got a better idea?" She turned back to the Blazer and held the pack out with its front flap open. Fee nosed at it, meeowed, and jumped in. It was "his" pocket when they went on hikes. Sarah sniffed. The mercaptan smell was sharp. The gas was definitely leaking out.

"You're taking the cat with us?" Red asked.

Sarah was shocked. "Of course! Feline P. Cat isn't just a cat! He's . . . Fee! He and I have a contract. I give him food, shelter and affection, and change his kitty litter; and in return he sometimes rubs himself against my leg. If he feels like it."

Red cocked a speculative eye at her. "Does what he likes, when he likes, eh? Answers to nobody but himself. Some people are like that, too."

She had hitched the pack onto her back and was making her way up Strain Gulch. "Are you going to stand here flapping your lips just to feel the breeze? Let's go. Those shoes you have will have to do."

133

# XII

Red spared a look back down the gulch while Sarah began the climb. Crayle was a thin figure in the distance, still coming implacably onward. *Like a force of nature*, he thought. He gave in to impulse and waved at their pursuer. Crayle paused and raised an arm in reply, but Red didn't think he was waving with all five fingers. He laughed and turned to follow Sarah.

Scrambling up the draw where Strain Gulch came down the mountainside, Red found himself face to face with Sarah's cat. Fee's head stuck out of his pocket, surveying the scenery —and Red's struggles—with serene indifference. Red made a face at the cat. Then he slipped on a loose rock the size of his fist and stumbled to his hands and knees. He cursed and brushed himself off, scowling at the cat.

"What good is that stupid cat, anyway?" he asked in annoyance.

"Keep climbing," Sarah answered without turning around, "and stop wasting breath. And if you have to ask what use a cat is, you don't deserve to know the answer."

Red grinned at her back and ran to catch up. The ground became steeper and the sides of the draw closed in upon them. The slopes on either side were lightly forested with evergreen trees and bushes. Looking up, he could see rounded peaks on either side with a third and higher peak directly ahead. The ascent in that direction seemed more gradual. Sarah zig-zagged across the draw taking advantages of local variations in the terrain. Red followed. He hoped she knew where she was going.

At one particularly steep stretch they crawled on hands and knees to keep their balance, holding onto shrubs and outcroppings to pull themselves along. Red grabbed a plant and it came out of the dry, dusty soil by its roots. He slid three feet down the embankment, scraping the skin on his hands and cheek, and striking his knee on a rock. He winced at the pain. Sarah turned and, gripping a sapling with her right hand reached down to him with her left. He flushed and took it.

He looked into Sarah's calm, brown face. *So this climb is just a brisk walk for you,* he thought. *I'm a city boy and you're a backpacker, but I'll make it. I'm at my best when I'm challenged.*

He pulled himself up by her arm and they resumed climbing. Red threw himself into the effort with renewed energy. He began watching what Sarah did. Where she placed her feet. How she chose the route. He followed doggedly. His breath came hard and ragged. Once, he looked back and was surprised to see how high they had come. The Blazer was out of sight behind the trees and rocks, but they were easily eight hundred feet higher up.

He slipped a couple more times on rocks and loose gravel but managed to grab something each time to keep his balance. Sarah never looked back to check on him again and he set his jaw grimly.

After a while, he realized what he was doing. He was pushing himself because *she* expected it of him. It was such a startling revelation that he stopped climbing for a moment and stared at her back. He admired the assurance with which she moved, the lithe grace and suppleness of the muscles. There were dark stains on her shirt, at the armpits and at the small of her back. He had been sent to bring Sarah in, for her own safety and that of the Associates; but it was working out the other way. Somehow, somewhere along the line, he had lost mastery of the situation, and he couldn't quite say where or how. Sarah was the kind of person who, once she had chosen her direction, couldn't help but draw others along with her.

Red wasn't sure how that sat with him. He never liked being subordinate. He liked being in charge. *Maybe that's why Sarah and I were so immediately* simpatico *when we met,* he thought. *Although I was never the kind of loner that Sarah seems to be. I like being part of a team. I like it when everything clicks together.*

135

He resumed climbing. Sarah's weakness, he decided, was that, while she gave help with no questions asked, she had difficulty accepting help. That could be dangerous. At crucial times, it was always better to have someone to watch your back.

*Why is it that we've never been able to find a stable social order that balances the individual and the group? The loners and the toadies. The pendulum keeps swinging from side to side, but doesn't spend much time in the middle.* A social pendulum. He could envision the equations. He could even picture the equilibrium manifold. A simple pleat, or maybe a swallowtail. Not like some of the strange attractors they had to deal with. Just shift the splitting parameter a bit and it would damp the cycle. The memes for it were there, in the cultural pattern. The very fact that he could imagine the possibility at all meant that they were part of his mimetic heritage. All that was necessary was that the Associates adopt it as a goal, then maintain a constancy of purpose for five generations. Five friggin' generations. Dream on. It was *maintaining* the commitment that was hard. Like everything else in life, the Associates would change over the years. Develop new goals and outlooks. He didn't think any group could maintain a commitment that long. One generation's heartfelt goals become another generation's hoary fables.

Hell, kids never believed how deep the snow was in their parents' time.

"What does the P. stand for?" he asked impulsively.

Sarah stopped, turned, and gave him a puzzled look. "What?"

He took the advantage and caught up with her. "The P. Feline P. Cat."

"Oh. P. as in Pussy. Feline, the Pussy Cat."

He winced. It figured. If she'd been a dog person, she would have called her pet Canine H. Dog.

The sound of a crack distracted him. He turned downslope.

"It's Crayle," Sarah told him.

Red could make out the gunman's figure at the bottom of the draw. He was firing uphill at them, but the shots were falling well short, making puffs of dust in the ground below them.

"Even a good marksman has a hard time firing up or down hill," Sarah commented, "but I'd rather not wait until he gets the range."

"He's only got a pistol," he pointed out.

136

"I'd rather not wait until he gets lucky, then."

Red grunted. She had a point. He watched the man reload his gun, holster it, and start up the draw after them. He wasn't giving up; but at least he'd need both hands to climb the rough spots. Still, when it came to Crayle, it was best not to make assumptions.

The rest of the climb was easier than the part they had just gone through and another half-hour brought them out on the relatively flat area atop the mountain. The main peak rose another three hundred feet on their left. The regular trail from Morrison lay to their right.

Red felt lightheaded and dizzy. Nauseous. He stopped and squatted beside the trail. Sarah looked at him.

"What's wrong?"

"Don't know. I feel like I'm going to throw up."

"Mountain sickness," she told him. "If you're not used to the thin air, exerting yourself like we've been doing can bring it on."

"Great. What's the cure?"

"Move to Colorado."

He gave her a sour look. She probably made jokes about seasickness, too. "Just give me a minute to catch my breath," he said.

She scanned the slope behind them. "It's a lot worse when you go up one of the really high mountains. You want to give Crayle a minute, too?"

"Hell no. He lives here. He's probably a mountain goat like you."

"Come on, then. The trail's for the *turistas*. It can't be as bad as coming up the gulch."

"Yeah." He looked around. They were on a high ridge. Several peaks lay to their left and right, separated by draws where the runoff water ran down to the high plains. The ruins of a stone building peeked through the evergreens to their west. The Walker Mansion, he thought. Falcon Castle. Then that peak over there on the right, about a mile away, must be where Walker started building the Summer White House, just before the First World War. He shook his head. Walker had been a man of dreams, a sentimentalist at heart.

Sarah dropped back and they walked the trail side by side. She pointed to the wreckage of the mansion. "He was quite a personality," she said. "Newspaperman and realtor, just like me."

137

Red smiled. "You as rich as he was?"

She laughed. "Not yet."

"He was a military adventurer, too; did you know that? He served in the Chinese army."

"Yes, I did know that," she replied. "But I read up on him because we had some careers in common. How do you know about him?"

"Oh," he said vaguely, "I heard things here and there. How he proved the feasibility of dryland farming on his model Berkeley Farm; how he turned *Cosmopolitan* into a prestigious literary magazine by featuring writers like Crane and Wells and Tolstoy and Clemens; how he bought the Stanley Company to push steam-powered 'locomobiles.' "

Another half-dozen strides and Sarah asked, "Was John Brisben Walker one of your people?"

Red stopped short. "What?"

Sarah kept walking and Red double-timed to catch up.

"And Ford and Edison and Firestone and Burroughs and Dewey and Taylor and, oh, dozens of others who changed or tried to change the course of history."

He grinned. "Why do you ask?"

"Because *you* seem to know a lot about Walker and . . . Dammit, Red, why don't you ever answer my questions?"

"Habit. Alright, I'll answer you: Yes and no."

She twisted her lips. "Meaning some of the people I mentioned were members and some weren't. Okay. We don't have to get into that now. I just wondered how many of our modern problems were caused by your people."

Red grunted noncommittally. "Today's problems are often yesterday's solutions. Our grandparents yearned for what we condemn. Don't blame us for everything you don't like in life. We aren't that powerful. Besides, Utopian Research Associates doesn't tinker much anymore."

She gestured toward the mansion. "Even back then, at the turn of the century?"

"Even back then," he said. "Quinn laid down the rule. He felt we didn't know enough to make large scale changes without risking unacceptable side-effects. Observe and study. Those were his watchwords. Over the years, they became 'Observe and study and make a bundle.' " He grimaced. "Not everyone liked the rule. Not everyone went along with it. But Quinn had strong, personal reasons for it; and the Associates have never taken concerted group action." He wondered if

138

Sarah would be the catalyst. He grinned. Cam Betancourt and the other Council members were in for a big surprise if they managed to recruit her.

"Hunh. Sometimes running doesn't work, either. Doing nothing is also a choice."

He was surprised to hear his own words coming back at him. "Are you trying to tell me something?"

"You want to start tinkering again."

He grinned at her. "It's in a good cause, though."

"Isn't it always?"

They had reached the ruins. Walker's house had been struck by lightning in 1918. It had burned and Walker, disillusioned, penniless, and heartbroken by his wife's death two years earlier, had never rebuilt. All that was left now were the stone walls, broken and gaping, with the tall chimney towering above, still improbably intact. A split rail fence surrounded the ruins.

The building was laid out in a U-shape, with the open courtyard facing roughly southwest. The chimney was at the northeast corner. They walked around the south wing to the courtyard. There was a signboard there for the tourists, telling all about Walker and his "Castle" and the summer White House he had started to build with pennies pledged by the schoolchildren of Colorado. Red ignored it and walked past into the courtyard. He surveyed the ruins. A fair defensive position. He'd been under worse cover that time in Jacksonville.

"Let's get behind the wall," he told Sarah. "It's too exposed out here." There was no point in going any further. The parking lot was too open and flat. Crayle would catch them with no shelter.

The wall before them had a doorway flanked by two windows. On their left was another wall, its middle section almost entirely tumbled down. They climbed the fence and ducked through the doorway. Red went immediately to the left-hand window and, standing off to one side, he studied their past route. He unzipped his coveralls so he could reach his gun quickly; but he didn't take it out in case ordinary tourists approached.

He scanned the trees to the east. He could see the plains beyond the mountain rim, where they stretched in perfect flatness to meet the sky. There was no sign of Crayle. That worried him nearly as much as seeing him would have. With Crayle, either way was bad news.

139

There was no sign of Janie, either; he checked his watch. They were early. He wished she would hurry.

He glanced around their surroundings. The remnants of walls, about waist-high showed where the different wings had been. Faded scorch marks discolored some of the stonework. It was all broken up. He couldn't tell what the original floorplan had been. "Why did you say that? About the tinkering, I mean."

Sarah squatted against the wall and shrugged out of her backpack. She took Fee from his special pocket and scratched his head. The cat narrowed his eyes in pleasure. "I don't know. The way you talk. Your body language. You want to change things. You don't like sitting back and getting rich off of other folks' miseries."

"The getting rich part is okay; and folks will be miserable anyhow. But you're right. It's past time the Associates stopped being so gun-shy."

She shook her head. "I still don't like it."

He stifled a spasm of annoyance. Why couldn't she see it? If they didn't do something to blunt the Society's efforts now, their grandchildren would suffer in poverty and serfdom. Was she too thickheaded? Or his arguments too weak? He turned his back on her and concentrated on his vigil. Damn. He wished he had binoculars. He asked Sarah if she had a pair in her backpack.

"They're back in the Blazer."

"Fat lot of good they'll do us there. What'd you bring along besides a stupid cat?"

"A stupid man."

He grunted. She was right. Who was he to complain? After all, he had brought nothing. It wasn't good to stay in the same place too long. Red crouched and crawled to another vantage point.

"Do you see him yet?" she asked.

"No. I wish I did."

"Where's your friend, Janie?"

"She'll get here when she gets here." He glanced quickly at his watch. She was already late. And she knew Crayle was loose, too. He wondered if They had intercepted her. No, not likely. If Crayle was coming after them personally, he had no one else to spare. Unless it was simply for the challenge. *Mano a mano.* He patted the gun under his jacket. Maybe he could pay Crayle back for Jacksonville.

Sarah shifted to a more comfortable position and drew patterns in the dirt with her finger. "I'll answer your question for you now," she said.

He looked at her, puzzled. "What question?"

"About the boy and the bus. For me, the answer is simple. Save the boy. Not for his sake. *But for my sake!* Do you understand that? You don't hurt people for things they haven't done yet and may never do. If I didn't try to save him, I would lose myself."

Red nodded. "You would have made a hell of a recruit," he said.

"Yeah. Red, what happened to Dennis?" Red glanced at her and she paused and swallowed. "God, it seems like that was another planet! Do you think he's dead?"

Red searched her face and saw the pain there. He had to remind himself that she had lost friends in this gambit. That made him more anxious than ever to get Crayle in his sights. There were rules to the game. If you weren't a player, you weren't a target. "It wasn't your fault," he told her. "It was nobody's fault."

"It was Their fault."

"I don't know. The message said that he had vanished completely, even from the hospital records." He scowled. "That doesn't make sense. Why bother? If They wanted him dead, it would have been easier to short circuit one of his life support units. Or even start a fire in the hospital."

She shivered. "They're vicious," she said. "Evil."

"That's why we have to stop Them. We have to start spreading anti-memes."

"Fight fire with fire?" she said.

"Don't be cynical. Have you ever fought a forest fire? Sometimes a backfire is the only way to stop one."

She shook her head violently. "No! You say They've attached puppet strings to us and They're pulling us the wrong way. But your only answer is to attach another set of strings!"

"What would you do?"

"Cut the strings. All of them."

He grinned at her. "Have you ever seen a puppet without strings?"

"Yes. Pinocchio."

He blinked, startled by her answer. Metaphor was always suspect; but frequently it provided insight as well. Almost, he

141

could see what her remark might mean; how to translate it into action.

"Maybe They didn't want him dead," she said. "Dennis. Maybe They found out about the List he had. Suppose he had figured out what it meant and had hidden it. They would need him alive then, wouldn't They?"

Sometimes people's needs were very basic. "That's probably it," he told her.

"Sure. Until They found the List. They'd want to know about the factor analysis that Carson and Quinn did on the entries, wouldn't They?"

"Sure. That must be it." He looked back out at the forest. Crayle had not yet made his appearance. That was trouble, because by now he should have. The back of his neck prickled. *Where was Crayle?* He took his gun from its holster. He didn't think any tourists were going to show up. "Directed behaviors leave 'footprints,' " he commented for want of anything else to say. "They create statistical anomalies in the data." A movement at the eastern rim of the plateau? Or was it the wind stirring the tops of the trees? He shifted position and stared intently through the broken window hole.

"Sure," Sarah babbled on. "And the mutual correlations define factors, like the axes of a coordinate system. The entries on the list were numbered one, two, and three, so Dennis and I figured . . ."

He wasn't particularly listening to her, so it was a moment before her words registered. He jerked his head around. "What did you say? *Three?* Are you sure?"

"Yes. Why? Is it important?"

He opened his mouth to answer her, but the words never came out.

# XIII

Sarah watched with horror as Red pitched backward against the stone wall. He slammed against it and fell forward on his face. Behind him a red splash decorated the stones. He didn't move. The whisper of the muffled shot echoed in the ruins.

A low, partial wall ran at right angles to the wall with the doorway in it, and Sarah hugged the ground behind it. The smell of the dirt was heavy in her nostrils. From the way Red had fallen, the shot must have come from the northwest. Crayle had apparently worked his way through the trees behind them while they had been watching the east.

Now she was trapped. Red had the only gun and he had fallen on top of it. Besides, his body was almost certainly within Crayle's field of fire. She looked behind her. Could she crawl out without being seen? Not through the door, that was exposed, but through another break in the masonry? Maybe, maybe not. But it was better than lying here and waiting for a bullet. She began to inch backward until her boots touched the wall. She probed back and forth with her feet, searching for a hole.

Yes. There was another way out. It was small, but she thought she could fit. She pushed herself into the hole feet-first, pulling her pack after her. Fee sat curiously atop it, like a king being borne on a processional float. *I wonder what he thinks of these antics.* Her squirming had pulled her jacket and shirt up and stones ground into her stomach and ribs. She tried not to think about getting stuck halfway through.

Her hips gave her a bad moment. For a moment, she couldn't move. She bit on her lower lip. Then she pushed as

143

hard as she could and came free. A stone raked her ribs on the left side and she stifled a cry of pain.

Finally, she was through. She gasped, rolled to the side and sat with her back to the wall. She felt her side where the stone had cut her and her hand came away bloody. No time to relax, she thought. Crayle was coming.

She glanced at the doorway to her right. Red was partly visible through it. She wondered if he were dead, or just unconscious. It had all happened so fast, but she thought he had been hit in the shoulder. She studied his muscles. In art class, she had learned what the body looked like in life and death. A dead man did not lie like a sleeping or unconscious one. All opposing muscle groups should be equally relaxed.

The sphincters relaxed, too; but she couldn't see his pants from where she sat. She took a deep breath, but she couldn't smell anything, either.

She opened her pack and dug inside. She came out with a mirror and her hunting knife. "Come on, Fee," she whispered.

Crouching, she ran to the corner of the ruins, keeping a tall wall between her and where she thought Crayle was. There she lay flat again and cautiously pushed the mirror out beyond the edge. She was careful to keep it in the shadow of the wall so it wouldn't reflect the evening sun. She tilted it this way and that, viewing the "inside" of the ruins.

She could see the low wall that she had lain behind. Red was beyond it, on the other side; but she couldn't see him.

There! She saw the reflection of a man approaching the ruin. She backed away from the corner, keeping the mirror in view. It was Crayle, just as she remembered him from the library. When he reached the wall, he swung his gun over, holding it in two hands. Then, seeing there was no one there, he ducked back, his eyes darting.

She saw him go around the back side of the building and smiled, because that meant Crayle couldn't read signs. The drag marks in the dirt showed clearly which way she had gone. Sarah edged around the corner. She left her mirror in place, but turned it so it now reflected the "outside" wall where she had just been.

She saw Crayle jump out with his gun aimed straight down the wall. Again, there was a moment of hesitation while he took in the empty scene. Then he let the gun drop and looked around.

144

"I know you're around somewhere, little lady." Pause. "Don't make this hard on yourself. We only want to question you."

Incredibly, Sarah found she had to suppress a giggle. How stupid did he think she was?

She watched him in the mirror as he walked toward her position. *When he reaches the doorway,* she thought, *he'll jump back through to this side.* It was an obvious gambit to try. She readied herself to jump around the end of the wall at the same time. *And what if he doesn't do it?* She swallowed and watched his feet carefully. A man about to jump holds himself a certain way.

Yes. He jumped and Sarah jumped at the same time. Her heart was pounding at this cat and mouse game, but she felt strangely exhilarated, as if she were somehow more alive. Every sense seemed stretched to the limit. She could hear Crayle's shoes where they crunched the gravel.

*This can't go on forever. I'll have to do something. How long till sundown?* She knew these hills. In the dark she might be able to escape. Crayle was not a woodsman.

She kept her eyes glued to the mirror, not daring to glance away even to check the sun. It felt strange knowing that she actually had her back to Crayle. Fee crept up to her and rubbed against her calf. Fee. Maybe he could help. She blocked out a plan in her mind.

"It's no use, little lady. You're all alone up here and I'll get you sooner or later. Just like I got your friends. You should have heard him beg for his life."

He had to mean Abbot. She couldn't imagine Morgan or Dennis begging.

Her plan had an element of the desperate in it. Crayle was a professional and it wouldn't be easy to trick him. But he thought he was dealing with an amateur—witness his attempts to get her to talk and reveal her position—and that gave her an edge. She pulled the hunting knife from its scabbard, and taking a deep breath, picked Fee up. "Forgive me, Fee," she whispered.

"And once I've taken care of you," said Crayle, "I'll head back to Denver and finish the job on your queer friend."

Turning her back on the mirror, she *tossed* Fee underhanded as far as she could along the outside wall. Fee, terrified and astonished, squealed and landed with a crash, and ran into the trees, scattering leaves and twigs.

Sarah jumped to her right with her knife cocked for throwing. She saw Crayle thirty feet away staring through the window hole in the direction of her cat. He was aiming his pistol out the window, but her movement must have caught the corner of his eye because he turned back to face her just as she threw.

The knife was a blur of motion that buried itself at the base of his throat. Crayle staggered and arterial blood spurted from the wound. His right hand made an abortive motion toward the handle and his left tightened convulsively on the pistol. The gun went off and sparks ricocheted across the stones. A look of infinite surprise crossed his features. He dropped the gun and collapsed like a deflated balloon.

She started to run toward him, but hesitated. Don't take Crayle for granted. She approached cautiously, ready to bolt for cover.

Crayle lay on the ground next to Red, his legs kicking in jerks. He turned his eyes toward her in what looked like disbelief. Then they filmed over and he sagged and was still.

Sarah began shaking and her knees felt weak. She sat on her haunches and covered her face with her hands. It was over. She sobbed and tears ran down her cheeks, leaving muddy trails in the dirt there.

How could you explain someone like Crayle? A man empty and vicious. Yet, once upon a time he had been a child, with a child's innocence; and surely his parents had never thought he would come to this. He had suckled and played with his toes. He had delighted his parents with his hesitant first steps. Now he was dead. Where along his path from toddler to corpse had the soul leaked out of him?

On hands and knees, she crawled past Crayle to where Red lay. She felt his throat for a pulse. Was there one? She thought she could feel something, but that might only be her imagination. "Oh, Red," she sighed sadly.

There was a sharp click behind her and she whipped around. A spare, older woman stood there, dressed in denim with a telescopic rifle cradled in her left arm. "Nice work, missy," she said.

There was something familiar about her windburned face. For a moment, she couldn't place her. Then she remembered. "You! You were in the library with Crayle!"

"Yup." She walked over and stared at Crayle's face. "He shore does look surprised. Can't say I blame him. It's always

146

supposed to be the other one. His kind never think it's going to be themselves that git it." She looked at Sarah. " 'Specially not from the likes o' you, missy. I'm a might surprised myself."

"You're . . ." Sarah stood up and stared at her. "You're Jane Hatch!"

She nodded, still looking at Crayle. "How's Malone? He gonna make it?"

*"How long have you been watching?"*

She shrugged and spat tobacco. "Long enough. You're one cool lady. Most folks would have been paralyzed with fear." She put her rifle aside and knelt over Red. Her hands probed expertly. "Shoulder wound," she said. "And concussion. He must've hit his head against the wall. Good thing his skull's so thick."

*"How long have you been watching!"*

Janie turned and looked at her. In her calm eyes, Sarah thought she could see more than a touch of Crayle's eyes. A detachment. A distancing from the world around her. "Why d'you want to know, missy?"

Sarah pointed at the rifle with the telescopic sights. "You could have shot him, couldn't you? But you let him stalk me like an animal! What's wrong with you?"

Janie shook her head. "It's nature's way, missy. We don't interfere. It's always up t' the bird whether the snake strikes it or not."

All during her conversations with Red, Sarah had thought that trying to guide the course of history took supreme arrogance. Now she saw that the opposite was also true. There was something equally arrogant in those who stood by and watched and did nothing.

She turned her back on Janie, her arms straight down at her sides, eyes and fists clenched shut. The tears on her cheeks felt hot. It had to end. There had to be a finish of it. The Society and the Associates both. She hated them. She hated their secrecy, their callousness. Even their good intentions were callous.

Her worm would start it. Crippling their data banks would throw both of them into confusion. Maybe give her time to think. And the worm had a stinger, too. A codicil that she hoped would shatter their smug little world forever.

When you know someone's deadly secret, there was only one way to be safe. Tell everyone. If it weren't secret anymore, there'd be no point in singling her out. So she had

147

instructed her worm to copy whatever it found and download it anonymously into every TV network, newspaper, police, and government system it could find. And that included Morgan's files, as well.

She knew that both organizations had heavily infiltrated the various information and intelligence groups. They were rich, powerful, and they'd do everything they could to ridicule and silence the truth. And maybe they could, this time, but Sarah didn't think so. The facts would be dispersed too widely; too many of them could be verified independently; and, ultimately, the two societies must be too small to block every possible avenue. Otherwise, they could not have kept themselves secret for so long. Perhaps millions would scoff; but millions would believe.

It would be, as Red had claimed, interesting times.

You can never do just one thing. Red had said that, too. Along with blocking their selfish machinations, she would also be blocking whatever good they could do. The Founders had ended slavery, had forestalled an atomic war. Red had intended to block the Society's attempts to create a Docile Society. Noble goals, every one. Was she right to sabotage that?

She didn't know. Time enough tomorrow to worry about that.

She walked to Crayle's body and stared down at it. She suppressed a feeling of revulsion, knelt on one knee, and pulled her knife from his throat. His unfocused eyes stared at her and she looked away. *The second time will be easier,* said a voice inside her head. Crayle's ghost? There wouldn't be a second time, she vowed. Not if she could help it.

She looked up. It was growing dusk. Janie had picked up her rifle. "I'm goin' down t' the pickup to git my first aid kit. Why don't you come along? You can sit and wait in the cab 'till I'm ready t' carry him down."

Sarah stabbed the knife into the ground to wipe the blood off the blade. Red would recover. She was glad. She didn't agree with him; at least, not entirely; but she was glad he'd be around to argue with. There was more than a touch of Morgan in the man. "No. Thanks," she said. She stood up and stuck the knife through her belt. "I've got something else I've got to do."

She walked through the broken doorway to the outside and climbed back over the fence. She squinted her eyes at the gathering gloom. The trees were tall and black and the wind ran through their needles with the sound of a distant crowd. *I had to do it*, she thought. *He'll understand*. She faced the brush and squatted.

"Fee?" she called into the night. "Fee? Come back. I need you."

# PART 2

# A ROSE BY
# OTHER NAME

# Then

Davis Belleau's day began slowly, lying abed savoring his morning coffee. Partly that was his temperment. He had been bred in Louisiana, and was accustomed to taking things at their unhurried, natural pace. Partly it was his age. His bones were brittle and his joints protested at every move. Later during the day, he knew, movement would come more easily; but the morning was always bad.

Sometimes he longed for his lost youth, for the time when he had been strong and fleet. The quickest lad in three parishes, they had said; and meant quick not only in the body. Sometimes the memories rose up so strongly he could almost smell them. (It was odd how, of all the senses, smells triggered the most potent memories.) Riding to hounds on his father's plantation, the pungent smell of horseflesh in his nostrils; or punting in the bayous, the odor of magnolia or cypress like a mist around him. Creeping through the thickets to spy on the old, black witch lady who lived in the swamp. The ferns brushing his face and the black delta mud squishing between his toes. The smell of brackish swampwater. The old woman could see the future, the older boys had told him. She could read it in a ball of mud and chicken bones that smelled of the graveyard and Belleau had been possessed by an overwhelming desire to see the future himself.

Now, of course, he only wished he could not; because the future *was* mud and bones and graveyards.

There were other times when he remembered that the world of his youth was gone past all hope of recall; and he lived now in an alien land. It was not merely that he had grown old; but that the world itself had died. Drowned in blood at Pittsburg Landing and at Gettysburg, and offered as a holocaust in the flames of Atlanta.

The new, revised world was truly alien and Belleau felt like a visitor from a far country, which in a sense he was. A stranger in his own land. A relic, like those strange, massive, stone skeletons unearthed in the West. The new world was better; the equations proved that. This present was better than the future that would have been. Yet, Davis Belleau found himself ill at ease in it.

It was not the technology, strange and wonderful though it was. Rails might now span the continent, and iron horses had replaced the keelboats of his youth. That was nothing more than Man's growing mastery of nature. No, it was the inner life that had changed and left him behind. Of all the passions that had once roused men to action—that had roused Belleau himself and moved him to anger or to tears—not one would today stir a flicker of emotion. The rallying cries of the past were muted; and men flocked to new standards. To causes that seemed of little moment. Silver coinage? Railroad rates? What were such trivia when measured against States' Rights or Nullification; the Tariff Question or Abolition? All the great issues have already been decided. *I have outlived my own life,* he thought.

Someone had taken a shears and snipped off the past and it was gone. And the fact that Belleau's hand had helped with the cutting mattered not at all. We knew we would change the future, he reminded himself. But we didn't know we would lose our own past with it.

The smell of age was in Belleau's room. The curtains, heavy and musty, blocked the sun and shrouded everything in shadows. Belleau set his coffee aside. He closed his eyes and relaxed on the pillows. Behind his eyelids, he could see the equations. The ones that had started it all; that had changed a harmless society of natural philosophers into—Into what? Saviors? Masters? The equations were simple, brutal. A judgment on a world. He heard again forgotten voices, arguing fearfully over those abstract symbols. Eli protesting that they knew too little to take any action; 'Diah arguing that delay could lead to catastrophe; Isaac keeping his own counsel, but staring fixedly at the chalkmarks on the board as if, by sheer concentration, he could will them into a more congenial configuration.

*My God, how young we all were!*

"No action at all is incumbent upon us," Phineas had protested. His hand had flashed, the chalk scrawled a mathematical curve across the slate. "Those are the figures for the last few decades. I've run them through the engines and fit them to an equation. Here is the projection." The chalk whispered. The curve grew. "Slavery is dying. Soon it will be dead. The border states are already talking of manumission. Virginia had 300,000 slaves in 1790; today, she has but 400,000 when the natural increase should have produced a million and a half. Only in the Deep South has there been any growth—because of the cotton bubble. Mississippi's slave population has grown at double the rate projected by the census data: it was 30,000 in 1820 and shall be 150,000 come 1850. All the ambitious young men are seeking their fortunes in cotton; but that bubble shall burst and cotton slavery will go the way of tobacco slavery. If we do nothing at all, the next fifty years will see the end of the whole sorry business. Am I not right, Brother Eli?"

Eli shifted and shrugged. "Do we know even that much? How confident are we in our equations? In our very data? They may be grotesquely wrong. If we decide to act, do we know enough to choose our course wisely?"

Jedediah Crawford's cane had thumped the floor like a judge's gavel. "We know enough that to do nothing would be cowardice of the worst sort. Irresponsibility. Every year that slavery persists is another year closer to disaster." He pushed himself to his feet and hobbled to the slateboard. He slashed an S-shaped growth curve atop the slavery decay curve. "Slavery may well be dying—and good riddance to it; but the corpse is still too lively. It is stunting our technological growth. The growth curve starts slowly. If it starts too late, the United States will not have waxed strong enough in time, and the United Germanies will explode the Ultimate Weapon."

"The Ultimate Weapon." Eli's voice was heavy with skepticism. "There is one extrapolation to which I can give no credence. Extrapolation is chancy at best. The power of the explosive you forecast is too incredible. What could possibly be so potent?"

Isaac spoke for the first time. "A question your father may well have asked of guncotton. Who could imagine an explosive more powerful than black powder?" Irony edged his voice and Eli flushed. Isaac turned his gaze back to the board.

"No, Brother 'Diah is right. We can project its power—and it does seem truly incredible, I grant you. We can project its power; but as to its nature—" A shrug. "Who can say? It may not even be chemical."

Meechum snorted. "Not chemical, suh? Then what?"

Isaac took a deep breath. "Don't know. Don't want to. I shall be dust long before it is conceived and I am eternally grateful for that small kindness that God has shown me. Sometimes—" And he had gazed once more at the equations, looking for all the world like a Papist before his idols. "Sometimes, theah is comfort of a sort in these calculations."

Davis Belleau, watching with the inner eye of memory, saw his younger self shake his head. Not with the doubt of Eli or Phineas; nor with the dread of Isaac or Jedediah; but with another emotion entirely. Alone of those in that room that day, he had had an inkling of what was to come.

"We cannot wait for slavery to die its natural death. We must hasten it." That was Brother Jedediah again. A crabby Vermonter, brilliant, incisive, visionary. Hobbled from birth by a clubfoot. Crawford had been the first to see in Babbage's work the potential for a new science; a science that treated manufacture, economics, politics, indeed, all of society as a great, complex engine. A scientific riddle to be solved. He had built the first, crude calculating engine; and fashioned the wonderful wooden cards, with the holes drilled in them at strategic loci, that enabled the engines to store their statistics and instructions. In sum, Jedediah was a man whom his associates respected.

And now he was telling them that it was not science, but engineering that was required. That the equations were more than intellectual abstractions; they were disasters awaiting the lives of their grandchildren, and their great grandchildren.

"Suh," responded Meechum. "I do not deny the necessity. You will recollect that the first abolition societies were founded in the South, not the North. Slavery has impoverished my country. Cotton is crowding farm products off the land; yet we spin less than 2% of it ourselves. We have less than a quarter of the Federal Union's railroad trackage. Our banks contain less than ten millions of dollars in deposit. New York City alone has twice the liquid capital of the entire South. I fear for our future." He gestured toward the tangled curves they had drawn upon the chalkboard. "We have virtually no

156

manufactures. Our children are rocked in a Northern cradle; our dead, buried with a Northern spade."

"And it is not in industry alone that we lag," Davis had added. "Illiteracy among our white population is three times greater than in the North. We have 18,000 public schools to your 60,000. We have 100 public libraries, 70 daily news-papers. You have 1,000 libraries and 170 newspapers. And these figures will worsen with the passing years."

"But!" Meecham continued, "we cannot force abolition down the throats of our countrymen. Should we attempt to do so, the South will secede!"

"The South will talk of secession," said Phineas. "We have heard the bleat of secession since the Nullification Affair, and naught has ever come of it. Besides, of the five million plus Southrons, how many would fight for slavery? There are a mere 350,000 slave owners in the entire South, and half of those own less than five slaves apiece! Why would five million sharecroppers and yeomen bleed for the priveleges of the wealthy planters? It makes no sense."

Isaac had been scribbling on a scratchpad. He glanced up at the faces of the arguing men. "And if'n the South does go?" he said. "Good riddance, ain't it?" He pointed to the techno-logical growth curve. "Without that poor, feudal millstone, will we not achieve the acceleration we seek?"

Meechum colored and Davis felt himself grow angry. "Be warned, suh," he said pointedly. "You insult our honor."

"If the South secedes," Eli told Isaac, "the North will fight. And probably the West, as well. Not for abolition, but to preserve the Union. No good can come from that."

"Fight?" Meechum laughed. "If the South leaves the Fed-eral Union, the North will dare nothing. Southron gentlemen are trained to combat from birth. How can a nation of shop-keepers and mechanics stand up to them?"

"How?" asked Isaac, amusement in his voice. He rose and walked to the chalkboard. Taking the chalk, he wrote a set of equations on the board and stepped back.

Davis studied the equations and felt his heart grow cold.

Meechum snorted, recovered the chalk, and added another term. The solution changed. Southron victory.

Isaac shook his head. "Neither England nor France will join in the fight."

"They will, suh, for Southron cotton sustains them. Cotton accounts for nearly half of the Union's exports to the devel-

157

oped countries. They will intervene or go bare-assed." Phineas and he laughed, and Davis marvelled how close Mississippi and Massachussetts stood on some things.

"I fear you are wrong regarding that point, Brother Meechum," said Eli. "There have been reports of successful cotton culture from Egypt and India. The South is not so indispensable as you suppose."

"Gentlemen!" Jedediah struck the floor once more. "We waste time over remote possibilities. There can be war only if the South secedes. The South will secede only if she believes abolition will be forced upon her by the National Government. That can occur only if the Electors choose an abolitionist President and the State legislatures appoint abolitionist Senators. And since neither the Democracy nor the Whigs are in danger of abolitionist control, there is small chance of that. Multiply the probabilities yourselves, if you wish. The product is vanishingly small."

*But not zero.* Even now, decades later, Davis Belleau remembered that thought.

*Sir?*

Belleau stirred and opened his eyes to the present. "We acted indirectly," he told the figure before him. "Never a word of abolition. But something went wrong."

"Sir?" His manservant stood before him, polite puzzlement on his face.

"And they missed the real point. All of them. Meechum never understood why I voted the way I did. But I could see where slavery led; and that was to Hell. Not for the slaves— for with suffering comes Salvation—but for the slave owners. To become a morally depraved aristocracy, wu'ss than any in the Old World. To become damned for all time and never know it. John Randolph was right about that. The worst curse of all is to be born the master of slaves."

"Sir!"

"What is it, Georges?" he asked irritably.

"A message for you, sir. From the banking firm of Gorman and Stout. The boy has instructions to place it only into your hands."

Belleau sighed and shoved the bedsheets away. He sat upright in his nightgown and cap and pushed his legs at his slippers. He moved slowly, deliberately. "Very well. I shall take it in my morning room. Send Martin to lay out my clothes and dress me. Let the boy wait in the kitchen. Miss Loretta may serve him some iced tea."

But the packet, when he had opened it, made his hands to tremble.

After dismissing the messenger boy, he sat alone in the morning room, a plate of breakfast on the sideboard. Inside the packet was an envelope and a covering letter from the bankers. And on the envelope . . .

He held it up to catch the light better. That handwriting. It couldn't be; not after all these years! He reached out and turned up the gas mantle. The flames hissed and the room brightened. He inspected the handwriting once more.

Yes. It was Brady Quinn's.

How long was it now since Brady had resigned and vanished? A decade? More years than Belleau wanted to remember. Brady Quinn. Now, there had been a sharp mind! One of the best in the Society. But Brady had had no stomach for the Society's work. Too bad. Belleau had little stomach for it, either; but he had the shoulders for it. Not Brady.

Lincoln. That was it. He remembered now. That was the reason why Brady had quit. A regrettable action, but a necessary one. The equations had proven that. And it was expedient, as it said in the Book, that one man die for the whole people.

Some of the punched hole cards had vanished with Brady. Belleau rememebered making the discovery and telling Isaac. And Brother Isaac, who had never in Davis' memory shown any emotion but resolution, had hung his head and silently wept. It was remarkable how clear such ancient memories were; while those of yesterday were cloudy and indistinct. Isaac had been Brady's mentor; but Belleau had always suspected something more behind the sorrow. Something more than his protégé's resignation or the theft of some cards. As if Isaac had nurtured some terrible secret in his heart.

He hefted the envelope. And now here was news from beyond the grave.

Or was it? No one knew whether Brother Brady were alive or dead. He had gone West and that was all anyone knew. Unless Isaac knew more.

He remembered the cover letter and pulled his bifocals from his vest pocket. Hon. Davis Belleau, Esq. Salutations, etc., etc.. He skipped the verbal parsley and went for the meat of the message.

159

As he suspected. Brady had left the enclosure in the safe-keeping of Gorman and Stout in 1866, with directions that it be delivered on or about the 16th of May, 1876, "to which-ever of the following gentlemen be hale enough to receive it." Dr. Jedediah Crawford, Ph.D., The Hon. Mr. Isaac Shelton, Dr. Elias Kent, M.D., Col. Meechum Clark . . . Belleau's vision blurred with tears. His brothers, one and all. How he missed them! The comradeship; the sense of mission; even the arguments. All gone now, save only Brother Isaac, and he senile. A tear fell from his cheek and the ink on the cover letter blurred and ran.

He barely knew the current Council members. Had not attended a meeting in many years. He was retired now from the Society's Business. Councilor emeritus.

With a sudden jerk, he pulled the letter opener across the envelope. Two pages of closely written foolscap were inside. Belleau hesitated a moment, then pulled them out and read.

And read them again.

*My Dearest Comrades,*

*I do not know whether any of you will be alive when this message is delivered; nor do I know if I myself shall live. Yet, I know that you, my comrades, deserve an explanation for what I am about to do; and, please God, at least one of you shall read these lines and understand.*

*Brothers, the Society has made too many errors. Our actions have too often had consequences unforetold by the equations. Brother Eli was right when he warned that our knowledge was too sketchy for what we attempted. Yet, I have been unable to disssuade you from the path Brother Crawford set us upon. Very well. I understand the urgency and sincerity with which you pursue the Goal. The Ultimate Weapon must never be exploded.*

*Yet, it is the very pursuit of that Goal that disturbs me.*

*My protégé—his name does not matter—has uncovered a problem and, between the two of us, we may have devised a solution; but I must be free of the Society to implement it. If our own calculations have been free from error, the event we foresee is imminent even as you read this. We have allowed for a margin of* error in the delivery of this missive, so that you shall have some forewarning; though, there is some small probability—on the order of 5%—that it has already taken place.

The warning is this: the Society itself is subject to the very cliological laws which we have discovered. By this I do not mean that we ourselves share the ideals and beliefs of our age—such goes without saying—but that the Society is "an ideonic complex in the sense of Babbage" and thus is itself subject to evolutionary change. We have begun meddling—however poorly—in the pursuit of a noble Goal; but that Goal will not remain immutable; and in the future, the Society's efforts may turn toward less noble purposes.

Consider this: in the familiar schoolyard game, a young boy whispers a story to his neighbor, who in turn whispers it to his own neighbor, and so on around a circle. When the last boy recites the story aloud, it bears little resemblance to the original. Let us call this "ideon decay." Approximately 25% of the ideon content is lost each time the message is passed on and must be replaced with ideons created by each new hearer. (Tho' more "active" ideas may decay more quickly.)

Just so, has Jedediah Crawford whispered a set of ideons into the ears of Isaac and Phineas; and they, in turn have whispered them to others, among them myself. Soon enough, the original ideons of the Society will have evaporated. We have calculated that, in the pure situation, Br. Jedediah's original ideons will have decayed to a mere 25% at the sixth link in the chain of protégés. This means that the sixth "generation" of recruits will perceive its own original thoughts as having equal merit as those inherited from the Founders, and they will therefore chart a new course for the Society. We believe that the transformed Society will attempt to engineer the national complex to its own benefit rather than to the benefit of all. One of our future members—by which I mean one of your present members, brother—will endeavour to steer the course of the Society itself, using our own cliological tools against us.

I have taken some small steps to counteract this. I have formed in secret a daughter society, divorced from *you, my brothers. We have kept the Oath and the ceremonies; but have altered the Rules in a way which, we hope, will be less easily distorted. I only pray that we have succeeded. Our new Society will take no action. Too many mistakes have been made; and too much blood spilled. We will return to the original purpose of scholarly study and hope that in the process we may learn enough to rectify the mistakes of the past.*

*Many of us were once members of the Society; but I have removed all traces of us from the Cards. Forgive me for that; but it was necessary that we germinate in isolation.*

*In the event, I remain ever*
*Y$^r$. Obed$^t$ Ser$^t$*
*Brady Templeton Quinn*

The pages rustled as Belleau set them down. The Society? Abandon the principles set down by Brother 'Diah? No, that was not possible!

And yet . . . And yet, he could see it. Now that the possibility had been pointed out, the mechanism—and the equations describing it—were clear. And the cusp would come . . . He did the calculations mentally, cursing the slowness of his mind. Too long a reliance on Babbage engines had impaired the skills drilled into him in youth. He made some simplifications to the numbers. He only wanted an estimate.

The cusp would come . . . Soon!

He gripped the arms of his chair until the knuckles stood out large and white. The Council must be warned. Curse Brady! Why had he said nothing ten years ago? Why had he waited until now, to speak from the past?

Davis Belleau rose and hobbled to the desk. His fingers ran through the days on the calendar there. Yes. Next Thursday would be a Council meeting. As Councilor emeritus, he was eligible to attend. He would do so. Warned even this late, Grosvenor Weil might yet forestall the coup that Brady foresaw.

But, he had forgotten some vital facts about Grosvenor Weil, not the least of which was how many links in the chain lay between him and Jedediah Crawford.

# Now
## I

[Easton, PA] Captain Reilly gradually became aware of the commotion in the computer room. He laid his pen on his desk and walked to the door of his office and looked out. He was tall and ruggedly built; still slim and hard because he jogged every morning around the South Side. He saw the officers and civilian staff clustered around the printer, talking excitedly. The printer was racing like a machine gun. He opened the door and walked over.

"What's going on?" he demanded. He saw that the paper from the printer was piling up in the basket. The daisy wheel was a blur. "What is this?"

One of his detectives was reading the sheets as they came out. "I don't know, captain," he said. "A lot of it looks like gibberish to me; but I think . . ." And he pawed backward through the printout; found a page; and tore it off at the perforations. "I think we got a line on that John Doe we found dead three years ago in Riverside Park."

Reilly took the page from him and read it. Not much happened in this town and the John Doe had been a nine-day wonder in the *Express*. It had always galled Reilly that the case was still unsolved. There was something not quite right about it; something he could never put his finger on. For all that the papers had referred to the victim as a drifter, the dead man had not had the appearance of one who lived on the street.

960709.01 *T. Crayle to Council. B. Simpson deleted @ Easton, PA. Closefile.*

"That's not all, Captain."

He looked up. It was the computer tech who had spoken. A short, chunky woman who wore "granny glasses" and no make up. She had always seemed to him to be as much a part of the machine as the printer and the terminal. "What?"

"Well . . ." And she held up a handful of sheets. "You need to contact somebody; but I'm not sure if it's the FBI or the *National Enquirer*.

[New York City, NY] "Okay, okay; but where's it coming from?" Greg Houvanis looked at the other reporters crowded around the terminal in the *New York Times* city room.

"Who knows," said one with a wave of his hand. "Some hacker playing a prank."

"Yeah. Remember Captain Midnight? When was that, about ten years ago? And there was that virus plague about 1989 or so."

"Yeah," said another. "Every programmer who ever thought he'd get his ass fired was planting time bombs in their companies' data bases."

Houvanis was scanning some of the sheets. "What kind of prank is this? It looks like a dump of someone's entire computer files."

"Yeah. Like I was saying—"

"Clear it up! Clear it up!" The managing editor plowed through the sea of reporters like the Queen Elizabeth parting the waves. The city editor followed in his wake, wringing his hands and looking uncertain. "What's the party?" asked the M. E. He grabbed one of the pages from a reporter's hands and read it.

The M. E. balled the paper in his fist. "Shut that damn thing off!" he ordered.

"But—"

"Shut it off, I said. I'm not going to see the paper's office supply budget used up because some crazy hacker wants to tie up our terminal." Someone reached out and the chattering printer fell silent. "Ben!" The M. E. called the office boy over. He shoved the crumpled sheet into the young man's hands. "Take this and the rest of this trash down to the shredder and see that it gets burned. And the rest of you," he added to the city room reporters, "don't you all have deadlines you need to meet?"

Greg returned to his desk with the rest of them. He woke

his terminal and scrolled until he found the graf he had been rewriting. For a few minutes he lost himself in hunting and pecking on the keyboard. Then he sensed a presence by his desk and looked up and saw Ora Harris. She was new to the staff, and he barely knew her. "Yes, Ora. What is it?"

She looked left and right, then slipped him a torn page of computer paper. "Don't let the M. E. see this. But, didn't you say that Morgan Grimes was a friend of yours?"

He took the page from her and saw that her hand was trembling. "Yes." He hadn't spoken with Morgan in months. Then, two weeks ago, he had gotten a call from him, asking him to research some items in the Times morgue. Now Morgan was in the morgue himself—no, buried by now. Life was funny. He looked at the sheet Harris had given him. *990620.34 O. Crayle to Council. M. Grimes deleted @ Denver, CO. Close Subfile.* "What is this?"

"Not here," she said. "Take it home and read it. It's not much. Just the one page; but I was reading it when the M. E. came out and I remembered you talking about your friend's death and . . . And Mr. Houvanis?"

"What?"

"Ask yourself why the M. E. was so anxious to stop the printer."

[Montreal, QE] He scowled over the diagnostic readouts. What could have caused the application to stall? Not enough memory? *C'est impossible!* He clicked a few times and activated the catalog. He scrolled through the listing. *Voila!* An unidentified application. A rogue program. "Merde!" he said under his breath. What was a virus doing in his system? How had it entered? He tapped in a few more commands and studied the result. It took a few moments for the impact of what he was reading to sink in. Then he sat up straight and clicked on the emergency shutdown. "Merde!" he said again, with considerably more feeling.

[Langley, VA] The printer suddenly came to life and Jen Samuals jerked in her seat. She put her book aside and swiveled her chair around to face the terminal screen. She picked up the phone; and read the leader on the first graf to see which agency she was to notify.

"Oh, shit!" she said, and cradled the phone. She ran her eyes down the next few pages, speed reading. "Oh, shit," she

165

said again. She reached out and hit the emergency stop button. The terminal sighed and died. The printer froze in midline.

Working quickly, she pulled the already printed sheets from the strip and ran them through the shredder. The shredder buzzed briefly and fell silent just as Leslie emerged from the washroom. "What's going on?" she asked as Jen removed a back panel from the machine.

"Some sort of short or something," she told her as she pulled a wire loose from its connection.

[San Francisco, CA] "Yes, Prudence, what is it?"
"I'm afraid you're not going to like this, Mr. Kennison."

"Hello?"
"There's a better home a'waiting."
"The circle remains unbroken. Report."
"Have you seen it?"
"Seen what?"
"Lord, it's dumping out on every terminal in the country!"
"What is?"
"Summon the Six, Bradford. We've got to take counsel."
"It's that serious?"
"Serious? Everything is changed. My God, everything is changed."

[Austin, TX] "And in other news this morning, computer terminals all over the country were tied up by an unknown computer hacker. In a prank reminiscent of the famous Captain Midnight incident . . .

[St Paul, MN] "Hey, Fred, set up another round for me and my buddies." He turned to the other men at the bar. "So my boss, she says to drop the whole thing. That it will only encourage other pranksters. But I read some of those printouts and I think . . ."

[Seattle, WA] "Station KING has learned, through a confidential source, the name of the computer hacker responsible for last week's prank on the national DataNet . . ."

[Washington, DC] "What do you think it was all about, Vince?"

166

"Oh, nothing to get excited over, Senator. A hacker, they said on the TV. Some woman deranged by her boyfriend's death in a drug deal."

The senator scowled and jutted his chin forward in his famous pose. "Is it anything the Senate should consider?"

His aide paused and considered. He was covered with nervous sweat and he hoped the senator would not notice. There was no time to call Brother Ullman for instructions. He'd have to wing it. Later, he would get together with some of the other congressional aides. Even the ones from the Other Side. Work out a common strategy. This would definitely be a "bipartisan" issue.

"I believe," he said judiciously, "that we should not make too much of it. These prankster types crave publicity. If we make a Federal case of it, by next week there'll be a dozen incidents." *Perhaps that would be the best way*, he thought. Flood the system with nonsense printouts and blatant disinformation. The best place to conceal a murder, after all, is on a battlefield. Meanwhile, though, we don't want the politicos actually reading the stuff. "I think the bill that's been hanging in the Communications subcommittee should be reported out. It contains a provision to stiffen the penalties for computer crime."

"Hmm." The senator nodded. "Harry's been sitting on that thing for too long. I know he doesn't like some of the clauses. He calls them 'semantic garbage.' But he must realize now that it's better to get the law out, even if it is flawed. Let the courts straighten out any ambiguities later. We've got to do something about unauthorized entry into data bases."

Vince nodded in agreement. They would have to do something about "Senator Harry," too; someday soon. The man was entirely too inquisitive. He sighed. He knew he would not get bipartisan support on *that* operation.

[San Jose, CA, Associated Press] The Center for Computer Disease Control recommended today that universities and research facilities quarantine their computers and purge them of an infectious "virus" that ran rampant through the national DataNet last Wednesday and Thursday dumping false and libelous material into terminals across the country. The Federal Bureau of Investigation is launching an inquiry to determine if federal law was violated, calling the incident an "attack" on the integrity of the Net . . .

167

The man he knew as Bernstein was chuckling as he read the paper. "What is it?" he asked. Bernstein opened to an inside page and shook the paper to straighten it. The paper rustled with the sound of footsteps through dry leaves. "It's your friend," Bernstein replied. "You should see what she's done."

[Cape Girardeau, MO] "Yeah, I know Washington said to put a lid on it, but I been thinking . . ."

Mr. Koppel: But suppose we assume for a moment, Dr. Vane, that the Beaumont Dump is genuine. Wouldn't the fact that individuals have made themselves rich by forecasting the future convince you that such a science is at least possible?

Dr. Vane: Not at all, Ted. Success does not imply method. There is no shortage of people in this country who have made themselves rich by forecasting the future successfully. In the stock market. In real estate. What escapes our notice is that many more people have become poor by forecasting the future . . . unsuccessfully. [Laughter among guests.] Random chance dictates that some forecasts will be correct.

Mr. Koppel: Could you elaborate on that?

Dr. Vane: Certainly. Suppose I offer to forecast the sex of unborn babies for a fee of one dollar; with the fee fully refundable in the event I am wrong. All I need do is predict "male" in each case. I would make an average profit of 50¢ per baby; but would not have a valid science.

Mr. Koppel: I see.

Dr. Vane: Here is another, slightly less obvious example. During WWII Enrico Fermi was discussing military history with General Groves when the subject of great generals came up. Dr. Fermi asked how many generals qualified as "great." About three in a hundred, the general replied. And how did one qualify? By winning five major battles in a row. Well then, said Fermi, consider that in most theatres, the opposing forces are roughly equal. The probability of winning a bat-

168

tle would then be 50%. Of two consecutive battles, 25%. Of three, 12%. Of four, 6%. Of five, 3%. So you are right, General. About three generals out of a hundred; but it is probability, not greatness.

[Littleton, CO] "I saw her," said Pat, passing the mashed potatoes, "I think it was a week before she disappeared; when I was working the night shift at the bulk handling center down by Union Station. She came from under the viaduct. Not running, but walking real fast. She told us she was looking over a building nearby and thought maybe she was being followed."

"Followed?" Kevin frowned and laid his fork down on his dinner plate. He looked at his brother. "That was before Morgan was killed, wasn't it?"

"Yeah. And before that thing in the park. You know, with the gunman."

Kevin rubbed his moustache thoughtfully. "So, you think she was coming unhinged even before that? Everyone down at the *News* is saying that it was Morg' being killed so soon after he helped her that sent her around the bend."

Pat shrugged. "I don't know. It was just funny seeing someone like that—I couldn't remember her name at first. Then a couple weeks later, she's famous."

"Infamous," Kevin corrected him. He picked up his fork again, but didn't eat. He shook his head. "It doesn't jibe," he said. "Granted, I hadn't talked to her since she left the paper; but I knew her. And I knew Morgan. The whole story is out of character, for both of them. And when Morgan was killed, he passed a very mysterious message onto Sarah."

"Are you two still jabbering about poor Sarah?" asked Kathy.

"You say she was looking at a building? Which one?"

Pat shrugged. "Beats me. She didn't say."

Kevin looked thoughtful.

"What are you talking about?" his wife repeated.

"The Pulitzer," he told her.

169

## II

"But I don't *want* to become someone else!"

Red Malone was sitting on the fencepost, enjoying the mountain air and watching the horses graze in the corral. His left shoulder was heavily bandaged and his arm was bound up in a sling. He had hooked his feet around the lower rail of the fence to help himself keep his balance. The soft breeze falling down from the high country rustled his shirt and created waves in the grama grass of the horse pasture. The mares were clustered around the fenceline on the far side, cropping the grass. Their stallion stood nearby, watching Red suspiciously.

When he heard Sarah Beaumont behind him, he didn't turn. "None of us do," he answered her.

"The rest of you don't have to," she said bitterly.

He did turn and look at her, wondering if she could be so blind. She was dressed cowgirl fashion, in tight jeans and checkered shirt. The white straw Stetson contrasted sharply with her skin. Red was still wearing his city clothes. He returned his attention to the horses. "Sometimes," he said. "From time to time."

She threw herself at the fence rail next to him and rested her chin in her arms. Red looked down at her. She was gazing out at the horses, a scowl across her face. "Dammit, Red," she said. "I spent years making myself into what I am. I worked hard at it, and it wasn't easy, and I like the way I turned out!"

"Then you're lucky. Most of us would do major alterations if we could. What are you carping about? Your new persona will be wealthy, secure. We take care of our own. A little

170

plastic surgery, too. Maybe lighten your skin a shade or two. Your own mother wouldn't recognize you."

Sarah's eyes went dead and she looked down at the grass. "She wouldn't know me now," she said quietly.

He wanted to say, *Well, then it won't make any difference;* but he sensed it would be the wrong thing. He watched as the stallion came suddenly alert, ears twisting like twin radar antennae. The horse trotted a few paces to the high ground at the rear of the pasture and stared like a statue at the mountains above. After a while, he relaxed and resumed his station by his mares. Red wondered what vagrant scent the mountain air had brought to his nostrils.

"It's for your own good, Sarah," he said finally. "Haven't you been watching the news lately? Ever since you spilled the beans about the Babbage Society, the television newsreaders have been ripping you apart. 'Paranoid' and 'mentally unbalanced' are the kindest things they're saying. Why not become someone else? Being Sarah Beaumont can't be a pleasant prospect these days."

"It's a dirty job," she said wryly, "but someone's got to do it." She turned and looked him in the eyes. "And what would you have done if you had been in my place?"

Red looked at her, looked away, and shrugged. "The same, probably."

"Someone was trying to kill me," she continued, almost to herself. "And I didn't even know why. So I kept digging until I found out. And you know what's funny?"

"No, what?"

"If they had left me alone, I would never have stumbled onto their dirty little secret."

Red was not so sure. "Maybe. Maybe not. Genevieve Weil isn't very smart, and she panics easily. But let me ask you something: What would *you* have done about Sarah Beaumont if you had been in *Their* place?"

She scowled. "I would never have been in Their place."

"That's not a fair answer."

"That wasn't a fair question! I can no more imagine myself in their place than I could imagine myself in the Klan."

"You've got to admit They had legitimate fears."

"What? So did your people; but *you* didn't try to kill me."

Red grimaced and looked at the ground. Absently, he rubbed his wounded arm. "No, we're much crueler than that."

"Yeah, destroy my reputation. Who told the world it was

171

me who spilled the beans? I dumped those files anonymously, so someone must have leaked my name to the media. Now they mock the messenger so people won't listen to the message. It's an old tactic."

"It works. How do you think it got to be so old? Dammit, that part of it is for *our* good! I don't fancy being lynched any more than They do. Why shouldn't we squelch your message?"

"Because it's the truth!"

He shrugged and didn't bother to answer her.

"And because it's futile!" she insisted. "I don't care how many 'moles' you have planted in newsrooms and police agencies. You can't stop it completely. That computer program I wrote will keep on dumping copies of your files—and Their files—until someone figures out how to kill it. Too many people will have a chance to read them. For every hundred who laugh, there'll be one who wonders. And don't forget the businessmen and politicians."

He looked at her in surprise. "Why them?"

"Think of their pride! Think how long they've believed that *they* were pulling the strings. They won't like the thought that they're just variables in your cliological equations."

Red smiled thinly. "Less than that, really. Epiphenomena of the mid-structure. Haven't you been attending orientation classes?"

Sarah made a sour face and Red laughed.

"Aaron's quite a character, all right. He's a thousand years older than anybody. He's seen it all and done it twice. I remember when I was recruited . . ." He saw the guarded look cross her face and reminded himself that she was not fully recruited even yet. ". . . when I was recruited, he was already as old as Methusalah. Story was, he was one of the Founders who'd stuck around to see that the Plan was carried out." He chuckled.

"You're avoiding my point."

"You have a point?" He kept a cheerful-looking smile on his face and showed it to her.

"Yes. Even if only one person in a hundred decides to follow up on what was in my worm, that's still thousands of people, all around the country. Trying to stomp on me is *useless*. It won't change a damned thing!"

"Maybe not. But if you were bleeding from a fatal wound, wouldn't you try to staunch the blood anyway? Living systems defend themselves. Didn't I tell you that one time? It's an

172

automatic response, not hate, or vengeance. At least, not on Our part. When you wrote that program, you didn't know about Us. All you knew was that They were trying to kill you. That They had killed others, including some of your friends. You're a living system, too—"

"Thanks."

"—and We don't blame you for defending yourself, either. So We'll discredit your message; destroy your reputation. Sorry, but We'll give you a new reputation in compensation."

"Yeah, such a deal."

"It is a deal. A better one than most people get. Look, what is it you want most of all, right now?"

"My old life back."

Almost, that stopped him; her voice was filled with such longing. He found he couldn't look her in the eye. "You can't have that. You decided that the moment you decided to run your worm. Ask for something else."

"Alright. I want to destroy Them. I want to find Dennis and I want to make Them hurt for what They did to us."

Red nodded. "Okay. That's what I want, too. You know that. Why can't you join Us?"

She shook her head. "I don't approve of your methods."

"You know what They're trying to do to people, don't you? I told you that, didn't I?"

"Oh, sure. They're trying to domesticate us. Simplify us. Turn us into nice little technopeasants. Docile enough to take orders and educated enough to follow them."

He heard the bitterness in her voice and wondered how she could not have picked sides. "Don't you want to fight that? I do. That's why I've started my own group within the Associates. We've got to get off our kiesters and start fighting. Forget Quinn's Rule."

"The ends justify the means, eh?"

"Don't they? Do you want people to be domesticated?"

"No, dammit! But don't you see, Red? The means have become the end! Why do they want to domesticate us in the first place? To make us more predictable for their equations; to make us more receptive to manipulation. To simplify Their goddamned arithmetic! If you and your group start down the same path, how long before you adopt the same goals?"

"One hundred and twenty years," he told her. "Plus or minus eight years."

She stared at him. "I don't know you," she said.

173

*We don't know ourselves,* he thought. *I shouldn't shoot from the lip so much. Not with her, and not about this.* She was right, though, about the means becoming the end. That was why he wanted her so badly. She had insight.

"I'm sorry," he told her. "I didn't mean to sound so flippant. What I meant to say was that We've got to start fighting Them *now*. The danger you mentioned is real, but it's also more remote. We have more time to work on it."

She shook her head once more. "No, it's more than just that. It's the whole notion of trying to manipulate people—"

"That again? You know, I'd agree with you if you could show me how cliology is different from what people try to do every day, using nothing more than guesswork and intuition. Is it our success you hold against us? Tell me how we differ from the official government, or an advertising agency, or the NAACP. Doesn't everyone try to propogandize the views that they believe in? Is our crime that we have more foresight or that we work out the consequences more carefully?" He didn't know if Sarah were just being stubborn or if she really couldn't see it. The future was a branching tree of possibilities, and the decisions being made today would prune off branches years ahead, closing off some possiblilities, opening up others. Sometimes the action that seemed the wisest course at the moment, became monumental folly in retrospect. It was more than important to know which branches might be inadvertantly pruned; it was vital. And those of us who can see farther ahead have the duty to guide the rest in the right direction. *Don't we?*

Sarah was silent, staring morosely at the horses. Finally she sighed. "If I do decide to join you," she said without looking at him, "will you help me find Dennis?"

Sarah was an impossible woman. Why couldn't she be grateful for coming out of the affair with a whole skin? Which was more than he had. He rubbed his fingers across the bandages and felt the abused flesh and muscles twinge. He remembered the way the shot had thrown him back against the broken wall. *I was lucky.* Memories of that time in Jacksonville; only things had worked out differently then. He didn't want to think about Jacksonville. *She saved my life. I owe her for that.* The Chinese would say I was her slave now.

"No," he said; and she looked at him in surprise. "No," he repeated. "I'll help you find Dennis whether you join Us or not." He waited for her to say something; grew uncomfortable

174

under her gaze. "I'll not have a Sister join through coercion," he explained. "I'll not have you with me except through your own free will. You may choose the new identity or not. You may choose to join us or not. Those are both your choices. But I will help you locate Dennis. That is between you and me."

He turned from her gaze. *I sound like a pompous fool.* He hoped she would not laugh at him.

She didn't. She shook her head in wonder. "I don't know you at all," she said again.

"Are they treating you alright?" he asked after a while.

Sarah shrugged. "I can't complain."

"Sure you could. It just wouldn't make any difference."

She was silent and Red wondered what was going through her head. Then, she sighed. "No, it wouldn't." She touched him gently on the arm. "How's the shoulder?"

"Better, thanks. A little stiff." He moved it experimentally. "The cast will be coming off soon. But I'll never play the violin again." She shot him a look of surprise. "Not that I ever could before," he added with a straight face.

Sarah snorted. She watched the horses with him. One of the mares broke from the herd and galloped across the rolling meadow. Red watched it run, enjoying the beauty of it; the way the legs danced and the muscles worked beneath the tawny skin. The stallion charged after the errant mare, nipping at her flanks, driving her back into the herd. Red glanced down at Sarah and had a sudden impulse to whip her hat off and tousle her hair. *I wonder how she would react if I did?* He shaded his eyes and looked at the sky. Overhead an eagle circled. Shit. *I'd probably lose my balance and fall, and how would* that *look?*

Sarah pointed at the mares. "Why do you suppose they do that?"

He looked at her; at the mares. "Do what?"

"With this whole wide meadow to choose from, why do they stick their necks out through the fence to nibble the grass on the other side?"

He shrugged. "Maybe it really is greener. How would I know? I don't know anything about farms."

"Ranches," she corrected him. "You don't know anything about ranches. Neither do I, but I think I know the reason."

"Oh? And what is that?"

"Maybe they just don't like fences."

175

*   *   *

When Jeremy Collingwood returned to his apartment it took him less than an hour to realize that it had been searched; and only a little bit longer than that to realize that it had been searched twice.

He had paused in the foyer to remove his hat and gloves and to place his umbrella in the umbrella stand. As he did so, a nagging feeling stole over him that something was wrong, out of place. He frowned and glanced over the apartment; and saw nothing amiss, so he put it down to the general malaise he had suffered since Dennis' accident.

Dennis' accident.

Poor Dennis. And he had *been* there when it happened! In his whole life, he had never seen an unpleasant sight. Well, not death or injury, anyway. It was appalling how sudden and unexpected it could be. One moment they were walking along the sidewalk, discussing the play they had been to see; the next, Dennis was hurtling through the air and a car was disappearing down Arapahoe Street. And the way he had fallen so . . . loosely. Jeremy shivered at the memory. The sound of an engine racing or of tires laying rubber still caused him to spin about, heart pounding.

In the kitchenette, he mixed himself a vodka martini, five parts to one. He stirred the vodka and dry vermouth in a pitcher of ice, humming abstractedly; and before he had quite realized what he was doing, he had poured two highball glasses full.

He stood frozen for a while, contemplating what he had done. It was awful the way habit worked; how the past could turn and slap you across the face. Really, he only needed to pour one drink. Dennis was getting his drinks intravenously, if he was getting them at all, which Jeremy doubted.

The ice tinkled as he set the pitcher down. He stared at his hand, then gripped the countertop to steady it. Dennis would recover. The doctors all agreed he would recover. There had been a bad time when the hospital records had been mixed up and they told him that Dennis was no longer there; that he had never been there. At first, Jeremy had thought that the nurse meant that Dennis had died. And the room, when he had run down the corridor, had indeed been empty. But the phone call yesterday had assured him that everything was straightened out now, and that Dennis was receiving proper care. No visitors yet, however.

176

Meanwhile, it did no one any good for him to pour two drinks. He carefully poured the second drink back into the pitcher. But then he reflected that, by the time he took a second drink, if he did, the ice would have melted and watered it unbearably; so he poured the whole pitcher down the sink. Such a waste; but there was no help for it.

Before he did anything else, he rinsed and dried both the pitcher and the extra glass and set them away. Dennis and he shared the apartment; and Dennis was a meticulous man: in his dress, in his manners. Everything had a place and everything was in it. Jeremy was an accountant, careful by nature, and his habits had meshed quite well with Dennis'.

He walked with his drink to the living room, intending to tune in the all-news cable channel; but in the center of the room the feeling of out-of-placedness returned. He frowned and scanned the room, more carefully than he had done upon first entering. His eyes searched out everything: buffet, secretary, bergère chairs, chesterfield . . .

Why the pillows on the chesterfield were out of place! He selected a coaster and placed his drink on the sideboard. The ochre pillow went *there* and the rust, *there*.

He set them aright; but, having noticed one item askew, a dozen others leapt to his eyes. The corner of a paper peeked from the drawer of the secretary. He opened it and saw that the stationery was otherwise neatly arranged; but arranged wrongly. The Mondrian on the wall was hanging *upside down*, for Christ's sake! And the chairs were out of place. He went to hands and knees and explored the nap of the rug with his fingers. Yes, here is where the chair legs had always stood.

A coldness crept through him, starting in his stomach and creeping out to his limbs. He had certainly not misarranged his own rooms! Someone has been in here. Someone who had searched quite thoroughly and methodically and then tried to put everything back the way it had been.

But why? He made his way shakily to his favorite bergère chair and dropped himself into it. A casual thief or burglar would hardly have bothered to disguise the fact of his entry. Why was it so important, not only to search his quarters, but to conceal the very fact of that search? What had they been looking for? Had anything been taken?

Impulsively, he rose and inspected the Mondrian. Yes, it was the genuine article. And if *that* had not been taken would the thief have left with anything less valuable? Maybe. The

177

painting had been hung upside down, which implied that the thief lacked appreciation for Mondrian's geometric style. Perhaps he had simply not recognized its value.

Carefully, he went through the apartment. The silver was all accounted for; so was the jewelry. So was the cash that was hidden none too expertly in a bottom drawer.

When he had satisfied himself that everything of value was still in place, he returned to his chair and sat in it. He steepled his fingers, as if in prayer, and rested his chin on them. The break-in was no robbery.

Should he report it? He caught his lower lip between his teeth and worried it. He couldn't even prove that anyone had been inside the apartment. No one would believe him. The pillows were on the wrong side of the sofa? Really, Mr. Collingwood. They wouldn't understand about Dennis and his fussiness. They really wouldn't. And there would be the knowing smirks and not-so-subtle innuendos.

Yet, he had to tell someone. Someone who could help him make sense out of it. He was no good at that sort of thing. Give him columns of figures and ledgers of accounts and he could bring order out of chaos. But when he read mysteries, which was seldom, he could never figure out "whodunit." Now here was a mystery literally in his own front room. Who could he ask for help? Not Dennis. They still weren't letting him see visitors.

There was that Beaumont woman that Dennis sometimes worked with. She was really quite tolerable for a woman; not constantly playing those teasy, sleazy games that women often did. Dennis had had great respect for her.

But Beaumont was gone, vanished; and the TV was saying awful things about her. The television people were rather vague about the details of what she had done, but they were quite certain it was heinous. Unauthorized access to data banks or some such thing.

*This is all too complex.* Why would someone search his apartment and go to the trouble of straightening it up again; and then botch it by putting things back incorrectly. Anyone careful enough for the former would be too careful for the latter. Unless . . .

*There were two of them, of course.*

Of course. His head came erect and he stared off at the wall. Whoever had straightened up the room had misplaced things because they had found the room already disarrayed.

178

No wonder they had gotten some things wrong. Most people would not notice the arrangement of the stationery or the placement of some pillows. The really chilling thing was how much they had gotten *right!*

Somehow, though, that seemed an even deeper mystery. He could imagine that a burglar might try to conceal his tracks. But why would a second burglar try to conceal the tracks of a first burglar? And why was nothing taken? At least, nothing that he knew of.

Could it have something to do with Dennis? That hit-and-run. The more he thought about it, the less it seemed like an accident. Jeremy had turned when he first heard the squeal of tires and had gotten the faintest of impressions that the car had veered just a moment before. Had Dennis been involved in something illicit?

Come to think of it, hadn't Beaumont disappeared the same day that Dennis had been struck? That was what? Almost two weeks ago, now. She had called for Dennis, and Jeremy had told her what had happened, and she hadn't seemed terribly surprised.

Nonsense! He was building elaborate fantasies on very little foundation.

But what *had* Dennis been up to in the weeks before the accident?

He reached into his inner jacket pocket and retrieved his appointment book. He thumbed through it. He and Dennis often made notes of each other's appointments. He felt vaguely pleased with himself that he was reasoning this out so well. Maybe he did have the makings of a detective. There! There was the day of the accident. Dennis and he had gone to see a revival of *Lady Windemere's Fan* in The Space at the DCPA. The outing had been Jeremy's idea; and so, somehow, the accident had been Jeremy's fault. If only . . .

*No! I won't let myself fall into that trap!* He calmed himself and concentrated on the issue at hand.

Ah, yes, he saw in the book. Dennis had had a luncheon meeting that same day with a man named Morgan Grimes. Grimes. The name was oddly familiar. He had heard it recently. On TV? In the newspaper? Newspaper. That was it! Grimes was the newspaperman who had been killed in a drug deal.

A cold hand squeezed his heart. Dennis and this Grimes fellow had done lunch and by the next day one was dead and the other run over by a car. Later, Beaumont calls, frantic; reacts oddly; then disappears. And she had been shot at earlier, he suddenly remembered, by that madman in the Civic Center. Dennis had been very upset when Jeremy had shown him the news story. And hadn't Grimes written that story, too?

He had the sudden notion that he was surrounded by unseen menaces. Menaces who were striking down people around him, some of whom he barely knew; and who, today, had reached in and violated his very home. More anxious now, a flutter in the center of his chest, he searched through the appointment book, searching for other clues to Dennis' activities.

Daniel Kennison lounged in his high-backed leather chair and rested his elbows on the arms. He clasped his hands together and watched the others around the long mahogany conference table. *We're a fine crew,* he thought sourly. The other Councilors twittered and chattered and fluttered like birds whose nest had been disturbed. *Fools.* Kennison clenched his teeth and kept his peace. His darting eyes made a circuit of the table and caught Gretchen Paige watching him. She flashed him a wintry smile and he returned one a few degrees colder.

*A pack of damned fools. They bicker and plot while everything we've worked for lies on the verge of collapse.* The bucket brigade on the Titanic. The Founders would be ashamed of them.

There was no doubt in his mind that Genevieve Weil had mismanaged the entire Beaumont affair from beginning to end. She had panicked—always her first reaction to any problem—and had stampeded the rest of the Council with her. Certainly, the Intruder had been close to unravelling the Secret; but they should not have assumed so quickly that Beaumont was the Intruder. *He* had argued that she was only a casual researcher. Maybe he had been wrong, too; but hindsight showed him closer to the mark than the Chairman.

*Act in haste, Madam Chairman,* he thought, *Repent in leisure.*

Yet, there she sat at the head of the table, plumed and rouged like a Hollywood starlet, calmly assigning portions of the blame to everyone but herself. Not a sign of repentance on her bony model's face. He wished she would say "I'm sorry. I screwed up" so they could stop pointing fingers and get on with the business of salvaging the Society. But that, he suspected, was not in the cards.

Or it was not if he let things go on as they were.

He had slept with Genevieve once. Once had been enough. She had asked and he had not dared refuse. It had been a sobering experience. She was so fashionably thin that lying with her had been like hugging a pile of coat hangers. She had said all the right things and made all the right moves. She had writhed and moaned and clutched in a parody of passion. There was no doubt she was technically proficient; but Kennison had sensed it was all a sham, like an actress giving the two thousandth performance of a dull play. The plot had gone stale and the lines came out flat, but she insisted on performances every night.

At one time or another, Kennison knew, she had slept with every other member of the Council, male and female. And probably, he liked to tell himself, with not a few of their household pets. Kennison kept a boa constrictor in a terrarium just in case it was true.

"We have heard nothing of the Beaumont woman since Brother Crayle was dispatched. That would indicate that Crayle has succeeded in deleting her from the equations."

Kennison cast an eye at Genevieve. "Nor have we heard from Brother Crayle," he commented dryly. And what would *that* indicate? That Beaumont had bested Crayle? Impossible! But there were indications that Betancourt's people were after her, too. Red Malone had made contact that one time; had tried to convince Kennison that Beaumont was not the Intruder.

Had Malone taken her under the Associate's protection? Possible. Possible. Did that mean that Beaumont's actions had been part of an Associate operation? Did they really think they could expose the Society without exposing themselves? No, Betancourt was too shrewd for that. And Malone had seemed genuinely surprised when Kennison had told him what Beaumont had been up to: the topics she had researched, the files she had accessed. Besides, that damnable program of Beaumont's had dumped Associate files into newsrooms and police stations along with Society files.

He lit a long thin cigarillo and sent a cloud of acrid smoke toward the ceiling. Madam Chairman had been stupid to call a Council; and doubly stupid, having called it, to make such poor use of it. It was time to throw a few memes into the pot.

"How much longer shall we sit here and discuss spilled milk?" he asked.

The buzz of conversation halted and they all looked at him. Genevieve turned hard, dark eyes on him, like ranging radars for a gun turret, and she swiveled her mouth into position for an answering blast.

"Damn it all, Brother Kennison's right! We've been here for four hours and we have settled nothing. Let the dead bury the dead. Yesterday's gone; tomorrow's what matters." That, somewhat to Kennison's surprise, had been Gretchen Paige.

He looked at her and she gave a look back that said You Owe Me One. He wondered what her game was. The same as his? Possible. Possible.

The wonderful thing about memetic engineering on the micro level was that a few trite proverbs dropped into a discussion acted as seed crystals in a supersaturated solution. The connotations of the proverbs, the cultural baggage they carried, immediately triggered certain thoughts, sometimes below the conscious level. The fact that everyone at the table recognized—and used—the same techniques did not stop them from working. Spilt milk. Bury the dead. Yesterday's gone. Madam Chairman is wasting our time. Let's get on with it. Heads around the table were nodding like marionettes.

Genevieve's face was a mask of pure hatred. If looks could kill. The meme sprang quickly to mind and Kennison reminded himself that they were, after all, in Genevieve's mansion, surrounded by Genevieve's retainers. It was time for some salve.

"Gentlemen. Ladies," said Kennison. "Madam Chairman did the best that she could in a confusing and rapidly changing situation. She deserves our thanks for handling it as well as she did. We all supported her actions at the time. If the results have not been entirely to our liking . . ." He grinned crookedly and shrugged his shoulders. ". . . we have only to review our Society's history to gain some perspective. We all know how unexpected meme linkages can take us by surprise; all the more so when we are dealing with a handful of individuals, too few to comprise a statistical universe. Madam Chairman cannot deserve all the blame."

Since Madam Chairman had not been about to take *any* of the blame, it was left-handed praise at best. But he saw

Genevieve smile in satisfaction and sit taller in her chair. The stupid cow! The stupid, scrawny cow. She was like one of those zebu that roamed the streets of India, bones showing through shrunken flesh, not doing anything useful, but too sacred for anyone to touch. Well, Kennison was no Hindu!

He saw that his remarks had not been lost on other Councilers, at least. Ullman had raised an eyebrow; and Lewis was grinning openly. The connotations were more subtle, buried deeper than was the case with proverbs. They acted subliminally, but they acted nonetheless. ". . . supported *at the time*. . . ." ". . . did *the best she could* . . ." ". . . handling it *as well as she did*. . . ." ". . . *not entirely* to our liking . . ." It all added up to: "Madam Chairman is an incompetent bungler."

"Yes," said Sister Paige. "Let the minutes reflect a vote of confidence in our Chairman's past decisions." They all rapped their knuckles on the table, some with cynicism, but some— Kennison noted—with genuine conviction! He noted who the latter were. They would not be on *his* Council, if and when.

If and when. He counted votes. What if Madame Weil were deleted from the equations? Who could he count on besides Sorenson and Montfort? Not Ullman or Ruiz. And Huang was an enigma, as always. Lewis? Who could tell what went on inside that grinning, crew-cut, bullet head? That left Benton, Toohey, and Westfield. No, it was too chancy yet. Too chancy. He needed more feelers.

"The issue before us now," Paige began, and Kennison decided to let her continue to run the ball. If the discussion *should* trigger any of Madam Chairman's fabled anger, let Paige be the target.

"The issue before us now is how best to preserve the Secret. This is the most serious breach of security since Brady Quinn defected. The fact that our enemies were able to penetrate our data bases and release them to the world indicates the need for two-fold action. First: how do we close that particular barn door and keep it from being opened again. Second: how do we contain and redirect the flow of unwanted memes among the general populace."

Too late, Kennison saw his mistake. Paige's not-so-subtle digs at Kennison's handling of the data banks diverted the Councilers' collective subconscious away from Weil's competency and toward his own. That image of the barn door. It

183

connoted carelessness, inattention. He felt the tips of his ears redden, and was glad he wore his hair long. Perhaps Paige was his true enemy, not Weil. Defense. Counterattack. He wracked his mind for a strategy.

Before he could say anything, there was a knock on the door and Weil's butler entered. He was an old man who walked with a pronounced stoop. He looked like a resurrected corpse, and a not too successful resurrection at that.

Judd, of course, was an Initiate of the Society. "Stooled to the rogue," as Kennison liked to think of it. But he had been a Weil man since before Genevieve's time. Kennison wondered whether, if it came down to it, the old man's loyalties would lay with the Society or with his mistress. That might depend on whether the old man was lying with his mistress. Kennison suppressed a laugh and kept his face composed. Did Genevieve's escapades include old Judd? Perhaps that was why the man always looked so drained.

Judd bent over and whispered in Genevieve's ear. Madam Chairman's face paled. She looked around the table. "Judd tells me that there are two reporters from the *Sun-Times* loitering around the front gate. He has asked them to leave, but they have refused. They claim their car has broken down and they are waiting for help."

"Perhaps they are waiting to see who enters and leaves your mansion, Madam Chairman," said Frederick Ullman acidly.

Good! thought Kennison. Someone else thought of it. Under the circumstances, a face-to-face Council meeting had been a stupid idea. Part of the process of discrediting Beaumont was to propogandize the meme-set that none of the Councilors actually knew one another. That her tales of a secret cabal were the ravings of a disjointed mind. To be discovered, *en masse*, as it were, in Weil's mansion could destroy that meme-set and call into question the entire contra-Beaumont program.

But who could have tipped the reporters? Who? Or did they think of this on their own, and it was just chance that the Council was meeting when they staked the place out? Kennison did not believe in coincidences.

"Don't be too harsh on Madam Chairman," said Gretchen Paige. "She undoubtedly felt that a Council conducted on our data net would be even less secure than a meeting *in corpora*." Paige smiled at Kennison. "Brother Kennison is no doubt working around the clock to secure the breaches wrought by the Beaumont person; but for now we dare not risk meeting on the Net."

"Oh, yes," said Kennison pleasantly. "I am working to secure all of our weak points." And he smiled most broadly at them all.

# III

"It's nine o'clock, Brother Malone. Don't you think it's time
to hang 'em up?"

Red looked up from his reading and saw Janie Hatch hover-
ing over him. He marked an entry on the computer printout
with a flourescent marker; folded the sheet once through the
middle; then he capped the marker and laid it aside. "Nine
o'clock already? Time sure flies when you're having fun."

Janie snorted and pulled a chair from beneath the neigh-
boring table. She turned it backward and straddled it. "Library's about t'close," she announced.

"I just finished the file." He pointed at the printout, wondering what was on Janie's mind. What had brought her to
the library sublevel?

"You know it ain't like you're the only one checking through
the Dump. We each got assigned a block to check."

"I know that."

"Then why in tarnation are you going through the whole
thing?"

Red grinned at her. "Light reading," he said. "Helps me
sleep at night."

She snorted again. "It don't help nobody else. Keeps me
awake, wondering what your little buddy spilled to the world."

"She didn't know what she was doing when she wrote that
worm. She didn't know she would put us in danger."

"Or she didn't care. Don't get so consarned defensive,
Malone. I ain't blaming her. But that ain't the point. The
point is to read the Dump careful-like, so we'll know what
critical information got Dumped. You try to read too much of
it, you git tired. You git too tired, you might miss something."

186

"I won't miss anything."

"You're a stubborn jackass, Red. How would you know if you missed anything or not?"

"You're right," he said. "I think I will pack it in."

He started to rise from the table but Janie put a hand on his arm. "It's that Beaumont woman, ain't it? You're doing something for her."

Red looked into the old woman's weathered face. Years of wind and bright sunlight on the open range had narrowed her eyes into a perpetual squint. He could see nothing in them. No hint of emotion. No curiosity. No clue even as to why she had asked the question. "What of it?" he said. "Quinn's Rules allow private projects. Sarah wanted to know if there was anything in the Dump about her architect friend."

"The one that vanished from the hospital?"

"That's the one."

Janie regarded him silently for a moment. "All right. I'll tell Tex to pass the word along to the others to watch for anything in their blocks. What was his name, French?"

Red felt surprise. "Yes. Dennis French. He was at Porter Memorial." He toyed for a moment with his marker. "Why are you doing this?"

"Doing what?"

"Helping me help Sarah."

The ranch manager shrugged. "Anything we learn about Them is worthwhile. Why'd They bother kidnapping French after They just tried to kill him? Don't make no sense to me. And you shoulda seen the mess his apartment was in, the day I went over there. They fair to tore it apart a'fore I got there." She gave him a steady gaze. "Like They were looking for something."

He returned her gaze. "I wonder what."

She held him for a moment longer, then released him, muttering under her breath, "Only the mountains last forever."

Red figured it was time to leave so he rose; stuffed the computer printouts into his briefcase; and laid the sheet he had folded carefully on top. Then he closed the briefcase and pushed the snaps shut. He felt Janie's eyes on him the whole time.

"Do you know Mark Lopez?"

Red turned in surprise at the unexpected twist of subject. "Who?"

"Our station chief in San Diego. He just sent us that new recruit, Howard."

He shook his head. "I know who you mean. I never met him."

"You may never git the chance. Tex found his name and address in his block of the Dump. In clear. The Council has tried to contact him, to warn him; but no luck so far."

He felt a shiver of fear. Was it starting already? The mob reaction. The mad vengeance. What other names were in the Dump? What other deadly information? "Was there anything in the news?" he asked.

"You mean about a riot?" She shook her head. "They're doing a good job of suppressing interest in the Dump. But there's bound to be them as wonder. Could be the CIA got him stashed away somewhere."

He felt uneasy. Was Janie trying to ask him for a favor? "I could go back to Washington and see what I can dig up," he volunteered. "If one of the Agencies has him, I may be able to find out."

"You ain't going anywhere, Red. Not 'till we know your name ain't in the Dump, too."

That jolted him. He knew it was a possibility, of course. He had been hunting for any mention of his public persona as diligently as he had been for Dennis French or anyone else. He had joked about it with Sarah when he had first gone to see her. "Strung up to the nearest lamppost." A burlesque image, comically grotesque; a parody that insulated one from the reality. Reality was being shot from hiding. Or beaten with fists and baseball bats by an angry mob, delirious with joy that now, at last, they had found a scapegoat for all their troubles. Or simply disappeared, like Lopez; to be questioned with drugs and cattle prods by professionally-trained paranoids. Reality was lying a bloody ruin in some back alley, knowing that the pain would only cease when awareness itself ceased. He shivered. He had just gotten a glimpse of what drove Genevieve Weil.

He looked at Janie Hatch. "What about the Ranch? Are we safe here?"

She reached out and gave his briefcase a backhand slap. "That's why we're reading through every line of the Dump."

Red looked carefully into her eyes. He wanted to see fear there; the same fear that he felt. He wanted to see something more than academic interest. But Janie returned his scrutiny coldly. "Jest wanted to let you know, Red," she told him. "If'n your going to git friendly with her, you should know exactly what she done to Us."

188

* * *

"Can any of you cite an example of such a spin-off?" Aaron Gewirtz spun his wheelchair around and braked sharply. He was looking at Norris Bosworth, the one Sarah thought of privately as SuperNerd. Bosworth stammered as he tried to answer.

Aaron had that effect on most of his pupils. Sarah realized full well that Aaron knew exactly who he would call on before he turned his chair; but finding those sightless eyes staring straight at you had an unnerving effect. He had already tripped Sarah up several times.

"Ah . . . Automobile production and the Baby Boom?"

"Are you asking me or telling me?"

"Ah . . . I'm telling you. The spread of automobiles led to significant changes in courtship rituals. The, uh, backseat of the Chevy was a convenient place for, uh, impregnating young women." Bosworth blushed a deep and sincere red. SuperNerd was a gangly adolescent still fighting (and losing) the Battle of the Zits. He had been recruited into the Associates by his uncle. "That was a spin-off," he finished, "totally unexpected by the inventors of the automobile."

"Good. You have the courage of your convictions, however wrong they may be. Would anyone care to . . . Yes, Ms. Howard?"

It was uncanny. Maureen Howard had raised her hand silently; part of her ongoing campaign to fool the blind man. Howard was a plump woman from southern California and dressed habitually in voluminous muumuus and wooden clogs. Sarah thought of her as The Earth Mother. From time to time Sarah had caught her casting venomous looks in her direction.

"Bosworth is wrong," the Earth Mother said. "The automobile may have changed breeding practices, but I can't believe that any significant fraction of the Baby Boomers was conceived in that way. The Boom was simply an adjustment to the previous Bust. Birthrates had been low during the previous generation, due to the Great Depression. The pendulum simply swung from one extreme to the other."

Dr. Gewirtz shook his head sadly. "Perhaps it is time for me to retire. I have handled perhaps ten thousand of these orientation classes for my Associates; and each seems more stolid and foolish than its predecessor. Am I losing my touch? Are my words like the seed that fell on the hard ground? Have the birds of the air come and plucked them away?

189

Human behavior, Ms. Howard, results from human decisions. We are not robots. No one consults the statistical abstracts prior to copulation, crying, 'We must procreate more diligently so as to compensate for our parents' lackluster performance!' " The class tittered and he favored them with a harsh glance. There were five recruits in the class. Plus Sarah. "Very well. Mr. Bosworth claims that the changed sexual practices induced by the automobile resulted, through unexpected spin-off, in the Baby Boom of the Fifties and early Sixties. Ms. Howard claims that those changes did not have so large an effect. Which is right; which is wrong?"

"They are both wrong," Sarah said on impulse.

"Ah, Ms. Beaumont! The Sphinx speaks at last. Enlighten us with your too infrequent wisdom."

"*Did* the automobile change the sexual habits of teenagers?"

"Ah, very good! You answer me with a question; but—you will pardon the pun—a pregnant question. I am an old man. My father drove a buckboard. I am sure you all know what a buckboard is. Do I need to enlighten any of you on that point? Good. My father told me how he and his friends would 'spark the gals' in the backs of their buckboards and how many an early marriage or 'late-in-life baby' resulted from it." He paused and a smile chased itself across his face.

"Perhaps I should explain that, in less enlightened times, a baby born out of wedlock was considered a mark of shame. Quite often, the mother would take her errant daughter on an extended trip and return pretending the baby was her own." He waved a hand negligently. "No one was deceived, but the forms had to be observed. The buckboard, in fact, possessed a singular advantage over the automobile. Since it was pulled by an animal somewhat more intelligent than those it transported, there was no need to 'park' in order to accomplish one's intentions. Going back further, we find, by way of example, that the *Geburtsbüchen* of 18th century Rhineland parishes possessed printed columns labelled 'legitimate' and 'illegitimate,' in order to facilitate the recording of teenaged indiscretions. It seems likely, therefore, that these sexual practices have not become more common so much as they have become more public. A trend which I deplore, primarily on the grounds of good taste. However—" He turned his wheelchair around and faced the projection screen. "Let us return to my original question. The equations that I've written imply that chain reactions within a society may entrain results unanticipated by those who initiated the action. This is especially the case when there are significant time lags between stages. When the system has, as we say, high viscosity. Again: Can anyone cite an example of such a spin-off? Let us make it more challenging—since such examples abound for those with the wit to see them. Can anyone cite an example which includes Mr. Bosworth's Baby Boom?"

Sarah sighed, closed her eyes, and raised her hand.

"Ms. Beaumont?"

She opened her eyes and saw that Dr. Gewirtz had not even bothered to turn around. How *did* he know who to call on? "The Baby Boom," she heard herself say, "was an unexpected spin-off, but of the GI Bill, not the automobile."

Gewirtz turned and the sightless eyes bored into her. "Explain."

She stuck her chin out and answered in a confident voice. "People do not copulate with one eye on the birth trends; but they do with one eye on their pocketbook."

"Their pocketbook? Ah, you must mean their resources. You really must learn to speak more precisely. Explain, please."

Sarah flushed. Aaron Gewirtz was impartial and freehanded with his sarcasm, but she thought he aimed his barbs especially at her. She gathered herself and spoke. "The human breeding strategy is to raise the largest number of affordable children. Qualitatively, we might say that parents divide their net resources—whatever is not needed to sustain their own position in life—by the cost of rearing a child in that niche." She waited patiently. She thought she was on firm ground, since she was simply reciting material from the text. She didn't know if she agreed with it—it seemed simplistic to her—but you couldn't go too far wrong parroting the book.

Gewirtz made an exaggerated shiver. "Your answer, Ms. Beaumont, seems cold; inhuman. People base their family size on their finances? Always? Consciously? What about love, passion, romance? Is there no room in your world for human feelings?"

Sarah wondered how the textbook had become 'her' world. There was nothing for it but to plunge ahead. "No, sir. Not always. Not always consciously. And love and passion are there, at least when the couple are young. Yet, though there are always exceptions, wealthier people generally have smaller families; and poor people, larger. Statistical causality is an attribute of the system, not of the individuals within the

191

system. We can draw the parallel with tobacco and cancer. What is clear cause and effect for the entire population is only a probability for a particular individual."

Dr. Gewirtz pantomimed surprise. "What? Wealthier people have *smaller* families? Are you sure of your theory, Ms. Beaumont? Surely, if finance and resources were the root cause behind family size, poor people would have fewer children."

That one she could answer from personal experience. "No, sir," she told him. "Because it isn't a matter of gross resources; but net resources relative to the costs of child rearing. It simply doesn't cost that much to raise a child in poverty," she finished bitterly. *No, Sarah, you cannot have a new dress. Mama will let down the hem on your old one; it still has months of life in it.*

"And how does the GI Bill fit in?" Dr. Gewirtz' face was expressionless, giving her no clue as to whether she was on the right track or not.

Now she was not in the textbook. It was a question of applying the principle to the situation, to see if it worked. "Well . . . It costs more—in time and energy—to raise an urban child than a rural child; so city birthrates are always lower than country birthrates, other factors being equal. Another kid around the farm can contribute to income, come planting and harvesting; but another kid in the city doesn't help mom or dad in the office or factory. So, as the country urbanized, the birth rate declined. That trend goes back at least to 1820. Then, after World War II, the GI Bill subsidized the costs of modern urban life for a significant fraction of the population. Veterans' preferences made it cheaper and easier to buy a home, to secure a job, to go to school. Since that reduced the 'cut' the parents needed for themselves, it increased the residual available for child-rearing."

"Very good, Ms. Beaumont. Someone, I see, has actually read the assignment and thought through the implications." He bowed slightly to her. "If you would be so kind as to reduce your thoughts to the poor and clumsy medium of mathematics, your classmates and myself would be eternally grateful. Your transcript shows that you possess a sufficient mathematical background. Be sure to include intangibles in your formulation of costs and benefits. What is the value of an infant's smile? Many a mother—or father, for that matter!—would sacrifice much for such a payment. Show also how the process leaves room for free will, in the form of a probability distribution around the expected value generated by your equations. Use your equations to postdict past birthrates with a standard error of no more than 0.5% for any one year. We will expect your report in, let us say, two weeks."

Sarah sighed and nodded. "Yes, sir." It didn't do any good to answer correctly or incorrectly. Dr. Gewirtz handed out the assignments with cavalier impartiality.

"If we were to summarize the substance of today's discussion," Doctor Gewirtz told the class, "it would be a quotation from those wise philosophers, Gilbert and Sullivan:

*Things are seldom as they seem;*
*Skim milk masquerades as cream.'* "

Sarah found Red Malone waiting for her outside the door when Dr. Gewirtz dismissed the group. He was leaning against the wall, his good arm crossed over his sling, whistling a tuneless ditty.

"Carry your books for you," he offered.

Sarah made a face. "What, you with your arm in a sling? Don't be silly."

He looked hurt. "I'm not an invalid. I'll go halfsies with you."

"Oh, all right." She handed him one of the thick ringbinders that they used for textbooks. He juggled it under his good arm and walked with her down the hall.

"Are you sparking me?" she asked suddenly.

"What?" He stared at her. "Sparking?" He looked puzzled.

"Never mind."

"Hunh. How do you like orientation class?"

She rolled her eyes at him. "Lord God, Red. I swear I've never studied so much so hard in so short a time as I have for these classes. Is it always like that?"

"No, I think Aaron is taking it easy on you because you started late."

She snorted. Red would never die from an overdose of seriousness. Still, she reflected, the enormous inter-disciplinary reading schedule she had been given had kept her occupied for the past several weeks and had generally kept her mind off her problems. She wondered if, in part, that might not be the reason why she was in the classes in the first place. Strictly speaking, she was not yet a "recruit." Yet, regardless of the reason why they had asked her to attend, the classes would be valuable. Know thine enemy. She knew people who were "anti-communist" who had never read Karl Marx. People who campaigned against "greedy corporations" who had never studied finance.

Fortunately, she had always had a predilection for learning. Her mind had roamed freely and widely, in school and afterward. Her classmates had always been "bored" with school. But that was a positive feedback loop. A spiral that led steadily downward into apathy and oblivion. The less you knew, the more boring the world became. Learning was always more fun.

Well, maybe not always. Lately, she had learned things that made life distinctly less fun. But not boring. No, certainly not more boring.

"Tex Bodean," Red told her, "and some of the boys went down to the Widener Building last week to clean it out. You'll never guess what they found."

"That's right. I never will. So why don't you just tell me."

He gave her a quizzical look, then cocked his head. "Inside one of the desks."

"School books. McGuffey's Readers. Randall Carson's dirty French postcards. Can I stop guessing now?"

"A body."

A prickling up the back of her neck. She jerked to a stop. "A body? Who?" For a moment, the thought that it might be Dennis paralyzed her.

"Who. We wish we knew. It was just a skeleton. Very old, maybe a century. It had a nice round hole right here . . ." He touched his forehead. "And a much larger, irregular hole here . . ." And he patted himself on the back of the head.

She shivered and hugged herself. "How did it happen?" She remembered the dreadful feeling she had had the evening she had discovered the hidden room. The horrid notion that someone was in the room with her in the dark, just beyond the shadows of her flashlight.

"How?" Red shrugged. "Carson shut down those old offices in a big hurry. There was a lot of confusion. Weil's goons had tracked them down. The skeleton might be one of Them, someone who found the room; or it might be one of Ours, defending the place. What does it matter now? Everybody who was there is dead."

They walked along in silence until they reached the elevator. The ranch was a safe house that the Associates kept for training purposes and for hiding people that needed hiding. Above ground, it looked like a simple, wooden ranch building; but the underground was honeycombed with tunnels and hidden rooms. Sarah had been billeted in a suite on the third sublevel. Along the way to the elevator, she was given neutral stares by a number of passers-by.

"They don't like me here, do they?" she asked as the elevator door closed on them. For the past few weeks she had felt uneasy, surrounded by people who, if not exactly her enemies, were not precisely her friends, either.

"Should they? You've upset their cosy little world, after all. We've been getting rich these past hundred years, from Our preknowledge of historical trends. We haven't done any harm; not like Them. Yet, because of you, We've been exposed to King Mob. Why do you think I haven't gone back to my post in Washington? The official excuse is I broke my arm in a fall from a horse; and there's a dummy entry in Denver General Hospital's files to prove it. But the real reason is that some of my, ah, colleagues might be a tad suspicious of me if they've seen my cover name in your computer Dump."

"Maybe the Associates haven't done anyone any harm," she said, "but you haven't done anyone any good, either."

"Ye are lukewarm," Red quoted. "Ye runneth neither hot nor cold and therefore I spew ye forth from my mouth."

"Something like that."

The elevator dinged and opened on the third floor. They stepped out into the hallway and the doors closed behind them. "Do *you* hate me?" Sarah asked suddenly. "For exposing the Society and the Associates, I mean."

Red looked thoughtful. "Hate? No. You did what you thought you had to do in self-defense. I can't hate a Living System for performing a natural function."

Sarah felt like punching him. Living System! She would show him a living system performing a natural function!

"But," Red continued, "don't forget that when They tried to have you killed, They were another Living System, also acting in what They thought was self-defense. No, I guess I feel exasperated."

"Exasperated?"

"Yes. You see, I'm used to analyzing spin-offs before initiating action. Taking action can have unexpected consequences. Wasn't that the subject of Aaron's lecture today? Well, you didn't. Analyze spin-off, I mean. After all, when you wrote

195

that worm to strike back at the Society, you didn't intend to vandalize any synagogues."

She stopped dead in her tracks and stared at him. Red walked several paces ahead of her before he realized it. He turned and looked at her. "What are you talking about?" she asked him.

"Have you ever noticed how a story or rumor changes as it spreads from person to person? Memetic drift, due to random mutations."

"Get to the point!"

"You started a story, with your computer dump. A lot of people received—and read—those printouts. A lot of other people heard something *about* what was on them; and still others heard about hearing about it. Understand? There are an awful lot of people out there today who have heard only vague rumors about a secret cabal controlling the course of history. Who? Why the Jews, of course. Or the Masons. Or the Vatican. Or the Rosicrucians. Or the Trilateral Commission. You can fill in your favorite whipping boy. The news today reported several synagogues in the northwest and the south vandalized by neo-Nazis and Klansmen. Phone calls to TV stations made it clear it had been done to 'strike back at the cabal.'"

"No! That's not right, at all! I never said that! Look at me. I'd be the last to encourage anyone on the far right."

"I know. But it's dat ol' debbil Spin-Off. It's why Brady Quinn laid down the Law a hundred years ago. Study, but take no direct action. Even when you want to do good, you can wind up doing harm."

"But then, why do you—"

They had reached the door to her suite. Red handed her book back to her. Then, unexpectedly, he put his good arm around her and hugged her. He brought his lips to her cheek but, instead of kissing her, he whispered. "Meet me tonight. Nine o'clock, at the horse corral." Then he left her and retreated down the hall.

Sarah looked after him until he disappeared into the elevator. Then she raised her hand and touched her cheek where Red had not yet kissed her.

196

# IV

Jeremy watched the pudgy history professor draw on her corncob pipe and send an O of smoke drifting toward the ceiling. Through the office window behind her, he could see the campus of Denver University. A few, lone students ambled along the paths between buildings, books tucked under their arms. It was midsummer, and most of the students were studying Tan 101 in California or Florida.

"Yes, Mr. Collingwood. I do remember your friend's visit. Rather unusual, you know. A non-student making an appointment. He had some rather odd questions for me, too."

Jeremy leaned forward eagerly. "I've told you what happened to him; and what happened to our apartment. I'm convinced he was involved in something . . . Well, something dangerous. I've checked his appointments for the last month and yours is the only one that was out of the ordinary. I thought perhaps there might be a clue in it."

"A clue?" Professor Gwynneth Llewellyn raised her eyebrows. "Dear me, I wouldn't think there was much of anything about the study of history that would make one a target for hit-and-run drivers! I'm afraid you are barking up the wrong tree, Mr. Collingwood. Mr. French only wanted background information on a few historical incidents. I answered his questions as best I could and he left. I'm sure his accident was only an accident."

Jeremy felt oddly disappointed. Realistically, he knew he shouldn't have expected much from this meeting. Still, it had seemed rather curious. Dennis had never shown the slightest interest in history. At least, not beyond the "best seller" level. It was outside his roommate's regular orbit. And the

197

timing—so close to the day of the hit-and-run. He had hoped that perhaps . . .

Reluctantly, he nodded. "Well, I'm sorry to have bothered you, then, dropping in unannounced like this. I'll let you go back to your . . ." He thought in sudden panic: *What does a professor do during the summer recess?* ". . . back to your work."

He took his leave and backed out the door, closing it behind him. He paused a moment and closed his eyes in weariness. Who did he think he was fooling? Jeremy Colling-wood, private investigator? Ludicrous! It was worse than ludi-crous! Yet he had to know. About Dennis; about the break-in at their apartment. He shoved his hands into his pants pock-ets and trudged down the hallway.

He had gotten no farther than the front door of the build-ing, however, when he heard his name called. He turned and saw Llewellyn walking toward him down the hallway, waving him back with her arm. It was unkind to think so, but he was surprised a woman so chubby could walk so gracefully.

"Did I forget something?" he asked when he had met her halfway.

"No," she answered. "Come back to my office and I'll explain."

When they reentered her office he noticed that the tele-phone had been taken off its hook and the mouthpiece disas-sembled. A tape player was running, its output jack hooked into the opened mouthpiece of the telephone with alligator clips. He looked from the jury-rigged set-up to the professor and back to the set-up.

Llewellyn had a worried frown on her face. "Do you know what that is, Mr. Collingwood?" She pointed to a device in the phone's mouthpiece.

Dutifully, he looked; but the widgets and wires were just widgets and wires. He shook his head. "I'm no good with gadgets. I've never even seen the insides of a telephone."

"I have, Mr. Collingwood; and that doesn't belong there. It's a bug. It picks up and transmits anything that is said in this room. Unless I connect my tape player to its input. Whoever is on the other end is now listening to A Typical Day in an Historian's Office. Sounds of me reading, typing, lighting my pipe, and so forth." She took her pipe from between her teeth and smiled. "Not anything to threaten the Top 40, but I like it."

198

Jeremy raised an eyebrow.

"I was a student radical once, in my salad days," she explained. "Probably, I am still more radical than some people would like; but, be that as it may, I learned a long time ago to recognize tampering with my phones." She looked again at the bug. "I wish I knew who planted this one; and why. I discovered it about a month ago, shortly after I met with your friend. I didn't make any connection at the time between the meeting and the bug. Not until you showed up and told me what had happened to your apartment. That is too much coincidence; and I have never liked coincidence." She shrugged and seated herself behind her desk. She leaned forward on her elbows and pointed the stem of her pipe at him. "Now, Mr. Collingwood. Let's you and I have ourselves a little talk."

Two hours later, Jeremy was pacing the room and Llewellyn was jotting notes on a yellow legal pad. "Let me see if we've got this straight," she said, picking up the pad. "Your friend showed me a slip of paper that he had found somewhere, one that had a list of dates and events on it. He didn't tell you where he found it, did he? No? Me, neither. Or I don't remember if he did. I told him that, in my opinion, the list was one of historical turning points . . . No, not exactly turning points. What's the word the physicists use?" She waved a hand vaguely in the air. "Fulcrum? Yes, they were 'fulcra.' Occasions when the efforts of a comparatively small number of people had had a disproportionate influence on later events."

"Give me a place to stand," Jeremy quoted, "and a place to set my lever and I can move the world."

"Archimedes. Yes." She tapped her pen against the pad in an irregular rhythm. "I didn't think too much of it at the time. You see, there is an on-going battle among historians between the Great Man theory and the Mass Movement theory. And I took the notes to be someone's attempt to prove the importance of individuals on the course of history." She pursed her lips before continuing. "But now you tell me that Mr. French was a partner of this Sarah Beaumont who's been in the news lately. I don't pay much attention to the television, I'm afraid. As an historian, the news doesn't interest me. Real history can't be condensed into catchy sound bytes. I had heard about her allegations, of course. This business about a secret conspiracy—" She paused and smiled crookedly. "Although who has ever heard of a *non*-secret conspiracy?" She chuckled. "Mostly talk around the department; but the conspiracy business is a growth industry. Every day someone announces the discovery of a new one: about Kennedy, about Lincoln, about the International Bankers. Mostly rubbish, of course; so after a while you learn not to pay attention. But now, if there is a connection with the list your friend showed me . . ."

"Yes. Perhaps it *is* true. This conspiracy. I'm not clear on the details, either; but I did understand that whatever the information was, it was dumped into every newsroom and police station in the country."

"Hmm. I'd like to read it. It shouldn't be too hard to lay hands on a copy. A study of its contents should tell us whether this whole thing is on the level." She frowned and drummed her desk with her fingers. "I have some grant money," she said, as much to herself as to Jeremy. "I was planning to use it for another project, but . . ." She laid her pen down. "I'm going to see the Dean about this," she announced. "I think we can put together a study team. Bring top scholars in from around the country. Either confirm what was in Beaumont's printout; or lay it to rest."

Jeremy tried to look interested. The Professor was getting off onto a side issue. But, then, her interest was not in Dennis' accident but in the list. She was concerned with larger issues. History, whatever that was. He wondered if it was possible to be interested in history without being interested in the people who lived it; and decided that it was. It was all too easy to view the past as abstraction. Germany did this; France did that. As if countries had free will. Still, whatever Llewellyn learned about this alleged cabal would probably shed some light on what happened to Dennis. Perhaps he could attach himself to the project, unofficially. Surely Llewellyn would not object to passing on to him any information she uncovered pertaining to Dennis.

It was as if she read his mind. Llewellyn pointed her pipestem at him. "Tell you what. I'll make you the project's administrator. You said you were an accountant, didn't you? You can handle the financial end while we academics drift around in the clouds, thinking great thoughts. Will you do it?"

"Well, I—"

"Look, Mr. Collingwood, if your roommate's accident was anything more than an accident, it was because of his connection with the Beaumont business. So, the only way we'll set your mind to rest is by resolving the larger issue."

*Please, Br'er Fox, don't throw me in the briarpatch.*

"Well, I believe I can accomodate you in my schedule. This is a slack time for CPA's. Tax season is over; and we're between quarters. And—" He paused, surprised at the depth of his own feelings.

"And?" prompted Llewellyn.

"And none of my current jobs are anywhere near as important as what happened to Dennis. If someone tried to kill him once, is he safe now?"

"Hmm. No, I suppose not." Llewellyn's face took on a curious look. "You know, from the sounds of things, it might be somewhat dangerous to dig into these matters." She sounded surprised and perhaps a little pleased.

"Yes," Jeremy replied soberly. "Dennis struck by a car. Beaumont shot at in the middle of downtown—"

"And now disappeared."

Jeremy nodded. "Dead, or hiding. And there was Beaumont's friend, that reporter."

"Grimes. I think his name was mentioned in this conspiracy business, too. Something about his files. You know—" She picked her pen up and fiddled with it. "If I remember correctly, there were three or four murders on that list your friend had. I didn't see how they fit in with the other items, but—"

Jeremy sucked in his breath. "Other people who got onto this conspiracy."

"Possibly. I don't recall the details. One or two items come back to me. I only saw the list that one time; but it seems to me that the dates of the murders ran well back into the last century." She shuddered. "If it is a conspiracy, it's been around for a Godawful long time." She looked at him. "What's wrong?"

Jeremy had stopped dead in his pacing. "The list! Maybe that's what was stolen. I wasn't looking for it, but I don't remember seeing anything like it when I searched the apartment." He shrugged helplessly. "Dennis would know where he put it; but they said he can't have visitors yet."

"There are ways around that," said Professor Llewellyn. She seemed lost in thought for a while. Then she pushed herself up from her desk and tapped the plug from her pipe. "Well, let's get on with it."

"Get on with it? Get on with what?"

"I said I remembered a couple of items from your friend's list. It may not be much of a start; but it's the only start we have. We're going to see a friend of mine in the English Department. He may be able to help us."

"English Department? How?"

"Oh. He's an expert on Ambrose Bierce. He has what may be the largest collection of Bierciana in the country. I'm interested, naturally, because I've just this minute decided to write a paper about Bierce and his connections with the Mexican Revolution. You're interested because Bierce's disappearance was on Mr. French's List. Although you may not want to mention that fact." She paused before she disconnected her tape player. "Oh, and one other thing. When you do go back to your apartment, check your phones. I think your first burglar may have been looking to take something— the List probably—but your second burglar I think left something behind."

When Kennison reached his offices it was close to noontime and he had to run a gauntlet of reporters. The elevator doors opened and a dozen questions formed a babble of sound; flashcubes went off like fireworks. Kennison steeled himself and stepped out into the hallway, where the reporters formed a cordon around him. *Like beaters trapping their prey,* he thought. He had a moment's wild fantasy in which they drove him over the edge of the elevator shaft, as their ancestors had driven mammoths over cliffs' edges. Involuntarily, he looked behind him and was oddly reassured by the solidity of the elevator's door.

He turned again and straightened his vest and tie. "I'm sorry," he told them, "but I still have nothing to say about that mad woman's accusations. I am surprised that any of you take her seriously." He smiled thinly. "I should think you would be interviewing psychiatrists rather than pollsters." The doorway to Kennison Demographics beckoned to him from the other side of the hall. He longed to be in there and away from this crowd.

"How did the meeting go on Friday?"

That jarred him, but he didn't let it show on his face. Curse Weil for holding that Council! He faced the *Chronicle* reporter. "I beg your pardon? What meeting was that?"

"The *Chicago Sun-Times*, they staked out the mansion of

that Genevieve Weil yesterday. You know, the woman who is supposed to head up this secret society. Well, nothing happened for a long time. Then the police came and hustled them away."

"A very newsworthy event, I'm sure."

"Right. So why'd the cops come and roust them? Somebody high up had to pull some strings, right? So they left, but they circled around and came back again and, whaddaya know? They see about a dozen limos leaving the place. Windows as black as a tax auditor's heart. And the license plates . . ."

Kennison was curious in spite of himself. "What about the license plates?"

"Funny thing. They only managed to copy three of them. They were too far away to read them clearly. But they did manage to trace the three."

"And?"

"One of them was registered to a rental car; but the agency swears the car wasn't rented that day, and anyway it belonged to a compact, not a limo. And the other two plates, according to the DMV computers, did not even exist."

Kennison grunted contempt. "Obviously your colleagues copied the plates incorrectly."

"Yeah. Well, it was awful funny all those rich people meeting like that; just like there really was a secret society and all."

"Sir, I do not know this Genevieve Weil. I never heard of her until that mentally unbalanced woman made these unsupported allegations. But I am sure that, if Ms. Weil is as rich as people say, she undoubtedly associates with other rich people and may even invite them over to her house for luncheon. She may even value her privacy enough not to want strangers hanging around her front gate. That hardly provides grounds for a conspiracy as vast as has been claimed."

"So, where were you over the weekend?" asked a reporter for the *Bee*.

"At my fishing cabin in Maine, if it is any of your business."

"Can anyone corroborate that?"

Kennison ignored the question.

"Is that your official statement, Mr. Kennison?" That was the West Coast stringer for the *Times*.

He shook his head. "I have no official statement. I am ignoring the entire sordid affair; and suggest you do likewise. I am surprised," he added disdainfully, "that a medium as respectable as the *Times* is pursuing a story more suitable to the front page of the *National Enquirer.*"

They began shouting more questions at him, but he pushed through them roughly. He yanked hard on the office door and twisted through it into the safety of his offices. The door closed, muffling the babel outside. He leaned momentarily against the door. There was a fine film of perspiration on his forehead and he fumbled for his handkerchief to mop it off. This was not going to blow over, he thought. It was not going to go away. People would keep digging at it. A detective here; a reporter there. Probably government agents, as well. And all of the obvious defenses—like scrambling the national data banks to erase all traces of Brady Quinn—were no more practical now than they were before. There were too many records. And too many records that were not in the Net; and even those that were in the Net, for the most part, were duplicates of paper records stored elsewhere. And the act of scrambling would be as revealing as anything else. Vincent Torino's idea seemed the only viable tactic. Although even that required careful study. Flooding the Net with blatantly incorrect data dumps might appear too obviously an attempt to cover up through confusion.

There is nothing more conspicuous than a man ducking for cover.

Like those license plates, dammit! They had to use dummy plates so the cars couldn't be traced to their true owners; but in the current atmosphere, the fact that the plates *were* dummies looked increasingly suspicious. Whether intentionally or not, Beaumont had created a situation in which the only possible defense was passivity. Virtually any active countermeasure would, in the end, support her allegations.

He became aware that the office staff were looking at him curiously and he straightened himself up. "Damned reporters," he muttered in explanation. The clerks and operators nodded in mute understanding. Since the scandal had broken, they had all been harrassed and questioned at one time or another.

Kennison knew that none of them had revealed anything important for the very simple reason that none of them knew anything important. They were employed only by Kennison Demographics, not by the Society. None of them were "stooled to the rogue" except his assistant, Prudence Baker. And the Night Shift, of course.

The key to analyzing and guiding the course of history, the "trajectory of the system," was the possession of reliable information on the state of the system. No one could act in ignorance—at least, no one could act effectively. That was where his Firm came in. No one questioned the motives of polling firms as they went about the country asking strange questions. The natural assumption was that some business or political party had hired them. And, in fact, Kennison Demographics did a great deal of such "outside" work. All survey data, regardless of auspices, was grist for the Society's information mills.

He liked to think of his operation that way: as a mill. Like the old-time water mills grinding grain into useful flour, the Firm ground data into useful information.

For a century, the Society had struggled along on what bits of information they could glean from public records and from "moles" secreted in various government and business offices. Then, fifty years ago, Kennison's father had established the Firm as an adjunct of the Society and data was collected and processed on a more systematic basis. For the first time, it became practical to gather nationwide, in-depth statistics on key variables. The Old Man had provided invaluable service to Galbraith and the War Production Board and helped them set up the centrally planned wartime economy; and, not incidentally, secured for the Society direct links into the Official Government. Since then, the Society's projections had increased fourfold in their accuracy and precision. That had made his father—and then himself—a Very Important Person within the Society.

Now it was all at risk. Everything his father had dreamed of and sweated to build; everything he himself had built upon it. Teetering now, like a house of cards. And all because of Beaumont and Weil!

Sometimes he almost wished there were no Society; or that K/D were independent of it. His Brothers and Sisters needed him a damn sight more than he did them!

Well, dream on. There was no realistic way to "pull a Quinn" these days. Oh surely, he could drop out of sight—he had created "Fletcher Ochs" for just such an eventuality—but he couldn't take K/D with him; and K/D was what gave him his power. It occurred to him—and not for the first time—that it also tied him down. Power gave rewards; but it also penalized.

He sat himself at his desk and placed his hands on it, palms down and fingers spread. He held that position, pressing down as hard as he could, for a few moments. Then he relaxed and allowed himself a moment or two to enjoy the view from his office window: a panorama that stretched from Coit Tower to the Presidio. An ocean mist was blowing in through the Golden Gate, and Kennison wished momentarily that he were on his yacht fishing for marlin, no cares to distract him. Then, with a sigh, he turned and picked the first of the reports stacked in his in-basket. His secretary brought him his espresso in a small china cup. He thanked her and asked her how her son was doing with his baseball. She said fine and left and he scanned the report's summary. He forced his mind to concentrate on the business at hand.

His desk and office were simple and simply furnished. A butcher block wood desk and swivel chair. A credenza with papers and bookmarked journals scattered over it. A small round conference table. The equipment—an EPIC tele-computer center—was plain and functional. Expensive, but not ostentatiously so. The room gave a message to everyone who entered: this was a no-nonsense operation. Straight, and to the point. Subliminal cues could be visual as well as verbal.

The report was a presidential opinion poll. His eyes darted over the essentials. Sample size. Stratification. Standard error. Together with previous polls this was building into quite a nice picture. Not that it mattered who won next year's election. But knowing who would win would enable Society members to position their assets and influence to greatest advantage. He penciled a coded notation in the corner so that Prudence would know to give a copy to the Night Shift. Given reliable estimates of the number of "partisans" for each candidate, and of the amount of wealth and media access each enjoyed, the Night Shift could run it through their model and forecast the equilibrium values for the vote-fraction for each candidate. Kennison could do it himself. He even remembered the equation, a tribute to his early trainers:

$$d\psi/dt = A(X - Y) + A_x X_O - A_Y Y_O - a\psi$$

where X and Y were the voters for the two candidates. A simple equation, based purely on psychological stimulus-response theory; yet, very powerful. Provided someone measured the variables and parameters accurately! Someone like K/D.

He suddenly became aware that he was being watched. He glanced up, startled, and saw Alan Selkirk standing in the office doorway.

"Yes, Alan?"

"Could I have a few words with you, Mr. Kennison?"

"Surely, come in and sit down."

Selkirk did so, closing the office door behind him. Kennison waited for him to speak.

Alan Selkirk was a Briton—Scots, actually—a brilliant, young statistician who had come to the U.S. five years before for the privilege of studying and applying new statistical theory at Kennison Demographics. When Beaumont's sabotage had disrupted the K/D system, all of the programmers and operators in the office had been annoyed, but Selkirk had taken it as a personal affront. It had taken several weeks, building on the last off-line save, to restore the system to partial operation; and, even so, they had lost the data for several current studies and had had to pay a performance bond to those clients who would now never receive their market surveys.

Selkirk had announced his intention of tracking down and eliminating the worm that had wrought the damage. Kennison was uneasy about that. After all, he didn't want the regular staff to learn too much about the K/D system. But he could not find any rational reason to forbid Selkirk from his crusade. It was obvious that, whatever slanderous reason Beaumont had given, the worm *had* penetrated the K/D database and scrambled it badly.

"Well?" Kennison asked. "What have you found? Don't tell me you've killed the worm."

"No, Mr. Kennison. At least, not yet. But I did find the key to the scrambler." When Selkirk spoke, there was very little trace of his Scots burr. Five years in the U.S. had Americanized his speech to such an extent that his accent had nearly vanished.

"Oh? And what was that?" Kennison sipped his espresso and felt the caffeine jolt run through him.

Selkirk ran his fingers through his straw-colored beard. "Well, it wore a lot of the usual hacker technology on its head. The worm did. Pretty well put together, considering it was encrypted in another program. I could have done a better job, given the time, but . . ." He shrugged elaborately. "The head only got the worm through the usual security locks. It had no discrimination. It poked into every system that accessed the Net. It may have been loose for days or even weeks before it got inside our system. By now, it's probably penetrated every database in the country."

"But it didn't scramble all of them." Kennison made it a flat statement.

"No. The number three segment of the worm was old JUGGERNAUT. A simple, foot-stomping program that was developed by Core Wars players back in the 70s. It rolls along from address to address, replacing data with random bits. No one ever actually ran it outside the universities, as far as I know; and there are easy countermeasures, like CLONE, if you know what to expect. Incidentally, our system is now protected against similar attacks in the future."

"Thank you, Alan. That alone earns you your salary for the next five years."

"But, it was the number two segment that was the most interesting. The head let the worm open the door and old JUGGERNAUT stomped whatever was inside; but Number Two told it whether or not to stomp."

It was coming. Kennison felt it. Selkirk had been leading up to it all along. He had found something he shouldn't have found. The sweat made Kennison's forehead cool and he forced his voice to remain calm. "And how did it do that?"

"It had a list of names that it compared against the database. If those names were in the base, it stomped; if not, it cancelled."

"Whose names?" he asked; but he already knew.

"Beaumont. Grimes. French. Someone named Abbot. Quinn. Belleau. Crawford. Penwether. McAuliffe. Should I go on?"

"Hmm, no. I don't think that will be necessary." Behind his calm demeanor, Kennison was frantic. He thought furiously. If this gets out, Weil and Ullman will have me. My own employee! The Council would never back me after this. Kennison swallowed and looked Selkirk in the eyes. The Scotsman was looking back steadily. There was a faint smile on his lips. Smug? Contemptuous? Kennison looked closer and saw the creases at the corners of the eyes, the stiffness of the lips. Selkirk was nervous. Frightened. He had hold of a tiger's tail, and he knew it. Kennison sighed inwardly. He had never ordered the death of anyone he knew personally. He wondered if Tyler Crayle was available. Or had he gone looking for his brother? "What were those names doing in our database? One of our surveys, maybe?" Bluff it out. Play dumb. Gain time.

"No, sir. That was the odd thing. Those names were the key that unleashed JUGGERNAUT, but those names were not in our system. Yet our system was attacked. Curious, I thought."

"Curious, indeed. Perhaps the worm malfunctioned?"

"Not a chance, Mr. Kennison. Maybe you don't understand this yet, but that Beaumont lady is *slick.* No, the obvious conclusion was that there was a secret part of the system." He grinned broadly. "Do ye know what a priest hole is, Mr. Kennison?"

"A priest hole. No."

"Back in England and Scotland, when the papish church was outlawed, some of the noble families who kept to the Old Religion built hidden panels and secret passageways into their houses for priests to hide in. Well, I found a secret passageway in our system architecture. Whoever wrote it was right canny and I salute him. There is an entire second system in there, piggybacked on K/D's system, like a parallel world from a science fiction book."

Kennison pasted a look of outrage on his face. "Do you mean that someone has been parasiting on our system without our knowledge? That is intolerable!"

Selkirk, still smiling, shook his head. "It won't wash, Mr. Kennison. I took a tour around that second system. I poked into things here and there. Turned over a few wee rocks to see what would crawl out. It was an education to me." He drawled his words out, beginning to enjoy himself. His Scots burr showed through from time to time.

Kennison gave up. He closed his eyes and rubbed his hand over his face. "All right, Alan. Get to the point. Quit the tap dancing."

Selkirk shrugged. "Everything Beaumont said is true. There is a secret society trying to direct history. And you're one of the executive directors." He flashed perfect teeth at him.

"You understand, Alan," Kennison said wearily, "that I can't let you go to the newspapers or the police with this."

For the first time Selkirk looked surprised. He sat up suddenly straighter in his chair "Oh, no, Mr. Kennison. You don't understand me at all. I don't want to *expose* you. I want in!"

# V

Sarah found Red by the horse corral. The summer sun was just setting and the Western sky behind him was a burst of color. The clouds drifted in echelon, low in the sky, seeming just to graze the peaks above the ranch. The tops of the clouds were dark and gray with the coming night, but the bottoms glowed orange from sunlight beyond the horizon. A flock of birds—Sarah couldn't tell what sort—took wing and flew across the scene.

Sarah was amused to see that Red had finally abandoned his Eastern garb in favor of more sensible Western clothing. On Red, though, the Stetson looked incongruous, like a bow tie on a gas pump.

"Howdy, pardner," she said.

"Pardner," Red grunted. "You really get into this scene, don't you? The West. Cowboys, horses, mountains."

"Don't you? No, of course not. You don't even realize you're sitting with your back to the sunset."

Red twisted his head and looked at the clouds. "Nice."

She shook her head. "Nice, he says. You're a philistine, Red. You'll never see anything like that back east. I never did when I was a kid."

It was too dim to see his face clearly, but she thought she heard surprise in his voice. "I thought you grew up in Chicago."

"I did."

"Chicago isn't in the east."

"Really? Which way is it? Point."

Red's arm stuck out.

"What direction are you pointing?"

"East."

210

"I rest my case."

Red sighed heavily. "All right, but I still don't get it. You're not from here. You're a city girl. What makes you so much at home?"

"I'm still a city girl most of the time. Denver isn't such a small town. It just isn't a sprawling *mass* like most of those Eastern cities. Sure, I grew up in Chicago. I knew every alley and hidey-hole on the South Side. But this is home for me, now. I knew it when I first laid eyes on it."

Red glanced at his watch, she could see the numbers glowing faintly on his dial. It was, she noticed, an old fashioned analog watch. "Tell me about it," he said.

She shrugged and stuffed her hands into her jeans pockets. "There isn't much to tell; not really. One day I just walked into my job at the *Trib* and told 'em I quit. Quit cold. I had no plans; no new job waiting for me anywhere. But Chicago was getting to me; closing in. I wanted . . . I didn't know then what I wanted. Something different. Wider horizons, maybe. A break with the past."

"Most young girls would have headed for New York."

"And Broadway. Yes, I know. But I wanted substance, not glitz. Besides, New York is just a bigger Chicago. A middle-class Calcutta. It's dirty and run-down and unbelievably primitive. People actually throw trash out in the streets." She shook her head. "No. I tossed everything I owned in the back of my old Chevy and headed for the Interstate. I didn't really have any notion of where I was headed. Just out of Chicago. I went south on the Dan Ryan and, when I came to the turnoff for the Skyway, I went west instead of east. Well, then I kept turning west and before I knew it I was on I-80, heading God-knew-where . . ."

She paused and sat on the lower fence rail, bent way over, her knees pressed against her chest. She leaned out and pulled a stem of grass from the ground and began tugging and tearing at the leaves. "I drove through Illinois and Iowa and the flatlands of Nebraska without really seeing them. All along the way I kept asking myself if I were doing the right thing and telling myself that I was being stupid. On impulse, I took the cut-off onto I-76 and headed for Denver. And then, one day—I think it must have been maybe midafternoon—somewhere between Julesburg and Sterling I first saw that magnificent, snow-capped wall of mountains marching across the horizon. 'Purple mountains' majesty.' I never knew what that meant before; but I knew what it meant then. I knew I was home for the first time in my life."

Red nodded silently. "To each his own," he said after a while. "Me, I couldn't imagine life without the bright lights and action, without the grit and reality."

"Red, between Broadway and the Sangre de Christo Mountains, which is reality and which is fantasy?"

He hopped down from the fencepost. "You'll get no argument from me. I never said I had no fantasies." He gathered himself up. "Well, it looks like a nice evening for a walk." Then, in a whisper, he said, "Behind the barn. The others are waiting."

She looked at him quizzically, but he was already ambling off. Others? What was Red up to? Why did he ask me to come out here? And why did he ask so secretively?

And why did I come?

There were three of them behind the barn: SuperNerd and two men she didn't know. They looked at her curiously, indistinct shapes in the dusk. One of the men was middle-aged and somewhat far gone into swivel-chair spread. The other man was younger, flat-stomached and lounged against the barn wall with unselfconscious assurance. He was dressed like a cowhand.

"Well," said Sarah, in a low voice, "who has the cornsilk?"

The older man chuckled, but all she got from the other two were blank looks.

She hunkered down by the wall and pulled a stem of wild grass. She began twisting and knotting it. "You friends of Red?"

There was no answer so she decided the hell with it. She settled in to wait with her own thoughts.

Red reappeared a few minutes later, and introduced people around, speaking low and quickly. The older man was Walter Polovsky; the younger was Tex Bodean. He was Janie Hatch's *segundo*. Sarah shook her head. She couldn't believe anyone was really named Tex these days.

Tex and Walter knew each other. They had never met SuperNerd. They had heard of Sarah, and what they had heard hadn't pleased them too much. "I know what you done," said Bodean. "And I suppose that, if'n it'd been me I'da done the same. But I don't expect I gotta like it."

"Never mind that now," said Red. "Listen up. Sarah, here, found a very interesting piece of paper in Carson's old mansion down in Denver. Tell them what you told me, Sarah. About Dennis' List."

The List? Her mind went back to the day on Mount Falcon when Orvid Crayle had caught up with them. She and Red had been talking about this and that, waiting for Janie to pick them up. The subject of the List had come up. She hadn't thought about it since then, because she hadn't wanted to think about anything connected with Dennis or with that awful day on the mountain. And Fee, her cat. She had lost Fee that day, and missed him terribly.

So, don't think about that part of it. Just concentrate on the List.

She explained how Dennis and she had come across the handwritten list of events and how the historian at DU had told him that they were turning points of history. Red interrupted to add: "One of the, entries was the assassination of Lincoln."

Walter nodded as if that explained a lot. SuperNerd listened eagerly. Tex simply waited. "What else was on the list?" Red prompted her.

"I don't remember. A lot has happened. Let's see . . . Frederick Taylor and his management system. Dewey and his teaching methods. Henry Ford. I remember those names because they were subjects that Dennis and I had talked about. Oh, and Brady Quinn's death, and a couple of others."

"Davis Belleau? Agatha Penwether?" That was Walter. She told him yes, and he nodded again. He looked questioningly at Red.

"Sounds like some of Quinn's and Carson's early work, when they were trying to identify what the old Society was up to. That's how We got onto Their plans for a Domesticated Society. So, what's the point? We already know about it. Hell, it was Quinn and Shelton engineered Lincoln's assassination, even before the Schism."

"Tell them what else, Sarah," Red said.

"Well . . ." She wracked her memory, trying to recall fragments of conversation with Dennis. "Teddy Roosevelt being made vice president. Umm. Winfield Scott's military appointments." She saw Walter's head jerk around and Tex stood up, away from the wall. "And, oh yes, Lincoln's election, too. And—"

213

"What is this, Red?" demanded Tex. "They don't belong on that list!"

"And neither did von Kluck's Turn or the sinking of the *Lusitania*," said Red

"Hell, those were in Europe and neither group . . ." Tex's voice petered out and he stared at Red. "You mean to say? . . ."

"At the bottom of the page, Sarah told me, there was a note that read 'Try orthogonal factor analysis.' " He paused and looked around the group. "The entries in the list were numbered with 1's, 2's, and 3's."

"Jesus H. Christ on a Harley," said Tex. It sounded like a prayer, not a curse.

"That's right," said Red. "We know who #1 and #2 are. That's the Old Society and Grosvenor Weil's perversion of it. But who the hell is #3?"

Sarah saw it, too. She laughed and the others looked at her. "All that sweat," she explained, "and all that anxiety to keep your Secret from leaking out. And all along someone else has had it, too! That's rich; that's really rich!"

Walter scowled. "I don't see how it's funny, Miss. As if we didn't have enough on our hands fighting Them and pulling the wool over Cam—"

Tex tried to shush him but Sarah laughed again. "Don't worry, Tex. I know all about Red's disagreements with Cam Betancourt. It's obvious you're all part of the cabal within the cabal." She turned and saw the mute appeal in Red's eyes, so she decided to say nothing about her own reservations. Could you really fight evil with evil means? Could you do it without taking on the very attributes of those against whom you struggled?

"And that's not all," Red said. "Can any of you read French?" Sarah told him she could and he reached into his shirt pocket and took out a piece of paper. "Tell me what this says. It's off of a Quebec City node of the DataNet."

Sarah looked at him, then unfolded the paper. She saw it was a sheet of machine paper. A copy of a memo.

"It says," she told them, "that there is a string of suspicious murders that bear looking into. Then it gives a list of names and dates. Jesus, it looks like Morgan's list!"

Red nodded. "I recognized the names."

Walt reached out and took the sheet from Sarah. He studied it while Tex and SuperNerd hung by his shoulders.

Sarah looked at Red. "Quebec?"

Walt looked up. "We don't have a station in Quebec; but They do."

"In Montreal," Tex reminded him. "Not Quebec City." Walt shrugged.

"Branch office?"

"Since when do they conduct Business in French?" Red asked.

"It's the Law up there. No official business in English."

"Or look into murders that They committed Themselves?" Sarah said. "Don't fight it, Walt. It looks like my worm picked up one of Number Three's files."

"I've been going through the whole Dump looking for strays," Red explained. "Anything that I couldn't assign to Us or Them. This—" He flicked the sheet with his fingertips. "—is the only one I found. Being in French, it stood out."

Silence fell on them and they looked at one another uneasily. Sarah wondered what they were thinking.

"The question now," said Red, "is: what do we do about it? Do we tell Cam and the others? Do we tell Them? Or do we nose around on our own before deciding what the best course is?"

"Brother Betancourt'll find out soon enough," Tex decided. "Whoever's reviewing the block containing the Stray will notice it and pass it upstairs."

"Maybe," Red allowed. "But everyone's concentrating on plugging Our own leaks. The checker, whoever it is, may see it; note that it isn't Ours; and not give it any further thought."

"Either way," Walt said, "we should keep quiet. Figure out how this affects our plans. Is Number Three an ally or an enemy?"

"I've got a question," said SuperNerd. They all looked at him. "This third group. We know about them; but do they know about us?"

Walt looked at the printout; then he looked at Sarah. "They sure as hell do now."

SuperNerd rubbed his nose and toyed with a pimple there. "Then time is probably not one of our major resources."

Red walked her back to the complex. He walked with his hands stuffed into his jeans. The others had dispersed on their separate ways.

"Five people?" she asked him. "That's your secret cabal?"

215

He scowled. "Don't be silly. I've got at least twenty-five people. Not everyone is out here, obviously."

"Still, it doesn't seem like you have too many 'assets' to locate a group that's stayed hidden at least as long as you have."

"That wasn't why I organized the group. You know that. But . . ." He shrugged. "We should have thought of it ourselves. Nature keeps no secrets. What one person learns, anyone can learn. Crawford couldn't have been the only one who read Babbage's book."

Silence closed down as they approached the ranch building. Sarah stopped on the porch and looked up at the stars. Somehow it was always the Big Dipper that caught her eye first. She remembered one time camping out above the tree line and gazing up at this same, slowly revolving sky and feeling—really feeling—what an immense distance it was from here to there.

She leaned on the wooden railing that ringed the porch, feeling the cool night breeze. There were animal sounds floating in the distance, muffled by the spruce forest around them. Red coughed and she turned and faced him.

"You're going to hear this tomorrow, but I thought you'd like to hear it from me."

"What?"

He seemed embarrassed. He shuffled his feet. "Your house in Applewood. Somebody broke into it and vandalized it. Smashed everything. Spray-painted the walls. Set fire to the drapes."

She hadn't thought there was anything left in the world that could reach her. Shock after shock had annealed her emotions until they lay numbed and hardened. The close brush with death; the loss of friends; the flight from everything she knew and loved . . . She closed her eyes and tears forced themselves through. "What?" As if repeating the message would change it. "Why?" She knew why. She opened her eyes and looked at him. He was blurred. "It was Them, wasn't it?"

He shook his head. "No. Just some of the locals in an uproar. From what was painted on the walls, the vandals thought you were the one directing history."

"That's absurd! I'm the whistleblower, remember?"

"You know that and I know that but you also know how information gets distorted as it spreads."

"Everything?" she said to herself. "The piano?"

"That was smashed. But, no, they didn't get everything. One of Us went down there a couple times over the holiday weekend to save what we could. It was easy to forecast something like this would happen."

"Easy to fore—?" She turned on him and stood with her arms stiff at her sides, her hands curled into fists. "Then why didn't you stop it?"

"How? Post armed guards twenty-four hours a day? There was no way."

"Dammit, Red," she said, fighting tears. "I loved that place. It was just right. I picked out each piece for it."

"We've got a piano here. A whole music room."

"That's not the point, Red. It's not *my* piano!"

He scuffed a boot. "I'm sorry. We did what We could. Here." He took her by the arm and led her inside. "I'll show you what we saved." She followed him in a daze, angry with herself for letting the news affect her so. *I thought I was going to be strong from now on.* But there was a limit to the shocks a person could take. When they reached her door, she tried to open it, but somehow she couldn't get the key to go into the lock. Red took it from her and opened the door.

And she stepped into the past. She stopped and looked around, not believing what she saw. It was all there. The furnishings from her house. Oh, not the piano or the sofa or the drapes. But the wall hangings and the photographs and the lamps and even the big stuffed chair that she sometimes fell asleep in reading. The painting she had done herself fifteen years ago, when she had thought about taking up art. She remembered how she had felt to layer the colors onto the canvas. And her books! Conrad, and Trevor, and Block, and Heinlein. Well worn and dog-eared. Faithful companions, all of them. A chime made her turn around; and there was the grandfather's clock behind the door. She gripped it with both hands, like an old friend long lost and stared at her reflection in the glass, remembering as she did so what she had seen there the last time. Behind her, on the countertop in the kitchenette, she could see the reflection of Fee's food dish.

And that was one piece she didn't want to see. Tears came. She had used her precious Fee to distract Crayle during that terror on the mountaintop. She had thrown her cat into the bushes for a single split-second advantage. It had saved her life and lost her Fee.

*Who am I kidding?* she thought. *These things don't matter to me. I was never crying over a house and furniture. I was crying over the memories and the struggles that they represent. Everything that brought me to where I was. Everything that I've lost now, forever.* She didn't think she could stand seeing that food dish.

"They found something else on the last trip," said Red, opening the bedroom door.

And Feline P. Cat strutted out, looking regal and arrogant. He hopped to the countertop and attacked his food dish.

"Fee!" Sarah rushed to him and hugged him and the cat endured her patiently. "Fee! I looked all over that mountain for you. You ran off. Not that I blame you after the way I treated you." She looked up at Red. "Where'd you find him?"

"Our people found him at your house. After combing Mt. Falcon for three friggin' days. He'd gotten in through the cat-door, and boy, was he a mess. So was the litter box." He shook his head. "Found his way back, somehow. I've heard of dogs doing that, but never a cat." He edged toward the door. "I'll leave the two of you to get reacquainted."

"Red Malone! Hold it right there, sucker!" Red froze in the doorway and Sarah stuck a finger at him. "My house must have been under pretty close surveillance. Neighbors, if no one else, would be wondering if I was coming back. Whoever went there to salvage my things was taking a terrible risk. Especially since he had to go back more than once. Whoever it was was a damn fool because none of this is worth his idiot neck. Except Fee." She stroked the cat and heard the familiar purr. "For that, I'll forgive him his stupidity." She looked back at Red. "You wouldn't happen to know the name of whoever it was, would you."

Red blushed. It was the most amazing thing Sarah had ever seen. His entire face turned a deep crimson that ran down his neck and into his shirt. That was the great thing about white folks. You could tell a lot just from their skin.

"Yeah, I thought so. Why'd you do it, Red?"

He looked at the carpet. "Because we owed it to you."

"Nice try. Try again."

"Because it seemed the right thing to do."

"Better. Once more."

"All right! Because I *wanted* to do it! Me! For my own reasons!"

She picked Fee up and cradled him in her arms. "Now, why would you want to do a fool thing like that?"

"Because I wanted to see you smile, just once before I died."

Her mouth dropped open and she stopped stroking Fee, who twisted in her arms to find out what had happened. "Red, you—"

"And besides, I left my plumber's van at your place."

The next day Sarah decided to ride up into the High Country.

She was walking along the underground corridor toward the elevator, on her way to the orientation class when she thought she heard her name spoken. She stopped and looked around, but there was nobody there. Frowning, she started on her way. Then she heard muffled voices coming from a small side corridor and, becoming curious, she turned into it and looked around.

There was a door on the right-hand wall. It was closed, but there was a vertical glass panel that paralleled it, and, through the panel, she could see men and women seated around a broad mahogany table. She recognized Red (who was not sitting at the table, but was perched on a credenza that ran along the far wall) and Jane Hatch, the old woman who ran the safe house. The others were strangers.

She backed away before anyone noticed her. Then she leaned cautiously forward and put her head close to the door.

". . . make up her damned mind!" (she heard)

"Give her time. It's not an easy decision." (That was Red's voice.) "We're asking her to erase an entire identity. To become another person. I'm not sure how I would feel about it myself."

"That from a man who keeps a dozen personæ! Brother Malone—"

"That's different, Brother Betancourt. Certainly, I maintain several different identities, but one of them is *me!* I may wear a new persona for a particular op. But when the op is terminated, I can shuck it. We're telling Sarah Beaumont that she can never be Sarah Beaumont again. Ever."

When Sarah heard that, she closed her eyes and hung her head. There was an empty feeling in her upper chest. As if something vital was missing. Red had not been pressing her for a decision on the change of identity, but the issue had not disappeared.

She continued to listen.

". . . know what 'd happen if folks outside knew who she was. Not jest Them; but the general public. There's a lot of hoorah going on, and a passel o' folks hold her to blame. This name change, it's for her own good."

"The old argument, Sister Hatch. Do as we say, because we know best."

"We *do* know best!"

"What's that got to do with it? If freedom means anything, it's the freedom to be a damn fool. To do something irrational or even dangerous. To be stubborn and cussed and downright muleheaded. To flip the bird at the inevitable fucking tide of history."

"Like someone else in this room I could name," said Betancourt.

There was a ripple of laughter before Red continued. "Now you know and I know that if she goes on being Sarah Beaumont in public, she will be killed. Maybe by one of Them, for revenge; maybe by some nut case with a fantasy about what she did or didn't do; maybe by Tyler Crayle, if he finds out it was she who did for his brother. It doesn't matter, except maybe to her. The logical thing for her to do is to change her identity. *But who are we to tell her she has to do it?*"

"We're the ones who rescued her. We saved her ass."

"No, Sister Hatch," said a new voice. "Brother Malone is right. We saved her ass, but we don't own it."

"Wish I did," said another voice, a male.

There was another ripple of laughter and Sarah's ears burned. She wondered who had said that.

"Wait your turn, Al. You'll have to stand in line behind Brother Ma—"

"I think you better close your teeth while you still have them, *Brother* Hollister."

"I invoke Rule 19!" That caused more laughter.

Someone banged on the table. "That will be all, gentlemen, if I may employ the term loosely. Brother Malone is a professional. He will assist our ward in making the right decision, I am sure. Isn't that so?"

Red's reply was slow in coming. "Yes, that's so. I'll help her make the right decision."

"Then, if there are no further agenda . . . ?"

220

Chairs scraped against the floor and Sarah backed hastily away from the door. She returned to the main corridor and scampered to the elevator. She pressed the button and fidgeted, then stabbed it several more times, although she knew rationally that that would not make the machine come any faster.

The overheard meeting preyed on her mind all through Aaron's class. What *should* she do? She had thought that she had severed all her ties to the past years ago, when she had put Chicago in her rear view mirror. But now, when the need came to obliterate them entirely, she found the hand with the scissors shaking. Erasing "Sarah Beaumont" and becoming— who? Jane Doe?—was a little too much like dying. It came to her suddenly that she needed to be in wild country with nothing around her but the sky. She needed to be alone with her thoughts. Through the window, she could see the snow-capped peaks of the Front Range and she thought about the tundra and the wildflowers and the krummholz and . . .

"We are waiting, Ms. Beaumont."

She jerked her attention back to the class. "I'm sorry. I wasn't paying attention."

Gewirtz stared at her with his rheumy, white eyes. "Is that a fact? I had thought you were perhaps engaged in astral projection."

"I said I was sorry. Could you repeat the question?"

"The First Rule of Thumb, if you please."

She sighed and took a deep breath. "The First Rule of Thumb of Cliology is: Evaluate the action, not the actors. That is, the results, not the intentions."

"Very well. Can anyone explain the meaning of this rule?" He scanned the class almost as if he could see them, then stabbed a bony forefinger. "Mr. Bosworth."

SuperNerd had been trying to slump down in his chair. He jerked up and looked around. "Ah, only that, uh, direct action seldom achieves its alleged objectives. Sometimes it achieves the exact opposite."

"Hmph. Is there another sort of opposite, Mr. Bosworth? Never mind. Can anyone cite an example in which the actual results of an action or policy were the 'exact' opposite of the stated intentions? Ms. Beaumont?"

"The attempts by the Babbage Society to preserve the Secret led directly to the exposure of that Secret."

221

There was a moment of embarrassed silence in the room. SuperNerd looked surprised and nervous. The Earth Mother bridled openly. The others glowered at Sarah.

Slowly, a smile spread across Aaron Gewirtz's face. His head bobbed up and down. "A truly creative response, Ms. Beaumont; if a trifle provocative, considering the venue. It does have—shall we say?—exceptional poignancy to those of us here in this room. Being engaged in the inspections of the motes in the eyes of others, we did indeed overlook this particular beam in our own. Alas, one needs more than good intentions in order to accomplish a goal. Are there any further examples?"

The Earth Mother spoke. "American government support for anti-communist dictators led, in 80% of the cases to communist, or at least anti-American regimes. Case examples: Cuba, Iran, Nicaragua, Chile, South Africa, Haiti, the Philippines. Only one of those post-revolutionary regimes could be regarded as friendly to American interests."

"Thank you, Ms. Howard. And why do you suppose that is? Ineptitude? Or perhaps secretly pro-communist sympathies in the State Department?"

"The size and strength of the middle class in the countries in question."

"Correct, Ms. Howard." Gewirtz wheeled away from her and spoke to the class at large. "Direct action frequently has the singular drawback of accomplishing its opposite. I refer you to Æsop's fable of the Dog and the Bone. Any engineer could weave tragic tales of the Promising Design that never quite worked in execution. Cultural engineering, whether done intentionally or not, is, if anything, even more difficult than mechanical or electrical engineering. I could cite pedagogical methods that somehow produce less-educated students. Or Ms. Howard's example of stroking every cur with an anti-communist bark. Usually, this unfortunate reversal of effect is unintended. It is the blind working out of millions of conflicting free wills, each intent upon its own betterment, colliding and ricocheting in an intricate statistical dance. But, occasionally it is deliberate, the subtle machinations of our friends on the other side. Yes, Mr. Reynolds?"

Reynolds was one of the two other men in the class. Sarah had never particularly noticed him. He was a gray young man with a gray personality.

"I don't understand what the middle class has got to do with whether a country goes communist."

Aaron thinned his lips. "Do you know what the middle class is, Mr. Reynolds?" he asked testily.

"Sure. It's the ordinary joes, like you and me. You know, not rich, but not poor."

"An inadequate description, Mr. Reynolds! One rife with hidden assumptions. I am not at all sure that you and I are 'joes' of the same class. Wealth has little to do with middle class status. Some members of that class are quite well off; others are poor. Mr. Bosworth?"

"Uh. The middle class, they were the merchants, the bankers, the lawyers . . ."

A pained expression crossed Gewirtz's face. "Do you intend to define the class extensively, through an endless recitation of occupations? I shall provide you with a hint. In an agricultural society, there are only two classes of importance. What are they?"

"Uh, the land owners and the land workers. Lords and serfs."

"Most astute, Mr. Bosworth. You will present us with a paper, using the calculus of diffusion, showing how such classes arise. Hint: the equations are similar to those describing dispersion of a population over a landscape. Initial conditions: egalitarian agricultural villages; boundary conditions: the usual range of soil fertility and climate plus a minimum caloric level needed to sustain life. Show how the development of classes is inherent in the random variation of crop yields and in the triage concept, given that we possess a sociobiologic tendency toward altruism." He wheeled his chair around on Reynolds.

"Nor have I forgotten you, Mr. Reynolds. Your assignment shall be to analyze the emergence of the middle classes—note my use of the plural form!—and show how it was inherent in the evolution of industrial society. Use the algebra of analogic to compare the industrial, 'middle' classes with their agricultural predecessors. Analyze the course of the Modern Revolution in the following categories of countries. Category 1: England, France and the United States. Category 2: Germany and Italy. Category 3: Russia and China. For each category, compare the outcome of the Revolution with the relative size and power of the middle classes *vis a vis* the aristocracy."

"Wait a minute! We never had aristocrats and serfs in this country!"

"No? I am sure Ms. Beaumont's ancestors would be pleased and comforted to learn that. I submit to you that the Revolution in this country climaxed at Appomatox, not at Yorktown. True, the plantation owners of the South bore no elaborate titles. They were not styled 'Duke of Roanoke' nor 'Baron of Selma.' They were called only 'Massah.' But they needed no other title. They constituted less than 4% of the white population of the South, yet controlled virtually all the wealth. They were landlords no less so than those of Europe."

Sarah paid only half a mind to the discussion. The answers were straight out of the text. The middle class in nations of the first category had been powerful enough to win armed conflicts against their upper classes, creating free enterprise capitalism and parliamentary democracy. Where the middle class was not so strong, the aristocracy co-opted the middle classes and modernized from the top down, developing sham parliaments and finally Fascist states. In Category 3 states, the middle class was weak, or even non-existent. In their desperation to modernize, the aristocracy created imitation bourgeoisie, called *intelligentsia* by Tsar Peter. But artificial bourgeoisie never quite match the accomplishments of the real thing. Ultimately, the forces of modernization exploded from the lower classes, the workers and the peasants, leading to communist dictatorships. Which was why propping up feudal aristocracies in banana republics always seemed to backfire.

As the class droned on Sarah became aware of a new sound. It was faint and squeaking and seemed to be coming from the heat vent. She frowned in puzzlement. The sound bordered just on the edge of familiarity, but on the wrong side of the edge. It swept up and down in pitch several times then stopped abruptly. After a pause it began again. It repeated this cycle several times while she listened.

All of a sudden, it came into focus. It was the clarinet solo from *High Society*. Someone was practicing the racing cadenzas over and over again, tripping up each time on the syncopations in the high register. Yet whoever it was was patient and determined. She realized that the sound had been going on for some time before she had become fully aware of it.

"Ms. Beaumont!" Sarah started, like a child caught with her hand halfway in the cookie jar. Aaron Gewirtz had swung his chair to face her again. "Once again, I have asked you a question without obtaining gratification. If you do not know the answer, please say so; so that one of your classmates may experience the benefit of my scrutiny instead."

"Oh. I'm sorry, Doctor. Could you repeat the question?"

"I could but I shall not. Instead, you will prepare an essay for our education in which you will demonstrate that the middle class origins of revolutionary leaders and thinkers is a necessary result of continued population growth. Adduce whichever cases seem relevant; but do not ignore those which seem to contraindicate your conclusion."

She tightened the cinch on the saddle while Red looked on unhappily.

"You *are* coming back, aren't you?"

"Of course, I'm coming back. I just need to be alone for a while. Somewhere where I can think things through. My whole life is going to be different from now on. I need to decide how much different, and in what ways."

Red handed her the bedroll and saddlebags. "I could get in big trouble for this, you know."

She tied the baggage down. "No you won't. Sure, all us 'recruits' are supposed to be incommunicado; but we've all taken short rides in the mountains before now."

"This isn't exactly a short ride you're planning."

"No, it's not. But I'm not going to make this decision under pressure, yours or anyone else's, or on the spur of the moment."

Red scuffed a boot in the dirt and straw of the stable. "You going to be okay up there? I mean, do you have everything you need?"

Sarah patted the horse on the neck and the horse whuffed in reply. It was a grulla mountain horse, mouse-colored and surefooted. She had fallen in love with it the first time she had walked through the stables. "Don't worry about me. Everything I really need, I carry up here." She tapped her head. "The stuff we salvaged when we went back for my car is just bonus."

"You don't need food?"

"No, there's plenty of food up there. You just have to know how to shop for it. I'm only packing a little jerky and some coffee."

"Janie said you could have some things from the kitchen."

Sarah shook her head. Red was like a mother hen. "What does Janie think of my little excursion?"

"She thinks you're nuts. She says there's only one sane choice."

"Easy for her to say. It's not her identity you're talking about erasing."

Red grunted something in reply. She led the grulla from the stable out to the corral. The day was cool. The sun was hiding behind occasional clouds and a fresh wind was blowing from the west. Sarah paused before mounting, twisting the reins in her hands. She looked at Red. "Well," she said. "Wish me luck."

Red stuck out his hand. "Luck," he replied.

Sarah hesitated a moment, then took the hand. "Thanks." Then she shoved her boot into the stirrup and lifted herself up. Western boots had pointed toes so the foot could enter the stirrup easily; and high heels so it couldn't slip all the way through. That way the rider could keep her seat, even under rough conditions.

"You know, Quinn did this once himself."

She looked down at him. "What?"

"Rode up into the mountains to be alone. It was just after he came West. He had some soul-searching of his own to do. He stayed up there for several months. Wandered up to Central City and down to the San Juans. Story goes that he built a log cabin with his own hands somewhere around here and lived in it for a while." He looked at her searchingly. "You won't be gone as long as he was, will you?"

She laughed shortly. "No, this is the twentieth century, not the nineteenth. We do things faster nowadays. Even soul-searching." She kicked the horse in the flanks and pulled on the reins. The grulla's head came around and she left the corral at a fast walk. At the edge of the property, she twisted around in the saddle and looked back at Red. He waved an arm at her and she waved back.

When Beaumont was out of sight, Jane Addams Hatch came out of the kitchen door of the main house and stood on the back porch watching. Her hair was white and her skin tanned. Red turned and saw her there. He walked over and stood beside her.

"She's gone," he said.

"I can see that," the small, wizened woman replied. "She gonna see sense?"

"I think so."

Janie grunted. "*You* gonna see sense?"

Red looked her in the eyes. "What do you mean?"

Janie snorted. "You shook her hand, Red. If'n I was her, I'da let you have one across the chops. Why didn't you kiss her?"

He turned and looked where the horse and rider had vanished into the trees. "She didn't say anything."

"Red Malone, you are a fool! She'll never say anything. Not her. Askin's not her style. An' she may not even know herself what she wants."

"Why, Jane Hatch! Are you trying to interfere with the natural course of history?"

The older woman snorted contemptuously. "I'm jest pulling a few stones blockin' the channel. That's all. Ain't nothin' wrong with that."

# VI

"Please try to understand," Jeremy told the nurse behind the admittance desk. "Mr. French is a dear friend of mine. I *know* he was brought here to Porter the night of his accident."

He shifted his feet and glanced around. Men and women in white passed by, intent in thought or conversation. One or two glanced curiously at the discussion at the desk. The air was ripe with the half-sensed odors of medicine and antiseptic. Behind him, in the waiting lounge, Gwynneth Llewellyn sat quietly, reading an ancient copy of *National Geographic*. She was listening without appearing to listen. She was even turning the magazine pages at reasonable intervals.

The nurse set her lips. "Perhaps the police report was in error. Are you sure he wasn't taken to Swedish or to Denver General or St. Joseph's; or perhaps even to General Rose or Colorado over on the east side?"

"No, don't you understand?" He gripped the edge of the admittance desk. "I came here with the ambulance. *I saw him here!* Now, his bed is occupied by someone else and your records show no trace of him."

"I'm sure there's been a mistake somewhere."

*Of course, there's been a mistake, you twit.* The angry thought formed in his mind but he stopped it before it reached his lips. Besides, he was no longer sure it was a mistake, at all. Dennis' vanishing had to be something deliberate. Like the searching of his apartment. Like the original hit-and-run. Like the bug he had found in his telephone after his visit with Professor Llewellyn.

"I received a phone call just last week from the hospital, assuring me that Dennis was stabilized. But no visitors. His

228

caller had been quite firm about that. Mr. French is unable to receive visitors just now."

The nurse shook her head. "No one here called."

It suddenly occurred to Jeremy that he might already have seen his friend for the last time. That he would never lay eyes on him again. Dennis had simply vanished into the memory hole, like a dissident in one of those dictatorial countries, leaving an unfillable void in Jeremy's life.

It was an intellectual realization, the knowledge of that void. His mind knew of it; but not his body. Like a tooth that had been extracted, like a limb that had been amputated, he still *felt* as if Dennis was there. Only gone on an errand. Back soon.

He was convinced now that Dennis—and Beaumont—had stumbled into something dangerous. Something that had reached out and whisked them both away. All because he had a scrap of paper.

He had searched the apartment carefully, looking for that scrap, but he could find no trace of it. And that meant either that it had been stolen (the objective of the first burglar?) or that it had been very cleverly hidden. And if Dennis had hidden it that cleverly, it argued that he had also become aware of its importance.

It was to discover whether that paper had been stolen or hidden that he and Llewellyn had come to the hospital, gambling that they could talk their way past the nurses and see Dennis. Dennis would know where he had placed the list; so at least they would know one way or the other.

Something of what he felt must have shown on his face, because the duty nurse hesitated, bit her lip, then nodded once. "Wait a moment. Perhaps the resident on duty that night remembers something. When did you say? The 19th of June?" She punched numbers into her terminal. Dennis glanced around idly while he waited.

Llewellyn was gone!

Panic ran through him. He tried to remain calm, but he could feel the trembling in his limbs. Had someone snatched her while his back was turned? Were they waiting even now to snatch him? He looked around the lobby searching for suspicious faces. What should he do?

Then he saw her returning to the lobby from the hallway and he closed his eyes briefly in relief. Llewellyn glanced at him without speaking and resumed her scrutiny of the *Geo-*

*graphic.* Jeremy sighed to himself. He was starting to imagine things.

"Here it is," said the nurse. Then, after a pause, "Well."

"What is it?" Jeremy turned and leaned forward on the admittance desk.

"Doctor Venn was on call that night. And Nurse Kilbright." She sniffed.

"How may I get in touch with them?"

"You can't. They ran off together, the Monday after. Now they're down in the Bahamas somewhere." Disapproval was plain on her face. "Doctor Venn was always making passes at the nurses; but no one ever suspected those two of being an item. Jane Kilbright was a married woman. We never thought she was like that. Though I'll say her husband is taking it rather well . . ." Abruptly, she seemed to realize she was telling tales out of school, and her lips closed into a thin line. "I'm afraid there's nothing more I can do for you."

Jeremy nodded and thanked her for her help; then he left the hospital and waited in the parking lot. It was late afternoon and the summer sun was seasonably hot. Heat poured off the automobile hoods in waves, creating a shimmering curtain of illusion in the air. Puddles of mirage water studded the parking lot. Jeremy pulled his handkerchief from his pocket and mopped his brow. What now?

He thought that the inside of the car must be like an oven so he fumbled in his pocket for the keys and opened all four doors. The hot air rolled out. He reached inside on the driver's side and started the engine. Then he flipped the air conditioner to maximum.

Llewellyn appeared while Jeremy was recording the gist of his conversation with the nurse in a pocket notebook. When she reached the car he started to tell her what had happened, but the chubby historian stopped him.

"I heard it all," she said. "Or all of it that mattered. While you were chatting I had someone look into the records for us."

"What? How? And why? There's no trace of Dennis in the records. Or . . ." A new expression crossed his face. ". . . at least that's what they've been telling me."

"And it's true. Dennis French is not listed in there. So I checked every emergency room admittance for the 19th. Then for a few days on either side." She paused and looked at him.

230

"There was a 'John Doe' hit-and-run victim admitted on the 18th, the day before your friend."

The disappointment was keen. Somehow, he had expected . . . "Oh. That couldn't be him, then."

Llewellyn smiled. "Funny, isn't it, how literally we take computer records. Unless the reality is right before us, we don't think to doubt them."

"Why, what do you mean?"

"Look, suppose you wanted to 'lose' someone; but he was in the hospital and couldn't be moved. How would you do it?"

He began to see what she was getting at. Why was it she always saw these things before he did? Was he that dull-witted? Or was it that he had lived so long in such a comfortable rut. "I would alter the records."

"Right. Those people directly involved in the original admittance would know better; but you can bribe them. Pay them off. With a permanent vacation in the Bahamas, maybe? Then you wait a few days and play musical chairs, move a few admittances and releases around and everyone else figures their memories must be at fault. If they bother to wonder, at all."

Jeremy felt the excitement knife through him. "You think that was him? John Doe was Dennis?" He turned and looked up at the hospital building. "You mean he was there all along, but just erased from the records?"

"Not erased exactly. Sort of relabeled. After all, he was severely injured, wasn't he? This way they could hide him without actually moving him. Which is encouraging, if you stop to think about it."

"Why is that?"

"They didn't want to hurt him." Jeremy brightened, but the professor added: "At least not until they could learn what he knew and who he had told."

Jeremy started back toward the hospital. "What are we waiting for? What room is this John Doe in?"

"Was. He was discharged last week. By your Doctor Venn, according to the records."

"But—Venn is gone. Was gone. He ran off with a woman friend on the 21st! He couldn't have authorized a release last week!"

Llewellyn shrugged. "The records are in order. And, unless someone goes looking for 'John Doe' and thinks about cross-checking dates, who will ever notice? Give them time and

231

they may even straighten that out. This has all the earmarks of being a jury-rigged operation."

Jeremy felt his hopes sink. Dennis had been there the whole time, but he was gone now. He banged his fist once on the roof of the car. Llewellyn waited silently. "Damn! What now?" He sighed and walked around to the driver's side and he sat there for a while, alone with his own thoughts. Llewellyn slid into the passenger's seat.

"Say," he said after a moment. "Why did they let you look at the records when they wouldn't let me?"

The professor smiled. It made her face look like the Pillsbury doughboy. "I found a candy striper who worked in the records office and I offered her a hundred dollars."

"You *bribed* a candy striper?"

Llewellyn sobered instantly. "Bribery's the least of our worries. Just after you left, a funny thing happened. I waited a few minutes, so it wouldn't be obvious that we were together. While I was waiting, I saw the nurse at the admissions desk suddenly stiffen, as if she'd been given an electric shock. A glassy look came into her eyes and she picked up the telephone. She punched a number, spoke a few words, and then hung up. I didn't hear what she said. Then her eyes refocused and she shook herself and looked around, as if she were mildly bewildered. I don't think anyone else noticed. It was a small thing and I noticed it only because I had been watching her."

Jeremy frowned. "Who do you think she called?"

"I don't know. I doubt she knows, herself. I think it was a post-hypnotic command. I think whoever altered the hospital records, and bribed or coerced the doctor and nurse to run to the Bahamas, also left an alarm system behind in case anyone got too nosy." She slammed the car door. "Let's go."

"Where?"

She pulled a slip of paper from her decolletage. "Before I left, I went back to my friend the candy striper and got the address of the doctor and the nurse."

"But he's gone. And so is she."

"But is her husband still around?"

Jeremy laid rubber leaving the parking lot.

An empty house has an air about it. A sense of abandonment. Jeremy stood by the fake-leather sofa in the Kilbright living room and felt the emptiness of the house. He ran a hand over the lampshade and his fingertips came away dirty. Nothing had been dusted for at least two weeks. He no longer felt nervous about breaking into the house. No one was coming back.

A creak in the stairwell. He looked up and saw Dr. Llewellyn returning downstairs.

"Closets are all empty," she announced.

Jeremy nodded. He had expected as much. A dead end. Perhaps in both senses of the phrase. Behind the romantic triangle and elopement, he suspected a bloodier tale. Nothing he had learned so far about the secret cabal suggested that they were in the vacation package business.

"Maybe we can locate them somehow in the Bahamas," Llewellyn suggested.

Jeremy shook his head. No one was ever coming back.

The phone call came just as Kennison had sat down to eat. Karin had served the dinner promptly on schedule, a veal timbale in a light Béchamel sauce and garnished with mace, and Kennison had just lifted the first forkful to his lips when Bettina, his butler, interrupted.

"There is a phone call for you, sir," she said with a small bow. She was slim and graceful and dressed mannishly in a black butler's outfit.

Kennison looked at his meal. Ruth Ann, his chef, was without parallel in the country and created dishes that truly whetted one's appetite. He had challenged her to produce a different meal each day for a full year and the year was now half gone without a single repetition. He sighed. "Can it wait, madam? I've just now sat down to my dinner."

"The caller says it is urgent, sir."

"Very well, madam butler. I will take the call in my study. Tell chef she must keep my meal warm for me. I will only be a moment."

His study was paneled in dark oak, set with bookshelves containing a discrete number of volumes. The matching desk was broad and totally clean, except for a small sign that read, in an intricate calligraphy: "A clean desk is the sign of a dirty mind." A single touch of understated humor which, coupled with his all-female staff, was meant to give his visitors a certain impression of Daniel Kennison, *bon vivant*. A man of power, financially and sexually. It was partly a lie, of course.

His financial power was vastly understated. He permitted only a fraction of his wealth to show under his own persona. Enough to be impressive and to open doors that might otherwise be closed, but not enough to make people wonder *however did he get it?* And the understatement of the one lie balanced nicely against the overstatement of the other.

The telephone and the reading lamp were islands of modernity in an otherwise conservatively appointed room. Deliberately so, since they, too, were supposed to deliver a message. With-it modernity. The lamp was programmed. It was sensitive to sound and movement, keyed to sensors placed strategically throughout the room. The lamp would "know" when he had entered the study and would turn itself on to exactly the brightness required and would *never* shine directly toward him. The telephone, too, was "smart" and had a number of interesting features, some of them legal.

He stood by his desk and picked the receiver up. "Yes, I have it now," he said. The light indicating the butler's extension winked out. He noticed that the call was coming in on the special line, one which, as far as the phone company's switching system was concerned, did not exist. "Lion, here," he said.

"Eggs, Paragraph seven."

Kennison's eyebrows arched. Gretchen Paige, calling him? And she wanted the call scrambled, did she? Which meant she did not trust the land line security, either. He cursed silently to himself. Didn't she realize that their best safety now lay in having no contact at all with one another? His fingers played over the phone buttons, setting up the scrambler for Paige's #7 code. Paige, on her end, would be doing the same.

"Yes?" he said.

"Watch the national news tonight. I caught the story on our local news here, which is an hour early. You still have a chance to see it for yourself. Call back."

The line went dead. There was no dial tone, not on that line. Instead, there was a silence infinitely deep. An empty universe, vast beyond comprehension. Then, somewhere inside that silence, Kennison thought he heard a tiny click.

He set the phone down shakily. That click. Had someone located and tapped the private line that he had set up with Paige and a few others? Weil, maybe? The Great Harpy? Did she suspect what Kennison was planning? Perhaps it was time

234

to move. Be done with the cautious feelers and double-layered conversations. Bring the others fully into it. Even Paige. *Especially* Paige, before she got the idea of striking on her own. His rivals, every one of them; but what of it? He remembered how Lincoln had formed his Cabinet from his greatest rivals; mastering them, manipulating them, and, finally, making them love him. Seward. Seward had thought to be puppet master to the ignorant backwoods president. Instead, he became his most loyal admirer.

Or maybe Betancourt? Had Cameron Betancourt finally begun to take active measures? Kennison had information that some of Betancourt's advisers were urging him to abandon Quinn's Rule. If the Associates ever awakened from their long sleep, they could be a formidable opponent.

Or maybe no one had been listening in at all, he told himself. Maybe he was just edgy after that business with Selkirk. Hearing things.

Abruptly, he recalled Paige's request. He looked at his watch and pressed a button on his desk. One of the bookcases swung around, revealing a television set. He pressed another button and the tube lit, showing the face of a well-known television newsreader. He was sitting behind a desk, looking serious and concerned, with a screen and a world map behind him. Kennison wondered how many of the countries on the map the man could name.

Kennison crossed his arms and half-sat on the edge of his desk. What was it that Paige had wanted him to see? If it had been on her local news, it would probably have an East Coast dateline.

He waited patiently through half a dozen "stories," really little more than headlines, with occasional cuts to one-sentence, "in-depth" comments by one of a handful of Officially Recognized Comment Makers. About one in twenty of these constantly interviewed personages were Society agents, or controlled by Society agents. A like number were no doubt manipulated by the Associates, although he did not know which ones they were. The remainder had no idea of what they were talking about.

He wondered, as he sometimes did, why no one ever wondered that the same small group of politicians and celebrities were constantly featured, mentioned, and interviewed while others, with perhaps more to say, went unsung; or were bundled quietly off-stage through patently set-up scandals.

The "news" stories themselves were unimportant. Portentous announcements by political and business leaders, who really thought they were making decisions of importance. Trivia about fires and car accidents and wars and movie stars and scientific inventions. Kennison shook his head. He was glad he did not depend upon television for either his news or his entertainment.

It was the last item, or close to the last item.

The newsreader picked up a fresh page of his script and pasted a look of concerned sorrow across his face. "A Tragic Death in New Jersey. The country estate of businessman John Benton in rural Sussex County was ransacked and burned today by a group of vigilantes calling themselves Free Americans. Mr. Benton, who was seventy-five and long retired, perished in the blaze along with two members of his staff. One of the vigilantes, an unemployed steelworker who refused to give his name, was captured by other staff members before he could escape the grounds. He had this to say . . ."

[Cut to disheveled, unshaven face. Dirty with soot. Baseball cap on head with name of local hardware store.] "We're gonna get every last one of those <beep> who been tryin to run our lives. I ain't had a <beep> job in two and a half years 'causa the <beep> auto industry. Thank God that Beaumont woman had the courage to blow the whistle on those <beep>!"

[Cut to anchorman.] "The man's mention of Sarah Beaumont is a reference to—" Kennison shut off the TV before the impeccably manicured newsreader could offer any inanities about the Meaning of It All.

Kennison sagged against the desk. He ran his tongue around his lips. So, they had gotten old Benton. He took out a cigarillo and lit it, fumbling once or twice with the match before he could get it to light. Benton. There was an irony in that. Of all the Councilors, Benton had probably deserved it the least. Not that he hadn't any blood on his hands, but he had been the most parsimonious at ordering deletions. And as for the man who had been out of work for two and a half years, who had ever told him that he could only work in an auto plant? Yet the world was full of people who yearned to slough the responsibility for their own lives. Whoever they blamed, gods or devils, it didn't matter. The important thing was that Someone Else was responsible. He wished that the Society did have the kind of power the man had implied. The kind of micromanipulation that fine-tuned every detail of life.

236

Smoothed out all the rough edges. In the right hands, that would bring an end to the chaos of history. Arrange all the parts of society to mesh smoothly, without the wasteful conflict of wars, strikes, competition, or crime.

Benton's death had been useless. There was something unbearably sad about that phrase. A useless death. A purposeless death. A man's death should count for something. He plucked the cigarillo from his lips and jammed it into the ashtray on his desk. Perhaps he could make use of Benton's death. Bend it to his own purposes. It was the least he could do for Brother Benton.

He picked up his phone and punched a series of buttons. When he heard the click on the other end, he said, "Eggs, Lion three."

When they had reestablished contact Paige asked him if he had seen the story.

"Yes. Do you suppose there will be mobs coming after all of us now?"

"Monkey see."

"A single swallow."

"How many Councilors can we lose before you would call it a trend?" Her voice was waspish and Kennison thought he detected a hint of tightly reined fear in it.

"Three," he replied without hesitation. "Three would be statistically significant."

"You're a cold-blooded bastard, aren't you?"

"Look, if we start to run, it will only prove the allegations to be true. We've got to stand fast."

"And be picked off one by one?"

"Ask for police protection." The idea came to him suddenly. A flash. "After today's incident, anyone named in the Beaumont Dump would have ample justification to do so, and the police would ask no questions."

"How can we conduct business with the police following us around? We can't depend on our own police moles being assigned to guard us."

"Most of our moles aren't patrolmen anyway. I'd suggest we suspend business for the duration of the emergency . . ."

"Impossible!"

"Necessary! If we invite the police and the reporters to follow us around—and we do nothing to contact each other or take any other action—how long will it be before they get tired and go home and tell the world it was all a false alarm?"

He could hear volumes in the silence at the other end. "A Potemkin village?" She was obviously thinking it over. "No good," she said at last. "We'd all hang separately."

Meaning they'd all have to hang together. Meaning she doubted they would.

"After all," she continued, "this is just what Madam Chairman has been bleating about since forever. The reason why she's had so many poor fools deleted over the years."

"Did you oppose any of those deletions? I don't recall that you did."

"Better safe," she told him. "I don't recall any votes that were not unanimous."

*Better safe*, Kennison reflected, pertained more to the dangers of voting against the Great Harpy than the dangers from some ignorant researcher stumbling on forbidden knowledge.

"No, Madam Chairman would never agree to have the police and the newpapers follow her around. Neither would Ullman or Ruiz or especially Lewis."

"Perhaps they would. If a *trend* were established."

There was another silence; this one longer and more profound. At last Paige spoke. "A trend could be established," she admitted, "if the conditions were right."

"Would you take care of that item for me? Thinking it over, I believe only one more incident would establish statistical significance. And, if it were the right incident, take care of any number of potential difficulties, as well."

"I will put your suggestion up to certain other Council members. About the Potemkin village, I mean. Also, that we pass word down to all Cells to suspend any and all business until further notice." There was a pause on the other end of the line. "Do you think we can carry it off, Brother?"

He wasn't sure if she meant the public or the private matter. "I am sure of it, Sister. I have complete faith in you." He cut the connection.

He did, too. Have faith in her. She would make an admirable Seward to his Lincoln. The thought pleased him, until he remembered what had happened to Lincoln in the end. Then he dismissed the thought brusquely.

"And if it doesn't work," he said aloud. "I can always call on Fletcher Ochs."

He returned to the dining room, where Karin was waiting patiently by the side board, his dinner plate sitting covered

238

under a portable heat lamp. Karin was solidly built. Smooth muscles under smooth skin, with no trace of fat on her, except the delicious padding that rounded all her edges. He allowed himself to admire her carriage for a moment, in her high heels and black mesh stockings and French maid's uniform. He imagined her without the uniform (which required little imagination) and the various activities they might engage in together (which did).

He sat down and placed the napkin over his lap, where it lay disappointingly flat. "I'll have my meal now," he said.

Karin brought it to him, bending deep when she turned around to pick it up and bending deep when she set it in front of him. She did that because she knew he liked it and because she knew very little would come of it.

*If I'm in danger, so are my people,* he thought. He remembered that two of Benton's household had perished with him. He didn't want that to happen here. He thought about sending them away to safety. He couldn't bear the thought that lovely Karin, or shrewd Bettina, or jolly Ruth Ann, or wholesome Greta, the parlor maid, would come to any harm. He thought about them, trapped in a burning building with him, like Benton's staff had been, crying and clinging to him, the flames licking close around them. Or chased and beaten by outraged mobs, toyed with by uncouth, lower class workmen.

Something stirred inside him and he looked down at his napkin. *Well,* he thought. *Well, well.*

When he finally tasted his timbale some time later, he found it to be somewhat dry.

# VII

Sarah rested with her back to a tall spruce and chewed thoughtfully on a strip of jerky, listening to the silence. The early morning sun slanted through the canopy overhead, piercing the forest with individual shafts of light. There was a stand of quaking aspen a little bit off to her left. That was how she'd built the fire to brew her coffee. The aspen is a self-pruning tree and there is always a fall of dead branches underneath one.

Well, it wasn't really silence, she admitted to herself. The trees were always busy from the frequent breezes. Especially the aspen, whose leaves shivered in the slightest breath. But the spruce and firs added their sound, also. The wind soughing through their needles produced a murmur like a distant crowd. Voices always on the verge of intelligibility. If she listened closely enough (or, perhaps, if she did not try to listen, at all) they might tell her something.

*Arbormancy*, she thought. Divination through the whispers of trees. And what would their advice be, she wondered? What did the forest say about the Associates and cliology and changing her identity? The breeze freshened and tree branches swayed in the wind. "Ssssssaraaaaah," they called.

A jay called and flew abruptly from one tree to another, not more than a hundred feet from where she sat. Farther away, something bigger scurried through the brush. A squirrel, maybe, or a porcupine. She took her coffee cup, holding it in both her hands to let the warmth of it work through her, and sipped from it. She glanced at the angle of the sunbeams.

*Time to move on.*

She poured the rest of the coffee on the fire. Then she carefully stamped all the embers into the ground. She walked to where the grulla had been pinned and retrieved a folding shovel from the saddlepack. Then she dug a hole and buried the fire.

Satisfied that she had left no hazard, she packed up the pot and the jerky, rolled up her bedroll and strapped them and the saddle to her horse. As she was tightening the cinches, she heard a loud report, like a rifle shot. She started and the horse, sensing her fright, jerked on the reins.

She jumped behind a piñon pine and crouched there. She stroked the grulla's neck, speaking soothingly to it, watching the direction from which the shot had come. She held her breath, waiting.

The sound came again, clearer now, and she almost laughed in relief. Not a rifle shot, at all, but a seed pod bursting. Some flowering plant preparing for the next spring, spreading its seed as widely as possible before it could die.

"I *really* needed this vacation," she told the horse and the grulla bobbed its head in agreement. She swung herself into the saddle and headed upslope.

Later that day she broke from a stand of Englemann's spruce onto a wide alpine meadow. In the middle distance, the bare peaks of the continental divide shoved the horizon skyward, like a rocky wave breaking upon the Earth. The bones of the earth, thrust out by an unimaginably ancient collision. They were speckled with patches of snow that never melted. The Never-Summer Mountains, the Utes had called them. Closer in, a mule deer buck raised its head from drinking at a pond and watched her. Sarah reined in and kept still, waiting to see what the deer would do.

The pond was the creation of a beaver family that had blocked the flow of the stream with their stick-and-mud constructions. The backed-up stream was well on its way to covering the meadow. The Arapahoe had a legend that beaver had built the world. The wily Indians had seen with their own eyes how beavers changed meadows into swamps with their dams. Of all the animals, only beavers and men create their own environments.

And what is the difference between a beaver dam and a human dam? Echoes of the conversation she had had with Red the day of that terrible drive to Mount Falcon. What made one natural and the other not? Only a matter of scale? Of intent? Both change the environment, and not necessarily for the better. Unless you are a beaver. Or a human.

Perhaps the difference lay only in the ability to foresee the consequences.

And wasn't that just Red's argument? What do you do when you can foresee consequences that no one else can? Do you sit idly by and rake in the chips, like the Associates; because you know which way the little roulette ball is going to go? Or do you try to make the ball go where you want, like the Society? Or . . .

Or what? What about the Third Force that they had deduced from Dennis' list and the Stray? What was their philosophy? Were they another Society or another Associates, or something else entirely?

*That's a lot of metaphysics to find in a beaver's dam*, she thought. And how should she answer Red? Red claimed that tampering with the course of history was justified, provided your intentions were good. That everyone did it anyway, blindly and without expertise. That history was nothing but the cumulative blunders of millions of bungling amateurs. How did you answer that? Turn professional? She yanked on the grulla's reins and pulled off to the north. The mule deer, startled by the movement, bolted for the forest.

Valleys lay below her like giants' furrows, turned up by a great plow. Some peoples had gazed at the stars of the Big Dipper and called it the Plow. Perhaps they had seen furrows like these. Sharp-sided cuts gouged out by mountain streams as they fell toward the plains far below. Sarah checked her direction against the vegetation. At this altitude, Douglas fir marched on the north slopes and ponderosa pine on the south. The south-facing slopes received more direct sunlight, and hence were drier than the north slopes. Different plants had adapted to each niche. Farther down, the ponderosas moved over to the north slope, while grasses, brush and prickly pear cactus took over the south.

When she broached treeline onto the alpine tundra, the wind nearly knocked her off her horse and she took a moment to yank her poncho out of the saddlebag. It flapped around her like a banner. She pulled it over her head and cinched it tight. The wind blew constantly up here, often reaching a hundred miles an hour; and nothing stood up tall. Everything hugged the ground to survive in a world that was never frost-free and where snowstorms could occur any day of the year. The clouds seemed so close that she could almost reach out and touch them, and they raced across the sky as if chased by demons.

She was on an old Indian trail; probably Ute this high up. She kept to it, obeying the injunction, Leave No Footprints. Tundra plants were incredibly hardy, but they were so closely balanced between life and death that the slightest stress could tip the balance against them. This trail might have been untrod for a century; yet the vegetation had yet to reclaim it. She blew on her hands to warm them.

The tundra was ablaze with color. The purples and whites of marsh marigolds and Parry primroses. The three-inch golden blooms of the alpine sunflower, which, like the Moslem, always faces east, providing a reliable compass to the traveller. How did the old gag run? There are only two seasons in the High Country: winter and July. She was glad she had come in July.

Here and there, limber pine, bent and twisted by the winds, crouched and hid behind rocks and other shelter. This was the *krummholz*, the twisted wood, sculpted into weird dwarf forms, like some sort of natural bonsai garden. It was no earthly landscape. The cold, thin, high-velocity air. The strange, grotesque vegetation. The rocky, angular horizon.

She began to imagine herself as a star traveller, far from Earth. She had landed on an alien planet. She even named it: Altaflora. It orbited a G-type sun, but one that was hotter than Earth's. On Altaflora, it was possible to freeze and get sunburned at the same time.

A yellow-bellied marmot stood upright amid the flowers and she saluted it, using Spock's Vulcan hand sign. (She had heard somewhere that Leonard Nimoy had learned the gesture in Jewish Brooklyn.) "Take me to your leader," she requested. The marmot continued to look at her and made no attempt to comply. Just as well, she thought. Marmots were anarchists at heart and had no leaders to speak of.

The Altaflorans had a civilization, of course. Underground, away from their harsh climate. There were fabulous cities carved from the permafrost somewhere under her feet. Magic caverns of glowing crystal.

There was a rumble behind her and she twisted in the saddle to look. Dark clouds had gathered around the peaks to the southwest. There was a blur underneath them that meant rain. Lightning crackled, and smashed the boulders on a distant peak, and she could feel the hairs on her neck rise from the static carried on the moist wind. It was time to get back downstairs and into drier climes.

She found a rocky draw that led downslope and turned her back on Altaflora.

The cabin was made of lodgepole pines. It was old and tumbled down. The roof was gone and the door, dried and cracked, lay amid the wreckage. Sarah circled the place slowly, checking it from every angle. It was old, very old. Was it the one Brady Quinn had built? Red had mentioned it being somewhere in this country.

But there had been mountain men all over this region in the early 1800s and some of them probably left cabins behind, too. Yet the place could not be too old, or snow and rot would have done for it. It reminded her a little of the ghost towns she had seen in Summit and Park counties. Preserved in a precarious state of mummification. The wood dried and bleached into a kind of fossilization.

She dismounted and drove the grazing pin into the ground, so the grulla could wander in a circle and browse.

She leaned inside the doorway. There was a young piñon growing in the center of the cabin, but out the vanished back wall of the cabin she saw a magnificent bristlecone! She made her way through the wreckage of the cabin and stood by the ancient tree. She reached her hand out to it and ran her fingertips over the rough bark. How old was it, she wondered. A century? Half a millenium? Farther north, on Mount Evans, trees like this one marked the treeline. And some of those were two thousand years old.

That settled it. This was where she would camp and take out her soul and inspect it. The tree was a comfort, an anchor for her into the depths of the planet's history. While she sat in its shade she knew she could never lose her bearings.

She turned back to the doorway and saw the markings on the inner wall of the cabin. She ran her fingers along them. Tally marks. Someone had once kept track of the passing days. Her fingers encountered something hard buried partly in the wood. She pulled her knife from its sheath at her belt and worried at it until it fell into her palm.

It was a stone arrowhead. Ute? Arapahoe? In the movies, the scout or mountain man always knew the difference. She inspected the point closely. There was no way of telling, so far as she could see.

She turned it this way and that, imagining what might have happened; and for just an instant, she *felt* the history of the place. Only a thin veil of years hung between her and what had once happened here. The lone camper or trapper in a land he thought of as empty wilderness. The Indians, fearful and uncertain of the intrusion on hunting grounds which *they* saw as crowded. The attack. The fight. Arrows cutting the air. The answering barks of the rifle. Flintlock? Maybe. How had it ended? With the Indians fled, or the white man dead?

And who said it had been a white man! Jim Beckwourth, the mountain man, had been a black—and a founder of Pueblo, Colorado, as well! And later on there was Bill Pickett, "the greatest sweat-and-dirt cowhand that ever lived." From the beginning to the end, the West had swarmed with black men and women. So, as long as she was fantasizing, she could fantasize a black man defending this place.

She set up camp in the ruins of the old cabin, well away from the bristlecone. She cleared away the old wood and built herself a stone circle to hold in the fire. During the day, she wandered the rocks and canyons, exploring. She found a narrow cañon, cut by a cold mountain stream. The stream was sluggish, the spring run-off being long past. She found twin sentinels; two spires of rock shaped by millenia of patient sandblasting. She found an overlook above a vast untouched forest and spent many hours on that pinnacle wrestling with herself.

During one of her hikes she crossed paths with a bobcat. The cat backed up and snarled, and Sarah stood very still while the cat looked her over. Then the cat decided that she was too big a bite for dinner, gave her a parting snarl, and disappeared into the brush. Only then did Sarah relax and find that her hand gripped the handle of her knife. It was easy to forget that Nature was not a Walt Disney cartoon. These animals and plants ate each other.

In the evenings she returned to the cabin and sat in the shade of the old pine tree and watched the sun set. There was nothing to compare with a sunset in the mountains. The peaks remained lit long after the sun had fallen below the horizon. They were tall enough that atop them it was still daytime even though the slopes and cañons were shrouded in night.

Glowing white peaks, orange sky, black forest. The Indians had called these the Shining Mountains, and they were right about that as they had been right about so much else. Hawks floated quietly overhead, and once she thought she spotted a bald eagle.

At night, when the stars lit the sky with a splendor unimaginable in the bright lights of the eastern urban megalopolis, she sat before a crackling fire and sipped strong coffee from a tin cup. Western coffee, when properly made, should allow the stirring spoon to remain standing upright. There were city dwellers she knew of who had no concept of the number of stars or the immensity of the universe. Only a few pitiful lights pierced the neon gloom of their night skies.

Altogether it was as fine a place as any for soul-searching. She was as alone as she had ever been. The nearest other human being was who-knew-how-many miles away. She could sit down beside herself and talk it out. How exactly did she feel about the Associates? About Red and his group? About not being Sarah Beaumont ever again?

It was that last question that ate at her more than anything. The Now was always dying and if a person was anything, she was who she *was*. That is, she was the culmination of years of growth and development, from childhood through adolescence to adulthood and (hopefully) into maturity. You couldn't cut away your past without cutting away part of yourself.

Or could you? Some people did. They put on new names and new histories like others put on a suit of clothes. They could leave their past behind and never look back. Were they stronger than she was, or weaker?

One day she returned to her cabin and put some coffee on the fire. She sat tailor-fashion, her legs crossed, with her back to the old bristlecone watching the front door of the cabin. In a few minutes, the sunset would be framed in the doorway. She cradled the coffee cup between her hands, sipping from it from time to time. It tasted a little sweet, although she had put no sugar in it. She gazed at the dirt floor of the cabin, disturbed by something that she couldn't name. But there were no marks in the dirt, except her own footprints coming in.

She shrugged and looked back at the doorway.

*And there was someone standing there!*

Her heart gave a leap and she started to stand up, but

found that somehow her legs wouldn't support her. She sagged back into the dirt. A dreamlike lassitude seemed to have come over her. The figure in the doorway was a black silhouette, framed by the rays of the evening sun. A glowing shadow. She couldn't make out the features.

Then the figure sat down beside her and she breathed a sigh of relief.

It was herself.

She was dressed in her blue suit, the one with the red bow that she had worn in the Civic Center Park the day she had been shot at. She looked herself over. Successful, independent. She knew who she was and what she wanted. Maybe she was also a trifle smug. She didn't have any friends. At least, she had never let anyone close enough to become her friend. But, if she held the entire world at arm's length, at least she was on top of it. Respected. Admired. Magazines had done feature stories about her.

"Well, you certainly have come down in the world," she told herself.

Herself shrugged. "Not me. I'm what I've always been. On the fast track to Number One. You seem to be a little down on your luck, though."

"Am I?"

"Sure. You don't know what you want anymore. People are hunting you to kill you; and the whole world hates your guts. Tell me that's going up."

"Somehow, I thought . . ."

"You thought what?"

"After that business on the mountain. With Crayle—" *When you killed a man.* "Somehow, I thought that would be the end of it."

"Roll the final credits?" Herself was sarcastic.

"And everyone would live happily ever after."

"They only roll the final credits once, sister. No one ever lives ever after; and no one lives ever happily. Not all the time."

She didn't bother to answer. "Why are you here?"

"You need someone to talk to. Who better? Who else knows you as well as I?"

Sarah seemed to hear the hum of another voice underneath the words. As if other words were being spoken and answered. It was barely audible; like the base note of an organ,

247

it blended in with the other sounds. She tried to turn her head to look for the sound, but found she couldn't summon the energy.

She looked at the polished and professional image sitting next to her. "What makes you think you know me at all? You're what I used to be. Someone I can never be again. Even if this all blows over, I can never be what I was."

"Oh, blow me some more tears, sister! I'll need a raincoat before you're through. Who ever said you could be? Who in the whole history of the world ever could stay what they were forever? Not you; not me; not anyone. Look at me close and see if you can find Chicago's South Side. There's a little girl back there that *I* can never be again."

Sarah looked away, at the sunset framed in the doorway of the cabin. "That was a long time ago. It's not real any more. You're not real. I'm hallucinating." Somewhere in the back of her head she remembered that the difference between reality and hallucination lay in the information content. An hallucination could never tell you anything you didn't already know.

"What if you are hallucinating?" herself asked her. "What does it matter? Tell me that you've never re-created yourself before and I'll call you a liar. When did you last see Lulu or Geraldine? Or Big Martha?"

Names from the past. Names without reference. Small childish faces screaming on the playground. The grim Chicago skyline in the backdrop. She couldn't imagine them as adults.

"Or Daddy?" the vision persisted. "Do you even know if he's still alive?"

Sarah scowled. "He left us. When Mama died. He got in his rig and went on the road and he never came back."

"Maybe it was just too hard for him to come back, with Mama dead. We were all grown up by then, even little Frankie. He never cut out when it would have been easy; when so many other fathers did. When staying meant scrimping and just scraping by and doing without. Mama stood by him all through that; and then, when the job was over, when he had seen us well and truly started, when they would have had their own time together, she was gone. No, I don't 'spect he could have stayed."

"Maybe that's why I left, too."

Herself sneered. "What, so you might find him someday on the road? Have you ever gone back just to put flowers on Mama's grave?"

248

"No!" She buried her face in her hands. "And if I do what they want me to do, I never can!"

"Oho! That's the problem, is it? Not that you ever *did*; but that now you never *can*. That lifeline was always there, even if you never tugged on it. Like that ol' bristlecone pine there behind you, with his roots sunk deep into Mother Earth. It's nice to sit in his shade; but it's a comfort just knowing he's *there*."

She raised her head and looked at herself. "Tell me what I should do."

"No, child. No one can tell you that."

She blinked and looked at the figure. It wasn't herself anymore. It was Mama. The way she looked before she took sick, with the square-jawed face and the mischief in her eye.

"You always were a headstrong child. Never were a one for the apron strings, or strings of any sort. But, by God, you never did run wild. You had a compass in your head that always pointed you right. Your Daddy told me so one night. He said you could fall into a cesspool and come up with someone's lost diamond ring on your finger. You do what you need to do. You'll do the right thing."

"But I don't want to lose you, Mama."

"Oh, don't talk foolishness, child. There is no way on God's green earth you can lose me. Because you carry me here . . ." She reached out and touched Sarah's head. ". . . and here." She touched Sarah's heart.

Sarah leaned over and hugged the figure and cried.

In the morning she awoke with a start and looked around her. She was lying on the ground, not even on her sleeping bag, and she was chilled to the bone. She pushed herself upright, and her stiffened muscles protested at the abuse. She bent and stretched, trying to loosen up. After a few limbering exercises she felt a little less like an embalmed corpse and a little more like a human being.

She went to pour herself some coffee and stopped. The fire was burned down, but the coffee pot had been carefully set to one side, along with her cup. She picked up the coffee pot and saw that it had been thoroughly scrubbed. She couldn't remember doing that.

She remembered clearly her experiences of the previous

evening. How she had spoken with her prior self and with her mother. It had seemed so natural at the time, so matter-of-fact; but now the weirdness of it settled over her. What on earth had happened to her?

She looked around, at the cabin, at the old pine. Maybe it was the place. Weird was the old Anglo-Saxon word for Fate. Maybe there was something fateful about this place.

She began gathering her things together. It was time to leave. Like the old Indians, she had gone to a lonely spot and had a vision that told her who she would be from now on. That was how the Indians learned their adult names. It wouldn't be right to tarry in such a place.

She noticed the dirt. Perhaps she half-expected footprints, some physical sign of her nightly visitors.

There were no footprints.

And there should have been! Her own footprints. And now she remembered having noticed the oddness last night. The ground then had only held her own prints coming in; and they should have held her own prints going out as well. In and out several times, in fact. Now even those prints were gone.

And that meant . . .

And that meant that someone had been in the cabin while she had been out walking in the cañon. Someone who carefully brushed out his—or her—tracks. Someone who, perhaps, had drugged her coffee. Experimentally, she sniffed the coffee pot, but could detect nothing except the sharp smell of the metal itself.

She crouched down and studied the ground. Yes, she could see the signs now. Someone had used a leafy branch to brush the footprints away. She followed the sign out to the old Indian trail. There it vanished, but she found the broken branch that had undoubtedly been the tool. She looked up and down the trail. Which way had her night visitor gone?

Whoever it was must have had a horse, and must have stuck to the trails. Going off across country was a good way to get trapped in cañons or cliffsides or among impassable trees. Better to follow the paths left by the Indians and the forest animals. She cut for sign, walking slowly and carefully in a wide circle around her cabin, studying the lay of the land.

Five hundred feet down the trail she found a small hole in the ground and grass that had been cropped. This must be where he had staked out his horse last night. She found no hoofprints, but she remembered the old trick of bundling a horse's hooves in sheepskin so they would make no definable mark on the ground.

She knew he couldn't ride far with his horse hobbled that way!

She scampered back to where she had left the grulla and quickly packed and saddled the mare. Then she set off down the trail in the direction her visitor must have taken.

Two miles farther on, she found a hoofprint. Once away from the cabin, her visitor must have felt safe in unbundling his horse's hooves. She studied the print closely, noting the crack in the shoe along the left side so she would recognize it when she saw it again. Then, carefully, she followed the trail.

After several hours, the sun was beginning to get low and she was wondering whether to put off further tracking for the day. She pulled up on the reins and looked around for a campsite.

There was a likely spot off to the right. A grove of aspen and a clearing. She dismounted and walked into it.

Immediately she sensed the wrongness. It *was* a good campsite. So good it had been used frequently, and recently. She knelt and felt the ground. It was still warm where the fire was buried. There the grass was crushed where someone had slept. And there was an oft-used path between the campsite and . . . where?

She tied the grulla to a tree and walked down the footpath. She pulled her knife from her belt and licked her lips, stepping carefully so as to make no noise. No one was in the campsite now, but it was best to take no chances.

The trail led around a knob of rock that looked vaguely familiar. There was a sort of nest in the rock there with a wall-like ledge before it. She stepped into the nest and looked over the rocks.

And she saw the ranch spread out below her. The Associates' safe house.

The horses were gathered in the corral directly below her. The ranch house was a little further out and she could make out two figures on the back porch. With a decent pair of binoculars she knew she could identify them. With a parabolic mike, she could hear every word. One of the figures threw something to the ground and stepped off the porch stretching his arms.

The stallion in the pasture below stood still and looked up in her direction. She remembered how he had done the same thing not too long ago, when she and Red had shot the breeze on the fencepost.

*Someone's been spying on us!* she thought.

Us?

As simply as that, she had joined the Associates.

# VIII

"Ah, but Mister Collingwood, there is no such thing as an historical fact."

Jeremy sighed. Herkimer Vane was easily the most difficult member of Gwynn's study team. He was a short, bald man with a beak of a nose. His clothing was invariably rumpled and little sheets of notepaper protruded from his jacket pockets. He had the unpleasant habit of wagging his finger in one's face whenever he was making a point.

Such as now.

Jeremy resisted a crazy impulse to snap at the offending digit with his teeth. He shifted his vodka martini from his right hand to his left and looked around desperately for someone to rescue him. But the other study team members were locked in their own conversations here and there around the reception room.

Gwynn claimed that she had assembled some of the best names in historical research for her "Project Beaumont." Jeremy had never heard of any of them before, but that was hardly surprising. What was surprising was their behavior. He was used to bickering among accountants. The tax laws were ambiguous enough that one could honestly disagree over the validity of this practice or that; but he had always thought of history as a cut-and-dried subject. One presided over by a legion of Mr. Chips, stuffy and dignified. He had certainly not been prepared for arguments over the basic facts.

And he had mistakenly said as much to Herkimer Vane. *Help*, he thought. *I am being held prisoner by an historical philosopher*. Aloud, he said, "What do you mean, there is no such thing as an historical fact? What was it that they taught me in school, historical fiction?" He thought he had made a rather fine *bon mot* and almost sputtered his drink when Vane agreed.

"Yes, exactly."

"I beg your pardon? It was all lies? You can't be serious!"

Vane looked nonplussed. "Lies? Oh, no. I don't believe I said that."

Now Jeremy was totally confused. "Well, then . . ."

"I think you misapprehend the word 'Fact,' " he said, finger wagging once more. "You think of it as some sort of category of ultimate truth; but that is not the case. Oscar Wilde once said that the English were always degrading truths into facts. Like so many artistic people, he had intuited something vital."

Jeremy shook his head. "I don't see it. A fact is a fact. They are the building blocks on which everything else is erected. If you have no facts, you have no foundation."

"No, no, Mr. Collingwood." The finger wagged back and forth. "Your metaphor is faulty. You think there is such a thing as raw data. But no data is raw. It is always cooked."

Jeremy laughed involuntarily. "That's a good line, Professor; but what does it mean?"

"It means that there can be no facts without theory. Some notion of what sort of fact to look for in the first place; and some notion of what it might mean afterward."

"A fact means what it means. There it stands," Jeremy waved his arm in a somewhat grandiloquent manner. "There it stands, self-demonstrating."

"No, Mr. Collingwood. A 'Fact' is not a thing, a noun; it is the past tense of a verb. *Factum est.* A dynamic word, not a static one. *Facto*, I make. I create. 'Fact' was not used as a noun until the Late Middle Ages; and, when it was, it meant 'an accomplishment,' 'something done,' like the French *fait* or the Magyar *tény*. Or our English word *feat*. And 'Fact' retained that meaning of 'Feat' even in English until the early 1800s. When Jane Austen wrote 'gracious in fact, if not in word' what she meant was 'gracious in deeds, if not in word.' "

"That's semantics," Jeremy objected.

"Ah. Then, at least we agree on how important the issue is."

"I beg your pardon?"

"Semantics is the science of the meanings of words; and

254

words are how we communicate. What, then, can be more important than a matter of semantics?"

Jeremy opened his mouth to object, then thought better of it. Vane was right. Jeremy sipped his drink. The little historian was irritating but intriguing. The way he had explained it, 'A matter of semantics' was indeed a most serious matter. So why did the phrase have such negative connotations?

"Still," Jeremy said, "you can't deny that the word Fact is no longer used in that way."

"True." Vane appeared to be greatly saddened by the degradation of the language, but Jeremy suspected that was for show. "I prefer the word Event. Lukacs once said that 'Event' is a far lovelier word than 'Fact'. It is neither dry, definite, nor static; but suggests life, flow, and movement. 'Event compares to Fact,' he once wrote, 'as Love does to Sex.' "

Jeremy felt frustrated. He thought Vane was playing an elaborate word game with him, taunting him with forgotten derivations. "Events or Facts, I don't care. What has that to do with my being taught fiction in school?"

"No, no, no. Events are not Facts. Events are Facts in motion. Events have momentum; but Facts have only inertia. No Fact exists in isolation. It is always connected with other Facts. We cannot even think of a Fact without associating it with others. For example: we cannot state the height of Mount Everest without relating it to other mountains. We cannot measure the body's temperature without some thought as to what that temperature ought to be. Now, 'Fiction' comes from the Latin *fingere,* which means 'to construct.' A Fact cannot be separated from its associations—which are constructions of the mind. Thus, not only is *fictio* of a higher order than *factum;* but every Fact is in some sense a Fiction, a construction of associations. That is what I meant when I said you were taught historical Fictions. Every attempt to reconstruct history is exactly that, a re-*construction*, and therefore a Fiction."

Jeremy thought that Vane might have a point. 'Fiction' did not mean 'untrue.' In fact—and he chuckled to himself at his use of the phrase—in fact, one found a great deal of truth in fiction. He began to suspect that Vane phrased his statements in a deliberately provocative manner. That it was his way of getting his listeners' attention. The academic equivalent of a two-by-four.

"Herkimer! Are you pestering poor Jeremy?" Jeremy

breathed a sigh of relief as Gwynneth Llewellyn sailed between them like a tugboat separating two ships. She put her arm through Vane's elbow. "Have you met everyone yet, Herkimer?"

"No, wait, Gwynn," Jeremy said. "Professor Vale and I have been having an interesting—if rather peculiar—conversation. He claims there are no facts in history."

Llewellyn gave Vane an elfish grin. "Herkimer! Have you been teasing him? You've got to realize, Jeremy," she added over her shoulder, "that history isn't all cut-and-dried, like accounting. History is what we make it."

"*Historia facta est*," said Herkimer Vane solemnly.

Jeremy laughed and the two historians looked at him in puzzled amusement, not sure of his reason. Jeremy wasn't sure himself. It wasn't just that Vane had made a pun in Latin (at least, Jeremy thought he had) but that he himself had earlier compared the ambiguities of accounting to the certainties of history, and now here they were making precisely the opposite comparison. *I suppose that one's own profession always appears more nuanced than the other person's. Your job is simple and straightforward; but my job is complex and difficult.*

"Well, fun is fun," he said. "But it all amounts to word games. You are debating 'What is a Fact?' rather than 'Are There Facts?'"

Vane pursed his lips and appeared to give the matter some thought. "Perhaps. Why not do as the scientists do and try an experiment? Let us take a Fact. Something as numbingly basic as simple chronology . . ."

"Now, wait, I realize that sometimes the exact date of an event is unknown—"

"Oh, no, Mr. Collingwood. I would not pull a stunt as vulgar as that. That a Fact has not yet been discovered is no proof that it does not exist. Let us take a Fact whose existence is allegedly indisputable. Tell me when and where the Second World War began. I don't mean anything as subtle as the roots of the war. They go back into the Middle Ages. I mean the actual hostilities."

Jeremy hesitated. Start talking with a professor and, sooner or later, you'd get a pop quiz. "I guess it started in, what? 1939? Germany attacked Poland."

"In September," finished Vane. "So you say. But might it not have started in Belgium in the summer of 1701?"

"What?"

"Certainly," said Vane complacently, "The French and the British fought four world wars between 1689 and 1763. The last one, variously called the Seven Years' War or the French and Indian War, was fought in India, as well as in Europe and North America. Surely, considering the geographical scope of the Great Wars for Empire, they deserve to be called world wars."

Jeremy sputtered. "That was a trick question!" he protested. He looked to Gwynn for support, but she was chuckling.

"The eternal student mind," she said. "You always think that the answers are more important than the questions. Don't you see? If words are anything more than labels, they must *mean* something? Just what do we mean by the label 'Second World War'? There are a host of preconceptions built into those three little words. Was it truly the Second? Perhaps it was only the continuation of the First? Some scholars contend that it should be called the Second German War. But, as Herkimer pointed out, there is the implicit assumption that world wars are a twentieth-century phenomenon. If it makes you think about all these things, why is it so reprehensible that it was a 'trick' question?"

"Because one usually must trick a student into thinking, I suppose," said Herkimer Vane. "But I'm afraid the question is even trickier, Gwynn, dear. I could argue that the 'Second World War' was never *a* world war at all, but two separate regional conflicts, the European and the Pacific, that happened to share a few combatants. After all, Germany and Japan never had a joint strategy and, while Hitler loyally honored his treaty with Japan and declared war on the USA, Japan did not reciprocate and declare war on the Soviets. There is an interesting contrafactual speculation that, if Hitler had kept his mouth shut, the USA would have gone off fighting into the Pacific and ignored the European war altogether. However, leaving such issues aside, we can legitimately ask whether the world war began in Manchuria in September, 1931; or in Hawaii in December, 1941. Surely those dates are as valid as the Eurocentric one you gave."

Jeremy started to answer, hesitated, then said, "Very well, Professor. I see your point. There was a European war and a Pacific war. Each one had a starting date and place. And you could argue that the *world* war, per se, didn't start until the Japanese attack on the American and British colonies involved those countries in both conflicts. But surely that does not invalidate the idea of historical facts. That only means we must define our facts more accurately."

Vale shrugged. "As I said earlier, the value of facts depends more on their relationships than on their accuracy. Perhaps it is more important to ponder whether there were two wars or one than it is to choose one answer over the other. Perhaps both answers are true in some sense. Now, understand, I am not saying that accuracy is unimportant. But I am saying that the more 'accurate' a fact is, the less *truthful* it may be. For example, I might say that the population of Denver on April 1, 1999 was—oh, let's say 657,232, to invent a number. That would be accurate. But if I were to say instead that 'Denver's population in early 1999 was between 650,000 and 660,000,' I would be more *truthful*, even though less accurate. Because the latter statement is a dynamic one, and the truth is always dynamical and relational. Who was or was not a resident of Denver at a particular moment is an abstraction, and a static one at that. What does 'the population of Denver' mean? People are constantly moving in and moving out. Does it include the hoboes down by your train station? The tourists in the hotels? Does it include the college students and business executives who are here for a few years and then gone? What of those who have two residences, one in Denver and one elsewhere? When you take motion into account, it is impossible to fix with any certainty the absolute size of the city."

"Heisenberg's Uncertainty Principle of History," said Llewellyn.

"Eh?" Vane turned on her. "What do you mean by that?"

"Heisenberg said that the velocity of a particle makes its position indeterminate, and *vice versa*. If you were as familiar with John Lukacs' œvre as you claim to be, you would realize that his conscious purpose was to apply Heisenberg's insight to historical thinking."

"Oh, yes." Vane waved a hand in dismissal. "Though it wasn't only Heisenberg, you know. The same *Weltanshauung* was emerging everywhere in those decades. In the writings of Pasternak and Ortega, for example; or in Guardini or Hantsch. What was Impressionism but quantum theory applied to painting? Or *vice versa*! And remember what Lukacs said. You can always study science historically; but you cannot study history scientifically."

Llewellyn looked at him speculatively. "Isn't that what we are here to decide?"

"My dear woman," Vane said, patting her arm. "It is already decided. The notion of a clockwork history is long discredited. Buckle was wrong. Our task is to discover the flaws in what has been claimed. Meanwhile . . ." He shrugged and put his empty glass on the tray of a passing waiter. "Meanwhile, we may generate a few interesting papers out of our researches." He stretched his arms and glanced quickly at his watch. "Well, it has been stimulating talking with you, Mr. Collingwood. We must do it again, sometime. Meanwhile, my jet lag is catching up with me; so, if you don't mind, I'll find my way back to my hotel."

Jeremy watched him leave. "It's been nice talking to me," Jeremy told Gwynn. "He means it's been nice talking *at* me."

"Oh, don't be too harsh on him. Herkimer means well, but he just can't resist lecturing people. Even his colleagues."

"Was he serious? About that fact and fiction business, I mean." Jeremy finished his martini and looked around for a place to discard the glass. He didn't see a tray nearby so he held onto it.

"Certainly! I know it seems rather esoteric to laymen— Did I say something funny?"

"No. It's just that 'layman' means 'a non-accountant.'"

Llewellyn chuckled briefly. "Yes. Every in-group divides humanity into two sets: Hellenes and Barbarians; Jews and Gentiles; Gaels and Galls. We Professionals and you Laymen. But, as I was saying, Herkimer's deliberate use of *fictio* in place of *factum* really is making a valid Heisenbergian point. He is saying that you cannot observe history without the act of observation affecting what you see. That we 'construct' history by making associations of fact."

"Then how can anyone predict history? Two people may look at the same events and reconstruct them differently. So how do you know when a prediction has come true? Hell's bells! How do you even know what happened in the past?"

"That is precisely Herkimer's point."

"If he doesn't believe it is possible to study history scientifically, why did you invite him to be on your study group?"

Llewellyn gave him a peculiar look. "He insisted, actually. When the word got out that I was forming the group, he called me and asked to be on it. But that isn't the issue. None

259

of us really believe that some secret cabal has reduced history to science; let alone that they have been controlling it for the last hundred odd years. No, that is quite impossible."

"But—"

"Oh, I am equally convinced that there is a group that has *tried* to do so. They might even believe themselves successful. We plan to investigate the claims with an open mind. To discover what would motivate this so-called Babbage Society."

"Why, for example, would they kidnap people or try to kill them?" Jeremy said, more heatedly than he had intended.

"Oh. Yes, sorry. Your interest is more than academic. It's easy to forget that. I admit there is something sinister going on. But understand, the existence of such a secret society does not prove that their beliefs are anything more than self-delusions, no matter how ruthlessly they pursue them. It is all too easy to reconstruct events so as to convince yourself that your predictions were borne out."

He and Gwynn were the last to leave the reception. In a sense, they were the hosts. Jeremy even managed to enjoy himself, once Vane had gone. Most of the team members were personable enough: Geoff Hambleton. Henry Bandmeister. Penny Quick ("Oh, no. I love my name. I would never dream of changing it!") Except for a lamentable tendency to throw out casual references to Significant Thinkers that Jeremy had never heard of, their conversation was interesting. In fact, Jeremy had to admit to himself, the talk of historical minutiæ was made more interesting by Vane's previous remarks. Whatever the topic, Jeremy would wonder whether it were possible to reconstruct the facts in a totally different way; and *pace* Vane, whether one reconstruction might be more true than another. If it weren't that his thoughts would occasionally return to the central fact that Dennis was missing, he would have said he was having a good time. Sometimes, though, a part of him wanted to *scream!* We're wasting precious time!

But the horror of any situation is that we soon grow used to it. Jeremy didn't recall who had said that. A Significant Thinker, perhaps. But he found it impossible to dwell constantly on Dennis' plight. (Or was it his own plight that concerned him? Was it really Dennis' fate, or his own loss of Dennis?) Regardless, life goes on, and he was prepared now to take things as they came. The frenetic urgency was dulling. A sense of fatalism, perhaps; or of confidence?

When they left the reception room, he and Gwynn were stopped by a stranger. He was lounging in an overstuffed chair, one of several that dotted the vestibule, and, when he saw them coming out at last, he leapt to his feet. He was a short, thin, Oriental man in rolled-up shirt sleeves. He wore dark frame glasses that seemed a little large for his face, and he had a felt-tip pen stuck behind his ear. A notebook and additional pens bulged his shirt pocket.

"Dr. Llewellyn?" he asked.

Gwynn looked at him. "Yes, I'm Llewellyn."

"My name is Jim Tranh Doang, from the mathematics department. Could I have a few words with you."

Llewellyn looked at her watch. "It's late. Can it wait until tomorrow?"

Doang puckered his face, causing a small crease to grow between his brows. "I suppose so. But you're here now and I'm here now, and we'll both be walking to the parking lot. It would be silly to walk out together in silence."

Gwynn shot Jeremy a glance and he shrugged an answer back to her. "Very well, Mr. Doang. What is it you want?" And, taking him at his word, she set off at a brisk walk toward the stairwell. Both Jeremy and Tranh Doang had to scurry to keep up.

"It's Dr. Doang," suggested the Oriental. "I am associate professor of operations research."

"I'm sure it's a very interesting field."

Llewellyn had made a habit of using the stairs rather than the elevator. Good for the circulation, she had told Jeremy. And besides it's only a couple of floors. The few times Jeremy had used the elevator himself, he had always found Gwynn waiting for him when he reached his destination, so he had given it up. Waiting time, Gwynn had told him, is part of the travel time. Stairs were faster, for short trips, because you never had to wait for one to come along.

"I was hoping it would interest you, Dr. Llewellyn."

"Operations research interest me? Why?"

Jeremy followed behind the other two. Gwynn walked straight, not touching the handrail. She barely glanced at the mathematician. Doang hovered at her side, trying simultaneously to face her as he spoke and to watch where he was walking.

"Please! Dr. Llewellyn. You're going about this Beaumont thing all wrong!"

His voice echoed eerily in the empty stairwell. Llewellyn stopped dead on the landing and Doang nearly crashed into her. Jeremy bit his lip to keep from laughing.

Llewellyn stared at Doang. "I'm not sure it is any business of yours how I go about my research." The little man seemed taken aback by the hostility and he looked from Llewellyn to Jeremy and back.

"Let him talk, Gwynn," Jeremy said and Doang shot him an appreciative glance.

"Thank you." He took a moment to compose himself. Llewellyn waited impatiently.

"As I understand it, Doctor, you have assembled a team to study the information contained in the Beaumont Dump."

"That's no secret. Chicago and Stanford have done the same."

"Yes; and like them, your team includes only historians."

"It's a question of history, Dr. Doang. Of course, I have assembled a team of historians."

"But . . ." Doang glanced briefly at Jeremy. "From what I have heard, Beaumont claimed that this secret society she discovered used mathematical models to forecast the course of history. The Dump contained information on the structures of these models. Not much, perhaps. I heard that the Dump was terminated in midstride. I suppose the owners of the database had discovered what was happening and pulled their system off the Net. But this technical data: Who on your team is qualified to pass judgment on it?"

Llewellyn cocked her head and looked at the mathematician. Jeremy could see her tongue running around the inside of her cheek, a sure sign, he had learned, that she was thinking things through. "And you think you are competent to do so?"

"I could show you reprints of my research articles."

"Never mind. They would only be nonsense to me." She looked at Jeremy. "What do you think?"

"How can it hurt? We probably should investigate the methodology of this Society. Is it mathematically valid? That sort of thing. If the whole business is a forgery of some sort, then surely Dr. Doang will be able to expose the inadequacies of the mathematics."

"Hmm. The mathematics are inadequate *a priori*. It is simply not possible to reduce history to abstract numbers."

"Please, Dr. Llewellyn, there are even eminent historians who would disagree with you. But that is not my concern. I am interested only in the mathematics. Many researchers, men like Rashevsky and Hamblin, have sought to model socio-politico-economic phenomena. Some schools of economics have created quite elaborate systems for forecasting the economy."

"Forecasts which are generally wrong," Llewellyn commented dryly.

"Perhaps not as wrong as the public media would have us believe. Weather forecasts are made with uncanny accuracy; yet it is the occasional, dramatic error that people remember. It is easy to mock. And, even so, perhaps the economic forecasts are inadequate because they model only the economy and not the other social subsystems that impact it. This alleged secret society has been working on their models for over a hundred years. Time enough to have refined and elaborated them."

"*Alleged* society?" said Jeremy with an edge in his voice. Alleged? Perhaps, Beaumont had only allegedly been shot at. Grimes allegedly killed. Dennis allegedly hit by a car. "Surely where there is smoke, Dr. Doang, there is fire."

Doang looked at him. "No, Mr. Collingwood. Where there is smoke, there is smoke. It may be fire; or it may be dry ice sublimating. Or only a cloud. Now we must discover which. That is the scientific method."

"All right, Dr. Doang," said Llewellyn. "I suppose you have a point. Whether or not their models are valid is an issue we shall have to investigate. If they are not, then it may all be a hoax. Still, a hoax worth studying. And even if they are *mathematically* valid, they may or may not be *historically* valid. Very well, Dr. Doang—dammit, I hate formality. Should I call you Jim or Tranh?"

"Jim is fine."

"Does anybody ever call you 'Ding'?" asked Jeremy.

Doang looked at him. "Never twice," he said. He waved his hand through the air like a knife and cocked an eyebrow at him. Jeremy swallowed.

"I'm Jeremy."

"And you may call me Gwynn," said Llewellyn. "The team meets tomorrow morning in the history department conference room—"

"If it is all the same with you, I'd rather not attend your

meetings. My work can be pursued independently; and discussions of historical philosophy I would find as tiresome as you would find differential equations." Doang did not say that the two attitudes were equally justified and Jeremy suspected from the look on his face that he considered anyone who could be bored by differential equations to be an odd fish indeed. "And besides . . ." Doang hesitated.

"Besides?" prompted Llewellyn.

"According to the rumors, people who have gotten too close to this matter have turned up dead or missing. They may not regard your committee as a threat. Especially if your historians are inclined to disbelieve the very possibility of historical science—oh, yes, I eavesdropped on your little party—but I have a feeling that if they knew *real* scientists were involved, they would become quite upset."

Llewellyn twisted her lips. "Real scientists. You have a pretty high opinion of yourself, don't you?"

"Of course. Doesn't everyone? But that's not the issue. The issue is the logical strategy to take. It is elementary game theory. Whether I am right or wrong, my strategy minimizes the risks. To all of us."

Doang bowed slightly, shook their hands, and departed. Jeremy and Gwynn remained on the landing after he had gone. "Risk," repeated Llewellyn.

Jeremy pursed his lips. The party had been fun; but as Doang had reminded them, they were treading on dangerous ground. Whether the so-called Babbage Society had a valid science or not was of academic interest. Whether they were prepared to kill to protect it was rather more personal.

# IX

His caller, Kennison observed with some surprise, was Benedict Ruiz. Bettina ushered him into the office, then left, closing the door behind her.

"Brother Ruiz!" Kennison exclaimed, rising from behind the desk. "What on earth are you doing here? It's too dangerous for any of us to meet *in corpora*." And Ruiz knew that, so what was he doing here?

Ruiz planted his wiry body in the visitor's chair. He pulled a handkerchief from his breast pocket and began mopping his brow. With his left hand, he kept a firm grip on his malacca walking stick. Kennison could see his knuckles bulging, white and prominent, against the dark wood. "Then you haven't heard?"

"Heard what? Can I offer you anything to drink?" He reached for the buzzer to call Karin but Ruiz held up a restraining hand.

"No. Nothing, *amigo*. *Gracias*. I came—"

"Were you followed?"

Ruiz struck the floor with his stick. "Damn it, Brother Kennison! I am trying to warn you for your own safety! And, yes, I am no fool. I was not followed." Ruiz jutted his chin forward, daring Kennison to deny it.

Kennison sank slowly into the chair behind his desk. Something was wrong here. Ruiz was genuinely worried. Kennison leaned his elbows on the desk, clasped his hands into a ball. "Warn me," he repeated. "Why? What's happened?"

"Genevieve. Her car was bombed. She's dead."

Kennison jerked upright. A thrill ran through him. The

265

Great Harpy, dead? He hadn't expected Paige to move so quickly. "Do you know the details?"

"Details?" Ruiz waved an irritated hand. The handkerchief fluttered like a flag of surrender. "Why do we need details? The mob has the scent now. They will pick us off, one by one." He resumed his face-mopping. "*Santa Maria*, what have we gotten into?"

"You mean, what has the Weil family gotten us into?"

Ruiz looked up and then glanced warily around the room. Then he laughed in self-deprecation. "You see? Her ghost still controls us. We are still careful what is said about her."

There was no doubt, Kennison thought, that three generations of Weils had left an indelible stamp in how the Society thought. Their ideas had been impressed into the Society's meme complex, sometimes ruthlessly. And yet, hadn't he read somewhere that when Stalin died, the Russians had wept? Not, perhaps, from genuine sorrow or affection, but only because a large and permanent part of their lives was now gone. He wondered if he should feel something at this news other than sheer delight.

He tried to keep that out of his voice when he spoke. "Do you know how it happened?"

Ruiz nodded spastically. "Yes. Yes. Sister Paige had gone to see Madam Chairman. She—Sister Paige, that is—had conceived a plan to protect ourselves during these trying days. She had already been to see me about it. But Madam Chairman—I heard this from Judd, himself—Madam Chairman refused to see her. She told Judd she was going to take a drive along the Lake. The next thing Judd heard was a thud from the garage. The whole mansion shook. When he ran to check, he found Madam's favorite Mercedes in flames. The heat was intense—petrol fires are extremely hot, you know; but he saw his mistress . . ." Ruiz paused, swallowed. He looked at the floor, refusing to meet Kennison's eyes, and his walking stick traced random curves in the carpeting. "He saw his mistress, a blackened husk; hands melted to the wheel; head thrown back, her jaws wide in a scream that never came." He looked at Kennison and his eyes were like tunnels into an endless pit. "Those were his exact words. I shall never forget them."

Kennison shuddered, and it wasn't altogether theatrics. A gruesome death. Sister Paige was far too given to extremes, too ready to let emotions rule her. *A less dramatic end would*

266

*have served my purposes well enough.* Then he remembered that Sister Paige didn't give two figs for his purposes; that she had purposes of her own. He made a mental note to watch himself more carefully around her in the future. Alliances of convenience lasted only so long as they *were* convenient. Aloud he said, "Those were Judd's exact words?" Ruiz nodded and Kennison considered that. The old man must have had a great deal of buried hatred toward his mistress to have described her death with such loving detail. One never knew what lay beneath the surface. He wondered if perhaps Paige had subborned Judd into setting the bomb.

"Do they know who did it?" he asked Ruiz.

Ruiz responded with an elaborate Latin shrug. "Who? The CIA. The KGB. The Camorra. The Associates. The Republican Party. *¿Quien sabe?* The country is filled with people who might want revenge for what we have done."

"For what they believe we have done," Kennison corrected him.

Ruiz threw his arm out. "Do not bandy words with me, *señor,*" he said through stiff lips. "I am no child. That meme of innocence may do for the public; but what end does it serve to delude ourselves? We have been guiding the course of this nation of ours for our own enrichment; and we have treated ruthlessly anyone who stumbled into our way. Can you deny it?"

"That was Grosvenor Weil and his get—"

"And we were only following orders," Ruiz shot back. "We labored under duress, crying all the way to the bank." He laughed humorlessly. "I am afraid that will be a poor defense against charges of this magnitude. No, we shall all hang, separately or together. The American government will see us as subversives. Confederate irridentists, as the ones who destroyed their society. Cultural genocide, isn't that the word they use nowadays? The Blacks will see us as those who kept them from their birthright. The Greens, as the ones who encouraged the Dæmon Technology. Oh, the list of our enemies will be an ungodly long one."

"And no one will blame us for the good things that have happened," said Kennison wryly. "We are not responsible for every jot and tittle of history. Name a politician or social reformer; name a businessman or revolutionary who has not attempted what we have done. Our abilities, our vision even, were limited. We have had better success than most only because our methods were more effective."

"You are singing to the choir, Brother Kennison. Who will take the trouble to study the matter so? To think it through? We have enriched ourselves on the misery of others. That is all anyone will ever need to know."

"I never saw you refuse the fruits of our labor."

Ruiz shrugged again. "And I never said my own hands were clean." He held them up and turned them this way and that, as if he could see the blood, if he stared hard enough.

After a moment he sighed. "What will you do now? Will you follow Sister Paige's plan? That we put on a dumb show before the public? A Potemkin village?"

Kennison was momentarily angry that his plan had now become Paige's plan. But he kept a stong grip on his emotions. There would be a reckoning some day; but not now, not with Ruiz. He was only the messenger. And the reckoning, when it came, would be carefully planned, not the spin-off of a moment's pique. "Paige and I discussed it some weeks ago," he said. "I thought it a good idea."

Ruiz twisted his face. "Better to be slain in public than in private, eh, *amigo*? But not I." He shook his head. "Not I."

Kennison's eyes narrowed. "And what will you do, *señor*?"

Ruiz pursed his lips and studied the heavy and elaborate ring he wore on his left hand. "*Señor*," he said after a long moment. "My family has lived in this country for three hundred years. We were *rancheros* and frontiersmen in Arizona and New Mexico long before the Anglos came. Later, we supported the Americans, because the *caudillos* in Mexico City gave us nothing and our natural trade was with our fellow frontiersmen from the east. We even managed to hold most of our property during the Land Grant Wars, because our *vaqueros* were better gunfighters than those the Anglos hired. It is a lovely country. Lonely and barren; pocked with *mesas* and wild *cañons*. I have not been back there in far too long. I think maybe I shall leave the business and retire to my *rancho*."

Kennison shook his head. "You will be no safer on your ranch than Sister Weil was in her mansion."

Ruiz flashed teeth at him. "But I will, Dan." His use of the nickname startled Kennison. "I will. Because my name is not Benedict Ruiz. It never has been. You see, when I was recruited, I was not as sanguine about the security of The

Secret as the rest of you. My true name was never entered into our database, so it has not been revealed by Beaumont's sabotage." He spread his hands wide. "So, I am safe. I can return to my home and live out my days and . . ." His face darkened. ". . . and study my soul."

Kennison didn't know whether to be angered or delighted. On the one hand, there would be one less Councilor to oppose him. On the other hand, Ruiz would be beyond the discipline of the Society. As Quinn had been.

He wondered how many others had had the foresight of Brother Ruiz. A secret persona outside the database; and, in Ruiz's case, at least, his true persona. In a way, he would miss the old chicano. Such foresight was precisely what Kennison wanted on his Council.

Then he wondered: *if too many of us do disappear suddenly, like Ruiz, will that not appear significant to the suspicious public?*

"Benedict."

Ruiz had risen from his chair, preparatory to leaving. He paused. "Yes?"

"The ship is taking water, but it is not sinking yet. Most of us will stay and do what we can. For the safety of those of us who remain, there must be no question about the disappearance of 'Benedict Ruiz.' Do you understand me? 'Ruiz' must die, in public. You do owe that much to the brothers and sisters you are abandoning."

Ruiz stared at him a moment, then nibbled on his lower lip. He obviously did not care for the connotations of Kennison's speech. "Yes," he admitted grudgingly. "I suppose I do owe you that much. What would you suggest?"

Kennison thought quickly. Nothing too complex. The more complex the plan, the more likely it was to go wrong. "When you leave San Diego, go by yacht and fall overboard in the Pacific. Drown. Can you manage that?"

Ruiz thought about it and nodded. "Yes. I have my loyal retainers. Men whose roots are entwined with my own family. They can arrange things properly and later make their way home. I—"

He stopped abruptly and cocked his head. He took two quick steps to the door and jerked it open.

There was no one there.

"Who else is in this house?" he demanded, his voice abrupt.

"Only my staff. Why?"

"I thought I heard a sound outside the door. As of someone listening. Do you trust them? Your staff?"

Kennison nodded indignantly. "I trust them with my life."

Ruiz nodded and smiled, and not without a certain savagery. "You may have to, my Brother. You may have to."

"The Secret Six," said Norris Bosworth.

Red Malone raised an eyebrow and looked from SuperNerd to Walter Polovsky. He marked his place in his book with a forefinger. "Is he making sense?" he asked Walt.

Polovsky shrugged. "Let's take a walk."

Red snapped shut the book he was reading. "All right." He rose from the reading carrel and turned the book in to the librarian. Polovsky glanced at the title.

"Refreshing yourself on the by-laws, Brother Malone?"

"I like to reimmerse myself from time to time in the ancestral ooze from whence we sprang."

Polovsky snorted. They left the library, Bosworth tagging along behind, like a lost puppy. In the elevator, Red touched the button for the ground floor. As the elevator rose, Bosworth started to say something, but Red held up a hand to silence him.

Once they were outside, Polovsky chuckled. "You really don't think that Cam has the place bugged, do you?"

Red thrust his hands into his pants pockets. "Game theory."

They followed him across the yard toward the corral. "Game Theory?" asked Bosworth.

"Sure," said Red. "We have two choices: either we yack in there or we don't. If we don't, then it doesn't matter whether Cam's gone paranoid or not. If we do, it matters a great deal. So, which strategy has the least probability of failure?" He wondered if Walt would notice that he hadn't answered his question.

It was late afternoon. The sun blazed down on them from just above the peaks. Red judged another hour or so of daylight. They reached the corral. The three of them leaned on the top rail of the fence and Red pointed to the herd, as if they were talking about the horses. "All right. What have you found?"

"The kid's a real hacker," Polovsky said. "He can mouse better than anyone I know."

*Then you don't know Sarah well enough,* Red thought.

Aloud, he said, "Save the testimonials for the awards banquet. Just tell me the results."

"The Secret Six," repeated Bosworth.

Red looked at him, then at Polovsky. "All right, I'll bite. Who or what are the Secret Six?"

"We think they're our competitors," answered Polovsky.

Red nodded and rubbed the palms of his hands together. "The Third Force. That was fast work. How'd you tumble to them?"

Bosworth answered. "It was a question of identifying historical anomalies. Mr. . . . ah, Brother Polovsky set up the equations. The nodes and yokes . . . I'm not up on all the math yet."

"I pulled the history PERT from just before Babbage's day to the present," explained Polovsky. "The kid here ran the programs to flag the low-prob nodes. We cleared all the nodes that we know were generated by Us or Them. Say . . ." Polovsky seemed struck by a new thought. "We can't say Us and Them any more, can we? There are too many Thems."

"Never mind that, now," said Red. "Tell me about this Secret Six of yours."

"Well, we looked at the low-probs that were left over. We figured some of them were things They had done that we hadn't tumbled to before; and we figured some of them were just random chance. So we did a little digging into the ones that had the greatest leverage."

"Sherlock Holmes and Watson. What'd you find?"

"We found the Rev. Thomas Wentworth Higginson."

"Wonderful. Who the hell was he?"

"An abolitionist. He wrote letters advocating armed raids into the South for the purpose of rescuing slaves." Polovsky examined his fingernails. "The idea was to set up a guerilla army in the hills of western Virginia and swoop down on the plantations from time to time."

"He wrote the letters to John Brown," added Bosworth.

Red perked up. "Oho."

"Oho, indeed," said Polovsky. "It seems the Good Rev was either a member of, or a tool of, a group that called itself the Secret Six."

"There were six of them," said Bosworth. Red looked at him.

"No shit."

"The Six," continued Polovsky, "were a group of Northern

271

businessmen and professionals who were trying to end slavery. We can't pin down the membership precisely, but certain names keep cropping up: Jabez Hammond. Gerrit Smith. Lysander Spooner. Like Higginson, they seem to have been connected somehow to the Six."

"Lysander Spooner?"

Polovsky shrugged. "Could I make up a name like that? There's some evidence that they tried to get Douglass in on it. The Brown Raid, I mean."

"Stephen Douglass? Lincoln's rival?" That didn't make any sense.

"No, Frederick Douglass. He was a slave who escaped North and became a spokesman for the abolitionist movement. He had a lot of cachet with the white abolitionists because he could testify from his own experience. He was a gifted orator and writer. And the other Free Blacks . . ."

"All right. All right," said Red. "I know who you mean. Go on."

"Well, the Secret Six set up a meeting between Brown and Douglass. In Rochester, New York, I think it was. Brown tried to talk Douglass into going to Harper's Ferry with him, but Douglass said no. Later, Brown's apologists tried to make it look like Douglass was a coward. But that wasn't it. Douglass thought Brown was crazy clean through. A Charlie Manson type. He thought that Brown's plans would set the Cause back. It would generate sympathy for the slaveholders and make them more defensive, so they would resist even moderate plans for manumission. Douglass favored expanding the Underground Railway. Get more slaves to run away, rather than kidnap them. He thought it was important that a slave freed himself, the way he had."

"So, the Six were behind Brown." Red nodded. It made sense. That sort of clandestine maneuvering had been the Society's forté back then. Back before better methods and mass communication were developed. There had been a civil war when the equations had predicted no civil war. No one had ever found an error in those equations; and Quinn had looked God-awfully hard for one. Two groups working at cross purposes . . . no, not cross purposes, but with "cross methods"; that might explain it. An interaction effect. Each group ignorant of the other's machinations. And Brown had been a key figure; both in Kansas and at Harper's Ferry. And hadn't

Robert E. Lee led the marines who stormed the arsenal? Definitely, a low-probability, high-leverage node.

"Have you run a simulation yet, incorporating the Six into the equations?"

Polovsky looked at him. "Sure, I got nothing but spare time on my hands. Rewrite the whole Master Program."

"Okay, Walt. I understand." *I wonder when Sarah will be back. This would be right up her alley.*

"One odd thing," said Bosworth.

Red looked at him. SuperNerd's forehead was creased in a frown. "What is it?"

"Well, based on what we learned of their early activities, I tried to trace the Six up to the present. Factor analysis. You know. Well, they left a pretty clear track of historical anomalies up until about the 1890s. Then, nothing."

"They broke up?"

"There were still anomalies afterward that couldn't be accounted for. Again, some of it must be just random chance; but there seem to be at least two sets of tracks after that."

"Two sets," said Red.

"Right. If we define a set as being a group of anamolies directed toward a common purpose."

"That's pretty hard to determine," commented Polovsky. "Even when we knew—or thought we knew—who the players were, and had some idea of their motivations. The outcome of a node might not be what the player intended. Both the Society and the Associates have made miscalculations in the past."

"I know," said Bosworth. "There are a couple of nodes dealing with Winfield Scott and Robert E. Lee that don't seem to fit in with either the Society's goals or with what we figure were the Six's goals. They may have been 'misfires.' And Sarah told us about two nodes in Europe that we haven't decided on. The Six may have tried branching out overseas. But I'm pretty sure there are at least two definable sets of anomalies that are neither Ours nor Theirs. Plus a scattering of random singletons."

"Sounds like the Six broke up, too," Polovsky told Red.

"Except the second track didn't last long," Bosworth said. "It petered out around the turn of the century."

Red nodded. "I'm sure they weren't immune to Carson's Dilemma, either." *And neither are the Associates.* The realization hit him suddenly. *We're acting out the same play*

273

*ourselves*. The meme complex inherited from Quinn had weakened over the years. Now he was trying to impose his own memes on the Associates. It was a disturbing thought, in its way. Even though he knew better, it smacked of determinism: As if he was only a puppet of historical forces and had had no choice in forming his little band of rebels.

That was nonsense. The equations only said that it would happen; not who or how. Still, it was an unsettling vision. Like looking through a microscope and seeing yourself waving back.

"Hey!" said SuperNerd. "Who is that?"

He was pointing up the mountain. Red shaded his eyes against the setting sun and looked. There was a figure on the edge of the cliff up there, waving an arm semaphore fashion and shouting. Red squinted, trying to see more clearly. Then he smiled quietly to himself. "Sarah's back," he said.

"Why, Jeremy, whatever are you reading?"

Jeremy looked up from his book just as Gwynn slid into the seat opposite. He was nursing a gin-and-tonic in a booth in the Campus Lounge. A large morocco-bound volume lay open on the table before him, and several manila folders were stacked neatly to the side. Gwynn had her corncob pipe clenched firmly between her teeth—unlit, for which Jeremy was grateful. Penny Quick sat on the edge of the seat beside Gwynn. She smiled briefly. "Hello, Jerry."

He looked from one to the other. "Is the meeting over already?"

"Jeremy, it's ten o'clock." Gwynn lifted the book and looked at the spine. "Henry Thomas Buckle? Oh, my." She raised her eyebrows. "I'm afraid he is more than a little out of fashion these days. No one reads Buckle any more. That florid, old-fashioned style."

Jeremy shrugged. "Herkimer said something about him at the get-acquainted reception last month and it made me curious. Buckle was wrong, he said. Well, who the devil was Buckle; and what did he get wrong? It obviously touched on the purpose of the study team, or else Vane would never have mentioned it. So . . ." He waved vaguely at the books and notes. He felt oddly diffident, an amateur explaining himself to the pros. "So, I checked up on him through the university library."

Gwynn eyed the manila folders. "And doing a respectable bit of research, I see." She touched Quick on the elbow. "We'll make an historian out of Jerry, yet. You wait and see."

"Oh, don't let her do that to you, Jerry," Quick told him,

flapping her hand. "It's a terrible life. Your eyes go bad; and you don't get paid well; and your friends simply can *not* understand how you spend your time." Quick was a thin, fine-featured woman who bubbled when she spoke. Everything she said and did bespoke enthusiasm. Jeremy thought she made a nice contrast to the other academics.

The waiter came and took their orders. Gwynn settled her bulk into the fake-leather seat. "How long have you been here, Jerry? I'm surprised. You don't seem the least bit tipsy."

Jeremy pointed to his highball. "That's my first."

"Oh? Then, I'm surprised the waiter hasn't thrown you out."

"Ah! Not if you know the Secret. I tip him generously every half hour or so. He leaves me alone, and I can concentrate on my reading. The bustle doesn't distract me—You wouldn't believe some of the places I've conducted audits—and I don't feel as . . . isolated here as I would in my apartment. *Besides,* he added to himself, *I try to be careful what I do in my apartment these days.*

Gwynn had advised him to leave the telephone bug untouched, but to say nothing aloud in the apartment that might interest anyone. Removing the bug would only alert whoever had planted it that they were on to him.

The waiter brought the women their drinks. "And what has your research told you about Buckle?" asked Quick. She had a pink, frothy concoction with an unlikely amount of fruit floating in it. Jeremy couldn't imagine drinking it.

"Well, he was certainly an original," he said. "Sickly. Educated at home by his mother. Then he spent fifteen years of his adult life living with her, escorting her around the continent. Nowadays, he would have been told to see an analyst."

"He was preparing his book," Gwynn said, tapping the volume on the table. *A History of Civilization in England.* Published in . . . 1857? Yes." She had turned to the title page. "It was 1857. Buckle was a typical nineteenth-century historian. He saw history as the story of Progress, from primitive beginnings to the very Pinnacle of Civilization; which, of course, meant nineteenth century England. Buckle was like most Victorians; he was a great believer in Progress." Gwynn and Quick traded knowing smiles.

*Sure, it's considered a naive attitude nowadays,* Jeremy thought. No one believes in progress anymore. Certainly not Progress-with-a-capital-P. People are more likely to deride it.

276

He wondered if people had grown wiser over the years, or only disillusioned. Why was cynicism considered a more valid outlook than optimism? Literature was like that, too. If the writing wasn't properly "ironic" it wasn't "literature." Occasional fire fights broke out in the New York Review of Books over the issue; but the Establishment was still firmly in control. Realism? But sometimes, Jeremy told himself fiercely, the hero does win.

"Did you also know," he said tartly, "that Buckle was convinced that history could be made into a science." He opened one of his manila folders and pulled out a photocopy. "Listen to what he wrote in 1856:

> 'In regard to nature, events apparently the most ir-
> regular and capricious have been explained, and have
> been shown to be in accordance with certain fixed and
> universal laws. This has been done because men of
> ability and, above all, men of patient, untiring thought,
> have studied natural events with the view of discover-
> ing their regularity: and if human events were sub-
> jected to a similar treatment, we have every right to
> expect similar results.' "

He looked to see their reaction; but all he saw was polite interest. He must have looked crestfallen, because Gwynn reached out and squeezed his arm. "Oh, don't be upset, Jeremy. It's only that we've heard that quote before. Buckle may be out of fashion, but he is not entirely forgotten."

"And besides," added Quick, "he was wrong. Don't you see? History can't have 'laws' like the physical sciences. History is evolutionary, like biology. Each event is dependent on what went before."

"There are laws in biology, too," Jeremy objected.

"Oh, yes; but they are different kinds of laws. Certainly you have the Theory of Evolution; but that isn't like the Theory of Gravitation. Astronomers can take their theory and calculate the future positions of the planets; but biologists cannot calculate what future species will evolve."

*Not yet, anyway.* It was a mental reservation. Jeremy was an accountant. He tried not to make categorical judgements until he had the figures in hand; and he certainly was not going to get sidetracked by Penny into a discussion in an area where they were both ignorant. But someone had told him once . . . When was it? At a party he and Dennis had gone to last year. Something about making a complete genetic map of each species. The Pan-Genome Project? *When we know what each gene does*, the young fellow had said, *we'll know what can happen when it's mutated.*

"You think I've been wasting my time, don't you?" he said, looking from Quick to Gwynn and back. "Why bother plowing through this turgid tome—" He picked up the book and let it drop"—when I could have just asked you to explain Herkimer's remark."

Quick reached out and touched his arm. "Oh, no, Jerry. I think you did splendidly. The whole idea of education is to discover things on your own. What kind of world would we have if everyone simply waited to be told things?"

"Too many people in the Managed Society do," said Gwynn.

Jeremy pulled his arm away. He flushed. She was right, of course. Still, it was a letdown to find that what you had discovered was already well-known. Like reaching the top of Mount Everest and finding a lemonade stand. No matter what they told him, they could not possibly think he had accomplished anything worthwhile.

"Cheer up, Jeremy," said Gwynn. "There are very few laymen who have ever even heard of Buckle."

"It's just that we've gone beyond that naive nineteenth-century view of history," Quick added. She flashed a smile at him. "I suppose that could be called Progress."

"Look," he said, "I know Herkimer dismissed the whole notion—a clockwork history, he called it. But isn't that the very axiom upon which the Babbage Society was founded? We should be interested in it. Regardless of whether it is correct or not." He added that last comment, because if he had not, Gwynn or Penny would have added it for him. For himself, he wasn't sure if he believed it was possible to reduce history to science. It wasn't a matter that concerned him a great deal. What did concern him was that the Babbage people believed it and that they had kidnapped Dennis to keep it secret. That was the central fact. Dennis. Everything else was academic nit-picking.

He gestured at the book. "Well, Buckle thought otherwise; and he was once a respected historian. Maybe you 'moderns' like to sneer at Victorian optimism. But maybe in the future others will sneer at your pessimism. Besides, Buckle wasn't

278

the only person who believed in the possibility of a social science. There was Adolphe Quetelet, too."

This time he received puzzled stares. "Who?"

Jeremy was secretly pleased that he had found something new that he could spring on them. He tried to keep his smile from becoming too broad. "Adolphe Quetelet was a rather famous Belgian astonomer," he told them. "A contemporary of Buckle's."

"An astronomer," said Gwynn.

"Oh. Well," said Quick.

"Yes, an astronomer. Intellectual categories weren't so neatly packaged and segregated back then. Perhaps that's something we could relearn from the Victorians. Quetelet and Buckle exchanged an extensive correspondence."

Quick looked at Gwynn. "I never heard that; but Buckle isn't my specialty."

"I was reading a collection of Buckle's letters," Jerry said. "It was in the University's rare book collection . . ." (A musty, tattered volume, half-falling apart, with ragged page edges and a sharp, dry odor. He had been required to read it in a special, climate-controlled room, under the stern and suspicious supervision of the Rare Volumes archivist. It had made him feel like a genuine Researcher. The archivist had seemed affronted that anyone would actually touch his precious volumes.) "Several of Buckle's letters referred in passing to 'my correspondences with M. Quetelet.'"

Gwynn traded glances with Quick. She took the pipe out of her mouth. "Why would Henry Thomas Buckle be writing to an astronomer?"

"I'll bet Buckle traded letters with Darwin, too," Quick said. "He was only a little younger than Darwin, I think." She turned. "Am I right, Jerry? Sure! I bet Buckle was really interested in Darwin's evolutionary theories. They were all the intellectual rage at the time." She leaned toward him across the table. "This sounds interesting. Tell us more. I never even knew Buckle's letters were ever collected."

It suddenly occurred to Jeremy that Penny Quick was trying to 'put the moves' on him. She might as well hang a sign out that said *I want you to impress me*. For a moment, he was flustered. He never knew what to do in situations like this. He thought of explaining that there was no point to her efforts; but that would cause embarrassment all the way around. On the other hand, to ignore her amounted to a put-down.

She really was quite charming, he supposed. At least, she met all the criteria that the media put forth for attractiveness. Still, for Jeremy, they were the "wrong specs." It was not that Penny left him cold; but that she affected him not at all. Still, she was a nice person and he did not want to hurt or embarrass her.

"Well," he said quickly, "I was intrigued, too. Because none of the Quetelet letters were in the collection. The editor explained in a footnote that none of them had survived, in either man's estate."

It occurred to him suddenly that he was doing precisely what Dennis had been doing in the days before his accident. Reading history. He had remarked to Dennis at the time that the sudden interest in history was unlike him. He saw now that it had been a condescending remark; not intended to hurt, but hurtful nonetheless. Now, somehow, by engaging in the same activity, he felt closer to him, even though his friend had vanished and might very well be dead.

Dead. He could think about Dennis calmly now. The frantic urgency, the kaleidoscopic need to Do Something, was gone; although at times he wished he could conjure it anew. Nothing the Study Team had done so far seemed helpful as far as locating Dennis went; and his present acquiescence to the status quo seemed almost shameful. As if he should be shouting from the rooftops or combing the back alleys of Denver. "High strung" some of his friends used to call him. Well, maybe so. Maybe he had always reacted in that "hyper," overwrought way. Perhaps he was only now learning to deal with crises differently. Gwynn, with her careful, plodding approach to life, had had a great calming effect on him. Maybe she could advise him on how to handle Penny.

He sorted through the meticulously labelled folders stacked on the table and found the one with Quetelet's name on it. He opened it and paged through the magazine articles, newspaper stories, and encyclopedia entries that he had copied. There were not many; Quetelet was hardly a household name. He chose an item from the *New York Review of Books* and passed it to Penny.

"This essay is concerned with the history of statistics, rather than with Quetelet himself," he told her. "but I've underlined the relevant passages." Penny nodded and ran her finger down the page, looking for the promised mention of the astronomer's name.

> " . . . Quetelet showed that variations in human heights conformed to this law of errors, and it was his perception of the wider applicability of the error law that provided the inspiration for the important work in statistics done in the late 19th century. His lasting contribution to science was to establish the concept of a statistical law—the notion that true facts about a mass can be discovered even when information about the constituent individuals is unattainable . . ."

She looked up. "This is marvelous. I always wondered who to blame for having to take stats in sociology. But who are . . ." She looked again at the article. " . . . Maxwell and Boltzmann?"

"I looked them up, too. They were scientists who applied Quetelet's concept of statistical laws to physics. But keep reading." He tried to keep from squirming in his seat from eagerness.

Penny smiled at him and read another passage.

> " . . . Beginning in the second quarter of that century, the collection of data became a wide-ranging enterprise. The motivation was often reformist; it rested on the belief that statistics would make it possible to erect a scientific basis for a progressive social policy. Adolphe Quetelet shared the concerns of the reformers but believed that more than just facts were needed. His aim was to erect a numerical social science that would bring order to social chaos . . ."

Jeremy spread his hands. "There. You see? There were quite a few people in those days who were considering the possibility of a social science. According to the Encyclopedia Brittanica, Quetelet studied the 'numerical constancy of voluntary acts.' Like crime." He showed them the copy of the biographical article. "That led to a lot of work in what they called 'moral statistics' and to a wide discussion of free will versus social determinism in human behavior."

Gwynn took the pipe from her mouth. "I should imagine," she said.

"Quetelet even wrote a book on the subject, entitled *Physique Sociale*, in 1835. No wonder he and Buckle corresponded so avidly. They shared the same vision. Too bad that none of their letters survived. The study team would probably have found them provocative."

"Provocative," said Gwynn, "is not the word for it." She looked at Quick and smiled wickedly. "Let's do tell Herkimer all about it at tomorrow's meeting."

"You tell him, Gwynn, dear. I'll hide under the table."

It was not until later that evening, as Jeremy prepared for bed, that he felt a prickling in his scalp.

Was it simply ill-luck that had lost the Buckle-Quetelet letters; or had it been something more? He paused with his pajamas half-on. In his mind's eye, he saw a mysterious, shadowy figure ripping apart the carefully tied bundles of letters and throwing them into a raging fire. He thought of Buckle dying so unexpectedly in Damascus. The young man had always been of frail health, but could it be . . . ?

He remembered Dennis flying through the air; the gunman who had shot at Beaumont; the dead reporter—what was his name? That Brady Quinn fellow he had read about in the printout. The Babbage Society killed those who drew near their Secret. Buckle had been a somewhat younger contemporary of Quinn's, hadn't he? Could Buckle have been poisoned?

He tossed the pajama top on the bed and strode to the living room, where he had left his materials. He fumbled with the clasps on his briefcase and then pulled forth a printout that Henry Bandmeister had compiled: An index to people, places, and things mentioned in the Beaumont Dump. He sat in the chesterfield with the printout in his lap. He flipped through the pages, looking for the B's; then he jumped further back, to the Q's. Finally he sighed and laid the sheets on his lap.

No, it was silly. A coincidence. Neither Buckle nor Quetelet were referenced in the Beaumont Dump. That was hardly surprising. In those days, Europe and the Americas had been separate worlds. Buckle had travelled extensively with his mother, but his travels had been confined to Europe and the Near East. There was nothing to indicate that he had ever been in contact with the Babbage Society; or even that the Babbage Society was aware of him. Or of Quetelet. No, the idea of a cultural science was simply "in the air" during the mid-nineteenth century. It was no surprise that several scholars had speculated about it.

Still, the prickling in his scalp would not go away.

# XI

It was a lot like falling off a cliff. Once the initial choice was made, everything else followed quickly and inevitably. The operation was performed like all Associate operations; quickly and quietly and with a minimum of disturbance. The surgeon that flew in made his suggestions and Sarah made her choices; and she came out of it with her head swathed in bandages, still wondering if she had made the right choice.

For several weeks she lay in the clinic bed on the lowest level of the underground warren; and SuperNerd and Tex and even Janie Hatch stopped by from time to time to see how she was doing. She told them she was doing fine and she couldn't wait for the bandages to come off and she didn't ask them where anyone else might be and why they hadn't stopped in.

After what seemed like an endless wait, the bandages did come off.

And then the real work began.

Sarah tried to avoid looking in mirrors. It became almost a habit with her since they had removed the bandages. When she walked down the hallway, past windows or other reflecting surfaces, she averted her eyes. When she washed up in the morning, she she would not look directly at her reflection. It wasn't that she was ugly or misshapen. Far from it. It was just that the woman in the mirror was a stranger.

She had studied her new face for a long time after the bandages had come off, turning the glass this way and that; trying to see it from all different angles. It was darker than her own had been. The brow seemed higher; the nose, a little

283

broader. Somehow, they had changed the shape of her mouth, so that her smile was wider than it had been. All in all, not a bad face. It would cause more than one head to turn. But, try as she might, she could see no sign of her mother in it.

Sarah closed the booklet she had been studying and leaned her elbows on the library table. She rubbed her face wearily. A long day. Too long. She glanced at the booklet, a three-ring binder with yellow cover. *The Life History of Gloria Bennett.*

*That's me now,* she thought. *Gloria Bennett.* She ran the name across her tongue to see how it tasted. Gloria Bennett.

She quickly suppressed the spasm of regret. It wasn't as if she had gone into it with her eyes closed. She had thought about it long and hard. She had agonized over it in her mountain retreat. She had made her decision, dammit, and there wasn't any point in dwelling on might-have-been's.

The left side of her brain kept telling her that. Really, it was the best choice—the only choice!—she could have made. And, regardless of how she felt, there was no turning back the clock. The left brain arguments were logical, reasoned arguments. But sometimes she was in her right mind and couldn't help glancing back a little wistfully at who she had been, and wishing that none of this had ever happened.

Well, if wishes were horses, beggars would ride.

At least, she was Gloria Bennett only when she was Outside. She had insisted on that before agreeing. Among the Associates, with Red and the others, she could still be Sarah Beaumont. A scrap of her old life that she could hold onto, like the ragged remnant of an old security blanket. She wondered now whether that had been an unspoken factor in her decision to join the Associates. The realization that the only way to retain a fragment of her old life was to live it here, in a Society she detested.

She picked up the booklet and gazed at its cover. The Associates were certainly thorough when it came to setting up false identities. She had to grant them that. There was nothing flimsy about the persona they had given her. Gloria had been a real person. She had had a real life; and people had really known her. But she wouldn't mind that Sarah would be using her name; because five years ago, in a light plane crash in the Canadian Rockies, Gloria Bennett had ceased to care about anything at all.

The accident had been a stroke of luck for the Associates, if not for the passengers in the Cessna. A chance combination of circumstances had enabled the Associates to co-opt the identities of all three people aboard and "bank" them as personæ for themselves. The crash had occurred in a remote area of British Columbia, and it had so happened that the area ATC was an Associate. She had managed to delete all traces of the accident from air traffic control records; and three other Associates had "completed" the ill-fated flight. Then they had "quit" their jobs at home and "moved" to remote areas, where old friends were unlikely ever to look them up.

There was a cruelty in that; that abrupt and unexplained severing of old ties with family and friends. It cast people adrift, loved ones who wondered why they had been left behind. It left voids in dozens of aching hearts that could not be properly filled with mourning, and remained as abcesses of inchoate resentment. It was kinder by far to let a person know she had been widowed than to let her believe herself abandoned. But, Sarah had grown used to—without accepting—the offhand callousness that marked the Associates' activities. When one is accustomed to the abstractions of meta-history, what do the lives of a few individuals matter?

Sarah had been concerned that someday she might run into one of Gloria's old acquaintances, but Tex Bodean had visited her in the clinic and told her not to worry. Those who had known the original Gloria well enough to matter had been out of touch with her for many years; and the plastic surgery had made the resemblance as close as was physically possible. Others had worn the Gloria persona for short periods; but they had made no close friends and, to casual acquaintances, would have looked much alike. The briefing booklet contained the details on all such contacts.

In one way, that was good news. It meant that she was unlikely to be unmasked by accident. In another way, though, it saddened her. If Gloria had been a person rather than a phantom, she would have been an intensely lonely woman, with no close friends and no ties to her family. It was necessary that it be so. To maintain the charade among close relatives and childhood companions would have been impossible. Yet, it seemed as if the persona they had given her was all too close to the life she had been living before. Putting on Gloria was like pulling on a worn and familiar dress. It was comfortable and it fit very well. But she noticed now how faded and drab it was.

She wondered if her prior life hadn't been something of a persona as well. A mask that she had put on for other people to see. A mask that she had put on even for herself.

The good news was that Gloria was rich.

She hadn't believed it when they told her, but she had hacked into the data bases herself and verified it. As "Gloria," she had enough money squirrelled away in various caches to support herself comfortably for the rest of her life. The Associates could well afford it. They were so wealthy that generosity meant nothing.

She remembered what Morgan had written in his notes: "They bought Xerox before it became a verb." For a hundred years the Associates, knowing which way the wind was about to blow, had trimmed their sails to catch it. Not that their forecasting was perfect. Far from it. The wind shifted frequently, for random or unknown reasons. The Associates had invested heavily in steam automobiles, for example. But, even a modest edge over the rest of the world had accumulated into a handsome return over the course of a century.

She wondered momentarily what was happening on the Outside, in the world beyond the walls of the safe house. She had been starved for information ever since coming here. She was Alice-down-the-rabbit-hole, living in an unreal world full of bizarre events; and every day she spent here was another day further removed from the life she had known.

Perhaps that was deliberate on the part of the Associates. A brainwashing tactic; so that, when she finally did emerge from this underground womb, she would be reborn, almost literally, as Gloria Bennett.

She rose from the table and walked idly around the library, stretching her back and arm muscles. She felt cramped from sitting at the table all day. As she walked, she glanced at the titles on the shelves. Sometimes pulling a book out and leafing through it. She was tired of studying Gloria every day. Tired of sleeping with earphones on. It was impossible to sleep that way and awake fully rested.

The library had an extensive selection of books on anthropology, systems engineering, statistics, psychology, economics, topology. All the topics that a good cultural engineer needed to master. Most of them, she saw, had been written and privately printed, by and for the Associates. She also knew, because she had asked, that the real library was much larger than this, with most of the "books" being in hypertext.

Hypertext was the coming thing. "Real twenty-first-century stuff," Tex had assured her. Still, there was something undefinably comforting about the smell of old paper and ink, about the heft of a morocco-bound volume in the hand. Some chord that had been engrained into human society since the first Egyptian brushed berry juice on papyrus. Without these rows of books, it just wouldn't have felt like a library.

Science fiction?

She paused at a short shelf of books and booklets and ran her fingers across the spines. Science fiction, the shelf label admitted. She read the titles. *Foundation. No Truce with Kings. The Squares of the City. Doomsday's Color Press.* Some of them were novels. Some were shorter fiction, privately copied and bound, in blatant disregard of the copyright laws.

Now why would the Associates enshrine a modest little collection of sci-fi, she wondered? She knew some of the stories, and browsed through a couple that she didn't. Then she chuckled to herself. Of course. All of them involved some attempt to direct or control the course of history. Psychohistory. Subliminal persuasion. The Great Science. The Kiersten Equations.

Evidently, no one else had ever thought to call it cliology.

She made a mental note to read the stories sometime and continued her slow circuit of the shelves. The librarian, a 250-pound man with a Mongolian scalplock, watched her without interest. He was cataloguing files intermittently, not a task that required his full attention. Sarah wondered what role he played on the Outside. The Associates tried to position their people at the critical nodes of the communications net, but this man looked more like a biker with a stomach ache than an opinion-shaper. Well, it took all kinds.

She came to a set of thin volumes on the upper left-hand shelf against the back wall. Their spines were too narrow for titles. She pulled one down and looked at the cover.

*Rules and By-Laws of Utopian Research Associates.*

The typing was crude; the letters, uneven, reminding Sarah of the old manual typewriters, with their dies at the tips of long, complex levers. It was signed in faded brown ink by Brady Quinn.

*Hello, Brady,* she thought. *Long time, no see.* Quinn was like an old friend now. She flipped the pages at random. *I*

287

*suppose I'll have to memorize these sometime.* She read a page.

---

Rule 24. "Associates making use of cliological data and projections for their own advantages must keep their brothers and the Council regularly apprised of their activities."

---

The entry was followed by a comment that it superceded Rule 4. There was a lengthy "Statement of Intent" and two amendments, one of which had, in 1887, changed "brothers" to "brothers and sisters."

*I suppose any organization must have its rules and by-laws.* But it seemed odd that people planning to control the world would bother with such commonplaces.

*I invoke Rule 19.*

Whoever had said that at the meeting she had overheard . . . When? A month ago? Whoever had said that had prompted a great deal of laughter, at her expense and Red's. Curious, she paged toward the front of the book.

The first item was Rule 21.

So where was Rule 19? Why would anyone start numbering their by-laws at 21?

Answer: They wouldn't.

"Excuse me," she called across to the librarian. The man looked at her and raised an eyebrow.

"Where can I find Rule 19?"

"Nineteen?" He scratched his double chin and ran his hand through his scalplock. "Say, aren't you Red Malone's friend? The one they just ran through a make-over?"

Make-over? Well, you could call it that. "Yes, I am."

The man grinned, as if at some secret joke. "I suppose Rule 19's pretty important to you, then."

"Are you going to tell me how to find it, or not?"

He flipped his hands out. "Don't get huffy. It's in Volume 1." He pointed vaguely toward the shelves where she was standing.

Naturally. Her ears burned. There were several other thinly bound folios where this one had sat. She pulled the others out, looking for Volume 1. *Correspondence of Jedediah*

*Crawford, Ph. D. Proposed Design and Construction of Babbage Analytical Engines. Constitution and By-Laws of the Babbage Analytical Society.*

Oh. Of course. When he had started his splinter group, Quinn must have kept most of the original rules. The second folio contained only the new ones.

She opened the volume and thumbed through it. This booklet, she saw, was much older, hand-written with a flat-nibbed pen in an elegant, curlicued script. That had been an era when penmanship was considered an art form, and a "good hand" was a mark of social distinction. The ink was brown, almost copper in color. The pages were brittle and cracked around the edges and smelled of more than a century of slow oxidation. The title page bore the signatures of J. Crawford, I. Shelton, and P. Hammondton. The Founders. She wondered what kind of men they had been.

She thumbed a few pages, noticed Rule 4, the one that had been superceded by Rule 24, and read it. *"Selflessness and the Common Good must be the Motivating Force of all Brothers."* The rule forbade members from using their researches for personal gain. She remembered Red telling her that this rule had been the original Society's undoing. That it went against human nature.

(*"Selfishness isn't human nature,"* she had protested to Red. *"No,"* he had answered with that irritating grin of his, *"but self interest is."*)

She wondered why Red had not come to see her during her convalescence. She had expected him; waited each day to see if he would show; but he hadn't. Was he out on an "op"? She hadn't seen him at all since the day she had returned from the mountains and told him of her decision to join. She had gone directly into the clinic the next day, before she could have second thoughts, and she had not seen him since. Perhaps, once her decision had finally been made, his task was done. Perhaps she had only been an "op" herself.

Brusquely, she turned her attention back to the book.

The three Founders had been sincerely altruistic; but their altruism was diluted in communicating it to new recruits; and diluted still further when the recruits recruited others. By the 1870s, the Society had become composed largely of men who considered their own, private interests to be at least as important as those of the Founders. And so much for Rule 4.

So, where was Rule 19? If Quinn had started with #21,

then #19 must be near the end of this volume. She turned the aged pages carefully. Yes, there it was. She read:

> "*Rule 19. In order to Assure that Our Brothers have a Vested Interest in the Felicitous Nature of future Social Conditions, it is Imperative that each Brother marry and sire Children, for Whose Well-being and Upkeep he assumes Full Responsibility.*"

She snapped the book shut. A sound behind her made her turn in time to see the librarian swallow a smile. She felt her face flush, but she kept a stony look on it until the librarian coughed self-consciously and returned to his cataloguing.

Sarah opened the book again and re-read the rule. Son of a bitch. No wonder those bastards had laughed so hard. She and Red? Nonsense. It was absurd!

She closed the folio carefully and replaced it. Returning to her reading table, she gathered up her things and walked out. The librarian watched her go, still trying to grin without being obvious. "Have fun," he said.

She didn't answer him. She wanted to slam the door instead; but it was one of those swinging doors that went both ways, so all it did was swish.

She turned and stalked down the hall. Male chauvinists, all of them. Even Janie Hatch and the other women she had noticed in that meeting. Sarah supposed that Red was under some peer pressure to fulfill Rule 19. One of the amendments had specified a time limit, and he might be approaching it. But that gave them no right to discuss her as if she were nothing more than a breeding cow!

Or, for that matter, as if Red were nothing but a stud bull. *Dammit!*

She had turned the wrong way down the hall. She was in a section of the underground warren she did not recognize. The walls were painted a muted pink, with green macro-designs in abstract geometric shapes. The plants situated here and there were artificial, but they lent an air of spaciousness to the corridor. Doors opened onto offices, some empty, some with people in them doing incomprehensible things. Farther along

290

she saw a canteen with three people sitting around a table drinking coffee from a vending machine.

An office complex, no different than thousands of other corporate offices anywhere in the world, except it was underground. But, what the hell, running the world was big business, wasn't it?

She decided to continue the way she was going. Sooner or later she would find an elevator bank or a manlift to take her to her own level. Meanwhile, she liked exploring.

The hall ended in a T-intersection and she flipped a mental coin and turned left. She wandered into a game room with chessboards and go-boards, some of them laid out in mid-game. One board had a sign: "Black's Move—Anyone Can Play." She glanced at the reverse side and saw that it announced White's move. She studied the board for a moment or two and saw that Black was engaged in a classic Philidor Defense. Not a very good position for Black. Well, that made it more interesting. She reached out and played P to KB5. She turned the sign around. Two women were musing over a complex gambit at another table. One of them was smiling, one frowning. They saw her and the smiling one waved absently. Her opponent scowled at the distraction.

She left the game room and resumed her explorations. She knew the Safe House was not nearly as big as it seemed. But there were so many levels and corridors and doublings back that, walking around inside, it seemed vast. That was intentional. This facility and the four others spotted around the country had been designed to house necessary Associate operations. Tasks that had to be done—even secret cabals had filing and paperwork—yet done privately. Some of it, Sarah knew, occurred in anonymous offices in high-rise towers in every major city. Often, on secret floors accessible only by means of special elevators. "Admittance to Authorized Personnel Only." There was a reason why so many office buildings lacked a "thirteenth floor." But the sensitive work was done in hidden Safe Houses. People lived here for months at a time and a feeling of spaciousness was essential to their mental well-being.

She saw an elevator ahead, at the juncture of another T-intersection, and hurried toward it. As she did, she heard music: the faint, squeaking sound of a clarinet drifting down the other leg of the T. She paused and listened. It was the same piece she had heard in the orientation class a month ago: the solo part from *High Society*. Whoever the secret jazzman was, he had finally mastered the syncopations. The music scampered and danced.

She tracked the sound to a small room thirty feet down the corridor from the elevator. The door was slightly ajar and she peeked through it, to see a man sitting on a metal folding chair with his back partly toward the door. He was dressed casually, in jeans and T-shirt. The T-shirt was burgundy and read "My Brother's Bar" across the back. He had dark hair and a long nose; but his fingers were short and his overall build stocky. His face . . .

His face! She stepped into the room.

"Never sit with your back to the door," she said. "That's how they got Hickock."

The man started and turned and faced her. She studied his eyes.

"Red?" she asked haltingly. "You are Red Malone, aren't you?"

"Would it matter much if I told you I was Jimmy Caldero?"

"You *are* Red! What have you done?"

"You of all people should know. Hey! You better sit down before you fall down."

She slumped into a chair like the one Red was sitting in. There were similar chairs and music stands scattered about the room. The metal was hard and cold against her back. Red cocked his head, seemed to see something in her face, and turned away. He toyed with his clarinet. Keys and pads clicked like tiny hailstones.

Sarah couldn't stop staring at his face. It was subtly different from the one she had known—in the shape of the nose and the chin and the ears; but she could see the old Red in there, peering out through the eyes, like a prisoner from behind bars.

"Red. Why?" It was silly, she knew, but she felt as if she had lost an old friend. That was the problem with people. As soon as you really got to know someone, they cut out on you. They died; or they went on the road; or they changed into someone else.

"Why? Why do you think? Same reason as you. Same reason as two dozen others in the organization. You didn't imagine you were the only one whose identity needed changing, did you?"

"You never mentioned it."

"You had your own problems."

292

Sarah realized that she hadn't given the matter much thought at all. She had been so wrapped up in her own crisis, she hadn't realized that others might be having one, too. "It's different for you," she said. "You do it all the time."

Red rubbed his hand over his nose and chin. "Not this. My face aches as much as yours. Sure, I've changed names and backgrounds before. Who hasn't? But I always managed to keep my own mug. What do you think?" He turned profile. "Am I more handsome than before? I didn't think it was possible to improve on perfection, did you?"

"Red. I'm sorry. It was my fault."

Red shrugged. "Hey. You gotta do what you gotta do. I'm just glad Our system was better protected than Theirs. Nearly all of your Dump was from Society files. Kennison was inexcusably lax. If he worked for me I would have fired him. You didn't even touch my own personal system—" He broke off suddenly. "You know what I mean."

Sarah knew he was talking about the parasite system he and his cabal were running. Red had already told her that it had been off-line while her worm was running. A coincidence, but one that had saved their system. Sarah wondered what Cam Betancourt would have done had he seen Red's secret files among the printouts. What did the Associates do with subversives in their own ranks?

"So, what do you do now?"

"We got word that my old employers—"

"The CIA."

He looked annoyed. "No. Don't try to be too clever. I was with the DIA. Defense Intelligence Agency. Not as "Red Malone," but as . . . Well, that persona doesn't matter anymore." He rubbed a hand across his face again. "The fact is, someone in the Agency saw my cover in the infamous Beaumont Dump. We got the word, from one of our people still inside, that the Agency was investigating. They backtracked my cover identity until they blew it apart." He looked at his clarinet and his fingers worked a few keys. "Do you know how hard it is to get a false persona past those bastards in the first place?" He shrugged. "Well, I'm out of it now. They knew my old face, so I changed it. But we can't change fingerprints—not enough to fool that crowd, anyhow. So here I am . . ." He blew a scale on his instrument. "On vacation."

"Then, not everyone is treating the Dump as a hoax."

"No, not everyone. There are some folks out there whose

job it is to take every possibility seriously. Maybe too many folks."

"You don't sound bitter."

"Bitter? No. I get unemployment. I'm rich, don't forget. Oh, don't get me wrong. The Agency was fun. It was important work. We need pipelines into those restricted databases and I liked what I was doing in that niche. The fact that I would have disappeared into Leavenworth if they'd caught on only added a little tabasco to the sauce." He put the mouthpiece to his lips and licked the reed. "I think I'll miss the rummy games as much as anything. Still . . ." And he shrugged. "I'm just as happy to be out of it. Try something new. Maybe get back into Adjusting." He began a C-major scale.

"Or raise a family?" asked Sarah.

The clarinet squawked like a duck on high F. He put it down again and inspected the mouthpiece. "Chipped reed." He tightened the embrouchure. "You know about that, do you." It was a statement, not a question.

"Rule 19," she said.

Red grunted. "Yeah."

"Do you plan to, ah . . . comply with it?"

"I told you. I'm the wild and independent sort. Being tied down isn't my style." He cocked his head and looked at the ceiling. "I wonder if I have any bastards around the country. That might satisy 'em." He looked at her. "Rule 19 applies to you, too, you know. You're one of Our Sisters, now."

"Uh-huh. Barefoot and pregnant. That's me. The Utopian Research Baby Machine."

"Don't be cynical." He was silent for a moment. Then he said in a different tone of voice, "Tell me. If you were organizing a group of people to 'design a future,' how would you assure that they went about it carefully and responsibly?"

"Well, I'd try to recruit only people with a sense of responsibility to the community."

Red shook his head. "It won't work. How do you measure it? How do you your recruiters screen for it? How do you assure its continuance, generation after generation? No, the mechanism must be something simple, measurable, and automatic. Something that makes responsibility self-enforcing."

"Every Brother and Sister must have someone they love held hostage to the future," she quoted.

Red smiled with half his mouth. "Exactly. The Rule isn't about giving birth. It's about accepting responsibility, and maintaining constancy of purpose. So Quinn and Carson built self-interest into it. Not altruism. Never trust an altruist. He'll sell you down the river for the sake of a Higher Purpose. It's negative feedback that makes responsibility self-enforcing. Like requiring landlords to live in the buildings they rent; or manufacturers to place their intake pipes downstream from their effluent pipes; or airplane mechanics to fly in the planes they repair. See? Compliance is easy to confirm; and that compliance assures that the businessman or the landlord or the mechanic acts responsibly. No rights without responsibilities. Self-interest is the key. Altruism is like building a dam. It doesn't last. Sooner or later, the river of history bursts through, with catastrophic results. Self-interest goes with the flow, but harnesses it; makes it do work. The Founders believed that the best protection against haphazard tampering with the future was to give the tamperers a stake in the outcome. Something that would make them more thoughtful regarding their plans."

"It's a good theory," said Sarah, "but I can think of two flaws."

Red grunted. "Only two?"

"What stops members from just going through the motions? Pop a kid; pay for its rearing; but otherwise ignore it. I've known plenty of parents who never did more. And even if they do care, will they build the best possible future for everyone, or only for their own children?"

"I won't argue with you. It's not a perfect system. Nothing is perfect."

His smugness irritated her. She was talking with a stranger. "Some things are," she said.

"Oh? Name one."

"The trio section of the Maple Leaf Rag."

He looked momentarily perplexed, then he laughed. "All right." He nodded at the spinet sitting against the far wall. "Prove it."

"What . . ."

"Want me to twist your arm? Come on." He stood and tugged her off her seat.

Red evidently was willing to discuss any subject but Rule 19 and how it might apply to himself. She allowed him to sit her at the old upright, where she ran up and down a few tentative scales. Her fingers felt huge and clumsy. "It's been a long time," she protested. "I haven't had time for play, lately."

Red shook his head. "You should always leave time for play."

She started the rag, stumbled over a chord, and started over. She was tentative at first, unsure of herself; but she soon found the tempo. Ragtime, Joplin had said, must never be played too fast. Her left hand beat out the steady bass rhythm while her right played with the syncopations. A classical rag followed a set pattern: AABBACCD; but she played the first two themes without repeating so she could get into the trio sooner. She rolled into the dancing strains easily, leaping up and down the keyboard. There was a bittersweet triumph about Joplin's music. Something at the same time sad and grand; as if some secret victory had already been won. The *Maple Leaf* had been his crowning achievement. "The King of Rags," they had called it. Every note in it was exactly right.

When she had finished, for some odd reason, she felt better than she had felt in a very long time; as if a terrible burden had been lifted from her. Her fingers wandered into another light rag, remembering how these tunes had formed the backdrop to her childhood. "Do you want to try it with me?" she asked Red.

He shook his head. "I'm not that good."

"You were doing all right on *High Society*. I heard you from the hallway. That solo you were playing is a test piece for jazz clarinetists."

"It's not that," he told her. "Not the technical difficulty. It's the . . . the Ear, I suppose. I can't play what I hear; I have to read it. Memorize it." Incredibly, he blushed and looked away. "I play notes, not music."

"You say that like you're admitting to pederasty."

"Play some more, would you? I kind of like that old-time sound."

She let her hands drift into *Panama*, then into the *Oklahoma Rag*. The Okie had been written by a white man, one of the few who had really understood. She was aware of Red watching her the whole time. She thought that should have made her nervous, that concentrated attention of his; but it seemed the most natural thing in the world. She closed her eyes and let the music lift her and carry her along. If she didn't worry about it, her fingers found the right keys without trouble. It was like falling off a bicycle; you never forgot how.

But when she opened her eyes at the end and looked at

him, she saw that he was not watching her hands at all. She ducked her head and stared at the keys. "I'm out of practice," she told him again.

"No, don't apologize. You were very good. They have a little jazz group here, you know. I play with them whenever I'm around. Chicago-style; a little Dixieland. Why don't you join? I think it'd be a good thing."

She turned her head and searched his face. The strange, new face. She didn't know how to read him any more. If she ever had. She realized suddenly how little she knew about Red Malone.

"For the group, I mean. They don't have a regular piano player."

She shook her head. "I don't play in groups. I just play for myself."

"You should try it. Really, you should. There's something about playing in a group." He walked back to one of the chairs and sat down. He wet his reed. "I can't describe what it's like. How it feels when everything clicks and harmonizes. I remember one time . . . Oh, this was ages ago, in high school. The band was rehearsing one day during lunch period. It was your typical high school piece: a medley of tunes from Tchaikowsky. We were tooting and scraping our way through it when, suddenly, it all came together. The notes, the timbre, the voicing. Everything, just right. It was as if Something was playing us like a single instrument. It sent shivers down my spine. We played the theme from *Marche Slav* in big, booming bass notes and segued into the quickstep from the *1812 Overture* without missing a beat. Our conductor, Mr. Price, swung his baton like a madman. Kids on their way to class, they stopped in the gym to listen. They crowded in from the hallway. And, when we finally climaxed, they cheered and clapped." He shook his head. "Not polite applause, like you get at a concert. They gave us an ovation. Because they could feel it, too. Someday, you might look up the root meaning of 'inspired.' "

Red was an ensemble player, Sarah thought, not a soloist. Yet, she had never met a man so much his own individual as Red seemed to be. Another contradiction in that bundle of contradictions.

"Well," said Red. "I guess I'll be packing it in here."

And Red was not the type for self-revelation. Like a flasher

297

in an alleyway, having exposed himself for a moment, he must button up and vanish. "Yeah. Should I close the piano up?"

"What? Oh, no. Don't bother. People wander in here at all hours, just to relax."

"Sure." She rose and picked up her books. "I guess I'll find my way back to my rooms." She hesitated, wondering if Red would walk with her.

"I'll give you a call tomorrow," he said, fiddling with his instrument case.

"Oh. Sure. See you around." When she left the music room, she did not walk to the elevator, but stopped in the hallway just outside the door, leaning against the wall. After a few moments, she heard him play again. This time it wasn't *High Society*, but the first movement of Mozart's *Clarinet Concerto*. The clarinet sang the throaty notes of the low register and the bright, crystalline notes of the high register with equal authority and technical precision. He played with grace and clarity. She closed her eyes and let the music take charge. In his own dialect, Mozart had achieved as much perfection as Joplin.

Then the elevator chimed and the doors opened and two people got off; and, rather than have them wonder why she was hanging around outside the music room, she got into the car and let the doors close her into silence.

298

# XII

Kennison often stayed late at the office, after everyone else had gone home. There were always hosts of details to attend to and never enough time to do it. Most of the staff left at five. In fact, some of them started leaving at four-thirty. Hired hands. Kennison never understood working by the clock. You spent as much time as necessary to get the job done right, and that was that. The new breed of worker he found strange and more than a little distasteful.

And knowing that the Society was partly responsible did not satisfy him. Granted that technopeasants were more easily manipulated; still, they did not have the inner dedication that Kennison wanted so badly. But then, the whole idea had been to breed a domesticated public; a simple public; a public that would react in predictable ways.

And a public that left work at five o'clock, if not sooner. Kennison made a face. *Ye have sown the wind*, he thought sourly. The same voices that were taught to whine *"What do we need to learn that for?"* to assure their dumb acquiescence to their betters, would also whine about quitting time. Yet he wondered if there might not be some way of achieving domestication without the whirlwind of passivity and apathy. It was an intriguing research problem, both in field work and in mathematical theory.

He reached for his espresso cup and found it empty. He sighed. With the Night Shift on indefinite leave, there was no one to look to his creature comforts after hours. Perhaps he should bring Karin in? Wearily he pushed himself from his desk and walked to his office door. The outer office was dim, only a few safety lights glowing. One work cubicle was lit, where the policeman assigned to guard him sat reading a magazine. Kennison wasn't sure what the magazine was. One of those popular do-it-yourself magazines. *Build a Space Shuttle in Your Basement!*

In theory, the policeman was young enough that his interests should have been more severely circumscribed. Music, women, cars, and sports. That was the meme complex the Society had been propagandizing at young males. Safe interests; with the music having a superficial veneer of rebellion to act as a bleeder valve for frustration. The technical magazine hinted at an unwonted curiosity about how things worked. But then, Kennison chided himself, perfect uniformity was a will-o'-the-wisp. There would always be those who ranged above and below the mean. A domesticated public would include domesticated technicians.

"Would you like another cup of coffee, Bill?" It never hurt to show the masses that you had the common touch. Be generous in small things and the great returns would follow.

"No, thank you, sir," the policeman replied.

Kennison nodded an acknowledgement and walked to the coffee station. There was no espresso left, so he poured himself a cup of decaf. As he sipped it, he glanced at the clock on the wall. He wondered if the policeman were sufficiently bored after all this time with no action. He could sympathize with the man's situation. Tagging around after Kennison certainly lacked for nothing but excitement. The local news organs had already given up. Kennison had performed nothing filmable, given no catchy sound byte; so they had gone back to their audiences with assurances of False Alarm, folks. And on to more important things, like fires and car wrecks.

The deaths of Benton and Weil and the apparent demise of Benedict Ruiz had had the desired effect. The various municipal governments had been more than happy to provide the obviously needed protection to their wealthy and important citizens. And it didn't hurt that many people having no connection with the Society had also asked for protection. The mob, once aroused, seldom engaged in fine distinctions of reasoning. Stories were garbled; and different pressure groups had their own axes to grind. Threats had been made against a great many people, diluting the attention paid to the Society. That had been another of Torino's ideas. The best place to hide a leaf, after all, was in a forest. Torino was sharp. A man to watch. Kennison decided to keep an eye on him, for all

300

that he was Ullman's man. Especially because he was Ullman's man.

Meanwhile, Kennison thought there was something amusing in having one of the sheep guarding one of the wolves.

"I'm finished now, Mr. Kennison. Will you be closing up?"

He turned with the coffee cup halfway to his lips. Prudence Baker was vice president of Kennison Demographics; and supervisor of the Night Shift. She was short and round-faced and wore her hair in an old-fashioned flip held in place with a plastic barrette.

"Yes, Ms. Baker. You may leave now." In a lower voice, he added, "Will I see you tonight?"

"Downstairs," she whispered. "Fifteen minutes."

"Little Girl Lost?"

She nodded and gave him the wide-eyed look that made her seem so much like a bunny rabbit. She patted her briefcase. "It's all in here."

"Very well, Ms. Baker," he said in a normal voice. "We will take that up on Monday."

He walked her to the door, while the policeman watched with both professional and male interest. That amused Kenninson. Prudence was somewhat older than the man appraising her, but she dressed younger than her years. She would not have seemed out of place on a college campus. Kennison found that rather enticing; perhaps even alluring; and liked to imagine all sorts of situations in which they might find themselves together.

Kennison busied himself at his desk for a few minutes, moving papers around. Then, when the fifteen minutes were up, he stuck his head out the office door and told the police guard that he would be in the washroom for a while. The officer nodded briefly and resumed his reading of the magazine.

The executive washroom at Kennison Demographics possessed a number of useful features. There were, of course, the usual facilities; but the most useful item of all was the small shower. Kennison locked the door behind him and entered the stall. He closed the glass and metal door and turned the knobs in a careful sequence.

There was a click, and the hiss of escaping air, and the floor of the stall slowly descended. Kennison hummed a tune.

The washroom on the floor below was virtually identical with the one he had just left. This one, however, belonged to

301

the import/export firm of Johnson and Cheng. J&C was modestly successful; did a pedestrian trade in bamboo and rattan furniture; and paid a reasonable amount of taxes.

It was also the main offices of the Night Shift.

Kennison paused before the washroom mirror and checked his appearance. He straightened his tie and ran a comb through his hair; brushed his jacket sleeves with his hands.

The offices outside were dimly lit by a single desk lamp that had been turned on to low. Prudence stood beside the desk, already dressed in her little girl clothing. The light cast her in curved shadows. He saw the knee-high socks, the matching green jumper.

Prudence was an occasional thing with him. She had distinctly odd notions of what constituted a good time, and Kennison found most of them tiresome, even degrading. He often wondered whether it were Prudence's conscious intention to degrade herself, and why; and what possible enjoyment she could get out of it. Participation was a burden, but Kennison was only too happy to assist another human being in her own pursuit of happiness.

To the extent he was able.

Memories of past sessions caused him to flush, and steeled his resolve to alter the game just a little.

"Oh, Mr. Kennison," she said when she saw him emerge from the washroom. She spoke in her high, squeaky, "little girl" voice. "I'm lost."

"Just a moment, Prudence," he said brusquely. "I'd like to try something a little different today." He reached the desk and turned off the light. The room fell into a dim redness, the only light coming from the emergency exit signs. Prudence was a soft, ruddy shape beside him. Her lips were twisted in a pout. The game pattern had been disturbed.

"You are not simply lost," he told her. "You're being followed." He pointed into the depths of the office: a jungle of file cabinets and partitions. "There's a bad man out there, waiting to get you."

Her eyes widened. She looked around at the surrounding office, nodded happily, and scampered off.

Kennison waited impatiently. It wasn't going to work, he scolded himself. It had only been a fluke before, with Karin. Now, here he was dragging himself down to Prudence's level. Dammit, it simply wasn't dignified. He hoped Paige or Weil never found out. Then he remembered that Weil was dead, which cheered him somewhat. The Great Harpy, at least, would now never gossip about his performances.

He toyed with the penholder on the desk, twisting the pens, pulling them out and reinserting them. He picked up a hemispherical paperweight and spun it. It wobbled like a top. He checked his watch. He couldn't stay "in the washroom" forever. Where was she?

He listened carefully. The office was hushed. The gentle background susurrus of building noises; fragments of traffic sounds that drifted upwards from the street below. "Prudence?" he called in a loud whisper. He waited. There was no answer.

"Prudence?" he called again. This was no time for jokes. He heard a cry, quickly stifled, and a crash, as if something had been knocked over.

Kennison stood stiffly, the paperweight in his hand. Something had gone wrong. Was there someone in the office? A burglar, perhaps? Had his innocent suggestion actually put her in danger?

He squinted into the ruddy gloom. Which way had she gone? He took a few tentative steps. If there were a burglar lurking in the dark, it would be foolish to stumble about blindly. He thought about the elevator concealed in the washroom, and looked over his shoulder at the door.

The sound of running feet jerked him around. He heard a chair spin and topple. A choked sob and the tearing of cloth. Kennison discarded the paperweight and pulled a letter opener from the desk organizer. He crept slowly in the direction of the sob, his ears alert for further sounds.

*Idiot,* he told himself. *Go back to the wall switch and turn on the lights.*

No, that would ruin the game.

If it was a game anymore.

If not, then turning the lights on would reveal his own location and Prudence's, as well as the burglar's.

He promised himself that he would look just in the first row of cubicles and that, if she was not in any of them, he would turn the lights on.

He could hear a whimper not too far off, but he could not tell its direction. *What if he's . . . doing something . . . to her?* He thought of the man—lower class, ill-clothed, probably rank of breath and filthy—fondling his little girl; and grew anxious. She needed him. Needed his protection. A soft man would run, seeking only his own safety; but Kennison was hard. He gripped the letter opener tight in his fist.

When he reached the opening for the first work cubicle, he leaped inside, suddenly and quietly, letter opener ready. His eyes searched the space. Nothing.

He crept his way silently down the aisle. The second and third cubicles were also empty.

In the fourth . . .

She was curled up in the knee space under the desk. Her blouse was torn and she was hugging her knees to her. When she saw him, she gave a little cry.

"Oh, Mr. Kennison," she said in her little girl voice. "I was lost, and there was a bad man following me, and he tried to . . ."

Kennison let out his breath. He laid the letter opener aside and crouched down in front of the desk. He held his arms out and she crawled into them and snuggled against him. He stroked her hair.

"Mr. Kennison," she said. "Look what he tried to do." And she showed him her torn blouse. Kennison looked and agreed that he had been a very bad man, but he was gone now. He continued stroking her.

"Everything is going to be fine, now," he told her.

Later, back once more behind his desk upstairs, he thought that Prudence was, by any rational measure, a sexual degenerate. Given the suggestion that she was being chased, she had actually lived the part. He thought of her stumbling and scrambling down the aisles of Johnson & Cheng, casting fearful glances toward her imaginary pursuer. Let's pretend. For a short time, she had managed to make it real for herself.

Kennison, of course, had not been fooled for a moment. Though even the pretense had been sufficient, and he had been able to give her something he had been unable to give for considerable time. He was quite pleased. It had been even better than with Karin; and Prudence, of course, had been delighted and surprised. If only it had . . . endured. But then, he had known the danger was only pretense.

What if it were *not* pretense? he wondered.

Time to close up shop, he decided. He unlocked a drawer in his desk, pulled out a disc, and carried it to the drive. He hummed abstractly to himself while he mounted the disc. The policeman glanced up once then turned his attention back to his magazine.

The disc was a new program, a virus detector, just delivered that morning from a software security company in Metuchen, New Jersey. He had placed the order himself through a dummy company having no known connection with Kennison Demographics. Kennison knew better than to order such things under his own company's name. It was easy enough to insert a virus into a commercial program, and there were plenty of hackers out there who would love nothing better than to emulate Beaumont's feat by piggybacking their virus into the system on commercial software.

Some years back, IBM had been nearly shut down by a Christmas card. The way Kennison had heard the story, one of IBM's programmers had sent an electronic card—a bit-mapped picture of a Christmas Tree—over the company Net to everyone on his inter-office distribution list. Buried in the code were instructions to copy the drawing to everyone on the *recipients'* distribution lists, as well. The virus had replicated itself through the system, consuming more and more memory in the process, until finally the system had been virtually paralyzed.

Then there was the incident on the ArpaNet, back in '88, when a computer science student had nearly paralyzed the Unix-operated military computers for no other reason than intellectual curiosity. Just to see if he could do it. And the British student—Singh?—who had broken into 250 sensitive military, commercial, and academic systems around the world, in a self-appointed mission to raise their security consciousness. The Official Governments had come down hard on them, of course. There was no greater sin than that the Great Unwashed should gain access to Official Secrets. But then, officialdom had always been more concerned with appearing foolish than with security.

And those incidents had been benign, or even unintentional; at least so far as Kennison knew. What might have been accomplished by the malicious? The Israeli government had once discovered a viral time bomb in their own data banks, just hours before it was set to explode and scramble everything. They had stumbled onto it only because a flaw in the code had caused the virus to continually reattach itself to the same programs, causing a perceptible increase in occupied memory space.

The virus detector he had just purchased could uncover much smaller increases. It compared the sizes of programs against their previously recorded sizes and flagged anything that had changed. If a virus had invaded the system and attached itself to a program, that program would occupy more space. It was a simple, but effective, countermeasure. It could not prevent system infection, but it could detect it quickly. Kennison had spent all day yesterday entering the program sizes as recorded in the original Master Logs. He had done it himself, not trusting the job to anyone else.

He activated the program with a staccato of keys. Then he leaned back in the operator's chair to watch the screen.

<Now checking system status. This could take some time.>

Could it, now? Kennison did not care for programs that pretended to talk to you. User friendly. He snorted. He felt like typing in, "Hurry up, damn you."

He spent a couple of minutes watching the screen. Every now and then the screen would blink and the message would repeat itself. Computers have destroyed our time-sense, he thought. *I've seen operators twisting impatiently in their seats waiting out delays of a few seconds.* We've grown so used to the Instantaneous that the merely Fast now seems intolerable. He knew that to compare the system dump against the Master Log would take many man-days and it would be prone to human error. So what did fifteen minutes or a half-hour matter?

He left the console and took his cup to the coffee station where he rinsed it out and set it there for his secretary's attention in the morning. Then he shoved his hands in his pockets and slouched around the room, pausing at various desks and work-stations to fiddle with the debris left behind at quitting time. Napoleon hadn't left this much behind on his retreat from Moscow. He found a personal letter that had been done on the WP application program. He found a confidential folder left atop a desk. He made a mental note to issue Stern Memos in the morning.

He heard a <beep> from his office. Did that mean the program was finished? He glanced again at the clock. Twenty minutes. He would have to plan for that twenty minutes every day from now on. Security meant taking extra pains. They backed up every day now; and Selkirk had designed a buffer system so that their own data banks were never directly plugged into the national Net. Kennison chided himself. He had been inexcusably lax in the past. Despite the stories about other people's systems, one never paid enough attention until it was one's own system that was hit.

He returned to his office and glanced at the screen. Then he froze and looked more carefully. The program was still running. The beep had meant only that a virus had been found. While he watched, it beeped again and a second log entry appeared on the screen.

Two viruses.

Kennison felt as if someone had just stepped on his grave. He reached out for the telephone and saw his hand was shaking. He pulled his hand back convulsively and balled it into a fist. Carefully, he lowered himself into his chair.

<Beep>

A third entry crawled across the display. Kennison felt the beginnings of panic seeping upwards from his gut. His bladder felt weak. *Who is doing this to us?* Beaumont was dead. *Or was she?* Crayle had never failed before. *But where is Crayle now? Why hasn't he reported in?* But it could be anyone who set those viruses. The CIA or the KGB would not be put off as easily as the local "action" news. He looked again at the screen. *It might be more than one someone.*

He grabbed the phone and punched up a number.

"Hello?"

"Alan? This is Dan. I'm at the office. You'd better come here right away. We've got a problem."

"Problem?" The voice at the other end was instantly alert. "What sort of problem?"

"The system is infected with viruses. I need a disinfectant."

There was a moment of silence. Then: "I'm on my way."

Kennison hung up the phone and scrutinized the screen once more. Maybe it wasn't as bad as it seemed. According to the log entries, all three viruses were attached to K/D programs. None had crossed the buffer into the Society's system. Fine. Let whoever is tapping in bore themselves with demographic surveys and statistical analyses.

Were they taps or time bombs? He didn't know. Kennison was computer literate, but he didn't trust himself on such a touchy job as this. If the viruses were time bombs, they might blow up in his face if he tried to disconnect them. His status in the Society would never survive that. If the data banks were scrambled a second time, he might as well pack it in and go join Ruiz in retirement. He hoped Selkirk would hurry.

He called up one of the infected programs and let the code

307

scroll across the screen. He didn't trust himself to do the surgery, but maybe he could palpate the body for lumps. He didn't really expect to find anything. He was just killing time until Selkirk arrived. *Dammit, I should have run the virus detector before Selkirk left the office.*

The phone rang and Kennison picked it up absently, thinking it was Selkirk calling back.

"Kennison?" It wasn't Selkirk. It was a woman's voice, an alto. It had a sly twist to it.

"Who is this?"

"That's not important. I see you found our little bug—"

*"Who is this?"* Kennison hit the Record button on the EPIC phone terminal and waved frantically at the policeman in the outer office. The policeman looked up and Kennison stabbed his finger emphatically at the telephone earpiece. The policeman nodded and picked up another line to begin the tracing. The K/D telephones were equipped with automatic call tracing. It would take only moments to discover the number of the incoming phone and only somewhat longer to find out where that phone was.

"Congratulations," the voice was saying. "I didn't really think you would find it so fast. It was programmed to report back immediately if it was detected, you know."

"Clever."

"Yes. We are, aren't we? You're finished, you know. You and your whole gang."

Kennison felt sweat on his forehead and there was a tightness in his chest. "What gang are you talking about?"

"Please, Kennison. Save that for the masses. We know better."

"Who are you?" Kennison felt himself close to tears and a tiny knot of fear twisted itself tighter in his stomach. He felt immeasurably cold.

"You're repeating yourself, Kennison. I didn't answer the first two times you asked me that. Why would you think I'd answer the third time?"

"Then *why* are you doing this?"

"Only to tell you that you *are* finished. We thought you'd like to know."

Anger replaced his fear with the suddenness of a storm. He felt his ears redden, and the coldness give way to heat. "Well, that's awfully considerate of you," he snarled.

"Yes. We are considerate, aren't we? I must go now; but, perhaps we shall speak again, you and I."

"Wait!"

But there was nothing but the dial tone in his ear.

Kennison slammed the phone down hard and the bells inside it jingled. He jerked his head up to look at the policeman, just in time to see him slam *his* phone down, too.

"What went wrong?"

The policeman made a disgusted sound. "We couldn't get the number."

"What do you mean, you couldn't get the number? It's an automatic readout. I pay Pacific Bell plenty each month for the service."

"No, it's not that, sir. Your caller used an old trick. He cut into the main trunk—physically cut in, I mean—down in the underground conduits. Opened up a cable and clipped on with a portable handset. He can dial anyone on the system; but no one can dial him. The system doesn't recognize his set as a legitimate port, so we don't get a number on him."

"Damn! No way to locate him, at all?"

"Well, there is a trickle power drain that can be traced electrically. We know he was calling from somewhere in the Tenderloin; but it doesn't matter. He'll be gone by the time we pinpoint him."

"Damn!"

"Was it a death threat, sir? We should report this."

Kennison waved to his recorder. "Just another kook, accusing me of running the whole world. He called to tell me he had planted a virus in my computer system."

"A virus. Is that serious?"

"It could be. I've asked my assistant to come in immediately to try to defuse it." Them, he reminded himself. There were three viruses. His caller had spoken as if she were a member of an organization. *But who?* The Associates? That would be crazy, with both of them exposed the way they were. But maybe Betancourt had gone off the deep end. He made a mental note to contact Malone and find out what was happening on the Other Side.

He sighed and put his head in his hands and found himself staring at the program code he had called up. Determination took hold of him. *Finished, are we?* We'll see about that. He pulled open the vertical file and grabbed the hard copy of the program. Carefully, he went through each line of code, comparing what was in the system to what was supposed to be in the system.

It was a half hour later and Selkirk was just arriving when he found the anamolous line: *Autocopy to Q File*.

What the hell did that mean?

The receptionist in charge of the meeting rooms was sitting at her desk across the room, amid a jungle of hanging and potted plants. She glanced up when Jeremy and Gwynn entered and checked something off in her logbook. "They're waiting inside for you, Doctor Llewellyn," she said, pointing to the room where the study team was meeting.

"Thank you, Brenda. There will be one more coming today. A Dr. Doang from the mathematics department."

"Drs. Hambleton and Quick just went in," Brenda said. "Dr. Vane called and said he would be a few minutes late."

"I'll wait out here and show Jim in when he arrives," Jeremy said.

Llewellyn smiled and pulled the pipe from her mouth. She pointed the stem at him like the barrel of a gun. "When you told them last week that Jim had been studying the math in the Dump, you created quite a stir. Half the team is scared to death that he will make them feel stupid with formulæ and jargon; the other half is peeved that a mathematician is even participating on the project."

Jeremy shrugged. "He didn't want to come to this meeting, either. He told me last week that he is personally satisfied with his conclusions and doesn't much care whether your study team agrees with them or not."

Llewellyn chuckled. "He does not have a very high opinion of us, does he?"

"He told me that philosophers have been arguing for more than four thousand years without ever answering a single important question."

"Hmmm. Then he doesn't understand philosophy. It's not the answers that matter, but the questions."

Jeremy chuckled. He liked both Jim and Gwynneth, but they were about as opposite as two people could be. It seemed as if he had spent most of the past month alternately explaining one to the other. "I don't think anything is quite real to Jim unless it can be measured and fitted to an equation. A question that cannot be answered is meaningless."

"Then he's missing half the fun of life."

"I suppose. As an accountant, though, I can see his point. When one deals with intangibles, nothing is ever settled. An audit can test whether someone followed an accepted accounting procedure; but how can it test for his state of mind when he did it?"

Llewellyn clapped him on the shoulder. "I wouldn't be too sure of the first, either, if I were you. As Herkimer would say, there is nothing so elusive as a Fact." They both laughed. "Bring Dr. Doang in as soon as he arrives, would you, Jeremy? I've got to get this circus started."

She entered the conference room and closed the tall, heavy doors behind her. The receptionist glanced up briefly and returned to her fashion magazine. Jeremy sighed and planted himself on the sofa. He opened the book he had gotten on Quetelet. The thick doors and walls, he knew, would allow no sounds from the meeting to distract him.

Jim Tranh Doang arrived shortly after. He stood in the entrance and looked about, blinking his eyes. He was dressed as Jeremy had always seen him: in rolled up shirtsleeves and open collar. Jeremy doubted whether the man owned so much as a sports jacket. He always looked as if he had been interrupted from his work. And that was probably an accurate assessment.

Jeremy closed his book and waved to him. Doang nodded and walked to the sofa. He lowered himself into the cushions; placed his briefcase on his lap and leaned his head back against the wall. He closed his eyes and sighed.

"They're waiting for you," Jeremy said, snapping the clasps on his own briefcase. "The meeting's already started."

"Let them wait," Doang replied, with his eyes still closed. "Let them have fun jabbering to each other in their self-important way. Time enough in a few minutes to tear their playhouse down."

Jeremy's eyes wandered to the briefcase on Doang's lap. He saw how the mathematician's hands stroked the smooth, brown surface. The fingers made rapid circular movements, as if they were massaging the padded leather; or as if their owner were nervous and agitated. Jeremy tapped the briefcase. "Give it to me straight, Jim. Is it what we thought?"

Doang opened his eyes and looked at Jeremy. The eyes were dead black coals. Tunnels into sunless depths. "You couldn't follow the math," he said.

"I don't need to follow. Just tell me where it leads."

"Death," he said and closed his eyes again.

Jeremy shuddered at the desolate way Doang had spoken. He reached out and shook Doang's shoulder. "What do you mean by that?"

Doang stared at the hand until Jeremy slowly removed it. "It's plain enough, isn't it? Do you want me to tell you who will win the next presidential election? When the first city will be built on Luna? The timing of the next stock market crash?"

"You mean the mathematical models in the Dump—"

"Were valid?" He toyed with the handle on his briefcase. "Yes. Yes, they were. Not the fragments that appeared in the Dump. They were incomplete. The system they were running in was pulled off the Net before Beaumont's Worm had finished downloading. But it was elementary to fill in the missing parts. By deduction. By analogy. Several of the equations were similar to models that we run in mathematical biology. The excitation of a nerve by a stimulus. The trajectory of a contagious epidemic. Child's work. Kitchen arithmetic." He waved a listless hand in dismissal. "The difficulty lay in discerning what real-world entities the variables stood for."

"What did they—"

Doang lifted his briefcase and dropped it in Jeremy's lap. "Read it yourself. It's all in there."

Jeremy felt his face go red. "Don't patronize me!" he said in a low voice.

Doang shook his head. He ground his fist into his palm. "You're right. I apologize. It is only that . . ." He shook his head again. "I had thought myself objective. Dispassionate. The true scientist. The idea of such elegant and powerful systems excited me." He flashed Jeremy a rueful smile. "But as I studied the models—as I completed them, discovered their meaning—I became . . . I became angry, and afraid. And lost. I ran simulations, using past data. I predicted the past. Postdicted? And always, always the equations rang true. The models were simplistic, incomplete, imprecise; but within their limitations they yielded answers consistent with the historical record, with the statistical abstracts and the almanacs. And where they did disagree I began to wonder whether the equations might not be correct and the official values a deception."

"Then you were successful. With your research, I mean.

Those Babbage people really do have a valid science?" He thought again of Buckle, of Quetelet, of Babbage and their dream. A science of history, lost for over a century. Forgotten; disparaged, except by a few. The viciously guarded secret of a small, elite clique. A secret they had killed to protect. *And now we know the secret.* He felt the thrill run though him. It was not fear, nor was it exactly eagerness. Perhaps it was only anticipation, an intuition of great events about to happen. The shaking of a racehorse in the moment before the bell rings. *We know Their secret; but do They know we know?* Once Jim reports his findings to the study team, the fat will be in the fire. "You don't seem too happy," he said aloud. No, of course not. Hadn't Jim already said that his conclusions led to death? "At least we know the truth," he offered.

Doang recovered his briefcase. He wouldn't look at Jeremy. "Ye shall learn the truth and the truth will set you free," he quoted and made a small, angry sound in his throat. "Does it? Or does it enslave you forever?"

Jeremy frowned and studied the morose, little mathematician. "What do you mean?"

"I mean that life is a sham, isn't it?" Doang spread his hands out, to the briefcase, to the meeting room, to the world. "I mean that, whatever our hopes and plans might be, what will happen will happen. I mean that all we really do is walk through life, speaking the lines, doing bits of business. And for what?" Doang clenched his hands tightly and pressed them against his briefcase.

"It's not as bad as that," Jeremy told him. "Now that we know what they are doing, we can take steps to counter them. We can break this Society of theirs—"

Doang threw his head back and let out a laugh, a harsh bark more despair than amusement. "You don't get it, do you?" he said. "The Babbage Society doesn't matter. They are as enslaved as we are. It's the equations themselves. Don't you see? Had the Babbage Society never existed, we would be as much prisoners as we are now. As we always have been."

So. It was not fear of the Babbage Society that was bothering Jim Doang; it was Fate. Wyrd. The Norns. The idea that his life was already woven inextricably into some divine tapestry. Jeremy felt surprised at the depths of the man's reaction. It seemed too abstract a concern to excite passion. Fear of violence, of death. Now, that was real. Real enough that

313

Jeremy could feel it in his own loins. But, fear of existential emptiness? "Dammit, Jim, you can't let it affect you this way."

Doang cocked an eye at him. "I can't let it? Are you so in control of your own feelings as that?" He rose to his feet, straightened his jacket, patted his hair. "Well, shall we go in and shatter their complacency?" He faced the doors. Then he grunted a single laugh. "More likely, they will not see it. They can not understand the math; and, lacking a knowledge of how the journey was made, they will deny the destination." He turned his head and looked at Jeremy over his shoulder. His eyes seemed empty and haunted. "There must be value in such ignorance," he said, "if it allows one to keep a sense of dignity. Perhaps our ancestors, with their belief in Destiny, were wiser than we."

"A pretty speech, Dr. Doang; but don't you think it is a trifle melodramatic?"

Jeremy turned and saw that Herkimer Vane had arrived. He was standing slouched, with his hands thrust into the pockets of his jacket. With his bald head, his smile and his stature, he reminded Jeremy of nothing so much as an elf.

"Herkimer," Jeremy said. "I don't believe you've met Jim Doang."

Vane extended a hand. "Our mathematical auxiliary. No, we haven't met; but I deduced who he must be." He smiled at Jeremy. "There, that's scientific enough, isn't it? Deduction."

"Actually," Doang told him, "science deals with inference more than deduction." Vane looked at him, but said nothing.

"I suppose you overheard what Jim told me."

Vane shrugged. "A little."

"Does it change your mind? About scientific history, I mean."

"Oh, my word, no. Doctor Doang has said nothing to change my mind."

"But . . ."

"Don't you see? Of course not. And neither does the good mathematician. It is just that long-range predictive systems are impossible, even in as simple a system as the Solar System, where there are only a few bodies and a single force, gravity, that must be considered. So how can the trajectories of social systems be predicted, when there are so many more interacting bodies and a multitude of forces?"

Jeremy looked at Doang, who was listening carefully to the

314

little historian. When Doang did not speak, Jeremy answered. "Now, wait a moment, Herkimer. I may not know much science, but I do know that they can predict the positions of the planets with great accuracy. Didn't someone once predict the existence of Neptune just from the equations of gravitation?"

"Either Adams or Le Verrier, depending on your patriotism. But they were wrong, don't you know."

"Eh? But they *found* Neptune, didn't they?"

"Surely, but not where they had predicted. Adams and Le Verrier predicted two different orbits for the unknown planet. It took them one, two years to perform the calculations. No one was going to spend a like time simply to check their arithmetic! Le Verrier predicted a planet with thirty-two times the mass of the earth, lying thirty-five to thirty-eight AU's from the sun, and having a period of 207 to 233 years. But Neptune is only seventeen times as massive; lies only thirty AU's distant; and circles the sun in a mere 164 years. Adams' calculations were even worse. Had Le Verrier made his calculations forty years earlier or forty years later, he would have missed Neptune completely!"

Doang spoke slowly. "You seem remarkably well-informed."

"For an historian? But remember, I am an historian of science and the philosophy of science. And I delight in pricking overinflated balloons." Vane beamed. "No, my friends. The predictive ability of Newton's equations have been vastly overrated. Poincaré saw that quite clearly."

"Yet," said Jeremy, "the equation worked well enough to put men on the moon. They aimed the ship at where the moon would be; and both moon and ship arrived together."

"Ah, but there are two difficulties. The first is the n-body problem."

"The n-body problem?"

"Ask your friend."

Jeremy turned to Doang. "What does he mean?"

Doang paused before answering. "Newton's equation is simple in principle; but it has a solution only in one special case: a single body of negligible mass orbiting another body of great mass. Now the Sun contains so much of the mass of the Solar System that, for all practical purposes, we can regard the planets as massless."

"I don't understand. Then what's the problem?"

"The problem," said Vane, "is that there are other bodies in the universe. Isn't that so, Dr. Doang?"

"Yes." A long, slow yes. "For example, after accounting for the effect of the Sun, the astronomers next add the effect of Jupiter. This will perturb the perfect Keplerian orbit in a way that depends on the positions of the two planets. Next, the effect of Saturn is added; and so on, until a suitable approximation is realized."

"But it doesn't stop there," Vane continued. "Every body in the universe exerts a gravitational attraction on the Earth. The effect may be minute; but it is cumulative. As a result, a planet's orbit cannot be forecast with any reasonable precision for more than a few millenia."

"Long enough," said Jeremy, "to satisfy my own personal needs."

Both Vane and Doang chuckled. "Yes," Vane said. "The time span of the forecast and its precision are also important. As a general rule, the longer the cast, the less precise it becomes. Projecting a planet's orbit over several millenia, who cares if it is off by a few hours? But in the case of a spacecraft flying to the moon, an error of a few hours is intolerable. Much greater preeision is required. But increasing the precision tenfold increases the necessary calculations a thousand-fold! One would quickly reach the point where, even with the swiftest computing machines, the computation would simply take too long. By the time you have pinpointed a spacecraft to a particular small region in space, the spacecraft would no longer be in that region."

Jeremy felt himself grow irritated. "The way you've explained things, Herkimer, makes any prediction seem futile."

Vane's finger wagged at him. "My point exactly. Long-range forecasts are impossible. In any system. That is what Chaos Theory is all about. A billiards player setting up a shot need take no account of the positions of the spectators who are watching. The gravitational potential involved is trivial. Yet, what I said about planets holds even here. The effects accumulate. If the player were to attempt a seven-ricochet cannon, the gravitational influence of the spectators would become vital in determining the final trajectory of the ball. Am I not correct, Dr. Doang?"

"Any billiards player who attempts a seven-ball cannon would be able to solve the equations in his head."

Vane threw his head back and laughed. "Yes. Now imagine how many collisions and ricochets there are in a society of millions of people! And, unlike gravity and elasticity, we do

316

not understand what the forces are and how they act. Even if there were scientific laws in history, they would be useless for making predictions. With the number of bodies involved, the solutions would become indeterminate much too quickly."

Vane looked at his watch. "Well, we must be getting in there, mustn't we." He turned to go.

Doang seized Jeremy by the elbow. "I know what I saw," he whispered fiercely into Jeremy's ear. "I ran the equations. They worked."

"They were approximate," Jeremy answered him. "You told me yourself. The precision was loose. Give me a wide enough hoop and even I can score a basket. Make up your mind. A few minutes ago you were upset because you thought the equations were valid. Now you're upset because they might not be."

"What do you think?"

"Me? I'm an accountant. I think that you are less right than you think you are. And so is Vane."

Doang released his elbow. "Dr. Vane!" Vane turned with his hand on the knob of the meeting room door. Brenda, the receptionist looked up from her magazine.

"Yes, Dr. Doang?" said the historian.

"I can make one forecast of the future."

"And what is that?"

"That in a few minutes I am going to set your study team into turmoil."

Vane shrugged. "Short range. Loose precision. You may be right."

Someone struck a bass drum next to Jeremy's ear. The room jumped and his vision blurred. The hanging plants by Brenda's desk swung crazily; and those on her desk top slid off and smashed to the floor. The plaster of the walls cracked and pictures fell off their hangers. The huge, thick conference room doors bulged and splintered and jumped nearly whole off their hinges, as if some giant had kicked them out from the other side.

The left-hand door struck Vane from behind like a monstrous fly swatter; and that was all Jeremy saw, because the room tumbled and he was looking at the ceiling, then at the entryway, then at the floor, which leapt up and smashed him in the face.

# PART 3

# THE ENEMY OF MINE ENEMY

# Then

The grass was still damp where the bearded man knelt by the grave. It soaked into his trouser legs, giving them a pungent, woolen smell. His knees felt cold. He placed a vase of freshly-cut flowers before the headstone, twisting it into the ground so that it would not topple. Then he pushed himself to his feet and made the sign of the cross. A brief gust of wind caught his open mackintosh and it snapped behind him. He pulled his western-style hat tighter down on his head.

Anyone watching—and he had to assume that someone was watching—would think that he was a friend of the person in the grave; that it was only a coincidence that he was in the graveyard on this particular day. That he was, at any rate, unconnected with the funeral now beginning a scant dozen yards away. That was what he hoped any observer would assume. But, when the ceremonies started, the bearded man glanced curiously at the cortege, as would be expected of any mortal man.

A small crowd, garbed against the imminent resumption of the rain, clustered around an open grave. A few precautionary umbrellas sprouted, mushroomlike, among them. Above, in the moist sky, the sun strove vainly to dispel the damp.

A spare, wooden casket rested beside the hole in the ground. Two men in work clothes flanked the nearby heap of freshly turned earth. The glistening clay was wet and heavy—the diggers could scarcely have had an easy time of it. They leaned on their shovels, watching the proceedings with professional detachment.

The bearded man turned back to the headstone and clasped his hands and bowed his head as if he were saying a prayer for his dear departed. As he was. His lips moved; and tears tracked the curves of his cheeks as he strained to hear the words the minister was speaking to the crowd.

"From the clay we came, and to it we return. Yet what lieth beyond the grave, my brothers and sisters? Yea, a better life, amen. We store up merits in our life on this earth against that day of glory and righteousness. Isaac Shelton was a good man. If we may presume on God's mercy, we might say with bold assurance that Isaac has gone to dwell among the angels. For all those who knew him can attest that here was a good and righteous man, who walked every day in the fear of the Lord, amen."

"Amen," said Brady Quinn. He kept his eyes fixed on the grave he had chosen to justify his presence in the cemetery. Rueben Judge had told him he was mad to go near Isaac's funeral. Grosvenor Weil, or his agents, would expect it. They would be watching. A disguise? The beard dyed black; the limp imparted by the pebble in his left boot . . . a flimsy charade, easily pierced. Of what value all the years of hiding if, when They most expected him, he exposed himself?

But the years of separation had lain heavy on Brady's shoulders. Isaac Shelton was his friend. He had nurtured him and trained him and counseled him; had given him all he had to give. And in the end Brady had walked out with never a backward glance. He had severed all ties; broken the old man's heart; thrown up in his face the value of his life's work. *How could I*, he had asked Randall, *not go?*

It was too late, they had argued. What value can your going have?

They had missed the point, all of them. What value? Inestimable value. Perhaps not to Isaac—although even that might be argued, if one searched amongst one's boyhood beliefs—but certainly to Brady Quinn.

Of Brady's inner circle, only Old Bill had understood that need. William Harrison Hatch had been a mountain man in the old days, before America came West; and he knew that even long separation could not weaken heartfelt bonds. You go, Bill Hatch had told him, and—despite the puzzled stares of the others—would not explain his reasons.

Brady gazed skyward and saw the dark clouds closing in once more. Rain. And not an honest rain, not like the epic

322

storms that broke over the western mountains. A mean rain, half-drizzle. He hated Boston. He hated the miserable weather, the mean-spirited people, the closed-in feeling of the city. He longed to be back in the West, where what a man did mattered more than who his parents had been.

Yet, Isaac had loved this place, and had never left it for long: a reminder to Brady that not all men shared the same passions. One man might love family and tradition where another would prize freedom and new horizons above all. His roots, Isaac had once told him, were sunk deep in New England's rocky soil. It was not conceivable—it was not even possible—that Isaac Shelton would lie in any other ground.

It was good to remember that this staid, well-mannered and manicured land had also been a raw frontier. And not very long ago, at that. Isaac's sires had tilled its barren hillsides with one hand on their plowshares and the other on their flintlocks; with a wary eye on the hostile forest before them and their backs to the cold, gray ocean, where they had drowned their pasts forever.

Boston would change, he reminded himself. Everything changed. Low-born Irish immigrants were already clawing their way out of the slums and stews of the south side and a flood tide of European peasants would soon be crossing that selfsame ocean to descend upon the hapless Yankee patricians. The New Boston would be quite different from the Old.

He realized suddenly that he had tarried at the grave far too long for his masquerade. He crossed himself once more, turned abruptly, and walked toward the cemetery entrance, where his horse stood tied to the hitching post, flicking its tail. A miserable nag, thought Brady Quinn. A city horse, rented from a stable. He was accustomed to better.

*Goodbye, Isaac. Vaya con Dios, as we say out West.*

It was odd. He had thought that his feelings would be much more intense; but what he felt most of all was an aching sense of loss, as of a limb that had been hacked off. Was that what sorrow was? Nothing more than regret and loss? A knowledge of wrongs that could never now be made right? If so, then the mourning was not for the mourned, but for the mourners. And perhaps that was good; for the mourners had at least the potential for change.

Isaac had had a long run of it. A full life that had accomplished much good. Even if his life's work . . . Ah, to what wickedness our good intentions drive us. What scales we lay upon our eyes. Well, Brady was done with all that, out of it well and truly. And now Isaac was, as well. Yet, Isaac had stuck with the work, knowing it was doomed. He had sold his soul for the chance to build a hopeful future; and even now, these many years later, Brady could not decide if Isaac's life had been a tragedy or not.

*Yea, the prophesies of Carson have come to pass, and a shadow has fallen over the land of the Founders.* He remembered warning Isaac of it, on that rainy night in Georgetown, so long ago. Ruthless men lacking the Founders' ideals would someday rule the Society. The high-minded ideals that had driven the Founders to terrible deeds would fade; leaving no residue but the terrible deeds themselves. What had he hoped for, telling Isaac that after Randall had begged him to keep it secret? That his mentor would forsake his life's work? No. He saw now it had been a foolish hope. Does not the captain go down with his ship, fighting to the last to save it? Fighting to the last, and losing in the end. Was there greatness in struggling against certain doom? The Vikings had had legends of doomed gods.

Had Isaac known, Brady Quinn wondered, who Grosvenor Weil was, before the senility reached out and took him? Had he known—as the Æsir had known—that the Cause was long lost, ground to powder in the jaws of his own cruel equations? Quinn offered up a prayer that the shades of the old man's mind had been drawn before that final heartache could be his.

Brady was brought up short by two men stepping between him and his horse. They were large men with the smugness of the bully. They wore checkered jackets and trousers and bowler hats. The one on the left held out a hand as large as a side of beef. "Hold up there," he said. "Mister Weil would like to have a word with you."

Brady looked at them. "Weil? I don't know who he is, and I have no business with him." He tried to step around them, but they moved to block his path.

"You don't understand, Quinn," the first man said flatly. "Mister Weil wants to talk to you; and what Mister Weil wants, Mister Weil gets."

Brady sighed and retreated two steps. "Does he?" Randall had warned him that this would happen. Still, he had owed it to Isaac to come. Now it looked like the problem of attending the funeral would be nothing compared to the problem of leaving it.

Brady had not fastened his mackintosh. The flaps of the long coat hung loosely. "I'll give you both one last chance," he told the two ruffians. "Will you let me mount?"

They exchanged amused looks. "You'll give us a last chance?" asked the one on the right. "I don't think you're in a position to give chances."

Brady's hands moved like lightning. "Now am I?" And the two looked down the barrels of twin Colts. So fast it had been, that the mackintosh had barely rustled. They licked their lips and their eyes darted, seeking escape. A moment ago they had confronted a victim; now they confronted death. They hadn't realized they were dealing with an armed man.

Randall and Bill had taught Brady many things after he had moved West. How to draw a pistol quickly and accurately, for one. Always to leave the other man a chance to back down, for another; but not to be a damned fool about it. When the time comes for action, they had told him, act; and act fast; and don't count the cost. In a fight, such a man has an advantage over those who harbor second thoughts.

"Well, now, this is right convenient, wouldn't you say?" he told the two.

They held their hands carefully in sight; made no sudden moves. They couldn't take their eyes off the guns. The one on the right was sweating.

The other scowled. "Convenient?" he asked.

"Why, this being a cemetery and all. You won't have too far to go, afterward."

He motioned with his pistols and they backed away slowly. Brady sidled past them to his horse. He holstered his left gun and used his free hand to unhitch the animal. "I know what you're thinking," he said, keeping the other gun trained on them. "You're wondering if I can get off two shots quickly enough to stop the both of you. Well, maybe I can and maybe I can't; but I'll surely get off one, and you might give some thought as to which of you will take that shot. Which of you wants to die to give the other a chance at me?"

He stepped up into the saddle and looked down on them. "I'm leaving now," he announced. "You can tell Mr. Weil that he needn't concern himself over me. I'm out of it. There's no reason for worry on his part. Meanwhile, my mind will rest a sight easier while I ride, if you two were flat on the ground."

The first man grinned nervously and knelt into the mud. He spread himself out, face down. The second man looked at his companion, then back at Brady.

"I ain't about to crawl in the mud for no man."

Brady shrugged. "Face down in the mud; or face up while they throw mud down on you. It's your choice."

The ruffian thought about it a moment longer, then he, too, lowered himself prostrate. "I'll get you for this someday."

"It's a big country. I doubt we'll ever lay eyes on each other again. But you are welcome to dream."

"Every man should have a goal in life," the thug said.

Brady gave him a surprised look. He grinned. "Yes, I suppose so. Then you can thank me twice, for I've given you both the goal and the life."

He yanked on the reins and applied the spurs. His horse bolted down the track to the main road. He kept his pistol ready to hand, in case the two men should be so foolish as to pursue him. He doubted they would. The two had been young and confident and Brady was no spring chicken. He imagined what Grosvenor Weil would say to them when they reported.

On sudden impulse, he turned the horse off the road, leaping the rail fence of a pasture. Weil could easily have stationed other toughs between the cemetery and the train station. From all that he had heard of him, Grosvenor Weil was a careful and meticulous man; not one to tolerate loose ends. He would not rely on this one try to take Brady Quinn. Not while Quinn had thrust himself so conveniently into harm's way.

Quinn's mouth drew back in a fierce smile as his horse cantered across the meadow. His knees gripped the animal's barrel. He had not felt this alive in years. The risks he had run in coming here seemed to have awakened him. The blood coursed in his veins. He was young again, daring great deeds. In a way, he did not care if he escaped this trap or not. It was important only that he had come.

That letter; the one he had left with Gorman & Stout. It seemed so foolish in retrospect; a rash and impetuous act. It had brought the wrath of Grosvenor Weil on him. Still, how could he have known that it would? And he could not bring himself to abandon his comrades with no word of warning whatsoever.

326

Was he making excuses to himself? Should he have forseen that the letter would reach the hands of the very Judas their equations had foretold? That Isaac's mind would have entered the shadows, so that he never saw the letter; and that Davis would so thoughtlessly reveal its contents? Should he have been that wise?

Weil's *coup* had come earlier than calculated; and he had been a far more ruthless man than either Randall or he had expected. *I was a fool.* And Davis was a fool. That fall down the stairs of his Washington mansion—that had been their first inkling of Weil's ferocity. That he had read into the Associates' existence his own fears and ambitions.

*Mea culpa,* he thought. The contents of an unwritten letter cannot be revealed.

Foolish, all of us. Isaac, Davis, myself. Even old Jedediah. Blind. Seeing only what we wanted to see. Weil, too. How could such foolish, fallible men ever believe they had the wisdom to guide the future? Sometimes he thought Elias Kent had been the wisest of the Founders.

He reached the farmstead just as the rain resumed its miserable drizzle. He found the farmer sitting on the front porch, an open Bible in his lap. The man sat in a canewood rocker, taking his allotted day of rest.

"Excuse me, sir," Brady said to him, reining in, "but which is the road to Providence?" Brady might believe himself a fool; but he was not so foolish that he would ride to the Boston depot with Weil's minions afoot.

The farmer's keen gaze took in Brady, the lathered mount, the Colt pistol—which Brady returned finally to its holster. He rubbed a hand across his stubble. "Well, stranger, the surest road to Providence be this one." And he held up the Bible.

Brady Quinn laughed.

# Now
# I

Red came knocking on her door early in the morning. It was a light, staccato rap and Sarah knew without checking that it was he. Smiling to herself, she set her coffee cup in its saucer. She straightened her robe, and walked to the door of her underground apartment, thinking as she did so that she would gladly pay any price, even the price of a new identity, for nothing more than a place to live that had windows and the morning sun. Fee followed her, dancing between her legs.

When she opened the door, he was leaning on one arm in the doorway. The New, Improved Red Malone. The not-quite-a-stranger with the eyes of a friend. "Hi," he said.

"Hi, yourself. What brings you around at this hour?" Fee circled Red's legs, staring at the boots and jeans; hackles raised and back slightly arched. Fee did not quite approve of Red—either edition. He felt a proprietary interest in Sarah that brooked no competitors. Red watched him with amusement.

"Do you feel like going out for pizza?" he asked. "I'm headed for Tony's."

"Pizza for breakfast?"

"No, we won't eat until later; but I'm leaving now."

"Well, I . . . Sure, why not?"

"Good," he said. He checked his watch. "You'll just have time to get dressed and pack a bag."

She checked herself in midturn. "Pack a bag?"

He gave her an innocent look. "Sure. Not too much. Just overnight."

"Overnight? Red, just where is Tony's?"

"In South Plainfield, New Jersey."

*"You're going two thousand miles for pizza?"*

Red didn't even crack a smile. "It's very good pizza," he assured her.

They threw their bags into the rear of the ranch's battered, old pickup and crowded into the cab with Janie Hatch. The older woman ground the engine into first and jerked onto the dirt road that connected the ranch to the state highway. Sarah had the shotgun seat. She twisted and looked back through the dust cloud at the receding buildings. The cool mountain wind whipped through her hair. Then she faced forward again, but left the window rolled down, resting her arm in the open frame. She could feel the rifle barrels in the gun rack cold against the back of her neck.

"You'll take care of Fee for me while I'm gone?"

"Cats take care o' themselves, missy; but I'll keep an eye peeled in his direction."

"Thanks."

Janie didn't reply; but then Sarah didn't expect her to. Janie never wasted a word when a shrug would do; or a shrug, when silence was enough. She was a puzzle Sarah had not yet solved. Aloof, detached, indifferent; the ultimate bystander. She would not hesitate to do a favor; but, so far as Sarah could determine, neither did she do favors from kindness. Sarah had to believe that there were emotions concealed behind the weathered and stoical exterior; but what those emotions might be remained elusive. Even after all this time at the safe house, Sarah did not know how Janie felt about her.

Sarah herself had mixed feelings about leaving the ranch. On the one hand, she was happy that she was finally leaving the safe house. She had been buried there, lost in limbo, like van Winkle among the elves. She half-expected to find that fifty years had passed in the Real World while she had been in that underground faerie land.

On the other hand, she was sad, in a curious sort of way. By entering the world at last as Gloria Bennett, she was forsaking her old life with a finality that was more than meta-phorical. She was relegating Sarah Beaumont to a dimly-remembered and half-mythical past; a faded snapshot, barely

329

recognized, in the scrapbook of her mind. And the fact that her own decisions had led her to this point was no comfort at all.

Sometimes, in spite of the drama and the crimes and the conspiracies in which she had found herself enmeshed, her biggest regret was that now she and Dennis would never complete Brady Quinn Place. The dream would whither and fade; but never be quite forgotten. It would lie in the attic of her memory, gathering dust and cobwebs; and every now and then, when she would happen upon it, it would remind her of all the things she had never done; and now never would.

And, on the third hand—if there was a third hand—she was apprehensive: because Sarah Beaumont was a Known Woman and a great many people were hunting for her; and here she was, going out among them. The vengeful, the celebrity-minded, and the merely curious. *They* were out there. And the Government. And the Secret Six that Red had told her of. And the talk shows and the newspapers. And the sheeplike crowd that followed anything famous. Fame groupies. Like the man—what was his name, Bob Ford?—who shot Jesse James for no other reason than the notoriety.

She said as much to Red, and he told her not to worry because she was Gloria Bennett now, and no one was looking for Gloria Bennett.

"But still," she said to him while Janie weaved through the morning traffic at the Mousetrap, "I don't *feel* safe. I feel . . . transparent. As if people could look right through me. I'm a black woman who has had plastic surgery. What if someone deduces from that that I must be Sarah Beaumont."

"People ain't that smart by half," said Janie.

Red looked serious. "I think you needed this trip for more reasons than one. Most of the scars aren't that obvious. Your hair or your makeup hides them. In another four or five months they'll fade out. Now me . . ." He ran a hand over his chin. "I look like I've been in a fight." He touched the bruises; reminders of his own surgery. "That's where you're lucky. Black and blue doesn't show on you."

"I didn't say it was a logical fear. But someone might figure it out."

"They will if'n you keep flapping yer gums about it, Gloria."

She turned on Janie. "Don't call me that! Not yet. Only on the Outside."

330

Janie Hatch didn't say anything. She shrugged and concentrated on her driving.

Sarah looked at Red and he shrugged with his eyebrows. Sarah twisted half-sideways on the seat so she could see the older woman. She was peering at the traffic on I-70 as if she were choosing targets. Sarah had watched her shoot targets once. Janie had stood off a good 500 yards with a telescopic rifle and put four out of five shots into the black. And she also remembered the time Janie had stood by with that same rifle and done nothing but watch while Orvid Crayle had stalked Sarah through the ruins atop Mount Falcon. "Janie, why do you have three rifles in your gun rack?"

"I hunt."

"I know that. I was asking why three?"

Janie paused and regarded her a moment. "Well," she allowed, giving her attention once more to the traffic, "the top one is for out'n on the prairie. Fires a high-velocity, flat trajectory round. But, up in the forest, you don't normally git a distance shot, so a fat, slow slug is best."

"Oh." Janie Hatch seemed better armed than some small countries. "What about the third rifle? What's that one for?"

Janie turned her cold, emotionless eyes on her once more. "Varmints," she said.

At the airport, a private jet was waiting for them at the general aviation terminal. The captain stood nearby talking with the ground crew, shouting to be heard over the whine of the engines. Red carted their overnight bags to the plane and the groundman broke off his conversation with the pilot to stuff them into the nose compartment. The pilot saluted Red, then shook his hand. A commercial liner roared down the runway in the distance.

Sarah turned to Janie to say good-bye, but Janie laid a hand on her arm.

"You be careful, missy. Y'hear?"

It was the same warning Janie had given her at the Denver library when Crayle had been nosing through her notes on Brady Quinn. Be careful, but don't expect me to interfere. Sarah brushed the hand from her arm.

"I can take care of myself."

"I know that. I wasn't thinking of you."

"Then, who . . ." She followed Janie's eyes. "Red? Don't be silly. He can take care of himself, too."

331

Janie gave Sarah a hard look. "He never told you about Jacksonville?"

She shook her head. "No, he's never mentioned it."

Janie shifted her chaw from one cheek to the other. She spat a stream at the ground. "Well, I never said anything, understand? And don't you go asking him. If he wants to tell you about it, he will."

Then Janie climbed back into the truck and closed the door with a slam. The gears shrieked in protest and the truck hopped into the flow of departing traffic. Red was waving to her. Time to board. Sarah walked toward the jet. Jacksonville? What had happened to Red at Jacksonville that worried Janie Hatch? And why did it mean that *she* should be careful?

It was a fast flight, and they were met at Newark by a limo with tinted windows and a uniformed chauffeur. As Red said, when she gave him a sardonic look: What's the point of being rich if you don't get to indulge yourself every once in a while?

The chauffeur drove them to a large mansion in a wooded part of the state, where the staff called them Mr. James and Miss Gloria. She barely had time to freshen up and change clothing before Red had a late model, mid-range car brought around from the garage and he and Sarah drove off through a maze of winding, wooded, two lane roads. Sarah wondered whether she could find her way back to the mansion in a pinch. Then she decided she couldn't, and decided not to worry about it.

Tony's Pizza was set in a small, older style shopping center. It sat in a line of small shops, flanked by a bakery and a gift shop. Farther off were a discount store and a supermarket. The parking lot was half full. Red parked the car and they stepped out into the gathering dusk.

A sudden screech. She jerked her head up in time to see a sea gull settle atop the lamppost in a flutter of wings. It was just light enough that the lamp couldn't make up its mind to glow or not. Dusk. The trip east had cost her two hours, and her peace of mind. She didn't believe for a moment that Red had brought her out here for pizza.

They stepped inside and the smell of freshly baked bread enveloped her. There were two men behind the counter calling to each other in Italian as they strewed cheese on their pies with the ease of long practice. Sarah took a deep, delicious breath of onions and peppers and tangy tomato sauce.

It was a narrow store, with the pizza ovens against the right-hand wall, behind the counter. Farther back were plastic booths for diners. Two of them were occupied, one with a crew of boisterous teenagers.

"He's waiting for us," Red told her quietly.

"Waiting? Who?"

Red nodded toward the booth farthest back on the right where were two men sat, side by side. The younger man sported a full, straw-colored beard. His older companion was well-dressed, with a pinched face and gray at the temples.

"Kennison," he said.

"Kennison?" She narrowed her eyes. "You mean—?" Red made a gesture and she kept her voice low. "Red, if I gave a party for everyone in the world, he wouldn't be on the guest list!"

"It never hurts to talk, even with the enemy. Perhaps, especially with the enemy."

"I've got nothing to say to him. Red—I mean, 'Jim.' *He killed my friend!* He tried to have me killed!"

"Then it sounds to me like you should have plenty to say to him." He took her lightly by the arm and guided her down the aisle to the booths. She went along reluctantly.

"I don't like it," she told him.

"You don't have to," he replied.

Kennison saw them coming. He stood and reached across the table to shake Red's hand. "It's nice to see you again, James. Mind your cuffs." He indicated the pizza sitting in the middle of the table.

Red slid into the booth, opposite the bearded man. "It hasn't been that long."

Kennison smiled. "Yes, quite." He looked at Sarah. "And this must be . . ."

"Gloria Bennett," said Red.

"Of course." His smile broadened and he took her hand and raised it. His touch was surprisingly gentle. Sarah thought he meant to kiss the hand and yanked it out of his grip as if she had been burned. Kennison took no offense. "I quite understand how you feel, my dear," he murmured. "Were I you, I should feel the same."

Sarah looked from Kennison to Red and saw no way out of it. She gathered her skirt and sat down at the table. Kennison

333

waited until she was settled; then he sat and placed his napkin carefully on his lap.

The bearded man was staring at her with a frankly appraising gaze. He had already taken a slice from the pan and held it steaming in his hand. "I've heard of you," he said before biting into it. "You're a bonny programmer."

"And from Alan, that is high praise, indeed." To Red, Kennison added, "This is Alan Selkirk, who joined my personal staff a while back. Alan, Miss Gloria Bennett and Mr. James Caldero." Selkirk waved distractedly while trying not to lose his cheese. Kennison gestured. "Would either of you care for a slice?"

Red studied the pizza. "What did you order? Pepperoni and anchovies? Anchovies, for crying out loud."

Kennison shrugged. "You can always remove them." He selected a piece for himself and transferred it to a paper plate. He picked up a plastic knife and fork and cut into it.

*Fastidious,* thought Sarah. How many people eat pizza with a knife and fork?

Kennison saw her looking at him, and paused with the fork nearly to his lips. He smiled across the table at Sarah. "A gentlemen never eats with his hands."

Red handed her a plate with a slice of pizza on it. "Here. Have some." He looked at Kennison. "Shall we get started?"

"My dear fellow," Kennison told him, gesturing with his fork. "Over dinner?"

"Why? Will there be port in the drawing room later?"

Kennison sighed and laid his utensils down. "Very well. I understand you have some information for me."

"To trade."

"Yes. To be sure." Kennison was brusque, all business. He looked for a moment as if he were sucking a lemon. "Since your young lady friend appears not to trust me, perhaps I should 'show my cards,' first."

Red waved a hand. "You gave me your word. Value given for value received."

"True; and a gentleman's word is his bond. I do not give mine lightly; nor to anyone." He patted his lips with his napkin and glanced quickly around the pizzeria. Then he folded his hands on the table. "Very well," he said. "My information is this: we are under attack."

Red nodded. "You've lost several Council members. Benton, Weil, Ruiz. We've been lucky. Most of Our names did not go public. Mark Lopez has disappeared. Louise Vosteen's house was vandalized, and I had to quit my job. But our system was not as vulnerable."

Kennison looked chagrined. "Yes. My fault, that. I was careless. But, I was not speaking of the random attacks of the ignorant mob. Something far more insidious is afoot." Quickly, and in a low voice, he outlined his situation: The viruses that had appeared in his system; the mysterious phone call.

Sarah listened without sympathy. She did not see why she should care that Kennison was being persecuted. He had ordered Morgan's death, hadn't he? And Paul Abbott's. And the other couple—she had forgotten their names. And the man in the park, who had been shot in the head. Kennison had tried to have her killed; and Dennis, as well. Sarah hadn't wanted anyone to die when she had written that worm; she had only wanted to expose her enemies to justice. Perhaps she had forgotten that the statue of Justice holds a sword; but, all things considered, she found it difficult to muster any compassion. If Kennison felt threatened, it was no more than he deserved.

And yet, it was a different matter to sit across the table from the man and look him in the face. Dammit, villains were supposed to be villainous. They were not supposed to be polite or well-mannered. They were not supposed to stare at you through eyes filled with fear and uncertainty.

Red rubbed his hand across his chin. "Viruses, you say? And there were three of them?"

"Three that we detected."

Red looked at Sarah. "You haven't been doing anything extracurricular, have you, Gloria?"

Sarah shook her head. She didn't care if Kennison's system was putrescent with bacteria. But it hadn't been she. As to whoever it was . . . Well, it said in the Book, "the enemy of mine enemy is my friend."

"I haven't heard of any such attack against our own system," Red said. "And I would have heard. I've been sitting in on the last few Council meetings, and none of our Council members have reported anything. Have your other Councilors received similar phone calls?"

Kennison took a deep breath and let it out. "I have been reluctant to contact my brothers and sisters. You know we've gone incommunicado, don't you know? There has been no contact among us during the last month, while we allowed the media and the police to watch us. A ploy to counteract the information in the Dump. I thought of calling Sister Paige, but . . . the caller may have intended to lure me into an act which, if revealed, would have nullified the entire ploy. I did not want to risk it. I am no Judas goat. I thought it best to consult with you, *in corpora* and *in camera*."

"You don't mind leading Us into danger, then."

Kennison smiled and spread his hands. "I am asking for help."

"I think it was the FBI," said Selkirk abruptly; and they all turned and looked at him. "The Official Government must be disturbed over what they've read in the Dump. I'm sure they have been trying to penetrate your system as well as ours."

"Perhaps, Alan. Yet, there were *three* bugs."

"FBI; CIA; KGB." Selkirk counted on his fingers. "I'm surprised there weren't more."

"Then why the phone call? Loose lips. A government agency would not indulge in such a foolish touch of bravado. They would quietly gather their intelligence and be done."

"The call was to spook you," Red told him.

Kennison didn't smile. "I must congratulate them on their success."

"The viruses were taps," Selkirk told them. "Not bombs like the one 'Gloria' wrote. They didn't hurt anything; they hadn't crossed the barrier I built, into the, ah, main system. There are physical locks that only Mr. Kennison controls. All they did was copy some files and download them outside."

"Someplace called the Q File," said Kennison. "At least, one of the taps had that destination. We're not sure yet about the others."

"Q for Quinn?" asked Red.

Kennison shrugged. "I assume so."

"Anyway," concluded Selkirk. "That's why I think it was just routine government surveillance."

Kennison looked at him. "But the call, Alan. What about the call?"

Selkirk frowned; looked at his pizza; shook his head. "I don't know." He sounded disturbed.

"The caller," Sarah told them both with a sense of savage glee, "wants to destroy you. She wasn't tapping your system to confirm a suspicion or to check out what she read in the Dump. She *knew*. Beyond any hope of doubt, she knew. And she wanted you to know she knew."

Kennison's eyes were tunnels of despair. "But, who was it? The Official Government? The Chamber of Commerce? The League of Women Voters? If we knew who it was, we could strike back. Defend ourselves, somehow."

Red leaned back and tapped his teeth with his thumb. He looked into the distance for a few moments, then he turned to Sarah. "I've got to tell him. I gave my word."

Sarah wondered if he were asking for her approval. "Go ahead then."

Red looked at Kennison. "Alright. There is another society. A third one."

Kennison looked puzzled for a moment. Then his eyes widened. "A third—"

"Yes. Not a daughter society, created by diffusion—we've both taken steps to assure ourselves against that possibility; but a genuinely independent development. One that is as old as we are."

Selkirk leaned forward. "No, that's not possible!" he said, his eyes wide.

Kennison glanced at his companion. He scowled, laid his forefinger aside his nose, and sat that way for a few moments. Then he pulled a pen from his jacket pocket and began scribbling on his napkin. Sarah watched partial differential equations skitter across the tissue. The Greek letters blurred as the fibers soaked up the ink. She recognized condensation equations from Dr. Gewirtz's classes. Ideas that were "in the air" condensed around suitable particles—human minds with high surface areas—and precipitated into the culture. Kennison was working through the solution set, counting the equilibrium points. Her estimation of his abilities climbed another notch.

Kennison studied what he had written. Then he screwed the cap on his pen and put it away. "Yes, Alan. I'm afraid it is possible." He passed the napkin to Selkirk. The young Scot took it with shaking hands.

"Damn it all," Kennison said to no one in particular. "We should have seen this possibility before." He turned impatiently and jabbed a finger at the blurred figures on the napkin. "There it is, Alan. And there. Yes, I know the usual solutions are 0 and 1. Most ideas never do 'catch on' or they have a single 'discoverer.' But, under certain, narrow conditions, there can be multiple, independent discoveries." He

337

turned to Red. "Are you sure suitable conditions existed at the time of the Founding?"

"They call themselves the Secret Six," Red told them.

Kennison frowned. "The Secret Six." Selkirk closed his eyes and laid his head in his hands. He took a deep breath and let it out. Kennison shook his head ruefully. "I'm afraid the Founders were rather too sanguine about the Secret. They assumed that they were its sole proprietors and never thought to look to their own contemporaries."

"Hubris," Sarah said. "The Greeks considered it the great tragic flaw."

Kennison considered that. "Yes. Pride always goeth before, does it not?"

Briefly, Red outlined what they had discovered. The list that Dennis and Sarah had found in Quinn's old mansion. The Stray he had found in the Dump. Bosworth's analysis of anomalies. The stranger who had been watching the safe house—and who had apparently drugged and interrogated Sarah. Kennison took notes in a small booklet he kept in his jacket pocket. Sarah saw that he wrote in a shorthand. She suspected it was a private code.

"And one other thing," Sarah added. She aimed a finger at Kennison. "Tell me straight out. Did your people kidnap Dennis French from the hospital in Denver?"

Kennison steepled his fingers against his lips, as if in prayer. "Why do you ask?"

"Because your man, Crayle, didn't seem to know about it."

"Ah. Yes. And where is Brother Crayle?"

"I'm here," she said shortly. "He's not."

Kennison nodded slowly. "I had wondered. You are a remarkable young woman, to have acted so resourcefully under such circumstances." His eyes glittered. "You must have been in considerable danger. Frightened." His tongue darted out quickly, wet his lips.

"You haven't answered my question."

Kennison blinked. "Oh, yes. Your question took me quite by surprise. You see, we had assumed that your people had rescued him."

Sarah closed her eyes and cupped her hands briefly over her face. That was why Red's search of the Dump had yielded no clues. Dennis had disappeared. Vanished without a trace. And maybe her enemy's enemy was only another enemy. She looked at Red. "Jim?"

338

"If this third group has him," he said grimly, "we'll find him."

"Indeed," said Kennison. "And I shall be pleased to assist you in any way possible." He paused and considered. "It may interest you to know that another intrepid band was also searching for Mr. French; at least, at second hand. His, ah, roommate, I believe."

"Jeremy Collingwood and the DU group. Yes. Jim told me." Jeremy as a man of action hardly seemed possible. Dennis' roommate had always struck her as an ineffectual sort of person. Still, who could predict how a crisis would affect somebody? One man may turn brittle and another hard, after his turn in the fire.

"It may also interest you," Kennison continued casually, "to know that he and his Team were wiped out this afternoon in an explosion."

Sarah looked up sharply. Her heart gave a thud. Jeremy, too? She struck the table with both fists; and the teenagers on the other side of the room glanced over at the noise. "How *dare* you sit across from me and—"

"Quietly, young lady!" He drew himself up. "It was not I."

Selkirk spoke. "The news blamed it on negligence. A reporter for one of the local stations found a two-month old work order in the building maintenance files requesting the repair of a gas leak. The maintenance super claims he never saw the work order; but he would say that in any case."

"Two months old?"

"Yes. That pre-dates the formation of the Study Team. So, even though the newsreaders did mention the Dump, they concluded that the explosion was a coincidence."

"And you may believe as much of that as you wish," said Kennison.

Red looked at him carefully. "It wasn't you."

"I don't believe in coincidence."

Red tapped his teeth again. He looked at Sarah. "I believe him." To Kennison: "Could it have been anyone else in your organization?"

He shook his head briefly. "Possible, but not likely. Not with the way we were being covered by the media."

"You're here," Red pointed out. "The media isn't."

"Hmm, yes. I see your point. My New York penthouse has a secret elevator. As far as the policeman outside my door knows, I am recuperating from my long flight out here."

339

"So, one of your brothers or sisters could have arranged it."

Kennison scowled and folded his hands as if in prayer. *What gods*, Sarah wondered, *could a man like that pray to?*

"Possible," Kennison admitted at length. "Denver is part of Brother Ullman's fief; but . . ." And he shook his head. "It was a monumentally stupid act; and, among Brother Ullman's many faults, stupidity is not numbered. Only . . ."

"Only what?"

"Only that one of those listed as killed was a mathematician. If the Denver team was actively investigating that aspect of the Dump . . . The other university teams are ignoring it as absurd, *prima facie*. Brother Ullman may have felt compelled to act without consultation. Still— I am familiar with his channel into the group; and I doubt that he would have sacrificed so useful an asset." He took a deep breath and looked at Sarah. "So, it appears as though we are to be allies of convenience. I will do whatever I can to assist you in locating your friend."

Sarah looked at him and wanted to deny him and his aid both. But Kennison seemed earnest; his face, open and sincere. And, what the hell? If it would help her find Dennis, she would accept help from the Devil, himself.

"Why?" she asked him. "Why should you help me?"

"Why, for the sheer pleasure of aiding another human being in distress." Kennison spread his hands guilessly. "And because the people who took your friend are threatening me, as well. So, for a little while, our paths converge on the same goal. Later, fortune may cause us to oppose one another once more; but for now . . ." An elaborate shrug. "Who knows? We may find we have more in common than you suppose."

Sarah tried to speak but Kennison held out a hand. "I understand perfectly, my dear. If it is any consolation to you, I voted against the Action of which you were the object. There was insufficient evidence, I told them. We may be taking aim at the wrong target. But, alas, Madam Weil was not to be deflected. A most impossible woman. She . . . well, *nil nisi bonum*. Later, your behavior took on a more sinister hue, and I am afraid I did allow myself to be persuaded. I hope you understand that there was no ill will toward you personally. As later events proved—at Mr. Benton's estate, at Ms. Weil's mansion—our fears of exposure were well justified."

He checked his watch briefly. "And now I fear we must

340

take our leave. In the meantime . . ." He turned to Sarah and said seriously, "If you should ever find yourself in danger, over this matter or any other, you may come to me for protection and you shall have it without reservation."

Sarah searched his face, trying to discern what Kennison was up to. But she saw nothing there but openness and sincerity. Almost an eagerness. Could it be that Kennison was trying to achieve a rapprochment with her? Was he trying to make amends of a sort for the hell that he had helped put her through? It was strange to think of this man as her would-be protector. But, either Kennison was a damned good actor, or he had meant exactly what he had said.

She glanced sidelong at Red and was surprised to see barely concealed hostility there. Red, who never took anything too seriously, did not like Kennison's offer of protection. Was Red jealous? Now, there was a thought for you!

They lingered for a while after Kennison and Selkirk had gone. Red said that he wanted to finish the pizza and Sarah sat quietly beside him, waiting. She leaned her elbows on the table and clasped her hands. She studied the smooth, dark skin of her arms. When she closed her eyes, she was acutely aware of her body and the position of all her limbs. She could feel her blouse and skirt hugging her figure. She could even sense Red sitting less than a foot away from her. His aura?

Finally, Red spoke. "It looks like the Secret Six is gunning for Cousin Daniel. I wonder if the mysterious lookout at the Safe House was theirs, as well."

She opened her eyes. "Don't forget," she told him, "that the Six split the same way that the Babbage Society did."

"I haven't forgotten that."

"I notice you didn't tell 'Cousin Daniel' that part."

"It must have slipped my mind."

"Slipped your mind."

"He's a bright boy. He'll figure it out. Carson's Dilemma is required study."

"Was he serious? About offering me his protection."

Red dropped the last pizza slice on the pan. "I hate anchovies," he said. He wiped his hands on a napkin. "Yes," he told her. "He was serious. Dan is a snake and a slimy son of a bitch; but he's an honest slimy son of a bitch. He'll never lie to you but once."

"Once?"

"When he's lying to himself, as well."

Outside, night had fallen. They paused a moment in the doorway to the pizzeria. Cars weaved about the parking lot in cavalier disregard for the marked traffic lanes. Sometimes, they roared past the store fronts at what seemed to Sarah dangerous speeds. To the right, at the far end of the lot, a gang of teenagers was clustered around two pickup trucks parked in front of the MacDonald's. Sometimes they cheered the drivers of the cars. The high intensity lamps threw everything into a peculiarly colorless sort of illumination, as if she were watching an old black-and-white movie.

"Well?" asked Red, zipping up his jacket against the September chill. "Was meeting Kennison as bad as you thought it would be?"

She shook her head. "It was worse."

"Worse?"

"Yes, dammit. He was charming."

Red shot her a look. "That's pretty wretched, all right."

"I think I was prepared for anything except that. 'Jim,' he *apologized* for putting out a contract on me and my friends. And he meant it."

"That's Dan. He oozes sincerity the way a slug oozes slime."

She looked at him. "You don't like him, do you?"

He grunted. "I didn't think it showed."

They stepped off the sidewalk and headed toward their car. As they did so, there was a screech to their left. She turned and saw another car accelerating toward them from the direction of the Bradlee's store. The wheels spun and the headlights weaved across the night, pinning her to the spot. Red shoved her hard with both his hands and they dropped behind the nearest automobile. Sarah scraped her knees and palms on the gravel. She hugged the ground. The smell of asphalt and motor oil was heavy in her nostrils. Small stones poked into her arms and thighs. *This is it,* she thought. *That bastard Kennison . . .* She heard three pops. One. Two. Three. Carefully spaced. The car lurched and a tire hissed like the audience at a bad play.

Tires squealed, and the other car spun 180°. It shot up the ramp onto Oak Tree, where it turned sharp left, cutting off a mini-van and forcing it off the road. The mini-van driver honked his fear and anger at the vanishing madman, leaning on his horn. Sarah heard a car door slam and ineffectual curses flung

342

into the night air. The teenagers at the far end of the parking lot were running toward them.

She became aware of Red's arm wrapped tightly around her, his body sheltering hers. She could feel his heat. Slowly, he relaxed his grip. She didn't move. Then he sat up and brushed at his clothing. "This is getting to be a nuisance," he said.

Sarah raised herself and was surprised to find she was not shaking. "What do you mean, a nuisance?"

He gave her one of his glances. "Every time you and I go out together, I get shot at." He stood and slapped at the knees of his trousers. Then he looked in the direction their assailant had vanished. "It's almost not worth it."

# II

Tex Bodean found Sarah in the music room playing a quiet blues number on the piano. She sensed his presence behind her, but did not let it interrupt her. Her eyes were closed; her head, held back. She let her fingers mourn: for her friends; for herself. Morgan, Dennis, Jeremy. *I'm a-goin' down that long lonesome road, yes I am.*

"Did you find it?" she asked without stopping the music. *I'm goin' where the water tastes like wine.*

"Yep." She heard him rustle inside a sack. There were dull, metallic sounds. "In the barn with the others. Woulda maybe found it sooner, 'cept it was in the discard pile. Horse musta threw it a while back." *Goin' down that road feelin bad, Lord, Lord.*

From the corner of her eye, she saw him place a horseshoe on the ledge of the piano. "Bad luck," she told him. "You should set it with the open end up. Otherwise the luck runs out of it." *I'm goin' where I've never gone before.*

She let the blues fade away on a minor chord. She held her hands poised for a lingering moment over the keyboard. Then, she sighed and reached out and took the horseshoe.

"Jimmy told me you played the ivories," Tex said.

She ran her finger down the left side of the shoe. There was a hairline fracture there. Just like the tracks she had found that day on the mountain. *Someone here*, she thought sadly. *It was someone here.*

"I play the 'bone, myself," Tex said.

"Do you?" Someone had watched and spied. And drugged her.

"Yep." He pushed his cowboy hat back and leaned against

the piano. He stuck his thumbs in his belt loops. "Hear tell your new persona had a field test."

"News travels."

"Did it hold up all right?"

"I'm here, ain't I?"

Tex nodded. "Told you not to worry. The cops don't normally investigate the complainants. But even if they had, your fingerprints woulda matched the ones on file for 'Gloria Bennett.' We try to be thorough."

She wasn't sure how to take Tex Bodean. He was friendlier than Walt or most of the others at the safe house. He smiled easily. Like Red, he seemed perpetually amused by life. Yet, she felt uneasy around him. It wasn't simply his off-hand confidence; a cool assurance that bordered on arrogance. She felt as if she were always on exhibit around him. That he was only waiting to see what she would do next. Perhaps that was it. Red was a player, ad-libbing his way through the script, while Tex was the audience, chuckling over the gaffes. Being Janie's segundo on the ranch, he had soaked up some of her awful detachment.

"Red doesn't think Kennison was behind the hit," she told him.

Tex considered that. "Hunh. Possible. What do you think?"

She paused. "I don't know." If not Kennison, one of his colleagues? From what she and Red had deduced, the Babbage Society was unravelling under the crisis.

"It might not have been a hit at all, you know. Maybe they just wanted to put you guys through the wringer with the cops."

Sarah shook her head. "No, they wanted to kill us." My God, how could she discuss it so calmly? Could it be she was getting *used* to it? "They tried to run us down, so the cops would think it was an accident. The kids race their cars in the parking lot at night. When that didn't work, they tried a few shots; but they took off because they didn't want to get caught themselves."

Tex smiled wolfishly. "Ah, but who were They? Kennison's friends? The Secret Six? The Six's daughter society, the one that seems to have vanished? Or . . . who knows? Jimmy's briefing the Council right now. Atlanta Office found the Stray, so he figured to bring Cam up to date on everything."

She handed him the horseshoe. "Do you know which horse wore it?"

Tex studied the shoe, turning it end for end. "This is the one, then?" he asked.

"Which horse?"

"I figure the sorrel. That's the only one threw a shoe last month."

"And who rode it?"

"The stablemaster gave me a list. Names and dates." He reached into his shirt pocket with his left hand and pulled out a sheet of paper that had been folded several times. He handed it to Sarah and she unfolded it and read, looking for the one date that mattered.

She found it, and chuckled sadly. "For want of a nail . . ." she said.

"What is that?" asked Tex frowning.

She took the shoe back from him and hefted it, open end up. "Good luck," she told him.

"How do you rotate the world?" asked SuperNerd.

Walter Polovsky sighed. "Move over kid; and watch how I do it." He rolled his chair in front of the terminal keyboard. Sarah stood behind them and watched over their shoulders. She sipped from a can of diet soda. The screen showed a complex tree diagram—they called it a weighted di-graph—filled with tiny bubbles, arrows, and logic gates. Her old friend, the "why—why" diagram—with a college diploma. "Trouble?" she asked.

Polovsky shook his head. "Nah."

"It makes me nervous," SuperNerd said, "to have people watching me like this."

Polovsky played for a moment on the keyboard. "See? You gotta make the gamma and kappa parameters go full circle. One revolution of gamma for each increment of kappa." Polovsky hit the return key authoritatively and sat back with his arms folded to watch. "You gettin' this, Bosworth?"

SuperNerd nodded. "What about her?" He pointed to Sarah.

Polovsky looked at her. "She don't need my help."

Sarah smiled at him, but he didn't smile back. *The hell with him*, Sarah thought. She turned her attention back to the screen. Bosworth clicked on one of the bubbles and a window opened, showing the details. *15.05.07. Sinking of the Lusitania.*

"That's the one," she said. "It was on Dennis' list."

Bosworth nodded and moused the cursor to an adjunct bubble and opened that one as well. The second window read: *German Embassy telephones* Lusitania *passengers, ad-*

346

*vising them to cancel passage; places advertisement in NY papers, announcing intention to sink ship.*

He scrolled into the menu bar and pulled down *Counterfactual*. Then he clicked on the *Lusitania* and selected the logic gate for negation. The di-graph flickered as bubbles burst, shifted, or were replaced by new bubbles. An automatic window opened with the heading: *Selected Events Altered by Counterfactual.*

Sarah set her can down and studied the list. Dates and events in two parallel columns. Everything seemed to track about the same; but the analog events in the Counterfactual ran later than they had in actual fact. U.S. troops did not arrive to stiffen the Allied line until May of 1918, nearly a year late, and after the Hindenburg Offensive was in full swing. The March, 1919 armistice declared the war a "draw."

Polovsky looked back over his shoulder at her. "Is this what you wanted?"

"What I wanted? I don't know. I'm just rolling over rocks. Why did the Germans sink a passenger liner, even if it was carrying war supplies? It was a stupid thing to do. It brought us into the war sooner."

"They didn't care if we came in or not," Polovsky told her. "The Germans rated our army about equal to the Rumanians; and Hindenburg thought he'd have it all wrapped up before any Americans could get over there."

Sarah pointed to the printout. "They would have gotten their wish if they hadn't sunk the *Lusitania*."

Polovsky waved a hand in irritation. "Sure, *we* know that; but they didn't have any cliologists to tell them so."

Sarah did not reply and there was a long moment of silence. Finally Polovsky turned and scowled at the screen. "Shit," he said.

SuperNerd jerked his head from one to the other. "What?" Polovsky looked at him.

"Wake up, kid."

SuperNerd's mouth opened into an O.

"Sure," said Sarah. "European scientists were no duller than American scientists. Crawford wasn't even unique in this country."

Polovsky took a deep breath and let it out. "Yeah. Yeah, I know. But the kid here, he found actual documents about the Six. From their early days, anyway." He scowled again at the screen. "This is just inference, though. Just because an event

347

was a turning point, doesn't mean it was planned that way. Every action has consequences; but that doesn't mean that it was a consciously directed action."

"All my actions," Sarah told him drily, "are consciously directed."

Polovsky made a noise in his throat. "You know what I mean. There are always residual anomalies in the data." He poked a finger at the bubbles and logic gates. "There are millions of unit events in the digraph. Some of them *have* to be improbable. It's like throwing a dart at a dartboard. What's the probability that the dart will hit a particular point by random chance? There's an infinite number of points on a disk, right? So the probability's one over infinity. Zero. No chance, *a priori*. But—" And he stabbed a finger at her for emphasis. "—the dart has to hit *somewhere*. That's the rub. Afterwards, we look where it hit and say how damned improbable it was. So we figure it must have hit there on purpose."

"When we see darts hitting around the same point, time after time, then maybe they *are* hitting there on purpose. Maybe a dart-thrower with good aim." Sarah felt a pang of irritation. Was Polovsky being deliberately obtuse? *It's only when we like the answer,* she thought, *that we accept the reasoning.* If we don't like it, we'll pick every nit there is. That was why the Catholic Church, in their canonization proceedings, always appointed a Devil's Advocate—to argue *against* the proposed sainthood. Maybe Walt was just taking a contrary view.

"Let's say some group wants Germany defeated. Maybe the same gang that convinced von Kluck to wheel his army short of Paris in 1914. But they need American troops to do it. So somehow they convince the High Command to sink a passenger liner." And over a thousand civilian men, women, and children. She set her mouth grimly. "Meanwhile . . ." She tapped the adjunct bubble. ". . . another group was working for German victory by trying to keep American citizens off the *Lusitania.*"

Polovsky looked at her. "How many groups do you want to find?"

"As many as there are," she answered.

"Don't forget Joffre and Viviani," said Bosworth, reading the detail window for another bubble. "It says here that Wilson wasn't planning to send troops until spring of 1918.

He wanted to use the Regular Army as cadre to train the National Guard and the newly-authorized National Army. But the French convinced him to send an expeditionary force right off."

Polovsky twisted his face. "I suppose you think Joffre and Viviani were part of a secret cliological society."

She shook her head. "Purposeful behavior creates patterns in the data; and factor analysis helps us identify those patterns. But, everything anybody does has a purpose behind it. If we analyzed events at a fine enough level of detail, we'd find that every person who's ever lived has been a cliological factor." She flashed, suddenly, on her living room, in a home she would never see again. Red sitting in the sofa, that big, stupid grin on his face, telling her how she and everyone else was "tampering with history." She hadn't believed him then. Now she saw that he had been right. Somewhere in the back of her mind a thought wriggled, trying to break loose. "What distinguishes the footprints of the Babbage Society and the Secret Six from those of other folks is that the patterns are in the *indirect* consequences of the events, not in the direct consequences."

"Are the consequences of any of our actions always what we intended?" Polovsky shook his head and looked away. "Three billion cliological societies," he said. "Jimmy's gonna love this." He ran a hand across his face and glanced at SuperNerd. "What do you think?"

"Why are you asking me? I'm just the dumb kid."

"I'm asking."

The teenager shrugged. "Okay. Then I think she's right."

"You think she's right. Great." Polovsky shook his head again. "They're just gonna love this."

The door to the computer lab opened and, thinking it was Red, Sarah spun around. But it was only Tex Bodean. He stopped just inside the door and looked around with lazy eyes. He pushed his cowboy hat back on his head and slouched against the wall. He stuck his thumbs in his belt loops. "So, here you are," he said.

"Yeah, here we are," Polovsky replied. "We been here all day. What is it?"

"Meeting. After Red finishes up with Cam."

"What meeting is this?" asked Polovsky. "Why wasn't I told?"

Tex looked at him. "Because I'm telling you now."

Sarah wondered how Red ever expected to bring his coup off. Even she, new to Red's cabal, could see that Walt and Tex rubbed each other the wrong way; that Walt thought Norris an adolescent freak; that SuperNerd thought the whole business was a computer game.

From the outside, she decided, a group always seems to be a seamless whole, with a single will. "The Secret Six" wants this. "The Babbage Society" did that. Giving the group a name, like "Labor" or "England," heightened the fancy. But from the inside it was patent nonsense. Every group was a cauldron of individual emotions, rivalries, and ambitions. People might make common cause over a single issue: to overthrow the tsar, or the Bourbons; but beyond that? Group solidarity always came to grief on the ugly realities of individuals.

Red wanted to repeal Quinn's Prohibition. He wanted the Associates to abandon their passivity; to fight the Society's efforts to create a docile nation of technopeasants. Yet, while Tex and Walt—and the others she had yet to meet—had joined him in this, had they really made common cause? They had agreed that it was time to stop drifting with the current; but had they agreed in which direction to lay the course? She herself felt as close to Red as anyone reasonably could. They had saved each other's lives; and that bound them closer than most lovers. Yet even she could not agree with his goal. The answer to manipulation was not counter-manipulation; it was no manipulation, at all.

She looked from Walt to Tex. And if she felt that way, what of the others? What personal ambitions did each one harbor? After the Revolution comes the Coup. Red had a vision; but visionaries were always discarded afterward, and the merely ambitious took over. Ask Trotsky. Ask Robespierre or Commandante Zero. Ask Sun Yatsen and Bismark.

Ask Brady Quinn.

Tex nodded to Sarah. "Did you find what you expected?"

Sarah glanced at the screen with its altered digraph. "Yes. I'm afraid so. There are at least five Europen horseshoe nails that we know weren't engineered by the Babbage Society; and they don't seem to fit in with what we know about the Six, either."

Tex grunted. "We didn't have enough troubles." He shook his head. "Life used to be right simple. Nowadays it seems like we need a damn program."

350

"It does have elements of farce, doesn't it?" Sarah said. Farce? Theatre of the absurd! Sartre could have written it. Everybody protecting the same Secret from everybody else.

No manipulation. She had vowed that while she searched for Fee in the long forest shadows that awful sunset at Falcon Castle. No more manipulation. An end to the Society and to the Associates. And now: to the Six and its offshoot; and to who knew how many others?

A noble resolution. Yet cliology and its attendant methods were a fact. Pandora's box was already open. How can you assure that no one will use a tool, when that tool has already been in use for generations? How could you even know it was being used? Cliology could be applied too subtly, over the course of decades. *We're too accustomed to rapid change,* she thought. We celebrate every ephemeral swing of fashion, while the generational trends go unnoticed. Cliologists were patient; their machinations could creep up on you like the tide. And there were too many cliologists.

She straightened slightly in her seat. Or were there? She remembered, suddenly, that Hope had lingered there in Pandora's open chest.

351

# III

There was a voice like a distant bell in an endless night. He floated in the darkness, turning slowly end over end while pulsating devil masks in red and orange laughed in a starless sky. A glowing face swelled until it stretched from one unseen horizon to the other. Behind it, another blossomed. And another. They trailed back like a chorus line to the vanishing point. They tried to tell him something in booming base notes just below the level of intelligibility.

"Jerry. Jerry, can you hear me?"

His eyelids fluttered and an explosion of light snapped them shut again. He groaned.

"I think he's regained consciousness," he heard a voice say.

He wished the voice would leave him alone. The darkness was peaceful. Floating was pleasant. The devil's mask kept tempo with the hammering in his head. Reluctantly, he forced his eyes open.

It was still too bright. He turned his face into the pillow. It was soft and cool. "Where am I?"

"You're in Porter Memorial Hospital."

Jeremy squinted for the source of the voice and found the face of Jim Doang floating above him. A bandage encircled Jim's head. His eyes were blackened.

Jeremy forced himself to a sitting position. He was lying in a bed, in a room that smelled of antisepsis and fresh linen. The room seemed to be slowly rotating. His head ached and throbbed. He saw Herkimer Vane sitting beside the bed. Vane's ribs were taped and his left hand was bandaged.

Gwynn Llewellyn was sitting in a chair by the wall. Her

hands were curled into a ball on her lap and tears glistened on her cheeks. Jeremy pointed at her.

"You're dead."

Vane blinked. "I trust not."

"But . . . The explosion . . . The conference room . . ."

He shook his head. "The others were all killed."

"All killed," Jeremy repeated. All of them. Torn apart like rag dolls. He tried to conjure up a feeling for Geoff, and Penny, and Henry and the other team members; but all he could feel was a vast relief that he himself had not been in there. He looked again at Gwynn. "All except you," he said.

The historian looked uncomfortable. "I had gone to wash my hands," she said.

"It was a gas explosion," said Doang carefully, "The television news blamed it on negligence."

"A gas leak." He remembered the noise, like a thunderclap. The physical blow lifting him up. The walls and doors bulging and splintering. Had they been any less thick . . .

"They interviewed Brenda this morning," said Llewellyn. "She vaguely recalled having told maintenance about the smell once before. She said she had written a work order."

"Brenda wasn't hurt, then?"

"Minor cuts and abrasions," said Doang. "She fell behind her desk and that protected her. She was lucky. We were all lucky."

"Yes," Jeremy said. "We all should have been in that room, you know." He looked from one to another and their faces told him that they knew that fact very well. Vane slowly rubbed his palms together. Llewellyn was looking at Doang, who left his post at Jeremy's bedside and found a chair against the wall. He sat there and leaned his head back and closed his eyes.

"Do any of you really believe," Jeremy asked, "that it was an accident?"

Llewellyn shook her head slowly. Vane gave him a bleak stare. "The news program did mention the Babbage Society and the fact that we were investigating the Dump; but they pointed out that the gas leak predated the formation of the study team."

Jeremy exchanged a look with Llewellyn. "If the records say that, it must be true." He heard the bitterness in his own voice.

"Nor were the study teams at Stamford and Chicago attacked—" Vane added.

353

"No," said Doang. He opened his eyes and challenged them. "But they did not have Jim Tranh Doang evaluating the mathematics, did they? Like all good humanists, they ignored the math." He looked away. "The wiser course, as events have shown."

"It was a stupid thing to do," said Vane. "The bombing. It was stupid. Regardless of the official explanations, it can only inflame suspicions." He shook his head. "How could a Society behave so foolishly and survive so long?"

" 'Foolish' is not the word I would use to describe them," Jeremy told him.

Vane glanced at him. "Foolish and vicious are not mutually exclusive," he said. "Often, they are correlated."

"Still the academic, eh, Dr. Vane?" Doang's voice was heavy with sarcasm.

"Has it occurred to any of you yet," said Llewellyn, "that, having survived the original attack, the four of us are now prime targets for another attempt? And that this is, in fact, the very hospital from which Dennis French disappeared?" She clenched and unclenched her hands.

"Since regaining consciousness," said Doang, "I have thought of little else."

Jeremy felt his heart thud. They would come for him here. He knew it. He had only to wait and they would come and he would be taken to wherever it was that Dennis had been taken. "They know where we are."

Vane rose from his seat and paced. Jeremy watched him. The little man's brow was beaded with sweat and he glanced nervously around. His right hand massaged the fingers of his left, where they protruded from the bandages.

"We've got to do something," Llewellyn said.

Vane stopped his pacing. He stood by the door to the room and ran his good hand up and down the metal door frame. "They won't find you," he said at last.

Doang watched dispassionately. Llewellyn pursed her lips. "How can you say that, Herkimer? We are sitting ducks here."

"I mean that they won't find you here." He turned and faced them. "The hospital records show that you were killed in the explosion."

There was a pause while they digested his words. "Clever," Jeremy said into the silence. "But aren't you afraid of going to that particular well too often?"

354

Vane looked at him and grunted a weak smile. "Bear with us. We aren't accustomed to this sort of thing."

Llewellyn looked from one to the other. "What are you two talking about?"

Jeremy nodded toward Herkimer Vane. "I think your friend is an agent of the Babbage Society."

Vane raised his eyebrows. "Oh, good heavens, no!" He seemed shocked.

"Jeremy, what are you suggesting?"

Doang spoke. His voice was harsh. "He is suggesting that Dr. Vane knows more than he admits." He turned his face to the historian. "He is suggesting that it was too damned convenient, the way Dr. Vane delayed entering that room."

Vane's brow darkened. "And I might point out with equal conviction that Mr. Collingwood and yourself also delayed entering that same room. And that Dr. Llewellyn *conveniently* left it barely in time. A more suspicious mind than my own . . ."

Gwynn rose suddenly from her chair. "Stop it, Herkimer!" There was an edge to Llewellyn's voice. "You're being offensive. We are all friends here." She hunched her back away from them and studied the instruments bolted to the wall. "When the explosion shook the building," Jeremy heard her say, "I hurried back and found . . . and found a shambles. Do you know the original meaning of a shambles? It meant the floor of a slaughterhouse." She turned and Jeremy saw her face was red and moist. "Herkimer, you were struck by the door. Do you want me to tell you what was on the other side of that door? What was *spread* across it like jelly on toast? I say 'what' because there was no hope of identifying 'who.' "

Vane blanched and turned his face away. "No."

Doang bowed without leaving his chair. His head dipped upon his chest. "Accept my apology, Dr. Vane. Mass murder is not a charge to be levied so lightly."

Jeremy noticed that Jim had not exactly withdrawn the charge. He struggled to sit erect. "Yet, we know the ruthlessness of the Babbage Society. They kill those who come close to their secret. Last week, I announced that Dr. Doang would present his mathematical analysis today—"

"Yesterday," Gwynn interrupted.

"Yesterday. And the room explodes shortly after we should have entered it. It seems clear that someone did not want us to hear Dr. Doang's report."

"Someone in the room?"

Vane looked at her. "Yes, Gwynn. Someone in the room. Who else would know of Dr. Do . . . of Jim's presentation? And, by extension, someone who survived; since I doubt that anyone would willingly throw his own life away like that."

Jeremy felt ill, nauseous. The effect of his injury, perhaps. Or just the idea that someone could kill himself over an abstraction. Like those people in the Middle East who drove cars packed with explosives into the midst of their target. Or the man in the park who had shot at Sarah Beaumont. Jeremy could not understand fanaticism. It made people behave irrationally; and irrational behavior was unpredictable and frightening.

"Do you know what you're saying, Herkimer? You're saying that one of us is a member of the Babbage Society. That one of us set that bomb, or caused it to be set. That one of us killed our friends."

"They were your friends and mine, Gwynn. Long-time associates. Colleagues. But Jeremy barely knew them; and Dr. Doang, not at all."

Doang stood abruptly, knocking his chair over. "If I had wanted to prevent you from learning the validity of those mathematical models, I had only to present a false report. Or present no report, at all. Had I not come to Gwynn with my proposal, none of this would have happened."

There was a silence, and Doang appeared to listen to his own words. "None of this would have happened," he whispered. He righted his chair and sank into it.

"No, Jim. It could have been you," Vane persisted. "To discover what we knew or suspected, you had to attach yourself to the Team somehow. As a mathematician, there was only one plausible way." Doang glared at him, but said nothing.

Jeremy laughed.

They turned and looked at him. "And what about me, Herkimer? How can you make me the villain of your piece? The Babbage people assaulted and then kidnapped my dearest friend. Make me the centerpiece of your scenario. I dare you!"

Vane smiled and spread his hands. "I am simply reconstructing history. The same facts, but with different fictions. You wish to be the centerpiece? Very well. This Dennis French was never your friend; only a convenient cover." He held up a hand. "You may say differently. You may say so

356

with great umbrage; *but how are we to know you are telling the truth?* We see only the surface behavior, not the motivations. Once you became aware of what Beaumont and your own roommate were up to, you took steps to eliminate them and others they may have spoken to. You went to Gwynn here because you wanted to know what Mr. French had told her."

Jeremy felt cold and frightened. It was plausible. It could have happened that way and only he could know otherwise. He saw Gwynn eyeing him uneasily. How easily the facts could be twisted!

"What about the study team?" he asked. "Why would I let her go ahead and form the study team?"

Vane shrugged. "Why, to unearth any other historians who took the Dump seriously. Why do you suppose I went to such pains to show that I did not? I am sure you had agents on the Chicago and Stanford teams, as well."

"Herkimer," said Llewellyn. "Do you believe any of what you are saying?"

"No, of course not. But I try to keep an open mind. Do you want to hear the scenario featuring yourself?"

Llewellyn looked at him for a long moment. "No," she said.

"Ah. So you see? Each of us can suspect the others. Each of us can lie awake in the dark wondering which of the others is a murderer." He shook his head. "A band of brothers," he said.

"But you did conceal our presence here in the hospital," Jeremy reminded everyone.

"An elementary precaution. It may not hold up in the long run. The doctors involved have accepted heavy bribes. Some may even see the need themselves; but—" A fatalistic shrug. "Sooner or later, someone will talk. In the meantime, no one searches for dead men."

"In the meantime," Jeremy said. "But what are we to do? Where are we to go? Obviously, none of us can return to our homes." He thought briefly of his possessions. Of the books; the *Mondrian*; the crystal. What would happen to them? Who would get them? He had never bothered to make a will and had no relatives who would own him. Well, it was all behind him now. If, under these conditions, a man wasn't prepared to abandon his baggage without a second thought, then he wasn't prepared to go on living. Life could always bring new possessions; but possessions could never restore life. He thought

357

of the ancient Benny gag: *Your money or your life*, demands the robber. *I'm thinking! I'm thinking!* replies Benny. It wasn't funny at all, Jeremy thought. It wasn't funny at all. "If we are officially dead," he concluded, "who are we now?" Curiously, the thought of walking away from his past life brought him a feeling of exhilaration, a sensation almost of liberation.

Vane looked at them. He stuck his right hand in his jacket pocket and hung his head. "There were four people who have died here in the hospital within the last two days. People without close relations; newcomers from out of the state. The records have been altered. You are now them and they, you."

"When my brothers and sisters come for my body," Doang told him, "they will know it is not me."

Jeremy shook his head. No one would come for "his" body. Did that make him lucky, or unlucky?

Vane hunched his shoulders. "It is a temporary expedient; only a ruse to get us out of the hospital safely. The sexes match; but not the ages or, in the one case, the race." He shrugged. "We must move quickly, now that Jeremy is conscious. Everything has been arranged."

"Everything has been arranged," said Jeremy. "By whom?"

Vane looked at him, but said nothing.

"If, as you say, you are not one of the Babbage people," Jeremy insisted, "who are you with? There was another Society mentioned in the Dump. A splinter group."

Vane shook his head. "Utopian Research Associates, they call themselves. I am afraid not, Mr. Collingwood." He walked slowly around the ward, picking things up and putting them down. He rubbed his good hand along the smooth metal of the bed rails. Finally, he appeared to reach a decision. He faced Jeremy. "I am a junior partner with Detweiler, Barron, & Stone."

"The investment firm?" asked Jeremy, surprised.

"The same."

"Who are Detweiler, Barron and Stone?" asked Llewellyn.

"They are an old-money Boston investment firm," Jeremy told her. "Founded in . . ."

"In 1848, by Adrian Detweiler," supplied Vane.

"Thank you. The Street claims they have 'the Midas touch,' an uncanny ability to identify new growth industries. I've steered several of my clients in their direction."

Llewellyn spoke from the other bed. "But, Herkimer, what

is your connection with Detweiler; and why should they care about hiding us from the Babbage people?"

Jeremy saw it an instant before the others did. He began to laugh. That resurrected his headache and he leaned back upon his pillows. "You're another," he said, pointing a finger at Vane. "Aren't you? Another group trying to guide the course of history." It made perfect sense. Hadn't Gwynn told him that Vane had invited himself onto the team? Hadn't Vane spent most of his efforts belittling the very idea of historical science? Damage control. Get a man onto any group digging into the secret and sabotage their efforts. And . . .

"You were trying to find out about the Babbage Society, too. Weren't you?"

Vane faced them. "We have a few minutes before the van comes," he announced. "So I will fill you in on what you need to know." His voice was harder, more authoritative. He paused, rubbed his hands together, thrust them into his jacket pocket. "The Firm has been always been successful in its investments; rather more so than the SEC suspects, because, as Mr. Collingwood has surmised, we have been making use of certain natural laws that occur in human affairs."

"Laws which you have always been careful to disparage," Jeremy pointed out.

Vane spread his hands in appeal. "Would you hand such an advantage to your competitors? Certainly, we sought to discourage others from discovering what we had discovered. How better?"

"Science applied to culture is dehumanizing," Jeremy quoted. "You cannot reduce people to numbers."

Vane nodded. "Exactly."

"Bastard," said Doang; and Jeremy looked at the mathematician's angry face with some surprise.

"I beg your pardon?" asked Vane.

"I said 'bastard.' If our lives are to be imprisoned by these laws of yours, at least we should be allowed to see the bars."

Vane shrugged. "I had hoped for deeper understanding from a man of your abilities. Is your spirit restricted by the law of gravity? Your soul enchained by thermodynamics?"

"Then your group has no connection with the Babbage Society?" Llewellyn asked. Vane turned to her.

"Oh, heavens no, Gwynn. They are barbarians; or at least they have become so. We were unaware of their very existence until lately. And, I daresay, they of ours. I begged onto

359

your study team, Gwynn, not only to protect our interests, but also to learn what I could about a potential danger." He paused and appeared to gather his thoughts. "We have always believed that the anomalies in our data were due to the complexity of cultural processes and to our own imperfect understanding. I am afraid that The Firm's own work was purely empirical. We lacked the computing machines and the theoretical framework that the Babbage Society seems to have had. In fact, our interests lay solely in the realm of finance. Save for discouraging a truly scientific exploration of such issues, we took no direct action of any sort. We were content to ride the financial trends and cycles." He smiled thinly. "We regarded the forces of history to be as unmalleable as the forces of the ocean. We could study them, analyze them, even forecast them within the constraints of precision and time span; but we could not change them."

"Yet the Babbage Society believed otherwise," Jeremy pointed out.

Vane pursed his lips and considered. "So they did. But then, they had a Mission. They had a need to believe in their ability to alter fate."

"Are you implying that they can't?" Jeremy could not say precisely why that prospect disturbed him so. Unless it was that killing to protect an error was somehow worse than killing to protect a truth.

Another shrug. "I am not prepared to say," Vane told him. "There are undeniably anomalies in the data. But might they not have occurred regardless? I wonder. The information we have is that the Society's efforts produced unexpected results as often as not. Perhaps they are simply deluding themselves with their own self-importance. Considering how elusive cultural 'facts' are, such self-deception comes easy."

"Facts are constructions you told me once," Jeremy said slowly.

Vane nodded. "I see that my impromptu lecture made an impression. Yes, facts are constructions—fictions—we make from our data. Yet, the same facts can be reconstructed differently. Did Wellington win the battle of Waterloo? Or did Blücher? Or did Napoleon lose it—which is not quite the same thing? Did not the poet, Simon, once say 'A man hears what he wants to hear and disregards the rest'? Everyone is a 'spin doctor,' reconstructing facts with utter sincerity. What does the Gross National Product *mean* when the martini an executive buys at lunch is added to the steel tonnage? It is not that such figures are meaningless; it is that their meaning might be quite different from what we suppose. How easy it would be for any group to construct the meaning they prefer. To convince themselves of their own potency. Listen to any president seizing the credit for some economic happenstance."

"Yet," said Llewellyn, "between 'powerless' and 'omnipotent' there is a wide range of possibilities."

"Indeed. Which makes it all the more important for us to learn what the Babbage Society knows. It may be that, having taken no actions during its life, The Firm has created no anomalies; and, therefore, left no 'footprints' that might be traced back to it. This is a point on which we would very much like to assure ourselves."

Jeremy felt an uneasiness growing in himself. Vane was affable and pedantic. Entertaining, even. Here they lay in a hospital room, hiding after a bomb attack on their lives, and they were discussing historical philosophy. His uneasiness, when he had prodded it awake, grew from the fact that Vane was telling them too much. And that must mean that Vane did not expect them ever to be in a position to reveal what he had told them. Images of the Man in the Iron Mask flickered through his mind. After all, Vane thought that one of them planted the bomb that destroyed the study team. And, come to that, Jeremy had to wonder if it might not have been Vane. Vane was waiting for someone to come and take them away. To where, he wondered? And would they ever return?

Run? Jeremy knew he would not get very far. He was weak, dizzy. And to where would he run? His apartment? Hardly.

So running was out. DB&S would take them where it would. And that meant, if they were ever to be free again, they would have to keep their eyes and their ears open. They must be ready to seize every advantage.

All this he considered and decided in an instant. A part of his mind, even as he listened to Vane's discourse, marvelled with self-satisfaction. He was making decisions, taking charge of his own life. The helpless funk he had experienced in the days following Dennis' accident (accident!) seemed to have happened to another person, a man of whom he was now vaguely contemptuous.

There was a tapping at the door. It must have been a code,

because Vane listened carefully, then opened the door to admit a lean, young man. He whispered to Vane, who listened nodding. The young man left and Vane addressed the group.

"The van is here," he announced. "Our Mr. Anderson will return presently to escort you out. In wheelchairs, as tradition demands. We will leave one at a time, so that no one will suspect we are together."

"Herkimer?"

He paused. "Yes, Gwynn?"

"Can we rely on you?"

"Gwynn! What a thought!"

"I want to hear you say it."

"Very well." He looked at them all. "I promise that no harm will come to any of you. We are not monsters. We have only asked to be left alone to our own interests. We have taken action in these last few months only because of our fears over the Babbage Society."

"You know," Jeremy told him, "the Babbage people could have been students of yours."

Vane blinked and gave him a puzzled look. "How so?"

"You've said all along that 'facts' are 'constructions.' The Babbage Society has taken that a step further. They've tried to set themselves up as the construction company."

"Our Mr. Anderson" shepherded them down the elevator and through the lobby. Jeremy felt conspicuous; but no one paid him any mind. His was, after all, a routine dismissal.

When it came Jeremy's turn at the desk, he was startled to recognize the nurse as the same one he had spoken to when he and Gwynn had come looking for Dennis. The nurse, however, showed no sign that the recognition was mutual, so Jeremy kept his mouth shut.

The van was parked in the driveway in front of the main entrance. The side doors were opened wide. Jim was already waiting inside and Jeremy climbed in and took a seat beside him on the rearmost bench. A few minutes later, Llewellyn was wheeled out and assisted aboard. She sat in the middle bench while Anderson returned to fetch Vane.

"Shall we hijack the van?" asked Jeremy. He was only half-kidding. How much of what Vane had told them was the truth? He leaned over Gwynn's shoulder and looked at the dashboard. No keys. "Does anyone know how to hotwire an ignition?"

"Jeremy, don't be ridiculous. I've known Herkimer for a long time. I can't believe he means us any harm. Besides, we have a more immediate concern."

Jeremy sat back on the bench. "What's that?"

"Your nurse friend at the desk?"

"She didn't recognize me."

"You think not? I came down just behind you. After you left, she made another one of her zombie phone calls."

Jeremy frowned and bit his lip. "She did?"

"Yes. And that means two things. First: she did recognize you."

"And second?"

"It would be a good idea to keep a watch out the rear window."

Jeremy glanced at the hospital entrance. Herkimer Vane was being helped from his wheelchair. "Will you tell Vane?"

"It's your decision, Jeremy."

"Mine? Why?"

"Because whomever the nurse called, they are no doubt the same ones who kidnapped Dennis. If they do follow us, they could well intend to capture us. In which case, they would take you to wherever your friend is."

# IV

"Yes, Alan?" Kennison looked up from his work as Alan
Selkirk entered his office. He laid his pen aside as Selkirk
dropped a sheaf of computer paper on his desk.

"I finished that analysis you asked me to do."

"Thank you, Alan." Kennison flipped through the sheets
and watched the numbers dance, as if in an animated cartoon.
"I will take this home and review it." It was a dismissal. He
retrieved his pen and returned to his interrupted work. He
checked the items one at a time, reviewing each one methodically. Slow and steady wins the race, after all. After a moment, he looked up again and saw Selkirk lingering by the
desk.

"Was there something else, Alan? The virus hunt is pro-
ceeding smoothly, is it not?"

"Yes, no problems there. Ms. Baker is an extremely capable programmer—although I told you I could have handled
the job myself. We've gotten all the viruses out of the system.
But . . ." He indicated the printout he had just delivered.
"Aren't you going to tell me what this is all about?"

Kennison raised an eyebrow. "Simply another job, Alan.
Another job. Kennison Demographics is a well-known, legitimate firm with many clients, who sometimes have odd
requests."

Selkirk leaned over the desk, bracing himself with his hands.
"Come off it! The 'client' this time was you! What are you up
to?"

Kennison stared at Selkirk's hands until the the young Scot
backed away and straightened up. That was better. Alan was

definitely becoming a problem child, Kennison decided. He had an inflated notion of his own importance. Sometimes he seemed to forget who was in charge. He behaved disrespectfully; and respect for one's betters was the *sine qua non* of civilization. A place for everything; and everything in its place. He would have to teach this young man his place. People always performed more efficiently when they knew their place and kept it. Craft unions knew that. It reduced friction and jealousy; and assured that work would be done by those competent to do it.

And yet, there was also something about Alan that appealed to him. Perhaps a wispy memory of his own youth. The young man was certainly not one of the docile sheep. Well, sheep needed sheepdogs, did they not? And kings, crown princes. Would Alan make a suitable crown prince? Perhaps. Perhaps.

"Yes," he told his protegé, "but what I said still holds. Some of our clients have unusual requests. This project of mine is very important to, let us say, our future security and peace of mind."

Selkirk shook his head. "I don't get it. What have the Spanish Land Grants in the Old Southwest to do with our peace of mind?"

"Loose ends," he told him. "Loose ends. Have you identified those Grants which came through the fighting essentially intact, and which remained thereafter in the possession of the same family?"

"Aye. I have. But shouldn't we be running a check on the Secret—"

Kennison cut him off with a raised hand. He nodded toward the main room where the policeman sat drinking coffee and chatting with the secretarial pool. "Tomorrow things will be back to normal, Alan. Ask me tomorrow about our plans. Prudence has been doing some investigations for me. She has not been idle, exactly."

Indeed not. In fact, Kennison mused, she has been rather energetic. He and Prudence had held "consultations" nearly every evening since his return from the meeting with Malone. It was, he admitted to himself, growing to be rather a bore. Although she was pleasant to the eye—and Kennison found himself contemplating this fact in his idle moments—her demands were growing harder and harder to fill. Perhaps the pretense of Little Girl Lost had become a shade too transparent, and had lost its savor; its ability to entice him.

He sighed and checked his watch. She would be calling any moment now, with her insatiable demands. The lips that never cry, *Enough!*

"So, all in good time, Alan. All in good time. Meanwhile, it is 1700 hours. Is it not time for the Daily Bug Hunt and Back-up?" The intercom buzzed and Kennison picked it up. "Yes?"

"Danny?" he heard a frightened voice say. "I'm in trouble. Hurry down here, please!"

Kennison covered the mouthpiece. "That will be all, Alan," he said, stressing the words evenly. It was important that the help know who was in charge. "And close the door when you leave."

When he was alone, Kennison uncovered the phone. "Now, see here—!"

"Please, Danny! I'll never ask you again. There's someone else down here. I need you." He could hear tears in her voice.

"My dear," he murmured. "What you need is more of the spice of life." Kennison wondered about that. Perhaps a new game . . . ? Prudence needed her shabby little charades the way an addict needed his "mothers' tears." Her mind was a cesspool of depravity. Each time he left her, Kennison felt unclean. He would scrub himself down with a hard brush in the executive shower until his skin tingled.

So, why did he always go to her? Perhaps he was overly considerate of her feelings. He had always been a soft touch. She would whine and wheedle him until he was induced once more to participate in her grotesque pretenses. Yet, she was a fellow human being, was she not? It would be callous of him to deprive her of her needs. The more so since she was one of his own people. Besides, Kennison was a great believer in the value of play. All work and no play, after all.

"Very well. I shall be there presently." He hung up before she could prattle her thanks. He stood and straightened his pants, which had become somewhat askew, and headed for the washroom elevator. *Noblesse oblige.* He sighed. No one ever said being the boss would be easy.

The offices of Johnson & Cheng were dark. *Tomorrow,* he thought, *things can return to normal.* And these nightly encounters would come to an end. The police protection would be withdrawn. The Night Shift would return to work and these offices would resume their wonted bustle. It made good sense for J&C to work a Night Shift, since that was daytime in China. (And, in fact, the Night Shift did conduct normal commerce, lest the perfectly legitimate Day Shift wonder why nothing was ever accomplished at night.)

He walked out to the middle of the main office, wending his way among the red-lit shadows. Let us get the squalid business over with. He stood still, listening.

Nothing.

There was a slight whispering sound that was either someone's breathing or the air conditioner. "Pru?"

No answer.

Perhaps there had been a burglar, after all? Perhaps Prudence had tried valiantly to stop him and had been struck down. Perhaps, even now, she was lying battered and bleeding, precious moments ticking away.

Kennison stode quickly up and down the aisles, glancing into each cubicle as he did. He remembered how she had cowered earlier in the knee hole of one of the desks. Perhaps the burglar had been real then, too; and now, frustrated, he had returned to the scene of his earlier, thwarted crime. Kennison found a pair of scissors on one of the desks and took it with him. He crept slowly, carefully. If the burglar were still in the offices, Kennison's own safety lay in silence.

He finished the last row of cubicles without finding Prudence's body. His pulse raced faster. He wondered if the burglar had raped her. Burglars came from the lower classes, and rape was always on the minds of that ilk. Prudence would have resisted, naturally; fought back gallantly as he ripped her clothes from her. He pictured her lying, bruised and naked, while the ill-bred brute had his will.

He entered Cheng's office and there she was. She was sitting in Cheng's high-backed, leather swivel chair, grinning at him. She was fully clothed.

It was a trick, after all.

Kennison felt a wave of anger like the heat from an open furnace. He laid the scissors on the desk and walked around to the chair in a few quick strides.

"Damn you, Prudence!" He spun the chair so she would face him and her head flopped loosely onto her shoulder.

Kennison noticed several things at once. The smile on her face never wavered for an instant. There was an awful smell as of an ill-kept restroom. And there was a large stain that covered the front of her dress from breasts to lap. The stain was black satin in the ruddy light that infused the room. He reached out and touched it and his hand came away wet.

He felt a grave sadness. "Oh, Prudence," he said, and there was no emotion he could name to put into those words.

"How touching."

He spun and faced the doorway to the office. A ghostly figure in shades of red and black. A .38 caliber pistol with silencer pointed directly at him. Kennison squinted into the gloom. "You!"

Genevieve Weil stepped inside the office. "Come around where I can see you, Danny Boy." She waved with her gun barrel. Kennison carefully stepped around the desk. Weil looked him up and down. Her eyes fixed on his trousers. "Well, well, you impotent piece of slime. I see you were finally able to get it up. Unbelievable. What has that fat slut got that I haven't?"

"More dead," Kennison said angrily, "than you alive."

Weil's face tightened and the gun came up and Kennison regretted the haste of his words. *Control*, he thought. *You must act with control.* Prudence Baker had never been the great love of his life. And yet, were the scene to replay itself, he knew he would speak the same words. Curious.

Weil grinned at him and lowered the gun a fraction of an inch. "No," she said. "Not quite yet."

Not quite yet! Then there was hope. Kennison's mind switched into high gear. "You survived the assassination attempt! We were all so worried—"

"Save the bullshit for the rose garden. Flowers like it. I don't."

"It may not yet be safe for you to show yourself. The mob hysteria that took Benton and Ruiz, and which nearly took you, has begun to abate somewhat, but—"

Weil laughed. Kennison could feel the sweat on his forehead, in his armpits. His knees felt weak. He knew he must smell of fear.

"You son of a bitch," she said. "I never did like you. You should never have gotten your father's Council seat."

"But—"

"Shut up and listen, you pompous, flaccid piece of shit. You want to know how I survived the car bomb? That's easy. I wasn't in the car. I knew what the public reaction to Beaumont's stratagem was likely to be. I knew there would be

368

mobs and violence. Mother told me often enough. And I knew that one or more of my devoted followers would try to take advantage of it. I had you and Ullmann and Paige on my list; so when Paige showed up on my doorstep with that asinine idea of hers, I knew she was up to something. It didn't take long to find out what. Judd is very good at what he does."

"She and I—"

The gun came up again. "I thought I told you to be quiet. Don't you obey your chairman? I know exactly what you said to her. I've got my own ears in your mansion."

Desperation made him speak. "Then you know I never said—"

"Of course, you never said. You never say anything. You're the only man I've ever known who could speak entirely in innuendo." She smiled coldly. "Do you want me to tell you how she screamed while Judd questioned her? It was pathetic. The sight of blood completely unnerved her. No one needs all ten fingers, anyway. She bawled. She whimpered. She offered to side with me, to betray you. It did her no good. I needed her information; I didn't need her. Who can trust a traitor?"

Slowly, Kennison's fear and desperation gave way to anger. Sister Paige had been his rival, his "Seward." But she had been acting for him when she had gone to Weil's mansion. He was responsible for her. "What did you do with her?"

"Don't be dense. There was a body in the car, you know."

"Was she . . ." *A blackened husk; hands melted to the wheel; head thrown back, her jaws wide in a scream that never came.* "Was she conscious when it happened?"

"Oh, certainly." Weil was matter of fact. Of course her victims knew. That was half the fun. Simple deletion was not enough for her. There had to be cruelty as well. Silently, Kennison cursed her; and spared a curse for her mother, too. If she had raised Genevieve differently . . . *Ah, well. Concentrate on the present, Daniel. On the Now. There might not be too much of the Now left you.*

"She watched us wire the device in place," Weil told him. "Judd even explained the circuitry to her and what it would do. Oh, how she squirmed and twisted; but the seat belt was welded shut. I can still see her eyes as I waved good-bye to her."

Kennison wanted to tell her she was an evil woman, but he clenched his jaw tight and wouldn't let the words out. He tried to imagine how Paige had felt, strapped into that car; knowing her fate, but helpless, helpless.

Weil could see something in his face, though. "What? Is it different when it's done at a distance? Are you somehow better than I because you've always hired those who hired those who did it?" She laughed at him

Her eyes went past his shoulder to the body in the chair. They looked thoughtful. "Your porcine playmate didn't whine. I'll give her that. She knew it was no use. I could have used her."

"Then why—"

"Why? You silly ass. Because she actually liked you. I won't use so bourgeois a word as 'love.' That's hard enough to imagine where something like you is involved. But there's no accounting for taste. She actually thought you would save her somehow, like some fucking knight in a goddamned fairy tale. Charging with your lance out straight. She threw it in my face, the bitch."

And he had failed her. She had waited for him to come and save her and instead she had gotten a bullet through her heart. Kennison was shamed. A man protects his own; and he had failed. Brave, brave little Prudence. His stalwart, gutsy aide, who went down heroically into the darkness. Somehow, Kennison knew, he would avenge her; even if it meant his own life.

"I'll be damned," said Weil. "So that's what does it for you. Danger." She aimed the gun at his crotch and Kennison stiffened. A .38 slug wasn't a .45. It would not stop the charge of a determined man unless it hit him in the heart. Tyler Crayle had told him that one time.

She uncocked the gun. "It seems a shame to waste it, don't you think? I mean, as long as we've got it, why not use it? I tell you what, Danny Boy. If that thing you've got lasts longer than the usual five seconds, I'll kill you quick instead of slow. And if it lasts long enough for me to get something out of it, I may not kill you at all. I may keep you as my bucking bronco. Then all I have to do whenever I want to saddle up is scare the living shit out of you. How does that grab you, Danny Boy?"

Sincerity was a word foreign to Weil's vocabulary. Kennison had no illusions of what was in store for him. What she wanted from him was not something she would want twice. There were, after all, plenty of roosters in the barnyard. But this was one rooster she'd been unable to have. Yet, her offer

370

meant a few moments more of life; and Kennison had discovered how precious those moments could be. "Yes," he said in a husky and cracked voice. "Yes."

"That was good, Danny Boy. You always did know how to crawl. Now come here and—don't forget—I've still got the gun. If danger is what does it for you, then as long as I've got my gun, you'll have yours." She laughed again, as if she had said something funny.

Kennison moved toward her, his mind working furiously. Weil was shorter than he; so her arms were shorter. If they were short enough . . . It was a desperate ploy; but this was a time for desperation. What was it Montrose had written?

> *He either fears his fate too much,*
> *Or his deserts are small,*
> *That puts it not unto the touch,*
> *To win or lose it all.*

He slid into her embrace and tried to repress a shudder of revulsion. He could feel the cold metal of the gun barrel against the back of his head. She turned her mouth up to be kissed and he pressed against her as hard as he could. She liked it hard and brutal, he remembered.

Her body remained sceptical, stiff in his arms. So he blanked his mind and imagined it was Prudence he was holding. He turned her around so he could press her against the desk. Over her shoulder, he stared into Prudence Baker's sightless eyes.

"What are you doing?"

"Permanent secretary," he murmured. It was an old joke. A secretary is not permanent until screwed on the desk.

She finally relaxed into him. Her arms snaked around his neck and shoulders. He could still feel the cold metal of the gun; but it was the butt he felt, not the barrel.

*Now!*

He grabbed the scissors from the desk and, with both hands joined in a fist, he rammed it into her back with all his strength. At the same time, he clamped down hard with his left arm, pinning her right to his side.

Weil jerked as if electrocuted, arching her back around the fulcrum of the scissors point. Her breath shrieked out in a hiss. He felt the blades scrape on bone and pushed harder. His hands grew warm and wet.

"You son of a bitch!"

He kept her tight in his grip. She couldn't bend her right arm far enough to bring the gun to bear on him. She twisted and squirmed. *Like Sister Paige must have done.* Her muscles contracted spasmodically and he heard the gun spit behind him. The muzzle flash singed his hair; the bullet grazed his back and buried itself in the far wall.

His grip on Weil grew slippery as her struggles became more frenzied. He could feel her arm sliding under his own. Wriggling free. If she could get the gun loose . . .

He twisted and batted her arm aside, and another silenced bullet shattered the elegantly framed diploma by the bookcase. He seized the gun arm in both his hands and twisted.

The third shot ran up his arm like a streak of fire and passed though the fleshy part of his shoulder. The pain was intense, but he knew that to lose his grip now would be death. *Pain means nothing to men like me.*

She was beating on him with her left fist, but he ignored it, twisting the right arm more and more until something snapped and the gun fell from limp fingers.

"My God!" she cried. "Oh, my God! It hurts! Call an ambulance!"

He pulled away from her, kicking the gun into the corner as he did. Madame Weil, he thought, should be the last person on Earth to call on God. She staggered away from him. Cheng's desk was covered with a black, glistening pool. The scissors were set in the back of her dress like a pair of eyebolts. Her arms twisted and flailed, trying to reach it. "Pull it out, God damn you!"

He stepped forward and grabbed the scissors; hesitated briefly, so she would cry again for his help; then he yanked them free. He tossed the scissors into the corner with the gun and turned her roughly around to face him. Her face was pale in the red light; her stance, less steady. She was crying.

The Great Harpy was crying!

He released her and she crumpled to the carpet. He had done it! He, Kennison, had been to the brink of the Great Abyss and had escaped! He had looked Death itself in the eye; put it all to the touch. He had bested Genevieve Weil.

He had it all now. With Weil and Paige both gone, the Society was his for the asking. No, not for the asking. For the taking. He would never again ask for anything. Everything that Weil had had was his.

Everything? No, come to think of it, there was one thing

that she had that he had never taken. He stood over her and looked down. She stared back at him with hopeless eyes. She knew he would never call an ambulance for her. She had given no mercy to others and could expect none in return. She knew she was going to bleed to death in the dark.

His lips pulled back from his teeth. "You were perfectly right, my dear," he said with precise politeness. "It does seem a shame to waste it. As long as we've got it, why not use it?"

Later, he used the phone in Johnson's office.

"Alan? Would you come downstairs, please. We've got a small problem to clean up."

373

# V

Anderson made a face in the rear view mirror. "You can't
be sure they're following us," he said.

Jeremy looked again out the back window. The blue sedan
was still there. "They're following us," Jeremy assured him.
"They're very clever about it. They don't ride our bumper,
like in the movies; they leave two or three cars between us."

"Well, don't worry," Anderson told them. "We're headed
for Stapleton."

"So are they," he said.

"That's not what I meant. Even if the men in that car are
Babbage Society agents, they wouldn't dare try anything. It's
too public." The traffic light changed to green and he turned
right onto Colfax. "What can they do?"

"Shoot us. Have you forgotten the gunman in the park?"

"They'd be caught!"

"They might not care." The gunman who had shot at Sarah
Beaumont had done so in the midst of a crowd. He had
opened fire in the sure knowledge that he, too, would die.
Jeremy shuddered. That sort of fanaticism was alien to him.
He could not imagine the state of mind of such a person.
Gwynneth had suggested that the man might have been "programmed" in the same way as the nurse. In some ways that
was worse. It was one thing to sacrifice yourself for your own
fanatic beliefs. It was something else entirely to be sacrificed
for another's.

Herkimer Vane turned around in his seat and looked at the
three in the back. His forehead was creased by a worried

frown. "What do you suggest we do? The Firm is unpracticed at such desperate games. We've never—"

"Yes, yes." Jeremy waved an irritated hand. "We know. You don't do such things. Why do you want my advice? Am I more practiced than you?"

"Jeremy?" Gwynneth Llewellyn spoke. "We've got to do something." Her voice was tight, controlled. Jeremy could hear the edge of hysteria in it.

"I know. I know." Jeremy fell silent. How had he become the leader? Why not Gwynn? Or Vane? Or Jim Doang? Or even Anderson? *I'm only an accountant. I don't do this sort of thing.*

It came to him that none of the others did, either. Leadership was his by default. The others had thrust it upon him, will he or no. Was that how it always happened? Were leaders only those who were slow in stepping back?

"How well armed are we?" he asked.

Anderson laughed. "There's a jack handle by the wheel well in the back."

Oh, fine. "No knives or guns?"

"They are usually not needed," Herkimer Vane said, "on an academic study team."

"But the bombing . . ." Good Lord, but Vane's people were babes in the woods! You would think that, after what had happened, they would have brought Uzis along on the rescue mission. Not one man and a mini-van. The hell with them. He looked at Jim Doang. "What about you?"

"Me?" Doang looked at him. "Do you have a plan?"

"Will you do what I ask you?"

The mathematician shrugged. "It is my karma."

"How good are you?"

"Black belt. But if the men behind us have guns . . ."

"Never mind that, yet." He clasped his hands together and frowned at the floor of the van. He could see a way. It was a desperate chance, but they might just barely pull it off. A lot depended on what their pursuers intended. If they had a Stinger missile in the car with them and were only waiting for a clear shot, it didn't matter what plan he came up with. He decided not to worry about contingencies like that. Start with the basics. Fight or flight. Pick one. Details to follow.

"All right," he said after a while. "Here's what we'll do."

\* \* \*

Kennison let his gaze wander across the bank of television monitors. The wall of his study was drawn back fully and seven phosphor-dot faces gazed back from the flickering screens. The faces wore a variety of expressions: impatience, doubt, barely-concealed hostility. Four other screens were blank, and Kennison kept his own face just as carefully blank as they.

Benton. Paige. Ruiz. Weil. Kennison wished that more of the screens were blank. It would be better to start his new regime with a *tabula rasa*. The current Councilors were tainted by their long association with the Great Harpy. Whether they had supported her or opposed her made no difference. She had been the origin of their coordinate system; and they had all defined themselves in reference to her.

All saving himself, of course.

Well, a man must work with the materials he has at hand. Kennison took a long swallow of the espresso that Karin had brought to his study. He had always prided himself on being a realist. He composed himself, joined his hands together on the desk top, and stared earnestly at the bank of screens.

"The queen is dead," he announced. And they could not help but finish the phrase in their own minds: Long live the king! Even as they looked into Kennison's face. Plant the seed. Plant the seed. He did not bother to update them on the timing of the queen's death. Only three people knew of that: He and Alan and Judd; and that was two too many. But Judd was safely stashed away in a cabin in rural Wisconsin, under strict guard, until Kennison could decide what to do with him. If he was as good an interrogator as Weil had claimed, there might be room for him on Kennison's staff. Otherwise . . . It depended on whether Judd were more loyal to his mistress or to his craft.

As for Alan . . . Well, Alan would keep quiet, for his own good. He was an accessory after the fact. Kennison shuddered. *What a grisly way to dispose of the bodies!* And so much blood. It was amazing how much blood the body held. Fortunately, the shower drain in the washroom had handled it. But the rest . . . The solid pieces . . . They had had to cut them small—a brutal, knife-dulling task—so they would not clog the toilet. Kennison had thought it a fitting end for Weil, and had helped both in the disassembly and the flushing. But when it had come Prudence Baker's turn, he found he had not the heart for it. Alan . . . Well, it could be useful to know how cold Alan could be.

"We know that," Frederick Ullman said acidly, bringing Kennison's attention back to the meeting. "The Society has been without a chairman for too long, while we play-acted that foolish game of Paige's." Kenninson saw Ullman's eyes flick to his left. He was looking at his own screens, wondering why Paige's was blank. Let him wonder.

"It worked, didn't it?" said Montfort. "It convinced the public that we were not what the Beaumont Dump claimed we were."

"I went along with it," Ullman admitted. "But I doubt it was necessary. The public will believe only what they are told to believe. What they want to believe."

A gaggle of geese, thought Kennison. Quack. Quack. "Our first order of business," he pointed out, "is to elect a new chairman. A center to hold us together." *Things fly apart! The center cannot hold! Mere anarchy is loosed upon the world.* He smiled and spread his hands. "The net is open to nominations."

"I nominate Brother Ullman," said Brigit Toohey.

"Second," said Westfield.

"Move the nominations be closed," said Toohey.

"Second."

"Call the question."

It happened so fast that it was over before Kennison knew it had started. Reynold Sorenson, who had been poised to nominate Kennison, looked back helplessly from his screen. Kennison gave him a look that said *why didn't you speak up faster?*

"Well, Brother Kennison? The question has been called." Ullman's thin, wrinkled face cackled at him from his screen.

Kennison reached forward and fiddled with the knobs on his transmitter. "I'm sorry," he said. "I lost the audio for a few seconds. What did you say, Brother Sorenson?"

Sorenson took the cue. "I said that I nominated Brother Kennison."

"What is this, Brother Kennison? What are you trying to pull?" asked Ullman. "Sister Toohey called the question."

Kennison shrugged for the camera. "A tree falling in the forest."

"I didn't hear her, either," said Sorenson. "There was static on the line."

"Nor I," said Peter Lewis. He was a big, broad-shouldered man with close cropped blond hair and a face ruddy from high mountain skiing. The window behind Lewis' shoulder opened on the snow-capped vista of the Bitterroot Mountains. Lewis' secret retreat was hidden somewhere in Idaho or Montana, no one knew where; and he left it only rarely. Kennison's staff had been comparing that vista against the Geological Survey maps for several years without success. Someday, perhaps— although Kennison had lately wondered whether the back-drop were nothing more than a hologram, a subtle lie.

Lewis smiled. "I no more doubt Brother Kennison's hon-esty, Brother Ullman, than I doubt yours." Lewis showed teeth that were white, even and plentiful.

Kennison admired Lewis' dental work. He wondered if this meant that Lewis would support him in the balloting. Possi-ble. Possible. It would be a close thing, he realized, if Toohey was in Ullman's pocket. He hadn't known that. Could he postpone a vote? Not likely, given the urgency of the situa-tion. See it through, then. Hope for the best and damn the fucking torpedoes. *If you can make a heap of all your winnings/ and risk it on one turn of pitch and toss . . .*

How did the rest of it go? He had forgotten his Kipling.

"No one has seconded Brother Kennison's nomination," Ullman pointed out.

Lewis shrugged. "Oh, I'll second it. Fair's fair, after all. There should be a contest."

"Are there any further nominations?" asked Kennison. He saw the eyes flit from screen to screen. The pygmies wonder-ing who might challenge the giants. None. They lacked the guts. They would never dare what he had dared; nor what Ullman had dared, come to that. Never risk it all on one toss. He and Ullman were cut from the same cloth; destined for greatness. He looked at Ullman's screen. *I salute you, my opponent. It will be an honor to destroy you.*

"I move the nominations be closed," said Toohey with a contemptuous look in Kennison's direction. "Did you hear it that time, Brother?"

"Loud and clear, Sister."

"Second the motion."

"Call the question."

"Then shall we vote?" Kennison reached forward and en-tered his own name into the net. He pressed the button and settled back to await the results.

It took only a moment. Ullman - 3; Kennison - 2; Not Voting - 4.

The look on Ullman's face would have been far more enjoyable had Kennison not known that his own face bore the same look. "Gee whiz," said Lewis. "Look at that. No one received a plurality." He smiled his smile again. Perfect white teeth against sun-reddened, Nordic face. Kennison thought what a pleasure it would be to smash the teeth. Not with his fists— he would break a knuckle. Perhaps with a pipe. Or one of Lewis' own Fiberglas skis.

He glanced at the special display that Alan had wired into the computer circuits. *For Ullman: Brigit Toohey, Frederick Ullman, Carl Westfield. For Kennison: Daniel Kennison, Reynold Sorenson. Not Voting: Roman Huang, Peter Lewis, Dana Montfort, Gretchen Paige.*

*Damn Montfort! She had betrayed him.* He looked at her image; but her face betrayed nothing of her thoughts. She might have been carved in stone. Who had bought her? And with what coin? Not Ullman. She hated that shriveled old geezer. She had promised to support Kennison to forestall Ullman's election. *Now I know what her promises are worth.* Kennison ground his teeth and smiled.

Ullman's eyes narrowed to slits. He worked his lips. "Give me a moment," he said and blanked his audio. Kennison watched him pick up a telephone and dial. Hastily, Kennison punched up another of Brother Alan's electronic gifts. *Tracing . . . his* screen told him. *Tracing. . . .* Ullman spoke a few words into his phone, then listened nodding. He spoke some more. *Trace completed. Port indeterminate.* A paper emerged from Ullman's fax machine. The old man pulled it, scanned it quickly and fed it back in. *Location . . . Location . . . Area Code 505.* Kennison's own fax machine rang and began printing. The other Councilors also looked to their sides, wondering what rabbit Ullman had produced to break the deadlock.

Area Code 505? Where was that? Even as the thought formed, his terminal screen blinked: *Location: Northern New Mexico. Further focus not possible.*

New Mexico? New Mexico! Ruiz! It had to be. Damn that greasy chicano bastard! How did Ullman know that Ruiz was alive? And how did he know how to contact him? It had to have been planned from the beginning. Ullman and Ruiz had been in it together. While Kennison had laid his plans with Paige and Sorenson and—he had thought—with Montfort; Ullman, Ruiz, Toohey and Westfield had been laying theirs. Ullman had let Kennison do the dirty work. Now he thought he could waltz in and pick up the marbles. Kennison clenched his fists out of sight of the camera.

The fax was Benedict Ruiz's proxy. Kennison gave it barely a glance. He knew what the contents would be. "Brother Ruiz is dead," Kennison told Ullman. "This proxy is worthless." Ullman knew better, of course. The comment was meant for the other Councilors.

"Not so," Ullman announced with a satisfied smile. "Brother Ruiz knew quite well that he was in grave danger as a result of the laxity exercised on our data net. (*Zap!*) So he took himself into hiding; much as Brother Lewis has done, only in a much more thorough manner. Brother Lewis wishes only to keep his location a secret—" A pause, and a smile that asked just how well-kept that secret could be from a man as wise and knowing as Ullman. Kennison enjoyed the discomfited look on the big man's ruddy face. "—as he has for these many years. Brother Ruiz wished for greater security than that, by keeping even his very existence secret. He has agreed to reveal himself now only to assure my election. To forestall, as he puts it, the further degradation of the Society."

Kennison hated the way their eyes all sought him out. He saw Montfort and the others counting votes in their heads. It was four to two to four, now. Ullman had a plurality. The Rules stated that, if a candidate and "not voting" were tied, the tie broke for the live candidate. It was bandwagon time.

"Just a moment," Kennison said. He blanked his own audio and picked up his phone. The private line. "Alan," he said.

"Yeah? How'd the vote go?"

"In case anyone breaks in—"

"No one can. I've been monitoring the net very closely."

"One cannot be too careful. In case anyone breaks in, can you make it appear as if I am talking to an unidentifiable port in the New York area?"

"Sure. 'Tis as easy as—"

Kennison didn't want to hear what it was as easy as. He cut Selkirk off. "You may send me that fax now."

The machine bells rang three times and a sheet emerged. Kennison checked it, to be sure of its contents; then he fed it back into the system so the others would receive copies. It was Paige's proxy, authorizing a vote for Kennison. There was an artistic symmetry to the ploy. Ullman had voted a live man whom everyone thought dead. Kennison was voting a dead woman whom everyone thought alive. *The returns from Chi-*

*cago*, he thought, *are coming in.* He was quite proud of the authorizing signature. It was one of his better efforts.

Ullman read the proxy, then gave Kennison a long, hard look. "Where is Sister Paige?" he asked.

"Need I repeat the tale you gave us concerning Brother Ruiz? These have been hard and frightening times. Sister Paige felt the same need for concealment as Brother Ruiz and Brother Lewis. I am sure none of us will blame them for their behavior. Prudence, after all, should not be confused with cowardice." (But juxtaposing the two words would plant that equation in their minds, especially with respect to Lewis, who had gone into hiding long before there had been any public outcry.) He saw that Lewis was angry; but unable to object, since Kennison had just said that he was *not* a coward. In addition, his phrase *the tale you gave us* might cause the others wonder about Ullman's veracity. Kennison was beginning to enjoy the election.

"In hiding, is she?" said Ullman. "I suppose we can accept that contention." Two can play at the game of innuendo. Ullman gazed steadily at Kennison. The calmness of his demeanor bespoke a more confident form of knowledge. *What does he know?* Kennison wondered. *How can anyone know what had happened at Weil's mansion? Judd had sworn— bragged—that no one else knew.* Ullman could have known nothing of Weil's deadly game of vengeance. Weil had hated him at least as much as she had hated Kennison and Paige. She would never have brought the Ancient One into her confidence. Kennison wished that Weil had chosen Ullman as her second target rather than himself. It would have solved so many problems. Ah, well. Spilt milk. Spilt milk.

The vote was four to three to three now. A plurality for Ullman, but barely so. Kennison watched Montfort's screen, daring her to continue her abstinence now. *If you sit on the sidelines, you little bitch, you'll guarantee that old fart's election.*

Montfort's head turned. She was looking at someone's monitor; but whose? *Damn it. She should take her cues from me.* His eyes darted from screen to screen, but if a signal were passed, he did not catch it.

Montfort reached forward and pressed a key. Kennison watched the tally. *For me!* He felt a great sense of relief and unclenched his hands. He hadn't realized how tense he had been, and it was another moment or two before he remem-

bered that he had achieved a tie and not a victory. Lewis and
Huang had not yet voted.

Lewis studied the returns on his own screen. Then he
shrugged. "Let's end this," he said, "or I'll miss the best
skiing." With a theatrical gesture, he dug into his pants
pocket and pulled forth a coin. He flipped the coin spinning
into the air; slapped it onto the back of his hand; and studied
the result. Then he entered his own vote into his terminal.
Kennison was astonished. It was the most contemptuous act
Kennison had ever seen. A slap in the face to both Ullman
and himself.

The vote was for Ullman. Which made the slap more bear-
able for The Geezer.

That made it five to four to one. A plurality for Ullman.
Kennison looked at Lewis' image and saw nothing there but
the bland smile he always showed.

Huang could still tie the vote. Kennison turned his attention to the lower right-hand monitor. Roman Huang lived on
a private island somewhere in the Hawaiian chain. Now he
lounged on his chaise, framed by bright sand and surf and a
smoldering background volcano. The ultraviolet sunglasses
concealed his expression. The Hawaiian could still save things
for Kennison. A tie would give him time. There were ways to
change people's votes. Persuasion. Or something.

He could not read Huang's face. *I will not beg,* he told
himself. *I will not crawl. Prudence did not beg; and I cannot
be less than she.*

Kennison was amused to see that the others were also
watching another monitor—presumably Huang's. So much
for the secret ballot.

Huang made no move, and the moment lingered. Finally
he said, "Will there be any further business at this Council or
have we concluded?"

And that was that. For whatever reason of his own, Roman
Huang remained in abstention. Kennison saw that Ullman
was also irritated. Once the decision is inevitable, why hold
out?

Kennison remembered a sound byte from a party nominat-
ing convention, when? 1984? A newsman had asked that of a
senator—from Montana, he thought. The nomination is
already sewn up, the newsman had asked. Why do you intend
to vote for a man who is sure to lose? The Westerner had
looked at the newsman as if he were an insect and replied that

382

the point wasn't to vote for the winner. The point was to vote for your principles. It seemed odd to Kennison to think of Roman Huang as a man of principles. What was his game? What was his game?

Kennison, as temporary chairman of the meeting, passed the gavel symbolically to Ullman as the newly elected permanent chairman. Ullman spread a few unctuous phrases around, thanking his supporters, praising his opponent, and telling everyone that it was now time to close ranks "in this the direst hour of the Society's history." Kennison smiled and congratulated him on his victory and pledged his support on his behalf. Everyone pretended to believe everyone else. *Enjoy yourself, Ancient One,* he thought at the monitor. *You're old. You won't last.*

"There are two items of business that we must conclude today," Ullman croaked. "The first is to propose nominees to fill the two Council vacancies of which we are aware."

*Cleverly phrased,* thought Kennison.

"I myself propose Vincent Torino whom many of you know and who, as you are all aware, has done excellent work for us in countering the Beaumont revelations."

*I must get one of my own in those slots. But who?* Who could he trust to be his man? Prudence. Yes, Little Pru would have been the perfect nominee. But she was gone. And that left . . . . "Alan Selkirk," Kennison announced. *Now why did I say that?* Whatever Alan might be on the Council, he was not likely to be Kennison's tool. An ally, perhaps. And perhaps an ally was better than a tool. Paige, after all, had given him greater service than Sorenson. "I propose Alan Selkirk. He was the Brother who finally tracked down and destroyed the Beaumont Worm. He has enhanced the security of our data base, immunizing it to the sort of break-in that we experienced." Kennison realized as he spoke that his praise of Alan also amounted to an indictment of himself.

Ullman nodded. "He is rather new to our ranks, but he comes highly recommended. You will forward his dossier to the other Councilors?"

"Certainly."

"Very well. Anyone with further nominations to make will please supply the appropriate dossiers to the Council by close of business tomorrow and we will consider the candidates at our next regular meeting. As our final order of business, I propose that we revive the office of Vice-Chairman, which my late predecessor regrettably allowed to remain dormant. I believe the events of the last several months have shown us how crucial it is that a vacancy in the chairmanship be filled quickly and automatically during an emergency."

*The Vice-Chairmanship*, thought Kennison. A meaningless post. A pitcher of warm spit. But it's mine by right. I came in second. If anyone deserves it, it's me. And the Vice-chairmanship would give him a foothold on the top post. A beachhead. It was only a matter of time before Ullman died—A very short time, if Kennison had any say in the matter—And then . . . Yes, he could humble himself in the Vice Chair for a while.

"Because of the close working relationship needed between a Chairman and his Vice," Ullman told the Council, "I feel it is appropriate that the Chairman nominate a suitable candidate for your advice and consent. In that way, we will be assured of uniformity in policy and execution."

Kennison felt a prickling in his scalp. Ullman would not nominate him. Kennison was sure of very few things in life; but that was one. He saw the prize receding from him. It wasn't fair! He had worked hard all his life for this. He would not be denied it now!

"While it would be highly appropriate for me to name Brother Kennison as my Vice, I feel that the data collection and analysis performed for us by Kennison Demographics is a full-time job, one too valuable to entrust to anyone else. Furthermore, Brother Kennison is in too exposed a position, being the only one among us who is publicly prominent. Therefore, I propose Benedict Ruiz for Vice Chairman. Being officially dead, he has greater freedom of action. And, if by chance some unexpected catastrophe should catch the rest of us unawares, Brother Ruiz would be well positioned to catch hold of the reins."

Kennison felt the blood drain from his face. Ullman had castrated him! The sly geriatric bastard! By claiming that the head of Kennison Demographics was too well-known to function effectively as Chairman of the Society, he had given the Council a rationale for voting against Kennison's candidacy in the future. Kennison could hear the door slam shut. He was finished. Ullman had blocked him forever from the top position.

Kennison kept his face perfectly still while the others registered their approval. Even Sorenson, the traitor. The relief on Sorenson's face was as disgusting as the triumph on Ullman's.

384

Kennison voted affirmative along with everyone else. No sour grapes, he; and the time for safe dissent had obviously passed. A thousand flowers had bloomed and quickly wilted.

Kennison and Selkirk sat in two high-backed chairs that faced each other over a low coffee table. The afternoon sun streamed through the window, bathing the dark wood paneling in rich, natural hues. Karin brought in the beverage cart. The crystal decanters tinkled against each other as she set them up on the side of the room. The diverse colors of the drinks showed splendidly against her black-and-white uniform. Kennison allowed the sight to soothe him. There were too many pleasures in the world—sights, colors, sounds, tastes, sensual experiences of all sorts—to waste much time in bemoaning his defeat. Water under the bridge. It's what comes next that matters. Revenge.

"Bourbon and branch for me, Karin; and whatever Mr. Selkirk will have."

"Scotch, neat, please." He favored Kennison with a smile. "I don't really like the stuff, but I feel it's my duty as a Scot."

Kennison chuckled with him. Karin served the drinks, bowed, and was dismissed. Selkirk tasted his drink. "My, but this has a bonny taste." He looked at his glass, then at the anonymous crystal decanter on the serving cart.

"It's a private distillery I own in the Orkneys," Kennison told him.

"Ah." Selkirk nodded. After a moment more of silence, he said, "It didn't go very well, did it?"

Kennison frowned into his glass. "No, it did not. To see everything I've lived for vanish in the blink of an eye. Well—" He tossed the drink back into his throat. It burned going down.

"Was it?" Selkirk asked.

"Was it what?"

Selkirk played with his glass. He ran his finger around the rim. The crystal sang. "Was it everything you've lived for?"

Kennison frowned at him. "I'm not sure what you mean."

Selkirk shrugged. "You have Kennison Demographics, do ye not?"

"And?"

"And is not K/D the tail that wags the dog? I'm not one for speaking up when it's not my place; but it seems to me that the Council needs you more than you need them."

Kennison rose from his chair. He walked to the beverage cart and poured himself another drink. He drank half of it. Then he turned and faced Selkirk. "What do you propose, then?"

Selkirk smiled at him. "They trust the data you give them, do they not?"

"This isn't going to work," Jim Doang told him.

Jeremy slapped him on the back. "Have faith." He glanced back down the dusty county road. "They can't hang back there forever. Most people in these parts, if they saw a van stopped by the side of the road, would stop and ask if they could help. So get on through there." He pointed to the culvert that ran under the road. Dank drainage water stood in the bottom of the corrugated metal tube. The odor of mold and decay.

Doang sniffed. "I promised to follow your directions; but—"

"Then do it!" Jeremy said harshly. Doang looked at him in surprise, and Jeremy did his best not to look surprised also. Since when had he become a forceful person? He clapped Doang on the back again. "Don't worry. I had Anderson park the van so that it covers us. As long as the blue car stays back there, they couldn't see us get out of the van; and they can't see us crawl through the culvert. Then, when they finally do pull up and get out, they'll have their backs to us. With your karate, my jack handle, and the element of surprise, we should be able to handle them—at least if there are no more than two of them."

"Three of them," said Doang. He made a fist of his hand and stabbed the air.

Jeremy laughed. "All right. Three of them."

Doang hunched over and began crawling through the culvert. Jeremy grasped the handle on the van's sliding door to close it, but Gwynn stopped him. "Leave it open, Jeremy. If they get out of their car with guns in their hands, I want to be able to jump out before they open fire."

"Maybe you should get out now. Hide in the ditch."

"No, Jeremy. You're our leader. Stick to your decisions. The worst thing a leader can do is to start changing his mind after setting things in motion. If they pull up and they don't see anyone in the van, they may suspect a trick."

"Well . . . If there is trouble, don't linger inside."

"I don't intend to."

386

"Because that car did not follow us into the sticks of Douglas County because they happened to be going our way."

"Good luck." She extended her hand and Jeremy grasped it. Vane stood before the opened hood of the van, ready to slide into the ditch at the first sign. With his ribs cracked from the explosion, he hadn't wanted to leap from the cab into the ditch. He licked his lips and nodded to Jeremy. Anderson looked down from the passenger's seat in the cab.

"I hope you know what you're doing," he said.

"Yeah. Me, too." Then he dropped to his hands and knees and followed Doang through the culvert.

The culvert was a corrugated tube that ran under the road from one side to the other. It was smaller than he had thought it would be. A tight fit. It was a good thing Anderson hadn't been the one to try it. He shoved the jack handle through his belt and squirmed his way through. His trousers became soaked in the fetid water. *I'll send the dry cleaning bill to the Babbage Society.* Stones in the water poked him. So did the jack handle, and he paused to adjust it as best he could.

Then he was through and found himself in the drainage ditch on the other side of the county road. He slid into it, rolled onto his back, and took a few deep breaths.

"Claustrophobic, wasn't it?"

He looked up and saw Doang. The mathematician was lying prone on the bank of the ditch, peering through a stand of weeds that allowed him to watch the blue sedan without showing his head. He spared a grin at Jeremy; and Jeremy grinned back. It wasn't bravado. It was sheer nervousness.

"Have they moved yet?"

"No."

Jeremy crawled beside Doang. "I feel like a doughboy in a World War I movie. About to charge from the trench."

"Not a movie," said Doang. "Wait!" He paused. "They're coming."

They both slid down below the lip of the ditch. It was not a very deep ditch and Jeremy found himself as close to Doang as he had ever found himself to anyone. "I hope your deodorant doesn't fail," he said.

"Is it traditional to make poor jokes at times like this?"

"Yes."

"Very well. Then I suppose now is the time to ask what if our followers' intend only to toss a bomb? What if they do not get out of their car, at all?"

"Then we never did have a chance; and we're no worse off than we were."

"You are an optimist, aren't you?"

"I think if they meant to do something like that, they would have done it already."

"Why did they wait so long back there? Why did they not simply pull up beside us when we stopped?"

"I think they were calling their boss for instructions. I think they were as interested in knowing where Vane was taking us as they were in . . . taking us." That was why Jeremy had had Anderson drive into Douglas County and onto the back roads. Not only was he looking for something like the culvert; but if he could make their followers think they were being led to a secret hideaway, they would wait just that much longer before acting.

"And what if their intentions are benign?"

"Then we'll apologize to them afterwards."

They fell silent as they heard the motor of the approaching car. It stopped almost on top of them and Jeremy realized that, if the driver looked down when he emerged, he would see him and Doang lying there. He laid a hand on Doang to keep him still; but Doang was like a rock.

Vane evidently noticed the same thing because, as the driver's door opened, they heard him call out. "Hey! You there! We've got a little trouble here. Do you fellows know anything about engines?"

Feet scraped on dirt. "Put your hands up, mister." Jeremy tapped Doang. Now!

They crept from the ditch and took cover behind their pursuer's car. Through the windows they could see two men in jeans and cowboy hats. They had revolvers in their hands. Vane stood by the opened hood of the car with his hands in the air. Jeremy cursed under his breath. The little man hadn't had time to jump into the ditch. Or had he hesitated because of the pain in his ribs? No matter. Should he change the plan?

No. Everyone knew what to expect. Even Vane. If he changed the plan, no one would know. They would begin to wonder. Maybe look around. Look in the wrong direction. Warn the two men with the guns. That must be what Gwynn had meant about leaders changing their minds.

"You can tell your friends," said one of the gunmen, "to get out of the ditch." Jeremy stifled a moment's panic; but the speaker had meant the other ditch, where Gwynn and Anderson had jumped.

"We aren't going to hurt you," said the other.

"Then you don't need those guns," said Vane; and one of the gunmen laughed.

Jeremy slapped Doang on the shoulder again. A prearranged signal. They ran around opposite sides of the car. Doang to the left; Jeremy to the right.

The gunman on the left must have seen something out of the corner of his eye. He started to turn just as Doang let loose with the most bloodcurdling cry Jeremy had ever heard. Doang had warned him of the cry. It was supposed to make the opponent freeze for a fraction of a second; and Jeremy could well believe that it would.

Jeremy was swinging the jack handle in an arc as he ran. His target was right-handed, so the gun arm was exposed to his swing. He saw Doang spin like a dervish, executing what ice skaters called a "camel." One foot kicked the gun from the man's hand; the other came around and connected with his temple.

The jack handle connected with the gunman's wrist. The gunman howled and the revolver dropped from his numbed fingers. He snatched at Jeremy with his left hand, but Jeremy danced out of the way, kicking the fallen gun before him like a soccer ball.

Then Doang landed with both feet on the man's back and it was all over.

Anderson had run from the ditch and had recovered the gun from Doang's man. Jeremy picked up the other. Their two assailants lay still.

"They're not dead, are they?" Jeremy asked. He began to shake from the adrenalin rush. The revolver was heavy; the barrel, long. A .45? He didn't know. The gun handle felt rough in his palm.

Doang shook his head. "My man is stunned from the blow to his head. Yours has had the wind knocked out of him. And we probably have a broken hand and a broken wrist, as well. Otherwise . . ." A shrug.

Jeremy said, "You did a good job, Jim."

Doang sat on the van's running board. He mopped his brow with a tissue. "Thank you. I have never attacked an armed man before; or, indeed, any man, except in sparring."

Jeremy looked at him. "I'm glad you didn't say so earlier. Dammit, where is the safety on this thing?"

Anderson stepped up to him and took the gun from him. "If you don't know that, you shouldn't have it in your hand. Let me see." A pause. "Well, I'll be damned."

"What?"

"The safety is already on." Another quick inspection. "So's the other one."

Jeremy looked from the guns to the men on the ground. The man he had attacked was beginning to stir. "They didn't mean to kill us, then."

"At least not immediately."

"That doesn't fit with what we know about the Babbage Society. They shoot first and ask questions later, don't they?"

"That's because," said the man lying at their feet, "we ain't the fucking Babbage Society." He hugged his broken wrist to himself.

Jeremy leaned against the van and began to laugh.

# VI

"Ah, Ms. Beaumont," said Aaron Gewirtz. "We are so pleased to have you back amongst us. I trust that you were able to complete your project during your vacation."

Sarah took her seat while the Earth Mother, SuperNerd and the others watched. Personally, she did not regard either surgery or target practice as "vacation." Especially when she was on the wrong end of the target practice. She settled in and opened her notebook without responding to his goad.

"Perhaps, Ms. Beaumont, you would care to enlighten us on the status of your project."

She looked up and into the old man's whitened eyes, and wished that the sight would not unnerve her so. "Actually," she admitted, "I've changed my topic."

"Indeed? Without my approval? I discern a commendable penchant for independent thought. I hope your new topic is as penetrating as the one originally assigned."

"I think," she told him, "that you will find it worthwhile."

"Would you be so good, then, as to enlighten the class with your findings?" Gewirtz motioned toward the chalkboard at the front of the room. He pulled on his wheels and backed himself away from the center of the room. "I ask the rest of you to follow her reasoning closely and be prepared to note any and all weaknesses therein. You will each be graded on the accuracy of your critiques."

Sarah picked up a piece of chalk and rolled it between her fingers. She had never cheated in school before. She had never found it necessary. But what she planned to do required more than a simple assertion, so Red and Tex and the

391

others had spent the entire night helping her develop her thesis.

"Very well," she said. She turned and began writing equations on the board, explaining them aloud for Gewirtz's benefit. She did not get far before he interrupted her.

"Just a moment," he said. "The Condensation of Memes is a well-understood phenomenon. Surely someone of your caliber intends more than a rehash of such a familiar topic."

"I believe you will find my conclusions stimulating. I intend to explore the conditions required for multiple and simultaneous centers of condensation."

Gewirtz pursed his lips. "I do not see the benefit of treading such a well-beaten path; but . . . go on. You titillate me with your promises."

Sarah continued, her voice covering the clicking of the chalk. She pointed out the population density needed to supply a sufficient number of susceptible minds. The need for high connectivity of the communications network. The cultural momentum, as described by the speed and volume of transport. The fraction of the population engaged in travel. She cited numerous examples of simultaneous discovery: Newton and Leibnitz; Wallace and Darwin; Edison and Bell; and so on. She noted that, in prehistory, agriculture had been "discovered" simultaneously by widely separated cultures; that fascism reared its head in several different countries at once; that the "population explosion" began during the sixteenth century in India, and China as well as Europe. She began to generalize from these examples.

"One moment," said Gewirtz. "You mentioned high connectivity of communications. Yet you cited the near simultaneous invention of agriculture in Mexico and Mesopotamia. Surely there were no communications between the two."

"No sir," she replied. "But both cultures were communicating with the common, global environment, which was then compressing the hunter-gatherer mode of production. Similarly, the global warming in the sixteenth century affected all societies. It opened more land to farming; and that opened more mouths, to consume the increased harvest."

Gewirtz chuckled. "Nicely put, Ms. Beaumont. I trust the other members of the class have been enlightened. Mutual communication of individuals with a common information source has many of the same features as communication among the individuals themselves. Mr. Reynolds, would you be so kind as to develop mathematically the analogy between the communication of information and of disease? Account for the analogs of environmental diseases such as the cholera, in addition to the usual communicable diseases." He nodded to Sarah. "You may continue."

"We come now," she told the class, "to a specific application. Namely, the condensation of the memes required for the formation of a Babbage-like Society during the early nineteenth century."

There was a stir among the class. A murmur. She kept her back to them and continued to write. "As you can see from the equations, the conditions during the 1830's were such that the formation of more than one such society is a virtual certainty." She listed the relevant parameters quickly. "Recent researches into the Data Base, CLIOSCOPE, have revealed the presence in this country of a group calling itself The Secret Six. The Six, of course, has since bifurcated, as predicted by Carson's Dilemma, but the daughter society's tracks have disappeared. Either it has ceased to meddle with the system—thus leaving no 'horseshoe nails'—or it has dissolved."

The murmuring in the class grew louder. Aaron Gewirtz's voice overrode them. "Young woman, are you quite sure of what you are saying?"

She faced him. "Yes, Dr. Gewirtz. Quite sure. May I go on?"

The old man's face appeared troubled. "This is disturbing news."

"The Council has already been briefed."

His eyebrows arched. "Indeed? Then—Yes, yes. Please continue."

The chalk skittered across the board. She could feel the eyes of her classmates on her back. The chalk dust tickled her nose; made her want to sneeze. "However, we must not neglect Europe. Conditions there virtually guarantee the precipitation of at least one, and possibly three additional societies. Given Carson's Dilemma, we may expect upwards to five or nine societies currently active, barring collapse, dissolution, or merger."

The class was silent now. She turned and faced them. Except for SuperNerd, who was smiling nervously, they were stone-faced. "Merger," she said, "is unlikely, however, since secrecy is a necessary condition for a Babbage-like society to operate."

"I see," said Gewirtz. "Then these putative societies are as mutually ignorant of each other as we have been of them?"

"There is no way to be sure. Certainly, they are now aware of Us, because of the Dump. One society recently used computer viruses to download the notes of a reporter named Morgan Grimes into something called the Q file. Grimes had stumbled across the murders committed by the Society; but he himself had no idea of what they meant. Somehow this Q group got wind of what he was finding and drew their own conclusions. Since all that took place *before* I wrote my worm. . ."

"This is absurd," said the Earth Mother. "I think Beaumont is simply trying to avoid responsibility for what she did to us." Others in the class murmured their agreement. Gewirtz remained silent and immobile.

"It is clear," Sarah said, "that someone is nosing around both ourselves and the Babbage Society. Jimmy Caldero —" She always felt a pang when she referred to his new persona. He was Red Malone, dammit. He always would be. "—who has experience in intelligence matters has assessed a number of these indications."

"Can you tell us what they are?" asked SuperNerd. Sarah thought he was hamming his part a little too much, but no one else seemed to notice.

"Dr. Gewirtz? I don't want to occupy too much of your class time on my project."

The blind man chuckled. "No, my dear. I am sorely tempted to accept your bluff; but I fear your classmates would rend me limb from limb were I to terminate the discussion at this point. By all means, finish." He waved a courtly hand toward her.

"Very well. Mr. Bosworth's researches into low-probability, high-leverage nodes have already identified the Secret Six explicitly." SuperNerd beamed at the compliment. "But there are other indications as well. I've already mentioned the Q-file tap on Morgan Grimes. In addition, the Q tapped into Kennison Demographics; and someone placed a threatening phone call to him. Third, the Stray, a lone file found by Dump searchers in the Atlanta Office. It was written in French at a Quebec node, urging an investigation of the murders in Grimes' files. I'm sure I don't need to point out that we have no Quebec station and that the Babbage Society would hardly need to launch such an investigation. Fourth, there is the bombing of the Denver University study team. That was *not* a Society operation. Not even Genevieve Weil would have been that foolish; and the surviving leadership of the Babbage Society has been 'playing possum' for the past month. They lost a valuable agent in the explosion and it couldn't help but inflame public suspicions, regardless of the conclusions reached by the news. By now, enough people have read about the Dump to be suspicious of any news pronouncements. And, finally, there is the fact that I was followed and drugged during my sabbatical in the mountains. All these events lead to what Jimmy called 'an assessment of capabilities.' He believes it would be imprudent to assume that all these activities were the product of a single organization."

She paused and looked over the class. They couldn't take their eyes off her. SuperNerd was grinning wide enough to crack his face. The Earth Mother was twisting her hands together. Reynolds was staring with narrowed eyes. Gewirtz was unreadable.

"Now, let's put ourselves in the place of one of these other societies, what is the first thing we would do once we knew about the Dump?"

That was SuperNerd's cue. He raised his hand. "Check for doors."

"Explain."

"A 'door' is information that can be used to gain entry into the Associates or the Society, either physically or through the DataNet, using taps, bugs, moles, or personal surveillance."

"A door. Exactly. And they found one."

Dr. Gewirtz spoke. "And what was that, if I may inquire?"

"I cannot answer for the Babbage people; but as far as our data, very little was leaked, which made our research easier. We tested each item in the Dump to determine whether it allowed access. For example: was the location of the ranch divulged?"

"It was not," said Dr. Gewirtz.

"Correct, Doctor." Sarah was beginning to enjoy the role reversal. See how he liked it. "However, Louise Vosteen was compromised. So, her home may have been bugged; or she herself put under surveillance."

"Sister Vosteen is safely under cover now," Reynolds said. "If she was being watched, she eluded them."

"And fortunately—or unfortunately," Sarah added, "her home

was burned by vandals, so it doesn't matter if it was bugged. Nobody learned anything."

"The point, Ms. Beaumont," said Gewirtz. "Get to the point."

"There was one open door. Mark Lopez. He was also compromised by the Dump. If the Six—or anyone else—acted quickly enough, he might have provided access, inadvertently or through coercion. Brother Lopez has not been located since then—"

"Thanks to you," said the Earth Mother.

"—but before he disappeared, he did send us a new recruit. Or *was* it before he disappeared?"

In the sudden silence, the eyes of the class turned to Maureen Howard. She looked from one to the other. "Now, wait a minute. This is ridiculous. Mark did a thorough background check on me before he sent me here."

"Did he?" asked Sarah. "Too bad we can't find him to ask him."

The silence in the room had grown deeper. "You don't have to. The Associates verified everything after I arrived."

"Oh, there's more," Sarah said with a smile. "If the ranch's location was not revealed in the Dump . . . who drugged me?"

Reynold's head jerked up. "You mean it's—"

"Someone at the ranch. Yes." She walked to her desk, opened her briefcase, and removed the horseshoe. She held it up. "This shoe was worn by the horse ridden by that spy. You can tell from the hairline crack that runs along it here." She pointed to the shoe. Maureen Howard reached out and took it. She studied the crack for some time then passed it to Reynolds.

"According to Tex Bodean it was worn by the sorrel gelding," Sarah continued. "The stablemaster checked the log sheet to see who was riding the horse that day. That person was Ms. Howard."

The Earth Mother jerked her head around. "That isn't true!"

"The stablemaster says different."

"I rode out on the horse; that part's true. But I tied it up and went hiking on foot. When I came back to where I left the horse, it was gone. I hunted around for hours and finally found it just before sundown. I didn't say anything to the stablemaster because I didn't want her to think I wasn't taking good care of my horse."

Sarah shrugged. "It's a good story, Sister. But I come from Chicago, where the dead vote early and often; so it's not too hard to imagine a dead man being used to validate your candidacy. Yet, what false identity is perfect? Especially one prepared hastily. Suppose others pick away at it? What overlooked flaw might they find? What chink in the paper trail of altered records? Believe me, no one has had more reason in the past few weeks to ponder that issue. So, when Brother Malone and Brother Polovsky began investigating your past, they found—"

She got no further. Howard leaped from her desk and ran for the door. SuperNerd rose on cue to stop her, but she toppled the last desk into his path and he fell in a howl and a tangle.

When Howard threw open the door, however, she found Red Malone and Walt Polovsky barring her way. She spun and glared at Sarah, a look of such hatred as Sarah had never seen before, not even in the white neighborhoods of Chicago. Then she clenched her jaws together.

"Watch it!" said Red.

Howard stiffened and her eyes rolled up in her head. She arched backward stiffly; sighed and fell. Polovsky caught her. She sagged limply in his arms. "Shit," he said and let go. Howard slid to the floor in a shapeless heap.

There was a moment of uneasy silence. Then Aaron Gewirtz said, "You were perfectly correct, Ms. Beaumont."

Sarah turned and looked at him. The old man nodded somberly. "As you promised, it was a most stimulating proof of your thesis."

"She . . . She wasn't supposed to do that," Sarah stammered. She could hear how foolish the remark was. "We couldn't break her cover. It looked flimsy when we checked it closely; but we couldn't break it. We were sure she was a mole, but we had no real proof. We hoped we could panic her into running."

Gewirtz turned his wheelchair to face the body. "Indeed. And she ran as far as anyone can."

"You want to what?" Kennison stared at Selkirk and dared him to repeat what he had just said.

The Scotsman leaned back in the conference room chair

and looked around the broad mahogany table. "I want to backup our entire system to a remote location."

"Alan. I made you supervisor of the Night Shift; not Chairman of K/D. Don't get above yourself."

"Above myself? After what I did for you, don't you think I should be treated as more than a kern?"

Kennison stiffened. *After what I did for you . . .* Bad form, really. One did not remind others of favors owed or given. A sign of low breeding. He glanced at Johnson and at Cheng, and they carefully avoided his eyes. They didn't know what had happened in their offices last week, and they didn't want to know. All they knew was that Prudence was gone and in her place was a stranger.

"We need to keep 'two sets of books,' " said Selkirk. "Once your former colleagues suspect that they are receiving suboptimized data, they'll mouse into our banks to check things out. We canna allow them to discover aught amiss. So we'll keep a false front here, and hide the correct information elsewhere, where they won't suspect."

"Perhaps," Johnson said slowly, "he has a point."

"Suboptimized data," said Kennison. "To lure them into poor decisions, while we prosper. Yes." He traced designs on the table top with his finger. "Perhaps that decision was rather too hasty." *Act in haste, Daniel, repent in leisure.*

Cheng nodded. "Too hasty. Yes, too hasty. We were in no danger from Ullman. What matter who sits at head of table, when we set table? Better to be the power behind throne."

Johnson rubbed his chin. "Hmmm. Uneasy lies the head, and all that?" He looked at Selkirk. "They have a point, too. Perhaps we shouldn't go through with this plan." He shook his head. "To go against the Society . . . I don't know that that's wise."

Cheng nodded again. "Act was fit of pique, not planning. Where is cliological analysis? What are consequences? We have never made decisions without such."

"It's too late." Selkirk told them. "The first burst of altered data went out this morning."

"Without my authorization, Alan?" Selkirk returned his gaze unflinchingly. Oh, yes. Alan would most definitely be a problem.

Selkirk shook his head. "I *had* your authorization; or don't you remember? Damn it all!" He struck the table with his fist. "Our situation requires boldness, not equivocation. Once

398

you make a decision, you see it through. You canna 'cut bait' forever."

Kennison pressed his palms against the table as hard as he could, and held them there until his arm muscles began to tremble. It was true. He had thought often of leaving the Society; of striking out on his own. His heart was with K/D, the fruit of his own loins; and not with the Society. Yet, it would be difficult, in several ways. Ullman would never let him leave; not with K/D in his pocket. The data K/D provided was too valuable.

And yet, there were possibilities. What if K/D were to swallow the Society whole? Possible. Eliminate the other Councilors. Make K/D into a New Society, shaped in his own image. A better Society. But, how to swallow such a lump without getting indigestion? Perhaps he should study Grosvenor Weil's career more closely. His case was not precisely parallel —Weil had only wanted to seize the reins of power, not re-string them—yet there could be much to learn.

Machiavelli had once observed that there were two sorts of states, the Turkish and the Frankish. In the former, all subordinates were servants of the Sultan and served at his pleasure where and when he chose. In the latter, the subordinates were barons in their own right, with their own loyalties and adherents. Then the clever Florentine had made a cunning observation. It was easier to seize control of a Frankish state; but more difficult to rule one.

Grosvenor Weil had absorbed that lesson. Crawford had built a Society on the Frankish order; a band of equals. That had made it possible for Weil to maneuver his way to the top; but once in power, he had bent every effort to transform it into a Turkish state. The Old Spider had acted patiently, cunningly. Spinning his web for years; casting it only when the tides were ripe. And, if he had not succeeded wholly, he had at least succeeded remarkably. Still, underneath the blanket of the Weil family's totalitarian rule were the faint fracture lines of the old baronies.

It might be possible, he thought. It might be possible. Did he have Old Weil's patience? Surely. He was the match for any man. Yet, he had already waited patiently far too long. He yearned for action; for the reward that he had so justly earned. *Aut Caesar, aut nullus.*

What else was there? Stay. Leave. Swallow. Or . . .

There was another possibility. A risky one; but he could cut

399

himself loose *and* keep K/D in the process. Selkirk's scheme had shown the way. He would need Selkirk to bring it off, damn the man; he would need his computer expertise. He glanced covertly at Selkirk. He could not afford to keep Selkirk around afterward. That would be too risky. Too bad, but cookies *did* crumble.

He made a decision.

"If we take this step, we are committed. The Red Flag of revolution. Are you each prepared to stay the course?" he asked.

Johnson hesitated, then nodded. Cheng shrugged fatalistically. Alan stared back unwaveringly. "It was my idea."

*Yes*, thought Kennison. *Your* idea. "Very well. Brother Alan: prepare a suitable plan for securing our data base elsewhere; but take no action until the four of us have reviewed it. In the meantime, no more doctored data. If anyone notices errors in this morning's burst, tell them there was a computer glitch. Brother Tsu-shih: conduct a cliological analysis of the effects of our actions. Yes, I know. Horses and carts have a strict order of precedence; but 'better late.' Use the Night Shift. Brother Alan: see that Brother Tsu-shih receives whatever manpower he needs for his assignment. Oh!" He held up a hand.

"And Brother. Be sure to include in your analysis the information Jimmy Caldero gave us regarding the other society; the Secret Six. And keep that information from contaminating the regular information pool. That may be our most significant edge over Ullman. That our analyses allow for their existence, while his do not. Consult Brother Alan for the details. He has discovered a number of things about them. . . . . Most diligent work, Alan. Thank you. . . . Brother Nate: You will be in sole charge of Johnson & Cheng while this operation runs. We will depend on you for the usual cover and for the security of whatever channels we need to access the daytime hours. Any questions?" He scanned the table. "Very well. Make it so."

He waited alone in the conference room after the others had left. There was no turning back now. *Jacta ilea est.* Was this how Caesar had felt? Perhaps. Even the great ones must have felt uncertainty when the moment of truth arrived. Elation, yes, at the chance of success; and perhaps even at the chance of failure. Gambler's High. The rush of adrenalin when the mind realized that one stood at the node of a cusp and the future could fall either way. Certainty bred few thrills.

What he envisioned was a far riskier operation than the conspiracy he had engineered against Weil. Had Weil discovered what he was doing, she would have killed him. *And she had; and she almost had! If he had been any less of a man. . .* Yet, risk has not to do with the dangers one runs, but with the chances of failure. He had been confident then of the eventual outcome. And the plan had failed. Perhaps this more daring operation would succeed. He remembered now the rest of that Kipling stanza.

> *"If you can make one heap of all your winnings*
> *And risk it on one turn of pitch-and-toss,*
> *And lose, and start again at your beginnings*
> *And never breathe a word about your loss . . ."*

Yes. That was what had been lacking before. Reckless daring. Too much caution. He had relied on weak reeds, like Montfort and Sorenson. Only Paige had proved her mettle, to her own misfortune. Poor Gretchen! Such a gallant end! He vowed to enshrine her bones properly, once Judd yielded the secret of her disposal.

And yet . . . too little caution was also dangerous. He and Selkirk had thoroughly mopped these offices and the conference room for electronic listening devices just prior to the meeting. They had found none, of course; but it was important to look. Just as it was important to look before crossing the street, whether one saw any traffic or no.

He doodled on the notepad before him. Weil. Ullman. Selkirk. The Secret Six. The three viruses. The phone call. He thought for a moment, then added: Beaumont and Caldero.

The Great Harpy had said, what? That she had an ear inside Kennison's organization. He drew an arrow from Weil to the viruses. As chairwoman, Weil had had access to the Johnson & Cheng offices. And she was surely capable of planting a virus in the system.

And Ullman had hinted at knowing more than he should have. He drew another arrow, from Ullman to the viruses; and then another, from Ullman to the phone call. He added several ornate question marks. The caller had been a woman. Could it have been Weil?

That would account neatly for the three viruses. Weil. Ullman.

The Secret Six. And the phone call would have been one of them, too. Probably not Ullman. Bravado was not his style. He sketched in the remaining arrows, studied the results, and sighed.

He tore the top two pages off the pad and ran them through the shredder. It was standard practice at the end of any meeting to shred any used pages off the fixed notepads at each seat; but only Kennison had the imagination to shred the blank sheet beneath that. Then he leaned back in his chair and stretched. He rose and walked around the table, tearing the top sheets off the notepads at the other places. Then he returned to his seat and rubbed each one carefully with the side of his pencil point.

Brother Nathaniel Johnson had, as usual, taken no notes. There were advantages to having a subordinate as stolid and unimaginative as Johnson; but there were difficulties as well. It was hard to discern what such a man was thinking; or if, indeed, he was thinking at all.

Cheng's pad revealed several Chinese characters. Ah, the Inscrutable Oriental! Kennison had once taken the step of seeking the translation for the characters he had found on Cheng's pad and discovered that, loosely translated, they read *Nosy, aren't we?* He smiled to himself. There were advantages and disadvantages also to having clever subordinates.

Selkirk's pad yielded a series of ornate and interlocked Q's surrounded by vines and flowers. Kennison loved expressive doodles and kept a practicing psychiatrist on retainer in case there were hidden meanings in them. One never knew when such information might prove useful.

Q? Mentally, he added 'Q File' to his own, now-shredded doodle. That was another fragment of information regarding one of the viruses. The Secret Six's? A "Quinn" file? Possible. Possible.

He folded the three sheets lengthwise and placed them inside his jacket.

When he left the conference room, the Night Shift was hard at work. He nodded to Cheng, who was in his office working at his terminal. Johnson was by the mainframe going down a checklist with the Head Programmer. Kennison knocked on the window of the computer room and waved to them. He stopped at a few workstations on his way through and exchanged pleasantries with the staff, asking after spouses or children or hobbies.

The common touch. It was a good thing to cultivate. People might not follow a leader with a vision; but they would follow one who remembered their birthdays and anniversaries.

The washroom elevator took him silently to his own offices. He walked briskly to the door of the upper washroom and froze with it only partway open.

Alan was using the EPIC terminal in Kennison's office, talking in a very animated fashion. Kennison closed the washroom door carefully and leaned his ear against it.

"We'll need an entire mainframe core, I tell you," said the muffled voice. Kennison had to strain to make out the words. "Yes. That's confirmed. They were headquartered in Oberlin, Ohio." Pause. "No, I don't know where they are now." Pause. "Yes, I know. It's too widespread, but I think we can salvage something . . . No, don't worry. I can take care of myself." Pause. "You did *what?* Was that wise?" A long pause. "I see. Och, aye. You were quite right. You didna ha'e a choice. What about Bernstein? Does he know? . . . Good. Let's keep it that way. And French? . . . Very well. *Adieu.*"

Kennison waited a decent interval. Then he went to the stall and flushed the toilet. At the sink, he cupped cold water in his hands and splashed it on his face. The icy water was a shock. He leaned his hands on both sides of the basin and gasped. Then he yanked a paper towel off the dispenser and covered his face with it. When he pulled it away, he looked at the dark designs the water had made, as if he could see in them the image of his own face. As if it were Veronica's veil.

He wadded the towel into a ball and slammed it into the trash can; yanked open the office door; and walked into an empty office.

He stood by the butcher block desk. *Carefully, Daniel.* He lowered himself into the chair—*his* chair, dammit. And *his* desk. Then he punched up a number on the terminal. Why had Alan been using his phone, and not his own? And to whom had he been talking?

"Yes. Bertie? Kennison here. Could you have my limo brought around? I'll be coming down in a few minutes. Thank you." He depressed the cut-off; punched in another number.

"Madam Butler? I will be leaving the offices shortly. Could you please inform Cook? Yes, thank you." This time, when he cutoff he continued talking. "Do you know what Cook is preparing?" he said into the silent handset. He quickly tapped in the code that displayed the most recent numbers called. A

403

glance at the screen confirmed what he had feared. There was no record of the call that Alan had just completed.

So, that was why Alan was using the EPIC. From the regular phone ports there was no way of erasing the records. They were tallied automatically by Pacific Bell. But the EPIC was smart and someone with Alan's talents could easily perform such an elementary trick.

"I see," he said aloud. "Well, it sounds delicious. I shall look forward to it. Good-bye, Madam Butler."

He replaced the handset.

He placed a mental question mark beside Selkirk's name. A very large question mark.

*I can take care of myself,* Selkirk had said. *Can you, now?* Kennison wondered. *Can you?*

# VII

"Miss Bennett!" said the concierge. "We're so glad to see you back."

Sarah looked at the slim, elegantly dressed white woman. She had never seen her before in her life. "Thank you, Helen," she said. "I do love San Francisco. I wish I could come more often; but—" A wave of the hand. "The press of business, you know." She turned to the bellman and handed him her key. "Take my trunks to the suite, would you please? The gray one goes in the sitting room; the black in the bedroom. Have I had any messages, Helen?"

The concierge pulled an envelope from a pigeon hole. "A Mister Caldero phoned. He wants you to phone him as soon as it would be convenient." The bellman was out of earshot, and the concierge added *sotto voce*, "Your suite is clean. The boy's name is José. He's not one of us, but you met him when 'you' were here last year. And Brother Caldero checked in three hours ago. He has the suite just below yours."

Sarah did not break character. "Thank you, Helen." She took the envelope. "Could you phone Mister Caldero and ask him if he would lunch with me in . . ." She checked her watch. "Oh, say forty-five minutes, in my suite. Have a light meal put together. Sandwiches and cold cuts. Mineral water. You know what to do."

"Certainly, Miss Bennett."

"Thank you." She walked quickly to her suite, where she removed her gloves and hat. The bellman was waiting.

"That's fine, José. It's nice to see you again." She tipped him ten dollars. He touched his pillbox cap with two fingers.

"It's nice to have you back with us, ma'am."

When he was gone she went to one of the plush chairs and sagged into it. She took several deep breaths to still the thumping of her heart. This was method acting with a vengeance. She wasn't just acting a part; or even living a part. She *was* the part. She *was* Gloria Bennett.

Only a handful of people in San Francisco knew that she wasn't. (Although, of course, she "really" was.) Helen was one; so was a man named Frank Chu on the building maintenance staff, who "took care" of the private suites. Both knew that Bennett had been a persona of convenience, used by several Associates but now assigned permanently to a single person. They had not been told Sarah's original identity; but they were certainly capable of guessing.

But she did not dare fall out of character with them. She would have to be careful to maintain the persona at all times, even among friends. She did not think she could switch the role on and off without becoming careless.

Sarah rose from the chair and wandered to the window. The bellman had opened the curtains and Sarah gazed out over the city. In the foreground stood Telegraph Hill and Russian Hill, the former crowned with the graceful, fluted, concrete pillar of Coit Tower. A cluster of trees formed a bush of greenery at the base of the tower. In the distance, the blue waters of San Francisco Bay lay tranquil and flat; and beyond them, in the morning mist, the hazy wilds of the Marin headlands. The panorama was framed on the right by the Bay Bridge and on the left by the Golden Gate Bridge, "the most beautiful bridge in the world." It was a vista she knew she could never tire of. Most of the houses were white, or light-colored, and the whole town seemed to shine in the sun. *"Thine alabaster cities gleam . . ."* Sarah didn't think she could ever leave Denver; but if she did, it would be to come here.

Then she remembered why she had come.

A knock on the door announced the arrival of room service, followed closely by "Jimmy Caldero."

Red set his bulky briefcase on the floor and threw his arms wide. "Gloria! It has been too long." Sarah stepped into his arms and he hugged her.

"Jimmy," she said. "You old scoundrel. What have you been up to?" Over his shoulder, she saw SuperNerd. "And who is this?" She disengaged from Red's embrace. *A pimple-faced chaperone, that's who. Red, you're a . . .* But she couldn't think of a word to describe Red.

"Do you remember that computer project we discussed over the phone? This is one of my star programmers. Norris Bosworth; Gloria Bennett." SuperNerd extended a hesitant hand.

"Glad to meet you," he said.

"That's fine," Red told the room service girl. "Leave it like that. We'll serve ourselves." He waved Sarah away. "No, Gloria, I insist." He tipped the girl generously and she left.

When the door had closed, Sarah started to speak; but Red raised a cautioning hand. He opened his briefcase and pulled out a contraption that looked like a tiny little satellite dish. He donned a set of earphones and began walking around the suite. Sarah waited patiently until he was through.

"The place is clean," he announced.

"Helen already told me that."

"So. It's better to be safe." He threw himself into the sofa and laid his arms out along its back. "I'll have roast beef, mustard, cheese and a slice of tomato, on rye."

Sarah handed a plate to Bosworth. "Make your own sandwich, Jimmy," she said over her shoulder. "I'm not your maid."

Red grinned and looked around the suite. "Okay, be that way. How do you like your digs?"

"They're very nice. I saw them so often on the training videos that it's like I've already been here."

"You have," Red reminded her. "Several times. Helen will cue you in on any of the little details that didn't make it into the training material." He roused himself and ambled to the lunch cart. He picked at the cold cuts on the platter. "Is this the best they could do? Maybe we should send out for pizza."

Bosworth sat in the plush chair and balanced his sandwich plate on his knees. Sarah found a chair by the writing desk and set her plate there. She watched Red pile things into his sandwich. "When do we meet with Kennison?" she asked.

"In a little while," he replied.

"Is he coming here?"

"In a way." He turned and bit into his sandwich. Juice from the tomato ran down his chin and he wiped it with his napkin. "Meanwhile, don't you want to hear what the kid found out?"

407

He gestured to Bosworth. "Go ahead. Tell her." To Sarah: "You'll love this."

SuperNerd glanced from Sarah to Red and back. "Well, Brother Polovsky and I finished the factor analysis on the European anomalies. We had a pretty good base to start from, using the items you remembered from the French List. But it turned out Carson was wrong after all. He thought he had identified a third factor; but it was really a confounding of two others: the Six's domestic efforts plus some European spin-off that impacted over here. You know how tricky factor analysis can be. You can't always go by the effects of an event. There are miscalcu—" He caught the look on Red's face. "Anyway, we think we've identified four sets of 'tracks' in the European digraph."

"Four?" Then she laughed. "Four? Oh, that's priceless!"

"Yeah," said Red sourly. "You might as well ask who was *not* inventing cliology back in those days."

"As nearly as we can tell," Bosworth continued, "one of them aborted almost immediately. Probably broke up from internal dissension. Two of the others fissioned sometime during the last quarter of the century. Carson's Dilemma."

"Hmm," said Sarah. "About the same time as the Six and the Babbage Society."

"That's right." SuperNerd nodded eagerly. "The distribution of times to failure is shaping up into a nice pdf. An extreme value distribution. I think—"

"Stick to the point, kid. Gloria can get the details later, if she wants to."

Bosworth flushed. "Okay," he said petulantly, "but you don't have to act so snot-castic about it."

Sarah smiled behind her hand. She had never heard Bosworth talk back to anyone before. Maybe the boy was beginning to feel more self-assured.

Red grinned. "Hey. I apologize." He waved his sandwich vaguely in the air. "But wrap it up, will you? The meet with Kennison starts pretty soon."

Bosworth turned to Sarah. "There were five tracks left going into the war era. I lost one during the first war; and two more petered out during the second. And guess what? The Nazis actually uncovered one of them and destroyed it."

"What?" Sarah saw that Red was surprised, too.

"You didn't tell me that," he said.

"My worm reported in just before we left," the teenager replied. "I thought I'd save it as a surprise."

"Yeah?" Red thought about it for a while. "I don't like surprises. Don't make a habit of withholding information."

"I wasn't with— Okay, forget it. You guys have no sense of drama. Anyway, I moused into the old Nazi files just to see if I could turn up a cross reference; and I found a thick dossier on a group called the *Gemeinschaft für der historische WiBenschaft*, or GHW. It blew my banana. They were headquartered in Vienna, and somehow Roehm and his SA goons got onto them. That's when the Nazis started their propaganda about the Jews and bankers running the world. I mean, they were always anti-semitic populists, but this really set them off. The GHW were wealthy and several key members were Jews; but Himmler rounded them all up, even the Aryan members. I think Roehm tried to make a deal with them, because Himmler grabbed the whole SA organization, too."

"The Night of the Long Knives," said Red. "Then there was more to it than intramural rivalry between the SA and the SS."

"It seems that way."

"And you found this file in the German archives?" Sarah asked.

"*Ganz bestimmt, gnädige Frau,*" Bosworth replied. "*Auf Generalstaatsarchiv Bonn.*"

She looked at Red. "Then the German government must know something."

Red frowned and looked uncertain. "Maybe," he allowed. "But those old records were scanned into Deutsche-BundesNet using automatic character recognition algorithms. Could be that nobody read them. A lot of Germans go three sides around the barn to avoid noticing anything from those days. In fact, I remember there was some fuss about putting Nazi-era records into the Net, at all. It was only pressure from France and Poland and Israel that forced them to do it." He shook his head. "Put it down as one more thing we're not sure of anymore. You sure have managed to shake things up, lady."

"Things were always this way, 'Jim'. You just never knew it."

"Yeah, I suppose you're right. I guess it's better, knowing

about them." Red turned back to Bosworth. "All right, finish up. Tell her about the last two societies."

Bosworth shrugged. "Nothing left to tell. One of the two surviving tracks vanished in the 1960s."

"And then there was one," Red announced with a flourish.

"It's hard to discover 'horseshoe nails' more recent than that," Bosworth reminded them. "It can take decades for the spin-offs to appear."

"Mmmm," Red nodded thoughtfully. He looked at Sarah. "Speculate."

"One of the survivors stumbled onto the other and wiped it out."

"Or vice versa. Yeah, that's what Norris and I thought." It was the first time Red hadn't called Bosworth "kid" and Sarah noticed how the teenager sat up straighter.

"And then the winner began wondering if there were any other rivals around," Bosworth said. "Like in North America."

Red pursed his lips. "Makes sense. They fished around for a couple decades until the various data nets started up."

"They must have planted a parasite inside the Net," said Sarah. "Something that randomly sampled police files, reporters' notes, things like that; and test for the sorts of patterns that a secret society would make. Like the trail of bodies the Weils left."

"Yeah. Then you turned the spotlight on, and they saw us, too. Well, at least we know how many others we're dealing with. The Secret Six, their daughter—if it's still around— and this European gang."

"Call them The Q," Sarah suggested.

Red was tapping his teeth with his thumbnail, looking thoughtful. He glanced at Sarah and nodded. "What? Oh. Okay. The Q. It's as good a name as any." He paused, looked down and rubbed his hands together. "You know Cam ordered an autopsy on Howard."

*The fat woman runs into Polovsky's arms. She struggles; then she jerks as if electrocuted, and slumps to the floor.*

"Hey," said Red. "What happened to her wasn't your fault. It was her decision to carry poison in a tooth. It was her decision to use it."

Sarah grimaced. "I know; but I feel responsible."

"You," said Red, "are too sentimental. Everybody dies, sooner or later. Howard just had the rare privilege of picking her own time." He looked at the last fragment of his sandwich; made a face; and laid his plate on the end table by the sofa. "At any rate," he continued, "the DNA analysis matched the one on record for 'Maureen Howard.' We expected that. Whoever she works for isn't stupid. But Bill Hollister says the DNA is more likely to be a European strain. There's so much overlap in the genomes of different human populations that he can't be certain where an individual sample belongs; but he did say that certain patterns in Howard's DNA were more common in Alsatian and Alpine populations than in American."

"So you think she was with the Q and not the Six?"

"It seems that way." He turned to Bosworth. "Norris, I want you to go all out on locating the Q when you get back to Buffalo Creek. If they do have a parasite in the Net like Gloria thinks, it must be pretty well camouflaged. I don't think the regulars will pick it out; so give them a hand."

"Sure thing, Brother Caldero. I think I'll start with a survey of the scientists who were around in the early 1800s. Find out who was capable of putting a show together. Those old records aren't camouflaged as well."

"Okay, but be discreet, for crying out loud. Don't let 'em trace the worms back to the ranch. They sound as dangerous as Weil was. Christ, the way that Howard woman killed herself . . ." He shivered.

"They must know where we are already," said Sarah. "Howard must have reported in, don't you think?"

Red glanced at her. "Maybe not. We watch recruits pretty closely. We didn't even let you get near a phone."

"You let her go riding up in the mountains," she pointed out.

"Sure, but there aren't any phones up there." He grinned and looked back at Bosworth. "Be discreet anyway, would you, kid? Game theory. Discretion is the optimal strategy. I don't like taking chances. The last time I took a chance was in the New York lottery in 1993."

The device Red attached to the window pane looked like a giant suction cup. Sarah watched him plug the wires into their sockets and run them to a speaker and cassette recorder.

"I don't believe it," she said.

"Believe it. Here, help me aim this thing." He stepped aside and Sarah came closer. "There. Look through that and tell me where the cross hairs are." Red bent over the dials on the cassette recorder.

411

Sarah closed one eye and squinted through the eyepiece with the other. Telegraph Hill swam into view. "I can see Coit Tower," she said.

"Too far east. Turn that knob. No, no, not that one. The third one in."

"You've got enough knobs on this thing."

"We're on Nob Hill, ain't we?"

She heard SuperNerd stifle a laugh behind her. "That's really funny, Jimbo," she told him. "You should be on the Leno show." She turned the vernier and her view shifted slowly. "What am I looking for?"

"That tall building on Greenwich. Thirteenth floor—except they call it the Fourteenth. Second window in from the right."

Sarah looked out the window and spotted the building. Then she put her eye back to the vernier. "So that's Kennison Demographics?"

"No," said Red. "It's an apartment he's rented under an assumed name."

Sarah shook her head. "I know I'm new to this game, but wouldn't it be easier if we just drove over there?" She got the cross hairs lined up on the window. "Got it!"

"Okay, lock it in." Red did something to the speaker and it began to hiss. "No, it wouldn't be easier. Because we don't know who is watching him. He doesn't want to be seen with us, because Ullman might 'ask questions later'; and, frankly, I don't want to be seen with him, either."

"Because of Ullman?"

"No, because I'm particular about who I'm seen with."

"Oh, come on, Jim. I only met him the one time, but he wasn't so bad."

"For a multiple murderer, you mean?"

"I didn't say I approved of him."

"Hell, Sarah. You've never said you approved of me."

She looked at him in surprise. He was hunched over his equipment. "You just broke character, Red."

Red scowled at his knobs. He made an adjustment. "So, Danny Boy is paranoid. He called me from a public phone booth. Says he doesn't have anyone else he can trust, and he has to talk to us right away. Can I come out here with a computer expert? How could I refuse such a touching plea?"

"I understand that, but why the parabolic mikes?" She gestured at the elaborate equipment Red had pulled from his briefcase.

412

"Kennison's mopped his apartment and it's clear of bugs, but he isn't sure about the telephone lines. This way, he can sit in his apartment and talk to thin air. Our mike reads the vibrations of his window and translates them into sound. We talk to him the same way. No one can listen in unless they've got parabolics and know which windows to aim them at."

He flipped a switch and a voice issued from the speakers.

". . . know you're there. I can hear you talking. Can you hear me. Answer, Goddamn it."

The speakers squealed and Red jumped to a knob and twisted it. "Feedback," he explained. "He's picking up his own voice from our speakers. And we're picking it up from him." He faced the window. "Cut in your filter, dammit!"

The squealing cut to a low hiss. "Is that better?"

Red found a seat on the sofa. He leaned back and put his arms behind his head. "Copacetic, Danny. Copacetic. No, Gloria," he added, "don't bother with the recorder. It's voice activated. Kicks in automatically."

"You're recording this?" Kennison's voice trembled ever so slightly.

"Sure. Aren't you?"

"I wish you would not."

"Okay." Red waited a beat. "There. It's off. Now, what did you want?" He ignored Sarah's accusing look, but scribbled something on a notepad he had placed on the arm of the sofa. He handed the pad to her and she read it.

*All's fair in love and war.*

*And which was this?* Sarah wondered.

Kennison told them everything. About the Council election —of which they had heard only rumors. About Selkirk's plan; and his apparent treachery. Red scribbled another note. *Carson's Dilemma: The Society is fracturing again.* He looked positively gleeful. So Sarah took the pad from him and wrote back: *So are the Associates. Red's cabal.* And Red didn't think that was nearly as funny.

"So why do you need the Associates, Cousin? You thinking of joining us?" Red made gagging gestures, pointing down his throat with two fingers.

"I don't need the Associates; only you and your friend."

"A shoulder?"

"To lean on, not to cry on. Just some temporary personal assistance."

"You'll get by with a little help from your friends, is that it?"

"Exactly."

"Gee, Danny. It would help if you had some friends."

"I know where Dennis French is."

Sarah jerked as if an electric shock had run through her. Dennis? She turned and faced the window. She could see Kennison's apartment on Telegraph Hill. The morning sun sparkled in the windows. She squinted her eyes against the brightness. "Where is he?" she asked. She felt silly talking to the empty air. Kennison was a ghost in the room.

"Ah, Miss Bennett. How are you? Are you the computer expert James brought?"

"Never mind that! Where is Dennis?"

"Will you help me?" Red was making warning motions with his hands.

"Yes. Now talk." Red gave an exasperated shrug, but Sarah ignored him.

"Very well. But first things first." There was a long moment of hesitation before Kennison spoke again. "I have decided to leave the Society and strike out on my own. And I plan to take my company with me."

Sarah looked at Red, who raised his eyebrows. "That would be a neat trick, Danny boy. Especially if you also plan to survive. How do you propose doing it?" Red was scribbling furiously on his notepad.

"I plan to proceed in four steps. Firstly, under a secret persona that I maintain, I will purchase an established firm dealing in, say, securities or market consulting. A company that might plausibly establish a public opinion subsidary. Secondly, I will copy the K/D data banks to that new base. Thirdly, I will corrupt the original data base so that it will be useless to Ullman and his ilk. Fourthly, I shall die and be resurrected in my new persona."

"After three days?" said Red.

"As long as it takes," said Kennison.

"And where do we come in?"

"I had originally planned to use my protegé, Alan Selkirk, for the computer work. His original plan, as I told you, was simply to feed corrupted data to the Council, while hiding a 'clean' data base in a secret location. He does not know that I plan to take it a step further, and I have no intention of telling him. I no longer trust him. I suspect he is in collusion with

414

either Ullman or your Secret Six. That's why I need your people; to verify the integrity of my system and to help me copy it into the host system that I select."

"But you trust us?"

"Yes."

That simple, flat answer seemed to disarm Red. He paused with his mouth open, and gave Sarah a helpless glance. She smiled at him with half a mouth. Sure, Kennison trusted Red. The question was: could they trust Kennison?

"The job sounds simple enough," Red told the window pane.

"I would also like your help," the window pane replied, "to set up the deal with the target company. In order to avoid attracting undue attention to myself, it would be best to create an arbitrage consortium with several partners."

"Hmmm." Red glanced at Sarah and Bosworth. "We could call it Caldero, Bennett, and . . . ?" He let the sentence hang, and there was a moment of tentative silence.

"Caldero, Bennett and Ochs," said Kennison after a while. "Fletcher Ochs will be the name of your junior partner."

"I look forward to meeting him," Red commented wryly. "Have you selected a target company, yet?"

"As a matter of fact, I have several in mind; but there is one that looks especially promising, an investment firm with an already impressive record of successes. It will not look unduly suspicious if we take it over and begin using cliological analysis to increase its earnings. No one is surprised when the rich grow richer. Nor would it be unreasonable for them to establish a market research arm. It would mesh quite nicely with their profile."

"Uh-huh. Does this firm have a name?"

"Yes. Detweiler, Barron and Stone."

"Never heard of them."

"They are an old Boston firm; but they trade in the New York and Chicago exchanges, as well." A long pause and a sigh. "Boston, alas, is not San Francisco; but it is as close as the East Coast can come to it."

Sarah drifted to the window. She looked out and across to Kennison's apartment. The hills, the sparkling white city, the Golden Gate. She had heard the catch in Kennison's voice. Genuine sentiment from a monster, she had not expected. "You'll miss San Francisco, won't you, Kennison."

"Who would not? There is not another city like her, Miss

Bennett. Not in all the world. Rudyard Kipling once said that her chief drawback was the difficulty of leaving."

Red was humming the old Tony Bennett tune. *I left my heart* . . . Sarah turned and scowled at him and he grinned and shut up. Somehow, Kennison seemed more human for the sentiment; less of a monstrous caricature. Red shouldn't make fun of anyone's private loves, not even Kennison's.

"Alright," Red announced. "I'll set up a lunch with the Detweiler people. How do you know they want to sell out?"

"I don't; but everyone has a price. We need only find it out and offer it to them."

"Yeah? No horse heads in the bed, though. Okay? That's not our style. How do we get in touch with 'Fletcher Ochs' to let him know about the meeting?"

"I'll contact you when it is safe."

"Look, it's your neck we're trying to save. There's nothing in it for us."

"There is Dennis French."

"Yeah. If you really know where he is."

"By the time we close the deal, I'll know."

They left the monitoring gear in place. Just in case, Red told them. However, he attached several small devices resembling mechanical spiders to the window. When he turned them on, their legs began tapping. Red explained that, by setting up a large number of unsynchronized vibrations in the window pane, he could frustrate any attempt to "read" conversations in the room. The net result of so many random patterns was that they cancelled each other out.

He asked Bosworth to stand watch while he took Sarah to dinner. If he got bored, he could work on the computer problem Kennison had outlined. Bosworth gave them a look but didn't object. "You kids have fun," he said. "But be sure to bring her back before midnight."

For some reason, Red thought that was funny.

Red took her by the arm and they walked together to the elevator. Sarah told Helen that "Mister Caldero" was taking her to dinner; and Helen told her to have a good time. However, when they entered the elevator Red pressed the button for his own floor.

Sarah looked at him. "Did you forget something?" she asked.

"No," he said.

The door opened and he led her to his suite, where there was a dinner table set up for two in his sitting room. A single red rose in a bud vase adorned the white tablecloth. The meals, under cover, sat under portable heat lamps. The drapes were drawn; the room lit by twin candles in golden holders.

Sarah looked at the arrangement. "I thought you were taking me out to dinner."

"I couldn't get a reservation."

"Isn't this a little intimate?"

"No, it's a lot intimate. Why, does that bother you? I could have the hotel staff serve us." He held a chair out for her.

She sighed and sat down. "Just don't get any ideas."

"Hell, I haven't had an idea like that since June of 1990." Sarah noticed how he suddenly stiffened, as if he had said something without intending.

"Why, what happened in June of 1990?"

"I took the veil."

He spoke lightly, but he wouldn't meet her eyes. Sarah watched him load a cassette into the player. There was an awful lot about himself that Red kept hidden. There was a wall of glass between them. She could see him, hear him, get as close to him as she wanted; but somehow, she couldn't touch him.

Red pressed the play button and a lone harp filled the air. Not a concert harp, with its thrumming resonances; but a curious, metallic-sounding harp. The music sounded old, almost medieval; and she thought immediately of cathedrals and kings. "What instrument is that?" she asked as Red took his seat.

"It's a *clairseach*. An Irish harp, strung in brass and played with the nails. The music is Ó Carolan. He lived in the late 1700s. The last of the old Gaelic harpers. At least, so they always say. He was blind—which for a musician, I suppose, is better than being deaf. This particular piece is called Ó *Flainn*, which he named in honor of Liam Ó Flainn, who brought him his last glass of whiskey as he lay dying."

She ate in silence, enjoying the food, and enjoying the music. Red broke the silence only occasionally, to announce a song title. This is *Sir Festus Burke*. That was *Brigit Cruise*. The music was hauntingly familiar. Ancient , half-remembered melodies passed along by country fiddle players; resurrected by mountain cloggers and Delta bluesmen. She glanced at Red across the table and he smiled and nodded to her.

417

Somehow, there was nothing uncomfortable in their lack of conversation.

She thought about Kennison's appeal for help. What a curious meeting that had been! Kennison was a strange bird. Repulsive; but at the same time attractive. Half devil; and half gentleman. But of course wasn't the devil always portrayed as a gentleman? He was a kingpin of the Society; yet now he wanted out. Not from a moral revulsion at what they had done, but simply because his ambitions had been thwarted. And Red would help him, not because he approved of Kennison's ambitions; but because he would do anything to thwart the Society's program. And so, for the moment, the three of them were curiously wary allies. The enemy of mine enemy is mine friend. She wondered if Kennison really did have a line on Dennis' whereabouts. When she had asked him again about that, he had asked her to bug his own telephone at Kennison demographics. How would that help locate Dennis?

The music paused and Red cocked his head to the speakers. "This next one's the one I wanted you to hear. It's called *Fanny Power*."

"Fanny power?"

He flashed her an irritated look. "No, not like that. Fanny was the daughter of Ó Carolan's patron. He wrote this piece for her wedding. I wanted you to hear it because I didn't want you to think that there was only one perfect melody in the world." He laid his silverware aside and leaned his arms on the table. He stared into infinity.

The music began simply. A melody of unaffected grace and beauty that floated through the upper registers. It was followed by a counter melody, pitched lower, that complemented it. Then the harpist began repeating the phrases, ornamenting them with grace notes and arpeggios of crystal-line elegance. Gradually, the music became fuller and grander, swelling to a great climax from which the original, simple melody emerged. Then the harp fell silent, the overtones shimmering in the air.

Red was still for a few moments; then, as the tape began another cut, he shook himself, rose and stopped the tape. "Well?" he asked. "What did you think?"

Sarah was surprised to see that his eyes were moist. "She must have been very beautiful."

He looked at her. "Who?" And his voice was sharp, wary.

"Why, Fanny." Sarah sighed. "There was magic in that old

418

man's music, if it can move us to tears for the beauty of a woman two centuries dead."

"Ah, yes. Fanny." There was a distant look in Red's eyes and she sensed the sadness in his voice. "I suppose she was. Beautiful, that is. But, beauty is in the eye of the beholder, you know; and Ó Carolan was blind. To him all women were beautiful."

# VIII

"Saudi Arabia?" Adrian Detweiler V worked his lips and
looked from face to face around the conference table. "Saudi
Arabia," the old man repeated.

Red kept his own face composed and decided to let Kennison
continue handling the discussion. Not that it mattered. It was
already obvious that the old man was not going to sell out;
that he never would sell out; that he had never had any
intention of selling out. Not when you were the fifth consecutive Adrian Detweiler, and the firm had been in your family
for a century and a half.

So then why had Detweiler agreed to the meeting at all?

Red glanced at Sarah, who was sitting on Kennison's far
side, and shrugged with his eyebrows; and she gave him a
'who knows' look in return. So. Sarah had drawn the same
conclusion as he. The negotiations were a charade. A waste of
time. Only Kennison seemed oblivious to that fact. But then,
of course, to "Fletcher Ochs," this was a life-or-death affair.

"Saudi Arabia," said Detweiler, "is considered to be quite a
safe investment by the community."

Now why, Red wondered, were they so taken up with this
one projection? Kennison had argued—and Sarah had agreed
—that they must prove themselves to be more astute than
the normal corporate suitor. A firm as successful as DB&S
was not going to sell out to amateurs. So, they had prepared a
number of cliological projections dramatic enough to impress
Detweiler with their insight. It was a good piece of work,
thanks to Sarah and Bosworth, and Red was proud of it; so he
was surprised that Detweiler and his people had become even
more reserved.

Kennison smiled. "Sir, we do not wish to divulge our methods. Suffice it to say that we rely on unusually keen intelligence of conditions there. A fundamentalist revolution is imminent; say within the next five years. We have been divesting ourselves quietly from our own interests there."

"Have you?" Detweiler smacked his lips. He frowned and turned to the man beside him. "Mister Stone, what have you to say?"

"Snake oil, sir," answered the younger partner in a high, nasal "Ha'va'd" accent. "And were Mrs. Barron heah, she would say the same, I am sure." He faced Kennison. "This is Boston, Mister Ochs. We do things differently down east. We don't care for your slick, Manhattan ways, with your fast money and your faster bankruptcies. DB&S has gotten along quite nicely for over 150 yeahs doing business the old-fashioned way." The gallery of portraits that lined the DB&S boardroom frowned their agreement. Stolid, dour New England paintings hung on stolid, dour New England walls. Adrian Detweiler, Marks I through IV, scowled importantly from the dark oak panels. Red wondered what it was like to have numbered ancestors.

Sarah leaned forward. "Is it part of the old-fashioned Boston way to gratuitously insult one's guests?"

Detweiler looked at her. "I beg your pardon, Miss Bennett?"

"What Miss Bennett means—" said Kennison, with a nervous glance at Sarah.

"I am quite capable of saying what I mean, Fletcher." She fixed her eye on Stone. "I agreed to buy in on this deal," she said, "because it looked like a good investment and a way of attaining certain objectives I have set in my personal life. We believe that, among the three of us, we have valuable resources that can enhance the position of this firm in the markets. I cut short a vacation trip to San Francisco to be at this meeting. It was a long flight and a tiring one; and I do not appreciate being called a 'snake-oil salesman.' And, Mr. Stone, I, too, made my money the old-fashioned way. But I started from ground zero. Did you?"

Detweiler did not take his eyes off Sarah. He rubbed his hand through his white, Commodore Vanderbilt beard. Red wondered what he was thinking. Then he nodded and smiled in a grandfatherly way. "Apologize to the lady, if you please, Mr. Stone. There's a good fellow."

Stone shot his partner a quick glance; then he bowed his

head. "I am sorry. I spoke unkindly. But it is our Firm's position that takeover mania has been the bane of American business. It squanders capital better spent in research and maintenance of equipment; and works to the benefit of no one but the Japanese and the Europeans. We refuse to be a part of it."

As an apology, thought Red, it had shortcomings; but he knew that Sarah had made the insult an issue only to put Detweiler on the defensive. *It's a good thing we have her.* She had spent more time in the rough-and-tumble of business than either he or Kennison, and knew more about the tactics of negotiating. *We should have made her the chief negotiator.* Detweiler, he was sure, had recognized her ploy and had decided to dispose of the issue quickly rather than wrangle over it. In fact, Red wondered if Stone's comment had been just as calculated.

Detweiler continued to watch Sarah, to Red's growing annoyance. Just what did the old man find so fascinating about her? He hadn't taken his eyes off her since she had first spoken. Was he a dirty old man? The thought that Detweiler might find Sarah attractive was vaguely unsettling.

*Forget it,* he told himself. These old-family, Boston brahmins never crossed the color line, except to diddle the occasional maid. And besides, what business was it of his?

He decided that there was only one reason to meet with a prospective buyer when you had no intention of selling. And that was an intense interest in the buyers themselves. *They didn't want to meet us to sell us their company. They just wanted to meet* us. But why? Perhaps to do some polite sniffing. Not interested just now, thank you; not in this deal. But maybe we can do other business together.

*If we can't buy DB&S outright; we might be able to form a joint venture, say in demographic polling.* A joint venture would suit Red; but he wasn't sure what Kennison would say. The man was vain as well as power-hungry. The symbols of power meant as much to him as the power itself; and the power meant a great deal. Red didn't mind if Kennison owned his own hidey-hole or just "rented" it from DB&S as a subsidiary, so long as he sabotaged the Society in the process; but Kennison probably minded a great deal.

Normally, of course, he wouldn't care what Kennison minded; but Kennison had some sort of lead on Dennis French's whereabouts, and that meant Sarah cared.

Dammit, he hated depending on Kennison for anything. There was something slimy about the man. Something unclean. And he was at his most repellent when he was acting the most charming. Other people didn't seem to feel that way; but the public didn't know him the way Red did.

Red decided he was liking Kennison less with each passing day. On a scale from one to nine, his rating was already well into the negative numbers. Familiarity, they say, breeds contempt; and, since forming their joint venture, Red had become all too familiar with Daniel Kennison.

Detweiler was polite, but firm. Stone was equally firm, and considerably less polite. Barron was not even present; and the other flunkies did not count. When Detweiler, at last, formally declined the proposal, Kennison started to raise the ante, but Red and Sarah both kicked him under the table. Never show your opponent how eager you are. Even Red knew that much about buying and selling.

Furthermore, he suspected that old Detweiler might be offended by an offer of more money. The suggested price had been a fair one. Both parties recognized that. But Detweiler's refusal had been predicated on principles; and people didn't sell those for cash. For other considerations, maybe; but not for cash. If cash could buy them, they had never been principles.

The meeting ended amicably at precisely two o'clock. Even Kennison managed to project affable good-losership. Detweiler had highballs served. They toasted each other's good fortune and parted in a flurry of handshakes. Detweiler—the old goat!—even gave Sarah a kiss on the cheek.

They walked down the hallway and through the large, open accounting department. Sarah had taken Red by the arm, as if he were her escort; and Red felt an odd tingle at the light touch of her glove on his sleeve.

He glanced back once and saw Stone and Detweiler in animated conversation, partly framed in the doorway of the boardroom. Detweiler was running his finger repeatedly down his neck, just behind the ear.

Then he felt Sarah's grip on his arm tighten. He glanced at her in puzzlement, but she said nothing. Yet, he could see from her face that she was alarmed at something. He scanned the office looking for the source; but there were only the staff accountants and analysts, displaying various degrees of disinterest in the departing guests.

423

He turned to her again and looked a question. "Later," she whispered.

They picked a small coffee shop on a side street just off State in Boston's downtown. Red ordered three cups, cream, no sugar. When the waitress was gone, he spread his hands out. "Well, it was a nice try. What's next, Fletch? You had some alternate choices, didn't you?"

Kennison didn't touch his coffee. "Several," he admitted, "but none as suitable as this one. Detweiler's record of success would have been admirable camouflage. With the other firms on my list, it would draw unwelcome attention if we became too wealthy too fast. Raise questions better unasked."

"Well, patience is all," Red told him. "The important thing is to get you set up on your own. Someplace where They won't think to look for you."

"No," said Sarah, "The important thing is to find out what Detweiler, Barron, and Stone are up to."

It was an unexpected remark. He looked at her and saw that she had her lower lip between her teeth. She was staring into her cup like a tea reader. "What is it?" he asked. Then he remembered how she had stiffened while walking through Detweiler's offices. "What did you notice back there?"

"I saw Jeremy Collingwood."

"Who?"

Kennison's head jerked up. "Collingwood? From Denver? But he was killed in the bombing, wasn't he? What was he doing there?"

*Because DB&S has a great retirement program?* Red fought the impulse to say that aloud. "He was Dennis French's roommate, wasn't he?"

There was a moment of silence. The cash register at the lunch counter rang and the cashier made some remark to a departing customer. The men at the counter laughed. The bells on the entrance door jingled. Kennison frowned and took a sip of his coffee. "Are you sure it was your friend?"

Sarah shook her head. "I didn't know him all that well, but I couldn't be mistaken."

"The reports may have been in error," said Kennison. "This Collingwood fellow may have survived the explosion and come out here simply to make a break with the past."

Sarah shook her head. "You don't know Jeremy. No, he was trying to find Dennis. He's still trying to find Dennis."

"At Detweiler, Barron and Stone?" asked Kennison.

Sarah reached across the table and grasped Red's wrist. "Jimmy. What if they're players?"

"Who? Detweiler?" That smiling grandfather in the three-piece suit? He couldn't imagine the old man as a player. He didn't have the demeanor for it. Stone. Now, Stone was a different matter. The younger partner had had a coldness about him.

"Yes. What if they rescued Jeremy from the bombing?"

"Why would they do that?" asked Kennison.

"Maybe because they don't like people being killed," she shot back at him.

"Then why," Kennison replied reasonably, "would they not rescue everyone?"

"Okay, maybe Jeremy survived the explosion on his own. The DU Study Team discovered something and were killed for it; but Jeremy has tracked Dennis to DB&S."

"Never mind that now," Red said. Christ, they could yack about this till the cows came home. They could create and demolish a thousand scenarios and none of them would be right. They needed some hard facts. "Okay," he decided. "Two things. We need to talk to Collingwood; and we need to know more about DB&S. Our people here in Boston can find out where Collingwood is living and plant a bug there; and I'll have Bosworth do a little mousing into DB&S's background."

"How soon?" asked Sarah.

"Let us not be hasty," said Kennison. "Haste makes waste. If they are players, we do not want to alarm them. And if your friend's, ah, roommate is with them incognito, we would not want to blow his cover."

Red smiled. Kennison was worried that they would get another line on French's whereabouts; and that if they did they wouldn't need him. He would lose his leverage with Sarah.

*Don't worry, Danny boy. I would never pass up the chance to corrupt your data base.* But he couldn't resist a chance to make Kennison sweat, either.

He downed the rest of his coffee in a gulp and stood. "How soon?" he said airily. "How about if I call Bosworth right now."

The cashier gave him directions to the nearest pay phone. He put a quarter in it and dialed an 800 number. The voice that answered wasted no time in pleasantries but asked him curtly for his number. Red gave his own code; Bosworth's code at the ranch; and the number of the public phone he was calling from. Then he hung up.

He waited impatiently for a few minutes, during which time he snarled at one lady who wanted to use the phone. Kennison was right about one thing. Haste did make waste. If DB&S were the Secret Six—or the European gang—it would not do to flail around at random. This called for some very discreet mousing. When the return call came, he picked it up on the first ring.

"Bosworth? Caldero, here. We've got a job for you. Priority One."

"Brother Caldero. I just left a message for you at your hotel—"

"Never mind the small talk, kid. I want you to dig—"

"This is an emergency, Jimmy."

Jimmy? Red held the phone away from his face and looked into the speaker. *This is an emergency.* He had a premonition. Whatever Bosworth was about to say, he wasn't going to like it. "All right, kid. You got my attention. Spit it out."

"The tripwires on 'Caldero' and 'Bennett' went off this afternoon."

"Say again."

"There was illegal activity on the Public DataNet. Someone was trying to mouse into your confidential files. You know. Social security. Birth records."

"Yeah, I know. What about 'Ochs'?"

"Was I supposed to alarm that file, too?"

"Yeah. Politics makes strange bedfellows." And they didn't get much stranger than Dan Kennison.

"Give me half a sec. I'll see if I can call it up."

"Where'd the balloon go up; and when?"

"I said just a sec." There was a pause. "It was a CPU in Boston. Where you are now. At, uh, 2:35 this afternoon. They didn't access anything sensitive."

Two thirty-five. Right after they had left Detweiler's office. Well, well. They didn't waste any time. He had to give them that. Curiouser and curiouser.

"Here it comes," said Bosworth. "Let me check this." A pause. "You were right. The same terminal tried to access the 'Ochs' files, too. Any idea who it is?"

"Yeah, I think so. A pretty good idea, at any rate. But I'm not sure why." Quickly, he briefed Bosworth on their visit to DB&S and the mysterious presence there of Jeremy Collingwood. "Can you worm your way into their system and mouse around for us? Without them knowing it?"

"Hey, does the pope wear a funny hat?"

"All right. Find out whatever you can. On the QT. Then meet us in the suite in San Francisco, say . . . Thursday."

"Can do, chief."

Red hooked the phone and stood quietly for a few moments, trying to get his thoughts straight. The traffic on State Street snarled and honked around him, but he shut it out. So, DB&S was checking up on them, were they? But why? A legitimate firm might want to check into the backgrounds of people they dealt with. Many businesses moused into the personal sectors of the Net despite the laws. But if that were the case, why do it *after* turning down their offer? No, there had to be more to it than that.

Something must have alarmed them, made them curious about Caldero, Bennett and Ochs. He didn't see how it was possible—their identities were legitimate and airtight; and Detweiler must get dozens of such feelers in a year from other firms—but that would explain the wariness during lunch and afterward. If DB&S were players, they might well be sensitive to any approach, especially since the Dump. Like a mafiosa family that had 'gone to the mattresses.' Hell, that Saudi projection Kennison had shown them. They might figure no one could draw that conclusion except through cliological analysis.

It was useless to speculate. Never go beyond the data on hand. Don't guess until the guess is reasonable. He had forgotten that precept only once, in Jacksonville; and look what it had gotten him. No, the only things to go on were the facts: A. Someone in Boston was poking into things. B. They had done so immediately after he and his companions had left DB&S. And C. Jeremy Collingwood was sitting in the accounting department there. And A plus B plus C equalled . . .

Who knew? He never was any damn good at algebra.

Collingwood. Red shook his head and started back to the coffee shop. How had Collingwood gotten from Denver to Boston? That must be a tale worth hearing, no matter what else came of this. Curiouser and curiouser? Alice hadn't known the half of it.

Jeremy was not precisely sure how he felt about being accepted into Detweiler, Barron & Stone. It had not been exactly a free choice on either part. Not only that, but by an odd travesty of reason, he had been accepted as a leader of some sort—which only confirmed his previous judgement that DB&S were tyros. If they could mistake *him* for a leader . . . Still, it did put him one step closer to finding Dennis. He had resources now. He had powerful help. People whose own uncertainties made them want to find out as much as he did.

But why had Detweiler called him upstairs and told him to sit in the bull pen with the accountants? Accounting was the last thing on his mind these days.

Like the others, he glanced curiously at the departing trio of arbitrageurs. A rumor had been going around the office about a takeover bid; but Jeremy didn't see how that was possible. DB&S was private; and, considering the true nature of their business, it was inconceivable that the old man would sell out.

Still, the three visitors made an interesting impression. A tall, distinguished-looking gentleman. A short, stocky man, who would have looked more at home on a construction site than a boardroom. And a tall, lithe, dark-skinned black woman with 'sculpted' hair. "Caldero, Bennett and Ochs," the woman at the next desk whispered to him. Jeremy nodded. He wondered which was which.

The black woman saw him looking at her and stiffened. *Don't worry,* he thought. *You're not my type.*

When they were gone, Peter Stone appeared in the hallway. He crooked a finger at Jeremy. "Collingwood, step in here a moment, please."

Jeremy stood. He shot his cuffs and straightened his tie. He didn't much care for Peter Stone and, he suspected, the feeling was mutual. The man always looked as if he used a lemon for chapstick. Stone stepped aside carefully as Jeremy entered the boardroom. Jeremy smiled to himself. *Don't worry, you're not my type, either,* he thought. Too dark and intense.

Old man Detweiler shook his hand briskly. No reserve there. No buried hostility. What was it about the old rich? Was it *noblesse* oblige; or was it just that they didn't have the insecurities of the *nouveau?* Detweiler was as obviously unafraid of being the target of a rabid homosexual attack as Stone obviously was. Maybe he and Stone just gave off the wrong pheromones. Rubbed each other the wrong way. That was the old saying, wasn't it?

He smiled and took a seat at the table next to Jennie

Barron, Detweiler's daughter. Stone took the seat on her other side. Barron glanced sideways at Stone and shifted a little in her seat, and Jeremy suppressed a chuckle. He wondered if Stone knew that he had the same effect on Barron that Jeremy had on him.

"Jeremy," said Detweiler. "Did you notice the tall black woman who just left? The one who calls herself Gloria Bennett?"

Jeremy turned to face the head of the table. He nodded cautiously. "Not particularly. But I did see her. Why?"

"Because my father is having paranoid fantasies," said Barron. Jeremy looked over his shoulder at her.

"Is that worse than having pollyannish fantasies?"

She sniffed and turned her head.

"I tell you she is Sarah Beaumont," the old man insisted. "Before she left, I gave her a peck on the cheek, just so I could get a closer look. She has a scar right here . . ." He ran his finger behind his left ear. "Typical of plastic surgery."

"Oh, Dad, thousands of people have had plastic surgery in this country! And she didn't look at all like her pictures."

"Isn't that the purpose of plastic surgery, Mrs. Barron?" Jeremy suggested.

"No, it isn't—"

"That will be enough, child. Jeremy, did she look at all familiar? Normal plastic surgery, as my daughter knows so well, simply removes wrinkles or bobs noses. There are limits to what it can do. The nose. The cheeks. The skin around the eyes. But the underlying bony structure cannot be altered, short of a disfiguring accident. Think, Jeremy."

Sarah Beaumont? Dennis' partner? His pulse hammered and he began to feel lightheaded. Was Detweiler right? He closed his eyes and conjured up Beaumont's face. Finally, he shook his head. "How can I tell? I didn't know why you wanted me out there or I would have—"

"I did not want to bias your perceptions. Ah . . ." He faced the door. "Did you get the photographs?"

Herkimer Vane and Gwynneth Llewellyn entered the boardroom. Vane was dressed incongruously in a doorman's uniform. He looked like a fleet admiral, splendid in ribbons and fourragére. Gwynn placed the glossies on the table. "We had a good look at them as they left the building. The other two are strangers, but there's no question that the tall gent was Daniel Kennison."

"Kennison?" said Stone. "Of Kennison Demographics? Why would he . . . Oh."

"Yes. Also Kennison, allegedly of the Babbage Society."

"Then the black woman could not have been Beaumont," said Jeremy. "She blew the whistle on The Society. They killed her friend and tried to kill her and Dennis. She wouldn't be with them."

Detweiler shrugged. "I can imagine off the top of my head at least five scenarios in which she and Kennison would appear together. What I don't understand is why they appeared here. Our cliometricians have assured us that there is no hint in the historical record of our existence. We have never attempted to meddle in affairs. And none of our records touching on cliology are accessible from the DataNet. So what is the Babbage Society doing at our door?"

"If the Babbage Society were at your door," said Gwynn, "your door would have been blown off its hinges."

A sudden, loud knock made them all jump, and Jennie Barron giggled in embarrassment. The door opened and Jim Doang entered together with another man whom Jeremy did not know. The latter was dressed in a white gown, the chasuble of the scientific priesthood. Doang and Jeremy nodded to one another. There was a bond among those who had faced danger together. A brotherhood.

The other man spoke. "The public dossiers on the three people you asked about are clean. They all have a paper trail straight from birth to today. Nothing looks funny."

"Of course nothing 'looks funny,'" said Detweiler. "It is only coincidence that Fletcher Ochs looks precisely like Daniel Kennison."

The boardroom telephone warbled. Doang, who was closest, walked over and picked it up. He listened for a moment then handed it to his companion. "It's for you." He took a seat at the board table next to Vane. "Hello, Herkimer. Gwynn."

Jeremy sensed a change in the atmosphere of the room. Barron and Stone seemed more reserved. They greeted Vane politely; but barely acknowledged Doang and Llewellyn. The new kids on the block. DB&S had been very comfortable for a very long time; and they didn't like the way their world had been turned topsy-turvy. And they especially did not like the threat of direct, physical action represented by Jeremy and his friends. Even Vane, because of his association with them, was tainted.

Only old Detweiler himself seemed unfazed, even exhilarated by the new uncertainty.

The computer man hung up the phone. "Bad news, chief. There's a mouse in our system."

Stone jerked around. "What? When? What is it doing?"

"What is it doing? It's mousing."

"Has it downloaded?" asked Doang.

"It's in realtime."

Stone pushed himself up from his chair. "Trace it, then!"

"We're on it. Don't worry. We sent a cat after it."

"Don't worry? And how long was it in there before your people stumbled on it?"

The computer man looked at Stone carefully and addressed his answer to Detweiler. "It couldn't have been in there too long, chief. There are safeguards. The mouser, whoever he is, is pretty damned good; but our cat should catch him."

While they argued over computer security, Jeremy reached across the table and took the still of Gloria Bennett that Gwynn had taken as they left. He studied it carefully. The jaws. The skull. He shook his head. He had met Sarah Beaumont only a few times, usually in Dennis' company. How could he hope to pick her out of a stranger's face? "Can we get a photograph of Beaumont to compare to this?" he asked Gwynn.

She looked thoughtful. "We had a complete rogues' gallery on the study team. Every name in the printout for whom we could secure a photograph. That's how Herkimer and I recognized Kennison. I know Beaumont's was among them. But that's all gone now." Her face clouded at the memory. "It shouldn't be too hard to find her picture, all things considered."

He looked again at the photograph. *Beaumont, is that you in there? Do you know where Dennis is?* He laid the picture aside and wondered if he was finally nearing the end of his quest.

431

# IX

Kennison's life had been turned upside down. At one time
he had been certain of everything, and his destiny had seemed
assured. Now he was certain of nothing. He had been in
control of affairs; but now affairs somehow controlled him. He
cut and chewed his food without tasting it. *Baked chicken
breasts a la Russe*. Marinated overnight in a sour-cream-and-
cayenne paste; then carefully breaded and baked. Ruth Ann
had excelled herself once more.

Ordinarily he would have praised the meal; sent his com-
pliments to Cook. He would have enjoyed Karin's presentation of the dishes. He would have smiled and joked. Now it
all seemed a pointless sham. Daniel Kennison, *bon vivant?*
Daniel Kennison, japing fool!

They had outmaneuvered him. All of them. Beaumont and
her worm. Ullman. Ruiz. Selkirk, damn his insolent, black-
mailing hide! Even Weil had fooled him for a time; until she
had succumbed at last to her lust for revenge and foolishly
shown herself.

He had, at least, that one victory to savor; and the savor
was sweet, even though it had cost him his beloved Prudence. He saw now that Weil had gone utterly mad. Beaumont's exposures; Ullman's and Ruiz' treachery; Paige's *attentat*.
They had driven her over an edge that had never been any
too distant. Even his own valiant attempts to salvage and
protect the Society had been misconstrued in her savage and
twisted mind.

And now, the ultimate comedy. After 160 years of carefully guarding the precious Secret, he found cliological societies

432

crawling out from under every rock he turned over. The Secret Six. The Europeans, the ones that Beaumont had called "the Q." The now-defunct GHW that Caldero had told him of. Even that Boston investment firm! Who would have believed it?

He shook his head sadly. Who would have believed it? The dikes were leaking and the fingers of a thousand valiant Dutch boys would not suffice. Protecting the Secret now would require such massive deletions that even Genevieve Weil might have blanched. Perhaps if all the societies cooperated . . . A sort of Cliological League. It would be difficult. Each society had an obvious interest in the continued ignorance of the masses; but each had also a deeply engrained fear of exposure, even to one another. Cooperation would be awkward and delicate. The way porcupines made love. It would require a man of exceptional talents to weld them all into a single force. A man such as himself? Perhaps. Perhaps. He allowed himself to toy momentarily with the scenario. *Capo di tutti capi.* Let Ullman chair the Babbage Society. He would represent but one member society in the league.

Yet, Jimmy Caldero seemed convinced that one society, the Q, had deliberately hunted down and exterminated its only surviving European rival. And perhaps it had also "blown the whistle" on the GHW, the one that the Nazis had destroyed. Were the Secret Six any less dangerous? Who could be certain?

But of one thing Kennison was certain. The Babbage Society was wide open. Not only to the assaults of the so-called Q, but to the Six, the CIA, the KGB; even the Boy Scouts, did they want to. Thanks to Beaumont. The public furor seemed to have died down for now, at least on the surface; though who knew what currents were flowing beneath? But then, the ignorant masses had always been the least of his worries. There was not much to fear from a public that thought Charles Lindbergh was a blimp, and could not locate Mexico on a map. It was the knowledgable elites that worried him. The government agents. The scholars. The nosy and inquisitive.

The Associates had sustained some minor damage in the affair. One mole, unmasked and deleted. A few public embarrassments. But they seemed to have contained things. Not so the Society. Weil's panic and Ullman's plotting had paralyzed any effective response. The Society sat dead in the water. Did he really want to become the captain of a target hulk?

No, of course not. It was better for Ullman to play that role. To sit in happy oblivion in the bull's-eye, while Kennison himself faded safely out of sight. Foregoing the chairmanship had actually been a stroke of genius on his part.

The more he considered it, the more attractive his new plan seemed. When you are in the bull's-eye, the first order of business is to *move*, and move fast. It was time to duck. Time to become Fletcher Ochs. Time to move his data base into a secret location, until it would be safe to reemerge.

He noticed that his palms were moist and wiped them on his napkin. Fletcher Ochs. Ochs Demographics? No, his new base of operations must have a markedly different name. Kennison Demographics must be scuttled. Buried forever. Too bad; but there was no help for it. What would Father have said? He glanced momentarily at the severe portrait that graced the fireplace. Then he took his crystal wineglass in his hand and sipped. A mediocre vintage. He must speak to Bettina about it.

Bettina. He wondered. Would it be possible to take his staff with him? Perhaps they could be persuaded into a change of persona. For their own safety.

He sighed. No, for *his* own safety, Ochs must live a lifestyle utterly different from that of Daniel Kennison. Ochs must be a different person, in all ways. Rough-hewn, rather than refined. Perhaps a touch less witty. There must not be even the whisper of a connection between Ochs and Kennison. Too bad. He would miss Bettina and Karin; Ruth Ann and Greta.

He watched Karin carry the now-empty plates from the dining room. *She walks in beauty . . .* The high heels forced her calf and thigh muscles into delicious shapes.

Karin must have sensed him watching, because she stiffened ever so slightly. Just a hint of fear. Kennison was pleased. She was learning. She would never be as adept at playing the lost, frightened girl as Prudence had been. But Kennison was teaching her. He was teaching her.

He reached inside his jacket and pulled forth a cigarillo. He struck a match and lit it. *Very well*, he decided. The Babbage Society is finished. It was dead and lacked only the formality of a funeral. Too bad. *Had I been her leader, this* contretemps *might have been avoided.* But now, her enemies knew of her; had her ranged and bracketed.

He laughed. He was in the bull's-eye, surrounded by

enemies. Surrounded. But if he ducked, they would wind up shooting each other!

There was a knocking on the dining room door. Bettina's knock.

"Enter."

Bettina opened the double door and stood inside. "Master Selkirk, to see you, sir," she said.

Kennison grimaced. The young man was growing more and more a nuisance. He pulled his pocket watch from his pants and studied it. Selkirk should be at the Office, managing the Night Shift; not here. But it was just as well. If he was here, he could not interrupt Beaumont while she installed the tap on Kennison's EPIC terminal. "Send him in, Madam Butler; but instruct Karin to serve no port until after he leaves."

"Yes, sir."

She left; and a moment later, Selkirk entered. He strode—arrogantly, it seemed to Kennison—to the dining table. He pulled a chair out; reversed it; and straddled it, leaning his arms on the back. Kennison watched him steadily. *Who are you, young man? Who do you work for? Ullman? The Six? The Q?* Or was Selkirk playing his own solitary game? He wondered if Beaumont-Bennett had made any progress in her investigation of Selkirk's background.

"What is it, Alan?"

"You were gone yesterday and the day before." It was a flat statement, but gravid with accusation. Kennison studied the other's visage—the cold eyes, the insolent twist to the lip—and bristled. Who did this person think he was, demanding an accounting from him?

"Why do you ask, Alan?" he asked blandly. "Did you encounter a problem you could not handle? I expect you to deal with any difficulties that occur during the Night Shift."

Selkirk seemed disconcerted by the implicit accusation and he stammered something in his own defense. Kennison steepled his fingers and kept the smile from showing. The best defense is a good offense. And vice-versa. Pride in his own abilities was Selkirk's weak point. Prick him there and it would throw him off course. It was best, in any confrontation, to keep one's opponents off balance.

". . . but I just don't think it's a good idea," Selkirk finished, "for you to go off that way without informing me."

"Indeed. And why is that?" Kennison stared closely at

435

Selkirk and saw the other's eyes narrowed in suspicion. Curious, edgy, nervous. It reminded Kennison of the day Selkirk had first entered his office with the damning evidence. *I don't want to expose you. I want in.*

"Because we're partners, you and I," Selkirk said, with overweening arrogance. Partners, indeed! "I helped you when you needed it; so I deserve a little consideration from you. I kept your encounter with Weil from becoming public, didn't I? I've kept word of your plan to corrupt the Society's database from leaking back to your friends on the Council."

Meaning he could let it leak if he wanted to. *Try to be a little more subtle, Alan.* "That was your plan, Alan," he said aloud, "not mine."

"You agreed. It's too late to back out now."

Kennison shrugged. "I have not backed out. But only fools rush in."

Selkirk's smile was condescending. "Yes," he replied. "But he who hesitates is lost."

"And so, *festino lente.* Let's be done bandying clichés, Alan. Why did you want to see me?"

"I wanted to discuss your plan for relocating the data base."

Kennison took the cigarillo from his lips and knocked the ash into the tray. "Yes, what about it? Have you found a repository that I can use without exposing myself to retaliation?" *It will be a cold day, my friend, before I use any scheme that you have engineered.* A cold day in Hell. Then he remembered that, in Dante's *Inferno,* the center of Hell was a vast frozen lake, imprisoning those who had betrayed their benefactors; and he nearly laughed.

Selkirk gave him an uncertain look. "I believe I have found a safe haven. Not only can you be secure from your former associates, but you can also be an important and honored man."

"And where is that?"

Selkirk took a deep breath and let it out. "I have run across evidence of another cliological society. Not the Six, but a European one."

"Ah." Kennison raised one brow.

"You don't sound surprised."

"Should I be? It was mathematically obvious, once the possibility was pointed out. In fact, there may be more than one." He dangled the bait.

"That could verra well be," Selkirk admitted. "I hadna thought o' that."

Was there a tightening of his eyes? A hesitancy in his speech? Kennison leaned back casually in his chair. "Go on," he said.

Selkirk nodded. "You see, I was puzzled by some residual anomalies. Even after I allowed for our own activities and those we've attributed to the Six, there were still more anomalous nodes than could be accounted for by chance."

"Horseshoe nails," said Kennison absently. "Gloria Bennett calls them horseshoe nails." He gathered himself. "And no one ever noticed these extra anomalies before?"

"No. And for two reasons. Firstly, no one was looking for them. But secondly, as long as the Six's activities were included among the residual anomalies, the value of P% was inflated and thus . . ."

"And thus the value of $\sigma_\%$ and the 'zone of reasonable doubt.' Spare me the details, Alan. My schooling was not deficient."

"All I meant was that by shrinking the error of the estimate, the other anomalies stood out like rocks at low tide. So I did a wee bit o' poking around among them trying to discover which were directed and which were really chance; and whether there were any second-order commonalities in their *sequelae.*"

"Very diligently, I am sure. And you found that some significant fraction of the anomalies were . . . ?"

"Eurocentric," Selkirk responded. "Meaning that the anomalous nodes were the outgrowth of European events. If I had to guess, I would say that the Europeans have been active as long as we or the Six."

*If he had to guess.* "I see. But what is the point? What has this European group to do with our plans for the database?" *And how does it make me honored and important?*

Selkirk stood. He paced the room. Kennison kept his gaze locked forwards, but followed him with his peripheral vision. "There are indications that these Europeans are moving into North America. Do you remember what Caldero told us that day in the pizza parlor? That one of the documents in the Dump was written in French? Well, we know it wasn't us and it wasn't Caldero's people. And the Six are strictly home-grown, so why would they communicate in French?"

"In Quebec, it is the law. But I take your meaning. Go on."

Selkirk rubbed a hand across his mouth. He toyed with the decanters on the sideboard. "I thought that if this gang wanted to expand into North America, they might give the franchise to someone with a ready-made infrastructure."

Kennison stiffened. "The franchise?"

Selkirk turned and faced him. "Aye," he said eagerly. "Put yourself in their place. Suppose you were planning to open branch offices across an entire continent and someone came to you, not only with a ready-made infrastructure, but a massively detailed database. It would cut years off their start-up time. How would you feel, if the alternative were to start from scratch?"

Kennison took a final drag on his cigarillo then snubbed it in the ashtray. "Gratitude?" he suggested. Kennison was a great believer in gratitude. It was the most useful of emotions. "And you believe that, if I were to approach this . . . What do they call themselves?"

"I don't know that yet."

"Ah. Yes. That if I were to approach them, they might offer me a job? As branch manager," he added wryly.

Selkirk approached and leaned on the table across from him. "Yes. And think. Would that job not be the equal of the one Ullman stole from you?"

The notion gave him pause. He hadn't thought of it in quite that way. Kennison allowed himself to look directly at Selkirk. "Indeed." He would be as powerful as Ullman. Wouldn't that be a delicious revenge? Deprived unjustly of the top job in one organization, to return with the backing of an even greater one. The look on Ullman's face when he found out!

"Very well, Alan. Take whatever steps you think necessary to locate this European association. But be careful that you do not alarm them; and take no steps to contact them until we have both reviewed your findings."

Selkirk nodded. "I'll do that." He turned to go.

"Oh, and one other thing."

Selkirk paused. "What's that?"

Kennison rubbed a finger by the side of his nose. He toyed with his wine glass. "Bennett's friend, the architect? It seems that she has a very good lead on his whereabouts."

He thought that Selkirk's eyes narrowed and his voice became wary. "Oh? And what is the lead?"

"I am not sure, but she now believes that he is held by another group and not by the Secret Six."

"Another group."

Kennison cocked his head and looked directly at him. "Yes. Do you suppose it could be the Europeans you've uncovered?"

"It could be," Selkirk said slowly.

Kennison nodded and pursed his lips. "We did promise to help her find him, after all."

Kennison smiled thinly after the Scotsman left. At least he knew now who Selkirk's employer was. The Europeans. Alan had probably come to America as part of an advance guard; searching out likely companies to acquire as fronts and "hidey-holes."

Much as Kennison himself had attempted to do with DB&S. Now that was a disturbing thought! Cartoons of bigger fish swallowing smaller fish swallowing tiny fish. Kennison reached out and siezed his wineglass and tossed off the dregs. He was accustomed to playing the predator, not the prey. He felt as if he were a tiger that had suddenly found itself being stalked. A new and unpleasant sensation, in many ways more frightening to a tiger than to a gazelle. Gazelles, at least, were accustomed to it.

But the Europeans hadn't known they were "stalking tigers," Kennison told himself. Not at first. Selkirk had been planted on him because a demographic firm was an invaluable resource. That was all. They had no doubt planted agents with Harris and Gallup and the others, as well. Selkirk could not have known that K/D was anything more than what it seemed. The Beaumont Dump must have taken him by surprise. Suddenly he had found himself with his head halfway in the tiger's mouth. No wonder he had been so shaken that day, when he had come into the office and asked for admission!

Well, one danger in finding a good "hidey-hole" was that something could already be hiding there.

He rose from the table and straightened his tie. Had Selkirk actually offered him the post of North American Coordinator for the Q? There were possibilities there. As much power as he had sought in the Society. A subordinate position, it was true; but in a larger concern than the one he was leaving. An ambitious man might make much of such an offer.

If the offer were sincere. Selkirk could not download the database without the keys that Prudence had fashioned. Only Kennison possessed those. *Once they have my database*, he thought, *they won't need me*. Would the offer still hold? It would depend, in the end, on their sense of honor; and Kennison had not achieved his present position by overestimating the honor of others.

Still, the bait that Selkirk had dangled was tempting. The Q would undoubtedly offer more scope for his genius than a two-bit investment firm like DB&S. If only he could be more sure of the dangers. He glanced at his watch. Beaumont had had quite enough time to install the tap on the EPIC terminal. She would be long gone by the time Selkirk returned to the offices. And Selkirk, Kennison knew, would try to contact his superiors as soon as possible.

And what of his "partners"? How would they react if he took Selkirk's offer?

Caldero would never agree. Kennison was not fooled by his old nemesis' protestations of friendly assistance. Caldero had not labored to help Kennison exit the Society only to help him enter a larger, more powerful society. Caldero would become an obstacle. Obstacles could be removed.

And what of Gloria Bennett? Selkirk and his organization was his lead to her friend—via the man called Bernstein. It was hardly likely that the Q would release French. Not after holding him for so long. But Bennett would not give up looking until she found him; and finding French meant finding the Q, a prospect which the Q would not find entertaining. So, either the Q must capture Bennett or delete her.

Which meant that she would be in very great danger.

Very great danger. Kennison's tongue darted out and he wetted his lips.

"Weren't you spooked?" asked SuperNerd. His face was wide and gaping, eager for stories of danger and suspense. . . . As long as they were vicarious.

"Of course, I was nervous," Sarah told him. "But it wasn't any more dangerous than that night on Mount Falcon." Sarah Beaumont, hardened veteran, spinning tales of past adventures. "If anyone had tried to come upstairs from Johnson and Cheng and had found the secret elevator shut off . . . Well, I kept a close ear on that contraption, let me tell you, so I could cut and run at the first sign."

Bosworth hugged himself. "I don't know if I could've done it. I'd be too nervous."

"Well, it's done now; and I'm back. That's it. No excitement, just another boring assignment." Sarah heard her own words and smiled to herself. She was coming across like an old pro. She broke in and installed phone taps every day.

She turned on the receiver and twisted one of the knobs. The suite was starting to look like a Crazy Eddie store. The pc terminal. The window tappers. The parabolic and its tape recorder. The receiver for the phone tap and *its* recorder. It was a good thing that Helen and Chu were taking care of things. Lord knew what the regular hotel staff would think if they could see all this.

"Nothing? No close calls or anything?" SuperNerd looked so distraught that Sarah felt obligated to supply him with some secondhand adrenalin.

"Just one thing," she said. "Not a close call or anything. Just . . ."

"What?"

"I don't know. A feeling. A creeping, dreadful feeling. I was in the washroom to shut off the elevator and . . ." She shook herself. "I can't describe it. Whenever I came close to the stall . . . It was a feeling of such incredible malevolence. I've never felt that way before." No, that wasn't true. She had experienced the feeling once, in the Widener Building; when she had gotten near that one rolltop desk, the one with the skeleton locked inside. Old bones, with a neat, round hole between the two eye-sockets and a not-so-neat hole in the back. But that intuition didn't explain the feeling she had had in Kennison's washroom. There hadn't been a body in the stall.

"Well? Has he used the phone yet?"

Sarah jumped, and she heard Bosworth suck in his breath. Kennison's ghost, speaking from the window pane. Sarah hunched her shoulders over the equipment. "Go turn off our tappers," she told Bosworth. She fiddled with the knobs until she heard the tiny, hailstone sound cease. Then she turned and faced the window.

"Hello, there, Cousin Dan," she said. "What are you doing in the city at this hour?" She knew she did not need to be facing the window to be heard; but it was bad manners to talk with your back turned.

"I expect our friend will want to make a call tonight. I was curious to hear what he has to say."

"Aren't we all," Sarah replied.

"Has Cousin James returned yet?"

"No," she admitted. "He's still in Boston, conducting surveillance on DB&S." A continent away. She wished Red were here. Playing the Old Pro was a lot easier for Red than it was for her. But he had been right. They had two leads to follow up on. It made sense for her to work this end, because of her computer skills. Still, she felt oddly vulnerable when he wasn't around. That wasn't a logical feeling. After all, she could take care of herself—and had for most of her life. There was no reason for her to feel dependent. And she had saved Red's life, too; so he had as much reason to feel dependent as she did. Then she remembered what Janie had said at the airport in Denver, and wondered what sort of feelings ran through Red at all.

"Have you heard from him?" asked Kennison.

"Not since yesterday. He thinks he'll be here tomorrow. They are on to you, you know. DB&S is."

"Yes. You told me. Regrettable. One of the drawbacks of being a public person, I suppose. But there was no time for plastic surgery; and makeup, close up and in person, looks like makeup."

"They are even wondering about me." All those assurances on the ride into Stapleton, and old man Detweiler sees right through me. That was another reason Red was working the Boston end. She didn't think she could deal with exposure. She would be too distraught to function effectively. "But what really has them concerned is that they don't know why we approached them."

"Why, we told them! We wanted to buy their company."

"They didn't believe you. They think there's some hidden purpose behind it all."

Kennison sniffed. "They are too subtle by half. Sometimes things are exactly as they seem." He seemed to catch himself; then he repeated, more thoughtfully, "Exactly as they seem."

"Detweiler is afraid that the Babbage Society has found them out. Jimmy was wondering if we shouldn't lay all our cards on the table. Explain what we want and see if they will give you shelter."

"No!" The answer was quick, immediate. "That is, DB&S may not be the best repository, after all. And we do not know how far we can trust them yet. Let us not be panicked into a hasty move."

Now who was being too subtle? Sarah wondered if Kennison would ever be made to move except by panic. Somehow, though his schemes seemed endless, his accomplishments were few. "What other repository do you have in mind?"

A series of flat, well-spaced tones interrupted Kennison's reply. Someone was punching numbers on the touch tone pad of Kennison's office phone. "Is that him? Is that Selkirk?" asked Kennison. But Sarah ignored him. The second tape recorder started automatically and she made a note on the log sheet. She had never realized before how much clerical work spying involved.

"Two-one-two," said Bosworth, cocking an ear to the pitch of the tones. "Manhattan." He scribbled down the rest of the numbers and slid into the chair by the computer terminal. "Let's see who he's calling."

The speakers warbled. A phone was ringing. Once. Twice. Dial tone . . .

"What?"

"He hung up."

"I know that."

"Do you think he noticed the bug you planted?" Kennison's voice was tight. "Perhaps you left some sign of your work."

Sarah shook her head. Then she remembered that Kennison was not in the room at all and said. "No. I double-checked everything." It was weird, holding a normal conversation with a man who was a mile away.

"Haste makes waste," Kennison told her.

Sarah suppressed a spasm of irritation. "I told you I double-checked everything."

"Maybe you—"

The touch tones sounded again. This time the phone at the other end was picked up on the first ring. "Yes?" said a voice in Manhattan.

"The first call must have been a signal of some sort," Kennison said.

"No kidding? Shut up and listen."

"This is the West Coast office," said Selkirk.

"Did you make the offer?" The voice was suave, assured. Underneath it, Sarah could hear muted background sounds. The rush of tires on pavement. The honking of horns. Fragments of talk; some old-fashioned rap music played on a passing "boom box." She could close her eyes and picture the setting. Bosworth looked up from his terminal.

"I've got it pegged," he said. "It's a public phone booth."

"I know," said Sarah.

"Upper East Side."

Sarah shot him a look that shut him up. She knew that she

could replay the tape any time she wanted, but she wanted to listen to what Selkirk was saying. He had made an offer. Of what? To whom?

". . . very cautious," Selkirk said. "Naturally, I was careful in what I said."

"Naturally. You are certain you cannot secure the data yourself?"

"No, I told you. There are certain access codes that only he—"

"Yes, yes." The voice from Manhattan was waspish. "Still, with your abilities—"

"Oh, I could do it." The assurance was serenely confident. "It wouldn't be easy, but I could do it. But 'tis so much simpler this way."

"Yes, I suppose so."

"Look here, Bernstein. The reason I called you instead of Control. Has there been any unusual activity around you?"

"Ah, and I had thought you yearning for the sound of my voice."

There was a short pause. Then Selkirk spoke in a low, tight voice. "We may not like each other, Bernstein; but we're in this together. So learn to live with it. Beaumont's still looking for her partner."

"I am not concerned with Beaumont. That has been taken care of."

*I've been taken care of?* How, she wondered. The comment seemed more menacing for its casualness.

"And Kennison is helping her."

"Nor am I concerned with Mr. Kennison. He is your responsibility." Sarah could almost hear the smile in his voice. "A summit meeting in a pizza parlor. Americans have so little class."

"Well, Kennison dropped out of sight for a few days last week. When I talked to him earlier tonight he said something that made me wonder if . . . But you say there's been nothing happening at your place?"

"What exactly did Kennison say to you?"

"Only that Beaumont had a new lead on French's whereabouts." Sarah jerked a look at the window. Why had Kennison told Selkirk that?

"I see. And how did the subject come up?"

"Kennison brought it up. We'd been talking about the other matter and he mentioned it just as I was leaving."

444

"He did." There was a silence at the other end. Then Bernstein hissed, "You fool. You bloody fool," and cut the connection.

She heard Selkirk gasp. "Oh shit." She heard fumbling sounds. Then there was a crackle of static; then nothing.

Sarah pulled the earphones off. She spun and faced the window. "Kennison! You damn fool! I spent a nervous hour putting that damn thing in! What did you tell him?"

"I? My dear lady, I told him nothing at all. I told him you had a lead on your friend's location. That is all. I said nothing of DB&S, or where we had been last week. I had no desire to wait until happenstance caused him to call his superiors and I thought that by dropping such a hint— I never thought that he would catch on."

"He didn't. Bernstein did." That had actually been clever of Kennison, to trick Selkirk into making contact. With Bernstein. Dennis' jailor? It seemed that way. And he was somewhere in Manhattan. Possibly on the Upper East Side; although the pay phone needn't be too close to wherever they were. Her pulse raced a little faster. Yes, it did. If the first call was a signal, Bernstein would have had to be nearby, to reach the pay phone in time. She was getting closer. She felt it.

She closed her eyes and tried to picture Dennis; but she couldn't. His face seemed faded, indistinct. She frowned and concentrated, but he still wouldn't come into focus. She couldn't have forgotten! She couldn't have. She felt an urge to look at his photograph and had actually fumbled with her purse for a moment or two before she remembered that Gloria Bennett carried no pictures of Dennis French.

She turned her face to the wall so Bosworth could not see her.

Later that night, after Bosworth had gone to his own room and Kennison's ghost had been exorcised, Sarah sat in the large wing chair watching the lights of San Francisco through her electronically enhanced window. Coit Tower was awash with spotlights. There had once been a telegraph station on that hill, Helen had told her, to send news of ship arrivals to the wharves. That was how it had gotten its name. Beyond the hill, the sky was lit garishly by the neon flash of Fisherman's Wharf and the Barbary Coast. The Golden Gate Bridge was a fairy web in the distance. Beneath it the running lights of some large vessel drifted out toward the open ocean. Bound for the China trade, she thought. San Francisco always made her think of Hawaii and China and the Pacific trade. The city seemed oddly closer to Honolulu and Shanghai than it did to Los Angeles. Despite the port of San Pedro, largest on the Coast, Los Angeles was a landlubber's town.

When the lights wreathing Coit Tower abruptly snapped off, she realized how late it was. She rose and stretched. She smothered a yawn. Things were happening; or about to start. Selkirk had made an offer to Kennison. She was sure of it. But what sort of offer? To join the Q? Perhaps that was why Kennison was not so wild to use DB&S any more. Yet, if that were so, why had Kennison tricked Selkirk into using the tapped phone?

She shook her head to clear the cobwebs. What was Kennison's game? Was he playing both ends against the middle? Or dithering, like the donkey standing halfway between two bales of hay?

*I am not concerned with Beaumont. That has been taken care of.*

She shivered to remember that smooth, confident voice. She wished again that Red were here.

She paused at the pc terminal on her way to bed. Idly, she ran her fingers along its smooth, plastic frame. Then she reached around back and powered it up. It chimed and the screen glowed. She pulled out the chair and sat down and, a few moments later, she was in the Associates' data base.

The data base was well defended—after the Dump, every base in the country was; but, of course, she now had her own key. Getting in was easy. As for the rest . . .

She had the system run a cross-correlation between Red Malone and Jacksonville, Florida.

A few moments later a folder appeared in the directory. A cue box asked for the entry code. Sarah leaned back in her chair and stared at the screen thoughtfully. She tapped her teeth with her thumbnail. Then she hunched forward again and typed in FANNY POWER.

FOLDER UNLOCKED, the screen told her, and she smiled to herself.

A list of sub-files appeared in the directory window. They bore anonymous alphanumeric codes. Except for one. That one was named SARAH, READ THIS.

She grunted in surprise. "I'll be damned." She moused

446

over and clicked it on and a bulletin board opened up. There was a single note on it.

*Sarah, the other files in this folder are unlocked. You can read them if you want; but I am asking you please not to. Red.*

She sat regarding the screen and its message for a while longer, drumming her forefingers rhythmically on the table top. Then she gave a hard, final rap with her knuckles; took a deep breath and blew it out through her nose. "You're a son of a bitch," she told the absent Red. She closed up the folder and quit the application. It was late and she was tired anyway.

447

# X

"They still haven't talked," said Herkimer Vane.

Jeremy inserted the key into the apartment door. "I don't expect they will." He opened the door and the others followed him inside.

It was a plain apartment, simply furnished; a hideaway until DB&S could decide what to do about them. For the moment, they were supposed to be dead; but that jury-rigged deception would not last too much longer. In the meantime, Detweiler had secured apartments for them in a building he owned in Charleston. Jeremy surveyed the worn, anonymous furniture and thought regretfully of his possessions in Denver —the books, the bergère chair, the Mondrian. He could not imagine ever regarding this place as home.

Jeremy closed the door behind them. "So we still don't know who they were working for," he said. Aside from the comment that they were not from the Babbage Society— which Jeremy was inclined to believe, if only for the spontaneity of the remark—the two men they had captured in Douglas County had given out no information, not even name, rank and serial number. They were being held on Detweiler's estate, which was as close as DB&S could come to a jail. As Vane had reminded them, DB&S had never had the need for safe houses and false identities.

Jeremy had heard that Jennie Barron was urging "more rigorous" questioning of the two; but that Detweiler had vetoed it on the grounds that nothing, not even survival, was worth the price of uncivilized behavior. Unless the luxurious surroundings and steady diet of caviar broke their captives' spirits soon, they would get no leads from that direction.

448

Vane dropped a manila envelope to the coffee table. He wandered into Jeremy's kitchen, where he poured himself a glass of milk. Gwynn picked up the envelope and pulled out the photographs of Gloria Bennett and Sarah Beaumont. She held them side-by-side and studied them carefully, working her lips. Then she overlaid them and held them up to the light. "How far would that surgeon commit himself?" she asked.

"He would only say," Vane replied, "that it was possible that the one face could be transformed into the other."

"Cautious."

"Wouldn't you be?"

"Jim. What about the mouse that got loose in the system yesterday?" Jeremy wondered. "What came of that?"

Doang answered. "Nothing. They chased it for about fifteen minutes before they caught it. Then they tried to follow it back, but it was booted through half a dozen intermediate terminals in the Net, so they lost it. It could have originated anywhere in the country." He shook his head. "Stone is really going to ride Tim's case over this. He'll regard it as a dereliction of some sort."

"Do you think there was any connection between the mouse and Kennison's visit?" *Of course, there was a connection— but what?* It was all a tangle, Jeremy thought. There were a thousand loose strands around them. Signs and portents. Yet, they couldn't seem to grab onto anything. They would yank on this strand or that only to pull out a frayed end, leading nowhere.

Doang shrugged. "I think that when we probed those identities—Bennett and Ochs and Caldero—it triggered an alarm of some sort. Apparently, that is standard practice on sensitive files that must be left in the Net. Tim told me that the next time he goes fishing, he'll masquerade his query as official government business. They can get in just about anywhere."

"Does anyone want pizza?" Gwynn asked from the phone. "I'm about to call one in."

"Make it two," said Jeremy. "Is pepperoni okay with everyone?" He looked around the little group. Vane shook his head and rubbed his stomach. "Make it one pepperoni and one plain. Gwynn, what's wrong?"

Llewellyn was frozen in place, staring at the telephone. Gradually, her eyes narrowed. She turned and jabbed her finger at the mouthpiece.

Jeremy crowded around her with the others. He glanced at her, saw the look on her face, and studied the phone carefully; but could not see anything peculiar. Gwynn had told him once—and, Lord, that seemed like an eternity ago!—that she had learned how to recognize tampering with her phones.

*And his mind skidded back suddenly to that day in his apartment, when he had discovered the break-in, just after Dennis had disappeared from the hospital. He remembered how helpless he had felt; how frightened and impotent. He never wanted to feel that icy knot in his stomach again. Now here it was. It had reached into his dwelling once more. Like a haunting; a ghost.*

*A ghost. With a shiver, he realized that he had not thought about Dennis in days. Yet, at one time, he had been unable to think of anything else.*

Looking puzzled, Doang started to speak, but Gwynn put a finger to her lips. She looked at Vane and asked a question with her eyes; but Vane only stared at the phone and shook his head.

For an instant, Jeremy was tempted to find four police whistles so they could all blast the ears off whoever was listening. Then anger took him with a surprising force. It was a red heat that surged up his neck and out his limbs. He grabbed the telephone from Gwynn and held it like a microphone.

"Look, whoever you are!" he shouted. "I'm sick of these games! Do you hear me? If you've got Dennis French, let him go! Or come and get me and take me to him! Beaumont? Kennison? Do you hear me? What gives you people the right to put me through hell?!" He slammed the phone down so hard the bells jangled.

Then he turned and faced his companions. "Sorry," he muttered. He felt his face flush, and the heat changed from anger to embarrassment. What if the phone were not bugged? He felt like an idiot. Gwynn patted him on the back.

"It's all right, Jeremy. We understand." The others looked away and would not meet his eyes. "It's all right," she repeated.

She led him to a chair and he sat. He wiped his cheeks with his coat sleeve. "It was so easy," he explained to them. "So easy to get lost in the intrigue and the danger. To forget why I started all this. Even to take pride in forgetting. Telling myself that I didn't need—didn't need—" He found he couldn't finish and covered his face with his hands.

450

He was not surprised when, a few minutes later, the telephone rang.

"Oh, I don't know," said Red Malone with a grin. He removed the paper-and-net delivery boy's hat and tossed it aside. "I thought it was a nice touch." He laid the two pizza boxes on the table. "You were calling out for pizza, weren't you?" He found the most comfortable chair in the room and sank into it with a sigh.

The others huddled around the dining table in a tight knot. Taking strength and comfort from each other's closeness, Red thought. The Four Musketeers. Well, facing danger creates bonds. Who should know that better than himself?

Collingwood was watching him with his fists clenched. Sarah had told him about Collingwood; yet the man returning his stare did not strike him as ineffectual. And he could tell from the way the others stood that they looked to him for their lead.

Gwynneth Llewellyn lifted the lids on each box in turn and inspected the contents. "You got the order right, too." She closed the lids carefully and faced him. "I suppose that was to demonstrate that you were listening in."

Collingwood read the logo on the lids of the boxes. "Where did you get these pizzas?"

Red grinned again. "You'd never believe me. I ordered out."

Collingwood crossed his arms. "Is this some big joke to you? Because I'm not laughing."

Vane snorted and strode to the phone. "I think I had better inform my partners."

"I wouldn't try that if I were you."

Vane paused with his hand on the receiver. "Why?"

"Because we disconnected your phone."

Vane made an impatient sound in his throat and picked up the phone. He punched a few buttons, paused, and jiggled the receiver hook. He scowled and faced the room. "The phone's dead," he announced.

Red twisted his face up. "Of course it is. Didn't I just tell you that?" Actually he thought Vane had showed good sense. After all, why should he have taken Red's word for it?

Vane sucked in his breath. He strode to the door and yanked it open. Two large men dressed in workman's coveralls stood on an oil-stained tarpulin stretched out on the floor before the open elevator door. Tools hung from their belt. A bright troublelight dangled in the dark, empty shaft. One of the workmen turned and faced the apartment. "I'm sorry, sir," he said, "but the elevator is out of service."

Vane chewed his lip. He looked at Red. "I suppose the stairs are out of order, too."

"We're working on them," Red told him. "They should be back in operation soon."

"Calm yourself, Herkimer," said Llewellyn. She closed the door softly, and took Vane by the elbow, leading him back into the room. "Mr. Caldero means us no harm, I'm sure." She looked at Red. "I assume that you are with that other group, Utopian Research Associates?"

"Loose lips sink ships." Christ. He was beginning to sound like that bastard, Kennison, the Cliché That Walked Like a Man. But he had let too much slip the first time he had met with Sarah. He had assumed, mistakenly, that she had known more than she had, and had almost gotten them both killed. He wasn't about to make the same mistake twice. The less anyone knew, the better off they were.

"I see," said Llewellyn after a moment of silence. "And the woman with you yesterday. Was she Sarah Beaumont?"

He had heard them speculating on the tape, so the question came as no surprise. He remembered telling Sarah not to worry about being identified and he wished he could be detached enough to chuckle over the irony. "Her name is Gloria Bennett," he said flatly. The Associates had gone to a lot of trouble to make that persona airtight. He wasn't about to poke holes in it just to satisfy their curiosity. If Sarah wanted to tell them . . . Well, he'd advise her not to. The best-kept secret is one that no one knows. "You can read all about her in *Who's Who*."

"She's a black woman," Llewellyn pointed out.

"That doesn't make her unique. There are more than one."

"She has a scar typical of plastic surgery," put in Collingwood.

Red shrugged. "So do I."

Llewellyn gave him a sober appraisal. "So might we all before this is over. But I'm sure you did not come here simply to refuse to answer all our questions. You could have done that at home."

Red decided that he liked her manner. He reminded himself that these people were not his enemies, even if they were not precisely his friends. The world did not consist exclusively

452

of friends and enemies. Most people were neutral or indifferent. They had their own drives and goals; their own circles of
friends and enemies. Sometimes the circles intersected a
little. "I came to do a little horse trading," he said. "I want to
know more about DB&S——"

"And why should we tell you anything?" demanded Vane.

Red kept a rein on his patience. He supposed that it was
natural for Vane to be reticent about his own organization; but
he was wasting time in ritualistic posing. They both knew that
they would be trading information in the end. What was the
point in putting it off? Red smiled at the historian but addressed his reply to Collingwood. "Because we have a lead on
Dennis French." There was an irony there. Red remembered
how Kennison had used the same bait to secure help from
Sarah and him.

Collingwood's mouth dropped open. He uncrossed his arms
and leaned forward. "Where is he?"

Red spread his hands. "I don't know exactly yet."

Collingwood flapped his arms out and turned away. "Great."
He stared at the wall.

"But I know someone who knows someone who might
know."

Collingwood looked back over his shoulder and gave him a
long stare.

Red twisted uncomfortably under his gaze. He hadn't meant
to sound flippant. It had just come out that way. Sarah was
always telling him that. That he never took things seriously
enough. Maybe she was right. Collingwood was hurting, and
there was no point in aggravating the hurt. "Sorry," he muttered. "It's not much of a lead; but it's the only one we've
got."

"Why do you wish to buy our help?" asked Doang abruptly.

The mathematician had been silent up until now and his
sudden comment surprised Red. He faced Doang. "Will finding Dennis French buy your help?"

Doang shook his head. "If you want our help, ask for it.
Don't try to buy it."

Red stretched his legs out and crossed them at the ankles.
He said nothing for a moment. People who spouted altruism
annoyed him. In a pinch, he wanted the people covering him
to be people who had a stake in his success; not people doing
a favor. That was an ironclad rule. Once—just once—he had
neglected it.

"It will buy mine," said Llewellyn. She stuck her jaw out and looked from one to the other. "Jeremy and I started this together. We will finish it together." She and Collingwood locked gazes for a moment, and Collingwood smiled at her. Llewellyn flushed and looked at the carpet.

"And I," Doang admitted. "Jeremy and I have fought together. And how else may I find my way back to my family?" He walked away from the table and stood before the window. The lights of Boston twinkled across the Charles. A helicopter made its way like a firefly across the estuary from Logan Airport. "I have no desire to disappear," he said. "I have no desire to have my life turned upside down. Never to see my brothers and sisters again." He turned and faced them. "I will not cower and hide my name or my face." He looked at Red as he said that.

Vane sighed. "And if I say I will not help, it will make me a false-hearted poltroon." He crossed his arms. "I will help Jeremy if I can; but not if it means going against my partners."

Red put his elbow on the arm of his chair and rested his chin on his fist. "That's the ticket," he said. "You want to know what's in it for you. How about this: we'd like to know who it was that blew your friends and colleagues to kingdom come. Would you?"

Vane jerked his head up. "Who? We already know who. The Babbage Society. Those damned murderers."

Red smiled thinly. "I won't argue whether they are damned, or why. But this particular murder wasn't theirs. The Babbage Society is practically paralyzed for the moment. Their Council is in disarray. A third of them are afraid that the other third is out to bump them off."

"And the third third?" asked Llewellyn.

"Already bumped off," he grunted. "They aren't the ones you need to fear." It seemed strange to him to think of his longstanding enemies as virtually powerless. If not exactly harmless, at least for the time harming only each other. "Besides, they had an agent on your Team. Someone named Bandmeister, of all things—"

That shook them. "Henry?" "I don't believe—" "You mean—"

Red held up a hand to quiet them. "That's right. He was one of theirs. And he was far too valuable an asset for them to sacrifice."

"Assets," said Llewellyn. "I've always hated people who

454

called other people assets." She heaved a sigh. "Christ, I miss my pipe."

"Besides," said Jeremy carefully, "they've sacrificed—assets—before."

Red shook his head. "Pawns, not bishops."

Vane protested. "I can't believe that a man like Henry Bandmeister was a spy for a secret society."

Jeremy leered at him. "How can you, of all people, say that?" And Vane had the grace to blush.

"If the Babbage Society didn't do it," said Llewellyn cutting them off, "then who did?"

He favored her with an approving glance. "You stick to the heart of the matter, don't you?"

"It saves wasting time," she said.

"All right. I'll take a chance. Here's some free information. There are other societies beside the ones you know of from the Dump. We suspect one of them destroyed your team."

"Why?" asked Llewellyn.

He shrugged. "If we knew why, we'd know who."

"We thought," said Doang hesitantly, "that because I had evaluated their mathematics . . ."

Red laughed. "And you think no one else has? You think that every mathematician and sociometrician in the country hasn't been pouring over those hints like a rabbinical student going over the Talmud?" He pointed to the boxes on the table. "The pizza is getting cold. I'll have some, if you aren't." Wordlessly, Collingwood pulled some paper plates from a cabinet. He put a slice on one and handed it to Red. No one else made a move.

"Thanks . . . No," he continued to Doang. "The validity of the mathematical fragments in the Dump is not a secret. Only a fool would think so; and, now that Weil is out of the picture, we are not dealing with fools." He took a bite—and flashed on the time he and Sarah had met Kennison at Tony's. The smell of the cheese and the tomato sauce; the voices of the men behind the counter. Kennison's rat-sharp face across the table. Sarah sitting beside him, close enough to sense; but not quite touching. He wondered briefly how she was managing out on the West Coast, and experienced a brief pang of anxiety that he could not quite pin down. "No, there had to be some other reason why someone wanted you out of the way," he continued, waving the pizza in the air as he spoke. "From what I know," he added, nodding toward the telephone, "we can do business together. What do you say? Do we trade information?"

Collingwood looked across to Vane. "I say we take Caldero to Detweiler's estate."

Vane looked like he was sucking a lemon. "Do you think it might do any good?"

Llewellyn shrugged. "It can't hurt."

"What are you people talking about?" Red asked in irritation. Take him to Detweiler's estate? Did they mean to take him prisoner, with his own people standing guard in the hallway?

Vane smiled thinly. "Trading information. Do you play poker, Mr. Caldero?"

"A little. Why?"

"Well, our Mr. Detweiler is holding a pair that we'd like to beat."


"Well," said Red Malone, looking through the one way mirror at the two men in Detweiler's library. "Well, well." One man wore a cast on his right wrist. He was walking around the room, picking out books and flipping through them in a desultory fashion. The other sat in an overstuffed Queen Anne chair playing a game of Canfield on the card table.

"They don't look like they're having a very good time, do they?"

Adrian Detweiler V cackled. "Boredom can be the cruelest torture of all. They don't even talk to each other for fear we are listening in."

Red refrained from pointing out that they *were* listening in. The two prisoners were playing it right, though. *Professionals*, he thought. *But whose?* "How can anyone be bored with all those books at his disposal?"

"I believe I judged them aright. Neither man is the bookish sort." The bray of old New England came through in the old man's clipped, nasal voice. Not for him the flavorless, pear-shaped tones of television English. Red wondered if he took special diction lessons. "Seen enough?" Detweiler reached out to close the shutters on the mirror, but Red laid a hand on his arm.

"Give me another minute." He studied the two prisoners. After a while the one playing solitaire squirmed in his seat. He squared the cards in his stock, tapping all four sides in

456

turn against the table, looking slowly around the room. When his gaze reached the mirror, he scowled and tapped the stock again nervously. Red grinned.

"Let me talk to the card sharp for a few minutes," he said.

The card player looked up suspiciously when Red entered the library. Red smiled at him and walked over, hand extended. "Well, I see they got you, too. Who are these clowns anyway?"

The card player pulled three cards from his stock and exposed the first. It was the eight of clubs. "Isn't that ploy just a little bit too transparent?" he asked.

"Hey, it was worth a try, wasn't it?" Red pulled one of the other chairs over and sat so that he faced the other over the card table. "Try playing it on the nine." He pointed to the tableau.

"Up yours." He played it on the nine anyway. "What'd you do with my buddy?"

"You mean the big guy with the bad case of tennis elbow? Does your buddy have a name?"

The man looked at him. "Yeah. Bud. Where is he?"

"Taking a potty break. Play the Queen there."

"Who's playing this, you or me?" He threw his cards down and shoved the tableau across the table. "Here, you play." He slouched in his chair and stared at Red with narrowed eyes. "I've seen you somewhere before."

Red gathered the cards together. "That's possible. It's a small world." He righted the cards and squared the deck. Then he shuffled the cards. "I was thinking the same thing myself." He cut the deck in two and riffled the halves together. He began dealing cards. "So what do you say, Charlie? A game of rummy?"

Charlie jerked suddenly. He stared intently into Red's eyes; then he screwed his face up. "Oh, Christ," he said. "Oh, Christ."

457

# XI

Of course, Detweiler called a summit meeting.

Red watched Charlie pick up the brandy snifter and swirl it
around. Charlie scowled into the glass, then he looked around
the table until he spotted Detweiler. "Say, you don't have any
beer, do you?"

Stone rolled his eyes up in his head; but Detweiler smiled
and crooked a finger to his manservant. "A beer for 'Charles',"
he said. "And 'Bud?' Yes, two beers. Will Sam Adams Lager
do?"

"Make it three," said Red.

"You know they came around and questioned me about
you," Charlie told him. "The DIA stiffs. Thanks." The servant
placed three tall pilsener glasses in front of them. The beer
was a nice golden color with a pure white, frothy head.
Charlie lifted his glass. "They wanted to know everything I
knew about you."

Red studied his own beer. Bubbles rose in columns from
the sides of the glass, becoming larger and farther apart as
they rose. He took a sip. The bubbles nucleated on minute,
invisible cracks and imperfections in the glass. *We wouldn't
even know the cracks were there if they didn't cause bubbles
to form.* He thought the hidden flaws were like the secret
cliological societies. A parable. He drank. "What did you tell
them?" he asked.

"What does it matter? You can't go back." Charlie took a
long pull and set his glass down. "I told them I didn't know
nothing, except you never cheated at rummy."

458

"Sure, I did," said Red. "You just weren't quick enough to catch me."

Charlie snorted. "That'll be the day." He turned to his partner. "Five years him and me sat in that room, close enough to kiss—if he were prettier and I was swish, which I ain't; and I never once caught on."

"You better watch what you say," said Bud. "We aren't among friends." He cast a dark look in Collingwood's direction and rubbed his wrist.

"Ah, don't worry about it," said Charlie. "Red, here is all right. I guess I gotta call you Jimmy now."

Red shrugged. "What's in a name? You know how it is." Five years together, and he had never suspected Charlie to be anything but a government spook, either. It was embarrassing. He wondered how Charlie felt about it. Looked at from a distance, it was almost comical.

Stone rapped the table with his knuckles. "Can we get down to business?" he demanded. "We want a full accounting from each of you. Who the hell are you and who do you represent?"

Charlie cocked an eyebrow and hoisted his glass. He looked at Red. "Amateur night, hunh?" Bud chuckled and Stone flushed. Red grinned at Charlie and saluted him with his glass. God, but it felt good to talk with professionals again.

He relaxed in his chair. "I suppose we might as well see where we stand." He looked around the table. Detweiler and his daughter. Stone. The Four Musketeers. Charlie and Bud. "My name is Jimmy Caldero," he continued. "and I represent Utopian Research Associates, the true heirs of the original Babbage Society . . ." Stone snorted and Red leaned forward in his chair. "There are over 150 years of background that we haven't time to go over right now, Stone; and which you do not have the need to know, in any case. If you haven't read the contents of the Dump, you have no business commenting."

Red had barely raised his voice; but Stone retreated a little into his chair, his eyes slightly wide, and Jennie Barron looked at him with a curl of contempt. She turned her face a little away from Red, but looked at him from the corners of her eyes with a coldly appraising gaze. *That's one hard bitch*, Red thought. He contrasted the grandfatherly geniality of old Detweiler with the offhand callousness he sensed in the two younger partners.

*Even here,* he thought. The rot has spread even here. Sarah was right. There was something about cliology that dehumanized its practitioners. There was something about the detachment. When people are the subjects, how easily they then become objects. And it was only a small step from detachment to dominance. The itch to make peope behave the way you knew they *ought* to; to make them subjects in quite another sense of the word. How often had psychiatrists taken advantage of their clients, or case workers abused the very people they were supposed to help? DB&S had a century and a half of profitable passivity behind them; yet he could sense that Stone—and probably Barron, as well— itched to intervene. To start pulling on the old puppet strings. What was it? The intoxication of power? How was it different from what he intended to do with the Associates? Because *my* goals are worthy?

The same old story, he remembered Sarah saying during that wild flight to the Walker mansion. The same old story. The end justifies the means. But it should count for something, he thought, that he took hold of the strings reluctantly.

"My old stable-mate here . . ." And he gestured toward Charlie, who was finishing his beer. "My old stable-mate represents the Secret Six."

It was just a guess, of course. Because it was either the Six or the Q. Or else it was some group he'd never heard of. And if that were the case, he might as well fold it up and go home.

Bud set his glass hard on the table. "How do you know that?"

Charlie let out a gust of satisfaction, set his glass down more gently, and wiped his lips with a napkin. "That's great beer," he told Detweiler. Then he folded his arms across his chest and smiled at Red. "He didn't know. He guessed. It was your people who accessed Lysander Spooner's files, wasn't it?"

Red saw the narrowing of the eyes. The wary look. *He doesn't know how far he can trust me, or the Associates.* Come to that, what did he really know about the Six? That Charlie was a member. So, who was Charlie? *Things are seldom as they seem/Skim milk masquerades as cream.* Gilbert and Sullivan capered through the back of his mind. "Our

460

real enemies," he told the others, "are not Charlie's people . . ." *At least, I don't think they are.* ". . . but a European gang that we call the Q." He filled them in on the Stray, on Howard, on the drugging of Gloria Bennett.

Charlie pursed his lips. "So, you know about them."

Bud spoke to Charlie. "You got a big mouth, you know."

Charlie jerked a thumb at Red. "He already knew."

"Yeah, but none of them others did."

Charlie pursed his lips. "No, Jimmy here's right. This 'Q' of his is our real enemy. Look what they did to our Oberlin office. Don't worry, Bud. I'll settle up with the Circle later, but I think they'll back me on this." He faced the group and put his hands flat on the table. "Let me start at the beginning. The Printout came as a shock to us. We always thought— Well, I don't need to tell you folks, I suppose. We decided to investigate." He looked at Red. "One of the taps your friend Kennison found was ours. So was the phone call." He twisted his hands into a ball and studied them. "That was Unauthorized—the phone call—but Ora . . . The Babbage people had killed a friend of hers—a reporter on the *Times.*"

Red cocked an eyebrow. "Houvanis?"

Charlie looked at him. "What, do you keep a scorecard?" He twisted and motioned to the servant. "Set up another round, would you, please?" He made circles with his finger. "I suppose your man here," he continued to Detweiler, "is privy to all this."

Detweiler smiled and spread his hands, but said nothing. Jennie Barron snapped, "Get on with it!"

Charlie chuckled. "Testy, testy. Well, like I said, we were sniffing around inside Kennison's data banks and what do you suppose we found? Three other taps. Isn't that a scream? Remember that scene in *Take the Money and Run,* when Woody Allen tries to rob a bank and there's another gang in there trying to rob the same bank?" He shook his head. The servant set the tall, pilsener glass in front of him.

"Kennison only found two other bugs," Red commented.

"Yeah? Well, we're smarter than he is." He took a long drink of beer and Red began to feel irritated at the way the man was stringing his story out. He saw that the others around the table were also waiting impatiently. Collingwood saw him looking and gave him a twisted smile. *Now you know how it feels,* he seemed to be saying; and Red felt himself flush slightly. He remembered how he had stalled with the Four Musketeers and, earlier, with Sarah. But, of course, that only made him more sympathetic to Charlie, because he knew the man was trying desperately to organize his thoughts; trying to decide what he could safely say and what he couldn't.

"We traced one of the other bugs back to an investment firm in St. Louis," Charlie continued.

"Global Investment Strategies," said Red.

"You know them?"

"It's a front for Fredrick Ullman."

"I know them," said Stone. He smirked. "If they are who you claim they are, they should be a great deal more successful than they seem to be."

Red looked at him and smiled. He scratched the side of his nose with his forefinger. "Oh, they are, Stone. They are." Stone flushed and Red turned back to Charlie. "I'll bet that bug was built into the system architecture, so Kennison's virus detector never saw it as 'extra' bits."

Charlie shrugged. "Who's telling this story?" He elbowed his partner. "There, you see, Bud? The Babbage clowns are spying on each other. There was something we didn't know before. We thought St. Louis was another independent group," he told the others. "Well, the third virus had been planted by the FBI, of course; so . . . What's so funny?"

Red wiped a tear from his eye. "Finally! The official government rears its head. I was beginning to wonder if there were anyone involved in this affair that wasn't connected with cliology, somehow."

"Cliology," said Charlie. "I like that word. We called it political meta-economy. Most of our founding fathers were college professors." He drank some more beer. "But what makes you think they aren't?"

"Eh?"

"The 'official government,' as you call them. What makes you think they aren't involved in cliology?"

"What are you talking about?"

Charlie grinned like a cat. "Do you know of any group of people anywhere that has engaged in social engineering on as massive a scale as the government? Or do you think the tax code is for raising revenue?"

"Teddy Roosevelt," said Llewellyn suddenly; and they all

looked at her. "Teddy Roosevelt and the Progressives," she said. "That's when this whole idea of government-as-manager first took hold. The Progressives' avowed purpose was—and I quote—'to apply rational, scientific techniques to the management of business, labor, and the government itself.' Funny, isn't it, that no one took them at their word."

Red rubbed the side of his nose. *Teddy Roosevelt's nomination as Vice-President.* That had been on the French List, hadn't it? And Walt had pegged it tentatively as a Six operation. But the Six had broken into two factions, just like the Babbage Society. So . . .

"One of your factions wanted to infiltrate the government," he said to Charlie, "and the other didn't." No wonder they had lost track of the Six's daughter! It was too big to be seen. Like the old cartoon of the hunter in the forest who can't see any game . . . but the reader notices that some of the tree trunks look an awful lot like legs.

"That's not important now," Charlie said waving a hand. "It's just a small clique inside the government; and we think they've forgotten most of what they once knew. It's the Europeans we have to deal with; and quick."

"And why is that, 'Charles'?" asked Detweiler. The brown upholstered wing chair seemed to engulf him.

Charlie turned his pilsener glass in quarter-turns. "The fourth bug in Kennison's system was theirs; the one that dumped into the Q file. We started tracing it back . . ." He shook his head. "That was a mistake. Sleeping dogs. When we found their virus, they must have found ours as well. We were running the op out of Oberlin. When we saw that security had been compromised, we skedaddled." He turned the glass another quarter-turn. "Two hours later, the building was in flames."

Red stirred uncomfortably. "They didn't even try to find out who you were? You should have kept the place under surveillance. Put a tail on whoever came by."

Charlie looked at him. "Are we amateurs? We did that. They never reported back." He frowned at his glass. "About the only intelligence we managed to uncover—which we got through their tap—was that they call themselves the SQPS."

"And what does that stand for?" asked Barron.

Charlie did not look away from his glass and Red wondered if the lost tails had been friends of Charlie. It was a hard life

that they led. Friendships were as unwise as they were un-
avoidable. Best to keep people at arm's length; so that, when
the time came to go to Jacksonville—

"The *Societé*," Charlie said at last. "The *Societé de Quetelet
pour le Physique Sociale.*"

"Quetelet?" said Collingwood. Red looked at him, and his
face seemed drained of color. "Quetelet? Oh, my God!"

Llewellyn looked at him with concern. "What is it, Jeremy?"

Collingwood hung his head and shook it slowly. "My fault,
my fault." He looked up. "Gwynn, what else was on the
agenda for that meeting, the day of the blast? Besides Jim's
mathematical report."

"Just your little bit on Quetelet and Buckle . . ." Her voice
trailed off. "Oh." Her voice sounded small and distant. "Oh,"
she repeated.

Red leaned forward. "Let me get this straight. You were
going to give a report of some sort about Adolphe Quetelet?"

Collingwood nodded. "Yes, after Jim was through. If there
was time."

Red sat back into the chair. He slid down until his head
rested on the back. It was possible. Quetelet had dabbled in
his "social physics." He had studied and written on statistical
regularities in crime data. He had created quite a debate
among European intellectuals over free will and determinism.
Had he inspired imitators the same way that Babbage had? If
only they had studied European events more closely! If only
they hadn't been so damned smug.

"I was going to report," Collingwood continued, "on Quetelet
and Buckle." He looked up, licked his lips, dropped his gaze.
"Buckle died unexpectedly, you know. He was still quite
young."

"It wasn't your fault," Llewellyn told him. "How could you
have known?"

For a wild moment, Red thought she meant Collingwood
was not responsible for Buckle's death; and he looked from
one to the other in confusion before recovering himself.

"You can't be sure," said Vane, "that the Team was destroyed to prevent them from discussing Quetelet."

They all looked at one another. "No," said Red judiciously.
"But it is a funny coincidence, and I've never liked coincidences. It's worth looking into."

"That's what we thought," said Charlie, "So when Penelope told us—"

"Penelope?" said Llewellyn. "Penny Quick?"

"Was there anyone on the Team," asked Collingwood of no one in particular, "who was legitimate?"

Llewellyn looked at him. "We were all legitimate," she said; and Collingwood bit his lip.

"Penelope told us what Collingwood here was up to," Charlie continued. "So we staked out the meeting. Our plan was to pick Collingwood up and find out what he knew. After the bombing, we stuck around, staked out the hospital, and followed you folks when you tried to sneak out. The rest—" He glanced at his partner's wrist. "The rest, you know."

"Wait a minute," said Collingwood. "The nurse didn't alert you?"

"What nurse? No. We were out in the parking lot the whole time."

Collingwood and Llewellyn explained about the nurse at Porter. Red saw how that made the others uneasy. If people could be hypnotically programmed, who could be trusted?

The nurse had called the Q, Red decided. That was the only thing that made sense. Except, it didn't quite make sense. If the Q had bombed the building at Denver University, they surely had local assets. So why hadn't the Q shown up when Collingwood and his friends left the hospital? They were ruthless. They had set that bomb at the first sign that the study team was even thinking about considering Quetelet. It wasn't like them to let the Four Musketeers elude their grasp.

There was a veranda that ran around two sides of Detweiler's mansion. Red stood on it, leaning against the railing, enjoying the cool night breezes. Well-manicured grounds rolled gently into the distance. A little ways off a stone staircase gleamed in the moonlight where it led through an embankment down into a landscaped garden. Red could not see the end of the property. Somewhere in the night a dog barked. He took a deep, calming breath and rubbed the palms of his hands together. The nights were colder in the northeast. He could see his breath.

The moon was setting, fat and tawny, shrouded by streamers of umber clouds. He wondered if Sarah were watching the same moon out there in San Francisco. A mystic link between them. Not likely, he decided. She was sensible. She'd be in bed by now.

There was a motion behind him and he turned suddenly. Jeremy Collingwood stood there with his hands stuffed into his pants pockets. "Chilly night," he said to Red.

Red faced the night once more. "It's getting late in the year. It always happens that way; but we're always surprised when it does. All the heavy clothes are still packed away and we have to go rummage through them."

"They told me you'd gone for a walk."

He pointed. "Hear those dogs out there? I don't go walking with Dobermans. How is the computer search going?"

"Not too badly. That number you got from . . . Who did you say was on the other end of the modem?"

Red looked back over his shoulder. "A kid. S— Gloria Bennett calls him SuperNerd. He's good. A hacker's hacker."

Collingwood looked at him for a long moment. Then he shrugged. "Well, the home address of that Howard woman that he gave us . . . There were several phone calls to Brussels and Paris that originated from public phones in San Diego on the day of the Dump. On the map, they make a nice little cluster around her home."

Red nodded. He had expected it. That had been a clever idea of Charlie's, doing a cluster analysis on phone calls to French-speaking regions against the time frame of the Dump. Correlating the data on Howard from the Associate files with the cluster analyses that the Six had already made had been tricky, though. Neither he nor Charlie had wanted to risk exposing each other's data base. In the end, they had set up an electronic neutral ground in a public library terminal in Omaha.

"I suggested they try analyzing calls between San Diego and San Francisco. To see if Howard was in contact with the mole that infected Kennison's system."

Red grunted. "Who didn't infect Kennison's system? Besides . . ." He turned and faced Collingwood, who was sitting on the porch swing, his arms spread out across the backrest. Red leaned back and half-sat on the railing. "Besides, you can infect a system from anywhere in the country. You just piggyback the worm or the virus on a commercial program, or on shareware or a bulletin board."

Collingwood shook his head. "I wouldn't know about that. I'm a simple man with simple needs. Oh, I use spreadsheets, of course; but not, I am sure, to their maximum potential. And Dennis . . . Well, he had—has a positive horror of computers."

"Silly attitude. They're tools. As well be afraid of T-squares or vacuum cleaners. Or quill pens."

Collingwood grinned crookedly. "The Decline of the West can be traced to the invention of quill pens. When people had to pound their writings into stone blocks they gave more thought to their words, I think."

Red smiled. "You could be right."

Collingwood kicked with his feet and the porch swing began to rock. "My grandmother had one of these on her porch. I feel like a kid again." He swung slowly, like a pendulum. "Are you going to tell me what you know about Dennis French?"

Red crossed his arms. "That's all this affair means to you, isn't it? Finding your friend. You don't care about the bigger issues at all."

"Don't I? I'd always thought friendship was one of the bigger issues."

"I didn't mean it that way. I meant . . . Well, *beyond* your concern for your friend. Don't the philosophical issues concern you at all? What about the political implications? Do you want your life controlled by some secret elite?"

Collingwood snorted. "Do you mean that it hasn't been?" The porch swing glided quietly. "Has there ever been a time since the pharaohs when some small clique of would-be managers hasn't insisted on running the show? As long as they do so in a reasonably competent fashion and leave me to my own devices, I have no quarrel with them. From all I've learned, the difference with you folks is that you've applied a little science to the task. Well, I don't see how that can be any worse than the trial-and-error we've always endured."

Red had expected anything but indifference. He uncrossed his arms and laid his hands against the railing. "You really don't care," he said, leaning slightly forward. He could not keep the surprise out of his voice. "You are deeper in the middle of this whole affair than just about anyone, and the fundamental issues mean nothing to you."

"Is that an accusation? Most of those who bleat about

467

removing the yoke of the oppressor are only those upset that the yoke isn't theirs." He stopped the swinging of the glider, his feet sliding against the wooden flooring of the veranda. "But I did add that one proviso. I said it makes no difference to me, provided you leave me to my own devices. And that you have not done."

Collingwood had not raised his voice; yet Red found himself flinching from it. He turned away from the man's accusing gaze and wrapped his left arm against one of the pillars. The paint was smooth and cool against his cheek. "No, we haven't, have we." And never mind that it had not been the Associates who had triggered the whole affair. That it was Genevieve Weil and her well-founded paranoia. It could have happened in any of a dozen ways. The whole structure had been rife with fractures; too many fractures to blame the one that had finally sheared.

"You aren't going to tell me, are you?"

Red looked back over his shoulder. "What?"

"You aren't going to tell me what you know about Dennis."

"I didn't tell you."

"No, you changed the subject. You let me 'twist slowly in the wind'."

He looked away again. "I'm sorry," he said. "It's second nature." He ran his hand up and down the post. There was a crack in the paint, and he picked at it with his fingernail. "You don't know what it's like," he told Collingwood, still keeping his back to the man. "To be sworn to a Secret like ours. You daren't let anyone know about it. Not even that there is a Secret. Not your parents. Not your closest friends. So, you learn to conceal; to hold things back; sometimes even to lie. To spout glib stories about your new "summer job," but never the real truth of it. Soon—" A long thin sliver of paint came loose and he turned it around in his fingers. "Soon, circumspection becomes second nature. To be safe, never say everything. To be safer, never say anything. But cliological distance is defined by the frequency of communications between two points." He smiled bitterly. "We learn that in training. So the distance grows between you and everyone you've ever known. And the worst of it is you know why it's happening. You can even work out the equations. Soon enough, your only friends will be others like yourself; locked away in a secret world apart from everyone else; secure in the knowledge that, after all, you are the world's true masters, and it is the round pegs who, in truth, don't fit." He flicked the sliver of paint into the night air; leaned forward on his elbows and clasped his hands. "Why am I telling you all this?"

"I don't know," said Collingwood. "Who should you be telling?"

Red glanced over his shoulder. He pursed his lips. "Are you sure you're only an accountant?"

"Tell me, Caldero," he heard Collingwood say. "How do you get into your line of work? You don't advertise in the employment sections, do you?"

Red ran his hand up and down the post. "No," he said. "No, we don't." He was remembering how he had been recruited. Emmett Blaine. How long since he had thought about the crusty old man, with his polka dot bow ties and his hair parted in the middle? The very antithesis of Cool; but a teacher who had made ideas come alive. "We're always on the . . . lookout, I guess you'd say. For people who show an interest. And a talent." *Like high school students, he thought, who don't quite fit in.* Shy, square pegs, awkward in a universe of round holes. The sort who might fall under the spell of a charismatic teacher. Independent enough to resist rounding off their own corners; and visionary enough to imagine squaring off the holes. Emmett Blaine. He hadn't thought about his history teacher in a good long time. Those long discussions about building a better world. About how one person could make a difference . . . *if* he could do the right thing at the right time. He was startled to realize how much of his own thinking echoed with Emmett Blaine's voice. And was disturbed, as well. Could it be that his current plans for the Associates were but the fruit of seeds planted long ago by his old mentor? That he was but a conduit by which Emmett sought to guide the future? Such patient subtlety was well within the ambit of cliological thinking. And wasn't that really the goal of every teacher and guru on the face of the planet? To shape the future through one's pupils?

No, dammit! Emmitt had not been that way! He hadn't had the eyes that Jane Hatch or Cam Betancourt had. We *learn* from our teachers; they don't *control* us.

"That makes twice," he heard Collingwood say.

"Twice what?"

"That you've avoided telling me about Dennis."

Red slapped his hands together. The night was getting colder. Autumn, he decided, was the saddest time of year. "The Q must have him," Red said. "I wasn't sure if it was the Six or the Q until tonight. Someone in Kennison's organization knows where he is. Kennison overheard him once on the phone. He hasn't told us who the mole is, but I have a guess. Bennett is back there now, tapping the phone so we can get a trace." He stood, turned, and faced Collingwood. "There. Was that open enough for you?"

Collingwood nodded. "It will do. Why is Bennett so anxious to help locate Dennis?"

Red shrugged. "It's her assignment," he temporized.

Collingwood seemed amused. "Circumspection, again? Never mind. I won't press you. As long as you promise that, when you do learn where Dennis is, you will inform me immediately."

He hesitated only a fraction of a moment. "Of course."

Llewellyn pushed the door open and light flooded the verandah. She squinted into the darkness. "Jeremy? Are you . . . Oh, there you are. And Mr. Caldero, too, I see."

Red sighed. "What the hell, call me Jimmy."

"Charlie has finished the correlation." She looked at Red. "Don't you want to check his work?"

"It's not necessary."

"You trust him?"

"I don't have to. SuperNerd is watching from the other end."

"I see. Well, they found a cluster of public phones in San Francisco that were all called by your Howard woman, or vice versa. The gentleman working at the other end of the modem checked through the data banks at Kennison Demographics and found that an Alan Selkirk lives smack in the center of the distribution."

Selkirk. He was not surprised. It made sense. Kennison had said that he didn't trust Selkirk any longer; but then Kennison seldom trusted anyone. But the shooting in the parking lot made sense now. Who else had known that they would be there except Kennison and Selkirk? He tried to imagine the young man as a ruthless assassin and couldn't. And didn't that make for the best kind? He remembered how shocked the Scot had been when they had told him that there was a third society. (Only three? Lord, how simple that seemed in retrospect!) And he remembered how relieved Selkirk had seemed when told of the Secret Six. Of course. He had probably been afraid that they had uncovered the Q.

"And Jeremy," Llewellyn continued, "Mr. SuperNerd had a personal message for you from Gloria Bennett."

Collingwood blinked slowly. "Oh?" He kept his face neutral. "What did she say?"

"Only that Dennis French was being held by a man named Bernstein somewhere in Manhattan."

Collingwood nodded. He looked at Red. "That was fast service on your part."

Red could not help grinning. "I keep my promises."

471

# XII

Kennison ushered her into the offices of Johnson & Cheng. "Don't worry, my dear," he murmured. "No one will be here at this hour."

*Two in the* A.M., thought Sarah. *But at least that Night Shift of his has gone home.* She yawned suddenly and stifled it behind her palm. "We couldn't do this by remote?" she asked again.

Kennison turned and looked at her. "By remote? Oh, of course not. There are physical safeguards we must deal with."

Resignedly, she followed him into the darkened offices. If it was hardware, SuperNerd would have been a better choice to go with Kennison. But he had insisted on her. He wouldn't trust anyone else.

Well, at least the late hour had given her a chance to enjoy that fabulous moon. Harvest Moon. Or was it still Satyr's Moon, this early in September? She had lost track. She had watched the moon last night from her apartment window; and, for some odd reason, the sight of it had soothed her. She had tried to recapture that solace earlier tonight, while she had awaited Kennison's call, but it had proven as elusive as smoke. It was the same moon; but . . . different.

The computer room was dimly lit; but the machine itself was powered up. The red and green lights winked at her in the darkness, a hydra restless in her not-quite-sleep.

"There are a few programs that run during the graveyard shift," Kennison explained, "but we don't normally keep people here the whole time." She looked at him but could see no expression on his face. It was too dark, and the man beside

472

her was only a black shape. Somehow, that frightened her. She tried to tell herself that that was illogical; but it *was* dark and Kennison *was* a bogeyman.

"Turn some lights on," she said. "So I can see what I'm doing."

"No. Someone might see from outside and wonder what was going on."

"There are no windows in this room," she pointed out. "And we can close the door."

"If we close the door, we might not hear it when someone comes into the main offices."

She looked at him. He sounded like a petulant child. "Oh, for Christ's sake! Who is going to come in at this hour?"

"A burglar?" It sounded like half a question, half a suggestion. She snorted.

"Don't be absurd."

He answered sulkily. "Oh, all right." And he touched the panel next to the door. The fluorescents twinkled and came on, bathing the room in a pearly glow. She saw that Kennison's lower lip was thrust out in a pout. His whole face had the puffy, pinched appearance of a disappointed child. *What is his problem?* she wondered.

They worked together for an hour. Kennison unhooked panels in the backs of the drives and disabled switches. Sarah followed him on the terminal screen. FILE UNLOCKED. FILE UNLOCKED. *He could have done all this himself*, she thought. *Once the physical locks were disabled, I could have worked from my own apartment.*

So why had he insisted that she accompany him? Because he's paranoid and needs someone to hold his hand?

Kennison emerged from the rear of the left-most cabinet. He had taken his jacket off, and his tie. He had rolled up his shirtsleeves. His top shirt button had been unhooked. To simulate hard, physical work? *Get real, "Cousin Daniel."*

"That's the last of them," he announced. "Anyone can get in now and highjack the files." He frowned slightly, bit his lower lip, and turned to stare at the drives. "Anyone," he repeated sadly. "*Jacta alea est.*"

"And this is your Rubicon?" she suggested.

He turned his head and smiled. "Ah, Ms. Bennett! Alas, so few are grounded in the classics these days."

"Yes? And whose fault is that?"

473

Kennison shook his head. "We can encourage and nurture a trend, Ms. Bennett, as you well know by now. We cannot force it." He looked again at the drives he had unlocked. "I am determined upon this course of mine. Yet, who can resist a glance backward? Who can abandon their past—their father's past, even—without some pang of regret?"

"Tell me all about it," she said, her voice heavy with irony. Kennison turned back to face her.

"Yes. You would know about that, wouldn't you? You and I are not Jimmy Caldero or the others like him. We cannot simply slough off everything we have been and might have been for the convenience of the moment. That is a bond between us. Brother and sister." His face brightened, as if struck by a new thought. "Yes, brother and sister."

*That will be the day*, she thought. She had to remind herself that this sad and sympathetic creature before her had ordered the deaths of people—of Morgan and Dennis. That he was interested in finding Dennis only because of his need to know who had taken him. Why couldn't he be a hard and arrogant psychopath, like the killers in the movies? Why did he have to be so wretched and pathetic?

She turned her face to the terminal screen. She had to study the system architecture so she could duplicate it quickly and dump it into Detweiler's system before anyone became aware of it. Only Selkirk, Johnson, and Cheng knew of the plan to secure a pristine copy of the files. If anyone else on the Night Shift detected the activity, the fat would be in the fire.

"Tell me, 'Brother.' You're sure that Detweiler has agreed to hide your system."

"Yes, Sister." (*Oh, Christ! He's taking it seriously.*) "Jimmy Caldero called this evening and confirmed it."

She wouldn't look at him. Why had Red called Kennison and not her? Too busy, maybe? According to Bosworth, there was quite a lot brewing out there in Boston, with DB&S and the Secret Six. He could have forgotten. He might have been distracted.

She did not have to make excuses for him.

Kennison caught her attention. He held his hands up. "I think I'll go wash up while you get started, sis." His hands were not dirty. She watched him leave the computer room. He turned the light off before he opened the door. When he had closed it behind him, she strode to the light panel and slapped the switch.

Sis.

It was an hour later before she realized he had not returned.

She paused in her work and looked around the room. The clock read three-thirty. Where the. . . ? She cocked her head and listened carefully; but all she heard was the subdued pings and murmurs of a building late at night. The hum of the terminal and the overhead lights.

She pulled on her mouse and put the screen to sleep. Then she walked to the door. She hesitated with her hand on the knob, remembering Kennison's paranoia. Then she sighed and turned the lights out.

In the darkness, her hand froze on the knob. She thought that, if she opened the door, there would be something horrible in the doorway, waiting for her. Freddy Kruger. Simon Ysidro. *No, don't be absurd.* Those were fictional. Imaginary. She was paying the price now for all those horror movies she had seen as a teenager. *You aren't in some schlock TV movie here,* she told herself.

No. The horrors were real. Drugged and hypnotized killers in the park. Anonymous automobiles with screeching tires. A knife in the ribs in a parking lot. Bombs that turned meeting rooms into charnel houses; or automobiles into infernos. An implacable killer with dead eyes. And where was Tyler Crayle? He had dropped from sight, according to Kennison. Was he hunting for his brother's killer? Was he hunting for her? *Was he waiting on the other side of the door, with his knife red with Kennison's blood?*

No, dammit, she chastised herself. Real life killers didn't do that. If Crayle were out there, he would not be waiting for her to open the door. He would have come in after her. To prove it, she yanked the door open.

And stifled a scream.

There was nothing there.

She leaned against the door frame. Go ahead, work yourself up into a state. A little hysteria is good for you. Helps purge the mind of an excess of rationality.

She stepped out into the main room. Dark. Dimly lit by a few EXIT signs. The partitions for the cubicles seemed like the walls of a maze. She could see over the tops of the cubicles. A large, open room broken up into nooks and crannies. The room creaked as the building swayed in the wind.

A large, open area, dark and empty. What was it about that image that seemed so terrifying? More so even than a small, enclosed space. She remembered feeling this way on the fourth floor of the Widener Building. The dread that had overwhelmed her when she had approached the one desk.

She remembered that they had found a skeleton in the desk.

*That's enough of this shit*, she thought, and reached around to hit the light switch in the computer room.

A pool of light spilled out into the room and threw the partitions into pale relief.

Kennison shot up from behind the nearest partition. "What are you doing?" he hissed.

This time she did scream.

In a moment, Kennison was by her and had his arms around her. "Don't worry, Sis," he said. "I'll take care of you." He pressed against her a little too hard for a 'brother.' She shoved him away.

"Don't you touch me!" she warned. "What do you think you're doing frightening me like that? Is that how you get your kicks, or something?"

He looked confused. "I . . . No . . . Of course not. That would be disgusting."

"Then what were you doing, hiding in that cubicle?"

He looked around and leaned toward her. Sarah backed away. "Selkirk is coming," he said.

Selkirk. "Then we'd better blow this joint before he catches us here. He mustn't see us together."

"No. No," Kennison protested. "He's looking for you. He knows that you know about him and about the Q. About Bernstein and French. He knows that you won't give up looking for your partner; and finding him means finding the Q."

She grabbed him by the shirt front. "Then why is he coming here?" she said into his face.

Kennison pulled her hands from his shirt. His grip was remarkably strong. "Because I called him and told him."

"You what!"

"Don't worry. I'll protect you."

"You're crazy!"

"No. Selkirk trusts me, because he offered me a job with

476

the Q. Well, not in so many words. But he wants me to download the Society's business into the Q's computers. In return, I get to be North American coordinator for their organization."

"So." She tried to pull her wrists from his grip and couldn't. "I told Red we couldn't trust you."

"I— Hush!" There was a noise at the main door. A shadow against the frosted glass. Kennison pushed her into the nearest cubicle. "Hide there. Under the desk." He slipped off down the aisle.

Sarah started after him, but checked herself. What was Kennison up to? Had he offered her to Selkirk as a token of good faith? Then why had he told her to hide? Did he think he could give her up to the Q and still protect her because they might give him an important office? She remembered that Red had told her that position was as important to Kennison as the power itself.

Red had never called him. It had all been a ruse, that business about Detweiler offering sanctuary. Why had she come here with him? How could she have let a vicious killer lull her into feeling safe? Because they were allies of convenience? And now, it was no longer convenient. . . .

There was too much she didn't know; but there was one thing she did know. Never hide anyplace where there is only one way out. Red had told her that. One of his secret agent aphorisms. And Red, even three thousand miles away, was a more reliable guide than Kennison.

She crept from the cul-de-sac of the cubicle and made her way silently down the aisle. She tried to pretend she was stalking game in the woods. Remain quiet and downwind. If she could position herself close enough to the door, she might be able to escape when Kennison led Selkirk to her "hiding place."

The door opened and closed quietly. Sarah heard the rustling of clothes and a shoe move on the carpet.

Then there was a sudden cry and a thud. Something crashed into a partition and shoved it a few inches across the carpet.

*Now!* She darted for the door.

But Kennison was there, at the light switch, and she brought herself up short. A single fluorescent panel lit like a spotlight over the entry foyer. Selkirk lay like a flour sack against the skewed partition. Kennison saw her and smiled.

"Hi, Sis. I figured you would try to sneak around in back of

477

him." He pointed to the motionless figure on the floor. "But I didn't really need your help. I told you I could handle it myself."

Sarah looked into his eyes. She had always wondered what a madman looked like. Now she knew. Completely and utterly sincere. She was suddenly afraid of Kennison. More afraid than she had ever been of Orvid Crayle.

She looked to Selkirk. For what? Help? Did one ask the scorpion for help against the rattler? Yes. Sometimes. But Selkirk could give none. He lay loose, his arms and legs askew, a smear of blood across his face where it rested against his shoulder. "Is he . . . ?"

Kennison held out a bloody paperweight. "I hit him with this," he said, as if expecting a compliment. "He was going to hurt you."

Sarah couldn't find any words to reply to that. Kennison stepped toward her and she backed away. A potted plant blocked her retreat and Kennison reached out and seized her wrist. "Don't worry," he said gently. "It's all over now. You're safe with me." He tried to pull her into his embrace and Sarah realized with icy certainty what he meant to do.

"Wait! No!" *Think, Sarah. Think!* "Not here. What if Selkirk comes to?"

Without loosening his grip on her wrist, Kennison twisted and kicked Selkirk hard in the rib cage. The unconscious man slid from his half-sitting position into a heap on the floor. "He won't. Not for a while. And besides . . ." He smiled weirdly. "Won't that add a little spice to it?"

*Oh, God.* "No. No, it won't. I . . . I won't be able to do it. Not with him here." She rubbed her hand up his arm. "Take me back to my apartment, brother. We'll be safe there." Safe with Helen and Chu. And Bosworth. And Polovsky, who had flown in that morning from Colorado.

Kennison might be crazy, but he wasn't stupid. He shook his head. "No, Sis. Too many people would see us. And what we have is . . . forbidden."

"Then, your place. Take me to your place."

He brightened. "Yes. Certainly. We'll go home." He put an arm around her shoulder and guided her into the corridor toward the elevator. His grip was like steel. "We'll go home."

She had planned to alert the cab driver somehow on their way to Kennison's apartment. But Kennison had driven himself into town, so there was no cab hailed. His car was in the building's parking garage, and there no one in the elevator or in the garage, or even at the toll booth. The metal gate was automatic. Kennison inserted his card in the slot and it rolled up out of their way. He pulled up the ramp onto Stockton and turned left toward Telegraph hill.

He laid his hand on her thigh and squeezed. "Don't worry," he kept saying. "You're safe now."

Polovsky and Bosworth were asleep when Red checked back into his suite in San Francisco. Bosworth was curled up on the sofa; but Polovsky had commandeered the king-size bed. He rousted them both awake.

"I just got in," he told them. "Missed my connection in Chicago. Weather in Boston delayed our takeoff and I had to wait for the next flight. God—" He yawned and stretched. "I'm beat. I was looking forward to a nice warm bed." He looked at Polovsky when he said it.

"So, sue me," said Walt. "You never showed. Why should I sleep on a daybed or a sofa? I get a crick in my back."

Red didn't bother to answer him. He wandered into the sitting room and the other two followed him like puppy dogs.

They had converted the sitting room into a command center and printout paper hung from the walls in streamers. Red scowled and tossed his flight bag onto the sofa. He walked to the nearest wall and inspected their work.

"Don't you know what tape does to the wallpaper?"

"Listen to him," Walt said to Bosworth, jerking a thumb. "Go ahead, read it. That tap that Kennison let us put into his phone terminal is something else. We've got complete transcriptions of everything that's gone in or out." Polovsky shook his head. "Cousin Dan must be serious about scuttling the Old Society. The kind of information we're getting . . ."

Red ran his finger down the transcripts of the messages. "Have you sent copies to the Council?"

"Oh, they're delirious with joy. Brother Betancourt thinks we can increase the values of our portfolios by a good fifteen percent by having advance knowledge of all Their moves."

Red looked at him. "If we *let* Them make Their moves. It'll also help us stop Them. Don't forget our Objective." *Or was it Emmett Blaine's objective?*

Polovsky returned the look. "Sure." Bosworth hunched his shoulders and concentrated on the terminal screen.

Red stuck his hands in his pants pockets and fiddled with

479

his key ring. The thumpers attached to the window made a tiny hailstone rattle. The late afternoon sun slanted through the slats of the blind. He walked over and pushed one aside with his finger. Street lights hung like strings of pearl on Telegraph Hill. Here and there a window glowed. "I thought Tex was coming."

"Yeah? Well you're stuck with me," Walt said. "Janie went off somewhere and left him in charge of the ranch." Red grunted but made no reply. "How was Boston?" Walt asked.

Red turned away from the window. "Wet. I met some of our competitors, though."

"Yeah, I heard." Polovsky gave Bosworth a nod. "The kid filled me in." He found a chair and eased into it. He rubbed his eyes. "So what do we do about them?"

"Which?"

"Any of them. All of them. What about that Boston group? Where do they stand?"

"They're harmless, at least for now. I was talking to their man, Vane, and he said that no one can really affect the course of history; but that everyone can convince themselves that they have."

Polovsky grinned and looked at Bosworth. "Yeah? You hear that, kid? Let's hope they keep thinking that way. If they think it's impossible, they won't even try to interfere. How do they explain our finding the Six and the Q? Or was that our imagination, too?"

Red walked slowly around the room. "Oh, they had to admit that the Six was real enough. They had two members for houseguests." He shook his head ruefully. "I worked with one of them for years while I was on the NetWatch. I'm starting to wonder if there's anyone in the official government who actually works for the government."

"What do we do about them?"

"Nothing, for now. We're allies in the search for the SQPS. First things first."

"What ever happened to the long-term perspective?"

"The long term's only an issue for people who survive the short term. And that means surviving the Q, the Quetelet people. I think Genevieve Weil would have felt right at home with that crowd. Hell—" He waved his hand in the air. "Just think about that Howard woman that they slipped in on us."

He remembered the way the woman had suicided. A stupid

480

waste. A stupid fanaticism. What could possibly drive people to believe that such measures were rational?

"Well . . ." Red stretched again. "I'm for sacking out. If I can find a place," he added pointedly.

Polovsky jerked upwards with his thumb. "Try upstairs, why don't you. There's a nice warm bed up there."

Red gave him a sharp look. "Watch your mouth, Walt. Your parents spent too much money on the orthodontia to have it go to waste now."

Polovsky shook his head. "Naw. She's not up there. She went over to Kennison Demographics about one-thirty or so. He wanted her to go over the architecture for the mega-worm she's designing to corrupt his data base."

Red scowled and looked at the blind-shaded window. "She went? This late?"

"They had to wait for the Night Shift to go off."

"I wish she hadn't gone."

"Why? Kennison's with us on this one, ain't he?"

"I just don't like the idea."

"Jealous?"

Red scowled at him. He drifted to the window and pushed the slat aside again. "Maybe I should go over there."

"Ah, hell. Maybe she's back already. We've been asleep and she wouldn't check in with us anyway."

Kennison's apartment seemed to glow in flickering lights and shadows, as if from a fire. A cold fire. She could feel no heat; but there was a smell as of cinders. Sarah stood on the threshold, not wishing to enter, resisting the persistent pressure of his hand against her back. She sensed a strangeness about the place. Weirdness—in the old Anglo-Saxon sense. Kennison was the Devil and this was Hell. She would not see, not feel the flames until she entered.

Kennison pushed against the small of her back and she staggered into the flickering twilight.

And it was only an apartment, bathed in an odd, sourceless light. Her eyes darted about the room. The apartment did not seem lived in; but that made sense because Kennison did not actually live there. Still, it seemed to her that there should be something personal in it. A photograph. A book. Anything. Instead it was bare; anonymous and devoid of personality. All she could see from the doorway was the electronic gadgetry set up by the window and the busy little window tappers "jamming" the vibrations of the glass. Still the feeling of weirdness stayed with her.

He locked the door behind them, leaned against it, and let out a deep breath. "There. Now, we're safe."

Not until he had closed the door could she see what was behind it. When she did, she sucked in her breath and took a step toward it.

A shrine.

A bank of votive candles in red and blue glass cups sat in a brass stand of curled metal. All the candles were lit, and the flames danced within their containers, casting halos on the wall and ceiling. It had been that that had given her the sense of a cold fire burning in the apartment.

Above the votive candles was a framed photograph of a round-faced white woman. Some of the candles cast halo shapes above her head. Her eyes smiled at Sarah. The photograph was surrounded by vases bursting with sprays of colored blossoms, some of them on the verge of wilting. A small, blackened cup in the center held the remains of incense cones.

*Oh, Sweet Jesus,* she thought. *What have I walked in to?*

She jerked her head around to stare at Kennison. He was still leaning against the door. His head and shoulders sagged. He held that pose for a long moment, while Sarah backed slowly away from him. The back of her heel caught the leg of the coffee table and the sound brought Kennison's head up.

There were tears in the corners of his eyes. He looked like a small child.

"It's gone," he complained. "It's gone already." He closed his eyes tight and clenched his fists. "We'll get it back," he said in what sounded almost like a normal voice. "I know how. It will be . . . hard on you; but worthwhile. You'll see. You'll understand." His voice was the calm, reasonable voice of a madman. He began to advance toward her.

She didn't understand at all. She wasn't sure she wanted to. She darted suddenly around the coffee table, intending to outflank him and reach the door. But he vaulted the table with surprising agility and cut her off.

"Now, Sis, that's no way to act. If you cooperate, it won't hurt very much."

"I'm not your sister!" she cried. He reached for her and she danced back toward the sofa. "What's wrong with you?" She had to stay out of his grasp. She remembered how strong he was.

"Are you afraid?" he asked with a peculiar smile on his face. "That's good. I'll protect you."

"Afraid?" She reached the end of the sofa and pulled it out into his path. "You bet your ass, I'm afraid." She threw one of the pillows at his face and he batted it aside. Her eyes cast about the room for something to throw at him.

She faked left and cut right toward the window. She ran both hands across the glass pane and brushed aside the little mechanical spiders. They fell in a cascade to the floor, where they clattered and danced in the nap of the carpet. She grabbed a double handful of the tiny devices and dashed around the other end of the sofa just as Kennison reached the window.

She turned and threw one of the spiders as hard as she could at his face. He ducked but it struck him in the cheek and he howled. He cupped his cheek with his hand and brought it away bloody. Sarah hurled another tapper at him and ran for the door.

"Walt!" she yelled over her shoulder. "Norris! Someone help!"

Helen shook her head. "She hasn't come back, Brother Caldero. "I've been here since she left, so I would know."

"Damn. I don't like it." Red chewed a thumbnail, thinking. "Let me into her suite, would you?"

Helen looked uncertain, and Red lost his temper. "Dammitall, sister, I'm no voyeur. This is business. Our sister went out without backup and she hasn't reported or returned yet. So will you let me into her suite?"

Helen stiffened under his lashing. "How will letting you into her suite help you find her?" she asked reasonably.

But Red was in no mood to be reasonable. He leaned far over the concierge desk, so that Helen backed up deeper in her chair. "I don't know," he told her. "Maybe she came back while you were in the john. I just want to see." He held the pose for a moment, staring into Helen's face. Then he straightened and looked away. "Please?"

Helen snatched her key ring from the desk drawer. She stood and straightened her skirt. "Follow me," she said.

Red trod on her heels. "I know where her suite is," he

said. *She's probably there, fast asleep, dreaming the dreams of the innocent.* Sure, that was it. She had come back late. Helen had been away from her desk and she hadn't wanted to waken the others. So she had tiptoed off to bed. If she was there, he would wake her up and give her a good tongue lashing on running ops without a handler or backup; and on the need to check in and out.

And if she wasn't . . .

Well, she was a big girl, wasn't she? She could take care of herself. Just ask Orvid Crayle.

But, no. None of us can really take care of ourselves. That's the whole idea of brotherhood and sisterhood. The French hadn't stopped at liberty and equality; two diametrically opposed sentiments. They had added fraternity to make it work. We need each other. Or maybe what is more important, we need to need each other. It's not that one's back must be guarded; but that, when it was, life was a hell of a lot less lonely. I am my sister's keeper; and she is mine. Otherwise, what was the point?

She wasn't in the suite.

Red prowled from room to room, calling her name. Helen waited patiently by the door. When he returned to the front room, he looked at her helplessly.

"I told you she wasn't back yet."

"But where is she?" He threw his arms out.

"With Cousin Kennison." Helen's pinched lips showed what she thought of Cousin Dan. "At the Demographics offices." She pointed to the phone. "You could just call over there, you know. If it would make you feel better."

"I—Red wondered if he looked as stupid as he felt. "Well, sure. Jet lag and late nights, right?" He grinned and picked up the phone. He punched three numbers. "Frank? What? Yes, I know what time it is. This is important. Do this one thing for me; then you can go home. Put me through to Johnson & Cheng. Right. So nothing shows up on the suite's regular hotel bill." He put a hand over the mouthpiece. "I suppose by tomorrow night every Associate in the country will know about this."

Helen shrugged. "You won't be the first one of us who's been flustered by Rule 19."

Red gave her a warning scowl. The phone was ringing. Ringing. "Dammit. No one answers." But who would? Neither Kennison nor Sarah were supposed to be there. They might just let it ring rather than answer. Yet, Sarah could glance at the readout and see who was calling. She would recognize her own number. He pushed the phone into its cradle.

Maybe they had gone to Kennison's apartment. Why, he couldn't imagine; or refused to. But it was a possibility. He squinted through the eyepiece on the eavesdropper. Kennison's apartment window swam into view; but it was too far away for him to see anything. "Still on target," he said.

He checked the speakers, but all he heard were the tappers on Kennison's window. Dueling drum sets. He hunched his shoulders and stayed by the window. "I still don't like it." Helen said nothing. He ran his finger up and down the phone handle. "Tell me. Was Brother Walt checked in before Sister Sarah left?" He looked up at Helen.

Now the concierge looked worried, too. "Why . . . Yes, he was. He arrived about mid-afternoon."

Red swatted the telephone and it flew from the table with a crash of bells. The dial tone buzzed like a bagpipe. "Dammit! He knew better! He should have set himself up as handler. Made sure she knew to check in and when. He should have arranged for backup. Chu, probably. And he should have kept watch! He let her go out by herself!"

Helen didn't say anything. She seemed to close in on herself. She chewed on her lip and wouldn't meet his eye. "He . . . he didn't like her. Because of what she did. You know. The Dump."

"Because of . . . My God, what has that got to do with the price of eggs? This was Associate Business, straight from the Council. You don't have to 'like' someone to do a job with her! If that were true, no orchestra would ever play a note." Brother Polovsky would have a lot to answer for. But to Betancourt, not to himself. If he called Polovsky to task everyone would think it was a personal thing. No, this had to go by the book. Later, he could invite Walt outside and make it personal.

An insistent beeping from the floor reminded him that the telephone was off the hook. He bent down and gathered it up. "Jeez," he said, fumbling it into place. "They sure do build these things rugged."

"I suppose a lot of people throw theirs across the room."

He glanced at Helen. "Yeah." He let out a deep breath. Then he turned and sat against the back of the sofa. Outside the window, San Francisco slept. The window tappers keeping up a constant drum-roll, as if announcing the imminent arrival of the star of the show. He crossed his arms and watched them paradiddle on the glass.

"Should I leave you here?" Helen asked.

"Hmm? What?" He looked over his shoulder. "Oh. Yeah. I'll wait for her here. Maybe I'll toss out on the sofa. Buzz me in here when you see her get off the elevator."

Helen shut the door gently and the room darkened. Red thought about turning a light on; but that would mean stirring from his spot and he didn't feel up to it. He was tired. If he just held tight, she would show up. Tomorrow, they'd both have a good laugh over it.

How long he sat there, he didn't know. The tiny hailstone sounds faded in and out. He dozed.

The sudden change in the sound jerked him awake. The speakers rushed liked a wave crashing on a pebble-strewn beach. The recorder clicked on and there were sounds: feet running; a howl of pain. Then a voice: "Walt! Norris! Someone help!"

The world seemed to freeze for an instant; and an icy hand seized his heart and squeezed. Jacksonville. It was Jacksonville all over again.

Kennison beat her to the door. Sarah threw another spider at him, but she missed and its tiny legs struck in the door like miniature daggers. There was another one fixed to the back of his hand, but he ignored it and came toward her again.

"No," he pleaded. "This isn't right. You've got to be afraid. You don't know how to play the game at all."

"You're crazy, Kennison. Walt! He's trying to rape me!" The recorder in her apartment, she knew, would kick in automatically; but what if no one was there to monitor it? They thought she was at the Demographics office, not here. They were probably asleep.

Well, at least she could leave a message with them. Tell them what had happened. She threw the spiders at Kennison's eyes, keeping him at bay, and gasped the story out in short bursts.

486

"He lured Selkirk over. Ambushed him. Without warning."

Kennison seemed oblivious to the fact that she was talking for the eavesdropper. He paused in his pursuit and gave her a puzzled look. "But he was Q, Sis. He was coming to hurt you. I protected you. Aren't you grateful?"

Grateful! She was running low on weapons. She ran back towards the window to grab some more from the carpet; but Kennison was too close behind her and she couldn't stop. The tappers crunched and popped under her shoes.

Kennison's fingers closed on her shoulder. She spun on her heel and slapped him hard, boxing his ear. She pulled away and her blouse ripped at the right sholder.

"This isn't right," Kennison complained, holding his ear. "You're not supposed to run away from me."

"You're sick, Kennison. You're very sick. And pitiful." And it was true. She was still afraid. Kennison was strong and, if he once got a hold of her, he could do whatever he liked. But she no longer felt numb with terror. This wasn't the dapper, well-mannered foe she had known. This was a sad and pathetic wretch. She couldn't hate him; she couldn't hate a man for being ill.

She saw her remarks had struck home. Kennison paused. A tiny crease appeared between his brows. His mouth parted. "Sick?"

She threw words now, instead of metal spiders. She saw the wounds each one opened, deadlier than any inflicted by stick or stone. "Yes, sick. You are vile and disgusting. Degraded." She turned suddenly and pointed toward the votive shrine by the door. "What would *she* have said?"

Kennison howled and covered his face with both his hands. "No! Prudence! She saw everything. But, I had to . . . . Everything was out of control. Weil; Ullman; Selkirk; Beaumont. Nothing was happening right. I had to show that I could still make things happen." He dropped his hands. "Prudence understands. She helped me. It was degrading—yes. I loathed it. I loved it. I loathed loving it." He took a step toward her. His eyes pleaded with her.

"Stop me. Please."

She kicked forward with all her strength and caught him squarely in the groin. He gasped and doubled over, clutching himself. He made retching sounds in his throat.

"Always glad to oblige a friend," she said. She jumped for the door and threw it open.

And screamed.

It was Selkirk, and he was very, very angry.

# XIII

Red jammed the elevator button with his thumb. The down arrow lit immediately, but he kept pressing it. The more often you pressed an elevator button the faster it came. Or maybe not; but he couldn't just wait for the car to come.

"Helen," he told the concierge. "Get Bosworth and Polovsky here. Tell them to man the listening station. Sarah's in Kennison's apartment and there's some kind of struggle. I'm going straight over."

Backup. Never run an op without backup. Walt was too fat; and the kid was a kid. The door chimed and opened and Red stepped in. Who had time for backup? He turned and faced front. Helen was already talking into the phone. Red caught the door as it closed. "Tell Frank Chu he's backing me. Give him the details."

When the elevator opened on the lobby, he ran out past the startled night clerk and the dozing bellman; but he skidded to a stop in front of the hotel. He needed a cab. Waiting for a cab seemed almost criminal. He felt like running all the way down Kearny to Telegraph Hill. It was absurd, of course; but he needed to be in motion.

The night bellman had followed him out, curious. "May I help you, Mr. Caldero?" He knew his name, of course. The staff always made it a point to know the names of their richer guests. Red turned to him.

"Call me a cab," he said.

*You're a cab.* Every doorman and bellhop in the world has

wanted to say that at one time or another. The young man looked into Red's eyes and stifled whatever impulse toward humor he might have had. He pulled the doorman's whistle from his pocket and stepped into the street. The whistle echoed from the steel and glass. Red stepped into the street behind him and laid a hand on his shoulder. "Keep blowing, son. This is the most important cab you've ever hailed."

*What's black and blue and red all over?* The old joke shot through Sarah's mind. Answer: Selkirk's face. The bruise where Kennison had struck him covered most of the right side of his head. Sticky, half-dried blood created rivers and tributaries down his cheek and chin, staining his shirt collar. Hard, angry eyes squinted through puffed and blackened flesh.

He held a pistol in his hand.

"Out o' my way, lassie," he snarled. "Where is that snakin', crowlin' ferlie?" He shoved her aside and stepped into the apartment. "Ah, there ye be." He grinned, but the smile broke open a half-healed cut in the lip and blood dripped onto his chin. He raised the gun.

"No, don't do it!" Sarah grabbed him by the gun arm and tried to hold on. He twisted and pulled.

"First things first. I'll treat wi' ye next, lassie. Ken wha ye've learned o' the Societé." Sarah could barely understand him. Selkirk lifted his leg and shoved against her abdomen. She staggered back and Selkirk pointed his pistol at Kennison.

Her hand felt something sharp in the carpet. One of the spiders she had thrown at Kennison. She seized it and threw it hard at Selkirk's face. He cried out; half turned toward her.

And—incredibly—the elevator chimed.

The apartment door was still open from Selkirk's entry. Sarah made a flying leap out into the hall, pulling the door closed as she did. She heard Selkirk's startled, "Hey! Wait!" Then the door slammed shut.

"Hold that elevator!" she said and ran for it.

A young man had just stepped off the elevator, a dozen paces down the hall. He stood unsteadily and favored her with a bleary-eyed stare. He grinned. "Hey, baby," he said. "You wanna—"

Kennison's door opened. Selkirk stepped into the hall. He saw Sarah and the young man and raised his pistol. The man stared at him, bug-eyed. Sarah almost rolled into the elevator car. She seized the man as she went in and pulled him after her. He staggered and fell against the back wall. Sarah hit the button that said LOBBY.

The doors slid shut just as something like an angry hornet ripped through the air and shattered the plastic panel by the young man's head. "He's got a gun," he said.

"No shit," said Sarah.

"What's a white man with a gun doing shooting at a sister?" He sounded angry, defiant. His use of the word 'sister' reminded her of Kennison and his sick game.

"I think he was shooting at you," she said.

"Oh. Well." The elevator hummed and they rode down together in silence.

Selkirk could have shot her easily, when he first came into the apartment. But he hadn't. Because he wanted to question her? Then, why hadn't he shot when he saw her escaping?

The thought struck her, irresistably, just as the elevator sighed to a halt. The undertones of wounded pride were so farcical that she giggled suddenly; and the young, drunken man beside her ceased his fascinated study of the bullet hole in the back wall and stared at her, bemused.

*Aren't I important enough to be a target?*

When they reached the lobby, Sarah pulled the red switch that shut off the power to the car. A ringing like a small alarm clock issued from the panel. Sarah wondered how long it would take before anyone ventured forth to investigate. There was a staircase, of course, and Kennison's apartment was only five flights up; so Selkirk could still pursue her. But this would give her a lead.

The apartment house had no night doorman. Sarah saw the splintered wood and bent metal where Selkirk had kicked his way in past the locks. She ran out to the sidewalk.

The cold night air struck her like a knife, sucking her breath from her. She threw her arms around herself. The chill sea breeze worked its way through the tear in her blouse, freezing her arm. She looked around, disoriented, at the dark and empty streets. Her breath was cotton in the air.

"You a'right? Who was that honky?" It was the man from the elevator. "What wuzzit, drugs?" He eyed her warily; sobered by the night, suddenly aware of his vulnerability.

"No," she said, casting about for a short, plausible

491

answer. "Espionage." She couldn't wait here. Selkirk was coming.

"I'll come with you," the man declared; and the offer was so sincere and so patently foolish and suicidal that she paused just a moment to touch him on the arm.

"No, thank you. I'm . . . I'm used to this. (God help me, I am.) Wait here. Hide. Someone will come."

So saying, she sprinted up the street without looking back. He's probably killed Kennison by now, she thought. The idea depressed her. There had been a time when she had wanted nothing less for Kennison herself. But between the rage and the reality, she had softened. In her memory she could see Orvid Crayle's glassy and unbelieving eyes, staring at the clouds, the night skies, the stars, and beyond. *The next time will be easier*, his ghost had whispered. Easier to resist. Defense was one thing; execution, another. She didn't want anyone dead.

Least of all herself.

There was a glow ahead of her. The false dawn backlighting the buildings. The fog rising off the Golden Gate was a ghostly lover caressing the city. The foghorn in the straits moaned like a lost soul.

Thank God she had kept herself in shape. Those weekends in the mountains. The survival training. Who would have thought? Her breath came in short, rapid gulps as she ran; but she sped rapidly and smoothly up the street.

A staccato clicking. What was it? She stopped and the sound stopped. She listened, breathing heavily. Then she started running once more. When the clicking resumed, she knew what it was. Her shoes striking the pavement. Echoing in the foggy night air and the deserted street.

Between one stride and the next she kicked her shoes off—first one, then the other—and ran barefooted in the dark. It seemed she ran faster that way, at one with her warrior ancestors in the steaming jungles of Africa. Hard-soled, enduring. They shored her up and carried her along. The steam was the mist of a Pacific morning; the jungle was concrete. The pavement was damp from the fog and cold, chilling her feet.

She heard his footsteps behind her. The slap of shoeleather on cement. They ran away from her; and she closed her eyes and allowed herself a moment of relief. She broke stride and halted, bending way over, hands on her knees, breathing in great gusts.

Then she heard his footsteps change direction and follow her up the street and she resumed running without even thinking about how tired she was.

She thought about shouting, awakening some of the people in the sleeping houses, calling for help. But she knew she couldn't. It would reveal her position to Selkirk; and he would reach her more quickly than any befuddled householder might. And no one might respond anyway. And, even if someone did, confused and half asleep, they would be no help against Selkirk.

An open space to her right. A park. She crossed the street and darted into the grass. The wet blades whipped at her calves and ankles, soaking her feet, numbing them with the cold dew. She stepped on a rock; and the sudden, unexpected pain caused her to let out a high squeak, quickly stifled.

But it had been loud enough in the silent night air to cause her pursuer to change direction. She cursed herself silently and forced herself to push on, hobbling slightly now because the rock had cut her foot.

Unexpectedly, she came out into a parking lot and found herself staring up into the noble and farsighted gaze of Christopher Columbus. Then she looked past the twelve-foot bronze and saw the tall, fluted pillar of Coit Tower. She was at the dead end of Telegraph Hill.

Red paused at the door to Kennison's apartment and put his ear to it. Nothing. No sounds of a struggle. Which meant it was over. *But how did it end?*

Someone had left the building, afraid of pursuit. The elevator grounded on the first floor proved that much. *Let it be Sarah,* he thought. *Let it be Sarah who escaped.*

He reached inside his jacket and his hand closed on nothing. *I really am tired,* he thought, *to go on an op unarmed.* He knew exactly where his gun was. In the sealed and bonded suitcase the porter had left in his suite.

The lock on Kennison's apartment door was a Rabson but it took Red only a moment to pick it. He was through the door in no more time than if he had had a key.

Two legs protruded from behind the door. Red faltered and steadied himself on the knob. He took a deep breath and stepped into the room, closing the door behind him.

493

Two quick strides and he was beside the body on one knee. He peered into the face. It was Kennison. He lay staring at the ceiling. The front of his shirt was stained red and the carpet beneath him was wet and sticky. Curiously, Red felt no sense of relief. He had come over intending to thrash Kennison within an inch of his life; but to find this . . . He wondered if Sarah had shot him. *She never needs my help.*

He rose and brushed his knee and turned on the speakers for the eavesdropper. "Bosworth, what happened?"

"We're playing back the tape now, boss—"

Polovsky's voice cut in. "Hey, Jimmy. I'm sorry this happened. I really am. It's all my fault. I was senior man on station and I shoulda taken charge; but—"

"Save it. Just tell me what happened." Red quickly inspected the rest of the apartment. When he came to the shower stall, he hesitated a moment before drawing the curtain, afraid of what he might find behind it. But there was no body. No Sarah. He closed his eyes briefly and gave thanks.

"We played back the tape," Polovsky told him when he returned to the living room. As near as we can figure, Selkirk barged in while Sarah was fighting Kennison." Walt's voice plunged. "Jesus, Jimmy, you should hear the kind of crap Kennison was spouting at her. He's a real piece of work, he is. But this Selkirk had some private grudge against Kennison, and Sarah gave him the slip while he was plugging our boy. He took off after her. Fired a shot down the hall, we figure. Anyway the acoustics sound different."

"There was a bullet hole in the elevator. No blood. He must have missed. She must have gone east, up Lombard. I would have seen her if she'd gone the other way. Where's Chu?"

"He already left for home. We called him on his car phone and he's on his way back. Make it half an hour."

"Shit. I can't wait."

"Let the kid man home plate, Jimmy. I'll get a car and be over."

"Alright. I'm not waiting, though. Seconds may count here." He started back toward the door; but Kennison's hand reached up and grabbed his pants leg. Red cried out in a moment's terror and pulled frantically. He looked down into Kennison's eyes.

494

"James." It was a hoarse, breathy whisper. "James. I'm so sorry."

"Shit! The sunuvabitch is still alive!"

"Who?" asked Polovsky. "Kennison?"

"How many dead sons of bitches do we have over here? Of course, Kennison. Tell Helen. Get some medics over here right away." He shook loose from the iron grip. "Take care of the Scene, Walt. You and Helen. You know what to do. Don't let the regulars find anything." And what was the use? Ever since the Dump they had been bailing water frantically. But there were people like Doang and Llewellyn all over the country. Probing. Wondering. Historians and mathematicians finding themselves together as odd bedfellows. Why bother concealing what had happened here?

Because, by God, you finish the course.

"I didn't hurt her, James." Red stared at the man. He wondered if he was dying. "I wanted to. I tried. But I didn't."

"Yeah, I'll give you a medal." He turned to leave.

"No." The hand reached out again, faltered, dropped. "Jacksonville."

Red wanted to run; to catch up with Sarah and Selkirk. But he was frozen in place. He would not turn and look at Kennison. "What about Jacksonville?"

"I'm sorry for that, too."

"I'm no damn priest. If you want absolution, apologize to Alice. I'd say you'd be seeing her soon; but you're probably not going to the same place."

"I am sorry."

He turned and lashed out at him. "Dammit, we play by rules! She was under my protection. She wasn't a target anymore. But you forgot to call off your man. She trusted me and, because of you, *I failed her!*"

Bubbles formed at the corners of Kennison's lips. "You hate me. You should. I once . . . I once left an enemy to die," he confessed. "Alone. In the dark."

*What does he want from me?* Red turned to the door. *Sarah needs me more than he does.* He paused with his hand on the knob. "Help is coming. I don't hate you that much, Dan."

The head turned to follow him. "Then. Stay with. Me."

Red opened the door. "I don't like you that much."

\* \* \*

495

When Red emerged from the apartment building, a young, black man leapt from the bushes and blocked his way. The man had a knife, which he held up so Red could see it. He had also been drinking heavily, and his breath was sour. "Your cab's gone, mister. They don't wait around, you know."

Red was in no mood for petty delays. He took a step back and fell into a fighting stance.

"You the one she was expecting?"

"What?" It was such an unexpected question for a mugger to ask that Red hesitated before kicking out.

"The lady that ran out of here. She told me someone would be along. Is that you?"

Red slowly relaxed. "Tall, black lady?" A nod. "That's me. I'm her friend."

A suspicious glare. "You're white."

"So what? Shouldn't more of us be friends?"

"Man chasing her was white, too."

"Short and young? Shaggy yellow hair and beard?"

"Yeah, that's the one. He come running out a minute or two after her. The mother had a gun. Shot at me in the elevator. Shit. I never got sober so fast." He grinned and hefted the knife. "Tell me, whitey. Does this have anything to do with drugs? With Mothers' Tears?"

"With . . . No. We're, ah, spies. Want to see my badge? Genuine US Goverment."

"That's what she told me. Spy shit. No, I don't need to see your badge." He put the knife away. "White people been killing us with drugs for a hundred years. But I believe you. She pulled me into the elevator. She was running for her life and she pulled me into the elevator. She could have left me to die."

"She wouldn't do that." Red thought of Kennison upstairs. "Listen. Go up to 510. I left the door open. There's a man up there, gunshot. He might be dying. He . . . He shouldn't be alone. I have some people coming. Big, white guy. Tell him 'Jimmy' posted you. His name's Walt. He'll handle things." He turned to go.

"Hey, wait. I followed them. The bearded guy and the sister. They went across Pioneer Park toward the Tower."

Red paused. "You followed them?"

"Yeah, just far enough to see which way they went. Then I

496

came back here and waited. I figured, shit, why not? It wasn't much to do; but I figured, shit, she saved my ass."

"Yeah," said Red. "She does that a lot."

She was cold and wet and the sole of her foot was bleeding. Her breath came in gasping heaves and she knew she could run no farther. She needed a place to hide. Coit Tower loomed above her, massive and graceful. The fluted concrete soared; the lines drew her eyes upward and she stared into the concrete statue of a bird, wings outspread, taking triumphant flight. Phoenix, rising from her bed of ashes. Death and Resurrection. She staggered up the stairs. Death and Resurrection.

The entrance was a revolving door. She grabbed the handle and shook. It was locked. She sobbed in frustration and drew back and threw herself at the doors. They rattled but did not budge. Pain shot up her shoulder and she staggered back. She hunched over, holding her arm, and looked over her shoulder for Selkirk. But he was not yet in sight.

When she looked back at the doors there was a man standing there watching her through the glass, and she gave a little cry and shoved her fist in her mouth. He was an old man, dressed in a Park Guard uniform. He had a thermos in one hand. "What the hell do you think you're doing, lady?" His voice sounded distant, muffled by the glass.

She pressed her face to the door. "Let me in, please. He's got a gun."

"What?" The old man frowned. He looked past her shoulder; then he studied her again. "What's the matter?" She turned her face up in mute appeal. The guard made a decision. He pulled out a key ring and unlatched the main entrance door. Sarah pushed her way in. The air rushed; the rubber stiles slapped against the housing. She staggered out and fell to her hands and knees. "Lock the door, quick."

"What's wrong, miss? Where are your shoes?"

"There's a man chasing me. He's got a gun. Is there a telephone?"

The guard straightened and blinked rapidly. He pointed with his thermos. "In there. To the right. Hey."

Sarah paused. "What?"

"Here." The guard dug into his pocket and pulled out a quarter, which he pressed into her hand. "It's a pay phone."

"Thanks. Look. If he bangs on the door, don't answer. If he thinks there was no one to let me in, he'll go somewhere else."

"Miss, you said he had a gun. Parks and Recreation, they put me here so's kids don't break in and damage the frescoes. I ain't about to get in no gunfight. That's police business. If this guy comes along, I'll lie low." He grinned a gap-toothed smile. "Learned that in 'Nam a long time ago."

She clenched his quarter in her fist and stepped inside the Tower.

And paused. The inside walls were covered with murals. Men larger than life toiled sweatily. They guided plows, swung hammers, packed oranges. The colors were somber; the faces, brooding and angry. To her right, a weed-grown shipyard, with sullen, out-of-work stevedores. Directly ahead, two farming scenes flanked a doorway. On the left, an idyllic landscape of nineteenth-century farmers. On the right, in sharp contrast, modern, mechanized farming, with a steam shovel devouring a hillside. A pair of all-seeing eyes, surrounded by sun, moon, rain, lightning, stared back at her from the center panel above the doorway.

She had never seen anything like it in her life. The murals encircled the Tower, covering both the inner and the outer walls of the hallway.

*Socialist realism*, she thought. The glorification of work by those who did no manual labor themselves. Would the painter have depicted pre-industrial farming in so idyllic a fashion if he had ever had to sweat on such a farm?

Through the doorway ahead of her, she could see an elevator and a set of stairs; the latter cordoned off by a metal gate. She stepped forward to try the doors and saw that they only opened outward. She cupped her hands and peered through the glass. Craning her neck, she could see a turnstile and an alcove.

"I said the phone was to the right." The guard had come up behind her. He guided her to a small alcove in the inner wall of the corridor. "I'll be in the Gift Shop if you need me," he said.

Sarah inserted the quarter and dialed her room at the hotel. Bosworth answered on the second ring. "Norris? Norris!" She held the phone in both her hands. It was so good to hear a friendly voice. "This is Gloria. I'm—"

498

"Sister Bennett! We've been worried. Is Brother Caldero there yet?"

"Red? He's back?" Why did that thought make her feel so irrationally relieved? It wasn't as if she were there with her. "What do you mean is he here yet? How does he know—"

There was a loud banging on the doors of the Tower. Someone rattled the locks. Sarah backed deeper into the telephone alcove. She dropped her voice to a whisper. "Listen, Norris. "I'm in Coit Tower. Alan Selkirk is after me. I think he killed Kennison—"

"No, Brother—"

"Norris, listen!" Her whisper was harsh, urgent. "He may not have seen the guard let me in—"

Two muffled shots. Whining, spitting sounds. The glass in the doors sang. "Or maybe he did. He just shot out the doors."

Sarah dropped the phone and ran from the alcove, cutting to the right, away from the door. A giant steelworker watched her impassively; a surveyor ignored her. She ran past joyless foundry workers.

"Hsst! This way." The guard beckoned from the Gift Shop entrance. She ducked inside with him. There was a counter directly ahead of her. To the right was a token booth: Ride the Elevator to the Top. To the left, the turnstile to the elevator. She and the guard crouched together in a nook where they could not be seen from the entrance.

"Where's the back door?" she asked in a whisper.

"There isn't any."

"Isn't any?" Then they were trapped. "I'm sorry I got you into this."

He shrugged. "I didn't have to let you in."

Or were they trapped? The corridor was circular. If they could avoid Selkirk until he was on the north side . . . She remembered how she had played the game with Crayle on Mount Falcon, ducking back and forth to keep the assassin always on the other side of the brick wall. Would it work again? She remembered how terrified she had been at the time; and cold sweat sprang again on her face and arms. Her foot throbbed where she had cut it.

The inner doors rattled. Selkirk was trying them just as she had. But they were exit doors for people returning from the top of the tower. The entrance was where she and the guard were hiding.

The old man crouched beside her, his eyes white and wide against his dark face. His breath was shaky and irregular. Sarah touched him on the arm. She pointed to where Selkirk was and made a circling motion. Then she pointed to the two of them and arched her arm toward the turnstile. The man swallowed, licked his lips and nodded.

She listened carefully to the quiet footsteps, trying to follow his route in her mind. A pause. A sound. He had found the telephone dangling and hung it up. *Now he knows for sure.*

A door opened. Which door? She closed her eyes and thought. The men's room was directly across from the phone alcove. *Methodical*, she thought. *He's checking all the hiding places closest to the main entrance.* Would he actually step inside the men's room? No. He would leave the door open and look inside. He wouldn't give anyone a chance to slip past him.

Sit tight, Sarah. Sit tight. Women's room next. On the other side of the entrance. And then . . . Around the corridor, clockwise. Which would bring him to the gift shop entrance last. She exhaled carefully. Had he gone widdershins, he would have found them before they had a chance to make their move.

She waited until his footsteps faded. Then she scampered barefoot across to the turnstile and hopped over it, landing on the balls of her feet. The jar of landing reopened the cut and sent a lance of pain through her left leg. The guard followed her, squeezing through the turnstile arms.

Now, a straight shot through the exit doors to the revolving door and down the stairs. Barefoot across broken glass. Could they do it before Selkirk heard them and raced around from the antipodes of the corridor? They would never have a better chance.

Softly, but quickly. She tiptoed to the doors and pushed them gently open. Then she dashed for the front entrance.

And Selkirk had her in his grasp before she had taken three steps.

The revolving doors had been shot out. Small, saw-like teeth of broken glass rimmed the empty frames. Red studied the door, trying to guess the caliber of pistol Selkirk might have; and wondering what the hell difference it would make anyway. You were just as dead from a .22 slug as from a .38.

The smart move would be to wait for Walt to catch up. Walt would come heeled and that would help even the odds.

It would certainly be a lot smarter than storming Coit Tower barehanded.

"Hell, I never was very smart," he growled aloud. Before he could think twice about it, he bounded through the two shot-out panels, hit the floor inside the tower, and rolled. He came to his feet, looked both directions, and took cover in the phone alcove.

No shot. Good news or bad news? It might mean that Selkirk was no longer inside. He might have come and gone already. And, if that were the case . . .

A shudder ran through him. He didn't want to think about that possibility. He had to believe that Sarah was still alive; and that meant he had to believe that Selkirk was inside the Tower, armed and waiting for him.

*He didn't know I'd be unarmed.* If he stayed in front to cover the door, he'd be just as exposed to my return fire. Some people just didn't have the sand to stand there and take it. So if he hadn't been covering the front door, where was he? Think, Malone! Three possibilities: Around the back; up the top; not here. Which was the more dangerous? Around the back, because he could come at you from either direction.

He glanced down and saw blood on the floor and his heart skipped a beat. Someone had stood by the telephone and dripped blood on the floor. He knelt and examined the spot. It was a partial footprint. Sarah's, by the size of it. He played his light along the floor and saw two more.

She came in the door, her foot was already bleeding. She came to the phone. Of course, she would have called in at the first opportunity. That means that Bosworth knows she's here and he would have called Walt on the walkie-talkie. Chu will head straight here as soon as he gets in.

Meanwhile, though, I am the man on the scene.

He lay on his stomach and peeked around the corner. Nothing. Another glance behind him was equally reassuring. He wished he knew Selkirk better; so he would know what to anticipate. Well, here goes. He stepped around the corner and flattened himself against the inside wall. You are crazy, Malone. You know that? Wait for Walt. How can it help Sarah if you get your fool head blown off?

He inched his way along the corridor until he came to the Gift Shop entrance. Then he leapt inside, rolling to his right.

He rolled into a body.

# XIV

He kept a hand clapped over her mouth, even though she
hadn't made any attempt to scream. They were on the observation gallery, about three-quarters of the way to the top. The
night wind whipped through the open arches that ringed the
Tower, grabbing at their clothes and hair. Sarah felt chilled
and hugged herself. Her teeth chattered. Selkirk had picked
the arch that faced the front side of the Tower, and kept
looking over the balustrade toward the parking lot, a hundred
feet below. "Don't worry," he said. "He'll leave as soon as he
sees no one is here."

That was exactly what she was worried about, but she
didn't see what she could do about it. Selkirk had used the
guard's keys to shut off the elevator; and the steel grate still
blocked the stairs. So, Red would figure that no one could
have gone upstairs.

Selkirk took his hand from her mouth. "I'm sorry, lassie.
What did you say? Softly, now." He waved his pistol
meaningfully.

"You didn't have to kill the old man," she said, biting the
words out. *And why him and not me?* Selkirk had known that
the Tower had no rear exit; so he had waited by the side of
the exit doors, knowing that Sarah would come out that way.
He had grabbed her and threatened the guard with his pistol.
But, dragging her toward the door, he had spotted Red approaching across the parking lot. Whereupon he had returned
and very cooly shot the old man through the heart.

Selkirk looked surprised. "Of course I did. Be reasonable. I
couldn't bring him up here with us. If Caldero didn't find the
guard somewhere on the first floor, he would conclude that

503

we had come up here. But I couldn't leave him behind, either; or he would simply have told Caldero where we had gone. Even if I left him unconscious, I couldn't take the chance of him reviving. This way . . ." And Selkirk paused and glanced once more over the balustrade. "This way, Caldero will conclude that I came here, shot the guard and took you away before he showed up. There was no other logical course of action for me. We're not monsters, you know. We don't kill people for no reason."

The most horrifying thing about Selkirk's speech, Sarah decided, was the utter sincerity with which he uttered it. Of course, they didn't kill without reason—but their reasons were evil. Of course, he had had no other logical course of action—but from wicked premises, logic produced wicked conclusions. We had to destroy the village in order to save it. Very neat, very logical; and utterly terrifying. Security and civilization rested upon shared assumptions. When someone reasoned from alien premises, their conclusions had the terrifying aspect of madness. She looked into Selkirk's eyes and saw the childlike innocence of the sociopath.

"Then why," she asked, "didn't you kill me, too?"

He looked at her. "There's no need for that, lass. You're going to help us."

"Never."

"Ah, but we're going to help you rescue your friend."

"What?"

"Hush, lassie." He clapped a hand over her mouth and looked around. "Your friend, French? Bernstein has him in Manhattan; but we can't get near him. His penthouse is like a fortress. But you, he might allow inside."

"I don't get it. Why should you care about rescuing Dennis?"

He shrugged. "I don't. I care about getting to Bernstein. He's dangerous. He's been defying the *Cabinet Cachette*. Operating contrary to policy. You'll help us get to him; and we'll free your friend as a reward."

It was an easy choice. Bernstein was Selkirk's opponent in some sort of power struggle within the Q. That didn't make him one of the good guys; but it made him the enemy of someone who had shot an old man through the heart because it was logical. "What makes you think I would want to help you, for any reward?"

"It's easier if you want to," he responded cryptically, "but it isn't necessary."

\* \* \*

The body was that of an aged, black man in the gray and black uniform of a security guard. One glance at the wound was enough to tell Red that the man was gone. A heart shot. The floor and the wall behind him was a scarlet backdrop. Red pushed himself upright, feeling sick. The guard was unarmed, dammit; but Selkirk had shot him anyway. Why? And where was Sarah?

Damn Kennison! This was all his doing.

He quickly checked through the rest of the alcove: the Gift Shop and the Token Booth. He was afraid of what he might see when he looked behind the counters. His arms shook and would barely support him when he leaned over.

When he saw that she was not there, he slumped against the Token Booth, half-relieved, half-distressed. *Get ahold of yourself, Malone. You'll be in no shape to help her, if you do find her, the state you're in.*

He walked past the body of the guard and ducked through the turnstile into the elevator vestibule. Selkirk wasn't a homocidal maniac. He'd had a reason for killing the guard. Not self-defense; not against a sixty-year-old, unarmed man. Then, why? Because the guard had seen something that Selkirk didn't want revealed. Selkirk's identity? Perhaps. His connection with the Q? He shook himself angrily. He was speculating in a vacuum; and it wasn't getting him any closer to his quarry.

Back to basics. Downstairs, upstairs, or outside. Downstairs was out. What about upstairs? Two means of access. He shook the gate. It was locked shut. He pressed the elevator button. Nothing. No lights at all; so the elevator was turned off. The Parks people must do that at the end of the day.

That left outside. *Selkirk must have left before I got here.* Either with Sarah or after her. He had reached the exit doors before he froze, one hand on the handle. He looked back over his shoulder. Then he returned softly to the elevator and went to his hands and knees.

Yes. Another partial footprint in blood. Several of them. In front of the elevator. And some of them had been over-stepped by a shod foot. He returned to the guard's body and searched it. No key ring on his belt or in his pockets. He sat on his haunches with his arms resting across his knees. Then he looked toward the ceiling; wiped his palms on his pants legs, the back of his hand across his mouth. She was up there.

505

He knew it. And Selkirk. Lying doggo. Trying to avoid a fight. *Not as brave, are you, if you think your opponent is armed?*

If only he were. All right. Think it through. Correlation of Forces and Means. The outcome of a battle, according to von Clauswitz, was determined by the product NxQxV: the number of combatants; their fighting qualities; and all variables affecting the circumstances of the battle. Whoever had the higher NQV emerged the victor. Von Clauswitz had even expressed his theory in the form of a mathematical equation; and Red wondered momentarily if the old general had been a closet cliologist. The only trouble was that damned V. All variables affecting the circumstances of the battle.

So what have we got? Liabilities. I'm unarmed. Selkirk is armed and has no compunctions about killing. He's got the high ground and both means of access are blocked. He's got Sarah as a potential hostage.

Assets.

He stifled an involuntary chuckle. *My good looks.* And a lock-pick. He glanced at the metal grate that blocked the stairs. If he could open the grate without making a noise, he might have the benefit of surprise. Selkirk wouldn't be expecting that.

He dug his jimmy out of his pants pocket and went to work. It was a large lock and not meant to resist a clever assault. The pins clicked easily into place.

Selkirk shifted rapidly from one foot to the other. He checked his watch. "When is that SOB going to leave?" he asked. He didn't really expect an answer, and Sarah didn't supply him with one. She didn't know what she wanted more: Red to come upstairs to rescue her; or Red to leave so he would not be hurt.

Behind them. A motion at the head of the stairs, barely sensed out of the corner of her eye. A figure creeping silently toward them. Oh God, it's Red. Sarah turned suddenly away, lest she betray his presence. She pointed over the balustrade. "Oh," she said in a voice heavy with disappointment. "He's leaving."

And Selkirk, of course, looked.

It was all the advantage Red needed and he ran and leaped suddenly at Selkirk. Seizing the gun arm with both hands, he pushed it down and away. A shot whined and sprayed stone off the balusters. Red ignored Selkirk's pummeling with his left hand and slammed the right repeatedly against the rail until the gun fell from his fingers. Red kicked it. It spun, bounced off a baluster and skidded down the walkway. Sarah ran and picked it up. She trained it on them, holding it in both hands. She was not a good shot with a pistol. She disliked handguns and had never practiced with them to the extent she had with knives.

Red and Selkirk were a tangle of limbs. She didn't dare risk a shot. She saw Red wrap a leg around Selkirk's legs and they both went down, grunting. Selkirk worked an arm loose and tried to gouge Red's eye; but Red twisted away and gave him a head butt that bounced Selkirk's skull against the paving.

Then Selkirk glanced at Sarah, saw she had them covered and went unexpectedly limp. He relaxed and held both his hands up, grinning broadly.

Red disentangled himself and backed away, keeping his eye on Selkirk. "It's about time you showed up," Sarah told him. He shot her a glance.

"Yeah? Well, we've just got to stop meeting like this."

She barked a laugh and Red frowned at her. "Are you all right?"

"Aside from assorted bruises and contusions? I've nearly been raped by a sick maniac. I've been chased, kidnapped and terrorized. I've seen a gentle old man murdered in cold blood because he did me a favor. Aside from that, I'm fine."

Red grunted. He studied Selkirk, who still stood grinning with his hands clasped atop his head. The grinning bothered Sarah. What did Selkirk have to be so cheerful about? "Where's your gun?" she asked Red.

Red grinned and shrugged. "I was in a hurry and I forgot it."

She glanced at him. "You came up here unarmed?"

"I thought you might need some help."

Her thoughts were confused. There was an aching in her chest. What if Selkirk had been quicker? What if he had been watching the stairs instead of the main entrance? "He expected you to give up and leave."

"I almost did; but you left footprints. Besides, he killed the guard. Why would he do that except to keep him from telling me where you'd gone? And if you'd left the Tower and vanished into the night, why bother silencing him?" He shrugged again. "It was a logical deduction. He might as well have left a note saying 'I've gone upstairs.'"

Sarah saw how that jarred Selkirk. The grin wavered slightly. "I never thought you'd be unarmed," he said. "I wanted to avoid a shootout."

"Yeah," said Red. "Gunning down bystanders is more your speed." He shook his head and turned to Sarah. "Now that we've got him, what do we do with him?"

"Turn him over to the cops. Murder One. I'm an eyewitness."

"A public trial? Too risky. Too much might get said. Besides, what's a trial for? To establish guilt. Do you have any doubt he's guilty? The only possible thing that could happen in a trial is that the twelve couch potatoes they pick for a jury could let him go free. I can think of two plausible scenarios that would let him off the hook and put you or me on it. Do you want to see that?"

Was Red trying to tell her they should execute him right here? Take justice into their own hands? "I won't shoot him down like he did the guard."

"It's more convenient that way," he said. "Tidier."

She narrowed her eyes, watching Selkirk across the gunsights. "It would be the logical thing to do," she said bitterly, and she saw Selkirk's lips twist into a smile. "But if I did, then I would be like him; and I can't do that."

"You gotta be you."

She glanced at him. "It's like I told you once before. It's a dirty job, but someone's got to do it." She looked again at Selkirk. "I made a promise once that I wouldn't kill anyone again, if I could help it."

"A promise? To whom?"

"Crayle's ghost."

Red grunted. "You're right. You don't break promises to dead folks. You've got principles. I like that. I don't know what I would've said if you had shot him. Tried to understand, I guess. Shit. If anyone had a reason to be quick on the trigger, it's you; after what you've been through."

"Touching," said Selkirk.

Red turned on him. "You shut up. We've got a place for you. It's very far away and you don't get much sunshine. The food is adequate, but plain; and the accomodations somewhat spartan. But it sure as hell beats twitching and kicking on the ground." He looked at Sarah over his shoulder and backed toward her. "We'll march him downstairs. Walt should be

508

here shortly. We'll fly him out to North House and throw away the key. Suits?"

"Suits."

"If he tries anything . . ."

"Red, you told me I had principles. One of them is not to be exceptionally stupid. I'll defend myself, and anyone else. I'll even kill him, if there's no other option; but I think losing a kneecap would be just as effective." She wasn't sure she could make a knee shot on a running man, but Selkirk wouldn't know that.

So why was he so cheerful?

When Red was about halfway between them, Selkirk spoke, clearly and distinctly. "Sarah. Sarah Beaumont. Quetelet requires your service."

His voice seemed to echo in her skull. The words resonated. She felt herself receding far, far away from the scene on the balcony. The two figures remained the same size; but they seemed tiny, tiny. She was encased in cotton. Her last independent thought was the realization that Maureen Howard had done more than interrogate her, that night in the mountains.

"Kill him," the voice rang. "Kill Jimmy Caldero."

Red saw Sarah stiffen at the command and knew instantly what had happened. She turned and shifted her aim to him. The pistol's muzzle was a cannon. Blank eyes stared at him over the sights; the first, golden rays of dawn reflected in them.

He had a chance. A leaping kick would send the gun sailing in an arc up and over the balustrade.

And Sarah, too.

That was the trouble. The move had a follow-through and he didn't know if he could perform the first part fast enough and still check himself in time.

A heartbeat went by. It took a long time.

Then Selkirk gave a cry of rage and said, "Throw me the gun, you bitch!"

Sarah turned like a zombie and tossed it to him underhand. Selkirk caught it deftly and pointed it at Red, freezing him in mid-dash. "I've got principles, too," Selkirk announced. "And one is to leave no witnesses. I don't know what went wrong with her programming; but she's no good to us now."

The sweat on his back was freezing cold in the wind. Over

Selkirk's shoulder, he could see the Golden Gate. "Wait," he said. "Release her first."

"Why?"

"So . . . So we can say goodbye."

Selkirk seemed oddly saddened by the request. He stopped smiling and backed away from them until he came up against the balustrade. The gun never wavered. "Aye. I'll do that. I'm no monster for a' that. I do what I must do; but I've no liking for it. *You* understand, even if she doesn't." He jerked his head toward Sarah.

He flinched. Selkirk appealing to their common background. And the most wretched thing of all was that he *did* understand. But he wondered what it would take for Selkirk to call something monstrous. "I've never killed anyone simply from duty," he said. Proudly? But was that really his own boast or was it only that circumstances had never faced him with the choice?

"You will. Or you would have."

Was Selkirk right? Was he looking at himself only a little ways farther down the road? Was this what it ultimately meant if he reactivated the Associates? "Will you release her?" he asked again.

He nodded. "Don't try any tricks. You'd never cover the distance." He coughed and looked at Sarah. "Sarah Beaumont. Quetelet releases you."

She started, looked at Selkirk; then turned and looked at Red. Then she burst into tears and covered her face with her hands. Red stepped toward her and gathered her up. She buried herself in his shoulder. "Oh, Red. I should have shot him, after all."

"No, no. You were right. It's one thing to die for a principle; it's another thing to kill for one. Revenge is for suckers. It validates everything your enemy has ever done to you and only tells him it's his turn again." He stroked her hair and the back of her neck.

She turned her face up. "Red, kiss me. I've . . . Morgan wanted . . . But I never . . ."

He saved her from her confusion.

The kiss was not like he had imagined it would be. Farewell kisses never are. Alice's lips had already been cold when he . . . But Sarah's were warm, yielding. The contact was overwhelming and his head seemed to whirl; yet, there was nothing erotic about it. It was stronger than that. He held her

510

for a long moment; and noticed that their heartbeats were synchronized. An odd, trivial, last detail to notice.

"I've always hated long goodbyes," said Selkirk.

Red held her tighter. "Don't look."

"No." She turned in his arms and faced the Scot. "No, you should always look."

He didn't want his last sight to be Selkirk. He kept his eyes fixed on Sarah. When the shot came, he jerked.

"My God," said Sarah. He squeezed her but she grabbed his sleeve and turned him toward Selkirk. "No. Look."

A scarlet flower had blossomed on Selkirk's shirt. His eyes were white and wide and his mouth had opened into a silent O. He put his hand to his chest and brought it away wet. He held it out to them in amazement. His lips moved, but no sound emerged. The color had drained from his face.

A second shot took him under the chin. His back arched and he flipped over the balustrade as if tossed by a careless giant. The sound of the impact came three seconds later, but it seemed to take forever.

Red dashed to the rail and looked over. Selkirk was a rag doll spread twisted over the steps. Chu and Walt stood there staring up at him in astonishment. Chu's station wagon sat in the center of the parking lot, its doors wide open. They had pistols in their hands. Walt saw him looking and put his back in his holster.

He turned and faced Sarah, who was staring at the anonymous apartment buildings that lined the hillside behind them. "Our ride's here," he said.

She didn't reply. Red came over to her and put his arm around her shoulder. "I don't get it," he said. "Those weren't pistol shots. And Walt didn't have the angle. What were they?"

Sarah hugged herself. "Varmint rifle," she said.

511

# XV

Jeremy looked toward the top of the building. How many stories was it? Too many. Manhattan depressed him. It was too cold. Too large. He checked the address on the slip in his palm and compared it to the building number. Four thirty-two. There was a bar-restaurant on the ground floor. He looked at Gwynn.

"Well, here goes."

She placed her hand on his shoulder. "Good luck."

He shrugged. "That Bosworth kid managed to contact this Bernstein fellow, using the same routine that Selkirk used. I understand he was surprised—but not too surprised—to hear from us. He admitted having had Dennis with him the whole time. Something about a difference of opinion with the *Cabinet Cachette*. I don't pretend to understand any of that stuff. That— What was it Caldero called it?"

"Carson's dilemma," said Gwynn.

"Right. Apparently, this crowd never went through it before. Just random chance, but they've never had a split-up until now. And why am I babbling like this?"

"This is where the message said to meet him?"

He checked the slip again. A hell of a thing if he got the number wrong. "Yes. Yes. This is the place. In the bar. Third stool from the right. Dash it all, Gwynn. I feel like a kid going on his first date."

"You haven't seen him for a long time."

"Not since the accident. We've . . . never been apart this long."

Gwynn gave him a push. "Then don't put it off any longer. I'll wait in that coffee shop there on the corner."

He pulled his handkerchief from his breast welt pocket and patted his brow. "You don't think it's a trap, do you?"

She shook her head. "No, there'd be no purpose to it. If Bernstein wanted to stay hidden, he'd have simply moved his headquarters. Either taken Dennis with him or . . . not." She gazed toward the penthouse. "I think maybe he's looking for allies."

"John Wayne types like us, I suppose."

The barroom was dimly lit; the clientele, a typical weekday afternoon, midtown crowd. Businessmen stretching their lunch hours to quitting time. Salesmen pitching to jaded buyers, more interested in the free drinks than in the product; talking a little too loudly and with a little too much enthusiasm. Jeremy paused in the doorway and looked around carefully. A few men here and there returned his gaze calmly. He had no idea what Bernstein looked like; but he had been told about his tight defenses. What was the phrase? He had "gone to the mattresses." The entire building was supposed to be a fortress. Some of the men in this room, Jeremy was sure, were bodyguards. Probably the ones who sat well back from their cocktail tables, with their jackets loose and unbuttoned and their right hands unencumbered with drinks.

One man was looking at him with sexual interest. Jeremy smiled at him and shook his head in the briefest of gestures, and the man shrugged and looked away. Jeremy tugged his gloves off and walked to the bar. The stools were small director's chairs on very tall legs. Most were empty, but the third from the right was . . . occupied.

From the back the man . . . No. He was much too broad-shouldered to be Dennis. Could it be Bernstein? Jeremy walked up behind him and touched him on the sleeve. "Excuse me, but—"

The man's icy stare cut him off. He looked down at him across a huge, cavernous nose, impaling Jeremy to the spot. He held the silence just long enough for Jeremy to feel fear; then he nodded. "I'm sorry. Was this your stool?" Without waiting for an answer, he gathered his drink and moved off. Jeremy had a glimpse of something black and shiny under his suit coat. Jeremy watched him join another man at a cocktail table near the entrance, where they watched Jeremy and the

513

doorway with equal interest. Jeremy took a shaky breath and perched himself on the vacated stool. The bar was clean and dry and Jeremy lay his gloves and fedora there. He clasped his hands on the bar top and waited.

The bartender was a slight, dark man with a scar over one eye. He saw Jeremy and limped over. "Can I get you something?"

Jeremy glanced over his shoulder toward the entrance. "Yes. Anything. I'm waiting for someone."

"Aren't we all?" said the bartender; but it was a rhetorical question. He moved off and reached for a bottle and a glass. Jeremy watched him pour, measuring each ingredient with punctilious exactness.

A motion at the entrance caught his eye and he turned. But it was only two young women, loaded down with bright bracelets and long, elaborate "Jersey" hair. They were whispering to each other and laughing. A few of the other men watched them settle into a booth; and one of the salesmen straightened his tie and walked over to them. It was all so normal, it was frightening.

When Jeremy turned back to the bar his drink was in front of him. He swirled the toothpick and its impaled victim, a pearl onion, in idle circles, watching the ripples in the icy clear liquid. He checked his watch and glanced again at the entrance. He felt uncomfortable and conspicuous. He had to twist in his seat to watch the door. The canvas cut into his thighs and back.

How would he know Bernstein when he walked in? Perhaps by the reaction of the others in the room. But, no. Most of them were legitimate citizens going about their legitimate business, padding expense accounts, trying to cheat on their wives. Jeremy didn't know them anymore. He felt as if he had lived the past few months in a secret world, hidden behind the wainscoting of reality. A world that existed in anonymous boardrooms and secret hideaways. Where decisions were made on the future; and politicians, the public, even large corporations were taught to carry them out. He had lived, for a little while, among the stagehands; and he didn't know if he could ever sit happily in the audience again, or even take his part in the play.

He took a sip of his drink. It was a vodka martini, and very good. He pursued the play analogy in his mind. He had told Caldero that he didn't care if the world were contrived or not;

514

that the play was scripted. But now he felt an odd passion for improvisational theater.

A footstep at the doorway. He turned and saw a slim, middle-aged man, gray at the temple, dressed in a Brooks Brothers suit of dark, worsted wool. He wore kid gloves of contrasting silver, and carried a walking stick with a knob of chased gold. He tucked the walking stick under his arm like an officer's crop and locked gazes with Jeremy.

Jeremy swallowed. He felt the other's detached interest, his mild sexual appraisal. Cold and aloof. Not at all a friendly gaze; but not unfriendly, either. The man—was it Bernstein? —nodded cooly and took a seat at an empty table. Jeremy saw that the table was surrounded by large men nursing their drinks left-handed.

He turned back to the bar and took a hasty swallow. Was that Bernstein? Was the nod an invitation? What should he do?

He stared at the remains of his cocktail, rotating the glass slowly back and forth between his palms, like a boy scout with a hand drill. Suddenly, he froze. A vodka martini? He had told the bartender to give him anything and he had given him this?

He raised his head and stared at the bartender who, he saw, was staring back at him. He studied the scar, the dark complexion, the limp; and the man walked over and stood before him. He wiped the counter with a bar towel. "Another one, sir?" he asked.

"Dennis?" He whispered it, half afraid he had guessed wrong; half afraid he had guessed right.

The bartender nodded. "Hello, Jerry. It's been a long time."

"You've . . . changed."

"Jerry. Clichés? Of course, I've changed. We all change. We only notice it when we've gone away and come back. Or . . . when we remember." His eyes seemed to turn inward as he spoke. "You've changed, too. Paul told me you had."

"Paul?"

Dennis nodded to the man who had come in moments before. "Paul Bernstein." The man had his hands clasped on the table watching them. He bowed his head, once.

Jeremy faced Dennis again. "Maybe I have changed, but not like you. You've . . ."

"Had surgery? Yes. It was quite dreadful; but you realize

that, after my accident, they were working almost from scratch as far as my features went. You haven't asked me how I've gotten on."

Jeremy choked on the words. "How have you gotten on?"

Dennis wiped his hands on the bar towel. "It was awful at first. I woke up and I wasn't in the hospital. I was in some private clinic, and I hurt all over. After a while the pain died away and people came and questioned me. What did I know; how did I know it; who had I told. That sort of thing. I thought it was the Babbage Society that had got hold of me." He shook his head slowly. "They had that list I had gotten from the Quinn mansion on Emerson Street. They were very interested in it; and very worried. They thought it meant that their existence was already known, that they might be walking into a trap. Here." He took the martini glass. "Let me freshen that." He walked off a short distance and refilled the glass from a pitcher. He brought it back and set it down. Jeremy watched him silently.

"Well, I suppose you know some of this; maybe even most of it. Paul's organization is expanding into the United States. They are very ruthless. One faction wanted to—" He bit his lip and dropped his eyes. "They wanted to dispose of me after they were done questioning me. They were the ones who tried to kill you, as well. But Paul managed to slip me out and stash me here where they couldn't— Well . . ." He rubbed his hands brusquely on the bar towel. "That's the main reason for the new face."

Jeremy toyed with his onion. "Why should Bernstein protect you?"

Dennis' eyes flicked over Jeremy's shoulder. "Why? A lot of reasons, I suppose. He has a grudge of some sort against the *Cachette*. Something about his grandfather and the Holocaust. I don't know all the details. He hasn't told me; but I have the impression that he has been nurturing his plan for a long time."

"And why would that lead him to defy his *confréres?*" Jeremy shook his head. "He didn't have to help you at all."

Dennis looked away. He shrugged.

Jeremy grunted. He glanced at Bernstein, who smiled thinly. So, it was like that. He supposed he should feel jealousy; but it was difficult to harbor resentment against the man for saving Dennis. He turned back to his drink and glowered into

516

it. He didn't like the idea of people behind him watching his every move. "This isn't working out at all the way I'd supposed."

"What did you think would happen? That I would run into your arms?" Dennis shrugged again. "People change. I had to survive, Jerry. And to do that, I had to cut loose from everything in my past."

"Everything?"

"Yes."

"Do you . . . ever miss it?"

"What? The past?" Dennis twisted the bar towel into a knot. "Every day. You. The apartment. Sarah. My practice. All gone. Everything I ever knew; or owned. Or loved. Do I ever miss it?" He looked down at the towel, unknotted it. Smoothed it out. "Well, that's all done."

"I see."

"Don't think I don't know what you've gone through. And why. I'm grateful, and touched. It's just that . . ."

"Never mind that." Jeremy slid off the bar stool. He took his hat and gloves. "I'll be going now. I won't bother you any more."

"Wait." Dennis laid a hand on his forearm. "You will come back. Paul wants it."

He looked at Bernstein. "Well, if 'Paul' wants it . . ."

"Don't be that way. He wants a liaison. Paul does. Someone who can act as a contact between his faction and . . . well, the group you've been associating with."

Jeremy twisted his lips. "Which is that? There have been so many."

"That's part of it. We need to find some concert of interests."

"Do we? And why me, particularly?"

Dennis looked him in the eye. "Paul feels that you and he have certain interests in common."

"Why should I not stay out of it entirely?"

"Because there are those who would run down harmless architects or blow up history professors; and there are those who want to stop them."

"The problem is that those who want to stop them have different reasons."

"All the more reason to open channels."

Jeremy tugged his gloves on. He picked up his hat. "Very well. I'll discuss it with . . . my friends. Good-bye, Dennis. I'll take your regards to Sarah." He turned to go.

"Jerry."

"What?"

"You've changed, too, you know. If we had broken up last June, you would be a complete wreck by now. You're different, now. More confident. Less dependent."

Jeremy paused and looked back. Dennis was twisting and untwisting the bar towel. "Yes, I suppose I am. You're right. People do change. Sometimes they become less dependent." He settled his hat upon his head. "We'll be in touch."

In the coffee shop on the corner, Gwynn asked him how it went.

Jeremy gazed wistfully at the building down the block. "I met a man who once was Dennis French."

# XVI

The piano wept. It was slightly out of tune, and the blue notes ripped at her heart. She let her hands slide easily over the keys, wringing out the melancholy chords. She hummed along with it, shaking her head slowly from side to side. Fee sat atop the piano listening with half-closed eyes. The rest of the underground safe house seemed far away.

"I sing because I'm happy," she sang, but not too loud, because she was only singing for herself and that did not require volume. "I sing because I'm free." And she stretched out the last word, holding the note and letting it tremble just a little at the end. "Oh, His eye is on, is on the sparrow, 'cause I know He watches me."

"Oh, He sure does that. Either He or Janie Hatch."

Sarah struck a dissonant chord. "Red, how long have you been listening?" She twisted around and saw he was assembling his clarinet. "It's embarrassing," she said. "I don't sing well. I don't like people listening to me."

"Oh, you'll never play the Met, that's for sure; but sometimes heart counts for as much as art." He stuck the reed in his mouth to moisten it. "Like me." He took the reed out and gestured with it. "Like that song you were singing. You hit it dead right. By all rights we should be dead." He replaced the reed in his mouth. "You explain it."

"Janie won't admit to being in San Francisco. She claims she was out hunting."

"Hunting." Red grunted. "And you can take that any way you want it."

"Red, can you explain Janie Hatch? Because I can't."

519

"No one can. She does what she wants and then she thinks up reasons for it. Maybe she's taken a shine to you."

"It's ironic, don't you think? Selkirk didn't have to grant your last request. It was probably the first genuinely kind act of his life, and it killed him."

"The good die young," said Red philosophically. "What are you trying to say? If he had been a kinder man he would have died a lot earlier?"

"If he'd been a kinder man, he would never have been on top of that tower." Her hands wandered through the rest of *His Eye is on the Sparrow*. "I think he needed to prove that he wasn't a monster, after all."

"Why bother to prove anything to us? He was going to kill us, wasn't he?"

"No. Prove it to himself."

"Oh." He took the reed from his mouth and strapped it to the emboucher. "Well." He blew a few experimental scales; removed his instrument; studied its keys. "Why didn't you shoot me?"

"Now, that's a hell of a question."

"On the tower. When Selkirk triggered your program. You didn't shoot. Don't misunderstand me; I'm glad you didn't. But I don't understand it. I *know* how deep conditioning works."

She played a few bars of *Good Blues*, then stopped with her hands elevated. "It's funny, you know. I can remember everything that happened. Every detail. The cold breezes. The salt smell of the ocean. How the dawn made everything seem to shine. But it's like a dream. Unreal, as if I wasn't there at all, but watching from a long distance." She turned on the bench and looked at him. "He ordered me to kill Jimmy Caldero; and I remember looking and looking. But all I could see was Red Malone."

Red jerked slightly. "Semantic trickery," he said. "That shouldn't have subverted a ductifacient drug."

"It wasn't semantics, Red. I never could see 'Jimmy Caldero,' not deep down. Selkirk ordered me to kill a man who, as far as I was concerned, did not exist."

"Ah." He toyed idly with his keys. "Well."

"What's wrong?"

"I was hoping that it was the power of love overcoming the power of the drug."

"Are you serious?"

520

"No. Not really. It would have made a hell of a story, though, wouldn't it?"

She turned her back on him and played a chromatic scale, slowly and softly. "The power of love," she said. "Maybe it was. Have you ever been in love?"

"Yes. Once."

She paused a moment, then resumed the scale. "I see. Jacksonville, wasn't it?"

"Someone told you."

She shook her head so he would see it. "No. But when the wind is nor'-nor'east, I can tell a hawk from a handsaw. And I can recognize the scab of an old wound when I see one. What was her name? Not Fanny Power."

"No," Red told her, "Alice McAuliffe. Her name was Alice McAuliffe."

Alice McAuliffe. A name from a list. "What happened?"

"Oh, she was someone like you. Someone who learned more than was good for her. A system analyst with an interest in history. She did a little of this and a little of that, and before she knew it, she knew too much. Weil had hysterics and ordered her dead; and Cam sent me to warn her. The two of us holed up for a few weeks in a cabin in the Smokies while Cam negotiated with Them to bring her Inside. Those were . . . long weeks; and we came to know each other pretty well. The negotiations went well. Everything seemed copacetic; but Kennison forgot to call off the dogs. Or he didn't bother to. They caught up with us in Jacksonville."

He was silent and she looked back over her shoulder. "And?"

"And what? It didn't work out so well as it did with you and me. She didn't have your background or abilities. I trusted some people I shouldn't have had to trust; and we . . . Things just didn't work out. Leave it at that."

"So that's what Janie meant."

"What?"

"The day she dropped us at Stapleton. She told me that my safety was more important to you than to me. It didn't make any sense at the time."

"It doesn't make sense now," he complained. "Janie's always been an enigma. Why do you have to know all this, anyway?"

"Because I need to know why an otherwise intelligent man

would climb Coit Tower unarmed, knowing that there was an armed, ruthless killer at the top."

"It seemed like a good idea at the time."

"Nothing is too serious for you make a joke, is it?"

He looked at her and smiled sadly. "Some things are too serious for anything else."

"Who did you think was on top of the Tower, Alice or me?"

"That's a fool question. Why do you care? You're the one who never needs any help. The solo player."

She looked at Fee; reached up and scratched him between the ears. A flicker of faces flashed before her eyes. Mama. Daddy. Abe. Morgan. Dennis. "Sometimes I do. Sometimes I even know it. You aren't the only one with scabs."

"Maybe . . ." He hesitated and she turned again and looked at him.

"Why haven't you ever tried to kiss me?" she asked.

He looked surprised. "I . . . Janie asked me that once. About you, I mean. I don't know. What if you had pushed me away?"

"What if I hadn't?" Sarah wondered suddenly, irrationally, whether Janie had set up the whole scenario atop the tower just to get them to kiss. *What if we hadn't? Would she still have shot Selkirk?* No, that was crazy. "Red, if it had been Walt Polovsky held hostage at the top of the tower, would you still have come charging up, unarmed the way you did?"

He grinned. "Well, maybe not quite so fast."

She laughed. "But you would still have done it. Good. Doing the right thing should never depend on who you're doing it for. Come and see me tonight, about seven, and we'll see about that other unfinished business. Fair's fair. I owe you a dinner. Janie promised me the run of the kitchen. Meanwhile . . ." And she nodded toward his clarinet. "Is that licorice stick for showin' or for blowin'?"

Red stopped and looked at his instrument. "Give me an A." She tapped the key and Red played a note, frowned, and cocked his head.

"You're sharp," she suggested.

"I know that; but the note wasn't quite right." He twisted the emboucher. "Try it now."

"Sounds better. What did you want to play? *High Society?*"

"I thought we might do your favorite. *The Maple Leaf Rag.*"

"I didn't know you'd learned it."

"I've studied the score; but I want to try it your way. By ear."

She smiled at him. "That's quite a departure for you."

"Yeah. Do me a favor, though. Play it through once on the piano, so I can hear it."

She started into the first theme. Red leaned forward in his chair, frowning intently. After a minute or two, she said matter-of-factly, "I'm going to see Dennis next Tuesday." Red grunted an acknowledgement. "According to Jeremy, he's changed a lot since I last saw him. Captivity, I suppose. The hostage learns to love his captor. I don't know. Pay attention to this transistion." She played it twice so he could learn it. She saw him fingering the clarinet.

"I don't know," she repeated. "Maybe it was his free choice. Maybe his gratitude became something else; and maybe this Bernstein had more in mind than a gambit against his colleagues. Or maybe Dennis was brainwashed; programmed like I was." She shook her head. "I think that was the most horrible experience I'll ever have. The whole idea of slavery has overtones for me that it can't possibly have for you. And this was the ultimate slavery, chaining the mind as well as the body."

"It's a wicked practice. I don't approve it."

She stopped playing. "And how is it different from what They do, and the Six; and what you want the Associates to do? It's control and manipulation. Is there some moral difference between wholesale and retail?"

He looked away from her. "I don't know. I used to know; but I'm smarter now."

"The smarter we get, the less we know. Or the less certain we are that we know it. That's why fanatics are so successful. They sell certainties. Are you ready? Okay, follow me." She started the rag, played the first phrase, and Red joined in on the repeat. He hit a few wrong notes, and Sarah tried not to wince too obviously; but he managed to stay in the right key.

"At one point," she continued over the music, "I thought that there were too many cliological societies around. The Society; the Associates; the Q; the Six; DB&S; even the U.S. government, or a faction within it, if we can believe your friend Charlie. But lately I've been wondering if maybe there aren't enough."

He stopped playing. "Not enough?"

"Not enough. What if everyone knew how to do it? What if

523

cliology were taught at MIT and Cal Tech? You told me once that everyone tried to alter the future. What if we all had the tools to do it better?"

"It would be chaos. People have different ideas about what the future should be. You'd have everybody pulling in different directions."

"So what? At least everyone will play the game with the same equipment. And whatever direction society does move, it will mean that a lot of people were pulling in that direction. When there are millions of players, the variations cancel each other out. That's basic probability theory, isn't it? The normal distribution of errors. Maybe the Society made so many errors because its thinking had become so inbred. Something like genetic drift must have taken place."

He stood and walked closer. He put a hand on her shoulder and leaned over. "Play that rag again. I hit too many clinkers the first time. Play it loud," he added in a whisper.

She looked at him and he put a finger to his lips. She hit the keys hard and he leaned close and whispered in her ear. "Let's not talk about it here. Tomorrow, we'll go horseback riding. You can show me that Altaflora of yours."

"Don't be ridiculous. It must be under a ton of snow by now."

"Then show me something else." He leaned closer and kissed her on the cheek.

"I'll come back later," said Tex Bodean from the doorway, "if this isn't convenient."

Sarah waved at him without losing the beat. Red held up his clarinet. "What the hell, Tex, why don't you join us?" he said. Sarah kept up the melody but softened the sound.

"Sure. Just let me make a phone call." He went to the wall phone by the door and spoke into it briefly. Then he went to the closet and pulled out a trombone case. He assembled it with a few quick moves and worked the slide a few times experimentally. "What are we playing?"

"Ragtime," said Sarah. "Maybe some Dixieland."

"Do you play Chicago-style?"

"Maybe later, if you're a good boy." She closed out the *Maple Leaf* and played the intro to *High Society*. Red looked at her and grinned. "Thanks," he said.

"Always put your best foot forward," she replied.

The three of them played for a few minutes, Tex laying a decent bass line with his 'bone even though Sarah thought he was hearing the tune for the first time. He had a good ear for improvisation, she thought. While they were playing, a bald-headed man with a curly, chest-length beard scampered into the room, carrying a trumpet in his right hand. He slapped Tex on the back and settled into the chair next to him. He listened for a while, tapping his foot; then his put his horn to his lips and puffed his cheeks out. The bright trumpet sound blended perfectly into the music.

Red got through his complex solo without a single error, which caused Tex to whoop a cowboy yell and brought a scatter of claps from the doorway. Sarah looked back that way and saw that a small crowd had gathered there.

As they concluded the piece, she heard someone say, "Excuse me. Coming through." And she saw Walt Polovsky pushing his way in with SuperNerd in tow. Polovsky pointed him toward the drums in the corner. "There, I told you we had a set. Now, put your money where your mouth is. You come in after Jimmy there." Bosworth looked around, blushed, and took a seat behind the drums. He picked up the sticks and waited, testing the reach to the various drums in the trap set. He rapped out a paradiddle.

"Thanks for the call, Tex. Hi, Stosh, Jimmy, Glo— Sarah." Polovsky hoisted a battered old tuba to his lap. *"Joe Avery,"* he announced. "Any objections?"

"Better do as he says, Sarah," Red told her. "It's his big chance to shine. Come on, Cam. You want to sit in, too?"

A man Sarah hadn't met yet seated himself against the wall. He was thin-faced and sharp featured; and his hair must have been white for a long, long time. He plucked a chord progression on his banjo. "Depends. You folks posing or playing?"

*Joe Avery* began with a strong, jaunty bass line and Polovsky played it with clear authority. The notes boomed and danced with an agility not normally given to the tuba. When the trumpet player took over, Polovsky dropped back and kept up a steady background rhythm.

They traded the melody around, each instrument giving it a twist all its own. The trumpet, bright and brassy, suggested the melody as much by the notes it omitted as by those it played. Tex's trombone was sweet and mellow; and no riverboat ever heard as fine a banjo as the one Cam Betancourt played. When it was her turn, Sarah closed her eyes and pretended she was playing solo. Her hands danced back and forth across the keyboard. She soared with the music.

Red went by the book, improvising very little; but that was all right because he had two registers to play in. When he played the low register, he carried the main theme; but he switched over to a counterpoint in the high register. The long, sweet notes above the treble clef hung in the air, contrasting with the bouncing, persistent rhythm that Walt kept up.

When he finished, it was Norris' turn, and the teenager hit the skins just as if there were not an easy two dozen onlookers and his face were not the color of choice, Grade A beets. His riffs were more rock than jazz, but he went through them without a fluff.

While he played, Sarah saw Janie Hatch standing in the crowd, watching them with her usual stony look. She turned up her mouth and shook her head slowly. Sarah caught her eye and mouthed the word "Thanks," but Janie only shrugged in reply. Then she rubbed her hands against her pants legs and stepped into the room.

There was a big double-bass lying on its side along the back wall. Janie set it upright and ran her hand up and down the fingerboard. Then, when Norris finished his drum solo, she leaned into it, slapped out a reprise of the tuba part with stoic precision. It was almost comical, the contrast between the rollicking melody and the calm, unmoving look on her face.

Sarah watched with her fingers poised over the keyboard. When Janie gave the nod, they all jumped in, playing *tutti*. Walt's bass, Red's counterpoint, all the parts blended into the joyous cacaphony typical of Dixieland. The crowd in the doorway and the hall beyond burst into spontaneous applause while they played and Sarah felt a thrill shiver up her spine.

When they had finally finished, they sat there looking at each other while the onlookers clapped and whistled. Sarah had lost herself in the music. She sat staring at the keyboard for a few moments longer, still hearing the ringing chords in her mind. Then she closed her eyes and relaxed. She let out a deep breath.

She turned around and the clapping doubled. She couldn't understand why. She had played no better than she usually did. And it hadn't been her alone, but all of them, that had somehow made the magic. But she smiled and acknowledged the kudos anyway.

She heard Tex say, "Wow," and the trumpet player, Stosh, pounded him on the back. Walt shook Norris' hand and waved an arm at him, inviting the crowd's applause. Bosworth couldn't stop grinning. He stood up and gave a short, jerky bow, and quickly sat down again.

Janie Hatch was leaning across her 'dogbox.' She caught Sarah's eye and looked at her. Then she looked at Red, and back to her. She raised an eyebrow. Sarah nodded once, and Janie Hatch, for a fraction of an instant, smiled.

# WINNER OF THE PROMETHEUS AWARD

## VERNOR VINGE

**Technology's Prophet**

*"Vinge brings new vitality to an old way of telling a science fiction story, showing the ability to create substantial works in the process."*
—Dan Chow, *Locus*

*"Every once in a while, a science fiction story appears with an idea that strikes close to the heart of a particular subject. It just feels right, like Arthur C. Clarke's weather satellites. Such a story is Vernor Vinge's short novel, TRUE NAMES."* —Commodore Power/Play

---